select
editions
Reader's
Digest

The names, characters and incidents portrayed in the novels in this volume are the work of the authors' imaginations. Any resemblance to actual persons, living or dead, events or localities is entirely coincidental.

www.readersdigest.co.uk

The Reader's Digest Association Limited
11 Westferry Circus Canary Wharf London E14 4HE

For information as to ownership of copyright in the material of this book, and acknowledgments, see last page.

Printed in Germany
ISBN 978 0 276 44436 4

THE READER'S DIGEST ASSOCIATION LIMITED, LONDON

contents

author in focus

Marina Lewycka is a reminder that success can come at any time, and it's always too soon to stop trying. For thirty years she nurtured a dream of becoming a writer, but received only rejection slips until she was fifty-eight. Then Penguin published *A Short History of Tractors in Ukrainian* and suddenly she was propelled into the limelight. *We Are All Made of Glue*, her third best seller, is funny, insightful, and stars an eccentric and feisty octogenarian who has a solution to all life's challenges, big and small. It also demonstrates vividly that despite differences in age, race or creed, we're united, ultimately, by the things that make us human.

in the spotlight

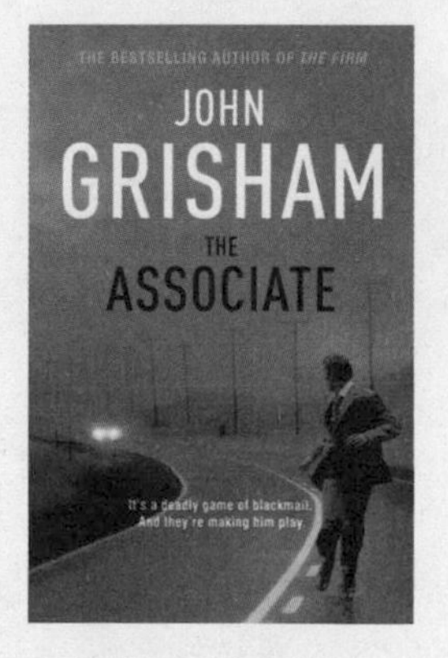

With the current media focus on corporate greed and the determined pursuit of wealth, this new David-and-Goliath tale from John Grisham is particularly relevant. The author takes us to the core of imaginary New York law firm Scully & Pershing, where huge salaries and bonuses are deemed just reward for round-the-clock dedication to making big money. Into this dog-eat-dog environment steps idealistic young lawyer Kyle McAvoy, whose decision to take the job of associate at Scully & Pershing is strangely out of character. What's more, all is not quite as it seems at the firm, and McAvoy is about to find himself trapped between a rock and a very hard place.

NEW YORK STOCK EXCHANGE

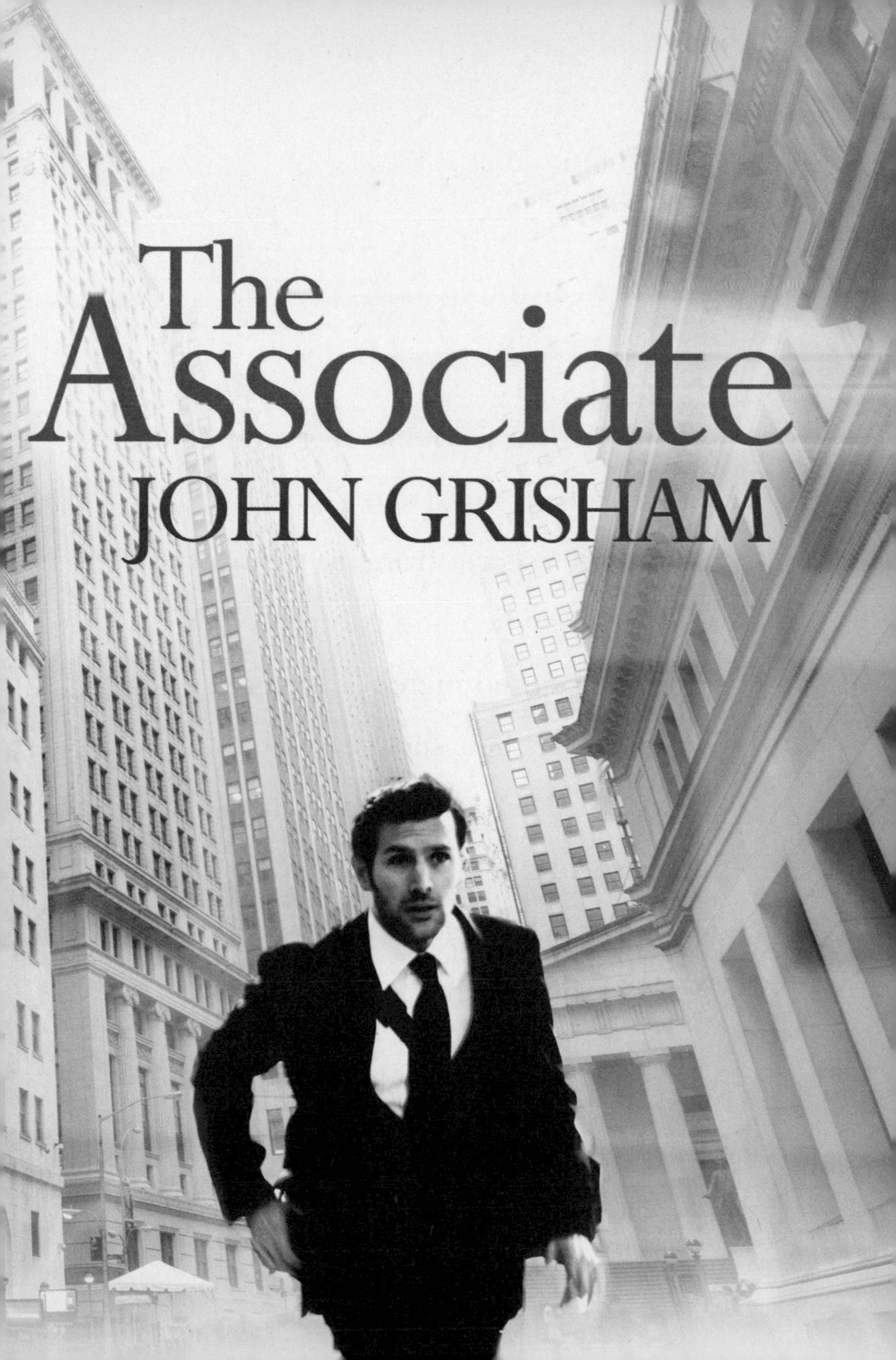
The Associate
JOHN GRISHAM

Kyle McAvoy is a young law graduate with a brilliant mind and a glittering future. But a secret from his past catches up with him when he's confronted by some dark-suited men in a back alley. The price for their silence will be Kyle's complicity. He must become an associate at the world's biggest law firm.

The only catch is that he won't be working for them, but against . . .

1

The rules of the New Haven Youth League required that each kid play at least ten minutes in each game. Exceptions were allowed for players who had upset their coaches by skipping practice or violating other rules. In such cases, a coach could file a report before the game and inform the scorekeeper that so-and-so wouldn't play much, if at all, because of some infraction. This was frowned on by the league; it was, after all, much more recreational than competitive.

With four minutes left in the game, Coach Kyle looked down the bench, nodded at a sombre little boy named Marquis and said, 'Do you want to play?' Without responding, Marquis walked to the scorers' table and waited for a whistle. His violations were numerous: skipping practice, skipping school, losing his uniform, foul language. In fact, Marquis had broken every one of the few rules his coach tried to enforce. Realising that any new rule would be immediately violated by his star, Coach Kyle had trimmed his list and fought the temptation to add new regulations. It wasn't working. Trying to control ten inner-city kids with a soft touch had put the Red Knights in last place in the 12 and Under division of the league.

Marquis was clearly the best player on the court, and within two minutes he had scored six points. But the game was out of reach. Kyle McAvoy sat on the bench, waiting for the clock to wind down. One game to go and the season would be over, his last as a basketball coach. In two years he'd won a dozen, lost two dozen, and asked himself how any person in his right mind would coach. He was doing it for the kids, he said to himself, kids with no fathers, kids from bad homes, kids in need of a positive male influence. And he still believed it, but after two years of baby-sitting, and arguing with parents when they bothered to show up, and hassling with other coaches who were not above cheating, he was fed up.

He looked around the empty gym, an old brick building in downtown New Haven. A handful of parents were scattered through the bleachers, all waiting for the final horn. Marquis scored again. No one applauded. The Red Knights were down by twelve with two minutes to go.

At the far end of the court, a man walked through the door under the scoreboard and leaned against the retractable bleachers. The guy looked out of place. He wore a dark suit with a white shirt and a burgundy tie, all under a trench coat. Coach Kyle thought he was probably a cop or agent of some sort. It would not be the first arrest in or around the gym.

The agent/cop cast a long suspicious look at the Red Knights' bench, and his eyes seemed to settle on Coach Kyle, who returned the stare for a second before it became uncomfortable. For a twenty-five-year-old law student with no criminal record and no illegal proclivities, the presence and attention of a man who gave all indications of being employed by some branch of law enforcement should have caused no concern. But it never worked that way with Kyle McAvoy. Street cops didn't bother him. But the guys in dark suits, the investigators and agents, the ones trained to dig deep and discover secrets—those types still unnerved him.

Thirty seconds to go and Marquis made a dumb foul that stopped the clock and prolonged the misery. Coach Kyle yelled at his star, who never listened. He ran his finger over the side of his neck, then flicked off the perspiration. It was early February, and the gym was, as always, quite chilly.

Why was he sweating?

The agent/cop hadn't moved an inch; he seemed to enjoy staring at Kyle.

The horn finally squawked. The game was mercifully over. Both teams lined up for the obligatory high fives, and as Kyle congratulated the opposing coach, he glanced down the court. The man was gone.

What were the odds he was waiting outside? Kyle wondered, acknowledging the paranoia.

The Red Knights regrouped in the visitors' cramped locker room, and Coach Kyle said all the right things—nice effort, our game is improving in certain areas, let's finish on a high note this Saturday. The boys were changing clothes and hardly listening. They were tired of basketball because they were tired of losing, and of course all blame was heaped upon the coach. He was too young, too white, too much of an Ivy Leaguer.

The few parents who were there waited outside the locker room, and Kyle knew there would be the usual complaints. It was those tense moments when the team came out that he hated most about coaching.

From the locker room, another door led to a narrow hallway that ran behind the home stands and out into an alley. Kyle was not the first coach to discover this escape route, and on this night he wanted to avoid not only the families but also the agent/cop. He said a quick goodbye to his boys and made his escape. In seconds he was outside, and walking quickly along an icy sidewalk. The temperature was somewhere far below freezing. It was 8.30 on a Wednesday evening, and he was headed for the law-journal offices at the Yale Law School, where he would work until midnight at least.

He didn't make it.

The agent was leaning against the fender of a red Jeep Cherokee that was parked on the street. The vehicle was titled to one John McAvoy of York, Pennsylvania, but for the past six years the true owner was his son, Kyle.

Though his feet suddenly felt like bricks and his knees were weak, Kyle managed to trudge on. Not only did they find me, he said to himself, but they found my Jeep. I have done nothing wrong, he said again and again.

'Tough game, Coach,' the agent said when Kyle was ten feet away.

Kyle stopped and took in the thick-set young man with red cheeks. 'Can I help you?' he said, and immediately saw the shadow of Agent No. 2 dart across the street. They always worked in pairs.

No. 1 reached into a pocket. 'That's exactly what you can do,' he said, pulling out a leather wallet and flipping it open. 'Bob Plant, FBI.'

'A real pleasure,' Kyle said, as all the blood left his brain.

No. 2 wedged himself into the frame. He was much thinner and ten years older. He, too, had a pocketful, and he performed the badge presentation with ease. 'Nelson Ginyard, FBI,' he said. 'Got a minute to talk?'

'Not really.'

'You might want to,' Ginyard said. 'It could be very productive.'

'I doubt that.'

'If you leave, we'll just follow,' Plant said, as he stood from his slouch position and took a step closer. 'You don't want us on campus, do you?'

'Are you threatening me?' Kyle asked. The sweat was back, now in the pits of his arms, and despite the arctic air a bead or two ran down his ribs.

'Not yet,' Plant said with a smirk.

'Look, let's spend ten minutes together, over coffee,' Ginyard said. 'There's a sandwich shop just around the corner. I'm sure it's warmer there.'

'Do I need a lawyer?'

'No.'

'That's what you always say. My father is a lawyer. I know your tricks.'

'No tricks, Kyle, I swear,' Ginyard said, and he at least sounded genuine. 'Just give us ten minutes. I promise you won't regret it.'

'What's on the agenda?'

They looked at each other, and both shrugged. Then Ginyard turned and said, 'Duquesne University. Five years ago. Drunk frat boys and a girl.'

Kyle's body and mind had different reactions. His body conceded—a quick slump of the shoulders, a slight gasp, a noticeable jerk in the legs. But his mind fought back instantly. 'That's bullshit!' he said. 'I've already been through this. Nothing happened and you know it.'

There was a long pause. Kyle's mind was spinning. Why was the FBI involved in an alleged state crime? Should he shut up? Should he call his father? No, under no circumstances would he call his father.

Ginyard took three steps closer. 'Let's cut to the chase, Mr McAvoy, because I'm freezing. There's an indictment out of Pittsburgh, OK. Rape. If you run to get a lawyer, then the indictment comes down tomorrow and the life you have planned is pretty much shot to shit. However, if you give us ten minutes of your valuable time, right now, in the sandwich shop around the corner, then the indictment will be put on hold, if not forgotten altogether.'

'Why should I trust you?' Kyle managed to say with a very dry mouth.

'Ten minutes.'

'You got a tape recorder?'

'Sure.'

'OK, I want every word recorded because I don't trust you.'

'Fair enough.'

They jammed their hands deep into the pockets of their trench coats and stomped away. Kyle unlocked his Jeep and got inside. He started the engine, turned the heat on high and thought about driving away.

BUSTER'S DELI was long and narrow with red vinyl booths along the wall to the right. To the left was a bar and a grill behind a counter, and a row of pinball machines. Kyle had eaten there a few times.

The last two booths were properly secured by the federal government. Yet another trench coat stood at the last table, chatting with Plant and Ginyard, waiting. When Kyle made his slow approach, the agent glanced at him, then offered the standard smirk before sitting in the next booth, where No. 4 was waiting, sipping coffee. Plant and Ginyard had ordered sandwich platters with subs and fries, all of it untouched. Kyle slid into the booth.

'It takes four?' he asked, nodding towards the booth behind him.

'That's just what you can see,' Ginyard said.

'Would you like a sandwich?' Plant asked.

'No.' An hour earlier he had been famished. Now his digestive system was on the verge of meltdown and he was struggling to breathe normally. He removed a pen and a note card from his pocket, and with all the nerve he could summon, said, 'Could I see a photo ID?'

'What the hell?' Ginyard growled.

'Photo ID, please. I'm not talking until I finish the preliminaries. Just show me your driver's licence. I'll show you mine.'

'We already have a copy of yours.'

'Whatever. Let's have it.'

Ginyard rolled his eyes as he produced a Connecticut licence.

Kyle examined it and jotted down the birth date and licence data. 'Which office are you guys from?' he asked.

'Hartford,' Ginyard said. He nodded at the next booth and added, 'They're from Pittsburgh.'

'Nice.'

Kyle then examined Plant's driver's licence, and when he had finished, he said, 'Where's that tape recorder?'

Plant produced a slender digital recorder and flipped it on.

'Please give the date, time and place,' Kyle said with an air of confidence that surprised even him. 'And please state that the interrogation has yet to begin and that no statements have been made before now.'

'Yes, sir. I love law students,' Plant said. He placed the recorder in the centre of the table and announced the preliminaries.

Kyle glanced at his watch. 'OK. You asked for ten minutes.'

Both agents leaned forward, all four elbows in a row, the booth suddenly smaller. 'You remember a guy named Bennie Wright, chief investigator, sex crimes, Pittsburgh PD?' Ginyard asked.

'No.'

'You didn't meet him five years ago during the investigation?'

'I don't remember meeting a Bennie Wright. Could have, but I don't remember. It was, after all, five years since the non-event did not happen.'

They both absorbed this, watching every nervous twitch of Kyle's eyelids. Then Ginyard said, 'Well, Detective Wright is here in town, and he would like to meet with you in about an hour.'

'Another meeting?'

'If you don't mind. It won't take long, and there's a good chance you can head off the indictment.'

'Indictment for what, exactly?'

'Rape.'

'There was no rape. The Pittsburgh police decided that five years ago.'

'Well, it looks like the girl is back,' Ginyard said. 'She's put her life back together, gone through some extensive therapy and, best of all, she's got herself a lawyer now.'

Since Ginyard stopped without a question, there was no need for a response, but Kyle couldn't help but sink an inch or two. Keep talking, he said to himself, but don't say anything.

'If the indictment has been issued, how can it be stopped?' he asked.

'It's under seal, by court order,' Ginyard said. 'According to Detective Wright, the prosecutor has a deal for you, one that the victim's lawyer cooked up, one that will allow you to walk away from this mess. You play ball and the indictment against you will never see the light of day.'

'I'm still confused. You guys didn't advise me of my Miranda rights.'

'This is not an interrogation,' Plant finally said. 'It's not an investigation.' Then he reached into the smoked-tuna basket and pulled out a greasy fry.

'What the hell is it?'

'A meeting.'

There was a long pause as all three considered the next move. Plant chomped on his second fry, but his eyes never left Kyle.

Finally, Kyle leaned forward on his elbows, and with the recorder just inches away he said, 'There was no rape, no crime. I did nothing wrong.'

'Fine, talk to Wright.'

'And where is he?'

'At ten o'clock, he'll be at the Holiday Inn on Saw Mill Road, room 222.'

'This is a bad idea. I need a lawyer. I'm leaving. Turn off the recorder.'

Neither made any move towards the recorder.

Kyle looked at it, then leaned down and said, very clearly, 'This is Kyle McAvoy. The time is eight fifty p.m. I have nothing else to say, and I am leaving Buster's Deli right now.'

He was almost out of the booth when Plant blurted, 'He's got the video.'

A horse kick to the groin could not have hit harder. Kyle clutched the red vinyl and looked as though he might faint. Slowly, he sat down again. He reached for a plastic cup and took a long sip of water.

The video. A fraternity brother, one of the drunks at the little party, had allegedly recorded something with his cellphone. Supposedly, there were images of the girl, naked on a sofa, too drunk to move, and admiring her were three or four Beta brothers, naked, too, or in the process of undressing. Kyle vaguely remembered the scene, but he'd never seen the video. The cops in

Pittsburgh hadn't found it. It had been destroyed, according to Beta legend.

'What video?' Kyle managed to ask, but it was lame and unconvincing.

'The one you boys hid from the cops,' Plant said, barely moving his lips. 'The one that places you at the scene of the crime. The one that will destroy your life and send you away for twenty years.'

'I don't know what you're talking about,' Kyle said, then drank some more water. Waves of nausea crashed through his stomach and head.

'Oh, I think you do,' Ginyard said.

'Have you seen this video?' Kyle asked.

Both nodded.

'Then you know I didn't touch the girl.'

'Maybe not. But you were there,' Ginyard said. 'You were an accessory.'

To keep from throwing up, Kyle closed his eyes and began rubbing his temples. The girl was a groupie, a wild little thing who'd spent more time in the Beta fraternity house than in her dorm room. The brothers of Beta passed her around. When she cried rape, the brothers had instantly gone mute and solidified into an impenetrable wall of denial and innocence. The cops eventually gave up when she proved too unreliable with the details. No charges were filed. She later left Duquesne and mercifully disappeared. The great miracle of the ugly little episode was that it had been kept quiet.

'The indictment names you and three others,' Ginyard said.

'There was no rape,' Kyle said, as he continued to rub his temples. 'If she had sex, I promise you it was by consent.'

'Not if she blacked out,' Ginyard said.

'We're not here to argue, Kyle,' Plant said. 'We're here to help cut a deal. If you cooperate, then this will all go away, at least your part of it.'

'What kind of deal?'

'Detective Wright will handle that.'

Kyle slowly sat back. He wanted to plead, to beg, to explain that this wasn't fair, that he was about to graduate and start a career. His future held so much promise. His past was unblemished. Almost. But they already knew that, didn't they?

'All right, all right,' he said. 'I'll be there.'

Ginyard leaned closer and said, 'You have one hour. If you make a phone call, we'll know. If you try to run, we'll follow, OK? You're making the right decision here, Kyle. Just keep it up and this will all go away. You'll see.'

Kyle left them there with their cold fries and bitter coffee. He made it to his Jeep, then drove to his apartment three blocks from campus. Then he locked his bedroom door, turned off the light and stretched out on the floor.

IT WAS AN OLD Holiday Inn, built in the 1960s, when motels and fast-food chains raced to build along the highways and frontage roads. Kyle had passed it a hundred times and never seen it.

The parking lot was dark and one-third full when he backed the red Jeep into a space next to a minivan from Indiana. He turned off the lights but left the engine running and the heater on. A light snow was falling.

In the past hour he'd thought of calling his father, but that conversation would take far too long. John McAvoy would provide sound legal advice, and quickly, but the back story had many complications. He'd thought of calling two of his Beta brothers from Duquesne, but then any advice they might give would be as unsound as the strategies racing through his mind. No sense ruining their lives. And in the horror of the moment he'd thought of the various schemes he could use to disappear. A mad dash to the airport, or the bus station. A long jump off a tall bridge. But they were watching, weren't they? And probably listening, too.

When the digital clock on the radio hit 9:58, he turned off the engine and stepped into the snow. He walked bravely across the asphalt. Could this be his last moment of freedom? He'd read so many cases of criminal defendants freely walking into the police station for a few quick questions, only to be charged, handcuffed and jailed. He could still run, to somewhere.

The glass doors slammed behind him. He paused in the deserted lobby and imagined he heard the clanging of cell-block iron at his back. As he rode the elevator to the second floor, he asked himself what kind of fool would voluntarily enter a motel room filled with cops and agents all hell-bent on accusing him of something that never happened. Why was he doing this?

The video.

He had never seen it. He did not know anyone who had seen it. In the secret world of Beta there were rumours and denials and threats, but no one had even known for sure if the 'Elaine thing' had actually been recorded. The reality that it had, and that the evidence was now in the possession of the Pittsburgh police and the FBI, made him ponder the bridge scenario.

Wait a minute. I did nothing wrong. I did not touch that girl, not that night anyway.

No one touched her. At least that was the sworn and battle-tested version within the Beta fraternity. But what if the video proved otherwise?

The noxious smell of fresh paint hit him as he stepped into the hallway on the second floor. He stopped at room 222 and knocked three times. The lock chain rattled, the door was jerked open and Special Agent Nelson Edward Ginyard said, 'Glad you could make it.'

Kyle stepped inside, leaving the old world behind. The new one was suddenly terrifying.

Ginyard had his jacket off, and strapped over his shirt was a shoulder harness, with a black pistol in a black holster snug under his left arm. Agent Plant and the two others from Buster's were staring, and all three were also coatless so that Kyle could get the full measure of their arsenal. Identical 9mm Berettas, with matching holsters and harnesses. Seriously armed men.

'Good move,' Plant said, nodding now.

Kyle was beginning to think that coming here was a very stupid move.

Room 222 had been converted into a makeshift field office. The bed had been pushed into a corner. The curtains were closed. Two folding tables had been hauled in and were covered with files and thick envelopes and notepads. Three laptops were open and on, and in the one nearest the door Kyle caught a glimpse of himself, from his high-school yearbook. Central York High School, class of 2001. Tacked to the bare wall behind the tables were colour photos of three of his Beta brothers and Elaine Keenan. Kyle felt light-headed as he observed the power of his government in action.

'Do you mind emptying your pockets?' Ginyard said.

'You think I'm armed? You think I might pull out a knife on you guys?'

One of the other agents saw the humour and broke the ice with a good laugh. Kyle pulled out his key ring, jangled its collection for Ginyard to see and put it back in his pocket. Then Plant began a very soft and quick frisk. When he finished he disappeared into the other room.

'Detective Wright is across the hall,' Ginyard said. Yet another room.

Kyle followed him out into the stuffy hallway, then waited as he tapped gently on the door to room 225. When it opened, Kyle entered alone.

Bennie Wright displayed no weaponry. He offered a quick handshake while spitting out, 'Detective Wright, Pittsburgh PD.'

Wright was in his late forties, short, trim, bald with a few strands of black hair slicked back just above his ears. His eyes were also black and partially concealed behind a pair of reading glasses perched halfway down his narrow nose. He closed the door behind Kyle, then waved at two cheap metal chairs facing each other on either side of a folding table.

'Let's talk, Kyle,' he said pleasantly, and Kyle realised he had a slight accent. English was not his first language. It was odd. A man named Bennie Wright from Pittsburgh should not have a foreign accent.

There was a small video camera mounted on a tripod in one corner. Wires ran to a laptop on the table. 'Please, sit down,' Wright said, waving at one chair as he settled himself into the other.

'I want all of this recorded,' Kyle said.

Wright glanced over his shoulder at the camera and said, 'No problem.'

Slowly, Kyle walked to the other chair and sat down. Wright was rolling up the sleeves of his white shirt. His necktie was already loose.

'Turn on the camera,' Kyle said. Wright punched the laptop, and Kyle's face appeared on the screen. He looked at himself and saw nothing but fear.

Wright opened a thick file and took out some paperwork. 'First, he said, 'we need to cover your Miranda rights.'

'No,' Kyle said softly. 'First we need to see your badge and ID.'

This clearly irritated the detective, but he fished out a wallet from a rear pocket, opened it and said, 'Had this for twenty-two years now.'

Kyle examined the bronze badge. Benjamin J. Wright, Pittsburgh Police Department, officer number 6658. 'How about a driver's licence?'

Wright yanked open his wallet again, fingered through some cards and then flung down a Pennsylvania licence. 'Satisfied now?' he snapped.

Kyle handed it back and asked, 'Why is the FBI involved in this?'

'Can we finish up with Miranda?' Wright was readjusting the paperwork.

'Sure. I understand Miranda.'

'I'm sure you do. A top law student at one of our most prestigious law schools.' Kyle was reading as Wright was talking. 'You have the right to remain silent. Anything you say can and will be used against you in court. You have the right to an attorney. If you can't afford one, then the state will provide one. Any questions?'

'No.' He signed his name on two forms and slid them back to Wright.

'Why is the FBI involved?' He repeated the question.

'Believe me, Kyle, the FBI is the least of your problems.' Wright spoke slowly, with authority. 'We have so much ground to cover, and time is slipping by. Did you ever play football?'

'Yes.'

'Then let's say this table is a football field. Not a great analogy, but one that will work. You are here, at this goal line.' With his left hand he striped an imaginary line in front of the laptop. 'You have a hundred yards to go, to score, to win, to walk out of here in one piece.' With his right hand, he laid down the other goal line, next to the heavy file. His hands were four feet apart. 'A hundred yards, Kyle, bear with me, OK?'

'OK.'

He pulled his hands together and tapped a fresh legal pad. 'Somewhere in here, at about the fifty, I'll show you the video that is the source of this conflict. You won't like it, Kyle. It will make you ill. Sick to your stomach.

But then we will continue your little march to the goal line, and when we get there, you will once again see yourself as the golden boy with an unlimited future and an unblemished past.' His right hand tapped the goal line. 'Now, we need to start with some background, OK?'

'Whatever.'

Wright pulled some papers from the file, studied them for a second, then picked up a pen. 'You were born on February 4, 1983, in York, Pennsylvania, third child and only son of John and Patty McAvoy. They divorced in 1989, and neither has remarried, correct?'

'Correct.'

Wright made a check mark, then launched into a series of quick questions about family members, their birth dates, education, jobs, addresses, hobbies, church affiliations, even politics. Wright had his facts straight.

'Your father is a general practice lawyer in York?'

Kyle only nodded. Then a barrage about his father, his mother, his life and career and interests. Kyle wanted to ask, 'Is this really relevant?' but he held his tongue.

Finally, the detective finished with the family and settled on Kyle.

'Honours from Central York High, star athlete, Eagle Scout. Why did you select Duquesne University?'

'They offered me a basketball scholarship.'

'But you didn't play much at Duquesne.'

'I played thirteen minutes as a freshman, then tore a knee ligament in the final minute of the final game.'

'Surgery?'

'Yes, but the knee was gone. I quit basketball and joined a fraternity.'

'You majored in economics and made near-perfect grades. What happened in Spanish your second year? You didn't make an A?'

'I should have taken German, I guess.'

'One B in four years is not bad.' Wright flipped a page, made a note. 'High honours, a dozen or so student organisations, fraternity secretary then president. Your academic record is impressive, yet you managed to also maintain a pretty active social life. Tell me about your first arrest.'

'Only one. A first, not a second. It was typical frat stuff. A loud party that didn't stop until the cops showed up. I got caught with an open container, a bottle of beer. I paid a fine of three hundred bucks and got six months' probation. After that, the record was expunged and Yale never knew about it.'

'I thought there was a second arrest.'

'No. I was stopped by the cops once on campus, but there was no arrest.'

'Why were you stopped?'

'A couple of fraternities were shooting bottle rockets at each other. I wasn't involved. Nothing went in my file, so I'm wondering how you heard about it.'

Wright ignored this and wrote something on his legal pad. When he finished scribbling, he said, 'Why did you decide to go to law school?'

'I always wanted to be a lawyer. My first job was running the copier in my father's office. I sort of grew up there.'

'Where did you apply to law school?'

'Penn, Yale, Cornell and Stanford.'

'Where were you accepted?'

'All four.'

'Did Yale offer scholarship money?'

'Financial incentives, yes. So did the others.'

'Have you borrowed money?'

'Yes. When I graduate in May, I'll owe about sixty thousand.'

Wright nodded as if he agreed that this was the correct amount.

'And you write for the law journal?'

'I'm the editor in chief of the *Yale Law Journal*.'

'That's the most prestigious honour in the school?'

'According to some.'

'You clerked last summer in New York. Tell me about it.'

'It was one of those huge Wall Street firms, Scully & Pershing, a typical summer clerkship. We were wined and dined and given easy hours, the same seduction routine all the big firms use. They pamper the clerks, then kill them when they become associates.'

'Did Scully & Pershing offer you a position after graduation?'

'Yes.'

'Did you accept or decline?'

'Neither. I have not made a decision yet.'

'Do you have other job offers?'

'I had other offers, yes. Why don't you just show me the video so we can skip all this bullshit? If it really exists, and if it implicates me, then I'll walk out of here and go hire a lawyer.'

Wright leaned forward and began gently tapping his fingertips together. The lower half of his face eased into a smile while the upper half was non-committal. 'Losing your temper, Kyle,' he said, 'could cost you your life.'

Life as in dead body, or life as in brilliant future? Kyle took a deep breath. The flash of anger was gone, replaced by the crush of confusion and fear.

The fake smile widened, and Wright said, 'Please, Kyle, you're doing fine here. Just a few more questions and we'll move into rougher territory. The other firms?'

'I was offered a job by Logan & Kupec in New York, Baker Potts in San Francisco and Garton in London. I said no to all three. I'm still kicking around a public-interest job down in Virginia, a legal-aid position helping migrant workers.'

'At a much lower salary?'

'Oh, yes. Much.'

'How will you pay back your student loans?'

'I'll figure that out.'

Wright looked as though he didn't like the smart-ass answer. Perhaps he already knew that Kyle's $61,000 in student loans would be forgiven by Yale if he spent the next three years working for minimum wage protecting the poor, the oppressed, the abused or the environment.

'Which way are you leaning?' Wright asked.

'I'm not.'

Wright reached for the file, frowning as if he'd been insulted. He flipped through some papers, then glared at Kyle. 'You haven't made a verbal commitment to accept a position with Piedmont Legal Aid, in Winchester, Virginia, beginning September the 2nd?'

A rush of warm air escaped through Kyle's dry lips. He almost blurted, 'How the hell do you know this?' but to do so would be to admit the truth. Nor could he deny the truth. Wright already knew.

As he was lurching towards some lame response, his adversary moved in for the kill. 'Let's call this Lie Number One, OK, Kyle?' Wright said with a sneer. 'Should we somehow arrive at Lie Number Two, then we turn off the camera, say good night, and meet again tomorrow for the arrest. Handcuffs, perp walk, mug shot, maybe a reporter or two. You won't be thinking about Wall Street then. Don't lie to me, Kyle. I know too much.'

Kyle almost said, 'Yes, sir,' but instead managed only an affirmative nod.

'What do you think of Scully & Pershing?'

'Big, powerful, rich. I think it's the largest law firm in the world. Some really smart folks who work very hard and put enormous pressure on each other, especially on their young associates.'

'Your kind of work?'

'It's hard to say. The money is great. The work is brutal. But it's the big leagues. I'll probably end up there.'

Wright chewed the end of his pen for a moment, staring at Kyle as if he were a psychiatrist, analysing the patient. 'Let's talk about your fraternity at

Duquesne. There were about ten members of your pledge class, right?'

'Nine.'

'The indictment names you and three others, so let's talk about the other three. Where is Alan Strock?'

The indictment. Somewhere in that damned file was the indictment. How could his name be listed as a defendant? He had not touched the girl. He had not seen anyone having sex. He had not witnessed a rape. He vaguely recalled being present in the room, but he had blacked out at some point during the night. How could he be an accomplice if he wasn't conscious? That would be his defence at trial, and a solid defence it would be, but the spectre of a trial was too awful to imagine. Kyle closed his eyes and rubbed his temples, and he thought about the phone calls home, first to his father and then to his mother. Other phone calls would follow: to the recruiting directors who'd offered him jobs. He would proclaim his innocence and all that, but he knew he would never shake the suspicion of rape.

'Alan Strock?' Wright asked again.

'He's in med school at Ohio State.'

'Any recent correspondence?'

'An email a couple of days ago.'

'And Joey Bernardo?'

'He's still in Pittsburgh, working for a brokerage firm.'

'Recent contact?'

'By phone, a few days ago.'

'Any mention of Elaine Keenan with Alan or Joey?'

'No.'

'You boys have tried to forget about Elaine, haven't you?'

'Yes.'

'Well, she's back.'

'Evidently.'

Wright readjusted himself in the chair. 'Elaine left Duquesne after her freshman year,' he began in a softer voice, as if he had a long tale to tell. 'She was troubled. Her grades were a mess. She now claims that the rape brought on severe emotional distress. She lived with her parents for a year or so, then began drifting. There was a lot of self-medication, booze and drugs. She saw some therapists, but nothing helped. Have you heard any of this?'

'No. After she left school, there was not a word.'

'Anyway, she has an older sister in Scranton who took her in, got her some help, paid for rehab, found a good shrink. Now she's clean, sober, feels great, and her memory has improved dramatically. She's also found herself a lawyer, and of course she is demanding justice.'

'You sound sceptical.'

'I'm a cop, Kyle. I'm sceptical of everything, but I have this young woman who is credible and who says she was raped, and I have a video that is pretty powerful evidence. And on top of that, her lawyer's out for blood.'

'This is a shakedown, isn't it? All about money?'

'What do you mean, Kyle?'

'The fourth defendant is Baxter Tate, and of course we know what that's all about. The Tate family is very rich. Old Pittsburgh money. Baxter was born with trust funds. How much does she want?'

'I'll ask the questions. Did you ever have sex—?'

'Yes, I had sex with Elaine Keenan, as did most of my pledge class. She was wild as hell, spent more time in the Beta house than most Betas, could drink any three of us under the table, and always had a purse full of pills. Her problems began long before she arrived in Duquesne. Believe me, she does not want to go to trial.'

'How many times did you have sex with her?'

'Once, about a month before the alleged rape.' The night Kyle had sex with her, he'd been in his own bed, sound asleep, when she crawled under the sheets naked and quickly got what she wanted.

'Do you know if Baxter Tate had sexual relations with Elaine Keenan on the night in question?'

Kyle paused, took a deep breath, and said, 'No, I do not. I blacked out.'

'Did Baxter Tate admit to having sex with her that night?'

'Not to me.'

'Where is Baxter?' Wright asked after a long, heavy pause.

'Somewhere in LA. He barely graduated, then went to Hollywood to become an actor. He's not too stable.'

'Meaning?'

'He comes from a wealthy family that's even more dysfunctional than most wealthy families. He's a hard partier, lots of booze and drugs and girls. His goal in life is to become a great actor and drink himself to death. He wants to die young, sort of like James Dean.'

'Has he been in any films?'

'Not a single one. Lots of bars, though.'

Wright suddenly seemed bored with the questions. He had stopped his scribbling. His hard stare began to drift. He stuffed some papers back into the file, tapped a finger on the table and said, 'We've made progress, Kyle, thank you. The ball is at midfield. You want to see the video?'

2

Wright stood for the first time, stretched, and stepped to a corner where a small cardboard box was waiting. It was white, and on it someone had printed, with a black marker, the words 'IN RE: KYLE L. MCAVOY ET AL.' Kyle McAvoy and others. Wright fetched something from the box, removed a disk from its sleeve, slid it into the drive on the laptop, punched a couple of keys, then took his seat. Kyle could barely breathe.

As the computer clicked and hummed, Wright began talking. 'The phone was a Nokia 6000 smartphone, manufactured in 2003, with ETI Camcorder software installed, voice commands, voice activated, state of the art for the time. A really nice cellphone.'

'Owned by?'

Wright shot him a smart-ass grin. 'Sorry, Kyle,' he said. 'Now, it's Friday, April the 25th, 2003, last day of classes, final exams start in a week. It's unseasonably warm for Pittsburgh, and the kids at Duquesne decide to do what all good college kids do everywhere. They start drinking in the afternoon and plan to drink all night. A crowd gathers at the apartment complex where you rent a place with three others. A party materialises by the pool. It's mostly Beta brothers and a few girls. Sometime after dark, the party moves inside, to your apartment. Pizza is ordered. The music is loud. More beer. Somebody shows up with two bottles of tequila, and this is mixed with Red Bull and consumed as fast as possible. Remember any of this?'

Kyle nodded, his eyes never leaving the screen.

'At some point, clothes start coming off, and the owner of the cellphone decides to secretly record this. Guess he wanted his own little video of the girls without their tops. Our best guess is he placed his cellphone on that narrow counter that separates the kitchen from the den, turned it on and hid it next to a phone book. The opening scene is pretty wild. We've studied it carefully, and there are six girls and nine boys, all dancing and in various stages of undress. Ring a bell, Kyle?'

'Some of it, yes. You gonna show it to me or just talk about it?'

'Don't be so anxious to see it.' Wright punched another key. 'It's eleven fourteen p.m. when the video begins,' he said, then hit another key.

The screen suddenly exploded into a frenzy of loud music and gyrating bodies. Somewhere in the back of his brain Kyle had hoped for a grainy, fuzzy clip of a bunch of Beta idiots drinking in the dark. Instead, he gawked at a remarkably clear video shot. The angle chosen by the phone's owner provided a view of almost the entire den at 4880 East Chase, apartment 6B.

All fifteen hell-raisers appeared to be very drunk. All six girls were indeed topless, as were most of the guys. Everyone held a drink in one hand; half had a cigarette or a joint in the other. The dance was a group grope. Bodies came together for a few seconds, then parted and moved to the next one. Some of the guests were loud and rowdy, singing along with the band, while others appeared to be fading under the flood of alcohol and chemicals.

'I believe that's you with the sunglasses,' Wright said smugly.

'Thank you.'

Sunglasses, yellow Pirates cap, gym shorts drooping low. A plastic cup in one hand, a cigarette in the other. Mouth open to sing along. A drunken fool. A twenty-year-old lunatic on the verge of another blackout.

Now, five years later, there was no nostalgia for those rowdy college days. But there was no remorse, either. Kyle felt embarrassed that he'd been caught on tape, but he'd partied no more and no less than anyone he knew.

'This goes on for about eight more minutes,' Wright said, glancing at his notes. 'As you can see, Elaine Keenan is not present. She says she was next door, drinking with some friends.'

'So she's changed her story again.'

Wright ignored this and said, 'If you don't mind, I'll fast-forward a little, to the point where the police show up. Remember the cops, Kyle?'

'Yes.'

The video scrambled forward for a minute or so, until Wright pressed a key. 'At eleven twenty-five, the party comes to an abrupt halt. Listen.'

In mid-song, and with most of the fifteen still in view, someone off camera clearly yelled, 'Cops! Cops!' Kyle watched himself as he disappeared from view. The music stopped. The lights went out.

Wright continued: 'According to our records, the police were called to your apartment three times that spring. This was the third time. Alan Strock, one of your room-mates, answered the door. He swore there was no underage drinking. He'd be happy to turn off the music and keep things quiet. The cops gave him a break and left with a warning. They assumed everybody else was hiding in the bedrooms.

'Most of them fled through the back door,' Kyle said.

'Whatever. The cellphone video was on voice activation, so it clicked off after sixty seconds of near silence. Its owner ran off in the panic, forgot about it, and in the melee someone knocked things around on the counter, the cellphone got bumped, so we can't see as much as we could before. About twenty minutes pass and all is quiet. At eleven forty-eight, there are voices and the lights come on.' Kyle moved closer to the screen. About a third of the view was blocked by something yellow. 'Probably a phone book,' Wright said. The music started again, but at a much lower volume.

The four room-mates, Kyle, Alan Strock, Baxter Tate and Joey Bernardo, were walking around the den, in shorts and T-shirts, holding drinks again. Elaine Keenan walked through the den, talking nonstop, then sat on the edge of the sofa, smoking what appeared to be a joint. A television, unseen, was turned on. Baxter Tate walked over to Elaine, said something, then put his drink down and yanked off his T-shirt. He and Elaine fell into a pile on the sofa, obviously making out while the other three watched television and milled about. They were talking, but the music and TV drowned out their words. There were no sounds from Elaine. Less than half of the sofa was visible now, but a tangle of bare legs could be seen.

Then the lights were turned off, and for a second the room was dark. Slowly, the glare from the television focused and bounced off the walls to provide some illumination. Joey Bernardo came into view, pulling off his shirt. He stopped and stared at the sofa, where some manner of frenzied activity was under way.

'Listen,' Wright hissed.

Joey said something that Kyle could not understand.

'Did you get that?' Wright asked.

'No.'

Wright stopped the video and said, 'Our experts have studied the audio. Joey Bernardo says to Baxter Tate, "Is she awake?" Tate is obviously having sex with Elaine, who's passed out drunk, and Bernardo stops by, takes it all in, and wonders if the girl is actually conscious. You want to hear it again?'

'Yes.'

Wright reset the video, then replayed it. Kyle leaned down, and with his nose six inches from the screen he watched hard, listened even harder, and heard the word 'awake'. The detective shook his head gravely.

The action continued, with the music and the television as a backdrop. Baxter Tate finally got off the sofa, stood, appeared to be completely nude, and walked away. Another figure, Joey Bernardo, quickly took Baxter's place. Some of the sounds could barely be heard.

A steady clicking arose from the scene. 'We think that's the sofa,' Wright said. 'Don't suppose you could help on that one?'

'No.'

Before long there was a high-pitched heaving sound, and the clicking stopped. Joey moved from the sofa and disappeared.

'That's pretty much the end of the movie,' Wright said. 'The video goes on for another twelve minutes, but nothing happens. If Elaine moved or got off the sofa, it's not on the video. We're almost certain that Baxter Tate and Joey Bernardo had sex with her. There's no evidence that you or Alan Strock did.'

'I did not. I can assure you of that.'

'Any idea where you were during the rapes, Kyle?'

'I'm sure you have a theory.'

'OK. Elaine says she woke up several hours later, around three in the morning, naked, still on the sofa, and suddenly had a vague recollection of being raped. She admits she was still very drunk, and wasn't sure where she was. She finds her clothes and gets dressed. When she sees you fast asleep in a recliner facing the television, she realises where she is and remembers more of what happened to her. There's no sign of Strock, Tate or Bernardo. She speaks to you, shakes your shoulder, but you do not respond, so she hurries from the apartment, goes next door and eventually falls asleep.'

'And doesn't mention rape for four days, right, Detective, or has she changed her story again?'

'Four days is correct.'

'Thank you. Not a word to anyone for four days. Not to her room-mate, her friends, parents, no one. Then she suddenly decided she was raped. The police were very suspicious of her story, right? They finally showed up at our apartment, and they asked questions and got very few answers. Why? Because there was no rape. Everything was consensual.'

'How could she consent if she was unconscious, Kyle?'

'If she was unconscious, how could she remember being raped? There was no medical exam. No evidence whatsoever. Just the blacked-out memory of a very confused young woman. The cops dropped the case.'

'The grand jury believe the video proves there was a rape.'

'That's bullshit. This isn't about rape; this is about money. Baxter Tate's family is filthy rich. The indictment is nothing but a shakedown.'

'So you're willing to risk the spectacle of a trial, and a conviction? You want the jury to see that video? You and your three roomies drunk out of your minds while a young woman is taken advantage of?'

'I didn't touch her.'

'No, but you were there, very close by, less than ten feet away. Come on.'

'I don't remember it.'

'How convenient.'

Kyle slowly got to his feet, then sat on the edge of the bed and buried his head in his hands. He found it impossible to think rationally. He had an image of himself and his three pals sitting in a crowded courtroom, judge frowning, jurors gaping, Elaine crying, his parents stoic in the front row as the video is played to a rapt audience. The scene made him sick. He felt innocent but he wasn't sure the jurors would agree.

'Is she awake?' Joey asked Baxter. How many times would that question echo round the courtroom before the jurors retired to consider the verdicts?

Wright sat patiently at the table, hairy hands folded on his legal pad.

'Are we at midfield?' Kyle asked, breaking the silence.

'Past midfield, around the forty and driving.'

'I'd like to see the indictment.'

'Sure.'

The detective began a series of movements that were immediately confusing. First, he pulled his wallet out of his rear left pocket, removed his driver's licence and placed it on the table. He produced his Pittsburgh PD badge and laid it beside the licence. From a box on the floor he pulled other cards and other badges and began arranging them on the table. He reached for a file marked INFORMATION, handed it to Kyle and said, 'Happy reading.'

Kyle opened the file and removed a stack of papers stapled together. The top one looked official. A bold title read: 'Commonwealth of Pennsylvania, Allegheny County, Court of Common Pleas.' A smaller heading read: 'Commonwealth versus Baxter F. Tate, Joseph N. Bernardo, Kyle L. McAvoy and Alan B. Strock.'

Wright produced a pair of scissors and methodically cut his driver's licence into two perfect squares, then started on the other plastic cards.

Kyle read on: 'This prosecution is in the name of and by the authority of the Commonwealth of Pennsylvania against the above-named—'

Wright ripped his bronze badge from its leather wallet and bounced it on the table.

'What are you doing?' Kyle finally asked.

'Destroying the evidence.'

'What evidence?'

'Read page two.'

Kyle, who was at the bottom of page one, flipped to page two. It was blank. He flipped to page three, then four, then five. All blank. Kyle held the bogus indictment and gawked at the detective.

'There is no indictment, Kyle,' Wright proceeded as if it all made sense now. 'No grand jury, no cops, no arrest, no trial. Nothing but a video.'

'No cops?' Kyle sat down.

'Oh, no. I'm not a cop. Those boys across the hall are not FBI agents.'

Kyle rolled his head back like a wounded boxer, then rubbed his eyes. The indictment fell to the floor. 'Who are you?' he managed to grunt.

'That's a very good question, one that will take a long time to answer.'

In disbelief, Kyle picked up one of the badges—Ginyard's. He rubbed it and said, 'But I checked this guy out online. He really works for the FBI.'

'Yes, these are real names. We just borrowed them for the night.'

'So, you're impersonating an officer?'

'Certainly, but it's just a small offence. We needed to convince you to come here and have this little meeting. Otherwise, you might have run away. Plus, we wanted to impress you with our resources.'

'We?'

'Yes, my firm. You see, Kyle, I work for a private contractor and we've been hired to do a job. We need you, and this is how we recruit people.'

Kyle blew out a chestful of nervous laughter. There was a rising thrill at the relief of not being prosecuted. But the anger was beginning to boil.

'You recruit by blackmail?' he asked.

'If necessary. We know where the girl is. She does indeed have a lawyer.'

'Does she know about the video?'

'No, but if she saw it, your life could get very complicated.'

'I'm not sure I follow you.'

'Come on, Kyle. Rape has a twelve-year statute of limitations in Pennsylvania. You have seven years to go. If Elaine and her lawyer knew about the video, they'd threaten criminal prosecution to force a civil settlement. Your life will go much smoother if you play along with us.'

'So you're recruiting me?'

'Yes.'

'To do what?'

'To be a lawyer.'

KYLE GLANCED at his watch. It was after midnight. He looked at Wright, or whatever the hell his name really was, and wanted to bolt across the table and punch his face with as much violence as he could generate. He vetoed the idea. Wright was fit and probably trained and could take care of himself. Kyle leaned back in his chair and relaxed for the first time in hours.

'So what's your real name?'

'Let's stick with Bennie Wright for now. It really doesn't matter, because you'll never know the real name.'

'I like this. Real cloak and dagger stuff. You guys are good. Really had me going there for about four hours. Already thinking about finding a nice bridge to wing it from. I hate your guts and don't ever forget it.'

'When you shut up, we can get down to business.'

'Can I walk out right now?'

'Sure.'

'And no one will grab me? No more phoney FBI agents?'

'Sure. Go. You're a free man.'

'Oh, thank you.'

A minute passed without a word. Kyle's mind raced through a hundred scenarios, but he never once thought of leaving the room.

'Let's talk about your future, Kyle,' Wright finally said.

'Sure. Now that I won't be arrested, the future has certainly improved.'

'This job you're planning to take. Piedmont Legal Aid. Why do you want to waste a couple of years saving the world?'

'I don't see it that way. There are a lot of migrant workers in Virginia, many illegal, and they're subjected to all sorts of abuse. They live in cardboard boxes, work for two bucks an hour. I figure they could use some help.'

Wright was not impressed. 'Let's talk about Scully & Pershing. They offered you a job, right?'

'Correct.'

'Beginning when?'

'September the 2nd of this year. I take the bar exam in July. Where the hell is this going, Bennie?'

'It's going to Scully & Pershing.'

'What if I don't want to work there?'

'You have little choice.'

Kyle leaned on his elbows and rubbed his eyes.

'Have you said no to Scully & Pershing?' Wright asked.

'I'm assuming you already know the answer to that question. I'm assuming you've been listening to my phone conversations for some time.'

'Not all of them.'

'No, I have not said no to Scully & Pershing. I've informed them that I'm giving serious thought to public-interest law for a couple of years, and we've even discussed a deferment. But I need to make a decision.'

'So they still want you?'

'Yes.'

'At a starting salary of two hundred thousand dollars?'

'Something like that. You know the numbers.'

'One of the largest and most prestigious law firms in the world. Come on, Kyle, it's an offer most law students would kill for. Why not take it?'

Kyle jumped to his feet and paced to the door and back. He glared down at Wright and said, 'Let me make sure I follow you. You want me to take the job at Scully & Pershing, for reasons that I'm sure will be against my best interests, and if I say no, then you'll blackmail me with the video and the rape allegations. Right? Is this where we're headed, Bennie?'

'More or less. Blackmail is such an ugly word.'

'I could go to the cops tomorrow and bust your ass. Impersonating an officer, attempted blackmail.'

'You want to run to the cops, go ahead. But you know what will happen, Kyle? I'll tell you what will happen. You'll never see me again. The boys across the hall, the FBI agents, are already gone. Before long, I'll go visit the attorney for Elaine Keenan, show her the video, provide her with the current addresses and phone numbers and emails for you, Alan Strock, Baxter Tate and Joey Bernardo, prod her to have a chat with the prosecutor in Pittsburgh, and before you know it things are out of your control. Maybe charges will be filed, maybe not. But trust me, I will destroy you.'

With that, Wright returned to his notes. Kyle sat on the edge of the bed.

'It could get really ugly,' Wright continued. 'Think about it, Kyle. Yale Law's brightest student arrested on rape charges. The video leaked onto the Internet. A brutal trial. Conviction. Prison. A career ruined.'

'Shut up!'

'No. So let's talk business. Let's take the video and lock it away so that no one will ever see it. How does that sound, Kyle?'

It sounded pretty damned good at the moment. 'What do you want?'

'I want you to take the job at Scully & Pershing.'

'Why?'

'Because I need information.'

'Great. That really explains things. Thank you so much.'

'Bear with me for a few minutes, Kyle. You need a little background here. There are two gigantic corporations who compete with each other. Both are worth billions, and they despise each other. Now they're about to square up to each other in the mother of all lawsuits. It will be filed in a few weeks in federal court in New York City. At stake is something in the neighbourhood of eight hundred billion dollars, and the loser might not survive. Nasty, vicious litigation. A bonanza for the attorneys. Each uses a huge Wall Street law firm, and guess what? The two law firms hate each other.'

'I can't wait to get in the middle of that.'

'That's where you're headed. One firm is Scully & Pershing. The other is Agee, Poe & Epps, otherwise known as APE.'

'I interviewed there.'

'Did they offer a job?'

'I didn't like the firm.'

'Attaboy. Now you can really dislike them.'

'I didn't go to law school to become a spy.'

'Let's not call it spying, Kyle. More a case of transferring information.'

'What kind of information?'

'Once the lawsuit gets cranked up, there'll be a million documents. We expect each of the two law firms to commit fifty lawyers to the case—maybe ten partners, the rest associates. You'll be in the litigation section of Scully & Pershing, so you'll have access to a lot of material.'

'Security at these firms is extremely tight.'

'Our security experts are better than theirs. We wrote the book, Kyle.'

'I'm sure you did. What are these two big companies fighting over?'

'Secrets. Technology.'

'Great. Thanks. Do these companies have names?'

'Fortune 500. I'll give you more information as we progress.'

'So you're going to be part of my life for a while?'

'I'm your official handler. You and I will spend a lot of time together.'

'Then I quit. I'm not spying and I'm not stealing. The moment I walk out of Scully & Pershing with a document or a disk I'm not supposed to have and give it to you or anybody else, I've broken the law and violated half the canons of ethics. I will be disbarred and convicted of something.'

'Only if you get caught. And we're much too smart for that to happen, Kyle. We do this all the time and we're very good at it.'

'Then go blackmail someone else.'

'No. It's all you, Kyle. Think about it. You take the job you've always wanted, at an obscene salary, living the fast life in the big city. By the time you're thirty, you're a senior associate making four hundred grand a year. Nice apartment in SoHo. A share of a weekend house in the Hamptons. A Porsche. Then one day the lawsuit is settled. We disappear. The statute runs out in Pittsburgh. The video is finally forgotten, and at the age of thirty-two or thirty-three you're asked to join Scully & Pershing as a full equity partner. A million or two per year. The pinnacle of success. Life is great. And no one will ever know about a little transferring of information.'

A headache that had been smouldering for the past hour finally matured and hit hard in the middle of his forehead. Kyle massaged his temples.

'Look, Bennie, I know you don't care about morals or ethics and such things, but I do. How, exactly, am I supposed to live with myself if I betray the confidences of my firm and its clients?'

'All we care about is getting the information. We don't spend too much time pondering morality.'

'That's about what I figured.'

'I need a commitment, Kyle. I need your word.'

'Do you have any Tylenol? I need something for a headache.'

'No.'

'I can't keep going. My head is splitting.'

'Whatever, Kyle. It's up to you. But I need an answer. Do we have an agreement, a deal, an understanding?'

'Do I really have a choice?'

'I don't see one.'

'If I have no choice, then I have no choice.'

'Excellent. A wise decision, Kyle.'

'Oh, thank you so much.'

Wright stood and stretched as if a long day at the office were finally over. He reshuffled some papers, fiddled with the video camera, closed the laptop. 'Would you like to rest here, Kyle?'

'Yes.'

'Shall I wake you in a few hours?' Wright asked pleasantly.

'No. Just leave me alone.'

'I'll be across the hall.'

When Kyle was alone, he pulled back the bedspread, turned off the lights, and soon fell asleep.

WHEN KYLE WOKE UP several hours later, his head was still hurting and his mouth was dry. He needed fresh air, and maybe someone to talk to.

He eased from the room and tiptoed down the hall, down the stairs. In the lobby some salesmen were gulping coffee, anxious for the day to start. Outside the air was cold and sharp, and he inhaled as if he'd been suffocating. He made it to his Jeep, started the engine, turned on the heater and waited for the defrost to melt the snow on the windshield.

The shock was wearing off, but the reality was even worse.

He checked his cellphone messages. His girlfriend had called six times, his room-mate three. They were worried. He had class at 9 a.m. and a pile of work at the law journal. And nothing—girlfriend, room-mate, law school or work—held the slightest interest at the moment. He left the Holiday Inn and drove east on Highway 1 for a few miles until New Haven was behind him. Then for the first time he wondered if someone might be following. He began glancing at the rearview mirror.

At the small town of Guilford, he stopped at a convenience store and finally found some Tylenol. He washed it down with a soft drink and was about to drive back to New Haven when he noticed a diner across the street. He had not eaten since lunch the day before and was suddenly famished. He could almost smell the bacon grease.

The diner was packed. Kyle found a seat at the counter and ordered scrambled eggs, bacon, hash browns, toast, coffee and orange juice. He ate in silence as the laughter and gossip roared around him. The headache was fading fast, and he began plotting the rest of his day. His girlfriend might be a problem: no contact in twelve hours, a night spent away from his apartment—unusual behaviour for someone as disciplined as Kyle.

Olivia was a first-year law student at Yale, a Californian, UCLA graduate, extremely bright and ambitious and not looking for a serious commitment. They had been dating for four months, and the relationship was far more casual than romantic. Still, he could not tell her the truth and did not look forward to telling her some stuttering tale of a night that simply vanished.

A body closed in from behind. Kyle glanced to his right and came face to face with the man he had once known as Special Agent Ginyard, now wearing a camel-hair sports jacket and jeans. 'Mr Wright would like to see you at three p.m., after class, same room,' he said, then disappeared.

Kyle had lost all interest in the food in front of him. Is this my future? he asked himself. Someone always watching, listening, waiting in the shadows?

He paid the bill at the cash register and called Olivia, who was sleeping.

'Are you all right?' she asked.

'Yes, I'm fine.'

'I don't want to know anything else. Just tell me you're not hurt.'

'I'm not hurt. I'm fine, and I'm sorry.'

'Don't apologise.'

'I'm apologising, OK. I should have called.'

'I don't want to know.'

'Yes you do. Do you accept my apology?'

'I don't know.'

'That's better. I expect some anger here. How about lunch?'

'No. I'm busy.'

'You can't skip lunch. Meet me at the Grill at noon. Please.'

'I'll think about it.'

He drove back to New Haven, refusing every half-mile to glance at his mirror for signs of a tail. He slipped quietly into his apartment and took a shower. By the time Mitch, his room-mate, finally staggered out of his bedroom, Kyle was sipping coffee at the kitchen counter and reading a newspaper online. Mitch asked a few vague questions about last night, but Kyle deflected them nicely and his room-mate went back to bed.

COMPLETE FIDELITY had been agreed to months earlier, and once Olivia was convinced Kyle had not cheated, her attitude thawed a little. The story he'd been working on for several hours went like this. He'd been struggling with his decision to pursue public-interest law instead of taking a big job with a big firm. He had no plans to make public-interest law a career, so why delay the inevitable? And so on. And last night, after his basketball game, he decided he had to make a final decision. He turned off his phone and took a long drive east on Highway 1 to Rhode Island. He lost track of time. After midnight, the snow picked up and he checked into a cheap motel.

He had changed his mind. He was going to Scully & Pershing.

He spilled this over lunch at the Grill. Olivia listened with scepticism but did not interrupt until he got to the sudden change in career plans.

'You must be kidding,' she blurted when he hit the punch line. 'You, Mr Pro Bono, Mr Public-interest Law?'

'I know, I know. I feel like a turncoat.'

'You *are* a turncoat,' she said. 'You're selling out. We have thirty years to make money. Why can't we spend a few years helping others?'

'I know, I know,' he mumbled lamely. 'But timing is important. I'm not sure that Scully & Pershing will defer.' Another lie, but what the hell.

She shoved her food away, crossed her arms and slowly shook her head. 'I don't believe this,' she said.

And at that moment Kyle couldn't believe it either, but it was important, now and for ever more, to give the impression that he'd carefully weighed the issues and had arrived at this decision. In other words, Kyle had to sell it. Olivia was the first test. His friends would be next, then his professors. Then he would muster the courage to visit his father and deliver the news. He knew John McAvoy detested the idea of his son working on Wall Street.

Kyle's selling job, though, did little to convince Olivia. They traded barbs for a few minutes, then forgot about lunch and went their separate ways. There was no goodbye peck on the cheek, no hug, no promise to call each other later. He spent an hour in his office at the law journal, then reluctantly left and drove back to the motel.

3

At the New Haven train station, Kyle boarded the 7.22 a.m. for Grand Central. He wore the better of his two suits, a plain white shirt with an utterly boring tie and black wing tips, and he carried a handsome leather attaché case his father had given him last Christmas. He also carried the morning's edition of the *Wall Street Journal*, and was indistinguishable from the other sleepy-eyed executives hustling off to the office.

After three days and many hours of talking, haggling and threatening, Bennie Wright had finally left town. He had receded into the shadows but, of course, would soon materialise again. Kyle hated his voice, his face, his confident, pressing manner. He hated everything about Bennie Wright and his firm or whatever it was, and many times during the past week he had changed his mind in the middle of the night and told them all to go to hell.

Then, in the darkness, as always, he could feel the handcuffs, see his mug shot in the newspapers, see the looks on the faces of his parents, and worst of all he could see himself afraid to glance at the jurors when the video was played to a hushed courtroom.

'Is she awake?' Joey Bernardo had asked while Baxter Tate had Elaine down on the sofa. *Is she awake?* The words would echo round the courtroom.

The countryside vanished as the train sped through suburbs and towns, then at some point it dipped under the East River and entered Manhattan. Kyle strolled through Grand Central and hailed a cab at the corner of Lex and Forty-fourth. Not once had he looked over his shoulder.

Scully & Pershing leased the top half of a building named 110 Broad, a tall glass edifice in the heart of the financial district. It was almost 10 a.m., and the elevator was empty. The lawyers had been at their desks for hours. He stopped at the thirtieth floor, the firm's main lobby, and paused to admire the massive bronze lettering that informed visitors that they were now on the hallowed turf of Scully & Pershing. Attorneys-at-law, all 2,100 of them, the largest law firm the world had ever known. Offices in ten US cities and twenty foreign ones. Magnet to the best legal talent money can buy. Power, money, prestige. Kyle already felt like a trespasser.

The walls were covered with abstract art; the furniture was rich and contemporary. A gorgeous little receptionist in stiletto heels took his name and asked him to please wait. After a few minutes of mindless gazing at a work of art so bizarre he had no idea what he was looking at, he heard the receptionist call, 'Mr Peckham is waiting. Two floors up.' Kyle took the stairs.

Like many Manhattan law firms, Scully & Pershing spent money on the elevators, reception areas and conference rooms—the places clients and other visitors might actually see—but in the bowels of the firm where the grunts worked, efficiency ruled. The secretaries worked in tight cubicles within reach of each other. The senior associates and junior partners were awarded small offices on the outer walls, with a view of similar buildings.

The rookie associates were stuffed, three or four of them together, in cramped, windowless cubicles, nicknamed 'cubes'. These were tucked away, out of sight. Lousy accommodations, brutal hours, sadistic bosses, unbearable pressure—it was all part of the blue-chip law-firm experience, and Kyle had heard the horror tales before he finished his first year at Yale. Scully & Pershing was no better and no worse than any other mega-firm.

At the corners of each floor, in the largest offices, the real partners anchored things and had some say in the decor. One was Doug Peckham, a forty-one-year-old litigation partner, a Yale man who had supervised Kyle during his internship the previous summer. They had become somewhat friendly.

Kyle was shown into Peckham's office a few minutes after 10 a.m. and they exchanged greetings and a few pleasantries. Kyle knew that Peckham billed $800 an hour, at least ten hours a day, and therefore the time that Kyle was now wasting was quite valuable.

'I'm not sure I want to spend a couple of years doing legal aid,' Kyle said, not too deep into the meeting.

'Don't really blame you there, Kyle,' Peckham said in a quick, clipped voice. 'You have too much potential in the real world. This is your future.' He spread his arms to take in his vast empire.

'I really would like to work in litigation.'

'I see no problem there. You had a great summer here. We were all impressed. I'll make the request myself. You'll be joining the best freshman class in years.'

The same was said about every freshman class at every major firm.

'Thanks. And I'd love to work in the litigation practice group.'

'Consider it done, Kyle.' And with that Peckham glanced at his watch—meeting over. As Kyle shook his hand and said goodbye, he decided he did not want to become another Doug Peckham. He had no idea what he wanted to become, or if he would in fact become anything other than a disbarred lawyer, but selling his soul to become a partner was not in the plans.

Two blocks away, he found a coffee shop. He sat on a bar stool in the window and for a long time looked rather forlornly at 110 Broad, at the tower that would soon become his home, or his prison. He knew the numbers. Scully & Pershing would hire 150 new associates worldwide, 100 in the New York office alone. They would pay them a nice salary that would amount to about $100 an hour, and the rookie grunts would have to bill a minimum of 2,000 hours a year, though more would be required to make an impression. Hundred-hour work weeks would not be uncommon. After two years, the associates would begin dropping out and looking for more sensible work. Half would be gone in four years. Ten per cent of his freshman class would survive, claw their way to the top, and be awarded with a partnership after seven or eight years. Those who didn't drop out would be squeezed out by the firm if they were not deemed partnership material.

Sure, the money was great. At least $200,000 to start with. Double that in five years as a senior associate. Double it again in seven years as a junior partner. Well over a million bucks a year at the age of thirty-five as a full partner with a future filled with even higher earnings.

Numbers, numbers. Kyle was sick of the numbers. He longed for the Blue Ridge Mountains and a nonprofit's salary of $32,000 without the stress and pressure and hassle of life in the city. He yearned for freedom.

Instead, he had another meeting with Bennie Wright. The cab stopped in front of the Millenium Hilton on Church Street. Kyle paid the driver, nodded at the doorman, then took the elevator four floors up to a room where his handler was waiting.

'The offer is still good,' Kyle said. 'I told Peckham I've decided to take the job. I'll start in September with the other associates.'

'Good. And you'll be in litigation?'

'Peckham thinks so, but there's no guarantee.'

Bennie had a file on Doug Peckham, as well as files on all of the litigation partners and many of the firm's other lawyers.

'You can make it happen. Have you thought about an apartment here?'

'No, not yet.'

'Well, we've done some homework and we've found a couple of places that will be ideal. Both are in Tribeca, fairly close to the office.'

'What makes you think I'd consider living where you want me to live?'

'Apartment hunting is a bitch in Manhattan. I'm just trying to help.'

'Thanks so much. No doubt these are places that can easily be watched, maybe even wired or bugged. Nice try, Bennie.'

'Where are you planning to live?'

'I'll figure that out, and I'll do so without any involvement on your part.'

'As you wish.'

'Damned right. What else do you want to talk about?'

Bennie walked to the table, picked up a legal pad and studied it as if he didn't know what he'd written on it. 'What about the girl? Olivia?' he asked.

'What about her?'

'How serious is the relationship?'

'Not sure where you figure into this, Bennie. Can you help me here?'

'Your life will be complicated enough without a romance. A serious relationship could pose problems. It's best if you postpone it for a few years.'

Kyle laughed in frustration and disbelief. He shook his head and tried to think of an appropriate retort, but nothing came to mind. Sadly, he agreed with his tormentor. And the relationship with Olivia was going nowhere fast. 'What else, Bennie? Can I have friends? Can I visit my parents?'

'You won't have the time.'

Kyle headed for the door, yanked it open, then slammed it as he left.

A BELIEF in public service runs deep at Yale Law. Admission is often determined by the applicant's record of volunteerism and his or her written thoughts about using a law degree to benefit the world. When an editor of the *Yale Law Journal* takes a low-paying job with legal services, he is a hero to the faculty. But when he caves in to Wall Street, he is viewed less favourably.

Kyle's life became miserable. His friends who planned to work in public-interest law were in disbelief. Those on the corporate side were too busy to care. Olivia said he had changed. He was moodier, gloomier, preoccupied with something, and whatever it was he couldn't tell her.

If you only knew, he thought.

She had accepted a summer internship with an anti-death-penalty group in Texas; thus she was full of zeal and big plans to change things down there. They saw less of each other but somehow managed to bicker more.

One of Kyle's favourite professors was an old radical who had spent most of the 1960s marching for or against something. When he heard the news that Kyle had flipped, he called and demanded lunch. Over enchiladas at a taco bar just off campus, the professor railed and hammered but got nowhere. He left Kyle with a disheartening 'I'm very disappointed in you.'

'Thanks,' Kyle retorted, then cursed himself as he walked to campus. Then he cursed Bennie Wright and Elaine Keenan and Scully & Pershing and everything else in his life at that moment.

After a few rounds of ugly encounters with his friends, Kyle finally found the courage to go home.

In 1975, John McAvoy had quit his job as a lowly paid pencil-pusher in a small real-estate law firm in York, Pennsylvania. He had marched across Market Street, rented a two-roomed 'suite' in a converted row house, hung out his shingle and declared himself ready to sue. Real-estate law was too boring. An ex-Marine who had served in Vietnam, John wanted conflict, courtrooms, drama, verdicts. He was looking for a fight.

He worked very hard and treated everyone fairly. He called himself a street lawyer, an advocate for clients who worked in factories, who got injured or discriminated against, or who ran afoul of the law. His clients were not banks or insurance companies or real-estate agencies or corporations. His clients were not billed by the hour. Often, they were not billed at all. Fees were sometimes delivered in the form of firewood, eggs and poultry, steaks and free labour around the house. The office grew, sprawled upstairs and down, and John eventually bought the row house. Mr McAvoy was demanding of his associates. He was kinder to his secretaries. One, a young divorcée named Patty, married the boss after a two-month courtship and was soon pregnant.

Through sheer volume, and an innate Presbyterian frugality, the firm covered its expenses and provided the McAvoy family with an income that was in the upper-middle class for York. Had he been greedier, or more selective, or even a bit firmer with his billing, John could have doubled his income and joined the country club. But he hated golf and didn't like the wealthier folks in town. More important, he viewed the practice of law as a calling, a mission to help the less fortunate.

Patty had twin girls in 1980. In 1983, Kyle was born, and before he started kindergarten he was hanging around his father's office. After his parents divorced, he preferred the stability of the law office to the strains of joint custody, and each day after school he parked himself in a small room upstairs and finished his homework. At the age of ten he was running the copier, making coffee and tidying up the small library. He was paid a dollar an hour in cash. By the age of fifteen he had mastered legal research and could hammer out memos on basic subjects. During high school, when he wasn't playing basketball, he was at the office or in court with his father.

Kyle always knew he would be a lawyer. He wasn't sure what kind, or where he would practice, but by the time he left York for Duquesne, he doubted if he would return. John McAvoy doubted it, too, though he often thought of the pride he would have if the firm name became McAvoy & McAvoy. He demanded hard work and excellent grades, but even he was a little surprised at Kyle's academic success in college and at Yale Law School.

KYLE HAD CALLED and told his father he would arrive in York late Friday afternoon. As usual, the office was busy at 5.30 when he arrived. Many of John McAvoy's clients got paid at the end of the week, and a few stopped by to write small cheques or see about their cases. Kyle had not been home in six weeks, since Christmas, and the office looked even shabbier. The carpet needed replacing. The bookshelves sagged even more.

Sybil, the ranking secretary, abruptly hung up the phone when Kyle walked through the door. She jumped to her feet, squealed and grabbed him. They pecked on the cheeks and enjoyed the physical greeting. His father had handled at least two divorces for Sybil, and Kyle knew that the current husband would soon be on the street. The firm had three secretaries and two associates, and he went from room to room, speaking to the employees as they packed their briefcases and tidied their desks. The boss might enjoy staying late on Fridays, but the rest of the firm was tired.

As Kyle drank a diet soda in the coffee room and listened to the voices and sounds of the office as it wound down, he asked himself why he didn't just tell his father everything. Start with Elaine, her allegations, the cops and their questions. Five years earlier he had come within minutes of hustling home and asking his father for help. But then it passed, and then it went away, and John McAvoy was never burdened with the ugly episode.

If he told his father now, the first question would be 'Why didn't you tell me then?' And Kyle wasn't prepared to face it, or the tougher questions that would follow. It was much easier for Kyle to keep his secrets and hope for the best. What he was about to tell his father was difficult enough.

After the last client left and Sybil said goodbye, father and son relaxed in the big office and talked about college basketball and hockey. Then family, the twin sisters first, as always, then Patty.

'Does your mother know you're in town?' John asked.

'No. I'll call her tomorrow. She's OK?'

'Nothing's changed. She's fine.' Patty lived and worked in the loft of an old warehouse in York. It was a large space with lots of windows that provided the light she needed to pursue her painting. John paid the rent, utilities and everything else she needed through a monthly stipend of $3,000. It wasn't alimony, but simply a gift he felt compelled to pass along for her upkeep because she could not support herself. Patty was severely bipolar, and the mood swings were, at times, astonishing. John still loved her and had never remarried, though he'd enjoyed a few girlfriends. Patty had been through at least two ruinous affairs, and John had been there to pick up the pieces. Their relationship was complicated, to say the least.

'I call her every Tuesday night,' Kyle said.

'I know you do.'

'So how's school?' John asked.

'Downhill. I graduate in three months.'

'That's hard to believe.'

Kyle swallowed hard and decided to get it over with. 'I've changed my mind about employment. I'm going to Wall Street. Scully & Pershing.'

John slowly lit a cigarette and studied his son from behind wire-rimmed reading glasses perched on his nose. He was sixty-two, thick but not fat, with a head full of wavy grey hair. 'Any particular reason?' he asked.

The reasons had been memorised, but Kyle knew they would sound flat, however smoothly they were delivered. 'The legal-services gig is a waste of time. I'll end up on Wall Street eventually, so why not get the career started?'

'I don't believe this.'

'I know, I know. It's an about-face.'

'It's a sellout. There's nothing that requires you to pursue a career in a corporate firm.'

'It's the big leagues, Dad.'

'In terms of what? Money?'

'That's a start.'

'No way. There are trial lawyers who make ten times more each year than the biggest partners in New York.'

'Yes, and for every big trial lawyer there are five thousand starving sole practitioners. On average, the money is better in a big firm.'

'You'll hate every minute of a big firm. You grew up here, around people and real clients. You won't see a client for ten years in New York.'

'It's a nice firm, Dad. One of the best.'

'I thought you wanted to try something different and help people in the process. Did I not hear these words from you just a few weeks ago?'

'I've changed my mind.'

'Well, change it back. It's not too late.'

'No. I don't want to spend three years in rural Virginia trying to learn enough Spanish so I can listen to the problems of people who are here illegally in the first place.'

'I'm sorry, but that sounds like a great way to spend the next three years. I don't buy it.' John shoved his chair back and jumped to his feet. He preferred to pace about when he was agitated. It was an old courtroom habit.

'I'd like to make some money.'

'For what? To buy new toys? You won't have the time to play with them.'

'I plan to save—'

'So it's all about the money, is it, Kyle?' His cheeks were turning colour. The Scottish temper was warming up. 'I don't buy it and I don't like it. You were raised better than that.'

'I've made my decision, Dad,' Kyle said softly. 'I ask you to respect it. A lot of fathers would be thrilled with such a job.'

John McAvoy stopped pacing and looked at his son. 'OK,' he said eventually. He seemed to have decided to back off. 'You're smart enough to know what you want, but I'm your father and I'll have some opinions about your next big decision, and the next. That's what I'm here for. If you screw up again, I'll damned sure let you know it.'

'I'm not screwing up, Dad. Can we go to dinner now? I'm starving.'

They rode together to Victor's Italian Restaurant, John's Friday-night ritual for as long as Kyle could remember. John had his usual end-of-the-week martini. Kyle had his standard drink—club soda with a twist of lime. He hadn't touched alcohol for years. They ordered pasta with meatballs, and after the second martini John began to mellow. Having his son at the largest and most prestigious law firm in the country did have a nice ring to it, he admitted. But he was still clearly puzzled by the abrupt change in plans.

If you only knew, Kyle kept saying to himself. And he ached because he couldn't tell his father the truth.

KYLE WAS RELIEVED when his mother did not answer the phone. He waited until almost eleven on Saturday morning before calling. He left a pleasant little message about popping in for a quick hello as he was passing through York for some vague reason. She was either asleep or medicated, or, if it was a good day, she was in her studio thoroughly absorbed in creating some of the most dreadful art never seen in a gallery. Visits with his mother were painful. She seldom asked about his life—law school, girlfriends, plans for the future. She was much too absorbed in her own sad little world. Kyle's twin sisters stayed far away from York.

He left the message on her recorder as he was hustling out of town, and the call was never returned, which was not unusual. Four hours later he was in Pittsburgh. Joey Bernardo had tickets for the Penguins–Senators hockey game Saturday night. Three tickets, not two.

The third ticket was for Blair, Joey's soon-to-be-announced fiancée. By the time the three of them had settled into a booth at Boomerang's, a favourite watering hole from their college days, Joey was gushing with the news that they were looking at wedding dates. Both were glowing with love and seemed oblivious to everything else. Kyle felt uncomfortable. What had happened to his friend? Where was the old Joey—the tough kid from South Pittsburgh, son of a fire captain, accomplished boxer, high-school fullback, the guy who'd vowed he wouldn't marry until he was at least forty?

Blair had turned him to mush. Kyle was astonished at the transformation.

They eventually tired of wedding plans and potential honeymoon destinations, and the talk turned to careers. Blair, a chatterbox who began every sentence with 'I' or 'my', worked for an advertising agency and spent far too much time detailing some of their latest marketing manoeuvres. Joey hung on her every word. As she prattled on, Kyle worked hard at maintaining enough eye contact to feign interest, but his mind drifted to the video.

'Is she awake?' Joey had asked as Baxter had sex with a dangerously intoxicated Elaine Keenan.

'Blair travels to Montreal quite often,' Joey said, then Blair ricocheted onto the subject of Montreal and its beauty. She was learning French!

Is she awake? Joey had no earthly idea that such a video existed. When was the last time he had even thought about the incident? Ever? And what good would it do for Kyle to bring it up now?

'Have you talked to Baxter?' Joey asked when Blair finally stopped for air.

'Not in a month or so.'

Joey was grinning as if a joke was on the way. 'He finally got in a movie!'

'No kidding. He didn't tell me.'

'That's because he doesn't want you to know,' Joey went on. 'He got drunk one night—and by the way, the drinking is now in no-man's-land—so he called and told me he'd made his debut. It was a cheap cable flick about a young girl who finds a human leg washed up on a beach, and for the rest of the movie she has nightmares about being chased by a one-legged killer.'

'Where does the great Baxter Tate fit in?'

'There's a scene on a boat when the cops are gazing out at the ocean, looking for the rest of the body, presumably. One of the deputies walks over to the sheriff and says, "Sir, we're low on fuel." That's our movie star.'

'Baxter is a deputy?'

'And a bad one. He has only that one line and delivers it like a frightened sophomore in the school play.'

'I can't wait to see it.'

'Don't, and don't tell him I mentioned it. He called the next morning, begging me not to watch it and threatening me if I told anyone. He's a mess.'

And that reminded Blair of one of her friends who knew someone who had landed a role in a new sitcom, and away she went. Kyle smiled and nodded as his brain switched compartments. Of the three room-mates, Joey was the only one who could possibly help, if indeed help was possible. Baxter Tate was in dire need of intensive rehab, and Alan Strock was thoroughly consumed with medical school at Ohio State.

For Joey, the stakes were high. He was on the tape, wondering aloud if Elaine was awake while Baxter did the deed, then Joey himself took a turn. He was currently handling accounts at a regional brokerage firm in Pittsburgh and had two promotions under his belt. He was goofy in love with Air Blair here, and any hint of an old rape charge would upset their perfect lives. Kyle was reluctant to drop the bomb on Joey at this point, but at the same time he felt as though he was taking the fall for his friend. He hadn't touched Elaine that night, yet it was *his* life and career now getting hijacked by Bennie Wright and his dirty little video.

During a break in the game, with Blair off in the ladies' room, Kyle suggested they meet on Sunday for breakfast. Just the two of them.

THEY MET FOR BAGELS at a chain-owned shop that had not existed when Kyle was at Duquesne. Blair was still asleep somewhere, and Joey admitted to needing a break. 'Sweet girl,' Kyle said more than once, and each time felt guilty for lying. He could not imagine a life with such a windbag.

They talked about New York for a long time—life in a big firm, the grind of the city, other friends who were there and so on. Kyle eventually brought the conversation round to the old Beta gang, and they played catch-up for a while. Several times, the 'Elaine thing' was at the surface, but Joey did not mention it. When they said goodbye, Kyle was convinced Joey had buried the episode, and, more important, no one had brought it to his attention recently.

He drove north to Interstate 80, then headed east. A few more weeks in the cosy world of academia, then two months prepping for the bar exam, and in September he would report for duty at the largest law firm in the world. There would be a hundred associates in his class, all bright kids from the finest schools, all anxious to jump-start their brilliant legal careers.

Kyle felt lonelier each day.

BUT HE WASN'T exactly isolated. His movements to, in and around York and Pittsburgh were closely monitored by Bennie Wright and his gang. A small magnetic GPS transmitter, the size of a man's wallet, was tucked away under some mud and dirt in the rear bumper of Kyle's red Cherokee, and his cellphone had long since been compromised. They listened to every conversation. The kid had yet to mention his predicament to anyone on the phone. They were also listening to Olivia's chatter, as well as that of Mitch, his room-mate. So far, nothing. They were reading Kyle's emails. He averaged twenty-seven a day, and almost all were related to law school.

Bennie was pleased with the progress. Kyle had hustled over to New York and cleared things with Scully & Pershing. He was seeing less of Olivia, and it was obvious, at least to Bennie, that the relationship was going nowhere. But the sudden trip to Pittsburgh was bothersome. Had he planned to confide in Joey? Had he in fact done so?

Bennie was listening and waiting. He had leased some office space in a building two blocks down from Scully & Pershing. The tenant's name was Fancher Group, a financial-services start-up domiciled in Bermuda. Its registered agent in New York was Aaron Kurtz, also known as Bennie Wright, also known as a dozen other men, all with perfect identification. In a few short months he'd be able to gaze out of his window from his new perch and see their boy Kyle enter and leave his place of employment.

4

The lawsuit was filed electronically in federal court in the Southern District of New York, Manhattan Division, at 4.50 on a Friday afternoon, a time chosen so that the filing would attract as little attention as possible from the press. A 'late-Friday dump'. The lawyer who signed it was a noted litigator named Wilson Rush, a senior partner with Scully & Pershing. Of the forty or so civil lawsuits filed that day in the Southern District, it was by far the most serious, most complex and most anticipated. The parties involved had been feuding for years, and most of the issues were too sensitive to bare in public. The Pentagon, many senior members of Congress and even the White House had worked diligently to prevent litigation, but all efforts had failed. The next battle in the war had begun, and no one expected a quick resolution.

The clerk, upon receiving the complaint, quickly rerouted it to a secure bin to prevent its contents from being exposed. This extremely rare procedure had been ordered by the chief district judge. A bare-bones summary of the lawsuit, also approved by the judge, was available to the press.

The plaintiff was Trylon Aeronautics, a New York-based defence contractor, a privately held company that had been designing and building military aircraft for four decades. The defendant was Bartin Dynamics, a publicly held defence contractor based in Bethesda, Maryland. Bartin averaged about $15 billion a year in government contracts—95 per cent of its revenue. It used different lawyers for its different needs, but for the biggest fights it was protected by the Wall Street firm of Agee, Poe & Epps.

Scully & Pershing currently had 2,100 lawyers and claimed to be the largest firm in the world. Agee, Poe & Epps had 200 fewer lawyers but boasted more offices around the world, so it also claimed to be the largest.

At the core of the dispute was the B-10 HyperSonic Bomber, a space-age aircraft that had been dreamed about for decades and was now closer to becoming a reality. Five years earlier, the Air Force had launched a contest among its top contractors to design the B-10, a sleek bomber that would replace the ageing fleet of B-52s and B-22s and serve the military through to the year 2060. Lockheed had been the expected front runner in the competition, but it was quickly outpaced by a joint venture put together by Trylon and Bartin. A consortium of foreign companies—British, French and Israeli—had smaller roles in the joint venture.

The prize was enormous. The Air Force would pay the winner $10 billion up front to develop the technologies and build a prototype, then contract for the procurement of 250 to 450 B-10s over the next thirty years. At an estimated $800 billion, the contract would be the richest in the Pentagon's history.

The Trylon-Bartin design was astounding. Their B-10 could take off from a base in the United States with a payload the same size as a B-52, fly at 7,600 miles per hour, or Mach 10, and deliver its payload on the other side of the world in an hour, then return to its home base without refuelling. The aircraft would literally skip along the edge of the atmosphere. After ascending to an altitude of 130,000 feet, just outside the stratosphere, the B-10 would turn off its engines and float back to the surface of the atmosphere. Once there, its air-breathing engines would kick on and lift the plane back to 130,000 feet. This procedure, a skipping motion much like that of a flat rock bouncing across still water, would be repeated until the aircraft arrived at its target. Because the engines would be used only intermittently, significantly smaller amounts of fuel would be required.

After three years of intense and often frantic research and design, the Air Force announced that it had selected the Trylon-Bartin design. It tried its best to downplay the B-10 programme, since the dollar amounts were staggering, the country was fighting two wars and the Pentagon decided it would not be wise to broadcast such an ambitious procurement plan. But as soon as the winner was announced, fighting erupted on all fronts.

Lockheed roared back with its senators and lobbyists and lawyers. Trylon and Bartin, historically fierce competitors, began sniping almost immediately. The prospect of that much money splintered any notion of cooperation. Each firm began corralling its own politicians and lobbyists to fight for a bigger piece of the pork. The British, French and Israelis eased to the sidelines but certainly did not go away.

Both Trylon and Bartin claimed ownership of the design and the technologies. Efforts to mediate succeeded, then failed. Lockheed loomed in the background, waiting. The Pentagon threatened to yank the contract and have another contest. Congressmen held hearings. Journalists wrote long pieces in magazines. Watchdog groups railed against the B-10 as if it were a shuttle to Mars. And the lawyers quietly prepared for litigation.

TWO HOURS after the lawsuit was filed, Kyle saw it posted on the federal court's website. He was at his desk in his office at the *Yale Law Journal*, editing a lengthy article on his computer. For three weeks he had been checking the filings in all the federal courts in New York, as well as the state courts. During their first session, Bennie had mentioned the upcoming filing of a massive lawsuit in New York, the one Kyle was now expected to infiltrate. Oddly, the online posting of the lawsuit revealed nothing but its title and the name, address and law firm of Wilson Rush. When Kyle saw the word SECURE after the title of the Scully & Pershing posting, red flags began to wave.

He searched Agee, Poe & Epps and studied their exhaustive list of corporate clients. The firm had represented Bartin Dynamics since the 1980s. Kyle forgot about the law-journal work and lost himself on the Internet. A search of Trylon soon revealed its B-10 HyperSonic Bomber project and all the problems it had caused, and, evidently, was still creating.

Kyle closed the door of his small office. It was almost eight on Friday night, and most of the crew had cleared out for spring break. He printed all available corporate info on Trylon and Bartin. There were several dozen newspaper and magazine articles on the B-10 fiasco. He printed them all and began reading the most serious ones.

There was a chance he was chasing the wrong lawsuit. He couldn't know for sure until Bennie confirmed it. But the timing was on schedule. Billions were at stake, just as Bennie had said. Two corporations that were old competitors. Two law firms that hated each other. Military secrets. Stolen technology. Corporate espionage. Foreign intelligence. Threats of litigation and even criminal prosecution. It was one monumental, sordid mess, and now he, Kyle McAvoy, was expected to insert himself into the fray.

Why couldn't he just go back to York and practise law with his father?

At 1 a.m. he stuffed his notebooks into his backpack. He looked around, turned off the light and locked his door, feeling certain that Bennie and his thugs had been there, probably with bugs and wires and mikes and other crap that Kyle tried not to think about.

And he was sure they were watching him. He'd seen them. They were good, but they had made a few mistakes. The challenge, he told himself, was to act as though he had no clue that they were watching. He never changed his routines, or routes, or parking lots. Same spot for lunch almost every day. Same coffee shop where he met Olivia occasionally after class. And because his habits remained the same, so did those of his shadows. They became lazy. Kyle, the innocent, lulled them to sleep, and when they nodded off, he caught them. One face he'd seen three times already, a young, ruddy face with different glasses and a moustache that came and went.

At a used bookstore near the campus, Kyle began buying old paperback spy novels. He kept the current one in his backpack, and when he finished, he tossed it in the wastebasket at the law school and bought another.

He assumed that none of his communications was confidential. His cellphone and laptop were compromised, he was certain. But if Bennie was listening, he heard not one word to indicate that Kyle was even remotely suspicious. Kyle told himself that to survive the next seven years he had to learn to think and act like his adversaries. There was a way out. Somewhere.

He began looking for a place to live. He looked at four apartments, all in SoHo and Tribeca. The cheapest was $4,200 a month for an 800-square-foot walk-up, and the most expensive was $6,500 a month for 1,000 square feet in a renovated warehouse. Whatever the rent, Kyle would be handling it himself because he did not want a room-mate. His life would be complicated enough without the strain of living with someone else.

BENNIE AND COMPANY had followed Kyle and the agent around Lower Manhattan and knew precisely where the apartments were located. By the time Kyle arrived at the Ritz-Carlton for their next meeting, Bennie's operatives were calling the same realtor, enquiring about the apartments and making plans to visit them. Kyle would indeed live where he chose, but the place would be infested by the time he moved in.

Bennie had some thick files on the table in the suite. 'The lawsuit was filed last Friday,' he began, 'here in Manhattan. The plaintiff is a company called Trylon Aeronautics. The defendant is a company called Bartin Dynamics.'

Kyle absorbed this with no expression. But Bennie knew he already knew. From his comfortable office on Broad Street, Bennie and his tech guys kept close tabs on Kyle's laptop and his office computer. They monitored nonstop, and knew that he was checking the court filings in New York and digging through the dirt on Trylon and Bartin.

Sit there and play dumb, son. I'll play along, too. You're smart as hell, but you're too stupid to realise you're in way over your head.

AS SPRINGTIME reluctantly arrived in New England, the campus came to life and shook off the gloom of winter. Plants bloomed, the grass showed some colour, and the students found more reasons to stay outside. Frisbees flew by the hundreds. Long lunches and even picnics materialised when the sun was out. Professors became lazier; classes grew shorter.

Kyle kept himself in his office, working feverishly to finish the June edition of the *Yale Law Journal*. It would be his last and he wanted it to be his best. Work provided an excuse to ignore virtually everyone else. Olivia finally got fed up, and they parted amicably. His friends, all of them third-year students and about to graduate, were either drinking and partying and trying to savour every moment of life on campus before being sent into the real world, or studying for the bar exam. Kyle found it easy to avoid them all.

On May 1, he sent a letter to Joey Bernardo that read:

Dear Joey: I graduate on May 25. Any chance you could be here? Alan can't do it and I'm afraid to ask Baxter. It would be great fun to hang out for a couple of days. No girlfriend, please. Correspond by regular mail at this address. No emails, no phones. I'll explain later.
Best, Kyle

The letter was handwritten and mailed from the law-journal office. A week later, the reply arrived:

Hey, Kyle: What's with the snail mail? Your handwriting sucks. I'll be there for graduation, should be fun. What the hell is so secretive that we can't talk on the phone or use email? Are you cracking up? Baxter is. He'll be dead in a year if we don't do something. Oh, well, my hand is aching and I feel like such an old fart writing with ink. Can't wait to get your next sweet little note.
Love, Joey

Kyle's reply was longer and filled with details. Joey's response was just as sarcastic and Kyle threw it away as soon as he read it. They swapped letters once more, and the weekend was planned.

JOEY BERNARDO arrived in New Haven Saturday afternoon, the day before the law school's graduation ceremonies, and, as directed, he proceeded to a dark and cavernous pizza parlour called Santo's, a mile from campus. At precisely 3 p.m. on Saturday, May 24, he slid into a booth and waited. He was amused and quite curious, and he was still wondering if his friend was losing his mind. One minute later, Kyle appeared from the back and sat across from him. They shook hands. Then Kyle glanced at the front door, far away and to the right. The restaurant was almost empty, and Bruce Springsteen was on the sound system.

'Start talking,' Joey said, now only slightly amused.

'I'm being followed.'

'You're cracking up. The pressure is getting to you.'

'Shut up and listen.'

A waitress paused at the table just long enough to see if they wanted anything. Both asked for diet colas, and Kyle ordered a large pepperoni pizza.

'Wasn't really that hungry,' Joey said when she was gone.

'We're in a pizza place, and so we need to order a pizza. Otherwise, we'll look suspicious. In a few minutes, a thug wearing faded jeans, a dark green rugby shirt and a khaki golf cap will walk through the door, completely ignore us, and probably go to the bar. He'll hang around for less than ten minutes; then he'll leave. When you leave, either he or one of his teammates will follow you and check your licence plates, and within minutes they'll know that I had a semisecret meeting with my old pal Joey.'

'These guys are friends of yours?'

'No. They are professional operatives, but because I'm not some highly trained thug myself, they're assuming I have no clue they're following me.'

'Great. That clears things up. Why, old buddy, are they following you?'

'It's a very long story.'

'You're not drinking again, are you? Not back on the smack?'

'I never did smack and you know it. No, I'm not drinking and I'm not losing my marbles. I'm dead serious and I need your help.'

'You need a shrink, Kyle. You're spooky. There's a glow in your eyes.'

The door opened and the thug walked in, dressed as Kyle had said.

'Don't stare,' Kyle whispered as Joey's jaw dropped.

The diet colas arrived, and they took a drink. The thug went to the bar and ordered a draft beer. From his stool he could see their table in the long mirrors behind the racks of booze, but he could not possibly hear.

'Please smile,' Kyle said. 'Please laugh. We're just two old chums reminiscing here. Nothing serious.'

Joey was flabbergasted and could manage neither a smile nor a laugh.

Kyle erupted in a loud cackle, then pulled off a slice of thin pizza as soon as it arrived. He was animated and smiling, and with his mouth full he said, 'Eat, Joey, and smile and please utter a few words.'

'What have you done? Is that guy a cop or something?'

'Or something. I've done nothing wrong, but it's a complicated story. You're involved in it. Let's talk about the Pirates.'

'The Pirates are in last place, and they'll be in last place come September. Pick another subject, or another team.' Joey finally took a slice and bit off half of it. 'I need a beer. I can't eat pizza without a beer.'

Kyle flagged down the lazy little waitress and ordered one beer.

There was a large screen in one corner showing baseball highlights. For a few minutes, they ate pizza and watched the footage. After about ten minutes the guy in the rugby shirt paid for his beer in cash and left.

When the door closed behind him, Joey said, 'What the hell is going on?'

'That's a conversation the two of us must have, but not here. It'll take an hour or two, and we'd get caught. If the bad guys see us engaged in serious talk, they'll know. It's important for us to finish the pizza, walk out the front door, and not be seen together alone, until you leave town tomorrow.'

'Thanks for inviting me up.'

'I didn't invite you for the graduation, Joey. Sorry about that. The reason you're here is to give you this.' Kyle slid across a folded sheet of paper. 'Put it in your pocket, and quick.'

Joey grabbed it and shoved it in a jeans pocket. 'What is it, Kyle?'

'Trust me, Joey, please. I'm in trouble and I need help. There's no one else but you.'

'And I'm involved, too?'

'Maybe. Let's finish the pizza and get out of here. Here's the plan. The Fourth of July is just around the corner. You come up with this wonderful idea for a rafting trip down the New River in West Virginia, three days on the river, two nights camping out. Me and you and some of the old gang from Duquesne. A boys' weekend while we can still do it. The list there has ten names and emails, stuff you already have. It also has the name of an outfitter in Beckley, West Virginia. I've done all the homework.'

Joey nodded as if nothing made sense.

Kyle pressed on. 'The purpose of the trip is to shake the surveillance. Once we're on the river and in the mountains, there's no way they can follow me. We can talk and not have to worry about being watched.'

'This is crazy. You're crazy.'

'Shut up, Joey. I'm not crazy. I'm dead serious. They watch me around the clock. They listen to my phone calls, and they've bugged my laptop.'

'And they're not cops?'

'No, they're scarier than cops. If we spend too much time together now, they'll get suspicious, and your life will get complicated. Eat some pizza.'

'I'm not hungry.'

Kyle kept eating. After a few minutes, he said, 'Look, we need to go. I have a lot to tell you, but I can't do it now. If you plan the rafting trip, we'll have some fun and I'll give you the full story.'

'You ever been rafting?'

'Sure. You?'

'No. I don't like the water.'

'They provide life jackets. Come on, Joey, have some fun. A year from now you'll be married and your life will be over.'

'Thanks, pal.'

'It's just a boys' trip down the river. Whatta you say?'

'Sure, Kyle. Whatever.'

'But when you email me, use the diversion.'

'The diversion?'

'Yes, it's written down. In your emails to me we're headed for the Potomac River in Maryland. We can't give these thugs too much notice.'

'What are they gonna do, follow us down the river in a speedboat?'

'No. It's just a precaution.'

'This is real strange, Kyle.'

'It gets stranger.'

Joey suddenly leaned forward on his elbows. He glared at Kyle and said, 'I'll do it, but you gotta give me a clue.'

'Elaine's back, with her rape scenario.'

Just as quickly as he had leaned forward, Joey shrunk back to his side of the booth and limply recoiled. Elaine? That was five, maybe six years ago, and the cops had closed the file. And why? Because there was no rape. Intercourse maybe, but it was consensual. He had a December wedding planned with the woman of his dreams, and nothing could screw it up. He had a career, a future, a good name. How could this nightmare be alive?

With so much to say, he managed to say nothing.

'This is something we can deal with, Joey,' Kyle said gently. 'It's frightening, but we can handle it. We need to talk, for hours, but not here, not now. Let's get away.'

'Sure. Whatever you say.'

THAT NIGHT, Kyle met his father for dinner at a Greek place called the Athenian. His mother could not be coaxed from her loft. They were joined by Joey Bernardo, who'd had a few drinks in preparation for the evening and seemed preoccupied. John McAvoy downed two martinis and was soon telling war stories about old trials and old cases. Joey matched him martini for martini, and the gin thickened his tongue but did not lighten his mood.

Kyle had invited him because he did not want his father to launch into a last-ditch effort to persuade him to resist the evils of corporate law and do something productive with his life. But after the second martini, John tried anyway. Kyle ate garlic crackers and hummous and listened.

Late that night, long after dinner, Kyle walked the Yale campus for the last time as a student. At twenty-five, he was now a fully grown man, nicely educated and all in one piece with no bad habits, no permanent damage.

At this point, the future should hold great promise and excitement. Instead, he felt nothing but fear and apprehension. Seven years of school, great success as a student, and it was all coming down to this—the miserable life of an unwilling spy.

OF THE TWO APARTMENTS Kyle was considering, Bennie preferred the one in the old meatpacking district, in a building that was 120 years old and had been built for the sole purpose of slaughtering hogs and cows. But the carnage was now history, and the developer had done a splendid job of gutting the place and renovating it into a collection of boutiques, offices and apartments. What impressed Bennie was the fact that the apartment directly above 5D was also available as a sublet. Bennie grabbed it, 6D, at $5,200 a month for six months. Then he waited for Kyle to lease 5D. Kyle, though, was leaning towards a second-storey walk-up on Beekman Street, near City Hall. It was smaller and cheaper at $3,800, still an obscene amount.

Scully & Pershing had paid him a signing bonus of $25,000, and he was thinking of using it to secure a nice apartment early in the summer when more were available. He would lock himself away in his new digs, study nonstop for six weeks, and take the New York bar exam in late July.

When it became obvious to Bennie that Kyle was ready to lease the Beekman apartment, he arranged for one of his operatives to offer the realtor more money. It worked, and Kyle was headed for the meatpacking district. When he verbally agreed to take 5D, for $5,100 a month for a year, beginning on June 15, Bennie dispatched a team of technicians to 'decorate' the place two weeks before Kyle was scheduled to move in. Listening devices were planted in the walls of every room. The telephone and Internet lines were tapped and wired to receivers in computers located directly above in 6D. Four hidden cameras were installed—one each in the den, the kitchen and the two bedrooms—Bennie and his boys could watch Kyle everywhere except the bathroom. Some things should be kept private.

ON JUNE 2, Kyle loaded everything he owned into his Jeep Cherokee and drove to Manhattan, where he planned to spend a few days with friends. He had yet to sign a lease on the apartment, and the real-estate agent was becoming irritated. He was ignoring her phone calls.

As scheduled, on June 3 he took a cab to the Peninsula Hotel in midtown and found Bennie Wright in a tenth-floor suite. His handler was dressed in customary drab attire—dark suit, white shirt, boring tie, black shoes—but that day his jacket was off and a 9mm Beretta sat snugly just below his left armpit in a shiny black leather holster. Kyle ran through all the sarcastic remarks he might make in the presence of such weaponry, but decided at the last second to simply ignore it.

'Congratulations on your graduation,' Bennie said, sipping coffee from a paper cup and standing by the window that overlooked Fifth Avenue. 'Did things go well?'

You were there, you asshole. When they took my photo in cap and gown, your goons were probably snapping away, too.

'Swell,' Kyle said.

'That's great. Have you found an apartment?'

Kyle listened carefully for Bennie's accent. It tended to come and go. He thought of the Mossad and the Israeli military and their talent for languages. Not for the first time he wondered whom he would be spying for and against. 'I think so,' he said.

'Where?'

'I thought we agreed that you would stay away from me.'

'Just trying to be polite, Kyle, that's all.'

'Why? I'm not chitchatting with you because I choose to. I'm here because you're blackmailing me. I despise you. Don't ever forget that. And stop trying to be polite. It goes against your personality.'

Bennie sipped his coffee and kept smiling. 'Well, moving right along. May I ask when you take the bar exam?'

'No, because you already know that. What am I here for, Bennie?'

'Just a friendly hello. Welcome to New York. That kind of stuff.'

'I'm touched.'

Bennie set down his coffee cup and picked up a notebook. He handed it to Kyle. 'These are the latest filings in the Trylon–Bartin lawsuit. Motion to dismiss, supporting affidavits, supporting exhibits and briefs. As you know, the file is sealed, so what you're holding there is unauthorised.'

'How'd you get it?' Kyle asked.

Bennie responded with the same silly smirk he always gave when Kyle asked a question that could not be answered. 'When you're not studying for the bar exam, you can bone up on the lawsuit.'

'A question. It seems to me that it's a long shot for Scully & Pershing to assign me to the litigation section that happens to be handling this case. What happens if I'm nowhere near it?'

'Your class will have about a hundred rookie associates, same as last year. Roughly ten per cent will be assigned to litigation, and you'll be the star of the litigation rookies because you're the brightest. You'll suck up and kiss ass and backstab and do all the things it takes to succeed in a big law firm. You'll want to work on this case, you'll demand it, and because it's the biggest lawsuit in the firm, you'll eventually be assigned to it.'

'Sorry I asked.'

'And while you're worming your way onto this case, you'll be providing us with other valuable information.'

'Like what?'

'It's too early to discuss. Now you need to concentrate on the bar exam.'

'Bless you. I hadn't thought about it.'

They sniped for another ten minutes; then Kyle left in a huff, as usual. From the back of a taxi, he called the realtor and said he'd changed his mind about living in the meatpacking district. The realtor was upset but managed to keep her cool. Kyle had signed nothing, and she had no legal ammo.

Kyle moved his junk into a spare room in the SoHo apartment of Charles and Charles, two Yale law grads who'd finished a year earlier and were now working for different mega-firms. The Charleses offered him their junk room for free, but Kyle insisted on paying them $200 a week. The apartment would be a great place to study because they were seldom there. Both were being thrashed by hundred-hour work weeks.

WHEN IT BECAME clear that Bennie's operation had just been stiffed for six months' rent at $5,200 per month for apartment 6D in the slaughterhouse, plus the costly 'decoration' of the apartment below it, plus $4,100 a month for a year for the apartment on Beekman, Bennie fumed but did not panic. The wasted money was not a factor. What bothered him was the unpredictability of it. For the past four months, Kyle had done little to surprise them. The surveillance had been effortless. But now Kyle was in the city, where watching him was more challenging. How much did he know or suspect? How predictable was he?

Bennie licked his wounds for an hour, then began planning his next project—research on the Charleses and an inspection of their apartment.

THE SECOND DETOXIFICATION of Baxter Tate began with a knock on his front door. Then another. He had not answered his cellphone. He had been driven home by a cab at four in the morning from a trendy nightclub in Beverly Hills. The driver helped him into his condo.

After the fourth knock, the door was quietly opened with no effort since Baxter hadn't bothered to lock it. The two men, specialists in retrieving wayward family members with addiction problems, found Baxter on his bed, still dressed in last night's get-up—liquor-stained white linen shirt, black linen jacket, bleached designer jeans. He was comatose, breathing heavily but not snoring. Still alive but not for long, not at the rate he was going.

They quickly searched the condo for weapons, then radioed to a waiting car. Another man entered. He was Baxter's uncle, a man named Walter Tate. Uncle Wally, brother to Baxter's father, was the only one of five siblings who had accomplished anything in life. The Tate family banking fortune was now three generations old and declining at a steady but not alarming rate. The last time Walter had seen his nephew he was in a lawyer's office in Pittsburgh, cleaning up after another drunk-driving episode.

Walter had long since assumed the role of the family boss. He watched the investments, met with the lawyers, handled the press when necessary and reluctantly intervened when one of his nieces or nephews flamed out. His own son had been killed hang-gliding.

This was his second intervention with Baxter, and it would be the last. The first had been two years earlier, also in LA, and they had shipped the boy off to a ranch in Montana, where he sobered up, rode horses, made new friends, saw the light. Sobriety lasted all of two weeks after he returned to his worthless career in Hollywood. Walter's limit was two rehabs. After that, they could kill themselves, for all he cared.

Baxter had been dead to the world for about nine hours when Walter Tate shook his leg long enough and hard enough to rouse him from his drunkenness. He backed away from the three men, scrambling to the other end of the bed before he recognised Uncle Wally.

Baxter rubbed his eyes, then his temples. 'Well, well,' he said. 'What brings you to LA?' He wrapped his arms round a pillow.

'We're taking a trip, Baxter. The four of us. We're gonna check you into another clinic, sober you up, then see if they can put you back together.'

'Where we going this time?'

'Nevada. There's a clinic near Reno, spectacular country.'

'It's not a dude ranch, is it? I can't take another thirty days on a horse. My ass is still raw from the last detox.'

'No horses this time. It's a different kind of place.'

'Can I just promise to stop drinking right now and skip the whole thing?'

'No.'

'And I'm assuming that if I say go to hell, get out of my house, then you'll simply bring up the trust funds. Right?'

'Right.'

The trust funds had been established by his great-grandfather in the days before private jets and luxury yachts and cocaine. Baxter's grandfather saw the warning signs. He changed the trusts so that a board of advisers could exercise a measure of discretion. Some of the money arrived each month and allowed Baxter to survive quite comfortably without working. But Uncle Wally controlled the serious money with an iron fist. If Uncle Wally said you were going to rehab, then you were about to dry out.

Suddenly Baxter bolted from the bed, shedding his jacket as he stumbled into the bathroom. The vomiting was loud and long and mixed with waves of profanities. Eventually he reappeared in the bathroom doorway.

'Let's go, Baxter,' Walter said.

Baxter waved his arms and looked around his bedroom. 'What about my place? The bills, the maid, the mail?'

'I'll take care of everything. Let's go.'

Baxter brushed his teeth, combed his hair, changed his shirt, then followed Uncle Wally and the other two outside and into a black van. They rode in silence for a few minutes, but the tension was finally broken by the sounds of Baxter crying in the rear seat.

THE BAR REVIEW COURSE was at Fordham University on 62nd Street, in a vast lecture hall that was filled with anxious former law students. From 9.30 to 1.30 each weekday, professors from nearby law schools covered the intricacies of constitutional law, corporations, criminal law, property, contracts and many other subjects. The volume of material was overwhelming. Three years of intense study would be reduced to a nightmare of an exam that ran for sixteen hours over a two-day period. The review course cost $3,000, but Scully & Pershing picked up the bill for Kyle and its other new recruits.

Scully & Pershing was typical in that it forgave the first flunking of the exam but not the second. Two bad tests and you're out. The fear of failure boiled just under the surface and often made it difficult to sleep.

Kyle found himself taking long walks, at all hours, to break the monotony and clear his head. He learned which coffee shops stayed open all night and which bakeries had warm baguettes at 5 a.m. He found a wonderful old bookstore in the Village and resumed his interest in spy novels.

After three weeks in the city, he finally found a suitable apartment. At daybreak one morning he was sitting on a stool in the window of a coffee shop on Seventh Avenue in Chelsea, sipping a double espresso and reading the *New York Times*, when he saw two men wrestle a sofa out of a door across the street and load it into a van. The door was next to a health-food store, and two floors above it a sign in a window advertised an apartment available for a sublet. Kyle quickly crossed the street, stopped one of the men and followed him upstairs to look around. The apartment had three small rooms and a narrow kitchen, and as he talked to the man, Steve somebody, he learned that Steve had the lease but was leaving town in a hurry. They shook hands on an eight-month sub at $2,500 per month. That afternoon, they met again at the apartment to sign the paperwork and transfer the keys.

Kyle thanked Charles and Charles, reloaded his meagre assets in his Jeep and drove twenty minutes uptown to the corner of Seventh and West 26th. His first purchases were a bed and table from a flea market. His next was a fifty-inch flat-screen television. There was no urgency in furnishing or decorating. Kyle doubted he would be having guests. It was an adequate place to start; then he would find something nicer.

Before leaving for West Virginia, he carefully set the traps. He cut several four-inch pieces of brown sewing thread, and with a dab of Vaseline stuck the threads to the bottoms of three interior doors. Standing and looking down, he could barely see the thread against the oak stain, but if anyone entered the apartment and opened the doors, they would leave a trail by displacing the threads. His counterintelligence tactics were rudimentary, but the basics often worked just fine, according to the spy novels.

THE NEW RIVER runs through the Allegheny Mountains in southern West Virginia. It's fast in some places, slower in others, but on any stretch of it the scenery is beautiful. With Class IV rapids in some areas, it has long been a favourite of serious kayakers. And with miles and miles of slower water, it attracts thousands of rafters each year.

They met at a motel in Beckley the first night. Joey, Kyle and four other

Beta brothers. They drank two cases of beer to celebrate the Fourth of July, and woke up with hangovers. Kyle stayed with diet soda and woke up pondering the mysteries of the bankruptcy code. One look at his five friends and he was proud of his sobriety.

Their guide was a rather rustic local named Clem, and Clem had a few rules for the twenty-four-foot rubber raft that was his livelihood. Helmets and life vests were mandatory. No smoking, period. No drinking was allowed in the 'boat' while it was moving down the river. When it stopped, for lunch or for the night, they could drink all they wanted. Clem counted ten cases of beer and realised what he was facing. The first day was uneventful. The sun was hot, and the crew was subdued, even suffering. By late afternoon, they were splashing water and began jumping in. At 5 p.m. Clem found a sandbar to settle into for the first night. After a couple of beers each, they pitched four tents and set up camp. Clem cooked T-bones on a grill, and after dinner the crew ventured off to explore.

Kyle and Joey followed the river for half a mile, and when they were certain they could not be seen, they sat on a log with their feet in the water.

'Let's have it,' Joey said, cutting to the chase.

Kyle loathed the idea of upsetting his friend's life, but he felt he had no choice but to tell the story. All of it.

Joey listened in rapt silence to Kyle's detailed replaying of the initial encounter with Bennie Wright. He was clearly stunned by the existence of the video, bewildered by the blackmail and terrified by the thought of some forgotten girl accusing him of rape and producing evidence to back it up.

Kyle unloaded everything but the background on the lawsuit. He had signed a contract with Scully & Pershing and felt an ethical obligation to protect firm business. This was silly in light of what he would be forced to do, but as yet his career was unblemished.

Joey's first reaction was a halfhearted attempt to deny any contact with Elaine, but Kyle waved him off. 'You're on the video,' Kyle said. 'You're having sex with a girl who's probably floating in and out of consciousness. If it's ever seen in court, the jurors would have no doubt that it's you. I'm sorry, Joey, but you're there. Don't you remember?'

'It was five years ago, Kyle. I've worked hard to forget it.'

'But you do remember?'

With great reluctance, Joey said, 'Yeah, sure, but there was no rape. Hell, the sex was her idea.'

'That's not clear on the video.'

'Well, the video is missing several important details. When the cops showed up that night, Baxter and I ran next door into Thelo's apartment, where there was a smaller and quieter party. Elaine was there, bombed as usual and having a good time. We hung around for a few minutes, waited for the cops to clear out; then Elaine tells me she wants to go back to our place for a 'session', as she liked to call it. With Baxter and me. That's the way she was, Kyle. Always on the prowl. Everybody knew she was the easiest lay at Duquesne. That's why we were stunned when she cried rape.'

'I know. And it's why the police lost interest.'

'Exactly. And there's something else. The night before the party, you and Alan and some others went to a Pirates game, right?'

'Yes.'

'Elaine was in the apartment then, too. And we had a three-way. Me, Baxter and Elaine. Twenty-four hours later, same apartment, same guys, same everything, she passes out, wakes up, decides she was raped.'

'I don't remember this.'

'It was no big deal until she cried rape. Baxter and I decided to keep it quiet in case she might claim we raped her twice. When the police started squeezing us, we finally told them. That's when they packed up and went home. Case closed. No rape.'

A small turtle stopped swimming by a log and seemed to stare at them. They stared back, and for a long time nothing was said.

'Do Baxter and Alan know abut this?' Joey finally asked.

'No, not yet. It was hard enough telling you.'

'Thanks for nothing.'

'I'm sorry. I need a friend.'

'To do what?'

'I don't know. Right now I just need someone to talk to.'

'What do these guys want from you?'

'It's very simple. The scheme is to plant me as a spy in my law firm, where I can extract secrets that the other side can use to win a big lawsuit.'

'Simple enough. What happens if you get caught?'

'Disbarred, indicted, convicted, sentenced to five years in state prison.'

'Is that all?'

'Bankrupted, humiliated, it's a long list.'

'You need more than friends.'

The turtle crawled onto the sand and disappeared into the roots of a tree.

'OK, Kyle,' Joey said after a while. 'You've lived with this since February. You've had plenty of time to think. Right now, I ain't thinking real clear. Tell me what we should do.'

'The big decision has been made. I'm officially employed by Scully & Pershing, and at some point I'll get around to the dirty work. But there are two things I want to know. The first concerns Elaine. Does she have a life, or is she living in the past? According to Bennie, she has a lawyer and she still wants justice. Maybe so, maybe not. Is she still capable of dragging this up again, or has she moved on? I'd like to know the truth.'

'Why?'

'Because Bennie is a liar by trade. If she's still angry, or if she's dreaming of squeezing money out of us, especially Baxter, it's important to know. It could impact what I do at the law firm.'

'Where is she?'

'She lives in Scranton, but that's all I know. For about two thousand bucks we can hire a private investigator to do a background on her. I'll pay it, but I can't arrange it myself, because they're watching and listening.'

'So you want me to do it?'

'Yes. But you have to be careful. No phones or emails. There's a reputable investigator in Pittsburgh. I give you the cash, you give it to him, he does the snooping, gives us the report, and nobody will know about it.'

'Then what?'

'I want to know who Bennie is and who he works for.'

'Good luck.'

'It's a long shot. He might work for an opposing law firm, or a client involved in a big lawsuit, or he might work for some intelligence operation, domestic or foreign. I'd like to find out who I'm spying for.'

'How?'

'I haven't got that far yet.'

'Great. And I'm guessing that I'll be involved in this plan, too.'

'I need help, Joey. There's no one else.'

'Why don't you just go to the FBI and tell them everything?'

'Oh, I've thought of that, believe me. I've spent hours upon hours walking through that scenario, but it's a bad idea. There's no doubt whatsoever that Bennie will use the video to inflict as much misery as possible on me, you, Alan and especially Baxter. You want Blair to know about it?'

'No.'

'This guy is ruthless, Joey. And he has an unlimited budget to do whatever he wants. He would watch us burn and have a good laugh, probably from someplace where the FBI can't touch him.'

'A real prince. You'd better leave him alone.'

'I'm not doing anything stupid. Look, Joey, there's an even chance that I can survive this. When I'm no longer useful, Bennie will disappear. By then, I've violated every ethic in the book and I've broken laws too numerous to mention, but I haven't been caught.'

'That sounds awful.'

And indeed it did. Kyle listened to his own words and was hit again by the folly of it all, and by the bleakness of his future.

They walked back to the campsite in silence. The sun had dropped below the mountains, and night was approaching quickly. Clem added wood to the fire. The crew gathered around and opened beers.

By 9.30 they were all sleepy. The beer and sun and red meat had finally caught up with them. Kyle and Joey shared a tent, and as they were arranging two rather thin air mattresses, Clem yelled across the campsite, 'Be sure and check for snakes.' Then he laughed, and they assumed it was a lame attempt at humour. Ten minutes later they heard him snore. The sound of the river soon put them all to sleep.

Breakfast was scrambled eggs and bacon with onions. Clem cooked over the fire while his crew broke camp and loaded the raft. By eight o'clock, they were floating leisurely on the New River, headed nowhere in particular.

After a month in the city, Kyle savoured the fresh air and open spaces. The thought of returning to New York made him feel ill. It was July 6. The bar exam was in three weeks. Scully & Pershing was two months away.

5

Tuesday morning, September 2, 8 a.m. sharp. A hundred and three nicely dressed and quite apprehensive new associates congregated on the law firm's forty-fourth-floor mezzanine for coffee and juice. After signing in and receiving name tags, they chatted nervously, introduced themselves and looked for friendly faces.

At 8.15 they began to file into the large meeting room, and on the way in each was handed a four-inch-thick notebook with the Scully & Pershing Gothic logo on the front. It was filled with the usual information—a history of the firm, a directory, pages and pages on firm policies, health insurance forms and so on. Each member had a small black-and-white photo with a short bio. The Ivy League dominated, but there was fair representation from other top schools such as NYU, Georgetown, Stanford, Virginia and Duke.

Kyle sat with a group from Yale and played with the numbers. With 103 associates at a starting salary of $200,000, there was now more than $20 million in fresh legal talent sitting in the room. A lot of money, but over the next twelve months each would bill at least 2,000 hours, charged to clients at $300–$400 an hour, generating at least $75 million for the firm. These numbers were not in the binder, but the maths was easy.

At 8.30, several older men entered the room and sat in chairs along the narrow stage. The managing partner, Howard Meezer, stepped to the podium and began an elaborate welcoming speech. Then he outlined the rest of the week. The next two days would be spent listening to various talks about all aspects of life at Scully & Pershing. On Wednesday, they would spend a day in computer and technology training. On Thursday, they would begin orientations in specialised fields. The tedium was rapidly approaching.

The next speaker talked about compensation and benefits. Next was the firm's librarian, who spent a long hour on legal research. A psychologist talked about stress and pressure. The monotony of the lectures was broken by the 'tech team', when they handed out shiny new laptops for everyone. Once the laptops were warmed up, the next technical adviser handed out the dreaded FirmFone. It was similar to most of the current smartphones on the market, but it had been designed especially for Scully & Pershing. It came with contact and biographical information for every lawyer in the firm, in all thirty offices, plus paralegals and secretaries. The database included detailed summaries of all S&P clients, a library of the most commonly used research and a registry of all New York and New Jersey judges and court clerks. The phone was equipped with high-speed Internet access and a dizzying assortment of bells and whistles. It was valuable and invaluable, and had to be kept at hand twenty-four hours a day, seven days a week.

In other words, the fancy little FirmFone now controlled their lives.

There were snide comments and soft groans from the crowd, but nothing too loud. None of the class clowns wanted to get too cute.

Lunch was a quick buffet on the mezzanine. The afternoon dragged on, but interest remained high. The orientation ended at six, and as they hurried out, there was a lot of chatter about heading to the nearby bars.

ON WEDNESDAY, Kyle passed his first test. He and eleven others were assigned to the litigation practice group and led to a conference room on the thirty-first floor. They were greeted by Wilson Rush, the firm's leading litigator and attorney of record for Trylon Aeronautics in its case against Bartin Dynamics, though that lawsuit was not mentioned. The great man told a few war stories, great trials from his illustrious career, then hurried away, no doubt off to sue another large corporation. More thick notebooks were passed out, and the next lecture was on the nuts and bolts of preparing lawsuits, responses, motions and other filings.

The first gunner appeared. There is at least one in every class. A gunner sits in the front row, asks complicated questions, sucks up to whoever happens to be at the podium, stabs backs to make law review, and arrives at the firm with every intention of making partner before anyone else in his class. Gunners succeed magnificently; most make partner.

His name was Jeff Tabor, and they immediately knew where he was from because in the midst of his first question he said, 'Well, at Harvard, we were taught that not all known facts should be included in the initial lawsuit.'

To which the fifth-year associate giving the lecture retorted, 'This ain't Kansas, Toto. It's our way or the highway.' Everyone laughed but the gunner.

At 9 p.m. on Wednesday, the twelve new litigation associates met at a three-star restaurant for what was supposed to be a nice dinner with Doug Peckham, the partner who had supervised Kyle the previous summer. They waited in the bar, and at 9.15 the first comment was made regarding Doug's tardiness. At 9.30 they debated the idea of calling him, but decided against it. Then at 9.40 he called Kyle on his FirmFone with a quick apology. He'd been in trial, things had run late, and he was tending to some urgent matter. They were to proceed with dinner and not worry about the bill.

The fact that a partner was working until 10 p.m. on a Wednesday throttled the enthusiasm for a fine meal, and as the wine flowed they began telling competing stories of associate abuse. The contest was won by Tabor the Gunner, who when lubricated with alcohol was not the asshole he'd been throughout the day. During a recruiting visit a year earlier, Tabor had dropped in on a friend from college, now a second-year associate with another megafirm. While they were chatting, Tabor's friend tried to shove a sleeping-bag under his desk, out of view. Tabor asked, 'What's that for?' and his friend sheepishly explained that he often found it necessary to catch a few hours of sleep during the night when he was overworked. Tabor pressed on and extracted the truth. The firm was a lousy place to work. Most of the rookies were on the same floor, and it was nicknamed 'the Campsite'.

LITIGATION WAS concentrated on floors 32, 33 and 34, and somewhere on the thirty-third floor, far away from the windows, was Kyle's cubicle. It was divided into four equal shares by canvas partitions so that it was possible for him to work at his desk with some small measure of privacy. However, if

Tabor to his right and Dr Dale Armstrong to his left rolled their chairs back no more than two feet, then they could see Kyle and he could see them.

His desk had enough surface area for his laptop, a legal pad, the office phone and not much else. A few shelves finished off the design scheme. He noted that there was barely enough room for a man to unroll his sleeping-bag. By Friday afternoon, Kyle was already tired of the firm.

Dr Dale was a female mathematics whiz who had taught at college before deciding to become a lawyer. She was thirty, single, attractive and frosty enough to be left alone. Tabor was the gunner from Harvard. The fourth member of their little cube was Tim Reynolds, a Penn man who had been eyeing Dale since Wednesday. Among the torrent of firm policies that had been carped on all week, the one that rang loudest was a strict prohibition against office romances. If a love affair blossomed, then one of the two had to go. If a casual affair was discovered, there would be punishment, though its exact nature was not spelled out in the handbook.

Week one was finished. Kyle found a cab and headed for the Mercer Hotel in SoHo. The traffic was slow, so he opened his briefcase and pulled out the FedEx envelope sent from a brokerage house in Pittsburgh. Joey's handwritten note read: *Here's the report. Not sure what it means. Drop me a line*. Kyle found it impossible to believe that Bennie could monitor the avalanche of mail in and out of Scully & Pershing every day, so he and Joey had decided to play it safe with snail mail.

The report had been prepared by a private security firm in Pittsburgh. Its subject was Elaine Keenan, now aged twenty-three, who currently lived in an apartment in Scranton, Pennsylvania, with another female. The first two pages covered her family, education and employment history. She attended Duquesne for only one year, and a quick check of her birth date confirmed that she was not quite eighteen when the episode occurred. After Duquesne, she attended classes off and on at a couple of schools around Scranton, but had yet to finish her degree. There were two minor incidents with the law, both involving underage drinking. The second scrape required counselling for alcohol and drug use. Her attorney had been a local female named Michelin Chiz, better known as Mike. This was notable since Elaine worked part-time in the law offices of Michelin Chiz & Associates. Ms Mike Chiz had a reputation as a fierce divorce lawyer, always on the side of the wives, and always ready to castrate wayward husbands.

Elaine's full-time job was with the City of Scranton as an assistant director of parks and recreation. Salary, $24,000. She had been employed there for almost two years.

Her living arrangement was not clear. Her room-mate was a twenty-eight-year-old female who worked in a hospital, had never been married and had no criminal record. Elaine was observed off and on for thirty-six hours. After work the first day, she met her room-mate in the parking lot near a bar favoured by the alternative crowd. Upon meeting, the two room-mates held hands briefly as they walked to the bar. Elaine had a diet soda and smoked skinny brown cigarettes. The women were very affectionate with each other.

Scranton had a women's shelter called Haven, a refuge and resource centre for victims of domestic abuse and sexual assault. It was staffed by volunteers, many of whom claimed to have been victims. In Haven's monthly newsletter Elaine Keenan was listed as a 'counsellor'.

The cab was at the Mercer. He returned the report to an inside pocket of his briefcase, paid the driver and entered the hotel. Bennie was in a room on the fourth floor, waiting as usual with his customary purpose and appearing to have been there for hours. They did not exchange pleasantries.

'So how was the first week?' Bennie asked.

'Great. A lot of orientation. I got assigned to litigation,' Kyle said as if he'd done something to be proud of. He had succeeded already.

'Very good news. Excellent. Any sign of the Trylon case?'

'No, we haven't been near a real case. This week was just the warm-up.'

'Of course. They give you a phone? A BlackBerry?'

'Something like that.'

'I'd like to see it.'

'I didn't bring it.'

'But the firm requires you to keep it on at all times, is this not true?'

'True. But you won't see it until I'm ready. It's of no value to you at this point, so the only reason you want them is to make sure I'm compromised, right? As soon as I give something to you, I've broken the law, violated ethics, and you own me. I'm not stupid, Bennie. We're going slow here.'

'We reached an agreement many months ago, Kyle. Have you forgotten? You've already agreed to break the law, violate ethics, do whatever I want you to do. And if I want something from the firm, then it's your job to get it. Now, I want the phone, and I want the laptop they gave you, too.'

'No. Not yet.'

Bennie walked back to the window. After a long pause, he said, 'Baxter Tate is in rehab, you know? For some time now.'

'That's what I hear. Maybe he'll clean up and get a life.'

Bennie turned and walked to within striking distance. 'If you don't follow my orders, Kyle, I'll provide a little reminder of who is in charge here. I'm giving serious consideration to releasing the first half of the video. Plaster it around the Internet, notify the folks at Scully & Pershing.'

Kyle shrugged. 'They'll probably think I was just another stupid drunk college kid, like many of them when they were younger.'

'We'll see.' Bennie picked up a thin file from the sideboard, opened it and pulled out a sheet of paper with a face on it. 'You know this guy?' he asked, handing it to Kyle, who glanced at it and shook his head. White male, thirty.

'Name's Gavin Meade, four years at Scully & Pershing, litigation. You'd probably have met him in a few weeks, but Mr Meade is about to be sacked.'

Kyle was holding the sheet of paper, looking into the handsome face of Gavin Meade, and wondering what sin he'd committed.

'Seems he, too, has a little problem from the past,' Bennie was saying. 'In college, ten years ago, he had a girlfriend he used to beat. One night he put her in the hospital. The police were invited in, and Mr Meade was arrested, jailed, formally charged. The girl wanted no part of a trial, so there was a settlement, money changed hands, and everything was dropped. Meade walked away, but he's got this record now. No problem: he just lied about it. When he applied to law school at Michigan, he lied on his application. When he went through the background check at Scully, he lied again. Automatic termination.'

'I'm so happy for you, Bennie. I know how much these little stories mean to you. Go get him. Ruin him. Attaboy.'

'Everybody has secrets, Kyle. I can ruin anyone.'

'You're the man.' Kyle slammed the door and left the hotel.

ON MONDAY, a senior associate named Karleen called them into her office and explained that for the next few days they would be reviewing some crucial documents, billing at least eight hours a day at $300 an hour. Eight hours was the minimum for now, and with lunch and coffee thrown in, that meant, roughly, a ten-hour day, starting no later than 8 a.m.

In case they were curious, Karleen billed 2,400 hours last year. She had been with the firm for five years and acted as though she were a lifer. A future partner. Kyle glanced around the office and noticed a diploma from Columbia Law School. There was a photo of a younger Karleen on a horse, but none of her with a husband, boyfriend or children.

She was explaining that there was a chance that a partner might need Kyle or Dale for a quick project, so be prepared. Document Review was certainly not glamorous, but it was the safety net for all new associates. 'You can always go there and find work that can be billed,' Karleen said. 'Eight hours minimum, but there is no max.'

How delightful, thought Kyle. If for some reason ten hours a day were not enough, the door to Document Review was always wide open for more.

Their first case involved a client named Placid Mortgage. Starting in 2001, when a new wave of government regulators adopted a less intrusive attitude, Placid and other home mortgage companies became aggressive in their pursuit of new loans. They advertised heavily, and convinced millions of lower- and middle-class Americans that they could indeed afford to buy homes that they actually could not afford. Placid sucked them in, collected nice fees up front, then sold the crap in the secondary markets. The company was not holding the paper when the overheated real-estate market finally crashed, home values plummeted and foreclosures became rampant.

Now the lawyers were trying to clean up the mess. Placid had been battered by lawsuits, but the worst one was a class action involving 3,500 of its former borrowers, filed in New York a year earlier.

Karleen led them to a long, dungeon-like room with a concrete floor, poor lighting and neat stacks of white cardboard boxes labelled PLACID MORTGAGE. It was the mountain Kyle had heard so much about: the files of all 3,500 plaintiffs. Each file had to be reviewed.

'You're not alone,' Karleen said with a fake laugh, just as both Kyle and Dale were about to resign. 'We have other associates on this review.' She opened a box, pulled out a file about an inch thick, and went through a quick summary of what the litigation team was looking for.

'Someday in court,' she said, 'it will be crucial for our litigators to be able to tell the judge that we have examined *every* document in this case.'

Kyle assumed it was also crucial for the firm to have clients who could pay through the nose for such useless work.

Karleen left them there. Kyle gawked at the boxes, then at Dale, who looked as stunned as he did. 'You gotta be kidding,' he said.

But Dale was determined to prove something, so she grabbed a box, dropped it on the table, and yanked out some files. Kyle walked to the other end of the room, as far away as possible, and found himself some files. He opened one and glanced at his watch—it was 7.50.

It took an hour to read every word in the file. One point two hours to be exact, as Scully & Pershing lawyers billed by tenths. Suddenly he had no reluctance in billing Placid for 1.2 hours, or $360 for the review. Not long ago, say about ninety minutes, he found it hard to believe he was worth $300 an hour. He hadn't even passed the bar exam. Now, though, he had been converted. Placid owed him the money because their sleaze had got them sued. Someone had to plough through their debris.

Dale left for ten minutes and returned. Probably a bathroom break. He bet she kept the meter running.

Lunch was in the firm cafeteria on the forty-third floor. They were free to leave the building and go to a restaurant, but few associates dared. There was an unwritten rule that the rookies ate in-house unless a client could be billed for a real lunch. Many of the partners used the cafeteria as well. It was important for them to be seen by their underlings, to brag about the great food, and to eat in thirty minutes as an example of efficiency. There was a clock on every wall, and you could almost hear them ticking.

Kyle and Dale joined Tim Reynolds at a small table near a vast window with a spectacular view of other tall buildings. Tim appeared to be shell-shocked—glazed eyes, vapid stare, weak voice. They swapped stories of the horrors of Document Review and began joking about their departures from the legal profession. The food was good, though lunch was not about eating. Lunch was now an excuse to get away from the documents.

But it didn't last long. They agreed to meet after work for a drink, then headed back to their dungeons. Two hours later, Kyle was flashing back to the glory days at Yale when he edited the prestigious law journal from his own office and managed dozens of other very bright students. His name was first on the masthead as editor in chief of a journal read widely by lawyers and judges and scholars. For one year, he was the Man.

How had he fallen so fast and so hard? It's just basic training, he kept telling himself. But what a waste!

Dale was seated fifty feet away with her back to him. It was a nice back, as far as he could tell, trim and curvy. What would happen, he reckoned, if (1) he slowly, over the next few days and weeks, put the move on her, (2) he was successful, and (3) he made sure they got caught? He'd be bounced from the firm, which at that moment seemed like a great idea. What would Bennie say about that? He would lose his spy. His spy would get the boot without getting disbarred. Interesting.

Of course, with his luck, there would probably be another video, this one of Kyle and Dale, and Bennie would get his dirty hands on that, too.

Kyle mulled these things over at $300 an hour. He didn't think about turning off the meter, because he wanted Placid to bleed.

He had learned that Dale earned a Ph.D. in mathematics from MIT at the age of twenty-five, and that she had taught for a few years before deciding to study law. Why she thought she could make the transition from the classroom to the courtroom was not clear, at least not to Kyle. He had just begun the task of trying to unravel her withdrawn and complicated personality.

He stood to go for a walk. 'You want some coffee?' he asked Dale.

'No, thanks,' she said, and actually smiled.

Two cups of strong coffee did little to stimulate his mind, and by late afternoon Kyle began to worry about permanent brain damage. To be on the safe side, he and Dale waited until 7 p.m. before checking out. They left together, rode the elevator down without a word, both thinking the same thought—they were violating another unwritten rule by leaving so early. But they shook it off and walked four blocks to an Irish pub, where Tim Reynolds had almost finished his first pint. He was with Everett, a first-year assigned to the commercial real-estate practice group. After they sat down, all four pulled out their FirmFones and put them on the table like loaded guns.

Dale ordered a martini. Kyle ordered a club soda, and when the waiter disappeared, Tim said, 'You don't drink?'

'No. I had to quit in college.' It was Kyle's standard line, and he knew all of the follow-ups it would provoke.

'You had to quit?'

'Yep. I knew I was drinking too much, so I saw a counsellor, went cold turkey and have never looked back.'

'That's awesome,' Tim said as he drained the pint of ale.

'I don't drink either,' Dale said. 'But after today, I'm hitting the bottle.' From someone with absolutely no sense of humour, this declaration was quite funny. After a good laugh, they toasted Placid Mortgage and the 400,000 foreclosures it had precipitated. They toasted Tabor, who had vowed to stay at his desk until midnight. They toasted Scully & Pershing and its wonderful beginning salaries. Halfway through the martini, the gin hit Dale's mushy brain and she began giggling. When she ordered a second, Kyle excused himself and walked home.

BY 5.30 ON TUESDAY Kyle was wrapping up his second day in the dungeon and mentally drafting his letter of resignation. He would happily tell Bennie to go to hell, and he would happily face Elaine and her rape claim in a courtroom in Pittsburgh. Anything would be better than this.

But then his FirmFone pinged with an email, from Doug Peckham, and it read, 'Kyle, need some help. My office. Now if possible.'

He forgot his letter of resignation, jumped to his feet and bolted for the door. As he dashed by he said to Dale, 'Gotta run and see Doug Peckham, a litigation partner. He's got a project.' She looked shocked and wounded, but he left her there in the Placid dungeon. He ran down two flights of stairs and was out of breath when he walked through Peckham's open door.

The partner was on the phone, and he waved Kyle into a leather chair across from his desk. After signing off with 'You're a moron, Slade, a true moron,' he looked at Kyle, forced a smile and said, 'So how's it going so far?'

'Document Review.' Nothing else needed to be said.

'Sorry about that, but we all suffered through it. Look, I need a hand here. You up to it?' Peckham began rocking in his chair, thrusting himself back and forth without taking his eyes off Kyle.

'Anything. Right now I'll shine your shoes.'

'They're shined. Gotta case here in the Southern District of New York. We're defending Barx in a class action filed by some folks who took their heartworm pills and eventually croaked. Big, messy, complicated case. We go before Judge Cafferty on Thursday morning. You know him?'

I've been here two days, Kyle almost blurted. I don't know anyone. 'No.'

'Caffeine Cafferty. His schedule's called the Rocket Docket because he moves things along. Good judge, but a pain in the ass. Calls up lawyers and screams at them when he thinks their cases are going too slowly. Anyway, this case has dragged on, and he's threatening to send it to another jurisdiction.'

Kyle was scribbling notes as fast as possible. At the first break in the narrative, he said, 'Heartworms?'

'Actually, it's a drug that eats away plaque in the major blood vessels, including the left and right ventricles. We have two partners with medical degrees handling that aspect of the case. Four partners total, as well as ten associates. I'm lead counsel.' He said this with far too much smugness. Then he jumped to his feet and lumbered over to the window.

Bennie's summary had been typically to the point. Peckham's wife was a lawyer who was a partner in a firm down the street. There were two small children. Their apartment on the Upper West Side was appraised for $3.5 million, and they owned the obligatory house in the Hamptons. Last year Doug earned $1.3 million; his wife, $1.2 million.

'Cafferty wants to get rid of the case,' he said. 'We, of course, will fight that. But truthfully, I'd rather see it in another jurisdiction. There are four possibilities—Duval County, Florida; downtown Memphis; a rural county in Nebraska called Fillmore; or Des Plaines, Illinois. Your mission, should you choose to accept it, is to research these four jurisdictions.' He fell into his chair again. 'I need to know what juries do there. How do big companies fare in these places? There are several jury research outfits that sell their data, and we subscribe to it all, but it's not always accurate. You gotta dig. You gotta call lawyers in these four places and find the dirt. Are you in, Kyle?'

As if he had a choice. 'Sure. Sounds great.'

'I wouldn't call it great. I need this by seven thirty Thursday morning. Have you pulled an all-nighter yet?'

'No. I've only been here for—'

'Right, right. Well, get to work. Memo form, but nothing fancy. We'll meet here at seven thirty on Thursday. You'll have ten minutes to do your summary. Anything else?'

'Not right now.'

'I'll be here until ten tonight, so zip me a note if you need something.'

'Thanks, and thanks for getting me out of Document Review.'

The desk phone was ringing as Kyle hustled out of the office. He went straight to the cube, grabbed his laptop and raced off to the firm's cavernous main library on the thirty-ninth floor. He could not remember being so excited over a research project. It was a real case, with deadlines and an angry judge and strategic decisions in the air.

Kyle almost felt sorry for the poor rookies left behind in Document Review. But he knew he'd be back there soon enough. He forgot dinner until almost 10 p.m., when he ate a cold sandwich from a machine. He left the library at midnight—there were at least twenty associates still there—and took a cab to his apartment. He slept four hours, then made the thirty-minute walk back to Broad Street in only twenty-two minutes.

His meter began promptly at 5 a.m. By nine he was calling trial lawyers and defence lawyers in Duval County, Florida, in and around Jacksonville. He had a long list of cases that had gone to trial, and he planned to talk to every lawyer he could get on the phone. There was no word from Doug Peckham, and Kyle was delighted to be given such a free rein.

He left the library at midnight on Wednesday, after billing Barx for eighteen hours. Six the day before. He added two more early Thursday morning as he polished up the fifteen-page memo and rehearsed his ten-minute presentation to Peckham and a team of senior associates. At precisely 7.30 he approached the partner's door and saw that it was closed.

'He's expecting me at seven thirty,' he said politely to a secretary.

'I'll let him know,' she said, without making a move towards the phone.

Five minutes passed as Kyle tried to settle his nerves and appear calm. He had a knot in his stomach, and there was sweat round his collar. Why? he asked himself. It's just a brief presentation before a friendly audience. Ten minutes, fifteen. He could hear voices in Peckham's office. Finally, the door was opened by one of the associates, and Kyle walked in.

Peckham appeared surprised to see him. 'Oh, yes, Kyle, I forgot,' he said, snapping his fingers and frowning. 'I should have emailed. The hearing's been postponed. You're off the hook. Keep the memo. I might need it later.'

Kyle's mouth fell open and he glanced around. Two associates were huddled over a small worktable, papers everywhere. And two more were seated near the desk. All four seemed to be amused.

The False Deadline.

Kyle had heard of this little manoeuvre, though he hadn't seen it coming. The hapless associate is run through the grinder to produce a time-sensitive memo or brief that will never be used. But the client will nonetheless get billed, so even though the research is not needed, it is at least profitable.

'Uh, sure, no problem,' he said, backtracking.

'Thanks,' Peckham said. 'See you later.'

Kyle was at the door when Peckham asked, 'Say, Kyle, where's the best place for Barx to try the case?'

'Nebraska, Fillmore County,' Kyle said eagerly.

Two of the associates laughed out loud, and the other two were highly entertained. One of them said, 'Nebraska? No one tries cases in Nebraska.'

'Thanks, Kyle,' Peckham said, patronising. 'Nice work.'

For $200,000 a year, plus treats, the job would naturally have its moments of humiliation. You're getting paid for this, Kyle kept repeating as he slowly made his way up the stairs. Take it in your stride. Be tough.

Back in the dungeon, he managed to smile. When Dale asked, 'How did it go?' he said, 'It's hard to say.' He sat down, opened a file, and re-entered the world of Placid Mortgage. It was known territory, and he felt oddly safe there. A career as a document reviewer would no doubt be dull, but it would also be much less hazardous than that of a litigator.

6

When Kyle left the office late Friday afternoon, he considered his first week to be a success, though a dismal one. He billed Placid thirty hours and Barx Biomed twenty-six, and though virtually all of this valuable time would eventually mean little to either client, he wasn't paid to worry about such things. He was there to do one thing—bill.

For the week, Tabor the Gunner billed fifty hours. Dale, forty-four. Tim Reynolds, forty-three. It was amazing how consumed they were with the clock after only five days on the job.

He walked to his apartment, changed into jeans, stuffed the FirmFone in one pocket, his own phone in another, and headed for the ballpark. The Mets were at home against the Pirates, who were already guaranteed another losing season. As he made his way to Shea Stadium, he picked up his surveillance as it was picking up him.

His seat was fifteen rows behind the third-base dugout. The night was hot; the Mets were in first; the place was packed. He timed his entrance perfectly and sat down as the first pitch was thrown. To his right was a young boy holding a baseball glove and eating ice cream. To his left was a real fan with a Mets cap, Mets jersey, even goofy Mets eyeglasses. Under the cap was Joey Bernardo, who had spent his entire life in Pittsburgh and hated the Mets.

'Do not acknowledge me,' Kyle said as he watched the field.

'Don't worry. Right now I hate your guts. And I hate the Mets almost as much as I hate you.'

'Thanks.'

They were talking out of the corners of their mouths, just loud enough to hear each other.

Joey took a sip of a tall beer. 'Are they really following you?'

'Oh, yes. Every day, everywhere.'

'But why?'

'Information is crucial. The more they watch and listen, the more they know about me. One day they might be able to use it to their advantage.'

A ball bounced off the left-field wall, scoring a run, and the crowd was on its feet. When things had settled down, Joey asked, 'How about the report on Elaine?'

'It worries me.'

'So what's next?'

'I think you should go see her. Just bump into her and see what happens.'

'Right! Drive to Scranton, a town I can't recall seeing in the last ten years, somehow find her, recognise her, assume she'll recognise me, then what? Have a friendly little chat about the last time we were together? Have a laugh for old times' sake? Hell, Kyle, she accused me of rape.'

'Shhhh,' Kyle hissed softly. The word 'rape' sort of hung in the thick air, but no one reacted to it.

'Sorry,' Joey whispered, and they watched the game for a long time.

A ferocious argument erupted at first base after a close call, and all 50,000 fans had an opinion. In the roar, Kyle said, 'It would be an interesting meeting. To see how she reacts. Is she bitter, angry, full of vengeance? You take the high road and say that the encounter has always troubled you, that you want to talk about it. See if she'll meet you for a drink and a serious conversation. You're not going to admit anything, you just want to see how she feels. Maybe you want closure. What's there to lose?'

'What if she recognises me, pulls out a gun, and bam!?'

'I'll take care of Blair.' Kyle managed this with a grin, though the thought of spending any more time with Joey's girl was not pleasant.

'Thanks. She's pregnant, you know. Thanks for asking.'

'Why is she pregnant?'

'Basic biology. But we're both surprised.'

'Congratulations, Daddy.'

'Getting married is one thing, but I'm not so sure about this fatherhood business. She said she was on the pill, but I don't know.'

This was not a topic Kyle wanted to explore. He changed the subject. 'Any word from Baxter?' he asked without moving his jaws.

'Nothing. I think they've locked him in a cave.'

'I know the feeling. I've been in a dungeon all week.'

'For the money they're paying you, no complaints.'

'OK, OK. They know he's in rehab, and they probably know where he is,' Kyle said as a long fly ball was caught on the warning track.

'They?'

'The goons. Their leader told me last week that he's in rehab.'

Joey sipped his beer. With the cup in front of his mouth he said, 'If they know about Baxter, are they keeping tabs on me?'

'It's possible. Play it safe. Vary your movements. Be careful with all correspondence.'

'Oh, this is just great.'

'My apartment is full of cameras and mikes. Everything I do there is being watched and recorded. But they don't know that I know, so I give them nothing of consequence.'

'So you're outsmarting these professional intelligence agents?'

'I think so.'

Another pause in the conversation as the Pirates changed pitchers.

'What's the endgame, Kyle?'

'I don't have one. I'm taking small, safe steps. Next, we make contact with the girl and see how bad things are there.'

Kyle reached for his vibrating pocket and yanked out the FirmFone. He found the message, and felt like cursing.

'What is it?' Joey asked.

The resignation of Gavin Meade, a fourth-year associate in litigation, had been announced. No details. Nothing but a quiet and quick exit.

'It's nothing,' Kyle said.

Everybody has secrets, Bennie had said. How did he do it? Perhaps an anonymous package mailed to someone in Human Resources. Affidavits, police records, the works. Poor Meade, ten years removed from his crime and hustling through the grind at $400,000 a year, when suddenly he gets a summons to a meeting with closed doors.

During the seventh-inning stretch, Kyle eased out of his seat and made his way to the gates. Joey stayed until the eighth, and finally he left as his beloved Pirates were losing their ninetieth game.

TANNED, FIT AND CLEAR-HEADED, Baxter Tate rode through the gates and left behind the safety of the Washoe Retreat, 105 days after he had arrived.

Following a series of tense phone calls between Uncle Wally and Dr Boone, Baxter's chief therapist, it had been agreed that Baxter was finally ready to be released. But before 're-entry' into the real world, he would spend three nights in a halfway house in Reno. An orderly was driving him there.

Not only had Baxter kicked booze and drugs, he had also quit smoking and had lost ten pounds. He exercised strenuously and was fanatical about his diet: no coffee, tea or sugar. He thoroughly believed he had conquered his demons and would henceforth live the sober life. He had confessed his sins and surrendered to a higher power, whatever that was. At the age of twenty-five, he was beginning a new life. But as the miles passed, Baxter became more apprehensive, even frightened. His confidence was rapidly disappearing. He had failed so many times in so many ways.

During the two-hour drive into Reno, little was said. As they approached the city, they passed a splashy billboard advertising an imported beer in a cold green bottle and fear hit Baxter harder. It consumed him, and beads of sweat lined his forehead. He wanted to turn round, to run back to the clinic, where there was no alcohol and no temptations. But he said nothing.

Hope Village was in a run-down section of Reno—abandoned buildings, cheap casinos and bars. It was the domain of Manny Lucera, the founder, pastor and leader of Hope Village.

A large man wearing dungarees and sandals was waiting at the kerb outside the church when Baxter stepped onto the hot sidewalk. He grabbed Baxter's hand and shook it violently. 'Mr Tate, may I call you Baxter?'

The question suggested its own answer. He was Baxter, not Mr Tate.

'Sure,' Baxter said.

'I'm Brother Manny,' he said, placing his thick left arm on Baxter's shoulder, completing a rather rough howdy-do. 'Welcome to Hope Village.'

He was about fifty, Hispanic, with a thick barrel chest, bronze skin, grey hair pulled back tightly into a ponytail that fell to his waist, warm eyes, big toothy smile, a small scar beside his left nostril and a larger one on his right cheek. His face was adorned with a soft white beard.

'Come, I'll show you around,' he said with a deep, melodious voice. 'We have you for just three nights, as I understand.'

'That's right.'

They began walking slowly. Brother Manny kept one arm across Baxter's shoulders. 'You look pale,' he said as they reached the front door of the mission church. 'Are you OK?'

'No.' It was refreshing to be so honest. A tear rolled down his cheek. He wiped it away with the back of his hand. 'I don't want to go back to LA.'

'You can't, son. You go back there and you'll be dead in five years. When you're an addict, you're powerless in the face of booze and drugs. Strength comes from somewhere else. For me, it comes from the Holy Spirit.'

'I don't feel very strong right now. Can you help me? I'm pretty shaky here, OK? I mean, I'm really scared.'

'Do you know Christ, son?'

'I guess. My mother took me to church every Christmas.'

Brother Manny smiled. 'Let's pray together, Baxter.'

'I'll try.'

SIX MONTHS after the Trylon–Bartin dispute went public with the filing of the lawsuit, the battleground had been defined and the troops were in place. Both sides had filed ponderous motions designed to capture the higher ground, but so far no advantage had been gained. They were, of course, still haggling over deadlines, schedules and who got to see what, and when.

A trial was nowhere in sight, but then it was far too early. With monthly billings to Trylon averaging $5.5 million, why would Scully & Pershing push the case to a conclusion? And with Bartin Dynamics paying just as much for a vigorous and gold-plated defence coordinated by the bare-knuckle litigators at Agee, Poe & Epps, the case just plodded along.

The hottest issue so far was no surprise to either set of litigators. When the forced marriage of Trylon and Bartin unravelled, there had been a virtual slugfest for the documents. Hundreds of thousands, perhaps millions of documents had been generated during the development of the B-10 HyperSonic Bomber. Researchers employed by Trylon grabbed all the documents they could. Researchers for Bartin did the same. Software was routed and rerouted, and some of it was destroyed. Thousands of secured files disappeared. Crates of printed documents were hidden. And throughout the melee each company accused the other of lying, espionage, outright thievery.

Because of the supersensitive nature of the research, the Pentagon watched in horror as the two companies behaved outrageously. The Pentagon and several intelligence agencies leaned heavily on Trylon and Bartin to keep their dirty laundry private, but they were ultimately not successful. The fight was now controlled by the lawyers and the courts.

A major task for Mr Wilson Rush and his Scully & Pershing team was to index, copy and store all documents in the possession of Trylon. A warehouse was leased in Wilmington, North Carolina, about a mile from the Trylon testing facility. A Washington security firm wired the warehouse with twenty closed-circuit cameras, and armed guards patrolled the empty warehouse long before any of the documents arrived.

When they did arrive, over a two-week period in mid-September, they came in unmarked tractor-trailer rigs, complete with more armed guards. The warehouse, nicknamed Fort Rush, came to life as ton after ton of paperwork was stacked neatly in white cardboard boxes, all waiting to be organised into a system understood only by the lawyers up in New York.

Ten of the most trusted associates from Mr Rush's litigation team were shipped to Wilmington. Under his direction, every document was copied twice and instantly scanned into the firm's virtual library. When the task was complete, the library would be accessible by a secured code, and once inside, a lawyer could locate any document in seconds. The firm's computer experts were supremely confident that the library's security was impenetrable.

To impress upon the associates the gravity of their seemingly mindless work, Mr Rush stayed for three days and was involved in the sorting, scanning, copying and repacking. When he left, two other litigation partners remained and directed traffic. Such mundane work was normally contracted out to a copying service, but that was far too risky with these documents. They had to be handled by real lawyers, all averaging around $400,000 in salary. They were forbidden to discuss any aspect of Fort Rush with anyone in New York. Security and confidentiality were paramount.

In the first six weeks, 2.2 million documents had been copied, indexed and added to the library.

By then, Bennie knew exactly where the warehouse was located and had a general idea of its security features, but his interest in these matters was only passing. What Bennie wanted, of course, was access to the virtual library, access only his spy could deliver.

JOEY BERNARDO stood outside a sandwich shop not far from the parks and recreation complex where Elaine Keenan worked. For another $1,000, the security firm in Pittsburgh had watched her long enough to determine her routine, and this was where she usually had lunch with some co-workers.

Joey wasn't sure he could sell a chance encounter with Elaine. Aside from the casual sex five and a half years earlier, he'd never really known her. After studying the three colour photos that the security firm had provided, he was not even convinced he'd ever met the girl.

Now, at the age of twenty-three, her dark hair was tinted a deep red and worn very short. There was no make-up, no lipstick, nothing but matching tattoos around her forearms. Somewhere under all the attitude was a cute girl, but if she had any interest in being attractive, it was not apparent.

Joey swallowed hard and entered the sandwich shop. He eased behind her as she waited to order, and after a few minutes, as the line moved slowly forward, managed to bump into her. 'Sorry,' he said with a wide fake smile.

She smiled back, but said nothing. He moved a step closer and said, 'Hey, you were at Duquesne a few years ago, weren't you?' Her two co-workers glanced back but were not interested.

'Briefly,' she said, eyeing him carefully, searching for any clue.

He snapped his fingers as if trying to recall something. 'Elaine? Right? Can't think of the last name.'

'That's right. And who are you?'

'Joey Bernardo. I was in Beta.'

A look of horror swept over her face, and she dropped her gaze to the floor. For a moment she was frozen. Then she shuffled a step to keep pace in line. She turned her back on him, obviously frightened.

Joey watched her nervously from the corner of an eye.

She turned halfway to him and hissed, 'What are you doing here?'

'I'm eating lunch, same as you.'

'Would you please leave?' Her voice was barely audible, but one of her co-workers turned round and glared at Joey.

'No. I'm just getting a sandwich.'

Nothing else was said as they ordered and moved down to the pick-up counter. Elaine hurried off to a distant table with her two friends. Joey ate alone at a small table near the door. The note was already prepared. It read: *Elaine: I'd like to talk to you about what happened. Please call my cell at 412-866-0940. I'll be in Scranton until 9 a.m. tomorrow. Joey Bernardo*. He hauled his tray back to the counter, then walked to her table, handed her the note without a word, and disappeared.

Two hours later, she called.

At 5 p.m. sharp, as agreed, Joey returned to the sandwich shop. He found Elaine at the same table she'd used for lunch. She was accompanied by her attorney. Icy introductions were made, and Joey sat down across from them with a knot in his throat and a strong desire to maim Kyle.

Elaine's lawyer was an attractive middle-aged woman whose business card proclaimed her to be Michelin 'Mike' Chiz, Attorney & Counselor at Law. She began matter-of-factly: 'My first question for you, Mr Bernardo, is, what are you doing here?'

'How many questions do you have?' Joey asked in his finest smart-ass manner. He had been assured time after time by his pseudo-lawyer, one Kyle McAvoy, that there was no danger in this chance meeting with Elaine Keenan. Any legal action she wanted to initiate could have been commenced long ago. Five and a half years had passed.

'Well, Mr Bernardo, I have just a few questions. I have represented Ms Keenan for some time now. She works part-time in my office, a fine paralegal, and I'm familiar with her story. Now, what are you doing here?'

'First of all, I don't have to explain a damned thing to you. But I'll try to be nice. I work for a brokerage firm in Pittsburgh, and we have some clients in Scranton. I'm here to see these clients. I got hungry around noon today. I chose this four-star restaurant at random, walked in, saw Ms Keenan here, said hello, she freaked, I wanted to chat, and now I'm taking questions from her lawyer. Why, exactly, do you need a lawyer, Elaine?'

'You raped me, Joey,' Elaine blurted. 'You and Baxter Tate, and maybe Kyle McAvoy.' By the time she finished, her eyes were moist. Her breathing was heavy, almost heaving, as if she might lunge at him at any moment.

'Maybe this, maybe that. You never got your story straight.'

'Why did you want to talk to my client?' Ms Chiz demanded.

'Because it was a misunderstanding, that's all. After she cried rape, we never saw her again. The cops investigated, found nothing because nothing happened, and by then Elaine had disappeared.'

'You raped me, Joey, and you know it.'

'There was no rape, Elaine. We had sex—me and you, you and Baxter, you and most of the other boys at Beta—but it was all very consensual.'

Elaine closed her eyes and began shaking as if chills swept her body.

'Why does she need a lawyer?' Joey asked Ms Chiz.

'She's suffered greatly.'

'I don't know how much she's suffered, Ms Chiz, but during her days at Duquesne she was too busy partying to spend time suffering. Lots of booze, drugs and sex, and there are lots of boys and girls perfectly capable of refreshing her memory. You'd better get to know your client before you pursue some bogus legal action. There's a lot of bad stuff back there.'

'Shut up!' Elaine snarled.

'You want to apologise to her?' the lawyer said.

'Yes. Elaine, I apologise for the misunderstanding, whatever the hell it was. And I think you should apologise for accusing us of something that did not happen. And right now, I want to apologise for even being here.' Joey sprang to his feet. 'This was not a good idea. So long.'

He walked quickly out of the deli, strolled to his car and left Scranton. Driving back to Pittsburgh, when he wasn't cursing Kyle McAvoy, he was hearing her voice again and again. *You raped me, Joey.* Her words were painful and free of doubt. She may not have known precisely what happened in their apartment five years earlier, but she certainly knew now.

He hadn't raped anyone. What began as consensual sex, at her suggestion, had now been transformed into something different, at least in her mind.

You raped me, Joey.

The mere accusation carried a heavy dose of suspicion, and for the first time Joey questioned himself. Had he and Baxter taken advantage of her?

FOUR DAYS LATER, Kyle stopped by the mail room at Scully & Pershing and picked up a letter from Joey. It was a detailed summary of the encounter. After setting out the facts, Joey concluded with the words:

EK has definitely convinced herself that she was raped by several of us, JB and BT for sure and 'maybe' KM. She is weak, fragile, haunted, but at the same time carries a certain smugness in her victimhood. Her attorney is a tough broad who wouldn't hesitate to start legal trouble if she could find any evidence. If that little video is half as damaging as you say it is, then by all human means keep it locked away from these people. Elaine and her lawyer are two cobras, coiled and ready to strike.

I think we should meet up and hash out our next moves. I have two tickets to the Steelers–Giants game on October 26. Shall I call you with this news so your goons will know about it? Your faithful servant, Joey.

Kyle read the letter and summary in the main library while hiding between shelves of ancient law books. It confirmed his worst fears, but he had little time to dwell on it. He quietly tore the sheets of paper into a hundred pieces, then dropped them in a wastebasket as he left the library.

The hotel nearest his apartment was the Chelsea Garden, a fifteen-minute walk. At eleven that cool, autumn night, Kyle dragged himself along Seventh Avenue, numb with fatigue, looking for the hotel.

Bennie was waiting in a suite on the third floor. 'You're two hours late,' he snarled.

'Sue me.' Kyle stretched out on the bed. This was their fourth meeting in New York since Kyle had moved there, and he had yet to hand over anything that Bennie wasn't supposed to have. His ethics were still intact.

So why did he feel like such a traitor?

Bennie was tapping a large white board mounted on an easel. 'This won't take long,' he said. 'Have some coffee if you'd like.'

Kyle poured himself some coffee, and sat on the edge of the bed. 'Go.'

'This is the Trylon team. At the top here is Wilson Rush, and below him are eight litigation partners—Mason, Bradley, Weems, Cochran, Green, Abbott, Etheridge and Wittenberg. How many have you met?'

Kyle studied eight squares with names scrawled inside them. 'Wilson Rush spoke to us during orientation, but I haven't seen him since. I did a memo for Abbott on a securities case, met him briefly, and I had lunch one day in the cafeteria with Wittenberg. I've seen Bradley, Weems, maybe Etheridge, but I can't say I've met them. It's a big firm.'

His supervising partner was Doug Peckham, and he was relieved that Peckham's name was not on the board.

There were smaller squares below the partners. Bennie tapped a finger near them. 'There are sixteen senior associates, and under them sixteen younger ones. The names are in that binder over there. You need to memorise them.'

'Sure, Bennie.' Kyle glanced at the binder. How Bennie knew the names of all forty-one lawyers assigned to the Trylon case was a question Kyle didn't even want to consider. How many sources did he have?

'How many of these associates have you worked with?'

Kyle looked back at the board. 'Five, six, maybe seven,' he said vaguely.

Bennie pointed to a smaller box. 'This is a senior associate named Sherry Abney. You met her?'

'No.'

'A rising star, fast track to partnership. Two degrees from Harvard and a federal clerkship. She reports to Partner Mason, who's in charge of discovery. Under her is a second-year associate by the name of Jack McDougle. McDougle has a cocaine problem. No one at the firm knows it, but he's about to get busted. His departure will be quick.'

Kyle stared at the board. How did Bennie know all this?

'And you want me to take his place?'

'I want you to schmooze it up with Sherry Abney. Get to know her. She's thirty years old, single but committed to an investment banker at Chase who works as many hours as she does, so they have no time for any fun. No wedding date, as of now. She likes to play squash, when she can find the time, and, as you know, the firm has two courts beside the gym. You play squash?'

'I guess I do now.' Kyle had played several times at Yale. 'Not sure when I'll find the time.'

'You figure it out. She just might be your entrée onto the Trylon team.'

Kyle planned to avoid Trylon and its litigation team as diligently as possible. 'Small problem here, Bennie,' he said. 'Nice homework, but you're missing the obvious. There are no first-year grunts anywhere near this case. The smart boys at Trylon probably told their lawyers to keep the rookies away from it. So, Bennie, where is plan B?'

'It takes patience, Kyle. And politics. You start angling for the Trylon case, kissing the right asses, networking, and we might get a lucky break.'

Kyle wasn't finished with the discussion about McDougle. He was about to pursue it when another man suddenly appeared from the sitting room adjacent to the bedroom. Kyle was so startled he almost dropped his coffee.

'This is Nigel,' Bennie was saying. 'He'll spend a few minutes on systems.'

Nigel thrust forward a hand to shake. 'A pleasure,' he sang in a cheery British way. He then moved to the easel and mounted his own display.

Kyle looked through the open double doors into the sitting room. Nigel had been hiding in there and listening to every word.

'Scully & Pershing uses a litigation support system called Jury Box,' he began quickly. All movements were rapid and precise. British, but with a strange accent. Forty years old. Five feet ten inches, 150 pounds. Short dark hair, half grey. No remarkable features. Thin lips. Brown eyes. No glasses.

'How much have they taught you about Jury Box?' Nigel asked.

'The basics. I've used it on several occasions.'

'It's your typical litigation support system. All discovery is scanned into a virtual library that can be accessed fast by all lawyers working on the case. It's fairly secure, pretty standard stuff. Scully also uses a more secure system for sensitive files and cases. It's called Barrister. You in on this one?'

'No.'

'Not surprised. They keep it quiet. Works pretty much like Jury Box, but much harder to access, or to hack into. Keep your ears open for it.'

Kyle nodded as if he would do precisely as he was being told. Since that awful night when he'd been ambushed after a youth-league basketball game in New Haven, he had met only with Bennie Wright. Or whoever he really was. Why was he being introduced to someone else with a bogus name now? Bennie was certainly capable of handling Nigel's little presentation.

'And then you have the Trylon case,' Nigel was singing. 'A completely different matter, I'm afraid. Much more complicated and secure. Whole different batch of software, really. But we've made progress.' He stopped long enough to allow himself a quick approving smile at Bennie.

Aren't we clever?

'We know that the program is code-named Sonic, as in B-10 HyperSonic Bomber, not very creative if you ask me, but then they didn't, did they? Ha-ha. Sonic can be accessed only from a secret, heavily secured room on the eighteenth floor of your building. Pass codes change every week; pass-words every day, sometimes twice a day. Sonic is probably a bastardised version of Barrister, so it will be incumbent upon you to master Barrister as soon as you're given the opportunity.'

Can't wait, Kyle almost said.

Slowly, through the fatigue, it was sinking in that Kyle was crossing the line, and doing it in a way he had not envisioned. Instead of delivering Scully & Pershing's secrets to Bennie like Judas for thirty pieces of silver, he was receiving firm secrets from an outside source. He had yet to steal anything, but he damn sure wasn't supposed to know about Sonic and the hidden room on the eighteenth floor. Perhaps it wasn't criminal and maybe it wasn't a violation of the canons of ethics, but it certainly felt wrong.

'That's enough for now,' Bennie was saying. 'You look exhausted. Get some rest.'

AT 5 A.M., the usual hour now, the alarm clock exploded at full volume and Kyle slapped it twice before it shut off. He hurried through the shower and the shave, and fifteen minutes later he was on the sidewalk, fashionably dressed because he could certainly afford fine clothes. His life was a mess, but he was determined to look nice as he stumbled through the day. He bought a coffee, a bagel and a copy of the *New York Times* at his favourite all-night deli, then caught a cab. Ten minutes later, he walked into the Broad Street entrance of his office building, and rode the elevator up.

He was not surprised to see another young lawyer at the cube. Tim Reynolds had been the first to sneak in a sleeping-bag, and now he was curled under his small desk, inside the sleeping-bag, dead to the world. Kyle kicked his feet and woke him up

'You look like crap,' he said pleasantly.

'Good morning,' Tim said, scrambling to his feet. 'What time is it?'

'Almost six. What time did you go to sleep?'

'Sometime after two,' he said, pulling on his shirt. 'I have a memo due for Toby Roland at seven and I have no idea what I'm doing.'

Kyle unpacked his briefcase. 'Just keep billing,' he said without sympathy.

Tim finished dressing and grabbed a file. 'I'll be in the library.'

'Don't forget to brush your teeth,' Kyle said.

When Reynolds was gone, Kyle switched on his laptop and went online to a website called QuickFace.com, which allowed amateur sleuths to put together composite sketches of faces. He began with Nigel's eyes, always the most important feature. Get the eyes right, and half the identification is over. The site offered over 200 different types of eyes—every race, colour, origin and blend. Kyle found the closest set, and began his face. He tinkered and sculpted until 6.30. When Nigel's face was properly put together, Kyle printed it and hustled off to the library, carrying a thick file. His private spot was a dead end in a dark corner on the third level of stacked tiers, a lonesome place where they stored thick tomes of annotations no one had used in decades. On the second shelf from the bottom, he lifted three of the books and removed a manila envelope. He opened it and added Nigel's face to the three composites inside—splendid renderings of his archenemy, Bennie, and two of the goons who were stalking him around New York City.

He hid the envelope and returned to the cube, where Tabor the Gunner was busy preparing for the day. The issue of whose career held the most promise had been settled weeks earlier. Tabor was the man, the star, the fast-tracked partner-to-be, who had proven his talents by billing twenty-one hours in a single day. He'd shown his skill by billing more the first month than all other litigation rookies, though Kyle was only four hours behind.

'Slept in the library last night,' he said as soon as he saw Kyle.

'Good morning, Tabor.'

'The carpet in the main library is thinner than the carpet in the twenty-third library. Did you know that, Kyle? I much prefer sleeping on the twenty-third, but it does have more noise. Which do you prefer?'

'We're all cracking up, Tabor.'

'Yes, we are.'

'Tim used his sleeping-bag last night. I woke him up an hour ago.'

'So you went home? Slept in your own bed?'

'Oh, yes.'

'I have two projects due at noon. I can't afford the luxury of sleep.'

'You're the greatest, Tabor. Go, Superman.'

And with that Tabor was gone.

DALE ARMSTRONG arrived promptly at seven, and though she looked a bit sleepy, she was put together as always. Evidently, the bulk of her fat salary was being spent on designer clothing, and Kyle, along with Tim and Tabor, looked forward to the daily fashion statement.

'You look great today,' Kyle said with a smile.

'Thank you.'

'Prada?'

'Dolce & Gabbana.'

'Killer shoes. Blahniks?'

'Jimmy Choo.'

Admiring her each day, Kyle was quickly learning the names of the high priests of female clothing. It was one of the few topics she cared to discuss. After six weeks, he still knew very little about her. When she talked, which was not very often, it was always about law-firm business. If there was a boyfriend, he had yet to be mentioned. She had dropped her guard twice and agreed to drinks after work, but she usually declined.

'What are you doing for lunch?' Kyle asked.

'I haven't had breakfast yet,' she replied coolly, and withdrew into her little section of the cube.

7

The lights in the shelter came on each morning at six, and most of the homeless awoke and began making preparations for another day. The rules did not allow them to stay past eight o'clock. Many had jobs, but those who didn't were expected to be on the streets looking for employment. Brother Manny and his staff were very successful in placing their 'friends', even if the work was often part-time and minimum wage.

Breakfast was served upstairs in the fellowship hall, where volunteers manned the small kitchen and prepared breakfast. It was served with a smile, a warm 'Good morning' for everyone, and a quick prayer of thanks once they were all seated. For the past month, the kitchen had been supervised by Baxter Tate. Baxter had scrambled eggs by the dozen, toasted loaves of white bread, prepared the oatmeal, washed the dishes, restocked the supplies and often said the prayer. He encouraged the other volunteers, had a kind word for everyone, and knew the names of most of the homeless he served. After they had eaten, he loaded them into three old church vans, drove one himself, and delivered them to their various jobs around Reno.

Alcoholics Anonymous met three times each week at Hope Village—Monday and Thursday nights and at noon on Wednesday. Baxter never missed a meeting. He was warmly received by his fellow addicts, and quietly marvelled at the groups' compositions. All races, ages, male and female, professionals and homeless, rich and poor. Alcoholism cut a wide, jagged path through every class, every segment.

Following the Twelve Steps to recovery, he made a list of all the people he had harmed and then made plans to make amends. It wasn't a long list and was heavily focused on his family. He did not, however, look forward to a return to Pittsburgh. He had talked to Uncle Wally. The family knew he was still sober, and that was all that mattered.

After a month, he began to grow restless. He did not relish the thought of leaving the safety of Hope Village, but he knew the time was coming. Brother Manny encouraged him to make his plans. He was too young and smart and gifted to spend his life in a homeless shelter.

'God has big plans for you,' Brother Manny said. 'Just trust Him and they will be revealed.'

WHEN IT LOOKED as if they might escape at a decent hour on Friday night, Tim Reynolds and others quickly organised a drinking party and hurried out of the building. Tomorrow was Scully & Pershing's annual family picnic in Central Park. Friday night was therefore cleared for serious drinking.

Kyle declined, as did Dale. Around 7 p.m., as they were both wrapping up the last details of an endless week, she said, 'What about dinner?'

'Great idea,' Kyle said without hesitation. 'Any place in particular?'

'My place. We can relax and talk and do whatever. You like Chinese?'

'Love it.' The word 'whatever' was bouncing around his addled brain. Was she picking him up? It was a startling idea. Dale was so shy and reserved it was hard to believe she would put the move on anyone.

'Why don't you pick up some Chinese and bring it over?' she said.

'Great idea.'

An hour later, Kyle was climbing the stairs of her Greenwich Village fourth-floor walk-up with a sack of shrimp-and-chicken fried rice. He knocked on the door and Dale opened it with a smile, and welcomed him to her apartment. Two rooms, a den-kitchen combo and one bedroom. It was small but nicely decorated. Her white cotton skirt was extremely short and revealed more of the slender legs that Kyle and the other vultures had been admiring. Her shoes were open toe, red leather, high-class-tart stuff.

Kyle glanced at them and said, 'Jimmy Choos?'

'Prada.'

The black cotton sweater was tight, without a bra under it. For the first time in many weeks, Kyle began to feel the excitement of sexual arousal.

'Nice place,' he said, looking at a photograph.

'Four thousand a month, can you believe it?' She opened the fridge.

'Yes, I can believe it. It's New York.'

She reached into the fridge and took out a bottle of chardonnay. 'I'm sorry, but I don't have any club soda. It's either wine or water.'

'I'll have some wine,' he said, with only a slight hesitation. And he decided that he would not torment himself about whether or not he should take a drink after five and a half years of sobriety. He'd never been to rehab, never considered himself an alcoholic. He had simply stopped drinking because he was drinking too much, and now he wanted a glass of wine.

They ate on a small square table, their knees almost touching. Even at home and completely relaxed, conversation did not come easily for Dale. He couldn't picture her in a courtroom in front of a jury.

'Let's agree that we will not talk about work,' Kyle said, taking the lead.

'Agreed, but first there's some gossip. Have you heard about the split?'

'No.'

'There's a rumour, I heard it twice today, that Toby Roland and four other partners, all in litigation, are about to split and open their own firm.'

'Why?'

'A fee dispute. The usual.'

'Have you met Toby?'

'Yes. And I hope the rumour is true.'

'Who's the biggest prick you've met so far?'

She took a sip of wine and thought about the question. 'That's a tough one. So many contenders.'

'Too many. Let's talk about something else.'

Kyle managed to shift the conversation around to her. Background, education, childhood, family, college. She had never been married. One bad romance still stung. After one glass of wine she poured another, and the alcohol loosened her up. She pushed the topics back to his side of the table, and he talked about Duquesne and Yale.

When the wine and food were gone, she said, 'Let's watch a movie.'

'Great idea,' Kyle said. As she looked through her DVDs, he glanced at his watch. Ten twenty. In the past six days he'd pulled two all-nighters and averaged four hours of sleep each night. He was physically and mentally exhausted, and the two and a half glasses of quite delicious wine he'd just consumed were thoroughly soaking whatever brain he had left.

'Romance, action, comedy?' she called out as she flipped through her collection. She was on her knees, the skirt barely covering her rear.

'Anything but a chick flick.'

'How about *Beetlejuice*?'

'Perfect.'

She inserted the disk, then kicked off her heels, grabbed a quilt and joined Kyle on the sofa. She wedged and wiggled and snuggled and pulled the quilt over them, and when she was finally settled, there was a lot of contact. Kyle sniffed her hair and thought how easy this was.

'Doesn't the firm have a rule against this sort of thing?' he said.

'We're just watching a movie.'

Warmed by the quilt, the wine and each other's bodies, they watched the movie for all of ten minutes. Later, they could not determine who fell asleep first. Dale woke up long after the movie was over. She spread the quilt over him, then went to bed. Kyle woke up at 9.30 on Saturday morning to an empty apartment. There was a note saying she was round the corner at a coffee shop reading the newspapers, so stop by if he was hungry.

THEY RODE THE SUBWAY together to Central Park, arriving around noon. The litigation section of the firm threw a family picnic on the third Saturday of each October, near the boathouse. The main event was a softball tournament, but there were also horseshoes, croquet, bocce and games for the kids. A caterer barbecued ribs and chicken. A rap band made its noise.

The picnic was to promote camaraderie and to prove that the firm did indeed believe in having fun. Attendance was mandatory. The weather was perfect, and the weary lawyers shook off their fatigue and were soon playing hard and drinking even harder. Kyle and Dale, anxious to avoid even the possibility of gossip, soon separated and got lost in the crowd.

Within minutes, Kyle heard the news that Jack McDougle, a second-year associate, had been arrested the night before when a narc team found a substantial stash of cocaine in his apartment. The firm was pulling strings to get him out of jail, but the firm's involvement on his behalf would only go so far. Scully & Pershing took a hard line on such behaviour. If the gossip turned out to be true, he would find himself unemployed in a few weeks.

Kyle paused for a few minutes and thought about Bennie. His second chilling prediction had come true.

LITIGATION HAD twenty-eight partners and 130 associates. Two-thirds were married, and there was no shortage of young, well-dressed children running around. The softball tournament began with Wilson Rush announcing the rules and declaring himself acting commissioner. Several lawyers had the guts to boo him, but anything was permitted on this fine day. Kyle found himself on a ragtag team with two people he had met and seven he had not. Their coach was a partner named Cecil Abbott (of Team Trylon), and it was soon evident that Coach Abbott had never run to first base in his life. But who cared? Kyle, easily the best athlete, was stuck in right field. In centre was Sherry Abney, the fifth-year associate Bennie was stalking as Kyle's entrée into the Trylon–Bartin case. As they came to bat, Kyle introduced himself and chatted her up. She was visibly upset by the McDougle arrest. They had worked together for two years. No, she had no idea he had a drug problem.

Mingling was encouraged, and after Coach Abbott's team was finally saved by the mercy rule in the fourth inning, Kyle plunged into the crowd and said hello to every strange face he encountered. The conversations were all the same—where'd you go to school, how's it going so far, life gets better after the first year. And, 'Can you believe McDougle?'

The tournament was double elimination, and Kyle's team distinguished itself by becoming the first to lose two games. He found Dale playing bocce, and they headed for the food tent. With plates of barbecue, they joined Tabor and his girlfriend at a table under a tree. Tabor, of course, was on a team that was undefeated, and he'd driven in the most runs so far.

You win, Kyle wanted to say. You win. Why don't they just go ahead and declare you a partner?

Late in the afternoon, Kyle eased away from the party and found a park bench under an oak. He watched the game in the distance, listened to the happy voices, smelled the last of the smoke from the grills. If he really tried, he could almost convince himself that he belonged at that party, that he was just another successful lawyer taking a quick break from his hectic life.

But reality was never far away. If he got lucky, he would commit a heinous crime against the firm and not get caught. But if luck went against him, then one day during this family picnic they would be talking about him the way they were talking now about McDougle.

TWO HOURS before the Giants–Steelers game began in Pittsburgh, Kyle and Joey settled into their seats at the forty-yard line and tried to stay warm. A cold front had chased away autumn and a freezing mist hovered above the stadium. It didn't matter. They welcomed the cold. This was real football weather.

Mercifully, Blair had little interest in football. Now five months pregnant, she had gained an enormous amount of weight and was not handling prospective motherhood too well. Joey was having second thoughts about marriage, but felt trapped. Kyle had little useful advice.

As the crowd settled in and the teams warmed up, Kyle was ready to talk. 'Speak softly, and tell me about Elaine Keenan,' he said.

Joey had a flask filled with vodka, his antifreeze. He took a swig, grimaced as if it tasted awful and said, 'She is one bitter young woman. But she's not nearly as mean as her lawyer.'

'Start at the beginning, and tell me everything as it happened.'

Another swig, then Joey launched into a thoughtful, detailed re-enactment of his trip to Scranton, finishing with the admonition, 'If they have the slightest opening, they'll attack us with a fury. Don't give them the opening. Let's just bury this little episode.'

They watched the game for a while and talked about nothing but football. During a time-out, Joey said, 'So what's the plan?'

'Can you come to New York next weekend? Steelers–Jets. Four o'clock Sunday at the Meadowlands. I'll get tickets.'

'Oh, boy. I don't know.' The problem was Blair, with money also a concern. Joey made a nice salary with commissions, but he wasn't getting rich. Now that he had a baby on the way and an expensive new condo to pay for, he couldn't afford to spend too much watching football.

'Why do you want me in New York?' he asked.

'Because I want to try to get a photo of Bennie.'

Joey took another sip and leaned close to Kyle. 'How, old buddy, do you plan to do that? This guy's a professional operative, right?'

'Something like that.'

'You're a lawyer, I'm a stockbroker. We have no idea what we're doing, and we could easily get ourselves in trouble.'

'Yes, we could.'

Kyle took a small package from a pocket of his bulky black and gold Steelers parka. 'Take this,' he said, keeping it low so that no one could see it.

Joey took it and stuffed it into a pocket of his own black and gold Steelers parka. 'What is it?'

'It's a video camera. But not one you're likely to see in a store window.'

The Steelers scored the game's first touchdown, and the crowd celebrated for five minutes. During the ensuing time-out, Kyle continued: 'It's not much larger than an ink pen. It goes in the pocket of a jacket, with a wire running to a control switch in your left hand. You can talk to someone face to face and video the conversation without their knowledge.'

'So I just walk up to Bennie, who's probably heavily armed, and introduce myself and ask him to smile.'

'No. There's a better way. But this week you need to practise with it. If things go perfectly, you'll have about three seconds to video Bennie.'

'And if they don't go perfectly?'

'I'll rescue you.'

'Great.' A long, nervous swig from the flask. 'So, Kyle, let's say we get Bennie on video. How do you go about identifying him?'

'I haven't figured that out.'

'There's a lot you haven't figured out.'

'I'll email you Tuesday, tell you I've got tickets. Are you in, old pal?'

'I don't know. I think you're crazy, and you're making me crazy.'

'Come on. You need to have some fun while you can.'

KYLE WAS HARD AT WORK in the main library when the FirmFone rattled softly at four on Thursday afternoon. The email commanded the first-year associates to congregate immediately on the forty-fourth-floor mezzanine, the largest gathering place at Scully & Pershing. The message meant only one thing—the bar exam results were in.

The ritual varied from firm to firm, but Scully & Pershing had a rather pleasant way of breaking the news. They gathered the lucky ones together and threw a party. Though it was supposed to be a surprise, by the second week of September every new associate knew the drill. The cruel part was that the unlucky ones were simply not invited. They were left to sneak out of the building and wander the streets for the rest of the day.

As Kyle ran up the stairs and raced along the hallways, he searched for his friends. He saw Dale and gave her a hug, and they walked quickly together to the mezzanine. The crowd was already in a raucous mood before Mr Howard Meezer, the firm's managing partner, stepped onto a small podium and said, 'Congratulations. Let's have a party.'

Champagne corks were soon flying. Bartenders were busy, and waiters began passing delicious antipasti. The general feeling was one of euphoria, even giddiness, because the nightmare of the past weeks and months was over and they were now lawyers for ever.

Kyle was enjoying a glass of champagne with Dale and a few others when Tim Reynolds approached them with a nasty smile. He had a drink in one hand and a printout in the other. 'Tabor flunked,' he announced proudly. 'Can you believe it? A Harvard casualty.'

Kyle wasn't as pleased. Sure, Tabor was obnoxious and opportunistic, but flunking the bar would kill him. He wasn't a bad guy.

Word spread; the body count rose. In all, there were 8 failures out of 103, an excellent pass rate of 92 per cent. Once again it was clear that they were the brightest stars and were now destined for even greater things.

They got as drunk as possible, then rode home in private sedans arranged by the firm. Kyle had only two drinks and walked to Chelsea. Along the way, he called his father with the wonderful news.

KYLE'S APPOINTMENT at noon Friday with Doug Peckham was described as a working lunch to review some discovery, but when Kyle arrived the partner said, 'Let's celebrate.' They left the building and crawled into the back of a Lincoln sedan, one of the 'black cars' that roam the city and keep the professionals out of the yellow cabs. The firm had a fleet of them on call.

'Been to Eleven Madison Park?' Doug asked.

'No. I don't get out much these days, Doug, because I'm a first-year associate and I'm either usually too tired to eat or I simply forget.'

'Whining, are we?'

'Of course not.'

'Congrats on passing the bar.'

'Thank you.'

'You'll like this place. Great food, beautiful dining room. Let's have a long lunch, with some wine. I know just the client we can stick it to.'

Kyle nodded. Two months in, and he was still uncomfortable with the notion of sticking it to clients. Overbilling. Racking up expenses.

The restaurant was in the lobby of the old Metropolitan Life Building, with views of Madison Square Park. Doug claimed to know the chef, and Kyle was not surprised when they were seated at a table looking at the park.

'Let's get your evaluation out of the way,' Doug said.

'Evaluation?'

'Yes, it's my job as your supervising partner to evaluate you after the bar results. If you'd flunked, we'd probably be stopping by one of those carts pushed by a street vendor, selecting a hot dog and having a bad conversation. But you passed, so I'm going to be nice.'

'Thank you.'

The waiter presented menus while the water was poured. 'Your billing is above average,' Doug said. 'In fact, it's very impressive.'

'Thanks.' No surprise that any evaluation at Scully & Pershing would begin with how much money one was raking in.

'I've had nothing but positive comments from other partners. At times, though, you seem to lack commitment, as if you're not fully on board. Fair?'

Kyle shook his head. 'I live, eat and sleep at the firm, like every other first-year associate, because that's the business model some guy came up with years ago. What else can I do to prove my commitment?'

'Good point,' Doug said, suddenly much more concerned with the menu. The waiter hovered, waiting.

'You ready?' Doug said. 'I'm starving.'

Kyle had yet to look at the menu and was still stinging from the criticism of his commitment. 'Sure,' he said. Everything looked delicious.

They ordered and the sommelier appeared. During the serious wine discussion that followed, Doug mentioned a 'first bottle' and a 'second bottle'.

The first was a white burgundy. 'You'll love it,' Doug said. 'One of my favourites.'

'I'm sure.'

'Any problems, complaints?' Doug asked, as if he were clicking off the items on the evaluation checklist.

'No, just the usual complaints of associate abuse. You've heard them before, and you don't want to hear them now.'

'You're right, Kyle, I don't. Look, we survived it, and now we reap the rewards. It's a bad business model because everybody's miserable. You think I want to push myself out of bed at five every morning so I can spend twelve crazy hours at the office so, at the end of the year, we can divide the spoils and be at the top of the rankings? Last year APE's partners averaged one point four million. We were at one point three million, and everybody panicked. We gotta cut costs! We gotta bill more! It's crazy. No one ever stops and says, "Hey, you know, I can live on a million bucks a year and spend more time with my kids, or at the beach." No, sir. We gotta be number one.'

'I'll take a million bucks a year.'

'You'll get there. Evaluation's over.'

'One quick question.'

'Shoot.'

'There's a cute first-year associate, and I'm growing rather fond of her. How big a deal is it?'

'Strict prohibition. How cute?'

'Getting cuter by the day.'

Doug took a breath and leaned forward on his elbows. 'There's a lot of sex around the place. You put five thousand men and women together and it happens. The unwritten rule is this: don't screw around with the employees. Secretaries, paralegals, support staff. As for your fellow associates—or partners, for that matter—no one really cares as long as you don't get caught.'

The first courses arrived and sex was forgotten. Kyle had a leek and cheese tart. Doug went a bit heavier with a salad of Maine lobster with fennel and black trumpet mushrooms.

'A bit of a shake-up is coming,' Doug said. 'I'm sure you've heard.'

Kyle nodded with a mouth full.

'It's probably going to happen. Five of our litigation partners are leaving with a bunch of associates and several clients. The mutiny is being led by Toby Roland. It will knock a hole in litigation. But we'll survive.'

'How do we fill the gap?'

'We'll raid another firm. They didn't teach you this in law school?'

They both laughed and returned to their food for a moment.

'Is Trylon leaving or staying?' Kyle asked between bites.

'Trylon is an old client, firmly within the protective custody of Mr Wilson Rush. What do you know about Trylon?' Doug eyed him closely.

'Just what I've read in the newspapers and magazines.' Kyle decided to push on, just a little. 'What's this Bartin dispute all about? The *Journal* said the court file is locked away because the issues are so sensitive.'

'Military secrets. The Pentagon is all over it. There's a lot of technology involved, not to mention a few hundred billion dollars.'

'Are you working on it?'

'No. I passed. There's quite a team, though.'

Fresh bread arrived to cleanse the palate. The first bottle was empty, and Doug asked for the second. Kyle was carefully pacing himself.

'The partners and associates who are leaving,' Kyle said, 'how many are working on the Bartin lawsuit?'

'I don't know. Why are you so interested?'

'Because I don't want to work on it.'

'Why not?'

'Because I think Trylon is a rogue defence contractor with a rotten history of making cheap products, screwing the government and the taxpayers, dumping dirty weapons around the world, killing innocent people, promoting war and propping up nasty little dictators.'

'The company is an extremely valuable client. And associates are not allowed to choose who they work for.'

'I know. I'm just sharing my opinion.'

'Well, don't. That kind of language will get you a lousy reputation.'

'Don't worry. I'll do the work that's assigned to me. But as a favour, as my supervising partner, I'm asking that you keep me busy elsewhere.'

'I'll see what I can do, but Mr Rush makes the final decisions.'

Their entrées arrived—braised pork shoulder and aged prime rib of beef—and they got serious about eating.

'You know your rate now goes to four hundred,' Doug said, chewing.

Kyle nodded. He was not sure he had the spine to bill a client $400 for an hour of his inexperienced legal work. Not that he had a choice.

'On the subject of billing,' Doug said, swirling his wine in the goblet, 'let's bill Ontario Bank for this lunch.'

'I was planning to get the cheque,' Kyle said, in a lame effort at humour.

'Of course not. I'll put it on a credit card and bill the bank. I'm talking about our time. Two hours for you, now at four hundred, and two for me at eight. The bank had record earnings last year.'

That was nice to hear. They would need healthy earnings to continue their relationship with Scully & Pershing. Twenty-four hundred dollars for lunch, and that did not include food, wine or tip.

'And now that you've passed the bar,' Doug said as he took another bite, 'you are entitled to use the black cars and bill clients for dinner. The rule goes like this: if you work until eight o'clock at night, then call a car. I'll give you the number and code, and be sure the client gets billed for the car. And if you choose, you can go to a restaurant, spend no more than a hundred bucks on yourself, and also bill the client.'

'You gotta be kidding.'

'Why?'

'Because I'm at the office almost every night until eight, and if somebody else is buying dinner, then I'll be damned sure I stay until eight.'

'Attaboy.'

'Seems kinda rich, doesn't it? Billing clients for expensive meals and cars.'

'Kyle, my boy, look at it this way. Our biggest client is BXL, the seventh-largest company in the world, sales last year of two hundred billion dollars. They have a budget for everything. Last year their budget for legal fees was one per cent of total sales, or about two billion. They use twenty different law firms around the world, but we got our share of that. Guess what happens if they don't spend the amount they budget? Their in-house lawyers call up and raise hell. Aren't we, their lawyers, properly protecting them? The point is, they expect to spend the money. If we don't take it, it screws up their budgets, they get worried, and maybe they start looking around for another firm, one that will work harder at billing them. You follow?'

Yes, Kyle followed. Expensive meals were necessary not only to keep the hungry lawyers going but also to properly balance their clients' financial statements. Now it seemed almost prudent.

'Yes,' Kyle said, and for the first time the wine made him relax.

Doug spread his arms and looked around. 'And look at where we are, Kyle. Wall Street. The pinnacle of success in America. We're smart, tough and talented, and we make a boatload of money to prove it. We are entitled, Kyle. Our clients pay us because they need us and we offer the best legal advice money can buy. Never forget that, Kyle.'

John McAvoy had lunch every day at an old café on Queen Street in York, and from the time Kyle was ten years old and hanging around the office, he loved having lunch with his father. The café attracted lawyers, bankers and judges, as well as mechanics and bricklayers. The gossip roared and the banter was nonstop. The lawyers always joked, 'Who's paying for lunch?' and boasted of sticking their clients with a $3.99 cheque. Kyle doubted that his father ever gave a passing thought to billing a client for lunch.

Doug insisted on dessert. Two hours after entering the restaurant, Doug and Kyle pushed themselves out of the door. Both nodded off during the ride back to the office.

FOR THE FIRST time in the nine-month life of the operation, Kyle contacted Bennie and suggested they meet. All prior meetings had been prompted by the handler, not the asset. Kyle gave no reason for wanting to meet, but it was assumed that he finally had something valuable to pass along.

Kyle emailed Bennie the instructions: 7 p.m. Saturday, room 42, Wooster Hotel in SoHo. So far, a different hotel had been used for each meeting.

On a desk phone, Kyle called Joey's new cell number and passed along the details. His flight from Pittsburgh would arrive at LaGuardia at 2.30 p.m. on Saturday. He would take a cab to the Mercer Hotel, check into his room, then kill time roaming the streets, browsing through bookstores, darting here and there in cabs. When he was certain he was not being followed, he would drop in at the Wooster Hotel and mill around the lobby. He had in his pocket a copy of Kyle's QuickFace composite of Bennie Wright. Joey had studied it for hours and was confident he could spot the man anywhere. Now Kyle wanted Bennie in complete digital colour.

At 7.30, Kyle walked through the hotel lobby and took the elevator to the fourth floor. Bennie had a small room, no suite this time. As Kyle tossed his trench coat and briefcase on the bed, he glanced into the bathroom.

'Just looking for Nigel, or perhaps another surprise,' he said. He could see no luggage or shaving kit or anything to indicate Bennie would stay in the room after he left.

'Just me this time,' Bennie said. 'You passed the bar. Congratulations.'

'Thanks.' Kyle sat on the edge of the bed. He noted Bennie's shirt—light blue cotton, no pattern, no necktie. The slacks were dark brown, wool, pleated. The jacket was evidently in the closet.

'Here's the scoop,' Kyle said. 'Five litigation partners are splitting off—Abraham, DeVere, Hanrahan, Roland and Bradley. They're opening up their own shop and stealing at least three clients in the process. As of last count, twenty-six associates are jumping with them. Of the partners, Bradley is the only one working on the Trylon–Bartin case. However, at least seven of the associates are assigned to the lawsuit.'

Kyle pulled out a single sheet of paper, tri-folded, and handed it over. It had the names of all the Scully & Pershing lawyers who were leaving. There. He'd done it. He'd handed over firm secrets, and there was no turning back.

Except that it was not exactly accurate. The gossip was changing by the hour, and no one seemed to know precisely who was planning to leave. Nor was it highly confidential information he was passing along. The *New York Lawyer*, the trade daily, had carried at least two brief stories about the spin-off. Besides, Kyle knew that Bennie already knew as much as he did.

Kyle watched as Bennie unfolded the memo and studied it carefully. Then he said, 'I need to use the bathroom.'

As he walked to the bathroom, Kyle passed the closet, its door half open, and hanging on a rack was a navy sports jacket and a grey trench coat.

'I'm not sure this means anything,' Kyle said when he returned. 'Trylon's in-house attorneys prefer more experienced associates. Those leaving are likely to be replaced with third- and fourth-year people. I'm still a long shot.'

'Patience, Kyle, patience. Good intelligence is based on long-term placement and relationships. You'll get there.'

'I'm sure I will, especially if you keep picking off the associates ahead of me. How'd you get rid of McDougle? Plant the drugs in his apartment?'

'Come on, Kyle. The young man had a serious problem with cocaine. Now he's on the road to recovery.'

'You asshole! He's on the road to prison.'

'He was dealing coke, Kyle. A menace to society.'

Kyle stood and began gathering his things. 'Gotta run. My old pal Joey Bernardo is in from Pittsburgh for the Jets game tomorrow.'

'How nice,' Bennie said, getting to his feet.

Kyle slammed the door behind him and hurried down the hallway. He ran down four flights of stairs and entered the lobby. He made eye contact with Joey, then went straight to the men's room. There were three urinals to the right. He straddled the centre one, waited about ten seconds, then was joined by Joey on the left. There was no one else in the men's room.

'Light blue shirt, no tie, navy jacket, all under a dark grey trench coat. No sign of a briefcase, hat or umbrella. He should be down shortly, alone. Good luck.' Kyle pulled the flush handle, and left.

JOEY WAITED two minutes, then returned to the lobby, where he picked up his newspaper from a chair and sat down. His dark hair had been cut short the day before and was almost entirely grey. He wore fake glasses with black frames. The camera, slightly larger than a pen but practically indistinguishable from one, was in the pocket of his brown corduroy jacket.

A hotel security agent in a smart black suit watched him, though not with any real suspicion. Thirty minutes earlier, Joey had explained to the agent that he was waiting on a friend who was upstairs.

Ten minutes passed, then fifteen. Each time an elevator door opened, Joey tensed slightly. He kept the newspaper low, on his knees, so that he could appear to be reading while the camera had a clear shot at the target.

The door to the elevator on the left opened, and Bennie was there all by himself. The composite of his face was remarkably accurate—slick bald head, a few strands of black hair greased down about the ears, long narrow nose, square jaw, heavy eyebrows over dark eyes. Joey swallowed hard, his head down, and squeezed the 'on' button in his left hand. For eight steps, Bennie walked directly towards him, then veered with the marble walkway towards the front door and was gone. Joey switched off the camera, breathed deeply, and became engrossed in his newspaper. He looked up each time the elevator opened, and after half an hour he feigned frustration with his tardy friend upstairs and stomped out of the hotel. No one followed.

KYLE WAITED NERVOUSLY at the bar in the Gotham Bar and Grill on 12th Street. He sipped a glass of white wine and chatted occasionally with the bartender. Their reservation was for 9 p.m.

Joey arrived promptly. There was no hint of grey in his hair now and he had exchanged the brown corduroy jacket for a more stylish black one. His smile told the story. 'Got him,' he said as he took a stool.

'So?' Kyle said softly as he watched the door for anything suspicious.

'Double Absolut on the rocks,' Joey said to the bartender. Then to Kyle, much lower, he said, 'I think I nailed him. He waited sixteen minutes, used the elevator, and I shot him for at least five seconds before he passed me.'

'Did he look at you?'

'I don't know. I was reading the newspaper. No eye contact, remember. But he never slowed down.'

'Good work, pal. Now we enjoy a fine meal—'

'And tomorrow we watch the Steelers kill the Jets.'

They clinked glasses and savoured their triumph.

BENNIE YELLED at the three operatives who had lost Joey after his arrival in the city. They had first lost him late in the afternoon, not long after he had checked in at the Mercer and hit the streets. Now he was having dinner with Kyle at the Gotham Bar and Grill—exactly where he was supposed to be. The operatives swore he moved as if he knew he was being followed. He had deliberately tried to shake them. 'And did a damned fine job, didn't he?' Bennie yelled.

Two straight football games, one in Pittsburgh, now one in New York. Joey was the only friend from college Kyle was now regularly in touch with. The warning signs were there. Something was being planned.

Bennie decided to beef up surveillance on Mr Joey Bernardo.

They were also watching Baxter Tate and his remarkable transformation.

AT 4.30 ON MONDAY morning, Kyle hurried off the elevator, alone, on the thirty-third floor and walked to his cube. As usual, lights were on, doors were open, coffee was brewed, someone was working. Someone was always working, regardless of the day or hour.

'Good morning, Mr McAvoy.' It was Alfredo, one of the plainclothes security agents who roamed the hallways during the weird hours.

'Good morning, Alfredo,' Kyle said as he wadded his trench coat and tossed it in a corner, next to his sleeping-bag.

'How 'bout those Jets?' Alfredo asked.

'I'd rather not discuss it,' Kyle shot back. Twelve hours earlier, the Jets had drubbed the Steelers by three touchdowns in heavy rain.

'Have a nice day,' Alfredo said happily as he walked away, his day obviously made better because his team had slaughtered the Steelers and, more important, he'd found a place to rub it in.

Kyle unlocked his drawer and pulled out his laptop. After making sure he was alone, Kyle slid the tiny T-Klip from the video camera into an adapter, which he plugged into his laptop. He waited a few seconds, clicked twice, then froze as the image appeared: Bennie in perfect colour. Rewind, watch it again and again. He chose the best shot, and quickly printed five copies.

He had his man, at least on tape. How about this little video, Bennie? Guess you're not the only one who can play games with hidden cameras. Kyle quickly fetched the copies from the printer and stared at the face of the rotten little son of a bitch who was currently in charge of his life.

There was a voice somewhere nearby, and Kyle put away his laptop, hid the T-Klip, and walked up six flights to the main library. There, lost among the stacked tiers, he added the prints to his hidden file.

The next step in his scheme had not yet been determined. He wasn't certain there was a next step. But for the moment, Kyle was content to take a breath, savour a small victory and tell himself there was a way out.

JUST MINUTES after the markets opened Monday, Joey was chatting with a client who wanted to dump some more oil stocks when his second desk phone rang. He routinely carried on more than one phone conversation at the same time, but when the second caller said, 'Hey, Joey, it's Baxter. How are you?' Joey got rid of the client.

'Where are you?' Joey asked.

'Here, in Pittsburgh,' he said. 'Clean and sober for a hundred and sixty days now.'

'That's great, Baxter. Wonderful. I knew you were in rehab.'

'Yes, Uncle Wally again. God bless him. You got time for a quick lunch? I need to talk to you about something.'

'Sure. What's up?'

'Nothing much. Just want to say hello. Grab a sandwich and meet me down at Point State Park. I'd like to sit outdoors and watch the boats.'

'Sure, Baxter.' Joey was becoming suspicious.

'Noon OK?'

'See you then.'

At noon, Baxter showed up dressed in old dungarees, a faded navy sweater and a pair of black combat boots. They embraced and swapped insults, and found an empty bench near the point where the Allegheny and Monongahela rivers merge.

'You seen Kyle?' Baxter asked when they were settled, and they spent a few minutes catching up about Kyle, Alan Strock and a few of the other fraternity brothers. When Baxter spoke, he did so softly and slowly and he gazed across the rivers, as if his tongue was working but his mind was engaged elsewhere. When Joey spoke, Baxter listened but did not really hear.

'You seem detached,' Joey said, blunt as ever.

'It's just weird being back, you know. Plus, now that I'm sober and all of that poison is out of my system, I look at things differently. I'm no longer the Baxter Tate you once knew.'

'Good for you, but the old Baxter wasn't such a bad guy.'

'He was a selfish, pompous, drunken pig, and you know it.'

'True.'

'He would have been dead in five years.'

An old barge inched along the river, and they watched it for a few minutes. Joey unwrapped his turkey on rye and began eating.

'I'm working my way through recovery,' Baxter announced quietly. 'My counsellor and pastor is known affectionately as Brother Manny. He's led me through the AA's Twelve Steps recovery process. Under his direction, I've made a list of all the people I harmed along the way.'

'And I'm on the list?'

'No, you didn't make it. Sorry.'

'Darn.'

'It's mainly family members. They're on my list, and I'd probably be on their lists if they ever got serious about life. Now that I've made the list, the next step is to make amends. It sounds frightening, doesn't it?'

'It does.'

'I assaulted a girl one time. She's on my list.'

'You don't say.' The turkey on rye froze halfway down the oesophagus. Joey kept chewing, but the food wasn't moving.

'Elaine Keenan, remember her? She claimed we raped her at a party in our apartment.'

'How could I forget?'

'Do you ever think about her, Joey? I tried my best to forget about it, and I almost did. But now that I'm sober and my mind is clear, I'm remembering things better. We took advantage of that girl, Joey.'

Joey placed the sandwich aside. 'What I remember is a wild girl who loved to party, loved to drink and snort coke, but what she loved the most was random sex. We did not take advantage of anyone. At least I did not. If you want to revise history, then go ahead, but don't include me.'

'She passed out. I went first, and while I was doing it, I realised she'd blacked out. Afterwards she claimed she was raped. Maybe she was right.'

'No way, Baxter. Allow me to refresh your memory. You and I had sex with her the night before. Evidently she liked it, because on the night in question we bumped into her again and she said, "Let's go." She consented before we got back to our apartment.'

Another long pause as each tried to anticipate what was next.

'You thinking about having a little chat with Elaine?' Joey asked.

'Maybe. I need to do something. I don't feel right about what happened.'

'We were all drunk out of our minds. The whole night was a blur.'

'Now I've finally sobered up, I feel compelled to at least apologise.'

'Apologise? Let me tell you what'll happen if you apologise, Baxter. There will be indictments, arrests, trials, lawsuits, prison. And not just for you, Brother Baxter, but for some of your friends as well. You get near her with some half-baked, feel-good apology and you'll find out what rape is all about when they lock you away.'

Baxter shook his head. 'I've got to talk to her.'

'Hell no! You're not going near her until the four of us—me, you, Kyle and Alan—have a long discussion. That'll be ugly, won't it?'

'I need to talk to Kyle. He has more sense than the rest of us.'

'Yes, he does, but he has a crushing workload. Tremendous stress.' Joey tried to imagine a meeting between the two. Kyle, thinking about the video, while Baxter confirmed the details. It would be a disaster.

He thumped his pal on the knee. 'You can't do this, Baxter,' he said with as much conviction as he could muster. He was thinking now about his own skin. How would he tell Blair, who was five months pregnant? *Hey, babes, just got a phone call. Seems they want me downtown, something about a rape charge. Could be serious. Might not be home for dinner. Someone said reporters are waiting. Catch it on Channel 4. Later. Hugs and kisses.*

'I'm not sure about what happened, Joey,' Baxter said, softly and slowly as ever. 'But I know what I did was wrong.'

'If you approach her and beg forgiveness, she and her lawyer will go nuts and drag in me and probably Kyle and Alan as well. You can't do it, Baxter.'

'If you did nothing wrong, you have nothing to worry about. I'm confronting what I did, and what I did was wrong.'

'This is crazy, Baxter. Look, you're clean and sober. Good for you. I'm very proud of you. The future looks great, yet you're willing to throw it all away and risk twenty years in prison. Come on! This is madness.'

'Then what should I do?'

'Go back to Reno,' he said. 'Give it some time. Pray about it. Talk to your minister. Look, you're in a state of transition right now. It would be a mistake to rush off and do something foolish.'

'Let's walk,' Baxter said, and slowly rose to his feet. They strolled along the river, saying little, watching the boats.

'I really want to see Kyle,' Baxter finally said.

8

In the four and a half months that Kyle had lived in his grim little apartment, he had managed to avoid having guests. Dale had asked about it a few times, but when Kyle described his place as a dump with almost no furnishings, lukewarm water and bugs, she let the matter drop. She was content to meet at her place. She had a fear of bugs. If you only knew, thought Kyle. My apartment has every kind of bug known to the covert world.

They had eventually managed to sleep together without actually falling asleep beforehand. Both collapsed shortly afterwards. They had violated firm policy on at least four occasions and had no plans to stop.

When Baxter called and asked if he could crash at Kyle's for a few days, Kyle was ready with a string of lies that were mildly convincing. Joey had sent a Mayday call from his desk phone to Kyle's just minutes after he'd said goodbye to Baxter. 'We gotta do something,' Joey said over and over until Kyle told him to shut up.

'Sorry, Bax,' Kyle said happily on his cellphone. 'I have only one bedroom, and my cousin has been sleeping on the sofa for a month. She's in New York looking for a job, and, well, I gotta say, the place is cramped.'

Baxter checked into the Soho Grand. They met for a late pizza at an all-night joint on Bleecker Street in the Village. Kyle picked the place because it had only one door in and out, large front windows that faced the sidewalk, lots of noise, and it was too small for one of the bloodhounds to enter without being noticed. Kyle arrived at 9.45, fifteen minutes early so he could secure a booth and sit facing the door. He pretended to be engrossed in a thick document, the tireless associate ever dedicated to his work.

Baxter was wearing the dungarees, sweater and combat boots that Joey had described. They embraced, then fell into the booth talking nonstop. They ordered soft drinks, and Kyle said, 'I talked to Joey. Congrats on the rehab. You look great.'

'Thanks. I've thought about you a lot in the past few months. You quit drinking during our sophomore year, right?'

'Right. I didn't have a serious problem, but one was definitely foreseeable. So I quit. Didn't touch a drop until a few weeks ago, when I had some wine. So far, so good. If I get worried, I'll quit again.'

'I had three bleeding ulcers when they took me in. I was a mess.'

They ordered a pizza and talked for a long time about the past, primarily Baxter's. Kyle listened intently while keeping an eye on the front door and the front windows. Nothing.

After an hour, when the pizza was gone, they eventually got round to more pressing matters. 'I guess Joey told you about Elaine,' Baxter said.

'Of course he did. It's a bad idea, Baxter. I understand the law, and you don't. You're walking into quicksand and you could take us with you.'

'But you did nothing. Why are you worried?'

'Here's a scenario,' Kyle said. 'You go see Elaine, looking for some type of redemption, forgiveness, whatever. You apologise to someone you once hurt. Maybe she turns the other cheek and accepts your apology, and you two have a nice hug and say goodbye. That probably will not happen. What is much more likely to happen is that she decides that what she really wants is justice. She wants vindication. She cried rape once and nobody listened. And you, with the best intentions, will vindicate her with your awkward apology. Things unravel quickly. There's a prosecutor in Pittsburgh who's tired of the mundane, the gang shootings, the daily street crime. Suddenly he has a chance to go after four white boys from Duquesne, and one just happens to be a Tate. Talk about headlines, press conferences, interviews. He'll be the hero, and we'll be the criminals. Of course we are entitled to a trial, but that's a year away, a year of absolutely terrifying hell. You can't do it, Baxter. You'll hurt too many people.'

'What if I offer her money? A deal with only two parties, me and her?'

'It might work. But offering money implies guilt. I don't know Elaine, and neither do you, so we can't predict how she will react. It's too risky.'

'I can't live with myself until I talk to her, Kyle. I feel like I harmed her in some way.'

'Got that. It sounds great in the AA handbook, but it's a different matter when other people are involved. You want to do something that will make you feel better. Well, good for you. What about the rest of us? Your life will be more complete; our lives could be ruined.'

'I can apologise to Elaine without admitting I committed a crime. I'll just say that I was wrong and want to apologise. I have to do something.'

'No, you don't,' Kyle said, raising his voice. He was surprised at the stubbornness across the table. 'You don't have the right to ruin our lives.'

'I'm not ruining your life, Kyle,' Baxter said. 'You did nothing wrong. I'll take all the blame,'

'Why are you so determined to get yourself into more trouble than you can imagine? You're toying with prison here, Baxter. Wake up, man!'

'I'll take the blame,' he repeated, very much the martyr now. 'You guys will walk.'

'You're not listening, Baxter. This is more complicated than you realise.'

A shrug. 'I'm listening to you, Kyle, but I'm also listening to the Lord. And he's leading me to Elaine. To forgiveness. I believe she will listen, and forgive.' Baxter was firm, and pious, and Kyle had little else to throw at him.

'Let it sit for a month,' Kyle said. 'Don't do anything hasty. Joey, Alan and I should have a say in the matter.'

'Let's go. I'm tired of sitting here.'

They roamed the Village for half an hour before Kyle, exhausted, finally said good night. He was dead to the world when his cellphone rang three hours later.

It was Baxter. 'I talked to Elaine,' he announced proudly. 'Tracked her down, called her, woke her up, and we talked for a few minutes.'

'You idiot,' Kyle blurted before he could stop himself.

'It went pretty well, actually.'

'What did you say?' Kyle was in the bathroom, splashing water on his face with one hand and holding his phone with the other.

'I told her I've never felt right about what happened. I didn't admit to anything other than some misgivings.'

Thank God for that. 'What did she say?'

'She thanked me for calling, then she cried and said no one has ever believed her. She still feels like she was raped. She's always known it was Joey and me, with you and Alan somewhere close by watching the action.'

'That's not true.'

'We're gonna meet in a couple of days, have lunch, just the two of us, in Scranton.'

'Don't do it, Baxter, please don't do it. She works for her lawyer, part-time. Did she tell you that? A lawyer who specialises in cases of this sort. You'll walk into a trap and your life will be over.'

'My life is just beginning, old pal. Faith, Kyle, faith. Good night.' The phone snapped shut; the connection was dead.

BAXTER FLEW back to Pittsburgh the following morning, retrieved his car—a Porsche he planned to sell—from the long-term parking area, and checked into a motel by the airport. His cellphone records showed numerous incoming calls and text messages from both Joey Bernardo and Kyle McAvoy that day, with no outgoing calls in return. He had two long conversations with Brother Manny in Reno, and some short ones with his parents and his brother in Pittsburgh. There were two calls to Elaine Keenan.

On the last day of his life, he left Pittsburgh before sunrise, headed for Scranton. Near the small town of Snow Shoe, he stopped at a rest area and went to the men's room. It was approximately 10.40 a.m. on a Friday in mid-November and there were only a few other vehicles at the rest area.

Mr Dwight Nowoski, a retiree from Dayton who was travelling to Vermont with his wife, discovered Baxter on the floor by the urinals, dying from a gunshot to the head. The young man was gasping and whimpering and thrashing about like a deer hit by a car. There was no one else in the men's room when Mr Nowoski stumbled upon the horrible scene.

The Pennsylvania State Police closed the rest stop, which was not equipped with surveillance cameras, and sealed the area around it. Six travellers, including Mr and Mrs Nowoski, were questioned at length at the crime scene. No one could recall seeing Baxter enter the men's room, nor did anyone see the murderer follow him in. No one heard a gunshot. A lady from Rhode Island recalled noticing a man standing by the door to the men's room, and upon further reflection she agreed that it was possible he might have been a lookout. Regardless, he was long gone, and her description was limited to: male white, between thirty and forty-five, at least five feet eight but no more than six feet four, wearing a dark jacket.

The autopsy revealed that Baxter had been killed by a single shot, at the base of his skull, from a 9mm pistol, a Beretta according to the lab.

Robbery was ruled out, as nothing appeared to have been taken. Baxter's wallet, containing $513 in cash and six credit cards, was untouched, as were his watch and the keys to his Porsche. The lab reported that there was no trace of alcohol or illegal drugs in his system, on his clothing or in his car. There was no evidence that the crime had anything to do with sex.

The investigators began scratching their heads. The apparent randomness of the act, plus the silent gunshot and the clean getaway, led them to conclude, at least at the scene, that they were dealing with professionals.

KYLE WAS AT HIS CUBE, chatting with Dale about their plans for the evening, when the call came from Joey. It was almost 5 p.m. on Friday. He had eaten a pizza with Baxter late on Tuesday night, but had not spoken to him since. As far as he and Joey could tell, Baxter had disappeared, or at least he was ignoring his phone.

'What's the matter?' Dale asked as she noticed the look of shock.

Kyle did not respond. He kept the phone to his ear and began walking away, down the hall, listening as Joey unloaded the details now being splashed across the television. News of the brutal death of a member of the Tate family was brightening up a dull news day in Pittsburgh.

He lost the signal in the elevator, and once outside the building he called Joey back and kept listening. The sidewalks along Broad were packed with the late-afternoon rush. Kyle plodded along without a coat to layer against the chill, without a clue as to where he might be going.

'They killed him,' he finally said to Joey.

'Who?'

'I think you know.'

THE INTERMENT of Baxter Farnsworth Tate took place on a damp and overcast day at the family burial plot in Homewood Cemetery, Pittsburgh. It followed an Episcopal service that was closed to the public and the media. Baxter left a brother, who attended the service, and a sister, who did not. Ollie Guice, a Beta from Cleveland who had lived with Baxter for two of their years at Duquesne, struggled through a eulogy that evoked a few smiles. Of the eight surviving members of their pledge class, seven were present. There was also a respectable showing from old Pittsburgh—some childhood friends and those required to attend because they came from the upper crust. No one from Hollywood came. Not a soul from LA. Baxter's agent sent flowers.

Unknown to Kyle and the others, Elaine Keenan had attempted to enter the church but was turned away because her name was not on the list. But Brother Manny managed to talk his way into the church, wearing his standard white uniform—baggy bleached dungarees and flowing shirttail. His only concession to the solemnity of the occasion was a black leather beret that adorned his tumbling grey locks and gave him an odd resemblance to an ageing Che Guevara. He wept throughout the service, shedding more tears than the rest of the hidebound and stoic collection combined.

Kyle shed no tears, though he was deeply saddened by such a wasted life. As he stood next to the grave and stared at the oak casket, he was unable to dwell on the good times they had shared. He was too consumed with the raging internal debate over what he should have done differently. In particular, should he have told Baxter about the video, about Bennie and the boys, about everything? If he had done so, would Baxter have appreciated the danger and behaved differently? Maybe. Maybe not. Baxter had not been thinking rationally. And Kyle himself had not foreseen the extent of the danger. But he certainly saw it now.

There were about a hundred mourners huddled round the grave site, all pressing close together to hear the final words from the rector. Kyle glanced away, at the rows of tombstones where the old money was buried, and beyond them to the cemetery's entrance, where a large pack of media types waited like vultures for a glimpse of something newsworthy. Ready with cameras, lights and microphones, desperate for a shot of the casket or the mother collapsing as she said goodbye.

Brother Manny wailed loudly from the edge of the tent, and this rattled everyone else. The rector missed a beat, then droned on.

Kyle stared at the hordes in the distance. Somewhere in their midst was at least one of Bennie's boys, maybe two or three, probably with a camera to record which of Baxter's friends had bothered to attend. Useless information, really, but then so much of what they did made no sense.

They knew how to kill, though. There was little doubt about that. The state police had nothing to say so far, and as the days passed it was becoming clear that there was simply no evidence.

When the burial was over, Baxter's parents and brother wasted no time in leaving. Kyle and Joey held back, and for a moment stood near the tombstone of another Tate.

'This will be our last conversation for a long time,' Joey said softly but firmly. 'I've got my hands full here, Kyle. I've got a life with a wedding and a baby in the future. No more of your silly spy games. You keep playing if you want, but not me.'

'Sure, Joey.'

'No more emails, packages, phone calls. No more trips to New York. One of us will be next, Kyle, and it won't be you. You're the one they need. So for our next mistake, guess who gets the bullet.'

'We didn't cause his death.'

'Are you sure about that?'

'No.'

'I'm going now. Please keep me out of it, Kyle. And be damned sure nobody sees that video. So long.'

Kyle allowed him to walk ahead; then he followed.

AT 6.30 ON THURSDAY morning, Kyle walked into Doug Peckham's office and reported back for duty. Doug was standing at his desk, which resembled, as always, a landfill. 'How was the funeral?' he asked without looking up from whatever he was holding.

'It was a funeral,' Kyle said.

'We have a hearing in federal court at nine. We'll leave here at eight thirty. Finish the Rule 10 memo and be here at eight.'

The prospect of a litigation associate getting near a courtroom during his or her first year was unheard of, and for Kyle a gloomy day suddenly improved. He hurried to his cube and was checking emails when Tabor appeared with a tall coffee and a haggard look. Since flunking the bar, he had worked hard to put himself back together, and though he was initially humbled, the cockiness was returning.

'Sorry about your friend,' he said.

'Thanks,' Kyle said.

Tabor was still standing and slurping coffee. 'Have you seen Dale?'

'No. I just got back from the funeral yesterday. Something the matter?'

'She got nailed with some heinous project Tuesday night, and I don't think she's slept at all. Let's keep an eye on her.'

'Will do.'

At 8.30, Kyle left the office with Doug Peckham and a senior associate named Noel Bard. They walked hurriedly to a parking garage a few blocks away, and when the attendant pulled up in Bard's late-model Jaguar, Peckham said, 'Kyle, you drive. We're going to Foley Square.'

Kyle wanted to protest but said nothing. Bard and Peckham climbed into the rear seat, leaving Kyle, the chauffeur, alone in the front.

'I'm not sure of the best route,' Kyle admitted, with a flash of fear at what would happen if he got lost and they were late for court.

'Stay on Broad until it becomes Nassau. Take it all the way to Foley Square,' Bard said, as if he made the drive every day. 'And be careful. This little baby is brand-new and cost me a hundred grand. It's my wife's.'

Kyle could not remember being so nervous behind the wheel. He adjusted the mirror and eased into traffic, cutting his eyes in all directions.

To make matters worse, Peckham wanted to talk. 'Kyle, a couple of names. Darren Bartkowski, first-year litigation associate?'

Kyle waited and finally said, 'So?'

'Have you worked with him? How would you evaluate him?'

'Uh, well, nice guy, I knew him at Yale.'

'His work, Kyle, his work?'

'I haven't worked with him yet.'

'The word is he's a slacker. Ducks the partners, late with projects, lazy with the billing. Have you heard he's a slacker, Kyle?'

'Yes,' Kyle said reluctantly. It was the truth.

Talking about colleagues was a contact sport at the firm, and the partners were as bad as the associates. An associate who cut corners or ducked projects was labelled a slacker, and the tag was permanent.

'What about Jeff Tabor?' Doug asked.

'I know him well. Definitely not a slacker.'

'He has the reputation of being a gunner,' Doug said.

'Yes, and that's accurate. He's competitive, but he's not a cutthroat.'

'You like him, Kyle?'

'Yes. Tabor's a good guy. Smart as hell.'

'Evidently not smart enough,' Bard said. 'That bar-exam problem.'

Kyle had no comment, and no comment was necessary because a yellow cab swerved in front of them, cutting off the Jaguar and forcing Kyle to slam on the brakes and hit the horn at the same time.

'You gotta watch these idiots,' Doug said.

The sound of important papers being extracted crackled from the back seat, and Kyle knew something was being reviewed.

'Will we get Judge Hennessy or his magistrate?' Doug asked Bard.

Kyle was shut out of the conversation, which was fine with him. He preferred to concentrate on the street ahead. After ten minutes of downtown traffic, he was wet under the collar and breathing heavily.

'There's a lot at the corner of Nassau and Chambers, two blocks from the courthouse,' Bard announced.

Kyle nodded nervously. He found the lot but it was full.

Peckham took charge. 'Look, Kyle, we're in a hurry. Just drop us off in front of the courthouse at Foley Square, then circle the block until you find a spot on the street.'

Kyle cut to the kerb in front of the courthouse, and both lawyers scrambled out of the rear seat. Peckham's final words were 'Just keep moving, OK. You'll find something.'

Alone, Kyle eased away and tried to relax. He headed north on Centre Street, drove four blocks, then turned left on Leonard and headed west. Every inch of available space was packed with vehicles and motorbikes. Nine o'clock came and went without a call from Peckham, not even a quick 'Where the hell are you?' The hearing was under way, but without Kyle the litigator. Kyle the chauffeur, though, was hard at work. It was obvious that every parking spot in Lower Manhattan was taken, and Kyle accepted the fact that he had no choice but to burn fuel.

Now confident in traffic, he picked up his phone and called Dale. She answered on the third ring and in a hushed voice said, 'I'm in the library.'

'Are you OK?'

A pause. 'I haven't slept in two nights. I think I'm delirious.'

'You sound terrible.'

'Where are you?'

'Right now I'm on Leonard Street, driving Noel Bard's wife's new Jaguar. What do you think I'm doing?'

'Sorry I asked. How was the funeral?'

'Terrible. Let's do dinner tonight. I need to unload on someone.'

'I'm going home tonight, to bed, to sleep.'

'You have to eat. I'll grab some Chinese.'

'We'll see. I gotta get out of here. Later.'

At 11 a.m., Kyle congratulated himself because he could now bill the client $800 for driving in circles. Ah, the life of a Wall Street lawyer.

The call came at 11.40. Bard said, 'We're leaving the courtroom. Pick us up where you dropped us off.'

'My pleasure.'

Minutes later, Kyle wheeled to the kerb like a veteran driver, and his two passengers jumped into the rear seat. He pulled away and said, 'Where to?'

'The office,' came the terse reply from Peckham.

For several minutes nothing was said. Kyle expected to be grilled about why he'd missed the hearing. But nothing. Sadly, he realised that he had not been missed. To create some noise, he finally asked, 'So how'd the hearing go?'

'It didn't,' said Peckham.

'We've just been waiting for the honourable Theodore Hennessy to shake off his hangover and grace us with his presence,' Bard said.

'It was postponed for two weeks,' Peckham said.

AS THEY STEPPED OFF the elevator, Kyle's phone vibrated. A text message from Tabor read: 'Hurry to cube. Problem.'

Tabor met him at the stairs. 'So how was court?'

'Great. I love litigation. What's the problem?'

'It's Dale,' Tabor whispered. 'She collapsed, passed out, something.'

'Where is she?'

'I've hidden the body.'

At the cube, Dale was lying peacefully on a sleeping-bag under Tabor's desk. Her eyes were open, she seemed alert, but she was very pale.

Kyle knelt beside her, gently took her wrist, and said, 'You OK?'

She nodded yes, but was not convincing.

Tabor, the lookout, glanced around and kept talking: 'She doesn't want anyone to know, OK. I say we call the nurse. What do you say, Kyle?'

'Don't tell anyone,' Dale said, her voice low and raspy. 'I fainted, that's all. I'm fine.'

'Your pulse is good,' Kyle said. 'Can you walk?'

'I think so.'

'Then the three of us will slip out for a quick lunch,' Kyle said. 'I'll take you home, and you're going to rest.'

With a hand under each arm, they slowly pulled her up. She stood, took deep breaths, and said, 'I can walk.'

'We're right beside you,' Kyle said.

They caught a curious glance or two as they left the building, but no one cared. Tabor helped her into a cab, then returned to the cube.

Kyle half carried her up the three flights to her apartment, then helped her undress and tucked her in. He kissed her forehead, turned off the lights and closed the door. She did not move for hours.

In the den, Kyle took off his coat, tie and shoes. He covered the small kitchen table with his laptop, FirmFone and a file full of research for a memo he'd been neglecting. Once he was settled, his eyelids became heavier and heavier until he walked to the sofa for a quick nap.

Forget the memo, forget the billing. To hell with the firm, at least for a few stolen moments. The funeral seemed like a month ago. Baxter was gone but not forgotten. He needed Joey, but Joey was gone, too.

The vibration of the phone woke him up: an email from Doug Peckham. It read: 'Kyle: Major realignment in litigation. Six partners and thirty-one associates departing effective as of 5 p.m. today. I've been added to the Trylon case. So have you. Office of Wilson Rush, 7 a.m. sharp tomorrow.'

WILSON RUSH'S OFFICE was at least four times larger than any Kyle had yet seen. Mr Rush evidently liked boats. His polished and gleaming oak desk was mounted on four rudders from old sailing yachts. Every painting depicted a grand vessel at sea. As Kyle walked in, he almost expected the floor to rock and salt water to splash across his feet. But he forgot about the decor when Mr Rush said, 'Good morning, Kyle. Over here.'

The great man was rising from a large conference table at the far end of his office, where a crowd had already gathered. Kyle sat next to Doug Peckham. Quick introductions were made. There were nine others present, excluding Mr Rush and Mr Peckham, and Kyle recognised most of the faces, including that of Sherry Abney. She smiled. Kyle smiled back.

Mr Rush, seated at the head of the table, launched into a quick review of the current upheaval. Two of the partners who had mutinied with Toby Roland, and seven of the thirty-one associates, had been assigned to the Trylon–Bartin case and it was imperative that the firm's manpower be shuffled immediately. Therefore, two partners, Doug Peckham and a woman named Isabelle Gaffney, were entering the fray, along with eight associates.

Isabelle, or Izzy behind her back, was somewhat notorious because she had once required two associates to wait in the delivery room while she was temporarily sidetracked giving birth to a child. Firm lore held that no one had ever seen her smile. And she wasn't about to smile as Mr Rush went on about the reshuffling and realigning of the legal talent at his disposal.

Two first-year associates were being added, Kyle and a quiet young man from Penn named Atwater. Of the twelve litigation rookies, Atwater was by far the quietest. Dale was a distant second, but she had warmed up nicely, at least in Kyle's opinion. He'd spent the night on her sofa again, alone, while she was dead to the world. The shock of being assigned to the Trylon case when he had been rather vocal in trying to avoid it, together with the horror of Baxter's murder, meant that he had slept very little—who could sleep with such nightmares rattling around?

Mr Rush was now going through the basics of the lawsuit, material Kyle had committed to memory months earlier. Kyle took notes because everyone else was taking notes, but he was thinking about Bennie. Did Bennie already know that Kyle had landed the prize position? Bennie had known the names of all members of the Trylon team. Was there another spy in the firm, another victim of Bennie's blackmail? If so, was this person watching Kyle?

After an hour of update and review, Kyle, Atwater and the other six new associates were led by Sherry Abney to the secret room on the eighteenth floor. Secret to some, but Bennie and Nigel certainly knew about it. Along the way they were introduced to a security expert named Gant. He stopped them at the door and explained that a coded plastic strip was required for entry and exit. Each lawyer was given a card, and every time the lawyer came or went, it was recorded. Gant nodded at the ceiling and informed them that there were video cameras watching everything.

They entered the room, which was about the size of Wilson Rush's office. No windows, bare walls, drab olive carpet. There was nothing in the room but ten square tables with a large computer on each one.

Sherry Abney took charge. 'This case now has over four million documents, and they're all right here in our virtual warehouse,' she said, patting a computer like a proud mother. 'The actual paperwork is in secured storage in a facility in Wilmington, but you can access it all from one of these. The main server is locked up in a room next door.' She kept patting. 'The computers are pretty fancy, custom-made. The software is called Sonic, and it's really just a variation of Barrister with some bells and whistles added for security reasons. Pass code changes every week. Password changes every day, sometimes twice a day. If you try to access with the wrong code or password, then all manner of hell breaks loose. You could be fired.'

She looked around with as much menace as possible, then continued, 'This system is self-contained and cannot be accessed anywhere else within the firm. This room is closed from ten p.m. until six a.m. Sorry, no all-nighters in here, but it is open seven days a week.'

At her direction, each associate sat down before a computer and was given a pass code and password. There was nothing on the screen to indicate who manufactured the computer or who wrote the software.

Sherry walked from lawyer to lawyer, looking at the monitors and chatting like a college professor. 'The documents are classified in three basic groups, with a hundred subgroups. Category A contains the harmless junk that Bartin has already been given—letters, emails and so on. Category B has important materials that are discoverable, though we've not handed all of them over. Category R, for "Restricted", is where you'll find the good stuff, the top-secret documents dealing with the technological research that's the heart of this little dispute. When you enter Category R, a record of your entry automatically registers with Mr Gant's computer right next door.'

All eight associates stared at their monitors, all thinking about the 4 million documents in there that had to be examined.

'Now, I'll be here for the rest of the day for a workshop,' Sherry said. 'The sooner you master Sonic and learn your way around our virtual library, the easier your life will be.'

AT 4.20 ON FRIDAY afternoon, Kyle received an email from Bennie. It read: 'Let's meet tonight at 9. Details to follow. BW.'

Kyle responded: 'I can't.'

Bennie responded: 'Tomorrow afternoon, say 5 or 6?'

Kyle: 'I can't.'

Bennie: 'Sunday night, 10 p.m.?'

Kyle: 'I can't.'

KYLE WAS SLEEPING when someone rapped on the door of his apartment at 7.10 on Saturday morning. 'Who is it?' he yelled.

'Bennie,' came the reply.

'What do you want?' Kyle demanded at the door.

'I've brought you some coffee.'

Kyle unlocked the door, and the man responsible for Baxter's death walked by him holding two tall paper cups of coffee. He placed them on the counter and looked around. 'What a dump,' he said. 'I thought you were making some money.'

'What do you want?' Kyle snapped.

'I don't like being ignored,' Bennie snapped back as he jerked round. His face was taut and his eyes were hot. He pointed a finger that came within inches of Kyle's face. 'You do not ignore me, understand?' he hissed. It was the first real display of temper Kyle had seen from him.

'Be cool.' Kyle brushed by him, their shoulders touching solidly, and walked to the bedroom, where he found a T-shirt.

When he returned to the den, Bennie was removing the tops from the cups. 'I want an update.'

Kyle took the coffee without saying thanks. 'I got assigned to the Trylon case yesterday. Big news, huh, or did you already know this?'

Bennie's eyes revealed nothing. He took a sip of his coffee, then said, 'And the secret room on the eighteenth floor? Tell me about it.'

Kyle described it.

'What about the computers?'

'Manufacturer unknown. Basic desktop models but supposedly custom-built for the project, all running Sonic, all linked to a server locked away next door, where there's a security expert monitoring everything. It's a dead end, if you ask me. There's no way to steal anything.'

Bennie grunted and gave a smart-ass smirk. 'We've cracked much bigger vaults, I assure you. Let us worry about that. How many documents?'

'Over four million.'

That brought a smile. 'What about access to the room?'

'Open seven days a week but closed from ten at night until six in the morning. There are at least three video cameras watching the door.'

'Does someone check you in?'

'I don't think so. But the key leaves a record of each entry and exit.'

'Let me see the key.'

Kyle reluctantly handed over the key.

Bennie examined it like a surgeon, then gave it back. 'I want you to visit the room as often as possible over the next few days, but don't arouse any suspicions. We'll meet at ten on Tuesday night, room 1780, Four Seasons Hotel on Fifty-seventh. Got it?'

'Sure.'

'No surprises.'

'Yes, sir.'

WITH 78,000 LAWYERS in Manhattan, selecting one should not have been so difficult. Kyle had begun the secret project not long after arriving in the city, and had abandoned it several times. He was never sure he would actually hire a lawyer, but wanted the name of a good one just in case. Baxter's murder changed everything. Kyle not only wanted protection, he wanted justice.

Roy Benedict was a criminal defence lawyer with a 200-man firm located in a tall building one block east of Scully & Pershing. The location was crucial, given the attention paid to Kyle's movements. Benedict measured up in other important areas as well. He had worked for the FBI before law school and after graduation spent six years with the Department of Justice. He had contacts, old friends, people on the other side of the street now, but people he could trust. The icing on the cake was his basketball career at Duquesne some twenty-five years earlier. On the phone, he said he wasn't taking any new cases, but the basketball angle opened the door.

The appointment was at 2 p.m. on Monday, and Kyle arrived early. Benedict was cordial and genuinely pleased to meet another New York lawyer who'd played for the Dukes.

Kyle cut off the basketball talk by saying, 'Look, Mr Benedict—'

'It's Roy.'

'OK, Roy, I can't spend too much time here because I'm being followed.'

A few seconds passed as Roy allowed this to sink in. 'And why is a first-year associate at the biggest law firm in the world being followed?'

'I have a few problems. It's complicated, and I really need a lawyer.'

'I do only white-collar crime, Kyle. Have you screwed up in that area?'

'Not yet. But I'm being pressured to commit a whole list of crimes.'

Roy bounced a pencil on his desk. 'My initial retainer is fifty grand.'

'I can't pay that much. I have five thousand in cash.' Kyle yanked an envelope from his pocket and tossed it on the desk. 'Give me some time and I'll get the rest.'

'What does this case involve?'

'Rape, murder, theft, wiretapping, extortion, blackmail and a few others. I can't give you the details until we reach an agreement.'

Roy nodded, then smiled. 'There's someone following you now?'

'Oh, yes. I've been under surveillance since early February, back at Yale.'

'Is your life in danger?'

Kyle thought for a moment. 'Yes, I believe so.'

The air was thick with unanswered questions, and Roy's curiosity got the better of him. He opened a drawer and withdrew some papers. He scanned them quickly—three sheets stapled together—added some notes with a pen, then slid them across. 'This is a contract for legal services.'

Kyle read it. The initial retainer had been reduced to $5,000, the hourly rate cut in half, from $800 to $400. Kyle signed his name and said, 'Thanks.'

Roy took the envelope and placed it in the drawer. 'Where do we begin?'

Kyle sank into his chair. 'I don't know. There's so much ground to cover.'

'Who's following you? Government agents of some sort?'

'No. Private thugs. Very good ones. And I have no idea who they are.'

'Why don't we start at the beginning?'

'OK.' Kyle began with Elaine, the party, the accusations of rape, the investigation. He introduced Bennie and his boys, his blackmail, the video, his covert mission to steal documents from Scully & Pershing.

He produced a file and spread out the photos of Bennie, along with the composites of Nigel and two of the street thugs who'd been following him. 'Bennie Wright is just an alias. The guy probably has twenty names. He speaks with a slight accent that's probably Eastern European. Just a guess.'

Roy studied the photo of Bennie.

'Is there a way to identify him?' Kyle asked.

'I don't know. Keep talking.'

Kyle removed another file and went through the basics of the Trylon–Bartin war, keeping to the facts that had been published in news stories.

Roy scanned the articles, then said, 'I've heard of it. Keep talking.'

Kyle described the surveillance and eavesdropping, and Roy forgot about Trylon and Bartin. 'Wiretapping carries five years, federal,' he said.

'Wiretapping is nothing. What about murder?'

'Who got murdered?'

Kyle raced through Joey's involvement, then the surprising arrival of Baxter and his desire to reach out to the girl. He handed over a dozen newspaper reports on the random shooting of Baxter Tate. 'I was a pallbearer at his funeral last Wednesday,' he said. 'I'm sure Bennie ordered the hit.'

'Why would Bennie kill Baxter Tate?' Roy asked.

'He had no choice,' Kyle said. 'If Baxter succeeded in making some harebrained confession to Elaine, then the events that follow are out of control. If the girl goes nuts, cries rape again, then I'm dragged back to Pittsburgh, my life is derailed. I leave the firm, and Bennie loses his asset.'

'But with Baxter dead, doesn't the rape case lose some steam?'

'Yes, but the video is still out there. And believe me, it's brutal.'

'But it doesn't implicate you?'

'Only for being a drunken idiot. When the sex begins, I'm nowhere to be seen. I don't even remember it.'

'And you have no idea how Bennie got the video?'

'That's the greatest question of all. I don't know which is more terrifying—the video itself or the fact that Bennie got his hands on it.'

Roy was shaking his head. 'How many interns did Scully & Pershing hire the summer before last?'

'Around a hundred.'

'So Bennie and his group get the names of a hundred summer interns, and they investigate them, looking for an Achilles' heel. When they get to your name, they snoop around Pittsburgh and Duquesne. They find out about the rape, lean on someone in the police department, hear the rumour about a video. Somehow, Bennie gets hold of it. He's got the resources.'

'Yep. So who's he working for?'

Roy rubbed his chin. 'I doubt if he works for APE. I cannot believe that a rival law firm would spend this kind of money to break so many laws.'

'Bartin?'

'Much more probable. Plenty of money, plenty of motive.'

'Any other suspects?'

'Oh, please, Kyle. We're talking about military technology. The Chinese and the Russians prefer to steal what they can't develop. That's the nature of the game. Bennie's probably a former intelligence pro who now hires himself out for a zillion dollars to do exactly what he's doing.'

'He killed Baxter.'

Roy shrugged. 'Killing doesn't bother this guy.'

'Great. Just when I was starting to feel better.'

Roy smiled, but the wrinkles never left his forehead. 'Look, give me a few days to digest this.'

'We need to move fast. I now have access to the documents, and Bennie's much more excited. I'm seeing him tomorrow night, at the Four Seasons Hotel on Fifty-seventh. Care to join the party?'

'Thanks. How long do these little meetings last?'

'Ten minutes if I'm lucky. We bitch and bark, and then I slam the door on the way out. I act tough, but I'm scared to death. I need help, Roy.'

'You've come to the right place.'

'Thanks.' They shook hands and said goodbye.

Long after Kyle was gone, Roy stared at his window and tried to absorb it all. A twenty-five-year-old former editor in chief of the *Yale Law Journal* being stalked on the streets of New York City by a deadly group of professional operatives who were blackmailing him into spying on his own law firm.

Roy smiled, and reminded himself of how much he loved his job.

9

For no reason other than sheer obstinacy, Kyle arrived forty-five minutes late for the Tuesday-night meeting at the Four Seasons. He was not surprised when Bennie's sidekick Nigel met him at the door.

'Kyle, old boy, how have you been?' he chirped with a fake smile.

'Marvellous.'

'Good evening, Kyle,' Bennie said, rising to his feet.

'So nice to see you, Bennie.' Kyle placed his briefcase on the bed.

'Tell us about the room on the eighteenth floor,' Bennie said, abandoning any more preliminaries.

'I've already described it.'

Nigel fired away: 'Ten monitors on ten tables, right? What about the computers themselves? Are they tall and thin, short and fat? Give us a hint!'

'More of a square box, sitting on the tables, to the right of each monitor.'

On the dresser next to the television there was a thin notebook, already opened. Nigel lunged for it and said, 'Take a look at these computers, Kyle. See anything remotely similar?'

Kyle methodically flipped through it. Each page had colour photos of eight computers, ten pages in all, eighty machines of wildly varying design. He settled on one that looked more like a colour jet printer than a computer.

'Yes, rather square,' Nigel observed. 'How many disk drives?'

'None. There are no disk drives, no ports, no way to transfer the data.'

'And the server?'

'Locked up next door. Out of sight.'

'Interesting. And the printers, Kyle?'

'None. If you need to print out a brief or a memo to be submitted to the court, or to the opposing attorneys, it's reviewed by your supervisor, then printed in a room next door. Every sheet of paper that's printed is coded and duplicated. It's impossible to print anything without leaving a trail.'

'Quite nice, really.' With that, Nigel took a sharp step back and relaxed.

Bennie took over. 'Kyle, how many people are normally in the room?'

'It varies. Sunday afternoon I was alone for about an hour. This morning there were five or six others.'

'Have you been there late at night when they close the room?'

'No, not yet.'

'Do it, OK. Be there at ten one night.'

'I can't go there just to hang out, Bennie. It's not a coffee room. There has to be a reason to be there, other than casing the joint.'

Bennie and Nigel studied each other, both minds hard at work.

'Will you go there tomorrow?' Bennie asked.

'Maybe. It depends on what I'm asked to do in the morning.'

'I want you to enter the room tomorrow, carrying your briefcase and wearing your jacket. As soon as you're settled in, take off your jacket. Keep the briefcase under the table.'

'Oh, sure. Anything else? What if I haul in a box of tacos and drop Cheddar crumbs on the keyboard? Where is this going?'

'Just trust us here, Kyle,' Nigel said gently. 'We know what we're doing.'

'You're the last person I'd trust.'

'Now, Kyle.'

'Look, I'm tired. I'd really like to go—'

'What are your plans for the next few days?' Bennie asked.

'I'll work tomorrow, leave the office around five, take the train to Philly, rent a car and drive to York. I'm having Thanksgiving dinner with my father on Thursday. I'll be back in the office Saturday. Good enough?'

'We'll meet Sunday night,' Bennie said. 'I'll pass along the details.'

'Happy Thanksgiving, boys,' Kyle said as he left the room.

KYLE KEPT two waterproof trench coats at the office, one black and the other a light brown. The black one he wore every day, to and from work and when moving around the city. The brown one was used rarely, only when he really didn't want to be followed. At 2.30 on Wednesday, he draped it over his arm and rode the elevator to the second floor. From there, he took a service elevator to the basement, put on the trench coat and ducked through the rows of thick plumbing pipes until he came to a metal stairway. He spoke to a technician, one he'd spoken to on several occasions. He saw daylight in a narrow alley that barely separated his building from the fifty-storey edifice next door. Ten minutes later, he was walking into the office of Roy Benedict. They had chatted briefly on the phone, and Kyle was uneasy about the plan.

Roy was not at all uneasy. He had studied the file, analysed the facts and was ready to move. 'I have a friend with the FBI,' he began. 'A friend I trust completely. We worked together years ago before I became a lawyer. He's a heavyweight here in the New York office. I want to meet with him and lay everything on the table. Everything.'

'What will he do?'

'Crimes have been committed. Crimes are in process. Crimes are being planned. And not small crimes. I suspect he will be as shocked as I am. I suspect the FBI will get involved.'

'So Bennie gets nabbed by the feds?'

'Sure. Don't you want him locked up?'

'For life. But he has a vast network out there in the shadows.'

'The FBI knows how to lay its traps. These guys are smart, Kyle. If I talk to them now, they'll move in quietly and lay the groundwork. When they want to, they can throw a whole army at the enemy. Right now you need an army.'

'Thanks. Is there a chance they'll take a look and let it pass?'

'Yes, but I doubt it.'

'When will you talk to your friend?'

'Maybe as early as this afternoon.'

Kyle barely hesitated. 'Let's do it,' he said.

IT WAS ALMOST midnight when Kyle quietly slipped through the unlocked kitchen door of his family home in York. All lights were off. His father knew he would be arriving late, but John McAvoy let nothing interfere with a night's sleep. Kyle kicked off his loafers, sneaked up the stairs to his bedroom, and within minutes was under the covers and dreaming.

Less than five hours later, John practically kicked in the door and boomed, 'Let's go, knucklehead. You can sleep when you're dead.'

In a drawer, Kyle found an old set of thermal underwear and a pair of woollen socks. From among the dusty old clothes in the closet, he pulled out his hunting overalls. His boots were where he'd left them last Thanksgiving.

John was at the kitchen table preparing for war. Three rifles with scopes were laid out, next to several boxes of ammo.

'Good morning,' John said. 'You ready?'

'Yep. Where's the coffee?'

'In the Thermos. Let's go.'

They loaded the gear into the pick-up, and fifteen minutes after crawling out of bed, Kyle was riding through the darkness of a frigid Thanksgiving morning, sipping black coffee and nibbling on a granola bar. The town was soon behind them. John was working a cigarette, the smoke drifting through a crack in the driver's window. He usually said little in the mornings.

Kyle was almost numb with the shock of open spaces, empty roads, no people, the great outdoors. What, exactly, had been the attraction of a big city? They stopped at a gate. Kyle opened it and John drove through it; then they continued deeper into the hills. There was still no trace of sun in the east.

The road went from gravel to dirt. At the edge of a wood, John parked and turned off the lights. They hiked for twenty minutes, then stopped under an elm tree just as the first hint of light fell across the small valley before them.

'Bill Henry killed an eight-point last week just over that ridge there,' John said, pointing. 'If he can get one, anybody can.'

A deer stand had been built in the elm, twenty feet up, with a rickety ladder leading to it. 'You take this stand,' John said. 'I'll be a hundred yards that way in another one. Nothing but bucks, OK?'

'Got it.'

As John walked away into the darkness, he said, 'You stay awake, now.'

Kyle tucked the rifle over his shoulder and crawled up the ladder to the small wooden platform anchored into the elm. He sat with his back to the bark, his feet dangling. He'd been in deer stands since he was five years old, and had learned the lessons of complete stillness. A soft breeze rustled a few leaves. The rifle was a Remington 30.06, a gift for his fourteenth birthday. He tucked it firmly across his chest and promptly dozed off.

The crack of a gunshot jolted him from his nap, and he swung the rifle round, ready to fire. To his left, in the direction of his father, he saw several white tails bouncing in a rapid getaway. Ten minutes passed with no word from John. He'd obviously missed with his first shot.

An hour passed without a sighting, and Kyle fought to stay awake.

Sounds were approaching, footsteps unconcerned with making noise. John was soon near the elm. 'Let's go,' he said. 'There's a creek just beyond the field, a favourite watering hole.'

Kyle lowered himself to the ground. John said, 'You didn't see that buck?'

'Nope.'

'I don't know how you missed it. It ran right in front of you.'

'The one you shot at?'

'Yeah, at least a ten-pointer.'

'I guess you missed it, too.'

They returned to the truck and went for the Thermos. As they sat on the tailgate, sipping strong coffee from paper cups, Kyle said, 'Dad, I don't want to hunt any more. We need to talk.'

HIS FATHER listened calmly at first, then lit a cigarette. As Kyle ploughed through the rape investigation, he expected an eruption, a series of sharp and painful questions. But John listened intently without a word.

The first flash of anger came when Bennie entered the narrative. 'They blackmailed you,' he said, then lit another cigarette. 'Son of a bitch.'

'Just listen, OK,' Kyle pleaded, and went full speed ahead. The video, Joey, Baxter, the murder, Trylon and Bartin. The meetings with Bennie, Nigel, the plan to filch the documents and hand them to the enemy. And finally, the hiring of Roy Benedict and the appearance of the FBI.

Kyle apologised repeatedly for not trusting his father. He laid open his soul, and when he finished, hours later it seemed, the sun was well into the sky, the coffee was long gone, the deer long forgotten.

'I think I need some help,' Kyle said.

'You need your ass kicked for not telling me,' John said.

'Yes, I do.'

'Good Lord, son. What a mess.'

They left the rifles in the truck and went for a long hike along a narrow trail through the woods.

THE FEAST OF TURKEY, dressing and all the trimmings had been prepared by a deli that sold the whole package to those who preferred not to be troubled. As John set the dining-room table, Kyle left to fetch his mother.

Patty answered her door with a smile and a long hug. She was up and, Kyle was relieved to see, properly medicated. She couldn't wait to show off her latest masterpieces. He eventually led her back to the door and down to his rental car, and they enjoyed a quick drive through York. She was wearing make-up, and a pretty orange dress that Kyle remembered from his teenage years. She chattered nonstop about local news, bouncing randomly from one subject to another.

Kyle's parents greeted each other with a polite hug, and the small struggling family worked its way through the gossip about the twin daughters, neither of whom had been back to York in over a year. One was in Santa Monica, the other in Portland. They called both and passed around the phone. As John sat the small turkey on the dining table, Kyle poured three glasses of wine, though his mother wouldn't touch it.

'You're drinking wine these days,' John said to Kyle.

'Not much.'

The two men fussed over Patty, worked hard to make her comfortable. She managed to ask a few questions about Kyle and his career, and he made his life sound enviable. The strain from events in New York was palpable, but Patty did not notice. She ate almost nothing, but her son and ex-husband devoured the lunch quickly. After pecan pie and coffee, she announced she wanted to go home. She was tired, she said, and Kyle wasted no time loading her up for the ten-minute drive.

ONE FOOTBALL GAME blurred into another. Kyle, on the sofa, and John, in a recliner, watched the games between naps, and said little. The air was heavy with things unsaid, plans that needed to be discussed. The father wanted to lecture and yell, but the son was too vulnerable at that moment.

'Let's go for a walk,' Kyle said when it was almost dark. 'I need to talk.'

'Can't we talk here?'

'Let's walk.'

They bundled up, and when they were on the sidewalk Kyle said, 'I'm sorry, but I don't like to have serious conversations indoors.'

John lit a cigarette. 'I'm almost afraid to ask why not.'

'Bugs, mikes, nasty little twerps listening to conversations.'

'Let me get this straight. You think these thugs have bugged my house?'

'No, but there's a chance. These guys believe in surveillance and have an unlimited budget. I play it safe and have the serious conversations outdoors.'

'Your apartment is bugged?'

'Oh, yes. I know of at least three listening devices hidden in the place. One is in the AC vent in the den. There's one hidden in the bedroom wall, just above the chest of drawers, and there's one in the kitchen in a door facing. I can't really examine them, because there are also three tiny cameras, at least three, that watch me continuously when I'm in the apartment, which is not very often. I've managed to locate these devices by pretending to do all sorts of routine chores around the place, cleaning vents, washing windows, scrubbing floors. The place is a dump, but it's pretty clean.'

'And your phone?'

'I still have the old one from law school, and they're listening. That's why I haven't switched. I give them enough harmless crap to make them happy. I installed a land line in the apartment, and I'm sure it's bugged. I use it just for harmless stuff—ordering a pizza, bitching at my landlord, calling a car service.' Kyle pulled out the FirmFone and glanced at it. 'This is one the firm gave us on day one. I'm pretty sure this one is bug-free.'

'The question is, why is it in your pocket on Thanksgiving Day?'

'Habit. It's turned off. For serious stuff I use the desk phone in my office. I figure that if they can bug the office phones, then we're all really screwed.'

'Oh, you're screwed, there's no doubt about that. You should have told me months ago.'

'I know. I should have done a lot of things differently, but I didn't have the benefit of hindsight. I was scared. Still am.'

The wind had picked up and leaves were blowing and landing around them. They made the block and talked about the future.

KYLE PUNCHED his clock at 8 a.m. sharp on Saturday when he entered the secret room on the eighteenth floor and settled himself at one of the workstations. Four other members of Team Trylon were there, lost in a virtual world of endless research. He nodded to a couple, but no one spoke. He wore jeans and a woollen jacket, and he hauled in his black Bally briefcase, six inches thick and showing some wear. He'd bought it at a shop on Fifth Avenue a week before orientation. All briefcases at the firm were black.

He placed the briefcase on the floor beside him, partially under the table, directly under the plain-vanilla computer that had so captivated dear Nigel. He withdrew a legal pad, then a file, and before long his workstation looked authentic. After a few minutes, he took off his jacket, hung it on the back of his chair and rolled up his sleeves. A quick look round the room revealed one other briefcase. All other jackets and coats had been left upstairs in the offices. The hours dragged by as Kyle lost himself in the futuristic world of the B-10 HyperSonic Bomber and the people who designed it.

The only good thing about the secret room was the prohibition against cellphones. After a few hours, Kyle needed a break, and he wanted to check his messages. Specifically, he was waiting to hear from Dale, who hadn't bothered to show up on such a beautiful morning. He walked to his office, and called her private cellphone.

'Yes,' she answered.

'Where are you?'

'I'm still in Providence.'

'Need I remind you, young lady, that this is the third consecutive day in which you have not billed a single hour.'

'I take it you're at the office.'

'Yes. Everyone's here but you.'

'Fire me. Sue me. I don't care.'

'You'll never make partner with that attitude.'

'Promise?'

'I was thinking about dinner tonight. There's a new restaurant in the East Village that just got two stars from Frank Bruni.'

'Are you asking me out for a date?'

'Please. We can split the cheque since we work for a gender-neutral firm.'

'You're so romantic.'

'We could do the romance later.'

'So that's what you're really after.'

'Always.'

'I get in around seven. I'll call you then.'

KYLE CLIPPED TRYLON for twelve hours, then called a sedan for the ride to dinner. The restaurant had twenty tables, a Turkish menu and no dress requirement. After the two-star review by the *New York Times*, the place was crowded. Kyle got a table only because there had been a cancellation.

Dale was at the bar sipping white wine and looking almost serene. They kissed, a peck on each cheek, then squeezed together, and Dale started talking about her Thanksgiving holiday as if she'd just had a month at the beach. Both of her parents taught mathematics at Providence College, and, though wonderful people, they had a rather dull existence.

Later, at their table and still sipping wine, she was quick to confess some exciting news. 'I had a job interview this morning.'

'I thought you had a job.'

'Yes, but it sucks. There's a boutique firm in Providence, downtown in a beautiful old building. I got a job there one summer when I was in college, doing the general gofer routine. About twenty lawyers, half women, a general practice. I talked them into an interview on a Saturday morning.'

'But you have a cherished associate's position with the largest firm in the world. What more could you want?'

'A life. The same thing you want.'

'So you're leaving?'

'I'm not cut out for this. I thought I was pretty tough, but you can have it.'

The waiter took their orders and poured more wine. They were side by side, in a narrow half-booth with a view of the restaurant.

'When are you leaving?' he asked.

'As soon as possible. I practically begged for a job this morning. If I don't get an offer, I'll keep knocking. This is madness, Kyle, and I'm checking out.'

'Congratulations. You'll be the envy of our class.'

'What about you?'

'I have no idea. I feel as though I just got here. We're all in shock, but it'll wear off. It's boot camp, and we're still sore from the initial bruising.'

'No more bruises for me. I've collapsed once. It won't happen again. I'm slacking off to fifty hours a week and I dare them to say something.'

'Go, girl.'

A platter of olives and goat cheese arrived, and they toyed with it.

'How was York?' she asked.

'The same. I had lunch with my parents, a quick deer hunt that killed nothing, and some long talks with my dad.'

'About what?'

'The usual. Life. The past. The future.'

ON A SMALL DESK in the hotel suite, Nigel had set up a computer that looked very similar to those on the eighteenth floor. Next to it was a monitor that was identical to the one Kyle had stared at for twelve hours the day before.

'Are we close here, Kyle?' Nigel sang as he proudly revealed his copycat workstation. 'Please have a seat.'

Kyle sat at the desk, with Bennie and Nigel watching every move.

'These look very similar,' Kyle said.

'Look hard, man, and find something different,' Nigel pressed. He was beside Kyle, bent and staring at the screen.

'The computer is slightly darker in colour, almost a grey, and it's sixteen inches wide and twenty inches tall.'

'You measured, Kyle?'

'Obviously. I used a fifteen-inch legal pad.'

'Bloody brilliant,' Nigel exclaimed, and seemed ready to hug Kyle. 'It has to be a Fargo,' he said.

'A what?'

'Fargo, Kyle, a speciality computer company in San Diego, big on government and military machines, big stout computers with more security and more gadgets than you can believe.'

As Nigel chirped away, he hit a button on the keyboard. The screen became a page unlike any Kyle had ever seen.

'Now, Kyle, tell me what the first page looks like. Anything remotely similar here?'

'No, not even close. The home page has one icon for the tutorial, but that's it—no other icons, format options, nothing but an index to the documents. You turn the computer on, get through the pass codes and passwords, then wait about ten seconds, and, presto, you're into the library.'

'Fascinating,' Nigel said, still staring at the monitor. 'And the index?'

'The index is a real challenge. It starts with broad divisions of documents; then it breaks down into subcategories and subgroups. It takes some work to find the documents you're looking for.'

Nigel took a step back. He was downright giddy with Kyle's information.

Bennie moved closer. 'Suppose you wanted to locate research materials relating to the B-10's air-breathing engines. How would you get there?'

'I don't know. I haven't been there yet. I've seen nothing about air-breathing engines.' The statement was true, but Kyle decided to draw a line at this point. With over 4 million documents in play, he could easily claim he had not seen whatever they were curious about.

'But you could find these materials?'

'I could find them quickly, once I knew where to look. The Sonic program is pretty fast, but there's a ton of paper to sift through.'

Bennie's movements were quick, his words a little more urgent than usual. 'You were in the room yesterday?' he asked.

'Yes, all day.'

'With a briefcase and a jacket?'

'Both, no problem. There was one other briefcase. No one checks them.'

'When will you return to the room?' Bennie asked.

'The team meets in the morning, and there's a good chance I'll get another assignment. Monday or Tuesday for sure.'

'Let's meet Tuesday night.'

'Can't wait.'

NOW THAT HE was an official member of Team Trylon, Kyle had the honour of beginning each week with a 7 a.m. Monday chalk talk in a huge conference room he'd never seen before. After three months in the building, he still marvelled at the meeting areas and tucked-away mezzanines and small libraries he was stumbling upon for the first time.

The room was on the forty-first floor and large enough to house many smaller law firms. Forty lawyers, give or take a few, crowded around a long central table, gulping coffee and settling in for another long week.

Wilson Rush stood at the far end and cleared his throat, and everyone shut up. 'Good morning. We'll have our weekly session. Keep your comments brief. This meeting will last for one hour only.'

Kyle was as far from Rush as possible. He kept his head low and took furious notes that no one, not even himself, could have read. Each of the eight partners stood in turn and gave updates on the latest motions filed in the case, the latest haggling over documents and experts, the latest moves by APE and Bartin. Kyle kept telling himself not to smile at the absurdity of the moment. He was a spy, perfectly planted by his handler, and now within reach of secrets that were valuable enough to cause men to commit murder.

He glanced up as Doug Peckham took his turn on the floor. Ignoring his words, Kyle looked at the far end of the table, where Wilson Rush seemed to be glaring at him, although it was hard to tell at such a distance. What would Mr Rush do if he knew the truth? What would Team Trylon and the hundreds of other Scully partners and associates do when they learned the truth about young Kyle McAvoy?

Suddenly he wanted to leap for the door, sprint down forty-one flights of stairs, and run through the streets of New York like a madman.

DURING LUNCH he used the basement exit ploy again and hustled over to the office of Roy Benedict. They chatted for a minute or two, then Roy said there were two people Kyle should meet. The first was his contact in the FBI; the second was a senior lawyer in the Department of Justice. Kyle nervously agreed, and they walked next door to a meeting room.

The FBI supervisor was Joe Bullington, an affable man with a big toothy smile and a hearty handshake. The man from Justice was Drew Wingate, a sour-faced sort who acted as though he preferred not to shake hands at all. The four sat at a small conference table, and Roy took charge.

'I've laid it all on the table, Kyle. I've had a dozen conversations with Mr Bullington and Mr Wingate, and it's important now for us to review where we are. Joe, talk about the background on Mr Bennie Wright.'

'Yes, well, we ran the photo of this guy through our system,' Bullington began. 'I won't bore you with the details, but we have some very sophisticated computers that store facial images of millions of people. We came up with nothing. No hit. No clue. We then sent it to the CIA, who conducted a similar search, different computers, different software, same result. Nothing. We're surprised, frankly. We were pretty confident we could identify this guy.'

Kyle was not surprised, but he was disappointed.

'Nigel might be a different story,' Bullington went on. 'We placed your composite of him into our system and came up empty. But the CIA got a probable hit.' He opened a file and pulled out an eight-by-ten black and white.

'That's him,' Kyle said immediately.

'Good. His real name is Derry Hobart, born in South Africa, raised in Liverpool, trained as a techie in the British intelligence services, got bounced ten years ago for hacking into the files of some rich folks in Switzerland. One of the most brilliant hackers in the world. Brilliant, but a real rogue, a hired gun, warrants outstanding in at least three countries.'

'How much have you told these people?' Wingate asked Kyle. It was more of an accusation than a question.

Kyle looked at his lawyer, who nodded and said, 'Go ahead, Kyle. You're not under investigation.'

'I've given them the layout of the computer room, general stuff like that. Enough to keep them happy, but no data whatsoever.'

'Anyway,' Bullington said, 'the other two composites turned up nothing. If I understand things, these two boys are just part of the surveillance and not that important.'

'That's right,' Kyle said.

'What's your next step?' Wingate asked him.

'We meet tomorrow night for an update. The plan is for me to somehow hack into the system, download the documents and hand them over. I have no idea how this is meant to be done.'

'When is this supposed to happen?'

'They haven't told me, but I get the impression it will be soon,' Kyle said. 'I have a question for you. Who are these guys? Who are they working for?'

Bullington flashed all of his teeth and said with a boyish shrug, 'We honestly don't know. Hobart is a whore who travels the world selling himself. We have no clue about Bennie. You say he's not American.'

'He doesn't sound like it. But all five of the agents involved in the first encounter, when I met Bennie, were definitely Americans.'

Bullington was shaking his head. 'Probably hired guns, Kyle, thugs brought in for the job, paid, turned loose. There's a whole dark world out there of former cops and agents and soldiers who got shoved out for a multitude of reasons. Most are misfits. They work for anyone who'll pay them.'

'What are the chances of catching the ones who killed Baxter Tate?'

The smile went away for a moment. 'First we have to catch Bennie, but it's obvious he's a pro, so the chances of squeezing him for names are slim.'

'How do you catch Bennie?'

'You'll lead us to him. We'll have enough warrants to arrest him ten times: wiretapping, extortion, conspiracy, take your pick. We'll probably move him to a secured facility far from New York so we can begin the interrogation.'

Roy glanced at his watch and said, 'If you'll excuse us, I need to talk to Kyle. I'll call you later.' And with that he stood, shook their hands again, and led Kyle back to his office. He closed the door. 'What do you think?'

'You trust those guys?' Kyle shot back.

'Yes. You don't?'

'There are at least eighteen intelligence outfits in this country, and those are just the ones we know about. What if Bennie works for one of them? Suppose his project is to procure and protect all the secrets? What if the supercomputers couldn't find his face because they weren't supposed to?'

'That's a pretty ridiculous scenario, Kyle. A rogue US operative, spying on a US law firm, killing US citizens? I don't think so.'

'Sure it's ridiculous, but when your skull might be the next target, it does wonders for the imagination.'

'Take it easy. Let's take it one step at a time. Don't panic.'

'I haven't panicked in nine months, but I'm getting close.'

'No, you're not. Be cool. We have to trust those guys.'

'I'll call you tomorrow.' Kyle grabbed his brown trench coat and left.

10

The Cessna 182 was owned by a retired doctor who flew it only in clear weather and never at night. He had known John McAvoy for over forty years and had flown him several times around the state for legal matters. Their little trips were as much pleasure as business, with John wearing a headset and taking the controls and thoroughly enjoying his time as the pilot. They took off from the York airport early on Tuesday morning and landed seventy-one minutes later in Scranton. John rented a car, and the doctor left in the Cessna to drop in on his son in Williamsport.

The law office of Michelin Chiz was on the second floor of an old building on Spruce Street in downtown Scranton. John walked in promptly at 9 a.m. and was greeted coolly by a secretary. He had never met Ms Chiz, never heard of her, but that was not unusual in a state with over 60,000 lawyers. A lawyer friend had told him that she ran an all-woman shop with a couple of associates, a couple of paralegals and the usual assortment of secretaries and part-time help. No men need apply. Ms Chiz specialised in divorce, custody, sexual harassment and employment discrimination, and had a busy practice. Her reputation was solid. She was a tough advocate for her clients, a good negotiator and not afraid of the courtroom. Not bad looking either, the lawyer had informed John.

And he was right about that. Ms Chiz was waiting in her office when John walked in and said good morning. She was wearing a black leather skirt, not too short, with a tight purple sweater and a pair of black and purple spiked-heeled slingbacks. She was in her mid-forties, with, according to John's source, at least two divorces under her belt.

They settled round a small worktable in a room adjacent to her office, and the secretary was sent for coffee. They played a few minutes of who-do-you-know, kicking around the names of lawyers from Philadelphia to Erie, then Ms Chiz said, 'Let's get down to business.'

'Great idea,' Mr McAvoy said. 'Please call me John.'

'Sure, and I'm Mike.'

'Mike it is.' So far she had exuded nothing but charm and hospitality, but John could already tell that just behind the smile was a very tough lawyer. 'Would you like to go first?' he asked.

'No. You called me. There's something you want, so let's have it.'

'Very well. My client is my son, not the best arrangement in the world, but there it is. As you know, he works for a law firm in New York. Law school at Yale, undergrad at Duquesne. I'm sure you know about the alleged rape.'

'Indeed I do. Elaine works here part-time, and we're very close. She wants to go to law school someday.'

'I hope she succeeds. As you know, the police in Pittsburgh closed the investigation not long after they opened it. Frankly, I knew nothing about it until very recently.'

Her surprise was obvious, and John continued. 'No, Kyle did not tell me when it happened. He was planning to, but the investigation was closed. This is upsetting because we are very close, but it's not important. I understand that you and Ms Keenan met with Joey Bernardo here in Scranton a few weeks back, and the meeting did not go well, according to Joey's version. I also know that Baxter Tate contacted your client, and was evidently on his way here to talk to her when he was murdered.'

'That's correct.'

'So it appears, Mike, that the episode five and a half years ago will not go away. My client would like to resolve things, to close this matter. It's a dark cloud hanging over these kids, and I'm here to explore ways to get rid of it. I'm representing only my son. The others know nothing of this meeting. The Tate family, of course, has no clue, and you can imagine what they're going through right now. Joey has a child on the way and is about to get married. Alan Strock, as far as we know, has forgotten the episode.'

Mike had yet to lift a pen. She listened intently as she softly tapped all ten fingertips together. Her hard hazel eyes did not blink. 'I'm sure you have something in mind,' she said, content to listen.

'I'm not sure what your client wants. She might be thrilled if all three surviving room-mates were convicted of rape and sent to prison. She might be satisfied with a quiet apology. Or she might entertain the idea of a financial settlement. Perhaps you could help me here.'

Mike licked her lipstick and rattled some bracelets. 'I've known Elaine for two years. She has a troubled past. She's frail, vulnerable and at times subject to some very dark moods, depression. She's been sober for almost a year, but she's fighting those demons. She has become almost like a daughter to me, and I believe her when she says she was raped. She is convinced that the Tate family leaned on the cops, who backed off.'

John was shaking his head. 'None of the four boys told their parents.'

'We don't know that for sure. Regardless, Elaine's problems stem from that episode. She was a healthy, fun-loving, vibrant student who had big plans. Shortly after the rape, she dropped out and has struggled ever since.'

'Have you seen her grades from Duquesne?'

'No.'

'Her first semester, she flunked one course, dropped out of another, and made horrible grades in the other three. She improved slightly the second semester and made straight Cs. She took all four exams after the alleged rape, then went home and never returned to Duquesne.'

Mike's eyebrows arched and her spine stiffened. 'How did you gain access to her student records?' she snarled.

'I didn't and it's not important. How often do your clients tell you the entire truth?'

'Are you suggesting Elaine is lying?'

'The truth is a moving target here, Mike. But what's certain is that we'll never really know for sure what happened that night. These kids had been drinking and smoking pot for eight straight hours, and your client was known to sleep around.'

'They were all sleeping around. That's no excuse for rape.'

'Of course not.'

Money was in the air. There were a few other obstacles to clear, but both lawyers knew they would eventually discuss the possibility of a 'financial settlement'.

'What does your client say about the episode?' Mike asked, her tone cool, the flash of anger gone.

'They had been by the pool all afternoon; then the party moved indoors, into the apartment. There were about fifteen kids, more boys than girls, but Elaine was not in the group. Evidently, she was next door at a different party. Around eleven thirty, the cops showed up and the party ended. Nobody was arrested, the cops gave them a break.'

Mike nodded patiently. This was all in the police report.

'After the cops left,' John continued, 'Elaine showed up. She and Baxter started making out on the sofa, and one thing led to another. My client was watching television in the same room, as was Alan Strock. My client was intoxicated, to say the least, and at some point he passed out. He is certain he did not have sex with Elaine that night, and at the time he was not certain if anyone else did either. He was too drunk to remember much the next morning, and, as you well know, no accusation was made by your client until four days later. Baxter Tate and Joey Bernardo both admitted to having sex with your client on the evening in question. Both were adamant that it was consensual. The police investigated the matter, but soon realised that they simply could not put together a case. There's still no case. There's no way to prove rape occurred. There was sex, sure, but you can't prove anything else.'

She finally wrote something. Lavender legal pad, elegant strokes. She took a deep breath and gazed out of the window for a moment.

For Team McAvoy, it was time for the biggest gamble. The one bomb that could wreck any deal had to be addressed.

'Have you talked to the detectives in Pittsburgh?' John asked.

'No, but I've read the entire file.'

'Anything mentioned about a video?'

'Yes, there were notes in the file. But the cops couldn't find one. Elaine even heard the rumour.'

'It's not a rumour. There is such a video.'

She took this without the slightest flinch. Nothing in her eyes, hands or body registered surprise. She simply waited.

'I haven't seen it,' he said. 'But my client saw it in February of this year. Don't know where it is now, but there's a chance it might surface, perhaps on the Internet, perhaps in your mailbox.'

'And what would this video prove?'

'It would prove that your client was drunk and smoking pot when she sat down on the sofa with Baxter Tate and began kissing and groping. The angle of the camera does not allow a full picture of the two engaged in sex, but it's obvious from the knees down that they're having a fine time. Baxter is followed by Joey. At times Elaine is not active; at other times she's obviously engaged. My client thinks it proves that she was in and out of consciousness, but he's not certain. Nothing is certain, except that neither he nor Alan Strock had sex with her.'

'Who has the video now?'

'I do not know.'

'OK, who showed it to your client?'

'He does not know the person's real name. He had never met the person until the person showed him the video.'

'Gotcha. I take it there's a complicated story behind this. Extortion?'

'Something close.'

'Is that why you're here? Your client is scared of the video? You wanna make peace with us so the extortion scheme goes away?'

'You're very astute.'

'Must be a helluva video,' she said, still not blinking.

'It clearly shows your client happily getting involved in a good romp on a sofa. Whether she blacked out at some point is not clear.'

'She is seen walking and talking and moving around?'

'Clearly. These boys didn't drag her in off the street, Mike. She had been in their apartment many times, drunk and sober, always looking for a party.'

'We could debate this for hours,' Mike said. 'And not settle anything.'

'I agree. Baxter was in New York three weeks ago today to see my client. In the course of a long discussion he told my client that he believed that he had forced himself on Elaine. The guilt was heavy.'

'And the rapist is dead.'

'Exactly. However, my client was there when it happened. It was his apartment, his friends, his party. He wants this thing off his back, Mike.'

'How much?' she asked.

'Is it possible to reach a financial settlement and have your client release all civil claims and agree not to prosecute?'

'Yes, assuming the settlement is sufficient.'

'My client does not have a lot of money. He has student loans, and it's not cheap living in New York City. I'll probably need to chip in a little, and a busy street practice in downtown York is not the road to riches.'

His honesty disarmed her for a moment, and she smiled.

'Yesterday, I spoke with an attorney for the Tate family, big firm in Pittsburgh,' John continued. 'Baxter had a trust that sent him six thousand a month, but that trust folded when he died. There's very little in his estate, so any contribution from his family would fall under the category of charitable giving and these people are not known for their charity.'

Mike was nodding in agreement. 'What about Joey?' she asked.

'He's working hard, trying to provide for a growing family. My client would like to keep both Joey and Alan Strock out of this.'

'That's admirable.'

'We propose two payments. One now, and one in seven years, when the statute of limitations expires on the rape charge. If your client gives up the idea of pursuing these guys, then she gets a nice payment at the end. Twenty-five thousand now, and for the next seven years my client will add ten grand to an investment account that will render a hundred thousand when Elaine is thirty years old.'

Same poker face. 'Twenty-five up front is ridiculous,' she said.

'He doesn't have twenty-five thousand. It'll come from me.'

'We're not too concerned about where it comes from. We're much more interested in the amount.'

'Well, right now you have zero, and if we don't reach an agreement, then it's very likely you'll stay at zero. Your chances of recovery are slim at best.'

'Then why are you offering anything?'

'Peace of mind. Mike, come on, let's put this baby to sleep so these kids can get on with their lives. Kyle had almost forgotten the incident, hell, he's working a hundred hours a week, then Joey bumps into Elaine, then Baxter shows up all consumed with guilt because he remembers more now than he did before. This is crazy. They were just a bunch of drunk kids.'

Yes, they were, and Mike couldn't argue the point. 'Let me talk to Elaine, and we'll make a counter offer,' she said.

'Fine, but there's not much wiggle room here, Mike. The up-front money will be a loan from me to my client, and he is obviously nervous about taking on a seven-year obligation.'

'I'll call Elaine.'

'I'm not leaving town until we have a deal. I'll just walk down to the coffee shop and kill some time.'

AN HOUR LATER he was back. They took their same positions, picked up their pens and continued the negotiations.

'I assume you're not taking our offer,' John said.

'Yes and no. The seven-year scheme is OK, but Elaine needs more up front. She is two years away from her degree at the University of Scranton. Her dream is law school, and without some help it will be impossible.'

'How much help?'

'A hundred thousand now.'

Shock, disbelief, amazement, rejection. John grimaced and allowed a lungful of air to whistle over his teeth. It was all an act, the long-practised pretence of utter incredulity at the other side's first demand. 'Look, Mike, we're trying to reach an agreement here. You guys are trying to rob a bank.'

'In two years, Elaine will still be earning what she earns now, twenty-four thousand a year. Your client, on the other hand, will be earning about four hundred thousand, with guaranteed increases. This is not a stretch for him.'

John stood as if he were leaving, end of negotiations. 'I need to call him.'

'Sure. I'll wait.'

John walked outside the building, put a cellphone to his head and called no one. A hundred thousand dollars was a bargain, under the circumstances, to keep Elaine quiet.

'We'll go seventy-five grand, and that's it,' John said, back at the table.

'Deal,' she said. They shook on their agreement, then spent two hours haggling over the paperwork. When it was finished, he offered to buy lunch and she readily accepted.

NIGEL'S LATEST workstation had been hastily assembled on a fine mahogany desk in the centre of the sitting room in a spacious suite at the Waldorf-Astoria. The computer was sixteen by twenty inches, an exact replica of the ten models on the eighteenth floor. The monitor, too, was a perfect mate. Next to it was an ominous navy blue box the size of a larger laptop.

Nigel went through a detailed description of the various cords and cables, then pointed to a spot behind the computer. 'Here we are, Kyle, the promised land, the USB port. Almost hidden but I know it's there because I have a contact with Fargo. It has to be there, trust me.'

Kyle grunted but said nothing.

'Here's the plan, Kyle,' Nigel said excitedly. From his neat little hacker's tool kit he produced two small, identical devices, three-quarters of an inch wide and about an inch and a half long. 'This is the wireless USB transmitter, hot off the press, not yet available to the public, no, sir.' He quickly plugged it into the USB port that was under the power inlet at the back of the computer. 'You plug it in just so, and, presto, we're in business. It's virtually invisible.' He waved the other device and explained, 'And this little bugger is the USB receiver that goes in the blue box there. With me, Kyle?'

'Got it,' he said.

'The blue box goes inside your briefcase. You park the briefcase on the floor, directly under the computer, flip a switch and the docs get themselves downloaded in a jiffy.'

Kyle sat in the chair in front of the monitor. 'So I'm supposed to somehow reach behind the computer, plug in the transmitter, leave it there, download, et cetera, while there are other people in the room and the video cameras are watching. How, exactly, do I pull that off?'

'Drop a pen,' Bennie said. 'Spill some coffee. Create a diversion. Go when the place is empty, and keep your back to the camera.'

Kyle was shaking his head. 'It's too risky. These people are not stupid, you know. There's a security tech on duty in a room next door.'

'We know security, Kyle, and the grunts who are paid to watch closed-circuit screens all day are usually half asleep. It's terribly boring work.'

'I'm supposed to be working in there, Bennie, ploughing through the documents. I'll have a project due and a partner waiting on it.'

Nigel charged in. 'It could be over in two hours, Kyle, assuming you can find the documents quickly.'

Bennie shook off all concerns. 'Priority one is the air-breathing engines that Trylon and Bartin developed together. The technology is so sophisticated that the Pentagon is still orgasmic. Priority two is the fuel mix. Do a search for "cryogenic hydrogen fuel" and follow it up with one for "scramjet". There should be a ton of research in the files. Priority three is called "waveriders". Do a search. These are aerodynamic designs used to increase the B-10's lift-to-drag ratio. It's the heart of the research, the crux of the lawsuit, and you can find it, Kyle.'

'Oh, thank you.'

Nigel withdrew the transmitter and handed it to Kyle. 'Let's see you do it.'

Kyle slowly got to his feet, leaned over the computer, shoved away some cables, and with some effort finally managed to insert the transmitter into the USB port. He sat down and said, 'There's no way.'

'Of course there is,' Bennie scoffed. 'Use your brain.'

Nigel bounced around to the blue box. 'When you have inserted the transmitter, you reach down and flip this little switch, and the script automatically locates the computer and begins downloading the database. It will happen very quickly, Kyle, and if you like, you can take a break, leave the room, go for a pee, act like nothing at all is happening, and all the while my little gismo is sucking up the documents.'

'Bloody brilliant,' Kyle said.

'You'll use this,' Bennie said, producing a black Bally briefcase identical to Kyle's, complete with a few scuff marks and Kyle's Scully & Pershing business card firmly in the leather tag.

Nigel carefully lifted the blue box and placed it in the centre compartment of the briefcase. 'When you unzip this divide,' he said, 'the receiver will already be in place. If for some reason you need to abort, just close the case and punch this button and it locks automatically.'

'Let me get this straight. Something goes wrong, maybe some alarm goes off in a supercomputer we know nothing about, and your plan is then for me to lock the flap on the briefcase, grab the transmitter that's almost hidden, and then do what? Sprint from the room like a shoplifter who's been caught? Where do I go, Nigel? Any help here, Bennie?'

'Relax,' Bennie said with a fake smile. 'This is a piece of cake.'

'No alarms, Kyle,' Nigel said. 'My software is too good for that. Trust me.'

'Would you please stop saying that?'

Kyle walked to a window and looked out at the Manhattan skyline. It was almost 9.30 on Tuesday night. He had not eaten since lunch in the cafeteria at 11.30. Hunger, though, was only a minor concern on a long list.

'Are you ready, Kyle?' Bennie said. Not a question, but a challenge.

'As ready as I'll ever be,' he answered without turning round.

'When?'

'As soon as possible. I want to get it over with. My best guess is that it'll be about eight tomorrow night, late in the day but with enough time to download, assuming I don't get shot.'

'Any questions about the equipment, Kyle?' Nigel asked.

Kyle walked stiffly back to the workstation and stared at the machines. He finally shrugged and said, 'No, it's pretty straightforward.'

'Super. One last thing. The blue box has a wireless signal so that I know precisely when you're downloading.'

'Why is that necessary?'

'Monitoring. We'll be very close by.'

Another shrug. 'Whatever.'

The blue box was still in the briefcase, with Nigel handling it as if it were a bomb. Kyle then added the materials from his own briefcase, and when he grabbed the handle and lifted it off the table, he was surprised at the weight.

Nigel had been watching every move. 'It's a bit heavier, isn't it? Not to worry. We've reinforced the bottom of the Bally. It's not going to drop out as you're walking along Broad Street.'

'I like the other one better. When do I get it back?'

'Soon, Kyle, soon.'

Kyle pulled on his trench coat and made his way to the door.

Bennie said, 'Good luck, Kyle. We believe in you.'

'Go to hell,' Kyle said, and left the room.

AT 6.35 ON WEDNESDAY morning, twenty minutes after Kyle had ridden the elevator to the thirty-fourth floor, Roy Benedict entered the same elevator with two fatigued-looking young men who were undoubtedly associates at Scully & Pershing. Roy knew half a dozen partners at Scully, but with 2,100 lawyers arriving for work, he figured the odds were slim that he would see a familiar face. And he was right. The two zombies riding up with him were just a couple of faceless souls who would be gone in a year or so.

The briefcase in Roy's hand was also a black Bally, identical to Kyle's, the third one required for this mission. He left the elevator alone on the thirty-fourth floor and walked past the vacant reception desk, down a hall to the office Kyle had been allocated when he was transferred to the Trylon litigation team. His client was sitting at his desk, sipping coffee, waiting. The exchange was brief. Roy swapped briefcases and was ready to go.

'Where are the feds?' Kyle asked, very softly, though no one was in the hall and the secretaries were just getting out of bed.

'Around the corner in a van. They'll do a quick scan to make sure there are no tracking devices. If they find one, I'll bring it back in a sprint and we'll concoct a story. If not, then they'll take it to their lab in Queens. When do you need it back?'

'Let's say seven p.m. That's twelve hours. Should be enough, right?'

'That's what they say. According to Bullington, they have a small army of geeks just itching to unwrap it. You good?'

'Great. Do they have arrest warrants?'

'Oh, yes. Wiretapping, extortion, conspiracy. They're just waiting on you.'

'If Bennie is about to be arrested, then I'm a motivated young man.'

'Good luck.'

Roy was gone, leaving behind the Bally with the same scuff marks and name tag. Kyle quickly stuffed it with files and legal pads and pens and went to find more coffee.

TWELVE LONG HOURS LATER, Roy was back with the second briefcase. He took a seat as Kyle closed the door. 'So?' Kyle said.

'It is what it is. It's a customised computer built along the lines of those used by the military. Designed for nothing but downloading. Two hard drives, with seven fifty gigabytes each. Basically, enough memory to store everything in this building and the three next door. Sophisticated software that the FBI geeks have never seen before. These guys are good, Kyle.'

'Tell me about it.'

'And there is indeed a wireless signal so they can monitor you.'

'Dammit. So I have to download something?'

'I'm afraid so. The wireless signal cannot indicate what you are downloading, or how much. It just lets them know that you're inside and that you've started moving the database.'

'Shit.'

'You can do it, Kyle. Do you know where you'll meet these guys?'

'No. It'll be a last-second notice. Assuming I download without setting off alarms, I'll call Bennie with the happy news, and he'll tell me where to meet. I'm going to the room in an hour, and I plan to quit at nine, regardless of the download. So, by nine fifteen, if I'm lucky, I should be on the street.'

'If you get a chance, call me at my office. Pretty exciting stuff, Kyle.'

'Exciting? How about terrifying?'

'You're the man.' Roy exchanged briefcases again and disappeared.

For sixty minutes Kyle stared at the clock; then finally he made a move. He loosened his tie, rolled up his sleeves, tried to look as casual as possible and took the elevator to the eighteenth floor.

Sherry Abney was in the room, and after he had said hello he chose a station as far away from her as possible. Her back was to him.

Despite his moaning, he foresaw little danger of being noticed by another member of Team Trylon. All ten chairs faced the outside walls, so that while doing research, he could see nothing but the monitor, the computer and the wall behind it. The danger was up above, lurking in the lenses of the video cameras. Still, he would have preferred to have the room to himself.

After fifteen minutes, he decided to visit the men's room. On the way out, he asked Sherry, 'Can I get you a coffee?'

'No, thanks. I'm leaving soon.'

Perfect. She left at 8.30, a nice breaking point that always made billing easier. Kyle placed a legal pad on top of the computer, then a couple of pens, things that could roll and slide and need retrieving. He scattered a couple of files beside the monitor and in general made a mess of things. At 8.40, he knocked on the locked metal door that led to the small printing room, and there was no answer. Then he tried a second metal door that led to places unknown, but he suspected it was the room where Gant hung out. There was no answer.

At 8.45, Kyle decided to plunge ahead in case another associate arrived. He walked to his table and bumped the legal pad on top of the computer, sending the pens flying against the wall. He threw up an arm, said, 'Shit!' then leaned over as if to retrieve things. He found one pen, couldn't find the other, but kept searching. On the floor, behind the monitor, under the chair, then again behind the computer, where he deftly inserted the tiny transmitter into the USB port just as he found the missing pen and held it up so the cameras could see it. Settled down now, composed, not cursing, he took his seat and began clicking away at the keyboard. He slid the briefcase closer under the table, directly under the computer now; then he flipped the switch.

No alarms. No virus warnings screaming from the screen. No sudden entry by Gant. Nothing. Kyle the hacker was downloading files, stealing at a dizzying speed. In nine minutes, he transferred all the harmless Category A documents that had already been submitted to APE. When that was finished he repeated the process and downloaded them again. And again, and again.

An hour after he entered the room, he again went through the charade of searching for lost pens, and plucked the transmitter from the USB port. Then he cleaned up his mess and left. He hurried back to his office, got his jacket and trench coat, and made it to the elevators without seeing another person. As he rode down, he realised that this was the moment he had always feared. He was leaving the office, with enough stolen files in his briefcase to get him convicted of numerous crimes and disbarred for life.

As he stepped into the raw December night, he immediately called Bennie. 'Mission accomplished!' he said proudly.

'Great, Kyle. Oxford Hotel, corner of Lex and Thirty-fifth. Room 551.'

'I'm on the way.'

Kyle walked to a black sedan, one duly registered to a well-known car company in Brooklyn, and jumped into the back seat. The small Asian driver said, 'Where to, Mr McAvoy?'

'And your name is?'

'Al Capone.'

'You're the man, Al. Oxford Hotel, room 551.'

Al the Agent called someone with the information. He listened for a few minutes, then said, 'Here's the plan, Mr McAvoy. We have a team on the move, and when they are at the hotel the supervisor will call me with more instructions. Would you like a vest? There's one in the trunk if you'd like.'

Kyle had been too preoccupied with his thievery to give much thought to the details of the arrest. Why, exactly, might he need a bulletproof vest? To stop bullets, of course. Baxter flashed through his overheated brain.

'I'll pass,' Kyle said, realising he was ill equipped to make such decisions.

'Yes, sir.'

Al looked for traffic, detours, anything to burn some clock. His cellphone rang and he listened, then said, 'OK, Mr McAvoy. I'll stop in front of the hotel. You'll walk into the lobby and take the elevator. Get off on the fourth floor, turn left, walk to the door leading to the stairs. In the stairwell, you'll meet Mr Bullington and several other agents. They'll take over from there.'

'Sounds like fun.'

'Good luck, Mr McAvoy.'

Five minutes later, Kyle walked into the lobby of the Oxford Hotel, his heart pounding furiously, and followed his instructions. In the stairwell between the fourth and the fifth floors, he met Joe Bullington and two other agents. Kyle was impressed with how large they were.

'I'm Agent Booth; this is Agent Hardy,' one said. 'Go to the door of 551. The second it starts to open, kick it very hard, then jump back out of the way. We'll be right behind you. We do not anticipate gunfire. We assume they're armed, but they're not expecting trouble. Once we're inside, you'll be removed from the scene.'

Kyle's knees were suddenly weak.

'Got it?' Booth growled at him.

'Got it. Let's go.'

Kyle entered the hall and walked to room 551. He pressed the button, took a deep breath and glanced round. Booth and Hardy were fifteen feet away, ready to spring, shiny black pistols drawn. From the far end of the hall, two other agents were approaching, also with guns visible.

Maybe I should have opted for the vest, Kyle thought. He pressed the button again. Nothing. Not a voice from within, not a sound. His lungs had ceased working and his stomach was a mess.

He frowned at Booth, who looked perplexed as well. Kyle pressed the button for the third time, then yelled, 'Hey, Bennie. It's Kyle.'

Nothing. He rang the doorbell for the fourth time, then fifth.

Booth motioned for some type of well-rehearsed formation and said to Kyle, 'Please step aside. Go right down there and wait.'

Hardy whipped out an electronic room key and inserted it. The green light came on, and the four FBI agents stormed in, guns aimed in all directions. Bullington was running towards them, and behind him were more agents.

The room was empty, of suspects anyway, and if anyone had been there recently, he'd left nothing behind. Bullington reappeared in the hall and commanded, 'Lock the building!' into a walkie-talkie. Agents hustled about, frantic with indecision and confusion.

An old woman in 562 stepped into the hall and shouted, 'Quiet!' but quickly lost her spunk when two frowning agents spun round with weapons. She retreated quickly, unharmed but awake for the night.

'Kyle, here, please,' Bullington said, waving him into room 551. 'Stay here for a few minutes. These two will remain with you.'

Kyle sat on the edge of the bed, putting the heavy briefcase between his feet, as his two guards closed the door and put away their guns. He thought of Roy, and called him. He was still at his office, waiting for the news.

'They got away,' Kyle said, his voice slow and weak.

'Whatta you mean?'

'We're in the hotel room, and it's empty. They're gone, Roy.'

'Where are you?'

'Room 551, Oxford Hotel.'

'I'll be there in fifteen minutes.'

WHILE THE HOTEL was being searched, three FBI agents entered Kyle's apartment in Chelsea and began a sweep that would take four hours and produce three hidden cameras, a wiretap on his wall phone and six other eavesdropping devices. Plenty of evidence to support indictments. A strong case for the feds, but what they really needed was some suspects.

11

At 11 p.m., when Roy arrived, Kyle was still seated on the edge of the bed, briefcase between his feet, trench coat on, staring blankly at the floor and ignoring the two agents who were guarding him.

Roy put a hand on his shoulder, then knelt down to face level and said, 'Kyle, you OK?'

'Sure.' It was somewhat helpful to see a trusted face.

Bullington was on the phone. He slapped it shut and said, 'There's a suite on the second floor. It's easier to secure and much larger. Let's make a move.'

As they filed out, Kyle mumbled to his lawyer, 'Did you hear that, Roy? Easier to secure. I'm being protected now.'

The suite had three rooms, one of which would work well as an office—desk, fax, wireless Internet and several comfortable chairs. 'This'll do,' Bullington said, as he ripped off his trench coat, then his jacket.

Kyle and Roy did the same. They took their seats and settled in. Two younger agents stayed by the door.

'Here's what we know so far,' Bullington began. 'The room was reserved this afternoon by a Mr Randall Kerr, using a bogus credit card. Around eight forty-five, Mr Kerr shows up to check in, alone, one small carry-on and a black briefcase. We've watched the video. It's Bennie, with no effort at disguise. He went to his room, and according to the electronic entry grid he opened the door to room 551 at eight fifty-eight. He opened it again eighteen minutes later, and evidently he left, because the door was never opened again. No one remembers seeing him exit the building. There are some video cameras in the hallways and lobby, but so far nothing. He's vanished.'

'Of course he's vanished,' Kyle said. 'You won't find him.'

'We're trying,' Bullington said.

'What did you download, Kyle?' Roy asked.

'Just the Category A documents. Five or six times.'

'And this went smoothly?'

'As far as I know. There were no problems inside the room.'

'What time did you start downloading?' Bullington asked.

'About eight forty-five.'

'And what time did you call Bennie?'

'Just before ten.'

Bullington thought for a second, then stated the obvious. 'So as soon as he knew you were downloading Bennie checked into the room. Eighteen minutes later he fled. That doesn't make sense.'

'It does if you know Bennie,' Kyle said. 'It's obvious someone informed him of our little plan. It wasn't me. It wasn't my lawyer. The only other parties involved would be you, Mr Bullington, the FBI and Mr Wingate and his gang over at Justice. We will probably never know. But Bennie got the tip and decided to have some fun. He's probably down the street watching a hundred FBI agents swarm around the hotel and laughing his balls off.'

Bullington's cheeks turned a dark red. He suddenly had a call to make and left the room.

'Take it easy, Kyle,' Roy said softly.

Kyle closed his eyes and tried to control his thoughts, but it was impossible.

Roy went to the minibar and pulled out two bottles of water. He handed one to Kyle. 'We should talk. We'll have to make some quick decisions.'

'OK. What do we do with this damned thing?' Kyle asked, patting the briefcase. 'Scully doesn't need it, because the documents are not confidential. I just stole a copy. Their files will appear to be untouched.'

'I'm sure the FBI will want it for evidence.'

'Evidence against whom?'

'Bennie.'

'Bennie? Bennie's gone, Roy. Listen to me. They'll never find Bennie, because he's a helluva lot smarter than they are. He won't be arrested. He won't go to trial. He's probably on a private plane right now, looking at his fifteen passports and deciding which one to use next.'

'Don't be so sure.'

'Bennie outfoxed us tonight, didn't he? Bennie has pals in high places, maybe not here in New York, maybe in Washington. Too many people got involved, Roy, and the network of gossip spread. It was a mistake.'

'You had no choice.'

'My choices were limited. Looks like I made the wrong one.'

'What about the law firm?'

'I'm sure I'll screw that up, too. What's your advice? God knows I'm paying for it, if at a discount.' Both managed smiles, but very brief ones.

Roy gulped his water, wiped his lips with a shirtsleeve and leaned closer. The two guards were still in the sitting room, within earshot. 'You could say nothing. Just report tomorrow for duty and act like none of this happened. The files are safe. Nothing has been compromised. Look, Kyle, you were forced to download some stuff to facilitate Bennie's arrest. The arrest didn't happen. The firm has no clue. If there's no prosecution, it will never know.'

'But the plan was to bust Bennie, tell the firm everything, and beg for mercy. Sort of like the bank robber who brings back the cash and says he's sorry, can't we just forget about it. With a few more twists, of course.'

'Do you want to stay at the firm, Kyle?'

'I took the job because Bennie had a gun to my head. At least now the threat of blackmail is gone. There's a chance the video may still cause some embarrassment, but nothing more. I'd like to get out of here.'

A radio squawked in the sitting room, jolting the agents. It came and went with no further news.

Kyle looked at his lawyer and said, 'You're a big partner in a big firm. What would you do if an associate pulled this stunt?'

'Fire him immediately.'

'Exactly. How can the firm ever trust me again? And there's something else, Roy, that Scully should know.' Kyle glanced at the sitting room, where his bodyguards were now watching TV. 'Bennie knew too much. I'm not the only spy. Someone else is planted there, passing along information to Bennie. I have to tell them.'

There was a commotion at the door, and the two guards quickly muted the television and hopped to attention. Kyle and Roy stood as Bullington swept in with a small, important group, the centre of which was a man of about sixty with short grey hair, a fine suit and the air of someone in complete control of all things around him. Bullington introduced him as Mr Mario Delano, director in charge of the New York office of the FBI.

He addressed both Kyle and Roy: 'Gentlemen, Bennie Wright has obviously left the building, and we have a serious problem. I have no idea where the leak was, but I assure you it was not my office. I doubt that's very comforting right now. Every agent under my authority is searching for him.'

Kyle shrugged. If he was supposed to be impressed, he was not.

Delano pressed on. 'It's urgent that you get out of town, Mr McAvoy. I suggest that we take you into protective custody for a few days, let the dust settle, give us some time to track down Bennie Wright.'

'And if you don't find him?' Kyle asked.

'Let's talk about that later. We have a small jet waiting at Teterboro Airport. You'll have protection around the clock until something changes.'

The crisp precision of Delano's plans left no doubt that the dangers were indeed substantial. Kyle could not argue. He was now the double agent, as well as the government star witness in the event Bennie got caught.

'Let's go,' Delano said.

'I need a minute with my client,' Roy said.

'Certainly,' said Delano. He snapped his fingers and the room emptied.

When they were alone, Roy said, 'I'll call Scully and put them off.'

Kyle withdrew his FirmFone and said, 'No need. I'll check in with Doug Peckham and tell him I'm sick. Bennie never got his hands on this phone.'

'Fine. It's best if I keep the briefcase and the computer.'

'Just don't let the FBI have it.'

'I won't.'

They shook hands. Roy said, 'You did the right thing.'

'Right or wrong, it didn't work.'

'You didn't hand over anything. You didn't breach a client's confidence.'

'Let's argue later.'

'Be safe.'

JOHN MCAVOY was enjoying a peaceful Thursday morning at his desk when a secretary rang in with the news that two gentlemen from the FBI had dropped by for a surprise visit. They were quickly shown in. Introductions were made, badges flashed, coffee declined.

'Is he all right?' John asked.

'He's fine,' the agent named Halsey said. 'Kyle has informed us that you are aware of the plans he had to help apprehend his handler.'

'Yes. I know what he had in mind. What's happened?'

Both agents shifted weight. The one called Murdock took over. 'Well, things didn't go as planned. Kyle secured the documents, and he was supposed to meet the handler last night in a midtown hotel. The handler didn't show, fled at the last moment. As of now, we have not apprehended him.'

John closed his eyes for a moment, then lit a cigarette. 'Where's Kyle?'

'He's with us, in protective custody. He's safe, and he's anxious to talk to you. That will not be possible at this moment.'

'Protective custody?' John repeated.

'Afraid so. He could be in danger.'

'Who botched the operation?'

'Not sure it was botched, or how or why. Let's just say there is a lot of investigating going on right now.'

'When can I talk to him?'

'Soon,' Halsey said.

'We're out of Philly,' Murdock said. 'But we're here in York for the next few days. Our job is to relay messages to you.' Both agents withdrew business cards. 'Cell numbers on the back. Please don't hesitate to call.'

KYLE SLEPT late into the morning, and awoke to the sounds of waves rolling onto a beach. He listened to the ocean and heard the distant calls of seagulls. There were no other sounds. No alarm clock startling him at some obscene hour. No rush to get to the office. None of that.

This was not an unpleasant way to begin the rest of his life.

The bedroom was one of three in a modest two-storey beach rental an hour east of Destin, Florida, on the Gulf, two hours and forty-eight minutes by Learjet from Teterboro Airport in New Jersey. They, he and his new friends, had landed at Destin just before 4 a.m. A van with armed drivers had scooped them up and raced along Highway 98, passing miles of empty condos and beach houses and small hotels.

The two windows were half open and the breeze blew the curtains. It was a full three minutes before Kyle thought about Bennie, but he fought the temptation and concentrated on the squawking of the seagulls. There was a knock at the door. 'Yes,' Kyle answered with a scratchy voice.

It opened slightly, and Todd, his new best friend, wedged through his chubby face and said, 'You wanted a ten o'clock wake-up call.'

'Thanks.'

Todd had joined the escape in Destin and was now assigned to guard their witness or snitch or whatever Kyle was considered to be. He was from the Pensacola office, was only two years older than Kyle, and talked far more than any other agent that he'd met so far in this ordeal.

Kyle, in boxers only, went next door to the large kitchen–den combo. Todd had been to the grocery store. The counter was covered with boxes of cereal, breakfast snacks and cookies, all manner of boxed foods. There were a few items of folded clothing on the kitchen table.

'Coffee?' Todd asked.

'Sure.'

Kyle's other new best friend was Barry, an older, quieter type with more wrinkles than any forty-year-old should have. Barry said, 'Good morning. We've been shopping. Bought you a couple of T-shirts, shorts, a pair of khakis, deck shoes. Don't worry, Uncle Sam paid the bill.'

'I'm sure I'll look fabulous,' Kyle said, taking a cup of coffee from Todd.

Todd and Barry, both in khakis and polos, were unarmed but not far from their weapons. There was also a Nick and a Matthew somewhere close by.

'I gotta call the office,' Kyle said. 'Check in, you know, tell them I'm sick and can't work today. By now they're already looking for me.'

Todd produced the FirmFone and said, 'Be our guest. We're told it's secure. Just don't give a hint as to where you are.'

With his coffee and his phone, Kyle stepped outside onto a wide deck that looked over some dunes. The beach was long and beautiful, and deserted. With great reluctance he looked at the phone. Emails from Doug Peckham, Dale, Sherry Abney, Tim Reynolds, Tabor and a few others, but nothing to alarm him.

He called Doug Peckham, got his voicemail, and reported that he was down with the flu, flat on his back, sick as a dog and so on. Then he called Dale, who was in a meeting. He left the same message.

Roy Benedict seemed to be waiting by the phone. 'Where are you, Kyle?' he asked, almost in a pant.

'Western Hemisphere. I'm doing well. How about you?'

'Fine. You're safe?'

'Safe. I'm hidden, stashed away, and I'm guarded by a posse of at least four, all anxious to shoot someone. Any news on our man Bennie?'

'No. They'll have indictments by noon, and they're adding one for murder. They'll splash these around the world and hope for a break. You were right. Your apartment had more bugs than a landfill. A transmitter in the rear bumper of your Jeep, too.'

'I never thought of that.'

'It's all being presented to the grand jury as we speak, so at least Bennie will have a thick indictment on record should he make a mistake.'

'Don't bet on that.'

'Have you talked to the law firm?'

'I left a message with Peckham, the flu routine.'

'No alarms, nothing strange?'

'No. It's weird, Roy. I'm a thousand miles away now, and looking back, I can't believe how easy it was to walk out with the files. I could have taken every single document and handed them over to Bennie. And I could have gone back this morning as if nothing happened. Scully has got to be warned.'

'So who tells them?'

'I do. I have a few things to get off my chest.'

'Let's talk about that tomorrow. I've been on the phone with Bullington all morning. Twice he's mentioned the witness protection programme. The FBI is pushing it hard. They are pretty nervous about you, Kyle.'

'I'm nervous about me, too, but witness protection?'

'Sure. They're convinced they can find Bennie. If they do, and they haul him back for a trial, you're the star. If you're not around to testify, then the government's case falls flat.'

'That'll take some serious thought and consideration,' Kyle said.

'Then start thinking.'

'I'll think about it and call you later.'

Kyle dressed in the khakis and a T-shirt, not a bad fit, then ate two bowls of cereal and read the *Pensacola News Journal*.

Todd joined him at the kitchen table. 'We have a few rules,' he said with a jovial face but a hard smile.

'What a surprise.'

'You can make calls, obviously, but only on that phone. Can't reveal your whereabouts. You can walk on the beach, but we have to follow.'

'You're kidding? I'm walking down the beach, and there's a guy with a machine gun tagging along. How relaxing.'

Todd caught the humour and enjoyed a laugh. 'No machine gun, and we won't be conspicuous.'

'You're all conspicuous. I can spot an agent a mile away.'

'Anyway, stay close to the house.'

'How long will I be here?'

Todd shrugged and said, 'I have no idea.'

'Am I in protective custody or witness protection?'

'Custody, I think.'

'Custody implies that I'm a suspect of some variety, doesn't it?'

Another shrug.

'But I'm not a suspect. I'm a witness, and I have not agreed to enter the witness protection programme. So, according to my lawyer, I'm free to walk out that door anytime I want. Whatta you think about that, Todd?'

'That machine gun you just mentioned? We have six on the premises.'

'So I should stay here, right?'

'Right.'

'OK, it's noon. What are we going to do?'

Barry had been hovering nearby, not missing a word. He walked to the table with a large basket of the usual board games the owners of all beach rentals leave behind. 'We have Monopoly, Risk, Scrabble, Chinese checkers,' he said. 'Your call, Kyle.'

Kyle studied the basket. 'Scrabble.'

THE TEMPERATURE hit eighty degrees in the early afternoon, and Kyle was bored with the beach house. He said to Todd, 'I'd like to take a walk. Would you please prepare the beach?'

'My pleasure. Which way are you going?'

'East, towards Miami.'

'I'll round up the gang. They're getting bored, too.'

Kyle walked for an hour, and passed fewer than ten beachcombers. Thirty yards behind were two of his guardians, a male and a female, a happy couple with receivers in their ears and handguns in their pockets.

He heard music, and saw a small crowd under a fake thatched roof. It was the Gator Hotel, a 1950s-style motel with a small pool and low rates. Just for the hell of it, he sauntered away from the water, walked between two small dunes, and pulled up a chair at Pedro's Bar. The bartender was mixing rum punch specials. The crowd numbered seven, all over the age of sixty, all overweight, all chatting in crisp northern accents.

Kyle sipped a rum punch and ordered a cigar. Between the dunes he saw his trailing couple stop and gawk and try to figure out what to do. Within minutes, another agent appeared from the front of the motel. He walked through the open bar, winked at Kyle and kept going. We're here, buddy.

He drank and smoked for a while, and tried to convince himself that he was relaxed. No worries. Just enjoying a few days at the beach.

But there was too much unfinished business in New York.

AFTER THREE DAYS of thorough protection, Kyle was fed up. The Lear landed at Teterboro just after 6 p.m. on Saturday, December 6. At Kyle's insistence, he was booked into a suite at the Tribeca Grand Hotel, near the Village. And at his request, all FBI agents remained below, in the lobby. He was tired of their overkill and silly rules—silly in his opinion.

Dale arrived promptly at eight. She was driven over by two agents and sneaked in through a service entrance. When they were alone, Kyle started with the fake flu and worked his way backwards. She listened with the same disbelief that had been shared by Roy Benedict and John McAvoy. They ordered room service, lobster and a fine white burgundy, compliments of the government, and kept talking. He was leaving the firm, and not sure where he was headed. She was leaving the firm, a nice lateral transfer to a better life in Providence. He wanted to talk about her future, but she was determined to finish up with his past. She said over and over, 'Why didn't you tell me?' The best response he could offer was, 'I didn't tell anyone.'

They talked until well past midnight. The back-and-forth was more a conversation between two good friends than between two casual lovers. They said goodbye with a long kiss and a serious promise to meet in a few weeks, as soon as Kyle settled some issues.

At 1.00 a.m., he called downstairs and informed the boys that he was going to sleep.

KYLE MCAVOY entered the opulent offices of Scully & Pershing for the last time at noon the next day. He was accompanied by Roy Benedict, Mario Delano of the FBI and Drew Wingate from the Department of Justice. They were led to a conference room on the thirty-fifth floor, where half a dozen of the firm's partners waited, all with sombre faces. All offered stiff introductions. Only Doug Peckham showed the slightest trace of warmth to Kyle, and only for a second. They took seats on opposite sides of the table like enemies glaring across the battlefield: Howard Meezer, the managing partner; Peckham; Wilson Rush, who looked particularly upset; a retired legend named Abraham Kintz; and two slightly younger partners from the firm's management committee, men Kyle had never laid eyes on.

Late Saturday evening, Roy Benedict had sent them a twenty-five-page, detailed summary of Kyle's big adventure, and there was little doubt that every word had been read more than once by all six of the partners. Attached to the narrative was Kyle's letter of resignation.

Meezer kicked things off. 'Mr McAvoy, your resignation is unanimously accepted,' he said pleasantly.

Kyle nodded but said nothing.

'We've read the summary prepared by your lawyer,' Meezer said slowly. 'It is fascinating, and troubling, and it raises a number of questions. I suggest we address them in order of priority.'

Fine, fine, yes, agreed all around the table.

'The first issue is what to do with you, Mr McAvoy. We understand the reasons behind your theft, but it was a theft nonetheless. You took the confidential files of a valuable client for purposes that had not been authorised by this firm. A criminal prosecution is in order, do you agree?'

Kyle had been told to keep his mouth shut unless Roy approved a response.

'A criminal prosecution is possible,' Roy admitted. 'But there is nothing to be gained. The firm lost nothing.'

'Loss is not a requirement, Mr Benedict.'

'But Kyle had no intention of turning over the documents. He did so only to stop a conspiracy to seriously harm this firm and its client.'

'The FBI will not cooperate in a criminal prosecution, Mr Meezer,' Delano said, the heavy hand of the federal government.

'Nor will the Department of Justice,' added Wingate.

'We don't need your help,' Meezer said. 'Theft can be a state charge. However, we are not inclined to pursue this as a *criminal* matter. We don't want our clients worried about confidentiality, and this little episode would make a wonderful story in the press.'

Wilson Rush was glaring at Kyle, but Doug occupied himself with a legal pad. He was there because Kyle fell under his immediate supervision, and because the firm needed a show of force at this unfortunate moment.

'As to the ethics,' Meezer was saying, 'this is a serious breach of a client's confidence. The state disciplinary committee should be notified.'

'I thought you were trying to avoid publicity,' Roy said. 'If Kyle gets reprimanded or disbarred, it becomes public record. A Scully & Pershing associate disbarred for taking confidential files. Is that the story you want splashed in the *New York Lawyer*?'

At least four of the six were slowly shaking their heads, and it dawned on Kyle that they were as nervous as he was. Their vaunted reputation was on the line. A major client might pull its business. Others could follow.

'Do you plan to stay in New York, Mr McAvoy?' Meezer asked.

Roy nodded, and Kyle said, 'No, I can't.'

'Very well. If you agree to forgo the practice of law in the state of New York, we will agree to forget the ethical violations.'

'Agreed,' Kyle said quickly. He couldn't wait to leave the city.

Meezer shuffled through some notes as if there were a dozen tough topics to cover, but in truth the meeting was practically over. 'In your summary, Mr McAvoy, you allude to additional security issues within Scully & Pershing. Care to expand on this?'

A nod from Roy, and Kyle began, 'Yes, but first I want to apologise for my actions. I hope you understand the reasons behind what I did, but I was still wrong. And I apologise. As far as security, I met with these thugs ten times while I was in New York. I took meticulous notes of each meeting—dates, places, duration, who was present, what was said, everything I could remember afterwards. My attorney has these notes. On three occasions, I was given information that could be known only by someone within this firm. I think there's another spy. For example, the man I knew as Bennie knew about the warehouse full of documents. During one meeting he hinted that they were making progress in breaching the security of the warehouse. They knew about the secret room on the eighteenth floor. Bennie knew every name of every partner and associate assigned to the lawsuit. He knew that a young lawyer named McDougle was leaving, that he worked under a senior associate named Sherry Abney on the Trylon case. Bennie handed me copies of pleadings, motions, rulings—I have over six hundred pages of the court file, which, as you know, is locked away and kept from the public.'

Three of the six jaws had dropped on the other side. It was a stunning blow. The nightmare of one lowly associate tapping into their impenetrable defences was bad enough. Now there might be another?

And just to give them more heartburn, Kyle added something he truly believed, but couldn't prove. 'And I don't think it's an associate,' he said.

Doug Peckham swallowed hard, cleared his throat. 'Are you saying—?'

Next to him, Wilson Rush quickly raised his right hand, partially in Doug's space. Like a king calling for silence.

Roy finally said, 'Anything else?'

'I believe that's all,' Meezer said. After an awkward few seconds, Roy stood, followed by Kyle and Delano and Wingate. The six partners sat frozen, with matching scowls, as Kyle and his little entourage left the room.

IN THE LOBBY of the building, they were met by the same three large young men who had brought Kyle from the hotel. The group made it safely outside, onto Broad Street, then walked one block east to the building where Roy worked, sixteen floors up. Drew Wingate decided that his job was over. He excused himself and promised to help in any way possible. After he left, Kyle, Roy and Delano gathered in Roy's office.

'What are your plans, Kyle?' Delano asked.

'Well, looks like I won't be practising law in the state of New York, that's for sure. I'll go home for a few weeks, take some time off.'

'I'm not sure that's a wise thing to do.'

'Thank you, Mr Delano. I appreciate your concern, but I'm not about to go into hiding. I'm twenty-five years old, stumbling but not falling, and I'll do just fine on my own.'

'Kyle, you can't be serious,' Roy said.

'Dead serious, Roy. No pun intended. I've just survived three days of protection, guards all around me, hiding and watching for bad guys. No thanks. I'm not going to live on the run.'

'These guys killed Baxter Tate without the slightest hesitation,' Roy said. 'What makes you think they won't do the same to you?'

'The operation was still hot when Baxter came barging in. That operation is now over. Bennie's gone. He might return with another plan—'

'I'm sure he will,' Delano said.

'But it won't involve me. What does Bennie gain by taking me out?'

'He takes out a material witness,' Roy said.

'Only if he's caught, which I seriously doubt. If Bennie gets hauled back for a trial, then we can talk about hiding.'

'Oh, it'll be too late then, Kyle,' Delano said. 'Believe me. The moment Bennie gets nabbed, there'll be a few guys headed your way.'

'The FBI can't force me into witness protection, and so I hereby officially, and respectfully, say no. Thank you, Mr Delano, but the answer is no.'

'I hope you don't regret this,' Delano said.

'So do I,' Kyle said. 'And please don't follow me around. I might go berserk and shoot the next person I see lurking in the shadows.'

'Don't worry. We have plenty of work elsewhere.' Delano stood and all hands were shaken. He said to Roy, 'I'll check in once a week with an update.'

Roy walked him to the door, and the FBI left Kyle's life. With the door closed, Roy took his seat and looked at Kyle as if he couldn't believe it. 'You're awfully brave.'

'Brave or stupid. The line is often blurred.'

'Why not disappear for a few months, Kyle? Let everything cool off.'

'These guys have long memories. If Bennie wants revenge, he'll find me sooner or later, and it won't matter where I happen to be.'

'You don't trust the FBI?'

'No. I trust you, me, my father, a girl named Dale and that's about it.'

'So you think it was an inside job?'

'We'll never know, will we? I have a hunch that Bennie works for the same government you and I send our taxes to. That's how he got away. That's why he'll never be found.'

'I still don't believe that.'

Kyle shrugged, and for a long time nothing was said.

Finally, Kyle glanced at his watch. 'Look, Roy, it's Sunday afternoon and you have a family. Go home.'

'What about you?'

'Me? I'm walking out the door, taking a long hike to my apartment, not once looking over my shoulder, and when I get there, I'll load up my Jeep with junk and drive home. I should get there in time for a late dinner with my father. Tomorrow he and I will draw up a partnership agreement—McAvoy & McAvoy, Attorneys-at-law—and I'll make partner faster than any graduate in the history of the Yale Law School. Real clients. Real people. Real cases. Deer hunting on Saturdays, Steelers on Sundays. A real life.'

'You're not kidding, are you?'

'I have never been more serious.'

'Come on. I'll walk you out.'

They rode the elevator to the lobby and walked out of the building. They shook hands and said goodbye, and Roy watched his client stride nonchalantly along Broad Street and disappear round a corner.

john **grisham**

While John Grisham is clear that the most satisfying thing about his time spent in the law was 'getting out of it', he also acknowledges that it was the foundation of his success as a writer. 'I seriously doubt I would ever have written the first story had I not been a lawyer. I've always preferred to tackle issues—death penalty, tobacco litigation, insurance abuse . . .'

He was born on February 8, 1955 in Jonesboro, Arkansas. His father, a cotton farmer and itinerant construction worker moved the family from town to town throughout the Deep South, eventually settling in Southaven, Mississippi, in 1967. Although both his parents lacked formal education, his mother encouraged him to read and insisted that he should aim to go to college. 'I read *Dr Seuss*, *The Hardy Boys*, *Emil and the Detectives* and lots of Mark Twain and Dickens,' Grisham remembers, despite the fact that all the way through high school and into university it was thoughts of becoming a professional baseball player that filled his mind. 'I was really an indifferent student and an athlete with delusions of adequacy and dreams of adulation,' he claims modestly.

For the first two years in higher education, Grisham drifted, attending three different colleges before obtaining a degree. Then, one evening, while watching an inter-college baseball game, 'it dawned on me that the players I was watching, though my age, also had a very slight chance of playing pro ball. I decided we were in the same boat and it was best to start studying.' He went to the University of Mississippi law school and settled down to learn accountancy and prepare for a career as a tax lawyer, but his interest shifted to litigation and criminal law.

After graduating in 1981, Grisham returned home to Southaven and and set up a small private legal practice, specialising in personal injury litigation and criminal defence. In the course of a decade he gained invaluable experience of the criminal justice system, and it was while observing the rape case of a young girl in the Mississippi court house that Grisham was inspired to write a novel exploring what would have happened if the girl's father had murdered her attackers. This would eventually turn out to be *A Time to Kill*, which he managed to complete in secret over three years, squeezing in time to write before going to the office and during courtroom recesses. 'The alarm clock would go off at five and I'd jump in the shower. I had to be at my desk, at my office, with the first cup of coffee and a legal pad and write from five thirty, five days a week.' Often he would write for two hours before he had to turn to his job as a lawyer.

After fifteen rejections, *A Time to Kill* was published to modest acclaim in 1988, but Grisham was undeterred. He was already deep into his next book—the story of a bright young attorney lured to an apparently perfect law firm that is not what it appears to be. *The Firm* sold over seven million copies, rocketed the 36-year-old lawyer into the best-seller lists, and was made into a hugely successful film. Suddenly Grisham was hot property. He gave up his law practice and devoted himself to writing full time.

Over the years he has branched out to write novels about life in the rural South, such as *A Painted House* and *Bleachers*, but *The Associate*, his twenty-first book, takes his loyal fans right back to what they love best: vintage Grisham, starring a high-flying Harvard law school graduate—who could so easily be a young John Grisham—with his idealistic heart set on 'giving something back' to the community.

Today, John and Renee Grisham (seen above at a gala), and their two children, divide their time between a farmhouse in Mississippi and a plantation in Virginia, where Grisham (pictured left, coaching junior baseball) now serves as the local Little League commissioner. Renee, whom Grisham married in 1981, takes a close interest in her husband's writing. 'I constantly inundate Renee with all sorts of story ideas, and she has an uncanny ability to spot a good one,' Grisham explains. 'Once I start writing, she is merciless as the chapters pour forth. She enjoys picking a good brawl over a subplot, a weak character, an unnecessary scene. I accuse her of looking for trouble—and, inevitably, I return to the typewriter and fix whatever troubles her!'

What To Do When Someone Dies

Nicci French

Affairs, like sudden death, happen only to other people. Or so Ellie Falkner thinks, until the chill autumn morning when she opens her door to two policewomen. Her husband Greg, they tell her, has been killed in a car crash . . . with a female passenger.

Was Greg having an affair? Devastated and drowning in grief, Ellie is determined to prove his innocence. Whatever it takes.

CHAPTER ONE

Moments when your life changes: there will always be a before and an after, separated, perhaps, by a knock at the door. I had been interrupted. I was tidying up. I had cleared up yesterday's newspapers, old envelopes, scraps of paper, left them in the basket by the grate ready to make a fire after supper. I had just got the rice bubbling nicely. My first thought was that it was Greg and he had forgotten his keys, but then I remembered he couldn't have because he had taken the car that morning. Anyway, he probably wouldn't knock but shout through the letterbox. A friend, perhaps, or a neighbour, a Jehovah's Witness, a desperate young man trying to sell dusters and clothespegs house-to-house. I turned away from the stove and went through the hall to the front door, opened it to a gust of cool air.

Not Greg, not a friend, not a neighbour, not a stranger selling religion. Two female police officers stood in front of me. One looked like a schoolgirl, with a fringe covering her eyebrows; one was like her teacher, with a square jaw and greying hair cut mannishly short.

'Yes?' Had I been caught speeding? Littering? Then I saw an expression of uncertainty, even surprise, on both their faces and felt the first small prickle of foreboding in my chest.

'Mrs Manning?'

'My name's Eleanor Falkner,' I said, 'but I'm married to Greg Manning . . .'. My words trailed away. 'What is it?'

'Can we come in?'

I led them into the small living room.

'You're the wife of Mr Gregory Manning?'

'Yes.'

I saw how the younger one looked up at the older one as she said the words, and I noticed she had a hole in her black tights. The older officer's mouth opened and closed but didn't seem synchronised with the words she was speaking so I had to strain to make sense of them. The smell of risotto reached me from the kitchen, and I remembered I hadn't turned the ring off and it would be dry and ruined. Then I remembered, with a stupid dullness, that of course it didn't matter if it was ruined: nobody would be eating it now. Behind me I heard the wind fling a few dry leaves against the bay window. It was dark outside. Dark and chilly. In a few weeks' time the clocks would go back. In a couple of months it would be Christmas.

She said, 'I am very sorry. Your husband has been in a fatal accident.'

'I don't understand.' Though I did. The words made sense. Fatal accident. My legs felt as if they didn't know how to hold me up any more.

'Your husband's car left the road,' she said slowly and patiently.

'Dead?'

'I'm very sorry,' she said. 'Sorry for your loss.'

'The car caught fire.' It was the first time the younger woman had spoken. Her face was plump and pale; there was a faint smudge of mascara under one of her brown eyes. She wears contact lenses, I thought.

'Mrs Falkner, do you understand what we have said?'

'Yes.'

'There was a passenger in the car. A woman. We thought . . . Well, we had thought it might be you. Do you know who that would have been?'

I stared dumbly at her. 'I don't know. Didn't she have her bag with her?'

'They couldn't recover much. Because of the fire.'

I put a hand against my chest and felt my heart beating heavily. 'Are you sure it was Greg? There might have been a mistake.'

'He was driving a red Citroën Saxo.' She looked down at her notebook and read out the registration number. 'Your husband is the owner of the vehicle?'

'Yes,' I said. It was hard to speak properly. 'Perhaps someone from work. He sometimes took them when he went to visit clients. Tania.'

'Tania?'

'Tania Lott. From his office.'

'Do you have her home number?'

'I don't think so. It might be somewhere. Do you want me to look?'

'We can find out.'

'I don't want you to think me rude, but I'd like you to go now.'

'Have you got someone you can call? A relative or friend? You shouldn't be alone.'

'I want to be alone,' I said.

'You might want to talk to someone.' The younger woman pulled a leaflet out of her pocket. 'There are numbers here of counsellors who can help you.'

'Thank you.' I took the leaflet she was holding out and put it on the table.

Then she offered me a card. 'You can reach me here if you need anything.'

'Thank you. Excuse me, I think the pan might have boiled dry. I should rescue it. Can you let yourselves out?'

I went into the kitchen. I took the pan off the hob and poked at the sticky mess of burnt risotto with a wooden spoon. Greg loved risotto; it was the first meal he had ever cooked me. Risotto with red wine and green salad. I had a sudden, clear picture of him sitting at the kitchen table in his shabby home clothes, smiling at me and lifting his glass in greeting, and I spun round, thinking that if I was quick enough I could catch him there.

Fatal accident.

Sorry for your loss.

This is not my world. Something is wrong, askew. It is a Monday evening in October. I am Ellie Falkner, thirty-four years old and married to Greg Manning. Although two police officers have just told me he is dead, I know that can't be true because it happens in a world meant for other people.

I sat down at the kitchen table and waited. I didn't know what I was waiting for; perhaps to feel something. People cry when a loved one dies, don't they? There was no doubt that Greg was my loved one, my dear heart, but I had never felt less like crying. My eyes were dry and hot. My stomach ached, and I put my hand on my belly for a few seconds and closed my eyes.

What had he said when he left? I couldn't think. It had been just another Monday morning. When had he last kissed me? On the cheek or on the lips? We'd had a stupid argument on the phone that afternoon, just a few hours ago, about what time he was coming home. Had those been our last words? Little bickering phrases before the great silence. For a moment I couldn't even remember his face, but then it came back to me: his curly hair and his dark eyes and the way he smiles. Smiled. His strong, capable hands, his solid warmth. It had to be a mistake.

I stood up, pulled the phone from its holster on the wall and punched in the number of his mobile. I waited to hear his voice and, after a few minutes, when I didn't, I put the phone back and went to press my face to the window. There was a cat walking along the garden wall, very delicately. I could see its eyes shining. I watched until it disappeared.

Perhaps I should pour myself a whisky. That was what people did when they were in shock, and I supposed I must be in shock. But I didn't think we had any whisky. I pulled open the drinks cupboard. There was a bottle of gin; a bottle of Pimm's, but that was for hot summer evenings a long way from here, from now; a bottle of schnapps. I twisted the lid off and took an experimental sip, feeling its burning thread in my throat.

The car caught fire . . .

I tried not to see his face on fire, his body consumed. I pressed the palms of my hands into the sockets of my eyes and the smallest sound escaped me. It was so quiet in the house. All the noises came from outside: the wind in the trees, cars passing, doors slamming, people getting on with their lives.

I don't know how long I stood there like that, but at last I went upstairs, gripping the banisters and hauling my weight from step to step like an old woman. I was a widow. Who was going to set the video for me? Who was going to help me fail to do the crossword on Sunday? Who was going to keep me warm at night, to hold me tight and keep me safe? I thought these things, but did not feel them. I stood in our bedroom for several minutes, gazing around me, then sat heavily on the bed—on my side, careful not to disturb Greg's space. He was reading a travel book: he wanted us to go to India together. His dressing gown hung on the hook on the door. There were slippers with their heels turned down under the old wooden chair, and on top of it an old blue jumper he'd worn yesterday. I went and picked it up, burying my face in the familiar smell. Then I pulled it over my head.

I wandered into the small room next door to our bedroom, which, for the time being, served as a junk room. It was full of boxes of books and stray objects we'd never got round to unpacking, though we had moved to this house well over a year ago, as well as an old-fashioned bath with claw feet and cracked brass taps that I had picked up from a reclamation centre and had planned to install in our bathroom once I had done something about the taps. We had got stuck carrying it upstairs, I remembered, unable to go backwards or forwards and giggling helplessly, while Greg's mother had shouted useless instructions at us from the hallway.

His mother. I had to call his mother and father. I had to tell them that their eldest son was dead. I felt breathless and had to lean against the door jamb. How do you break that kind of news? I returned to the bedroom and sat on the bed once more, picking up the phone on my bedside table. For a moment, I couldn't remember their number, and when I did, I found it hard to press the buttons because my fingers weren't working properly.

I hoped she wouldn't answer, but she did. Her high voice sounded aggrieved to be called at this late hour.

'Kitty.' I closed my eyes. 'It's me, Ellie.'

'Ellie, how—?'

'I've got some bad news,' I said. And then, before she could draw breath to say anything: 'Greg's dead.' There was complete silence from the other end, as if she had hung up. 'Kitty?'

'Hello,' she said. Her voice had dwindled; she sounded very far away. 'I don't quite understand.'

'Greg's dead,' I persisted. 'He died in a car crash. I've only just heard.'

'Excuse me,' she said. 'Can you hold on a moment?'

I waited and then another voice came on the line, a kind of gruff, no-nonsense bark. 'Ellie. Paul here. What's this?'

I repeated what I'd said, the words becoming more and more unreal.

Paul Manning gave a short, nervous cough. 'Dead, you say?' In the background I could hear sobbing.

'Yes.'

'But he's only thirty-eight.'

'It was a road accident.'

'A crash?'

'Yes.'

'Where?'

'I don't know. I don't know if they told me; maybe they did. It was hard to take everything in.'

He asked me more questions, detailed questions, none of which I could answer. It was as if information would give him some kind of control.

Then I dialled my parents' number. That's what you do, isn't it? Even though you may not be close to them, that's the right order. His parents, then my parents. Chief mourners. But there was no reply and I remembered that Monday was quiz night at the pub. I depressed the button and sat for a few seconds listening to the dialling tone. The clock on Greg's side of the bed told me it was thirteen minutes past nine. Hours to go before morning came. What was I supposed to do until then? Should I start calling people, telling them the news? Then it came to me.

I found her home number in Greg's old address book. The phone rang several times, four, five, six. It was like a terrible game. Answer the phone and you're still alive. Don't answer and you're dead. Or perhaps just out.

'Hello.'

'Oh.' For a moment I couldn't speak. 'Is that Tania?' I asked, although I knew it was.

'Yes. Who's this?'

'It's Ellie.'

'Ellie. Hi.'

I took a deep breath and said the nonsense words again. 'Greg's dead. In an accident.' I cut into the expressions of horror that came down the line. 'I rang you because I thought you might have been with him. In the car.'

'Me? What do you mean?'

'He had a passenger. A woman. And I assumed, you know, that it was someone from the office, so I thought . . .'

'Two of them died?'

'Yes.'

'Christ, Ellie, how awful. God, I can't get my head around this. I'm . . .'

'Do you know who it could have been, Tania?'

'No.'

'He didn't leave with anyone?' I asked. 'Or go to meet anyone?'

'No. He left about half past five. And I know he'd said earlier he was going to get home in good time for once.'

'He said he was coming straight home?'

'I assumed that. But, Ellie . . . It might not mean what you're thinking.'

'What am I thinking?'

'Nothing. Listen, if there's anything I can do, you only have to—'

'Thanks,' I said, and put the phone down on her.

What *was* I thinking? What might it not mean? I didn't know. I only knew that time moved sluggishly on, and there was nothing I could do to make it go faster. I crept downstairs and sat on the sofa in the living room, Greg's jersey pulled down over my knees. I waited for it to be morning.

THE SOUND of the newspaper hitting the mat was a reminder that the world was outside, trying to get in. Soon there would be things to do, duties to fulfil, responsibilities. But first I phoned Tania again. 'I'm sorry,' I said. 'I wanted to catch you before you went to work.'

'I've been thinking about it all night,' she said. 'I can't believe it.'

'When you get in, could you check who Greg was seeing yesterday?'

'He just spent the day at the office, then left to go home.'

'He might have called in on a client on his way, dropped something off. If you could have a look at his diary . . .'

'I'll do anything, Ellie,' said Tania, 'but what am I looking for?'

'Ask Joe if Greg said anything to him yesterday.'

'Joe wasn't in the office. He was on a visit.'

'It was a woman.'

'Yes, I knew that. I'll try.'

I thanked her and put the phone down. It rang instantly. Greg's father had questions he wanted to ask me. I wasn't able to answer any of them. I had already told him everything I knew.

I wasn't at all hungry or thirsty but I decided I ought to have something. I walked into the kitchen and the sight of Greg's leather jacket draped over one of the chairs hit me so that I could hardly breathe. I used to complain about that. Why couldn't he hang it on a proper hook, out of the way? There would be a lot of moments like that. As I made myself coffee there were more of them. The coffee was Brazilian, a kind he always chose. When I opened the fridge door, I was bombarded with memories, things he had bought, things I had bought for him, his preferences, his aversions.

I realised that the house was still almost as it had been when he had left it, but with every action I took, everything I used or moved, I was eliminating his presence, making him that little bit deader. On the other hand, how did that matter? He *was* dead. I took his jacket and hung it on the hook in the hall, the way I'd always nagged him to do.

My mobile was on the shelf there and I saw I had a text message—and then that it was from Greg, and for a moment I felt as though someone had taken my heart in their two hands and wrung it out like a flannel. With thick fingers, I called it up. It had been sent yesterday, shortly after I'd got upset with him for staying later at the office than he'd promised, and it wasn't very long: 'Sorry sorry sorry sorry. Im a stupid fool.' I stared at the message, then pressed the phone against my cheek, as if there was a bit of him left behind in the message that could enter me.

I took the coffee, his address book, my address book and a notebook and started to think who I should call. I felt as if my mind wasn't working properly and I had to write everything down, so that I didn't forget someone or ring someone twice. There were close friends I would have to try to reach before they left for work. First, though, I rang my parents.

My father answered and immediately called my mother so they were both on the line. I blurted it all out. There was a sudden outpouring of emotion and then of questions. Was I all right? Did I need any help? Should they come over?

I needed to speak to Joe, Greg's partner and his dear friend. But I only got through to his answering machine, and I couldn't bear to break the news like that. I imagined his face when he heard, his blazing blue eyes; he would be able to cry the tears I didn't yet seem able to. Tania would have to tell him for me. I thought she'd want to anyway; she was new to the company and adored Joe, as a schoolgirl adores a movie star.

I wrote out a list of forty-three people and started calling them roughly in the order they had come out of my address book and then out of Greg's. The first was Gwen Abbott, one of my oldest friends. When I heard her cry of shock, I felt I was experiencing it all over again, except it was worse because the blow was struck on bruised and broken flesh. After I had put the phone down I simply sat, almost gasping for breath, as if I was in thin air at high altitude. I felt I couldn't go through with it, reliving the moment through other people over and over again.

But it got easier. After a few times, I managed to steer each conversation and bring it to a fairly quick close. It was worst with his dearest friend Fergus who had loved Greg for much longer than I had. He'd been his running companion, confidant, surrogate brother, best man. He said, 'What will we do without him, Ellie?' I heard his dazed, cracked voice and thought, That's how I'm feeling too; I just don't know it yet. I felt about grief as if it was crouching out of sight in hiding from me, waiting to spring out and ambush me when I least expected it.

Halfway through the list, there was a knock at the door and I opened it to find Joe standing there. He was in a suit and carrying the slim briefcase that Greg used to tease him about, saying it was always empty and just for show. He looked like a man who had been in a punch-up and come off worst, reeling, pale and glassy-eyed. Before I could speak, he stepped over the threshold and enveloped me in his embrace. All I could think of was how different he felt from Greg, taller and broader, with a different smell as well: soap and leather.

I wanted so badly to break down and cry in his arms, but somehow I couldn't. Instead Joe cried, tears coursing down his lived-in face, as he told me how wonderful my husband had been, and how lucky he was to have known me. He said I was family to him and that I must lean on him. He kissed me on both cheeks and held my hands in his and told me very solemnly that I didn't have to be strong. He scoured the pan I'd burned the rice in, wiped the kitchen table and put out my rubbish. He even started trying to clear up some of the mess, lifting piles of paper and putting books on shelves in a frantic, utterly ineffectual way until I told him to stop. Then he left and I continued with my task.

By the time I got to Greg's part of the list, people had started leaving for work. I didn't phone mobiles. I couldn't bear the idea of talking to people on trains, of them having to keep their voice down, embarrassed about their reactions in front of strangers.

By then the phone had started ringing. People I'd talked to had digested the news and thought of things they needed to say, questions they wanted to ask. Friends had rung other friends and some of those friends immediately rang me, one expression of grief after another, so that they seemed to merge into a continual howl.

One of the calls wasn't from a friend or relative, but from WPC Darby, one of the women who had broken the news to me. 'I'm sorry to bother you,' she said, 'but did I say anything about identifying the body?'

'I can't remember,' I said.

'I know it's a difficult time,' she said, and there was a pause.

'Oh,' I said. 'You want me to identify the . . .' I stopped. 'My husband. But you came here. You told me about it. You know already.'

'It's a requirement,' she said. 'You could always nominate another family member. A brother or a parent.'

'No,' I said immediately. The idea was impossible. When Greg had married me, he had become mine. I wasn't going to let his family reclaim him. 'I'll do it. Where is he?'

'He is in the mortuary of the King George V Hospital. Do you know it? Is there someone who can take you?'

I phoned Gwen and she said she would drive me to the hospital, even though I knew it meant she would have to phone in sick. I realised I was still in the clothes I had put on the previous morning. I took them off and stood in the shower, my head lifted into the hot jet and my eyes closed. I dressed quickly, glanced in the mirror and saw that I was entirely in black. I took off my sweater and replaced it with a rust-coloured one.

Some people know instinctively how to respond to your moods. Gwen is like that. Greg and I once had a conversation about who of our friends never irritated us and she was the only name we both agreed on. She senses when to stand back, when to come close. Mary and I regularly argue, but Mary argues with most people, almost for the sake of it. But Gwen, with her soft mop of golden hair, her grey eyes, her quiet clothes, her calm and reflective manner, doesn't like to raise her voice. At university people who knew her called her 'the diplomat', a tag that was both admiring and sometimes slightly resentful, because she seemed to hold back from intimacy. But I had always liked her reserve; it felt like a privilege to be let into her tiny circle of friends. Now, when I answered the door to her, she didn't open her arms, inviting me to step into them to cry and be comforted. Instead she looked at me with a grave tenderness, putting a hand on my shoulder but letting me decide if I wanted to break down or not. And I didn't. I wanted, needed, to hold myself together.

As she drove me towards the hospital in King's Cross, she didn't speak and allowed me to stay silent. I stared out of the window at passers-by, doing today what they had planned yesterday. Didn't they realise it was temporary? It might all seem to be going smoothly, but one day, tomorrow or the day after or in fifty years' time, the charade will come to an end.

We arrived at the hospital and discovered that we had to pay to park. I got suddenly and pointlessly angry. 'If we were going to the supermarket instead of to the morgue, we wouldn't have to pay.'

'Don't worry,' said Gwen. 'I've got change with me.'

Once inside the hospital, I wasn't able to take in the instructions that the receptionist gave us but Gwen led me along corridors, down in a lift to a basement and another reception.

A man emerged from an office behind the reception desk. He was wearing a green coat. He was very pale, as if he spent all his time down there underground, away from the sun. He looked at us enquiringly.

'My friend is here to identify a body.'

He nodded. 'I'm Dr Kyriacou, senior registrar. Are you a relative?'

'He's my husband,' I replied. I wasn't ready to use the past tense yet.

'I'm very sorry for your loss,' he said, and for a moment I thought he really was sorry, as sorry as you could be when you expressed it every day.

'His name is Gregory Manning,' I told him.

Dr Kyriacou rummaged through some files piled in a metal tray on the counter until he found the one he wanted. He opened it and examined the papers inside.

'Do you have any identification?' he asked. 'I'm sorry. It's a regulation.'

I handed him my driving licence and he wrote something on his form. 'Your husband's body was badly burned,' he said. 'This will be distressing for you. But in my experience it's better to see the body than not.'

'Do you want me to come with you?' Gwen asked.

I shook my head. She sat down and Dr Kyriacou led me into a room that looked as if it were full of filing cabinets with drawers four deep, but with handles like old-fashioned fridges. He glanced at the clipboard he was carrying, then walked to one and turned to me. 'Are you ready?' he asked.

I nodded. He pulled open the door and there was a rush of cold air into the already cold room. He drew out a tray. There was a body lying on it, covered with a sheet. He lifted a corner of the sheet. I couldn't stop myself gasping because now I knew, finally, that there was no mistake and that he was dead, my darling Greg.

I made myself look closely. His face was blackened by the fire, some of his hair was burned away and his scalp scorched. The only real damage was above his right eyebrow where there were signs of a terrible collision. I reached out and touched some of his hair, then leaned forward and touched it with my lips. There was a strong smell of burning. 'Goodbye,' I whispered to him. 'My love.'

'Is this Gregory Manning?' said Dr Kyriacou.

'Yes, it is.'

'Thank you,' he said, and wrote on his clipboard.

He took me back to Gwen and then a thought occurred to me. 'The other person in the crash. Is she here?'

'Yes,' he said.

I paused. I hardly dared ask the question. 'Do you . . .' I began. 'Do you know her name?'

Dr Kyriacou rummaged through the files. 'Her husband came,' he said. 'Yes, here we are.' He looked at the front of the file. 'Milena Livingstone.'

Gwen looked at me. 'Who is she?'

'I've never heard of her,' I said.

MY LITTLE HOUSE filled with people. Friends made me cups of tea and pieces of toast that I tried to eat. The phone rang and rang. Gwen and Mary must have set up a rota between them, because as soon as one left it seemed that the other arrived. My parents turned up with a ginger cake. Joe came with whisky. He sat on the sofa, shook his head slowly in disbelief and called me 'darling'. Fergus arrived, his face ashen with shock. Everyone tried to hug me. I didn't want to be hugged. Or, at least, I didn't want to be hugged by anyone except Greg. I woke at night out of dreams in which he was holding me in his warm embrace, and lay with dry, sore eyes, staring at the darkness, feeling the space in the bed beside me.

I needn't have worried about what I had to do for at every stage there were plenty of people to tell me. I had become part of a bureaucratic process and was channelled smoothly and efficiently towards the end point, the funeral. But before there could be a funeral, the death had to be registered, and for that, I discovered, there needed to be an inquest to establish the cause of death.

We used to talk about dying. Once, while drunk, we answered an online questionnaire that provided you with your date of death (me at eighty-eight, Greg at eighty-five), because death seemed ludicrously far away. If we had ever thought about it seriously, we would have assumed that when it came we would be old, and one of us would be holding the other's hand. But I hadn't been holding his hand and someone else had been with him. Milena Livingstone. Who was she? Why had he been with her?

'Why do you think?' asked my mother, grimly, and I ordered her out of the house, slamming the door hard behind her.

'Why do you think?' asked Gwen, and I laid my head on the table on top of all the lists of what I had to do, and said I didn't know, I had no idea. But I knew Greg. He would never . . .

'TELL ME ABOUT HER.'

'Who?' Joe looked at me with a grave, attentive expression.

'Milena. Who was she?'

'Ellie.' His voice was kind. 'I've no idea. I didn't know about her.'

'She wasn't a client?'

Joe and Greg were partners in their own business. Accountants are supposed to be thin, grey men in suits and glasses, but that wasn't true of those two. Joe was flamboyant and charismatic. Women gravitated towards him, drawn by his blue eyes, his wide smile, his air of utter attention. He was handsome, but Greg and I used to say that the real secret of his charm was that he made other people feel beautiful, special. He was older than us, in his late forties, so he seemed like an uncle or an older brother. And Greg—well, he used to say that if I'd known what he did for a living, I'd never have gone out with him. But I couldn't have known. We'd met at a party, a mutual friend of a friend's, and if I'd had to guess, I would have said he was a TV director, a writer, an actor or a professional activist. He looked raffish and stylishly unkempt; there was a slightly dreamy, unworldly air about him. I was the one who was methodical and practical, whereas he was enthusiastic, untidy, boyish. Certainly not what I thought of as an accountant.

'No,' said Joe. 'I've looked through everything. Twice.'

'There must be an explanation.'

'Can't you think of anything?' This time his kind voice, pushing me gently to acknowledge the obvious, made me shudder.

'I would have known.' I glared at him. 'You would have known.'

Joe put his hand on my shoulder. 'Both of us know how wonderful and adorable Greg was but, after all—'

'No,' I repeated, cutting him off. 'It's not possible.'

'WHO WAS MILENA?' I asked Fergus.

'I have no idea,' he replied. 'He never mentioned anyone called Milena.'

'Did he mention . . .' I hesitated. 'Did he ever say he was . . . you know?'

'Having an affair?' Fergus finished the sentence I couldn't.

'Yes.'

'He adored you.'

'That's not the question.'

'He never mentioned he was having an affair. Nor did I ever suspect that he might be. Not for a single second.'

'And now? Do you suspect he might have been?'

Fergus rubbed his face. 'Honestly? I don't know, Ellie. You know I was in his office with him the day he died.' Fergus was some kind of computer whiz and he'd done freelance work for the firm several times. 'He seemed completely normal. He talked about you. He never said anything that would make me suspect. Yet he died in a car with a strange woman whom no one seems to have heard of. What can I say?'

THE INQUEST WAS SET for ten o'clock on Tuesday, October 15, in the coroner's court off Hackney Road. I could bring family and friends, if I wished. It was open to the public and to the press.

I asked Gwen if she and Mary would come with me. 'Unless it's difficult for Mary to arrange childcare,' I added. Mary had a young son, nearly a year old now. Until Greg's death, the conversations between us had been dominated by nappies, first smiles, teething problems, cracked nipples, the swamping pleasures of maternity.

'Of course we'll come,' said Gwen. 'I'm going to cook you something.'

'I'm not hungry and I'm not an invalid. Does everyone think she was another woman?'

'I don't know. It doesn't matter. What do you think?'

What did I think? I thought I couldn't survive without him. I thought he had betrayed me. I knew, of course, that he hadn't. I thought when I woke up at night that I could hear him breathing in the bed beside me. I thought a hundred times a day of things I needed to say to him, I thought I could no longer remember his face and then it returned to me, teasing and affectionate. I thought it was his fault because he had chosen to go with her, and I thought, too, that I would go mad with not knowing who the woman was and yet if I found out I should very likely go mad as well.

Milena Livingstone. How old was she? What did she look like? All I knew about her was that she had a husband who had identified her body at the same morgue as Greg was in. I went upstairs to my laptop and turned it on, then Googled her name.

I clicked on the first reference and the screen was filled with an advertisement for a business. Something about everything being taken out of your hands and no detail left unattended to. Venues. Meals. I scrolled down. It seemed to be a glorified party-arranging business for people with lots of money. A sample menu. Tuna sashimi, sea bass marinated in ginger and lime, chocolate fondants. And here, yes, were the people who ran it.

Two photographs smiled at me from the screen. The face on the left was pale and triangular, with dark blonde hair cut artfully short, a straight nose and a restrained smile. She looked attractive, clever, classy. It wasn't her. No, it was the other one, with a tawny mane (dyed, I thought spitefully), high cheekbones, white teeth, grey eyes. An older woman, then. A rich woman, by the look of it. A beautiful woman, but not the kind of beauty I'd ever expected Greg to fall for. Milena Livingstone had a glamorous, artful look to her; her eyebrows were arched and her smile knowing. A man's woman, I thought. But not my man. Surely not Greg. Bile rose in my throat and I turned off the computer and went into the bedroom where I lay face down on my side of the bed.

I don't know how long I lay there like that, but at last I got up and went to the wardrobe. Greg's clothes hung on the right-hand side. He didn't have many: one suit that we'd bought together for our wedding and he'd hardly worn since, a couple of casual jackets, several shirts. I started to go through everything in the wardrobe. I felt in each pocket, and found only a receipt for a meal we'd had in an Italian restaurant two weeks ago. I remembered: I'd been upset and he'd been patient and optimistic. I pulled open the drawers where he kept T-shirts and underwear, but I didn't discover any women's lacy knickers or incriminating love letters.

I stood in front of the mirror, examined myself and found myself wanting. I weighed myself and realised I was shrinking. It occurred to me that since he had died I'd barely cooked. Eggs are comforting, I thought. I boiled myself an egg, broke open the top, then dabbed my spoon into the yellow yolk. I made myself eat half of it before I felt so sick I had to stop. I had stomach cramps, a grim, familiar backache, so I ran a bath and lowered myself into it. I lay in the hot water and closed my eyes. Then I opened them and watched a curl of red blood run out of me and spread, then another.

So. It wasn't to be, after all. Once again, as with all the other months of trying and hoping, I wasn't pregnant. Greg had died in his car with another woman and left me alone, and what on earth was I going to do now?

CHAPTER TWO

It was drizzling. Gwen and Mary arrived early, when I was still in my dressing gown. Mary had brought some Danish pastries, and I made us a big pot of coffee. We sat round the kitchen table, dunking the pastries, and I was reminded of when we were students together, sitting just like this in the kitchen of the house we'd shared in our final year.

'I'm so glad the two of you could be here,' I said. 'It means a lot.'

'What did you think?' said Mary, heatedly. Her face was flushed with excitement. 'That we would let you go through this alone?'

I thought I might cry at that, but I didn't, although grief felt rather like a fishbone that was gradually working itself loose in my throat. I asked Mary how her son was and she replied in a constrained, self-conscious way, very different from the eager assumption she had made in the past that I would be interested in every belch and gurgle he made. I had crossed into a different country. No one felt able to have an ordinary conversation with me, no one was about to tell me their petty anxieties and daily fears in the way they would have done a week ago.

I went upstairs and chose my clothes: black skirt, stripy grey shirt, black woollen waistcoat, flat boots, patterned tights, hair tied back. I was so nervous that it took me three attempts to thread my earrings through the lobes of my ears; my hands trembled so that I smudged my lipstick. I felt as though I was about to be put on trial: what kind of wife were you, anyway, that your husband was with another woman? What kind of fool, that you never had the slightest idea?

WHEN WE REACHED the coroner's court, a low, modern building that looked less like a court than an old people's home, the feeling of unreality continued. We went into a corridor that led through a series of swing doors into a room where lines of chairs faced a long table. The air-conditioning hummed loudly and the fluorescent light shimmered overhead. I had been expecting something impressive, wood-panelled perhaps, with an air of formality, not this blandly cheerful room with louvred blinds. Only the crest of the lion and the unicorn, squeezed between the two windows, gave any hint that this was a court. Several people were already there, including a couple of police officers.

A grey-haired man in a suit was blocking our way. He had a moustache and the air of a sergeant major. 'Can I take your names, please?'

'I'm Eleanor Falkner. I'm Greg Manning's wife. These are my friends.'

He introduced himself as the coroner's officer and pointed us to seats in the front row. Mary sat on one side of me, Gwen on the other.

Just before ten, a group of three entered and were directed by the coroner's officer to the front-row chairs a few places along from where we sat. A middle-aged man with corrugated greying hair and a silk tie, a slender young woman, whose pale hair rippled down her back and whose aquiline nose quivered, and a young man with untidy dark hair, untied shoelaces and a stud in his nose. I tensed and clutched Gwen's arm.

'That's them,' I hissed. 'Her family.'

I stared at the middle-aged man. After a few seconds he turned and met my gaze. Someone near him murmured something and he turned round. It was his name. Hugo. Hugo Livingstone. The court officer asked us all to rise. I had expected a judge in robes and a wig but Dr Gerald Sams was just a man in a suit, carrying a large bundle of files. He sat down behind the table at the front and began to address us in a calm, deliberate tone. He offered his condolences to me and to Milena Livingstone's husband and two children. 'Stepchildren,' muttered one loudly.

He gave a brief talk about the process. He said there might be some details that family members would find upsetting, but that the inquest was often helpful to the next of kin, giving a clear account of what had happened and perhaps some sort of closure. He would call witnesses, but this was not a trial. Any interested person could question them and, indeed, ask questions at any point. He asked if anybody had legal representation. Nobody spoke.

I took a notebook and a pen from my pocket. I opened it and wrote *Inquest* at the top of a blank page. I underlined the word, then turned the underlining into a box surrounding it. Meanwhile a police officer had come forward to the little desk at the front of the room and swore, on a tatty copy of the Bible, to tell the truth. An unremarkable young PC, with reddish-brown hair combed flat against his head, he was the man who had found my husband.

He consulted his notebook and, in a strange monotone, gave a halting account of how he had driven to Porton Way in response to a call from a member of the public who had reported seeing a fire.

Dr Sams asked if the officer could describe Porton Way.

'There's not much to say, really,' he said. 'There used to be factories and warehouses there, but it's mainly derelict now. They're starting to redevelop it, though.'

'Is the road busy at that time of night?' asked Dr Sams.

'No,' said the officer. 'It's not a through route. Sometimes kids steal cars and drive them round there, but we didn't see anyone else.'

'Tell us what you found.'

'The fire had died down by the time we got there but we could see the smoke. The car had slipped down the embankment and turned over. We scrambled down and saw there were people in it but they were clearly dead. My partner called the fire brigade and an ambulance. I walked round just checking. I couldn't really get close. It was still hot.'

Dr Sams was writing notes on a pad of paper. 'Did you form an impression of what had happened?'

'It was obvious,' the officer said. 'The driver lost control, the car came off the road, rolled down the embankment, hit a concrete ridge, burst into flames.'

'I meant more why it happened,' said Dr Sams. 'Why the driver lost control.'

'That's pretty obvious as well,' the officer said. 'Porton Way goes straight and then it suddenly curves to the right. It's not very well lit. If a driver was inattentive—if he was talking to his passenger, or something like that—he could miss the turn, carry straight on and then be in big trouble.'

'And you think that was what happened?'

'There were no skidmarks, so it looks as if the car left the road at speed.'

Dr Sams asked the officer if he had anything else he wanted to add. The policeman looked at his notes. 'The ambulance arrived a few minutes later. The two bodies were pronounced dead at the scene, but we knew that anyway.'

'Is there any suggestion that another vehicle was involved in the crash?'

'No,' said the officer. 'If he crashed because he was avoiding another vehicle, there would have been skidmarks of some kind.'

Dr Sams looked towards those of us in the front row. 'Does anyone have any questions arising from this statement?'

I had many, many questions buzzing around my head, but I didn't think that the answers to any would be found in that officer's little black notebook. Nobody else spoke either.

'Thank you,' said Dr Sams. He then called Dr Mackay. A woman in a trouser suit came forward and sat in the chair. She was about fifty with dark hair that looked dyed. She didn't swear on the Bible. Instead she read a promise from a piece of paper.

Dr Sams looked at us again, especially me, the grieving widow, and him, the grieving widower. 'Dr Mackay carried out the post-mortem examination on Mr Manning and Ms Livingstone. It's possible that the details in her evidence will be distressing. Some of you might wish to leave the court.'

I felt a hand grip one of my arms. I shook my head.

'Very well,' said Dr Sams. 'Dr Mackay, will you give us a brief account of your findings?'

Dr Mackay laid a file on the table in front of her and opened it. 'Despite the condition of the bodies, I was able to undertake a complete examination. The police report stated that the two people in the car were not wearing seatbelts and the injuries were consistent with that: consistent with the head of each person being thrown forward and striking the interior of the car. The result was massive trauma. Therefore the cause of death was, in both cases, compression of the brain resulting from a depressed fracture of the skull.'

There was a pause as Dr Sams wrote notes. 'So the fire was not a factor?'

'I took blood samples from both Mr Manning and Ms Livingstone. Both tested negative for carbon monoxide.' Dr Mackay looked towards us. 'That suggests the two of them were not breathing after the fire started. I checked the airways and lungs and found no traces of carbon. Also, although the bodies had suffered burns, the sites of burning showed none of the signs of inflammation you would expect if it had happened while the person was still living. It may be of some comfort to the families to know that the deaths must have been all but instantaneous.'

I glanced across at Hugo Livingstone. He didn't look comforted. He didn't even look upset. He was frowning slightly, as if lost in thought.

Dr Sams asked Dr Mackay if she had checked Greg's blood-alcohol level. She said she had and that there was nothing untoward.

Dr Sams released Dr Mackay and she went back to her seat. He said he was calling no further witnesses and asked if anybody had any statements to make or any questions to put to the court. Once again there was an awkward pause.

I looked at my notebook. I had not written a single note. I didn't really have anything to ask but I had a lot I wanted to say. Greg had always been a careful driver. Blind drunk and engaged in animated conversation, he still wouldn't have missed a turn in the road. He wore his seatbelt even when moving the car ten feet. I could have announced this to the court, but then I would have been the person with questions to answer: what did I know about the way he behaved when he was with this other woman? Did I not know about this other relationship, this other life? And if I didn't, what did my knowledge about him count for? I stayed silent.

'Good,' said Dr Sams. 'There is obviously no confusion about the identity of the victims and the time and place of their death. If there is no objection, I would like to record a verdict of accidental death in the case of Gregory Wilson Manning and of Milena Livingstone. The deaths can now be registered and the bodies released for burial. Thank you very much.'

'RIGHT,' I SAID, out loud. I had noticed that I was beginning to talk to myself, like a mad woman, trying to fill the silence of the house with a human voice. I didn't care. I had a purpose. I was going to take Greg's life apart and find out what had been going on. He wouldn't escape me that easily. I was going to track him down.

After the inquest I'd persuaded Gwen and Mary to leave and assured them that, yes, I'd be all right. Gwen asked if I was starting work again and I said I was thinking about it. Probably it would have been a good idea. It would have been therapeutic. I restore furniture, from valuable antiques to worthless junk. Badly paid though it often was, part-time though it usually was, I loved it. I loved the smell of the wood and the wax and the feel of a chisel in my hand. It was where I'd always gone to escape. But not now.

I began with the tiny mezzanine room. It was next to the bathroom and overlooked the garden, which was small and square, dominated by the rickety shed at the end where I stored the furniture I was working on. This was a study of sorts. There was a filing cabinet full of things like accounts and insurance policies, a bookshelf that mostly held reference books, and a table I had found in the junk shop at the end of the road, then sanded and waxed, on which stood Greg's laptop. I sat down, opened the lid, pressed the start button and watched icons spring to the screen.

First, the emails. Before I started, I searched 'Milena' and 'Livingstone' and came up with nothing. I winced at the unopened messages that had arrived since Greg had died. There were about ninety, mostly junk mail and one sent by Fergus about half an hour before I had rung him and given him the news. He was suggesting they run a half-marathon that weekend before watching the football together. I bit my lip and deleted it.

I went through his mailboxes methodically. There was almost nothing to do with work; he had a separate mailbox for that. Deliveries, house stuff, bookings, confirmations of travel arrangements. Several were from me and I looked at those as well. They had an easy intimacy about them that seemed far away and unfamiliar now. Death had turned Greg into a stranger; I could no longer take him for granted. Dozens were from Fergus, swapping bits of gossip, sending references to websites they'd been discussing or continuing a conversation. Joe, of course. Other friends. Casual greetings and arrangements to meet. Sometimes I was mentioned: Ellie sends her love; Ellie's a bit down in the dumps (had I been? I couldn't remember). When there was anything remotely interesting or curious about the emails he had been sent, I pressed the little arrow beside them to see what he'd written in reply. He was normally quite terse—he always used to say that tone was hard to detect in an email; you should be careful about irony or sarcasm. He was careful and factual, even with me.

One of Greg's more regular email correspondents was a woman called Christine, the ex of an old friend, who he sometimes met up with; he wasn't so careful with her. I flicked between her messages and his. She lamented approaching her thirty-sixth birthday and he said she was more attractive now than when they'd first met. She thanked him for taking a look at her boiler and he said it was nice to have an excuse to see her again. She said he was a very nice man, did he know that? And he replied that she must bring out the best in him. He was tanned after his holiday; she was radiant after hers. He was looking tired—was everything all right at home? He replied that she, on the other hand, was as fresh as ever and blue suited her.

'But were things all right at home, Greg?' I glared at Christine's solicitous notes, his flirtatious, evasive responses. 'Come on, tell me.'

I moved to the SENT messages, but they didn't tell me. They showed me he had ordered woodchip for the garden, grey paint for the kitchen, and a CD by Howling Bells, which I'd never heard of. Maybe he'd given it to someone as a present. Milena? Christine? I called up his music library and scrolled down, and there it innocently was.

Greg was pretty efficient at getting rid of old messages and, anyway, they only went back a few weeks: the older ones were deleted at an even deeper level, somewhere in the mysterious circuitry of the computer. I ploughed doggedly through them, feeling I was simply wasting my time. There was a strange little message from Tania, in which she said she didn't really understand his query and he should ask Joe about it.

I got the phone from our bedroom—my bedroom—and called Joe on the office number.

'Yes?' He sounded unusually curt.

'It's me. Is that the way you usually talk to clients?'

'Ellie.' His voice softened. 'It's one of those days. I was going to call you this evening. Tell me about the inquest. Are you all—'

'Were there any problems with your business?'

'How do you mean?'

I mentioned the email I'd found on Greg's computer.

'What date did you say?'

'A week or so ago.'

There was a pause.

'I'm scrolling through my mail and there's nothing I can see from Greg about a worry.'

'So, everything was OK?'

'Depends what you mean. If you want me to bend your ear about clients who don't pay up on time, or dealing with the Revenue and the nightmare of bureaucracy . . . But that's just business as usual.'

'All the work Greg had to do late at the office, that wasn't because there were problems?'

'Did he often work late?' His tone was cautious, with an underlying note of sympathy.

I felt the blood flame into my cheeks. 'Recently. Later than usual anyway.'

'Did he seem stressed?'

'No. At least, not really. I keep thinking back and seeing things I didn't notice at the time—or, at least, thinking I can see things. Maybe he was a bit preoccupied. Or maybe I'm making that up.'

There was a silence at the other end. I knew what Joe was thinking: that perhaps Greg was preoccupied because he was having an affair.

'If he was worried, though,' I continued, 'I think he would have told me. That's the kind of marriage we had. We shared things.'

'I think you're right,' he said. 'Greg would have told you.'

'You mean about everything?'

Another silence.

'Ellie, I'm finishing up here. Can I come round on my way home? I'll bring a bottle of wine and we can talk this through.'

'I won't be here.'

I FOUND HER ADDRESS in his old address book and decided to walk, even though she lived in Clerkenwell and the drizzle outside was turning into a downpour. It didn't feel like something I could express over the phone.

As I arrived, I saw her coming from the other direction. She was wearing a belted mac and a scarf tied round her head, and looked like a Fifties film star in one of those classy, black and white French movies.

'Hello.'

I stood in front of her and she looked at me with narrowed, suspicious eyes, then gave an exaggerated little start. 'Ellie? My God. I meant to get in touch. I'm so very, very sorry. He was such a lovely—'

'Can I come in?'

'Of course. You're soaked.'

I looked down at myself. I was still wearing my inquest clothes and had forgotten to put on a raincoat. I was cold and wet and looked dreadful.

I followed Christine upstairs into a spacious kitchen. She took off her mac, pulled the scarf off her head and shook out her chestnut hair.

'Do you live alone?' I asked.

'Yes,' she said. 'Just at the moment.' Then she offered me tea.

'No, thanks. Is that the boiler Greg fixed?' I asked. 'He never managed to get ours sorted.'

'I'm sorry . . . Look, is there a particular reason you came?'

'I wanted to ask you something.'

Her face took on the eager, helpful expression I'd become so familiar with since Greg's death.

'You were friendly with Greg. Would you say you were close to him?'

'It depends what you mean by close.' Her tone was cautious now.

'I read your emails to each other.'

'Yes?'

'He thought blue suited you.' Her expression had changed: no longer eager but embarrassed. I pressed on. 'You told him he was very nice and complimented him on his tan and he said you looked radiant.'

'You mean . . .?' She stopped. 'You poor thing,' she said softly.

I stared at her. Shame flushed through me, leaving me clammy. 'There was nothing between you, then?'

There was a nasty silence, then she said, 'It didn't mean anything.'

'He never tried to make it go further?' I felt abject, and also disgusted by myself.

She gazed at me with a pity that made me want to crawl under a stone.

'Greg and I were just friends.'

A wave of nausea assailed me. 'I ought to go. I shouldn't have come.'

'Are you sure I can't get you anything?'

'Yes.'

'I'm sorry. About everything.'

IT WAS DARK outside, with rain still falling, so I flagged down a cab and sat with my arms wrapped round myself, feeling wretched. When I reached my front door I discovered I didn't have enough money to pay the driver so

I ran inside, then came back out to pay the driver with odd bits of money I'd discovered in various drawers and pockets. I'd found a five-pound note in Greg's old leather jacket, which was still hanging in the hall. When was I going to sort out his things? A list of tasks streamed through my mind: contact the lawyer, the bank and the building society; find out about our life policies; organise the funeral; cancel the appointment we'd made together at the fertility clinic; change the message on the answering machine, which still had Greg's voice saying 'hello' and 'please call back later' because Greg and Ellie weren't around just now. Ellie was around, but Greg wasn't and Greg would never be. Greg with his dark eyes and his wide smile and his strong, warm hands. He used to rub my neck at the end of a long day. He used to wash my hair for me. He used to tell me about his days, or so I had thought. He used to watch me as I got undressed, his arms behind his head and a grave look on his face, waiting. He used to lie on his back in bed and snore gently. He used to wake up and turn to me, smiling in welcome as I struggled out of sleep.

Who else's neck had he rubbed, who else's hair had he washed? Who else had undressed for him, under the gaze I had thought was for me alone? All at once, a jealousy so pure and visceral it felt almost like intense physical desire swept through me. I had to sit on the stairs for a few seconds, trying to breathe normally, before I could make it to the bedroom.

I peeled off my wet clothes and put on a pair of jogging pants and a thick sweatshirt. That night I worked hard, stopping only for a mug of tea at ten, a glass of whisky at midnight, a sandwich at two. I sat in the living room and went through his diary, though it wasn't his work one, just the old book he kept personal appointments in, and didn't find a single thing that made me suspicious. I went through all his papers. I went through the box of old letters in the junk room. I went through his photo albums. I emptied the contents of boxes onto the floor and examined them: old vinyl records, tapes, books, magazines. I pulled out each drawer in our bedroom and went through his clothes.

I opened the cupboard under the stairs and took out every object there—bike panniers, a squash racket, running shoes, an old tent we hadn't used since that trip to Scotland when it had rained non-stop and we had eaten fish and chips and listened to the rain hammering on the canvas. He had told me then that wherever I was that was his home. We had both cried.

At six, because it was too early to go out and I had gone through everything in the house, I started making a list of people I would ask to the funeral. At eight o'clock I made myself a bowl of porridge and a large pot of strong coffee, then I washed and got dressed. Because it was cold and grey, I put on a duffel coat and wrapped a red scarf round my neck.

Kentish Town Road was thick with cars and people on their way to work. I got onto the overcrowded Underground train that took me to Euston, then walked the last few hundred yards to Greg's workplace. It was on the second floor of a recently renovated office block. I rang the bell and before long Tania was ushering me in, taking my coat and scarf, too solicitously offering tea, coffee, biscuits, anything at all, gazing at me with her big brown eyes, shaking her head in horror and sympathy so that her ponytail bounced. She was like a puppy, an eager spaniel trying to please.

'Is Joe here?'

'He's in his office. I'll go and fetch him.'

At that moment, Joe came striding across the room towards me, holding his arms out well before he reached me. 'You should have told me you were coming,' he said. His eyes narrowed. 'You look exhausted.'

'I've been up all night. I was looking through Greg's stuff. Trying to find out what he'd been up to.'

'Here, come and tell me.' He took my arm and led me into his office. On the white wall behind his chaotic desk hung a photograph of his family: his wife, Alison, and his three children, who were teenagers now but in the picture were still small and childlike.

'There's nothing to tell,' I said, as I sat in the chair he pulled out for me. 'There wasn't anything strange.'

Joe's brow wrinkled. 'What were you expecting?'

'I don't know. That was why I was looking. I need to go through his things here as well.'

He seemed taken aback. 'There's not much personal stuff. I think Tania's already packed up most of it. There's nothing else except clients' files.'

'It's his work things I want to go through. His papers, his diary, his appointments. There must be something to show me he was having an affair with this Milena.'

'Ellie . . .' He sounded sympathetic but stern, too, and I dropped my eyes under his gaze.

'Because I'm telling you, Joe, there's nothing at home that suggests he was having an affair with her or anyone. You had no idea. Neither did Fergus. Or anyone. And nor did I. Even now I look back and can't see it.'

Joe nodded, then got up and stared out at the room beyond. Then he turned back to me. On his face was an expression of kind patience that made me squirm. 'Maybe he was just good at keeping secrets.'

'If he was having an affair, someone would have known. There would be evidence somewhere. He couldn't have left no trace.'

'Perhaps not. Perhaps you'll turn his whole life upside-down and investigate everything and eventually find something. But why do you want to?'

'Why? Because I have to. Don't you understand? I loved him. I thought he loved me . . .'

'He loved you.'

'I knew him, Joe. I knew our life together. Or I thought I did. And now he's dead and there's this mystery and I look back at our life and I can't see it any longer, can't trust it. If he was dead and that was it, no other woman involved, at least I could miss him and remember him with tenderness and feel good about what we had—but even that's muddied by this. I can't even mourn him properly. It's a mess.'

'But don't you see, Ellie? Whatever you do, however much you search, you can't prove he wasn't having an affair. He loved you,' Joe repeated. His voice was gentle, insistent. 'Even if he was having an affair, he loved you very much.'

'So you think he was, then!'

'I'm saying "if". Everyone has secrets. Everyone does things they don't want to be discovered.'

'Have you, then?'

'What? Had an affair? Do you think I'd tell you if I had? And if I had, would it somehow make it more likely that Greg had as well?'

'You have, haven't you?' Of course he had, I thought. All those women who crowded round him.

But Joe put his hand on my shoulder. 'Stop this, Ellie.'

'Sorry.' I bit my lip and sat for a while, composing myself. 'I still want to look through his things.'

He shrugged helplessly. 'If that's what you need. We didn't know you were coming so it's in a bit of a mess, I'm afraid.'

Joe installed me at Greg's old desk with his computer and his electronic organiser. Tania brought files and folders and I trawled through them as well. I looked at accounts, receipts, letters from clients, queries about trusts and power-of-attorney. There were yellow Post-it notes stuck on some, scrawled with Greg's slapdash writing. Meaningless. I had no idea what I was searching for and it was quickly apparent to me that I might as well have been reading a hieroglyphic script. I felt my brain throb as I searched for connections I knew I wouldn't find. Tania brought me a cheese-and-tomato bap and asked me if there was anything that needed explaining.

'One thing,' I said. 'You sent an email to Greg at home, saying he should ask Joe about whatever it was that was worrying him. Do you remember what it was about?'

Tania wrinkled her button nose and furrowed her smooth brow. 'No,' she replied eventually, 'so it can't have been important, can it?'

I made a list of all the clients Greg had visited over the last three weeks, with their phone numbers and addresses, and stared at them, the names blurring. My head buzzed with tiredness and a despairing frustration. Anything was better than not knowing. For how could I say goodbye to Greg when I no longer knew who he was?

I MEANT TO GO straight home. There were so many things that needed doing. Instead I took a southbound train and got off at Kennington. I knew that the Livingstones lived at number sixteen Dormer Road, so I went into a newsagent's and bought an *A–Z*. It took only a few minutes to walk there.

The Livingstones' house was large and white, set back from the road. I instantly disliked its pillared porch and raked gravel, and this helped me march up the short drive and ring the bell before I had time to think about what I was doing or prepare an explanation.

'Yeah?'

The youth who stood in front of me was tall and skinny. I thought he must be in his late teens. He had long, dark, unbrushed hair, eyes that were almost black. He was wearing boxer shorts and a faded T-shirt; as on the day of the inquest, he had a stud in his nose. I smiled cautiously at him but he stood blocking the doorway, arms folded over his chest, a flat, assessing stare on his face.

'Is Hugo Livingstone in?' I asked.

'No.'

'You're his son, aren't you? I saw you at the inquest.'

'Yeah, that's me.' He gave a mock bow, knees knobbly below his boxers, quite unembarrassed by his state of undress. 'Silvio Livingstone.'

'I'm sorry about your mother,' I said.

'Stepmother.' The way he said it was so contemptuous I was startled.

'I'm sorry all the same,' I managed. 'And I'm sorry to have bothered you.'

'You're his wife, aren't you?'

I didn't pretend not to understand who he was talking about, simply nodded.

'What do you want here, then?'

'I thought we should meet. Given everything.'

'You want to come in?'

'It was only if your father was here.'

He gave a shrug. 'Did you know about them?'

'No,' I said. 'Did you?'

'Not about your husband,' he said.

For a reason I didn't understand, I found I was more comfortable with this wretchedly sarcastic, angrily self-conscious young man than I had been with anyone else since Greg had died.

'I've changed my mind,' I said. 'Unless you think your dad would be angry.'

'It's my house too.'

'Just for a few minutes, then. Maybe you could make me some coffee.'

'And you can ask me questions about her instead of asking Dad. At least I'll be honest. I'm not the one she made a fool of.'

He led me through the hall and down a corridor lined with photos. I caught glimpses as I passed: there she was, white flesh glowing above a low black dress; there she was again, hair swept up and a tiny smile on her lips. The kitchen was enormous, glinting with appliances; double doors led out into the garden.

'So, you had no idea about Greg—my husband?'

'Why would we? The point of a secret affair is that it's secret.' He scooped ground coffee into a cafetière. 'Milena liked secrets. It was what she was good at, secrets, gossip, rumour.'

'What about your father?'

'I don't know. Didn't ask. Here, coffee. Help yourself to milk.'

I splashed in some milk and took a sip. 'So you're not really sure?'

For the first time a flash of interest, no, intense curiosity, crossed his face. His eyes narrowed. 'They died together,' he said. 'That's pretty intimate.'

'I mean, there's nothing you've found that shows your stepmother knew Greg?'

'I haven't looked. Why should I?'

'And your father?'

'My father?' He raised his eyebrows sardonically. 'Dad's been working very hard since she died. He's been busy.'

'I see.' I sighed and put down my cup, then stood up. 'Thanks, Silvio.'

'You're not what I'd expected,' he said, at the front door.

'What you expected?'

'Of my stepmother's lover's wife.'

'It sounds like you're making fun of me,' I said.

Suddenly he flushed and seemed younger. 'I didn't mean that,' he said.

A thought struck. 'What was she like as a stepmother?'

I thought he would shrug or say something sarcastic, but he went red and muttered something.

'I imagine she wasn't normal stepmother material,' I said.

'You shouldn't have come here,' he said. 'It's none of your business.'

He pushed the door shut so abruptly I had to step back quickly so my foot didn't get caught.

THERE WAS ONE THING I knew I had to do before the funeral. Since the inquest I'd been imagining what it looked like, and recently I'd even started dreaming about it—a deep pit, Greg's red car hurtling to the bottom, bursting into flames there. Porton Way.

And so, the day before the funeral, I headed east, getting off at Stratford. It took me about twenty-five minutes to walk to Porton Way. The sky, which had been grey, turned an ominous purple-brown; a storm was coming, and occasional raindrops splashed my cheek.

The entire area seemed to have been turned into a building site. Giant cranes punctuated the horizon and swathes of land had been turned into rubble and mud. There were Portakabins behind high fences, men in hard hats driving diggers. Porton Way, lying at the bottom of a steep incline, was dismal, abandoned, full of half-smashed warehouses and the remnants of old houses, brought to the ground in a pile of bricks and cement blocks.

What a drab, dreary, ugly place to come for a tryst. But private. Even now, in the middle of the morning, there was no one around; it looked as though work had been suspended for the time being. As I trudged towards the fatal corner, it started to rain properly. The bottoms of my jeans were soon soaking. Water squelched in my shoes. My hair lashed wetly against my face. I could barely see where I was going.

But there I was, at the steep corner. This was where it had happened. Greg had gone straight across and plunged down that embankment. I left the road and clambered down the slope, but the mud was like slippery clay and I half fell, putting out my hand to catch myself, ripping my sleeve on a thick bramble.

It seemed to take a long time to get to the bottom; by the time I arrived I was muddy and sodden. My forehead stung and when I put a hand up, it came away red with blood, which trickled into my eye. I took off my scarf and held it against the cut.

It was quite clear where the car had landed, although it had obviously been cleared away long ago. There was a charred patch of land, a small crater in the larger one of Porton Way. I made my way across and squatted. So, this was where Greg had died. I stared at the gash in the earth. I blinked away the streaming rain and pushed my hair back, as drops of blood escaped the scarf I still held to my forehead. The woman at the inquest had said that Greg wouldn't have suffered. Had he even known he was dying, that this was the end, or had it been too quick even for that?

At last I stood up, miserably cold and wet, my jeans sticking to my legs. There was nothing for me here. I turned my back on the site and trudged up the hill. At some point I realised I'd dropped my scarf, and when I turned I could see it, a wisp of colour on the muddy ground.

WHEN I ARRIVED HOME, it was midafternoon and my fingers were so numb I could barely turn the key in the lock.

'Ellie?'

I jumped at the voice behind me and turned. 'Joe—what are you doing here?'

'What do you think? I've come to see you. But what on earth have you been up to?'

'Oh, nothing. I just went out and it started pouring with rain,' I said feebly. I didn't really want to talk about my day, not even to Joe.

'You've got blood all over your face.'

'Oh, that. It's nothing. Come in.'

I managed to get the door open and we stepped into the hall. I pulled off my mud-caked boots and struggled out of my jacket, then stood dripping.

'Here,' said Joe. 'It's not important but I thought you'd want this. It was in the kitchen and we missed it.'

He'd brought me Greg's favourite mug. It had the photograph of him finishing his marathon last year printed on it.

'And I wanted to check if there was anything I could do for the funeral.'

'You probably just wanted to check, full stop,' I said.

He smiled ruefully at me. 'Well, I can see you're taking excellent care of yourself. Go and have a bath.'

'I'll do that.'

'While you're at it, can I do anything for you? Tidy up a bit or make you a warm drink?'

'That's kind of you, but no, thanks.'

'Ellie?'

'Yes?'

'You'll tell me if you're not all right?'

'Yes.'

AFTERWARDS, I remembered the funeral only as a collection of random moments, all of them bad. We had been told we had to arrive five minutes before the eleven thirty start because there were funerals before and afterwards. So, we found ourselves standing outside the North London crematorium waiting for our turn.

The hearse arrived, the back door opened and the wicker coffin I had chosen was exposed. It wasn't lifted by pall-bearers, but trundled into the chapel on a silly trolley that looked as if it should be moving packing cases into a supermarket. The funeral director had warned me about it in advance, saying it had been forced on them by their insurers. There had been reports of serious back injury.

A middle-aged woman, who must have been a relative of Greg's, asked if we should follow it in.

'I'm not sure if the group before us has finished,' I said. It was as if we'd booked a tennis court.

'I'm so sorry,' Greg's relative said.

I still hadn't worked out what to say when people said how sorry they were. 'Thank you' didn't seem quite right. This time I just nodded.

'It must be so terrible for you,' she said.

'Well, of course,' I said. 'It was such a shock.'

Still she didn't go away. 'I mean,' she said, 'the circumstances were so awkward. It must be so . . . well, upsetting.'

I felt as if I had an open wound and this woman had put her finger into it and was probing to see whether I would cry out or scream.

'I'm just sad I've lost my husband,' I said. I walked away from her.

Everyone, absolutely everyone, knew that Greg had died with another woman and that this meant they had been having an affair.

My next memory of the funeral places me inside, right at the front, next to Greg's parents. I could feel the crowd of mourners behind me, staring at the back of my head. They were sorry for me, but what else did they feel? A little bit of embarrassment, contempt? Poor old Ellie. She hasn't only been made a widow: she's been humiliated, her marriage exposed as a sham.

Greg's brother Ian came to the front and read some Victorian poem that was meant to be consoling but I stopped paying attention halfway through. Then Greg's sister Kate said she was going to play a song that had meant a lot to Greg. There was a long pause and then a rattling in some speakers on the wall and then what was clearly the wrong song came on, a power ballad I remembered having heard in a movie with Kevin Costner. It was completely alien to Greg, who had liked scratchy songs played on steel guitars by wizened Americans who had served time in prison, or looked as if they had. I saw panic on Kate's face. She was visibly wondering whether she could run out and switch off this awful song and put on the right CD, then deciding she couldn't.

It was the only bit of the funeral that really meant anything to me. For just one moment, I had a vivid sense of what it would have been like if Greg had been there, and how he would have looked at me, and how we would have struggled not to laugh, and how we would have cackled about it afterwards. It was the closest I got to crying all day, but even then I didn't cry.

Afterwards, everybody was invited back to my place where we had the worst party of all time. I was reminded of those awful teenage parties where the boys clustered in a corner, giggling among themselves, staring at the girls but not daring to approach them. Something tribal had happened. It was as if Greg had left me for Milena and there were those who were taking his side against me.

Gwen and Mary were there and, of course, they were entirely in my camp. They fetched drinks and food and hovered around me, murmuring words of support.

My parents were there, and then there was Fergus, whose eyes were swollen with grief; I envied him that. I got the impression from Jemma, his hugely pregnant wife, that he had been sobbing on and off since it had happened. There were people like Joe and Tania, who drifted between the camps, making heroic and doomed efforts to bring them together.

In a strange way, the people I took most comfort from were those I had never met before. There were several clients, who came up to tell me how much they had depended on Greg, trusted him, liked him, and would miss him now that he was gone. It was such a relief to be with people who didn't know the back-story to his death, and were there simply to say goodbye.

'He was a very dear young man,' said Mrs Sutton. She wore a black silk dress and seamed stockings, and had a creased face and silver hair in an immaculate bun. She looked very old and rich, with an aquiline nose and straight-backed bearing that seemed to belong to a different era. 'I always looked forward to his visits. I'm going to miss him.'

'I'm sorry,' I said absurdly.

'As a matter of fact, he was going to visit me the day after he died. That was how I heard—when he failed to arrive I rang his office to ask where he was.' She gave me a piercing glance. 'I'll be eighty-eight in two months' time. It doesn't seem right, does it? People dying out of their turn.'

I couldn't speak and she lifted a hand like a claw and placed it lightly over mine. 'You have my sympathy, my dear,' she said.

For the main part, however, it was a funeral party where nobody seemed able to do the sort of things that funeral parties are for. They couldn't offer their condolences without seeming embarrassed; they couldn't engage in uncomplicated reminiscences. Gradually they just peeled away.

Gwen and Mary stayed on and I opened some more wine and told them what the woman outside the crematorium had said, and Mary said, 'You don't have to fight it, you know.' I asked her what she meant and she said I had nothing to feel bad about. Men were bastards. My friends loved me and would support me. I would get through this. I just poured myself glass after glass of wine and drank it as if I was insatiably thirsty. They asked if I wanted them to stay and I said I wanted them not to stay, so they left.

When I was ten my grandfather had died. I didn't want to go to the funeral but my mother said funerals were where we went to say goodbye to people who had died. We thought about them and we cried for them and we said goodbye to them and then we went back to our lives.

As I lay on my bed fully clothed, drunker than at any time since my first year at university, I knew that on that day I hadn't cried for Greg, and, above all, I hadn't said goodbye to him.

CHAPTER THREE

In the middle of the night I suddenly sat up in bed. I didn't know what time it was. I had turned off the digital alarm clock because, over the past weeks, I had come to dread waking in the small hours and gazing at the time clicking past. I only knew that it was dark and something had roused me. A memory which must have wormed its way into my dreams.

Like most couples, I'm sure, Greg and I used to have conversations about which of our friends were unfaithful. After all, if one in three partners cheats on the other, or something like that, we figured we must be surrounded by people who were betraying each other. Now I remembered a conversation so vividly it was like being there again, and there we were in bed together, warm under the duvet and facing each other in the half-light.

'My parents?' he was saying, and I giggled.

'No way!'

'Your parents?'

'Please!'

'Who, then?'

'Fergus and Jemma?' I suggested.

'Impossible. He's not that kind of guy.'

'What kind of guy is that? And, anyway, it could be her.'

'She's too moral. And too pregnant. What about Mary and Eric?'

'She would have told me,' I said firmly.

'Sure? What about if it was him?'

'She would definitely have told me that too. Even if she didn't, I'd know.'

'How?'

'I just would. She's a very bad liar. Her neck goes blotchy.'

'What about me—would you be able to tell with me?'

'Yes—so watch it.'

'How would you know?'

'I just would.'

'Trusting fool.'

We smiled at each other, sure of our happiness.

I got out of bed, went downstairs into the kitchen, turning on the light. I saw from the wall clock that it was nearly three o'clock. It was windy outside and when I pressed my face to the window, I could still hear Greg's voice and see his smile, and the contrast between the intense comfort of that memory and this cold, empty darkness was like a blow to the stomach, making my eyes water. No one tells you how physical unhappiness can be.

I made myself a mug of hot chocolate and drank it slowly. Greg's face faded. I knew he wasn't here, wasn't anywhere. But I heard his teasing voice. Trusting fool, he called me.

'ELLIE?' Fergus's eyes widened with surprise. He was still in his dressing gown, unshaven and puffy with sleep. 'Are you OK? What's happened?'

'Can I come in?'

He stood back, pulling his dressing gown more tightly around him, and I walked past him into the kitchen.

'I know it's a bit early.'

'It doesn't matter. Coffee? Tea? Breakfast? Devilled kidneys? That last one was a joke. Jemma will be in bed for ages. She's on maternity leave now.' As he said this, I saw anxiety cross his face: Jemma was on maternity leave and I was childless, barren, shamed and alone.

'Coffee, please. Maybe some toast.'

'The funeral seemed to go off all right,' he said cautiously, as he filled the kettle and slid a slice of bread into the toaster.

'The funeral was crap. No one knew what to say to me.'

He smiled ruefully at me. 'It's over, at least.'

'Not really.'

He looked at me, eyebrows raised. 'What d'you mean?'

'I've decided to believe him.'

The kettle started to boil and, very methodically, he measured spoonfuls of coffee into the pot, then poured in the water. Only when he had handed me the hot mug did he look me in the eye. 'Come again?' he said.

'Greg didn't have an affair. On the one hand there's how it appears, him dying with this other woman. On the other is my trust. I'm keeping faith. I'm not abandoning him.'

'I see,' Fergus said, and picked up his mug, staring at me over the rim. 'Well, that's good, I suppose. I mean, if it lets you come to terms with what's happened.'

'No.'

'No?' Fergus frowned. 'Why don't you tell me what you're thinking, Ellie?'

'Look, Fergus, Greg died with another woman. But he wasn't having an affair with her. So, what were they doing together? That's the question, isn't it? For a start there are other possibilities. Just off the top of my head she might have been a hitchhiker.'

Fergus thought for a moment. 'Not wanting to be a devil's advocate, but this woman was some sort of businesswoman, no? Do they tend to hitchhike? In London?'

'Or just some business contact. That he was giving a lift to.'

'All right.'

'So you believe him?'

'Ellie, he's not here to believe. Your husband—my best friend, the man we both loved and miss like hell—is dead. That's what this is really about, isn't it? It's as if by somehow persuading yourself that he wasn't fucking another woman, he won't be dead after all. You'll go mad if you keep on like this. You're never going to find out what happened,' he said wearily.

I should have kept a tally of how many times that had been said to me. 'I trust him,' I said. 'That's enough for me.'

AT SUNDAY LUNCH with Joe, Alison and one of their children, Becky, I repeated what I'd said to Fergus. It was harder in front of three people. I sounded forced and over-insistent. I saw Joe's shoulders sag, and I saw him glance at Alison before he turned to me. 'Sweetheart,' he said.

'I know what that means,' I said. '"Sweetheart." It means you're going to tell me very patiently why you think I'm behaving in a wrong headed and self-destructive way. You're going to tell me I'll never find out the truth and must learn to live with that uncertainty and move on. And probably you'll tell me this is a form of grieving.'

'Yes. And that we love you and want to help in any way we can.'

'Do you want to put the kettle on, Becky?' Alison said, in a mild tone.

'You don't need to be tactful, Alison.' I smiled at her. 'We've known each other too long and too well for that. It's fine. I'm fine. Really. I just thought you should know that Greg wasn't being unfaithful.'

'Good.'

'It would be better if someone believed me.'

THE MAN STOOD on my doorstep, barely visible behind the battered wooden rocking chair he was holding.

'Terry Long,' he informed me. 'I've got the chair for you.' He looked at me expectantly.

'I don't—' I began.

'You said you'd repair it for us. I called you at the beginning of September. You said it would be fine.'

'Things have changed,' I said. 'I'm not taking on new work.'

His face had hardened. He put the chair on the ground.

'I'm sorry.'

'That's it? You're sorry? You can't just let people down like that.'

'I'm very sorry. I just can't. I really can't. I'm sorry.' I kept repeating the word: sorry, sorry, sorry. In the end he went, leaving the chair behind. Even his back looked angry.

I picked up the rocking chair, shut the door, and went through the house and into the garden where I unlocked my shed.

Inside, there were ladder-backed chairs, a corner cupboard in dark oak, an ash cabinet without a back and a Georgian desk and chair. They were waiting for my attention. I went in and ran my finger across the wooden surfaces. Even though I hadn't been in there for days, there was still the wonderful smell of sawdust and wax. Curls of planed wood lay on the floor. I picked up a pale rind, wondering if I'd ever come back to work here again.

Greg and I had argued about stupid things. Why he didn't rinse the basin after he'd shaved. Why I didn't know how irritating it was when I cleaned up around him, huffing loudly. We argued about clothes that shrank in the wash, burnt toast, careless words, trivial matters of mismanagement and mess. We never fell out over the big things, like God or war, jealousy or deceit. We hadn't had long enough together for that.

'So you don't believe me?'

Mary and I were walking on the heath. It was cool and grey. Our feet shuffled through drifts of damp leaves. Robin, her one-year-old, was in a carrier on her back, asleep; his head lolled on her neck as we walked.

'I didn't say that. Not exactly . . . Look, Ellie, Greg was lovely but he wasn't a saint. Most men stray if they get the chance.'

'Stray?' I said. I was beginning to feel angry and rattled. 'Like a sheep that's got out of its field?'

'It's all about opportunity and temptation. This Milena probably made the first move.'

'This Milena didn't have anything to do with him. Or him with her.'

Mary stopped. 'Because I don't agree with you, it doesn't mean I'm not on your side. It's rotten, what's happened. Really horrible. Listen, though.' She put a hand on my arm. 'I do have a bit of understanding of what you're going through. You know what happened just after Robin was born?'

A feeling of dejection settled on me.

'Eric slept with this woman at work. I was woozy and weepy and tired, my breasts were sore, I'd only just had my stitches out so I could hardly sit down; sex was out of the question. Yet I was happy. I was so happy I thought I'd melt. And it wasn't just once, a drunken mistake or something, it went on for weeks. He'd come home late, take lots of showers, be over-attentive, over-irritable. It's such a cliché, isn't it? Looking back, I can't believe I didn't realise what was going on. But I was blind, in my own little bubble of contentment. I had to practically see them together before I knew.'

'Why didn't you tell me before?' I remembered again the conversation with Greg, in which I had insisted I would have known if Eric had been unfaithful to Mary.

'Because I felt humiliated. And stupid.' She glared at me. 'So fat and ugly and useless and ashamed. You must understand that feeling now, after what's happened to you. That's why I'm telling you.'

'Mary,' I said, 'I'm so sorry. I wish we'd talked about it before. But it's not the same.'

'What makes you and Greg so different?'

'He wouldn't have behaved like that.'

'That's what I used to say about Eric.'

'I have an instinct.'

'Has it occurred to you that maybe Greg was sick of having sex to get you pregnant?'

I flinched in pain, as if Mary had slapped me across the face.

'Oh, Ellie.' Her face softened; I saw there were tears in her eyes, whether from the cold or emotion I couldn't tell.

WPC DARBY SHOWED me into a small room. I sat down and she sat opposite me. I looked at her face, weathered, shrewd and pleasantly plain under her severely cut hair, and was satisfied that she was the right person to tell. There was some meaningless chat and then I stopped.

'It's not the way it seemed,' I said. 'I don't believe he was having an affair with Milena Livingstone. Actually I don't think they even knew each other.'

She gave a nervous smile and when she spoke it was clearly and slowly, as if I was a small child. 'They were in the same car.'

'That's why I'm here,' I said. 'It's a mystery. I think you ought to look at it again.'

She leaned towards me slightly, her grey eyes on my face. 'Ms Falkner, your husband died in a car crash.'

'He wasn't wearing his seatbelt—but Greg *always* wore it. You have to investigate further.'

'The coroner was satisfied that it was a tragic accident. I understand that the fact he was with another woman is upsetting for you. As a matter of evidence, how they knew each other doesn't matter.'

'There's no evidence at all that he knew her,' I said. 'I'm telling you, he didn't know her.'

'No. You're telling me you don't believe he knew her. With all due respect, what you believe and what is true are not necessarily the same thing.'

'So you're just going to let things lie?'

'Yes. And I would advise you to do the same. You might consider seeing someone about—'

'You think I need bereavement counselling? Professional help?'

'I think you've had a terrible shock and are having difficulty in coming to terms with it.'

'If anyone says "coming to terms" to me again, I think I'll scream.'

I READ THROUGH Greg's emails so often that I almost knew them by heart. I thought they might give me a sense of his mood in the weeks leading up to his death. Was there a hint of anxiety? Anger? Apprehension? I couldn't find anything. Then I noticed something blindingly obvious, something that everybody in the developed world apart from me must have known. Every email showed the exact time he had pressed the SEND button. Each email was a fairly accurate guide as to where Greg had been at a particular moment.

Within half an hour I was back from the stationer's with two carrier-bags. I tipped their contents onto the carpet. There were poster-sized sheets of card in a roll, rulers, coloured pens and Magic Markers, highlighters, and sheets of little stickers—circles, squares and stars.

I spread four of the sheets of card in a row on the floor, using heavy books to hold the corners down. Then, using a ruler and a fine architect's pen, I started to rule grids across them, each representing a week in the last month of Greg's life. I traced seven columns, then drew horizontal lines until I had chopped each column into 120 rectangles, each representing ten minutes in a day starting at eight and finishing at midnight. I didn't bother about the nights because we hadn't spent a night apart in that last month.

From memory, I was able to cross out evenings I knew we had spent together. At the weekends there were days I eliminated with a bold stroke of black: the Saturday we had taken the train to Brighton, walked on the beach and bought a secondhand book of poetry; the day we had walked along the Regent's Canal from Kentish Town all the way to the river. Those were two days when he hadn't been having sex with Milena Livingstone.

Then I started on the emails. At work, Greg had written twenty or thirty a day, sometimes more. Based on each one, I wrote 'O' for office in the appropriate slot on the card. He had a habit of sending a flurry of messages as soon as he arrived at work, another just before one o'clock and another at around five, but others were dotted through the day. It didn't take me much more than an hour to work my way through the emails, and when I was done, the chart was already satisfyingly shaded in.

The next day I invited Gwen round. I said it was urgent but she was at work and didn't reach me until almost six. When she arrived I hustled her through to the kitchen, boiled the kettle and made a pot of coffee.

'Would you like a biscuit?' I said. 'Or a slice of ginger cake? I made both this afternoon. I've been busy.'

Gwen looked amused and a bit alarmed. 'Some cake. A tiny slice.'

I poured the coffee and gave her the cake on a plate. I wasn't hungry.

'So what's up?' said Gwen. 'Did you summon me here to try the cake?'

'No. I've got something to show you.' I steered her along the hall and into the living room. 'There,' I said. 'What do you think of that?'

Gwen stared down at the four large pieces of card, now covered with marks and stickers, all different shapes and colours. 'It looks lovely,' she said. 'What's it meant to be?'

'That's Greg's life in the month before he died,' I said.

I explained about the timed emails and my own memories and how I'd even found receipts from the sandwich bars where Greg had bought his lunch. All the receipts, whether for food or petrol or stationery, gave not just a date but an exact time when the purchase was made. 'So all these stickers show moments when I know exactly where Greg was. It's pretty amazing, isn't it?'

'Yes, but—'

'A couple of times a week Greg drove to visit a client. I pretended to be Greg's assistant, rang up and said that for tax reasons I needed an exact time for when the meeting had taken place. People were very helpful. I've marked all those in blue. Then I was left with the gap between him leaving the office and arriving at the client. But I found a website. If I type in the postcodes of the office and his client, it gives an estimated journey time. I've marked those in red. It's not an exact science, but even so it fits pretty well. It took me a day and a half—and look. What do you see?'

'Lots of colours,' said Gwen. 'Lots of stickers.'

'No,' I said. 'It's what you don't see. There's barely a gap over four weeks when I don't know where he was and what he was doing.'

'Which means?'

'Look at the chart, Gwen,' I said. 'It shows Greg working very hard, travelling, eating, buying stuff, going to the movies with me. But where's the bit when he's having an affair? Where's the space for him even to meet the woman he died with?'

There was a long pause.

'Ellie,' said Gwen. She looked at my charts almost with an expression of pity. 'I don't really know what to make of this.' She took my hand. 'I'm not an expert but I've heard that there are stages of grief and at the beginning it's anger and denial. It's understandable that you feel anger. I think the point of mourning is to get through that and reach a kind of acceptance.'

I pulled my hand away. 'I know all that,' I said. 'And you know what I was thinking when I was doing all this? What would make it easy would be to find just one deleted email, just one scrap of paper, that would show Greg had been having an affair. Or even just one occasion when he wasn't where he was meant to be, or a missing afternoon when nobody knew where he was. Then I could just get angry and be sad, and my life would continue. But there's just no space for this relationship. If I showed those charts to the police, do you think it would make a difference?'

Gwen frowned at the charts for a long time. 'Honestly?' she said.

'Yes.'

'I don't think the police would pay much attention to it,' she said, 'but if they did, they might say, "Perhaps he was seeing the woman while he was doing other things. Perhaps she met him while he was buying his sandwich. Or you might be right. Maybe they didn't meet in that month. She could have been away and they were meeting up again on the day they crashed."'

My first impulse was to be angry with Gwen, but I stopped myself. She might have humoured me. Instead she had said what she really thought.

'And if they said anything,' Gwen continued, 'it would be that you're ignoring the only piece of evidence that really matters, which is that Greg and the woman died together. What in the end can you really say to that?'

I thought for a moment. 'That it's difficult to be innocent,' I said. 'And to prove you're innocent is impossible.'

I KNEW BEFORE I rang the bell that no one was there: there were no lights on in any of the windows, no car in the driveway; the house had an unoccupied look. But I stood, stamping my feet in the cold, waiting to make sure. I wondered what Hugo Livingstone was feeling now. Did he think about Greg as I thought about Milena, with hatred, jealousy and puzzlement? Did he know something I didn't?

That morning, when I had sat over my breakfast of slightly stale bread and the last scrapings of marmalade, I had decided I needed to look at the picture from the other side. I had examined Greg's life and found nothing, but what about Milena's?

So there I was, on a damp November morning, staring at the blank windows of the large house and wondering miserably what to do next. Because I couldn't return to my own small, cold house and deal with the things that were piling up: bills, letters, phone messages, laundry, dead leaves, broken chairs, dust, dirt and drabness. I found myself consulting my map and walking the half-mile or so from the Livingstone house to the address of Party Animals, the business Milena and her partner had run together.

Tulser Road was a quiet residential street just down from Vauxhall Bridge. It didn't look like the kind of place for offices. Number eleven was just like the other houses on either side: large and semidetached, with a basement floor and bay windows. There was only one bell, and no sign saying this was where exciting and original happenings, tailor-made to suit every individual customer, were organised.

But there were lights on in the downstairs window. I raised my hand to ring the bell and saw my wedding ring. I looked at it for a moment, almost dispassionately, as if it had suddenly appeared. In fact I hadn't taken it off since Greg had pushed it over my knuckle in the register office. I had thought it would be difficult to get off but I'd lost weight and it made no resistance. It was an object now, not part of me. I put it into my purse and rang the bell.

The woman who answered the door was slightly older than I had expected, tall and slender, with long legs. Her dark blonde hair was cut short in a chic style with soft wisps framing her triangular face. Her pale skin was just beginning to line, and she wore thick, rectangular specs. She had on beautifully tailored black trousers and a pale blue linen shirt, tiny studs in her ears and a thin silver chain round her neck. There was a classy look to her, a restrained and intelligent attractiveness.

'Yes?' she said. 'Can I help you?' Her voice was low and husky.

'Is this where Party Animals is run from?'

'That's right. Are you planning an event?'

'No,' I said. 'I've come about Milena Livingstone.'

I saw her eyes widen and then she made a visible effort to control herself. I recognised the weary sense that the story would have to be told yet again.

'Are you a friend of hers?' she asked. 'Didn't you know?'

There was a moment when I could have said, 'Yes, I knew, because the man she died with was my husband.' But something stopped me. 'Know what?' I said.

'Come in for a second. Sorry, my name's Frances Shaw.'

She held out a hand and I shook it. Her grip was warm, strong. I stepped over the threshold and she shut the door.

'Better come downstairs into the office, if you can call it that. I'm in total chaos, I'm afraid.' She led me into the basement, a large room with a long table in the centre. On its surface were several roughly stacked heaps of paper and files. There was a sofa covered with brochures and a desk pushed up against the wall, also piled high with folders.

A phone was ringing and a young woman, with dramatically dark eye-shadow, very high-heeled boots and full breasts, came out of the adjoining room. 'Shall I get that?' she asked.

'No, let the machine answer it,' said Frances. 'I tell you what, though, Beth, perhaps you could make us a cup of coffee. If you want coffee, that is,' she added, turning to me.

'Coffee would be lovely.' I was a bit dazed.

'Have a seat.' Frances scooped up the brochures from the sofa, then laid them on the floor. 'When did you last see Milena?'

'I don't want to give you the wrong impression . . .' I said.

The phone rang again followed by her mobile, which was lying on the table. 'Damn. Sorry. I'll be with you in a second.' She flipped it open and turned away from me. I heard her murmuring something. I sat on the sofa, taking off my jacket. The warm, cluttered room was like a nest.

Frances snapped shut her mobile and sat beside me. 'I'm so sorry to have to tell you that Milena died. She died in a car crash.'

That was my last chance to say who I was, but I didn't. I wasn't even sure why.

'Oh!' I said, and rubbed my face because I wasn't sure what my expression should be. 'How terrible.' I felt like an actor, saying lines that made little sense to me.

'It was awful. She was with a man. Someone nobody knew even existed.'

'So young,' I said. The possibility of putting Frances straight receded, and then—as she told me Milena's husband and step-children were coping as well as could be expected and I expressed sympathy—it vanished.

'Hence the chaos,' said Frances, gesturing at the room.

'It must be hard for you,' I said. 'Were you close?'

'When you work together in the way we did, you have to be close.' She grimaced. 'For better or worse. She wasn't exactly . . .'

Frances stopped. I wondered what she'd been going to say. I wanted to ask what Milena had been like, but I was supposed to know that. So instead I nodded and said, 'Yes,' in an I-know-just-what-you-mean kind of way.

The door was flung open and Beth tottered in, carrying a tray on which there were a cafetière, two mugs and a milk jug. As she approached she stepped on a file and stumbled. She tried to keep control but disaster was inevitable. The cafetière banged onto the wooden boards and exploded, sending arcs of coffee everywhere; the jug shattered and a river of milk ran across the floor towards Frances; the mugs broke on impact and shards skidded across the room.

'Fuck,' said Beth, from the floor.

'Are you hurt?' said Frances. She didn't seem surprised, just very tired.

'Sorry,' said Beth, scrambling to her feet.

'Let me help,' I said.

'Don't be ridiculous,' said Frances.

I took Beth's arm. 'Come on. Show me where your cleaning stuff is.'

'Would you? That's really kind.'

We went upstairs into the kitchen and when we returned, armed with kitchen roll and a bin-bag, Frances was on the phone, protesting about something. After she'd hung up, she took off her glasses to rub her eyes.

'Trouble at work?' I laid wads of kitchen towel over the puddles of milk and coffee and started to pick up pieces of glass and china and drop them into the bag. Beth hovered round me, avoiding broken china.

'What I need,' said Frances, 'is the world to stop for about a week while I get the backlog sorted out and my life in some kind of order. Milena, may she rest in peace, wasn't the most organised of women. I keep discovering things she's done or promised that there's no record of. At least'—she glanced round the room—'no record that I can lay my hands on.' She watched me as I picked up the mass of sodden kitchen roll and dumped it in the bin-bag. 'You shouldn't be doing this.'

'I quite like clearing up mess,' I said. 'With your work, though, maybe you should get extra help in, for the time being at least.'

'I can't do any more,' said Beth, grumpily.

'I wouldn't expect you to,' said Frances.

I gathered some loose sheets of paper from the floor. 'What do you want me to do with these?'

'Nothing. You've done more than enough as it is. I'll sort them out later.'

'I can put them into piles for you, if you want. I'm quite good at organising stuff.'

'I couldn't possibly ask you to do that.'

'You're not asking. I'm offering. I'm not doing anything right now. I'm'—I hesitated—'between jobs.'

'You'd do that?' For a moment she looked as though she was about to burst into tears or hug me.

'Just to sort this lot out. After all, it wouldn't have happened if you hadn't offered me coffee.'

Beth pottered around to not very much effect while Frances and I sorted the papers: venues, catering companies that Party Animals used, parties being planned, quotations. There was nothing that gave me any hint of the personal life of Milena Livingstone, although there were papers with her dashingly scrawled signature.

Beth made coffee in a jug and brought it in mug by mug. I felt strangely, absurdly relaxed, even though I was there under false pretences. It was a relief to be helping someone instead of being the one in need. Maybe it also felt good to have a holiday from being me, the grieving widow and 'betrayed wife', pitied friend with a great big bee in her bonnet.

When the time came for me to go, Frances, seeming slightly embarrassed but also a bit desperate, asked if there was any chance I could pop back. I replied that I'd be glad to help out and suggested the next day.

'Yes, great,' said Frances. 'Oh Lord, that's amazing. You're my saviour. I was on the point of—Hang on, I don't even know your name.'

And I answered, without missing a beat, 'Gwen. Gwen Abbott.'

CHAPTER FOUR

As soon as I arrived home, I looked up Gwen's name in the phone book. It wasn't there, probably because she teaches maths in a secondary school. If her name was in the book her phone would never stop ringing: what's the homework tonight? Why did my child fail his exam?

I put a baking potato into the oven, poured myself a glass of wine and then another as I thought about what I had done. Had I committed a crime? I didn't think so. As long as I wasn't doing it to perpetrate a fraud or theft.

Was it morally wrong to give a false name, a name that belonged to one of my best friends? But, then, borrowing a name wasn't like borrowing a sweater. I wasn't depriving Gwen of it. I wasn't going to damage it or get it dirty. I had misled Frances and Beth. But if I had been open about who I was, they might have thought I was insane.

After an hour or so, I took the baked potato out of the oven and mashed it with lots of butter, then sprinkled it with salt and pepper. I ate the soft inside first, then the crunchy skin. It was delicious. The phone rang.

'Where the hell are you?' Mary said.

'What do you mean?'

'You're coming here for dinner,' she said.

'Am I?'

'I asked you several days ago. You said yes. We're all about to sit down.'

'Ten minutes,' I said. 'Fifteen at the most.'

I cursed as I had a thirty-second shower and pulled on a dress. I put a coat on, ran out of the house and got a taxi at the end of the road.

Mary greeted me rather frostily as she opened the door, but she couldn't shout at a widow in front of Eric and her four other guests. I knew two of them: Don and Laura were old friends of Mary. Then there was Maddie, who worked in Mary's office, and Geoff, who explained to me that he had met Mary and Eric on a cycling holiday in Sicily a couple of years back.

As Mary introduced me, I saw the now-familiar concern passing across everybody's face. It was clear that Mary had briefed them in advance about my situation. But I was grateful, in theory at least, to Mary for inviting me. She must have known I wouldn't be the life and soul of the party. The others seemed constrained as well, perhaps with the effort of avoiding any subject that might seem inappropriate: death, funerals, marriages. And I now knew rather too much about the state of Mary's marriage; I kept glancing at Eric, then looking away when he caught my eye.

At the end of the evening, I turned down Geoff's offer of a lift home. I wanted to walk to think, to sort things out in my head.

I'd half decided I wasn't going back to Frances's office, because it was wrong in every way, but looking back on the evening at Mary's, I also felt I couldn't continue like that. From the outside, I probably seemed all right, like a robot that had been fairly well programmed to behave like a human being: I hadn't made a scene, I hadn't cried, I hadn't embarrassed anybody. From my point of view, from the inside, it was a different story.

Perhaps it was a sign of success to make it through the day and then to the end of the evening without cracking up. But that wasn't what I wanted from my life, that horrible feeling of dissociation, of acting a part that didn't belong to me. If I could just discover if Greg and that woman had been having an affair or if they hadn't, I could start my new life as a real person.

So the next day I put on clothes that were business clothes, but not too much like business clothes because I didn't own any—you don't dress up for restoring furniture in the shed in your garden. I selected black trousers with a thin grey jersey, and tied back my hair in a bun, put on earrings, a silver chain round my neck, even eyeliner and mascara. Now I wasn't Ellie but Gwen: helpful, calm, practical, discreet, ever so mathematical. I went through my shoulder bag carefully, removing anything that identified me by name. I looked at my left hand. No wedding ring.

At five past ten, when I arrived at her house, Frances opened the door with a smile of such welcome and relief that it made me smile back. 'I thought you wouldn't come,' she said. 'I thought maybe I'd hallucinated you yesterday, out of desperation. It's such a disaster zone.'

'I'll help out for a day or two,' I said. 'I've got work of my own to get back to, but you're having a bad time, so if there's anything I can do . . .'

'I am having a bad time,' said Frances, 'a terrible time, and part of what's terrible about it is that I don't know what you can do to help, what anyone can do, apart from putting a match to it all.'

'I can't organise a party,' I said, 'or cook a five-course meal for forty, but if someone could give me a cup of coffee, I'll go through every piece of paper in this office and reply to it or do something about it or file it or throw it away. And then I'll get back to my own life.'

Frances smiled again. 'What have I done to deserve you?' she asked.

BETH ARRIVED just after eleven. She apologised, saying she had been out late, but she looked fresh and rested. And she was immaculately dressed, entirely different from the day before: a dark grey pencil skirt with a little slit up the back, shoes with very low heels, and a waistcoat over a crisp white shirt. Her skin glowed, her hair tumbled over her shoulders. She made me feel shabby, old and boring. She seemed surprised and not completely pleased to see me. 'Where's she going to work?' she asked Frances.

'She's going to hover,' I said, before Frances could reply. 'Just sort out a few things and not get in anyone's way.'

'I was just asking,' said Beth, and was interrupted by a merry tune from her mobile phone. She opened it and turned her back on me.

It was immediately obvious that it would take more than a day or two to restore order to the chaos of the office. It surprised me that Frances had let everything get into such a mess: she seemed the kind of person who would be calmly and instinctively organised.

'Did Milena do the organising and filing?' I asked, as we drank our first coffee of the day, poured from a new cafetière.

'That's a laugh,' said Frances. 'No. Milena was the gorgeous public face of Party Animals. It was her job to schmooze the clients, flirt with the suppliers and come up with the brilliant ideas.'

'What did you do?' I asked.

'We picked up the pieces,' said Beth, from across the room.

'She sounds quite a character,' I said.

'You must have seen that,' said Frances.

'I meant that you don't know what people are like at work,' I gabbled, cursing myself silently. 'You must miss her.'

'She's certainly left a gap,' said Frances, as she picked up her phone and punched numbers into it.

I found some space by a work surface at the back of the office. I began to add to the piles of paper I had created the previous day. I avoided speaking for a while, worried I might give myself away again. I felt startled and shifty every time Frances called me Gwen. Couldn't she tell that I was not a between-jobs Gwen but an out-of-control Ellie? That my black trousers, grey jersey and eyeliner were a disguise? I kept expecting a stern hand to fall on my shoulder.

'How did you know Milena?' Frances asked me.

'Oh.' My mind raced. 'I met her at a fund-raising event. For breast cancer,' I added. 'It was boring and she was fun so we kept in touch. Vaguely. I can't remember when I last saw her, though.' I glanced at Frances: she didn't seem to find my words incredible.

'What do you do normally, Gwen?' she asked.

'I'm a maths teacher at a comprehensive school.' So far so Gwen Abbott.

'No wonder you are good at this kind of thing. But why did you leave?'

'I'm just taking a break. I like teaching but it's so stressful.' Frances nodded sympathetically and I warmed to my theme, remembering things Gwen had said. 'I teach in an inner-city school and half the kids don't want to be there. Instead of teaching them, I try to keep order. I thought I'd take a few months out and think things over. Maybe I'll travel.'

'Lovely,' said Frances, staring at a brochure and frowning. 'Where?'

'Peru,' I said. 'Or I've always wanted to go to India.' Without warning, tears stung my eyes. Greg and I had talked about going to India together. I blinked furiously and pushed two receipts into the appropriate folder.

'Are you married?'

'No. I was with someone for a long time but it didn't work out.' I gave a rueful shrug. 'Between jobs and between relationships. So, you see, I have this rare moment of freedom.'

'No children yet?'

'No,' I said shortly. And then I added, without realising that I was going to, the words taking me by surprise, 'I always wanted children,' and for one fearful moment my defences were down and I was being me, Ellie, with a pain in her heart because she hadn't been able to have children and now . . . I sat up straighter, snapped a folder shut. 'Maybe one day,' I said—Gwen said—with brisk cheerfulness.

'I never wanted children,' said Frances. 'It seemed so time-consuming, so wearing, trading your freedom for someone else's well-being. That's not for me, I thought, And David agreed. But then, a few years ago, I thought how nice it would be to have someone to care for like that. Would have been, I should say. Too late now. Tick-tock,' she said, with a sad little laugh.

I DIDN'T GET much information about Milena from the papers I went through on that first morning, just slapdash signatures on copies of letters about the cost of finger food and the hire of champagne flutes, although I wrote down every relevant date and place in my little notebook. I decided to go for a more direct approach.

'Tell me,' I said, as we sat drinking another of the mugs of coffee that punctuated the day, 'this man Milena died with: who was he?'

Frances shrugged. 'I don't know anything about him. I never even knew he existed.'

'Strange,' I said.

'Not in Milena's world. Milena's private life was always a bit complicated. And mysterious.'

'You mean she was unfaithful?'

Frances's face was flushed with either embarrassment or distress. 'Basically, yes.'

'Oh,' I said. 'I didn't know. Didn't her husband mind?'

Frances gave me an odd look. 'I don't know if he even knew. People see what they want to see, don't they?'

'So she didn't confide in you?'

'When she wanted to. I guessed she'd met someone new. She had the familiar radiance about her.' She gave a small, sour smile. 'You probably think I'm being heartless, speaking ill of the dead.'

'You're being honest. Milena was a complicated woman.' I worried I'd gone too far. I didn't want Frances to think I was prodding her into being rude about her friend. 'And messy,' I said, standing and crossing the room to fetch another pile of unsorted papers. 'I'd better crack on with this lot.'

AT ABOUT FOUR O'CLOCK, when the day outside was thickening towards twilight, Beth answered the phone, then muttered something to Frances.

'Bloody hell,' said Frances. 'All right, we'd better go.' She looked at me. 'Gwen,' she said, 'something's come up. We've got to pop out. Would you mind holding the fort?'

I wouldn't mind holding the fort. I positively wanted to hold the fort. I waited until the front door closed and I saw them—or, at least, their lower halves—walking past the basement window. Then I jumped up and started to prowl. I didn't know what I was looking for, but I knew it probably wouldn't be in any of the folders and files I was ploughing through. Maybe in the desk drawers.

I yanked the first drawer open and came across two vodka bottles, one empty, the other half full. I pushed the drawer shut and turned my attention to the computer. I pinged it on and waited for it to load.

The doorbell rang, making me jolt in my chair, my heart pumping wildly in my chest. I turned off the computer, smoothed my hair, put on a Gwen-expression of calm enquiry and went to answer it.

The man standing on the step seemed surprised to see me. He was quite small and slim, almost gaunt, dressed in a grey suit with a white shirt. He had hollow cheeks, quick grey eyes and brown hair starting to thin.

'Can I help you?' I asked.

'Who are you?'

'Why do you want to know?'

'Are we going to go on just asking each other questions? Is Frances there? That's another.'

'No. I'm helping her out for a bit. I'm Gwen.'

'Johnny.' He reached out a hand and I shook it. He didn't meet my eyes but looked over my shoulder as if he didn't believe I was on my own. 'Did Frances forget I was coming?'

'She's a bit distracted by everything. She'll be back soon.'

'I'll wait.' He walked past me, obviously at home in Frances's office.

'Do you work with Frances?' I asked.

'I sort out most of the food for her.'

'You don't look like a chef,' I said. It came out sounding rather rude.

He looked down at his suit. 'You think I'm pretending? I've been kicked upstairs into management, in line with which I've brought her a menu for next week. Do you want to see it?'

'I'm not really the person to—'

'You're here, aren't you?'

We sat together on the sofa and he showed me the menu. He told me how to make soufflés in advance; he said he sourced his ingredients locally; he put his hand on my arm; he told me his restaurant was called Zest and I had to pay him a visit there soon; he listened attentively when I spoke; he laughed and looked me in the eye; he called me Gwen with each sentence—'. . . don't you think, Gwen?' and 'I'll tell you what, Gwen . . .' And Gwen flushed with self-consciousness and awkward, complicated pleasure.

When Frances came back, she looked at the two of us on the sofa with affectionate amusement. 'I see you haven't missed me.' She took off her coat and threw it on the back of the chair, then kissed Johnny on both cheeks.

'I always miss you,' he said, 'but I've been well looked after.' He put his hands on her shoulders and held her away from him, gazing at her seriously. 'You seem worn out, Frances. Are you taking proper care of yourself?'

'No, but Gwen is,' she replied, and they smiled at me with approval.

JOHNNY DROPPED ME at the Underground station. He took my hand in both of his and said it had been a real pleasure to meet me and we would certainly see each other again soon. I muttered something in reply, and avoided his bright gaze. Why should I feel guilty because a nice man was flirting with me—or, at least, with me pretending not to be me? After all, I was a free woman. But I didn't feel free: I felt that I was still in a relationship with Greg, and that to respond would be a betrayal.

It was dark and drizzly as I walked home from the tube. In a few weeks, it would be the longest night of the year; the days were closing in. I wondered drearily what I would do for Christmas. For a moment, the thought of waking up on Christmas Day alone made me gasp with pain.

As I went into my house I heard my mobile ringing. It was Gwen.

'I've been trying to get hold of you all day.'

'Sorry, I've been busy.'

'That's good. Have you forgotten it's your birthday in a few days' time?'

'No,' I said. 'I just haven't really thought about it.'

'It would be nice to have a little drinks party for you.'

'I'm not sure about that.'

'At your house. You don't have to do anything but be there. I'll do everything else. I'll even clear up for you.'

'You're making it sound as though you've already organised it.'

'Not exactly. But I've made sure that people like Mary can come.'

'What do you mean, "people like Mary"? Who else?'

'Just a few. Me, Mary and Eric, Fergus and Jemma, of course, Joe and Alison, Josh and Di. That's about it. And anyone you want to ask.'

I gave up protesting. 'I'll check my diary,' I said ironically, 'but I'm pretty sure I'm not busy then.'

'Good. That's settled. I'll come round at five, straight from school, and we'll get everything ready.'

WHEN I ARRIVED at the office, Frances was on the phone. She waved me in frantically. It sounded as if she was on the receiving end of a lecture. 'Is that really true? . . . Didn't we? . . . Is it serious? . . . So what do we do?'

I tiptoed across the room, made two mugs of coffee and handed one to Frances. She pulled faces at me like a silent-movie actress, signalling thanks for the coffee and, at the same time, frustration and exasperation. 'Yes,' she said. 'But things have been a bit difficult, you know . . .'

Finally she put the phone down. I thought she was going to cry.

'I never wanted to be a businesswoman,' she said, her voice a wail. 'That was our horrible accountant. Apparently we're late with our VAT. I thought the point of accountants was that they were meant to deal with that sort of thing. Oh, God, Gwen, I hate this—I'm out of my depth.'

I remembered a conversation with Greg, when we were getting to know each other and I'd teased him about being an accountant. Wasn't it just about adding up numbers and filling in forms? He'd laughed. It wasn't like that at all, not with the clients he had. It was a mixture of being a psychiatrist and magician, hostage negotiator and bomb-disposal expert, with a bit of form filling at the end.

'Beth's not handling this very well,' said Frances. 'The thing about Beth, who, incidentally, has not arrived yet, is that she's very young, very decorative and very confident. You can take her anywhere and she seems very busy all the time but at the end of a day it's never easy to work out exactly what she's done. She's good at events. The clients are keen on her. The male ones, I mean. It's to do with her being twenty-two. And her breasts.'

'They're very nice.'

'Well, breasts don't get the VAT done. Gwen, are you sure I can't give you a job? Or a three-month contract to get us through this?'

I shook my head and tried to think what Greg used to say about situations like this. 'What you really need is to know where you are just now. What you owe, what you're owed, what you've got, and what your plans are. We can sort that out in a couple of days and then you'll be fine again.'

'When I met Milena,' said Frances, 'it was all going to be fun. We liked going to parties, we liked having parties, so why not do it as a living? It didn't turn out like that. You know how you never properly enjoy your own party? You always worry that the drink's going to run out or that someone's not happy? It's like that all the time.'

'Was it like that for Milena?' I asked.

'No,' said Frances, with a sad smile. 'Milena didn't let the details get her down.'

'The details are my job now,' I said. 'At least for the next few days.'

Somehow, when it isn't your own life, it isn't so hard. For two hours, I piled up pieces of paper that looked alike. I made lists of dates. I checked receipts against bank statements. At eleven o'clock Beth arrived. I gave her a list of phone calls to make to check delivery dates. She was as shocked as if I had asked her to clean the drains. She glanced resentfully at Frances, but she did what I said.

Twenty minutes later, Johnny arrived; he nodded at me, then sat next to Frances and talked menus. I barely looked up. I was holding a lot of information in my head temporarily. If I spoke or thought about something else, even for a moment, it would dissipate and I would have to start again.

A short while later I felt a presence beside me. It was Johnny.

'You're doing all the boring bits of the job and none of the fun bits.'

'That's what seems to be needed,' I said, frowning at the distraction.

'Whereas,' said Johnny, 'my own strategy is to do the fun bits and leave the boring bits to sort themselves out.'

'That sounds like a recipe for going bankrupt.'

'All restaurants go bankrupt in the end.'

'That doesn't sound much fun.'

'It's great,' said Johnny, and added thoughtfully, 'until the end. And then you start again. It's got a sort of rhythm to it. But what I really wanted to say, really wanted to ask, in fact—you remember I mentioned my restaurant—was whether you might want to come over and I could show you the sort of food I do. Some time. Today or tomorrow or whenever.'

He was handsome in a louche sort of way, well dressed, a man who went bankrupt and didn't let it get him down. He was perfect, in a certain fashion. Perfect if I wasn't me—although, of course, the person he was talking to wasn't actually me. 'I can't,' I said. 'Not at the moment. I'm not in the right place for that. In my life.'

'Oh, no,' he said, unruffled. 'I wasn't suggesting a date. I'm not harassing you. I just thought, as one professional to another, it would be interesting and useful for you to see the kind of food we do.'

'My life's a bit confusing right now,' I said, 'but I will think about it.'

SHORTLY AFTER THREE I heard a visitor come in. Faintly surprised to hear a man's voice, I looked round, and was jolted.

It was Hugo Livingstone. A man I had seen just once, at the inquest. What on earth was he doing there? Then I cursed my stupidity. He was Milena's husband. Wasn't it natural for him to visit his dead wife's office? The idea of being recognised and forced to attempt an explanation was so terrible that I felt feverish anticipating the nuclear explosion of exposure and embarrassment.

I bent over some papers as if I was scrutinising them with particular attention. Other people had come and gone without paying me any heed. If

I could just sit tight, maybe he'd go away. I tried to make out what he was after, but he was speaking in a mumble of which I could only hear the occasional word. There was no such problem with Frances. I heard talk about the chaos she was in, and then I knew what was coming.

'Oh, that's Gwen,' she said. 'She's been an absolute treasure. She came from nowhere and she's sorting things out. Gwen?'

Frozen in panic, I grasped for something, anything, that could prevent me having to turn round. My mobile phone was on the desk. Switched off, so nobody could ring me. I picked it up.

'That's right,' I said into it. 'Could you check it? Yes, it is urgent. Yes.'

I turned my head about half a degree and raised my free hand in a gesture much like the one I'd seen from Frances earlier. I hoped it meant, *Sorry, I'd love to be introduced, but I'm caught up in this absolutely crucial phone call.* I decided I was talking to a builder who was doing some work on my bedroom. I continued to say yes and no, to murmur half-sentences. Even though I was becoming more and more used to living in a fantasy world, and now a fantasy world within a fantasy world, it still sounded unconvincing to me.

In the gaps between my fatuous outpourings, I tried to listen to what Frances was saying. My fear was that she would tell him I had been a friend of Milena's and then he might stay to find out how I knew her. But then Frances started talking about people I had never heard of, and after a few minutes more I heard the front door opening and closing. 'So we'll talk about the colours when we meet?' I said brightly, loudly. 'Great. Bye.'

'Everything OK?' Frances said sympathetically.

'It's my so-called builder,' I said. 'You know how it is.'

Frances just nodded. I don't think she wanted to find out too much about my life.

I really was organising the company's papers. I wasn't lying about that. But at the same time I was also surreptitiously jotting down in my notebook every reference to where Milena had been on a particular day. If I compared it to the chart I had constructed for Greg, perhaps I could find somewhere they had been together, or a route that had crossed. Indeed, as I worked I decided I would stop off at the stationer's on the way home for more card and coloured pens and that I would make a separate chart for Milena.

I worked with such concentration that when I heard Frances say my name it was as if I had fallen asleep and woken up to find the world dark.

She wasn't alone. A man was standing with her, tall, distinguished, rich. He must have been in his mid-fifties, with short, dark grey hair, silvering at the edges. He was wearing an overcoat with a navy-blue scarf.

'This is Gwen, my good fairy,' said Frances. 'This is my husband, David.' He gave me a slightly wry smile and held out his hand. It was beautifully manicured but, then, everything about him looked beautifully manicured, his hair, his black leather slip-ons. His handshake was dry and limp.

'David, you've got to persuade Gwen to stay.'

He regarded her coldly, then gave a small shrug. 'Don't you see how much you're valued?' he said, in a voice that managed to combine sarcasm with indifference.

'It's just a holiday for me,' I said.

'Funny sort of holiday,' he said.

'She's a maths teacher,' said Frances.

'Oh,' said David, as if that explained everything.

'Time to go,' said Frances. 'But wait a second.' She went to her desk and scribbled on something. Then she came back and handed me a cheque.

'I can't take this,' I said.

'Don't be ridiculous,' she said.

'No,' I said. 'I really can't take it.'

'Oh, you mean the tax? David, could you give me your wallet, darling?'

He sighed and handed it over. She riffled through it, pulled out some notes and offered them to me. I wanted to say no but I thought that a person who comes and works for you, sorting out your office, then refuses any payment, starts looking a bit creepy, maybe even suspicious. I took the money.

'Thank you,' I said.

'Tomorrow?' she asked.

'Tomorrow at least,' I said.

The three of us left the house together.

'You know how we all love you,' said Frances.

'Don't be silly,' I said.

'I mean, Johnny adores her,' she said to her husband, who smiled distantly and moved away from the hand she laid on his arm. I saw her wince as she registered the slight. She was too eager with him, I thought, and too anxious, while he treated her with something close to contempt. I felt a spasm of pity for Frances—a beautiful woman in her privileged life, yet she was clearly unhappy.

'DO YOU THINK,' I asked, 'that it would be a good idea for me to go through Milena's emails and check there aren't any more nasty surprises waiting to jump out at you?'

Frances had just discovered that she and Milena had been expected at a client's large house in Kingston upon Thames to discuss plans for her daughter's wedding. Even from the other side of the room, I could hear the woman's voice coming down the phone, high and irate.

'Milena never mentioned it,' said Frances, dejectedly, after she had ended the conversation and promised she would be there the following day. 'She was supposed to write everything in the office diary.'

'May I see the diary?' I asked. 'Just to double-check things.'

'Would you?'

I took the large, hard-backed book, which had a page for each day and was covered with scrawls, crossings-out and reminders, and tried to memorise appointments, but I soon gave up. I'd have to write them down later.

Frances had no objection to me sifting through Milena's messages, but the computer did. I found that to access her email I had to enter a password. 'What was it?' I asked Frances.

'I haven't a clue.'

'Oh.' I stared at the screen in frustration. Idly, I tried the names of her two step-children, with no success. 'No ideas?' I asked Frances.

'You could try her date of birth: the 20th of April, 1964.'

So she was forty-four, a decade older than me. I typed it in. Nothing.

'Oh, well, I guess we'll just have to hope there aren't other appointments waiting to be missed.'

THAT DAY I had told Frances I needed to leave early. Even so, when I hurried up the road, Gwen was waiting at my door, several carrier-bags at her feet. 'Happy birthday!' she said, kissing me on both cheeks. 'But where've you been? I was worried you'd forgotten or got cold feet.'

'Just trying to catch up with a few things,' I said vaguely.

She looked at me curiously. 'You're being rather mysterious.'

I felt flustered. 'I don't mean to be. It's just I've been having to sort out things, like—like money.'

'Horrible for you,' Gwen said sympathetically.

'It's got to be done.' I fished my key out of my pocket. 'Let's get inside out of the cold. I'll carry some of these. What's in here? I thought you said just a few people.' We went into the kitchen.

'That's right. Twenty at most.' She started unpacking a bag onto the kitchen table. 'Hummus with pitta bread, and guacamole. Tortilla chips with salsa, pistachio nuts. Nothing much to do except put them in bowls.'

'What time is everyone coming?' I was filled with panic. I was used to being Ellie-and-Greg facing the world together. I'd lost the ability to cope on my own—unless, that is, I was pretending to be someone else, in which case I seemed to be managing much better.

'About six, six thirty.'

'What shall I wear?'

'Calm down. It's just your friends. We'll have a poke through your wardrobe in a moment, but it's casual. People will be coming straight from work. You can wear what you've got on now, if you want.'

'No,' I said, with a sharpness that surprised even me. I was wearing my Gwen-clothes: black trousers, grey jersey. 'I can't wear these. I'd feel all wrong.'

'I've got something for you,' Gwen said. 'A birthday present.' She held out a small packet. 'Go on, open it.'

I tore off the wrapping paper and found a little box. Inside there was a plain silver bangle. 'It's beautiful.' I slid it over my wrist and held up my arm so Gwen could admire it.

Her face changed, but not in the way I'd expected. 'Ellie, you've taken off your wedding ring.'

I felt a terrible flush spreading over my face and down my neck as we stared at my bare finger. 'Yes,' I said finally.

'Is that because—'

'I don't know why,' I said. 'It's in my purse. I might put it back on. Shall I?'

'God, Ellie, I don't know. We'll talk about it when everyone's gone home. Now we're going to choose your clothes.'

In the end I dithered and fretted in front of the mirror until Gwen chose for me: jeans and a thin white shirt. I brushed my hair and piled it on top of my head. 'There, will that do?'

'You look gorgeous.'

'Hardly.'

'No, you do. I invited Dan. Is that all right?'

'Who's Dan?'

Gwen blushed deep crimson. 'Someone I met.'

'That's great,' I said. 'As long as Dan knows how lucky he is to be invited by you.' Gwen didn't have much luck with men. I always told her she was too good for them and, in a way, it was the truth. Men, I thought grimly, go for women like Milena, who treat them badly, who don't care. It's caring too much that's our downfall.

The doorbell rang.

'Who's that? Is it time already?'

'It'll be Joe. He said he'd arrive early with the drink.'

Sure enough, it was Joe, his car parked by the pavement with the boot open. He gave me a bear hug; his stubble scratched my cheek and his overcoat itched against my skin. 'How's the birthday girl?'

'Doing fine.'

'Right, I'll put it in the kitchen, shall I? Twelve bottles of champagne—well, sparkling wine, to be honest. Let's open a bottle now, shall we?'

He peeled off the foil and wire and eased the cork out of a bottle. Then he poured three glasses, which we lifted and chinked together. 'To our dear Ellie,' he said.

'To Ellie,' said Gwen, grinning at me fondly.

Why did I feel so much like crying? Why did my eyes sting and my sinuses ache and a block of sorrow lodge in my throat?

PEOPLE ARRIVED in dribs and drabs, and then a small flood. Soon my little house was full of people. They were in the living room, in the kitchen, sitting on the stairs. They'd all brought presents: whisky, plants, earrings. Josh and Di arrived with a rocket that they set up in readiness in the garden.

These are my friends, I thought, and this is my life now. Fergus was a bit subdued but very sweet and affectionate, Joe was in expansive mood, throwing his arms round people, pouring too much wine into their glasses. Gwen was talking to Alison, but glancing surreptitiously at her watch every few minutes because Dan had not yet turned up. Mary had cornered Jemma and was telling her what to expect from childbirth in every agonising detail. I went from group to group with a bottle in my hand; that way I didn't have to stay with anyone for long. I didn't drink and I didn't talk to anyone properly—and no one mentioned Greg. He was the ghost in the house.

At seven thirty—just after Gwen had answered the door and returned, shy and pink, with a man I assumed to be Dan—Joe clinked his fork against a glass. 'Gather round,' he roared.

'Oh, no.'

'Don't worry, Ellie, this isn't a speech, just a toast.'

'Good.'

Alison was standing beside me. 'You don't know what Joe means by "toast",' she warned.

'No, really—all I wanted to say was you've had a terrible time and I know I can speak for everyone when I say that we're always here for you, through thick and thin. Happy birthday, Ellie!'

'Happy birthday!' came the ragged chorus.

'Speech!' someone shouted.

'Just . . . thank you,' I said. 'All of you.'

'More wine,' commanded Joe.

'Here.' At the other end of the room, Fergus pulled a cork out of a bottle and a spume of froth flowed over its neck and onto the small table by the window. 'Oh shit, I've spilt it—what *is* this, anyway?'

'Oh,' I said, cursing myself for not having put it away. 'That's—well, it's my chart.'

Fergus bent over it, dabbing at the wine with his sleeve. 'It's very colourful. Is it work?'

'No.' I hesitated. 'Actually, it shows where Greg was during the last few weeks of his life.'

'Seriously?'

'Yes.'

'It's amazing, Ellie.' He seemed dazed. 'There's almost no time unaccounted for! It must have taken for ever. But why?'

'Because . . .' I was glad I hadn't put out Milena's chart: it was still a work in progress. I took a deep breath. These were my friends, after all, and suddenly it seemed important to make a public declaration. 'Because I wanted to work out when Greg would have been with that woman. And you see'—I waved at the chart— 'he wasn't. There are barely any gaps. He simply didn't have the time.'

I stared at them. Nobody was smiling or nodding; everyone was looking at me gravely, or with embarrassment. 'So, something else was going on,' I said ominously, hearing my words fall into the silence. 'Something bad. I think he was murdered.'

You could have heard a pin drop.

'Let me pour you some wine,' said Joe at last, taking the bottle from Fergus.

'No, thanks. You all think I'm mad, I can tell.'

'No!' said Fergus. 'We think you're'—I could see him searching for the right word—'tremendously loyal,' he concluded. Jemma, beside him, nodded urgently.

'I made a cake,' Mary said, into the awkwardness. 'Is now the right time to cut it?'

Everyone made over-enthusiastic noises; I blew out the symbolic candle on top of the coffee-and-walnut sponge, then slid in the knife.

'It's bad luck if we hear it touch the plate,' warned Di, just as the knife clinked audibly against the china.

Joe scowled at her and wrapped an arm round my shoulders. 'It's only good luck from now on,' he said, kissing the top of my head.

'Do you think I'm mad?'

'Not mad. Sad.'

'Meet Dan,' said Gwen, appearing beside me. 'Dan, this is Ellie.'

He was big and shy, with a quiet, rumbling voice. I liked him at once for the way he looked at Gwen.

'Josh is about to light the rocket,' said Gwen, tucking her arm through mine. 'Come out and see it and then I'll send everyone home. Right?'

'Right,' I agreed, for suddenly I felt tired and dejected. And lonely, too lonelier now, in this crowd of too-eager friends, than I did when I *was* alone.

BY THE TIME I got to bed it was after two. It didn't matter because the next day was Saturday. My plan, if it could be called a plan, was to sleep until I woke and then to go back to sleep. If I left my bed it would be to eat and then I would return to my state of hibernation. Instead, I was woken by the doorbell. I pulled on a dressing gown and went downstairs, muttering to myself like a bag lady. I found Fergus on the doorstep.

'Did I wake you?' he said.

I was still fuddled with sleep. 'What time is it?'

'Breakfast time,' he said, smiling. 'Can I come in?'

I was genuinely tempted to say no. But I stood aside for him, then went upstairs, had a shower and tugged a pair of jeans up over my tired, pale legs. I put on an old sweatshirt of Greg's and found some slippers in the back of a cupboard. I could already smell coffee.

When I came down to the kitchen Fergus had cleared the kitchen table and laid out mugs and plates. 'I found a muffin in the freezer,' he said. 'I'm defrosting it. Unless you want bacon and eggs.'

'I don't even want a muffin,' I said.

'Of course you do.' He took the muffin from the microwave and spread it with butter, then raspberry jam, and put it on a little side plate and gave it to me. He poured a mug of coffee for me and one for himself, then sat down opposite me. 'We've been having a conference.'

'We?'

'The usual suspects. Me and Gwen and Joe and Mary. I was the one delegated to come and see you.'

'It's the chart, isn't it?' I said. 'I should have put it in a cupboard.'

'We've not been looking after you properly,' he said.

'Everyone's been looking after me,' I said. 'You came to my birthday party. I've been invited to dinner. I think I've had enough help. Maybe it's time now to help myself.'

'I'm not allowed to take no for an answer,' said Fergus.

'Says who?'

'Says me and Gwen and Joe and Mary and no doubt other people too.'

'This is since the party?' I said.

'Some of it was at the party. But the lines have been buzzing as well.'

'I wish people would just talk to *me*. So what's the plan? Is someone going to take me to the seaside? Are you clubbing together to pay for a massage?'

'You shouldn't be sarcastic,' said Fergus. 'It's the lowest form of wit. The immediate plan is for you to eat your muffin, then show me round your house.'

I nibbled at the muffin, feeling like a child who has been told off. It was dry in my mouth, hard to swallow.

'That'll do,' said Fergus, after a while. 'Let's go upstairs.'

As I walked upstairs with him, it seemed to me that I had spent days and days dealing with my affairs, sorting out Greg's stuff, generally getting things ordered, but as I saw my bedroom, the junk room and the spare bedroom through Fergus's eyes, I had to admit that it didn't look like it. There were piles of Greg's clothes in the bedroom. The spare bedroom and the landing were piled high with files, papers, folders and books.

'It looks bad, I know,' I said. 'I'm in the process of getting it sorted.'

There was so much I couldn't say, starting with the supposed excuse that one of the reasons I hadn't cleared up the house was that I had been sorting out Milena Livingstone's office near Vauxhall Bridge.

'Don't worry,' he said. 'I've already heard about this from one of my spies.'

'Who? I bet it was Mary. If I live to be a hundred and spend the entire time doing housework, I'll never live up to her standards of cleanliness.'

'I'm not saying,' said Fergus. 'What I can do is tell you the plan.'

'The plan?'

'Are you at home today?'

'I hadn't thought of going anywhere.'

'Good. You might have some visitors. I think you'll recognise them. They'll help you deal with this. Some of it they'll do on site, but mainly we don't want to be in your hair. We can take things away, sort them out. If you trust us, that is.'

'This is lovely of you all,' I said. 'But it's something I should do myself. And I don't want to have Greg surgically removed from my life. I want his stuff around me. Not necessarily in piles on the floor. But for me to move on, I don't need to have all this stuff dumped in a skip.'

'That's not what it's about. We just want to help you deal with it. If it's a matter of privacy, if you don't want us nosing through your things, then just say so and we'll back off.'

'There's nothing I want to hide from you guys. It's too late for that. But it feels wrong.'

'It shouldn't,' said Fergus. 'Let us do it for you.'

An hour later Joe, Gwen and Mary arrived, looking a bit sheepish. I told them I felt terrible. This was their weekend. Didn't they have obligations, people to be with? They hugged me and made apologetic sounds. I wasn't sure whether it was more difficult to receive help or to give it.

Joe gave me a friendly nudge. 'It's not so bad. Just think of it as some decorating that needs doing and we've come round to hang wallpaper.'

'Do you want me to show you what everything is?' I asked.

'What we want,' said Gwen, 'is for you to go out and do some shopping or have a swim, anything, and we'll go through everything, and some of it we'll put in boxes and take away. In a couple of days we'll bring it back and then, at least, we'll have been able to sort out one bit of your life. We hope.'

I thought for a moment. 'I feel I should say no to all this, or feel resentful, but really it's such a relief.'

'Then go away,' said Mary, and I did, though not before I'd rolled up Milena's chart-in-progress and put it into my bag. There are some things even friends shouldn't know about.

I SWAM in the public pool, washed my hair in the showers afterwards and put on some clean clothes. I found a café, ordered a pot of tea and read the newspaper. When I got home, they had left. I went upstairs and it was miraculous. Almost everything was gone and everything that wasn't had been arranged neatly on a shelf or a desktop. Someone must have found the vacuum cleaner as well, made my bed and done the washing up.

The next morning, Joe rang. He'd gone through Greg's work stuff and most of it could be dealt with at the office. Anything personal he would drop back later in the week. In the afternoon, Gwen came round with a pile of household files under her arm. She had gone through them, reordered them and written a 'to do' list: people to be phoned, bills to be paid, letters to be written. She had drawn a star next to the ones that needed to be dealt with immediately. She was being Gwen to me in the way I was being Gwen to Frances, but I couldn't tell her that.

On Sunday evening I phoned Frances and told her I wouldn't be in on Monday. I wasn't sure I would ever be in again, but I didn't say so. On Monday morning I went into the workshop, put on the CD player with something baroque, and began to attend to that man's rocking chair. I sanded it down with far too much care, not because I wanted the job to be perfect but because I found it reassuring to be doing something so physical and precise that I couldn't think about anything else. Almost automatically, in a dream, I continued with the job, and when I woke from the dream, the chair was there, finished and perfect, almost too beautiful to part with.

When I got into the house, I rang the owner of the rocking chair and said that, after all, I had found time to mend it for him, and he could collect it whenever he wanted. Then I had a long bath and afterwards I remembered I hadn't checked my answering machine, as if I'd wanted to keep the world away, just for the moment. There was a message from Fergus. I rang him.

'Are you home for the next ten minutes?' he said.

'Yes.'

He hung up. I'd barely got dressed when the doorbell rang. It was Fergus, but he was different from Saturday morning, not meeting my eye.

He walked straight past me into the living room. He sat on the sofa and I sat beside him. Without speaking, he took something from his pocket and placed it on the low table in front of us. It resembled a large, narrow playing card. 'I think you should look at that,' he said.

CHAPTER FIVE

I picked the card up. My hands were shaking but, even so, I saw it was a menu with the date—September 12—scrawled across it. There was a choice between goat's cheese and walnut salad or watercress soup for starter, followed by either sea bass with roast Jerusalem artichokes or Welsh lamb with mashed sweet potato and steamed baby vegetables. Then, for dessert, chocolate fondant or fruits of the forest. I saw all of this, even as I was reading the bold, handwritten message across the top. *Darling G, you were wonderful this evening. Next time stay the night and I can show you more new tricks!* I didn't have to read the signature to know who had written it: I had spent days looking at the handwriting on bills, receipts, letters.

'Ellie . . .' Fergus began.

'Wait,' I said. I stood up and went to the chest where I'd put the chart. I took it out, unfolded it and examined the grid for September 12. An hour and twelve minutes was unaccounted for.

'Where was it?' I asked Fergus. My voice sounded quite calm. My hands were no longer trembling.

'Inside one of his running books. I was going through them this afternoon. Jemma said I shouldn't clutter up the house. I'm so sorry, Ellie.'

'Thank you,' I said politely, and folded my hands in my lap. I looked at the fingers laced together and thought I would be keeping my wedding ring off my finger after all.

'You were wonderful, the way you trusted him. At least you know now.'

'That's true.'

'Can I get you a cup of coffee?'

'No, thank you.' He looked so wretched that I forced myself to make an effort. 'This must be really horrible for you, Fergus. But I'm glad you told me. It would have been terrible not to. I'm grateful.'

'He was a fool. An idiot. But he loved you, Ellie, I know he did. You mustn't forget that.'

'It's nice of you to say so. If you don't mind, I'd like to be alone now.'

After he had gone, I continued sitting on the sofa with my hands clasped together. I don't know how long I stayed like that, or what I thought about. Perhaps those words: *I'll show you more new tricks.* What kind of love note was that, with its tacky suggestiveness? Perhaps I thought how extraordinarily, stunningly good he had been at keeping it secret from me. Perhaps I thought it didn't make sense, or that it made perfect sense, at last.

Several times, I heard the phone ring and voices leaving messages. Friends who must have heard on the grapevine. Soon everyone would know.

Finally I pulled out the chart again, staring at the gap that I could now fill in: Greg was with Milena. I unrolled her much less filled-in chart as well. Nothing for September 12 there either. So. She had wanted him to stay the night next time . . . Had he? I couldn't see when he would have done, but neither could I see why it should matter any more. I had the evidence I'd been searching for and dreading. As clearly as if she was in the room, I heard Mary's voice: *Now you can get on with the rest of your life*.

Right. I went upstairs to our bedroom; my bedroom. I opened the wardrobe and pulled out Greg's handful of smart shirts, most of which I'd given him over the years, and his jackets. They would do for a start. I had been going to share them out among friends but now that didn't feel right. On my way downstairs, I grabbed his old towelling robe from the back of the door. I wouldn't be snuggling up in it on a cold evening any more.

In the garden, I bundled them all into a pile and put a match to them. You'd have thought clothes would burn easily, but not those. It was nearly dark, and drizzling, which didn't help matters. I went into the shed, took paraffin from the top shelf and splashed a bit over the damp pile. I didn't even need to add another match; an ember must still have been glowing in the folds of a jacket, because there was a bang, and a violent orange flame roared several feet into the air. I could smell burning and realised my hair was singed. Who cared? Not me. I threw on Greg's leather brogues. They made a terrible smell. As I watched them blacken, I had a sudden picture of him buffing them with a soft cloth, that look of concentration on his face, and wanted to rush forward and rescue them, but it was too late for that.

The elation had drained away and I felt empty, bleak, grim, defeated. Tired of the whole sorry business of being angry, being ashamed, being sad, being lonely. Being me.

Perhaps that was why I returned to Frances's the following morning. Because there, for a time, I wouldn't have to be me. I could be Gwen: calm and in control, helping other people sort out the mess of their lives.

FOR A MOMENT I thought Frances was going to hug me, but she contented herself with a hand on my shoulder and a warm, relieved smile.

'Hello,' I said. 'Sorry about yesterday.'

'I'm just pleased you're here now. Come downstairs. Johnny's made us a pot of coffee.'

'Johnny?'

'Yes. Listen, I need you to do me a favour. Anyway, it'll be more interesting for you than just trawling through the papers.'

'What is it?' I asked. Trawling through the papers was exactly what I wanted to do: I hadn't finished with Milena Livingstone yet. Her chart was incomplete. My need to know about her had not been extinguished by that single coarse message scrawled so carelessly on the back of one of her menus. Now I wanted to know why—why had Greg fallen for her? What did she have that I didn't?

'I've got to dash out.' She waved her hand vaguely in the air. 'Crisis. But I'd promised Johnny I'd go to sample some of his suggested dishes, make the final choices. You can go instead of me.'

'I don't know anything about food.'

'You eat, don't you?'

'Kind of.'

'Then it'll be a treat for you. Are you hungry?'

I tried to remember when I'd last eaten a proper meal.

'Good. That's settled, then,' said Frances, as if she had read my mind.

Johnny arrived with the coffee. He kissed me on one cheek, then the other, and said I was looking lovely. I stammered something and caught Frances's amusement and something else. Tenderness?

JOHNNY'S RESTAURANT was in Soho, down a little side alley. I knew it must be exclusive because it was almost impossible to spot from the street. The dining room was small, maybe ten tables; only one was unoccupied as we came in. With its low ceilings and deep-red wallpaper, it had the air of being someone's house rather than a public place. There was the hum of conversation, the chink of cutlery on china; waiters padded through, hovering deferentially over diners, pouring wine.

Johnny whisked me through the door at the back and suddenly I was in an entirely different world: a brightly lit space of gleaming stainless-steel surfaces and scrubbed hobs. It was like a laboratory where men and women in white aprons bent over their work, occasionally calling instructions. I stared around me in fascination. Johnny pulled out a stool and sat me down at the end of a counter. 'I'll give you some things to try.'

'Am I meant to choose the menu for Frances?'

'No, I've already decided it.'

'Then what am I doing here?'

'I thought you were sad. I'm going to look after you. Wait.' He disappeared through a small swing door and returned holding a large glass with a tiny amount of gold liquid in the bottom. 'Drink this first.'

I took an obedient sip. It was sweet, pungent, like apricots.

'Now, some soup. Radek, soup for the lady here!'

It didn't come in a bowl, but a tiny teacup, and was frothy like cappuccino. I drank it slowly, finishing it with a teaspoon. 'What is it?'

'Do you like it?'

'It's delicious.'

'Artichoke.'

Lunch came in miniature portions: a sliver of sea bass with wild mushrooms, a single ravioli sitting in a puddle of green sauce, a square inch of lamb on a spoonful of crisped potato, a thimbleful of rice pudding with cardamom. I ate slowly, in a dream, while around me the bustle gradually died down as the restaurant emptied and the kitchen filled with racks of washed plates and glasses. Johnny fussed over me, wanting my approval. The mess of my life receded; in this warm space I felt I need never be Ellie again.

'I haven't eaten like this in my entire life,' I said, over strong black coffee and a bitter chocolate truffle.

'Is that in a good way?'

'I feel looked after,' I said.

'That's how I hoped you'd feel.' He put a hand on my shoulder. 'What is it, Gwen?'

Our eyes met. For a moment, I so badly wanted to tell him the truth that I could feel the words in my mouth, waiting to be spoken. Then I shook my head. 'Everyone has their sad days,' I said, smiling. 'You've cheered mine up.'

'That was what I wanted. Tell me, is there anyone?'

'There was,' I said. 'For a long time there was. But not any more. That's all over now.' I felt so sad as I said the words. Cocooned in sadness, tiredness, food, warmth and the admiration of this nice stranger.

I let him take me to his flat near the restaurant, up two flights of stairs and looking out onto a street market that was just packing up. It wasn't out of desire but need, and the raw, monumental loneliness that had engulfed me: to be held as the day faded, to be told I was lovely. I shut my eyes and tried not to think of Greg's face, tried not to remember and compare.

Afterwards, when he tried to hold me, stroke my hair, my body wouldn't let me stay still. I got out of bed and dressed with my back to him, so I couldn't watch him watching me. An hour later, as I opened my front door, I felt a sudden unease, as if the house itself would be angry with me for what I'd done.

'WHAT WAS IT LIKE with Johnny?' asked Frances.

I looked up from some files and wondered if she could see my cheeks going red. Had he blabbed? 'What do you mean?'

'The food,' she said. 'What did you think?'

'It was good,' I said. 'It was really nice.'

'Details, details,' said Frances. 'I need to know everything.'

Frances poured a cup of coffee for me and one for her, and I went through every dish Johnny had served me, the ingredients, the garnishes, the presentation. And as I talked, she leaned forward, her lips parted, as if she was tasting the food in her imagination. I suddenly saw her as a hungry woman—not just for the meals I was describing, but for intimacy, affection.

'Mmm,' she said, when I'd finished. 'Lucky you. Do you think it's stuff we can use?'

'Johnny never showed me a menu, but I guess it's expensive.'

'That's the whole point,' said Frances. 'In the bonus season, the problem for most of our clients is finding things that are expensive enough. And that look expensive as well, without being vulgar. But what I really wanted to talk to you about was Johnny. Did you see him at work in the kitchen?'

'That was where I ate.'

'On a first date?' said Frances.

'It wasn't exactly a date.'

'Whatever,' said Frances. 'But wasn't it wonderful, watching him cook? I remember the first time he made supper for David and me—it was a revelation. It was like knowing someone and thinking they're fairly normal, then discovering they can juggle or do magic tricks. The way he chopped vegetables or handled a piece of meat, he did it all so quickly and casually. Except it wasn't casual. Preparing a meal, tasting it . . . I think he misses that, being management rather than spending all his time in the kitchen, hands on.'

'I know what you mean,' I said. I was trying to think of a way to change the subject.

'David is one of the restaurant's main backers. I'm afraid it's all very incestuous.'

'Is that what David does for a living?'

'Sometimes. It's hard to explain—David is a rather mysterious man.' She gave a little frown, as if an unpleasant thought had occurred to her. I saw the way she plaited her hands together tightly, so her thick gold band cut into her wedding finger. 'He buys things, changes them a bit and sells them again, usually for much more than he bought them for.'

'What's that called?'

Frances laughed. 'I don't know. He earns a horrible amount of money from it, though. I'm not sure I'd like to be in one of those companies while he's doing the sort of things he does to them, cutting away the dead wood, whatever he calls it. Anyway, that's what gives me the freedom to do this.'

'You make it sound like a hobby,' I said.

'From David's point of view it is,' she said, a bit wistfully, I thought. 'Not mine. But he keeps an eye on me, for what it's worth. Matter of fact, I think he's having lunch with Johnny today.'

'Why?'

'I don't know,' said Frances. 'Just to talk things over, I think.'

IT MUST HAVE BEEN a very long lunch because it was late in the afternoon when the two of them wandered into the office, looking very relaxed. I didn't trust myself to meet Johnny's eye. I wondered if he would come over and kiss me or put his arm round me, do something to suggest what had happened, but he didn't acknowledge me at all, so far as I could tell with my head down and pretending to concentrate. Instead I detected another presence close by me. I smelled a wave of aftershave and alcohol.

'How do you take your coffee?' David asked.

I looked round. He was wearing a fawn-coloured suit made of a peculiar material that was probably expensive. 'No milk, no sugar,' I said.

'That's easy, then,' he said, and handed me the mug he was holding.

I expected him to join the others but he pulled up a chair and sat next to me. I sipped the coffee while he leaned over my desk. He picked up a piece of paper. It was just a summary of invoices with details of what had been received and not, paid and not, but he scrutinised it with a frown.

'Is something wrong?' I asked.

'Far from it,' he said. 'Looking at this, I can't imagine what Frances and Milena were up to. But you're in danger of turning this company into a going concern.'

'I'm just tidying up.'

He gave a languid smile. 'That's about ninety-nine per cent of what it takes to run a business.' He looked across at his wife who was huddled in conversation with Johnny. 'You're wasted here,' he continued. 'I could use someone who can do work like this.'

'It isn't what I do for a living,' I said.

'You mean you want to get back to teaching a class of young hoodlums? Let me tell you, they're not worth it.'

I felt I ought to leap to the defence of those kids, even if they didn't exist. 'I don't agree.'

'You like teaching logarithms and trigonometry year after year?'

'Um—yes!' I replied wildly, praying that he wouldn't ask me anything technical. I knew about addition, subtraction, simple multiplication and even simpler division, and that, more or less, was it.

He ran his fingers through his thick, greying hair. 'Johnny was talking about you at lunch. No, don't worry,' he said quickly. Perhaps he noticed an expression of alarm on my face. 'He's very impressed with you. He says you've got a flair for the job and that Frances was lucky to find you.'

I didn't reply. Like so many conversations I was having in that office, I didn't want it to go any further, any deeper.

'You're an enigma. That's what Johnny says. We lose Milena suddenly and tragically, and you appear like a white knight. It's Fate.'

I snatched the chance to push the conversation in a different direction.

'Milena feels so present here. And absent. What did you make of her?'

'You knew her, didn't you?' His tone was curt.

'Not well,' I said. 'Were you close to her?'

I expected David to smile and make a joke but his face took on a stony expression. 'No,' he said. 'I wouldn't say I was close to her.'

'But she was a remarkable character, wasn't she?'

He allowed himself a very small, very forced smile. 'In some ways, yes.'

'You don't sound as if you liked her very much.'

'"Liked" is rather a tepid word when talking about someone like Milena. People either found her whole act appealing and attractive, or . . . well, they didn't.' He looked at me more closely. 'It's funny to think of you as connected to Milena because you're as opposite to her as it's possible to be.'

And yet, I thought, she'd been involved with my husband. Perhaps what he had been looking for was someone as different from me as possible.

'You see?' he said. 'You've got me changing the subject, talking about Milena, when what I want to talk about is you. Milena would have wanted to be the centre of attention. To get back to you, what Johnny said is that he thought very highly of you but he couldn't make you out. Reserved, mysterious, those were the words he used about you.'

I tried to force a laugh. 'There's nothing mysterious about me,' I said. 'I just wanted to help Frances, that's all.'

'Why?' said David. 'Why did you want to help her? From a general love of humanity? A religious calling? Do we have a Good Samaritan here?'

'It's nothing complicated,' I said. 'When I was little I used to like clearing up my room, putting things in piles and arranging them. When I saw the mess this office was in, I wanted to sort it out. When the job's done I'll return to my old life.'

David glanced at me more sharply. 'We'll see,' he said. 'I reckon you'll find it harder to walk out on this than you think.'

He had used a silky, detached tone that made it difficult to decide whether he was paying me a compliment or threatening me. He looked at receipts, letters and invoices with me, made comments and suggestions. He was helping but it felt as if at the same time he was assessing me for a test I didn't know how to pass because I didn't know what the questions meant.

After a few minutes I felt a hand on my shoulder and Johnny pulled up a chair. I muttered a greeting without meeting his eye. I needn't have worried because the two men chatted casually as if I wasn't there. They were talking about a restaurant they were planning to revamp. Then they wandered around the room, making phone calls, chatting until it was five o'clock.

As I stood up to go, David said, 'Do you fancy coming for a drink with us?'

'I can't,' I said, deliberately not making an excuse, something that could be argued with.

'I'm about to drive in your direction,' Johnny said. 'I could drop you.'

I shrugged and he led me outside. We sat in his car.

'I thought you needed rescuing from their clutches,' he said.

'I can look after myself,' I said.

'That's probably true.' There was a pause. 'I meant it about driving you, though. Where shall we go? My place or yours? I'd like to see where you live. I'd like to learn something about you.'

The idea of Johnny prowling round my house trying to learn about me, about the real Gwen who wasn't Gwen, was unbearable.

'Let's go to your place,' I said.

HE WATCHED ME as I undressed, as if seeing me naked was a way of seeing me as I really was. But even with my clothes off, even when we were entangled in his bed, I tried to make myself believe I wasn't really there.

Afterwards, I lay with my back to him and felt his fingers running through my hair, down my spine.

'This doesn't mean anything to you, does it?' he said.

I turned to face him. Suddenly I felt hard and cruel. I had spent too long trapped in my own misery. 'I'm sorry,' I said. 'But I'm in the wrong place. Wrong place, wrong time. Working for Frances was meant to be an interlude. I need to get back to my own life.'

Johnny ran a finger down my cheek, the side of my jaw. 'I don't know what you're talking about. What's this if it's not your life?'

'I feel I'm filling in for a dead woman and it's not right. Milena was the one the company was built round, the one everybody talks about. She needs to be replaced, and that's not something I could do, even if I wanted to.'

Johnny laughed. 'You mean you're not a drama queen. You're not chronically disorganised. You're not totally self-centred. You're not manipulative. You know she thought she looked like Julie Delpy, the movie actress? She didn't at all, of course. It was about wanting to be French and Bohemian. You're not unreliable. You're not dishonest.'

I leaned forward and kissed him, but only on the forehead. 'I've got to go.' I climbed out of the bed and began to pull on my clothes.

'There was one thing, though,' Johnny said. 'She didn't leave in the middle of the night.'

I looked round sharply. Knowledge coursed through me, bitter and toxic.

'You didn't?' I said, though of course I knew he had—and how had I not understood before? Milena had got into everyone's lives.

'Is that a problem?'

'Why didn't you tell me?'

'You mean, tell you about an affair with someone who's not alive any more and that happened before you and I knew each other?'

I pulled my sweater over my head. 'You should have told me,' I said.

'Why would it have made any difference? It was before we met,' he repeated, pulling on a pair of jeans and a sweatshirt, then following me downstairs and out onto the street. We stood in silence until a taxi approached and I hailed the driver. Johnny handed me in.

The next morning, as soon as I arrived, I opened Milena's computer and clicked on the email. When the window appeared asking for a password, I typed 'juliedelpy'. I was in.

'WAS IT A DREAM? A mistake? Shall we do it again? J xx.'

I pressed the semicircular arrow beside Johnny's message to see what Milena had replied: 'Tonight, 11.30 p.m. your place. Light the fire.'

The following day: 'You left your stockings. Next time, can't you stay?'

Milena replied: 'Maybe you've forgotten I'm a married woman.'

Two days later: 'I can't leave the restaurant at 10, I'm afraid. Later any good? Thinking of you every minute of the day, J xxxx.'

And the reply, a terse 'No,' to which Johnny responded, 'OK, OK, I choose you over the crême brûlée. 10 then.'

Three emails she didn't answer. The first was anxious: 'Why didn't you come? Has he found out? Please tell me.' The second beseeching: 'Milena, tell me what's going on. I'm frantic.' The third angry: 'Fuck you, then.'

There were dozens and I read them all. Their affair had lasted weeks. They usually met late at night, but sometimes they grabbed an hour or two in the day. They used Johnny's flat, Milena's house, when Hugo wasn't there, a hotel a few times. I noticed that whereas Johnny's emails were often emotional—besotted, elated, angry or hurt—Milena's were almost always the same: short, practical, and often in the form of orders or careless ultimatums. She gave Johnny dates, times, places, that was it. I felt sorry and embarrassed for him: Milena was very sure of her power over him, and in his messages to her he was not the sardonic and assured man I knew but someone insecure, needy, painfully submissive. By the end his messages deteriorated into abusive accusations about other lovers, deceit and calculating cold-heartedness. To these, Milena did not bother to respond.

In her work, Milena had been untidy and disorganised. But her personal emails were scarily well ordered, almost businesslike in their arrangement. She had a special mailbox for her affairs, labelled 'Miscellaneous'. Johnny was in there, and so was a lover from the previous year, Craig, who had begun as a client. It struck me that she rarely addressed them by their name.

Gradually I came to feel a certain appalled admiration for the woman who'd taken my husband: she might have been predatory and cold, but she didn't pretend to feelings she didn't possess; she never used the word 'love'. I was struck by the apparent absence of pleasure, the energetic joylessness of her affairs. And she'd had so many. How had she managed it? All that planning, all the lies she must have told.

I searched for Greg by name, but wasn't discouraged when nothing turned up: if I'd learned anything over the past weeks, it was that their secret was buried deep. There was a mailbox labelled 'Accounts', which set my heart pounding ferociously, but it turned out to be just what it said: increasingly exasperated messages from Milena's and Hugo's financial adviser about her accounts, which were clearly in a mess. There were also several people who didn't sign off with their own names and whose addresses didn't give any immediate clue as to their identity—perhaps, I thought, one might turn out to be Greg, masquerading under an assumed name. And then, of course, there were other people who hadn't been given their own special compartment, but were scattered randomly through the in-box, or who had been moved to the catch-all 'Personal' mailbox, which also held messages from friends, acquaintances and family.

'What are you doing?'

I started. I had been so engrossed that I hadn't noticed Beth arrive. I felt as if I'd been caught with my hands in the till.

'Checking some stuff out,' I said.

'You want some coffee?'

'Great.'

I told myself I mustn't look at Milena's emails, that it was too risky while Beth was there, but I couldn't help myself. I arranged the screen so that she couldn't see it and opened a notebook, so that I appeared to be doing accounts, and returned to it with dread and overpowering curiosity.

First in the computer's memory there was Donald Blanchard, a barrister and colleague of Hugo's, who called Milena 'Panther' and suffered from bursts of anxiety about betraying his friend, which hadn't stopped him taking Milena to Venice for a weekend.

Another of the affairs, with a man who signed himself J, began, as several did, with memories of 'last night' and anticipation of the next time. Then it gradually petered out, although there was a flurry at the end, as the affair finished. The last message consisted of a single ominous sentence: 'Well, I can just phone her up, then.' Milena clearly didn't like being left.

This overlapped a more drawn-out affair with Harvey, who was visiting from the States. He went home and someone called Richard arrived on the scene. During her time with Richard, Milena had a couple of flings. After Richard there had been Johnny. And after Johnny, in the crucial month before Greg and Milena had died together, there was only one significant player: he never used a name, simply signed off with kisses.

Was the anonymous lover Greg? His hotmail address was 'gonefishing'. There were dozens of messages from him. They were love letters: they commented on her hair, her eyes, her hands, the way she looked when she smiled at him, the way he felt when he saw her before she lifted her head and saw him too. There was a lump in my throat and my vision blurred. If this was Greg, he had never written to me in that way. And if this was Greg, he was writing to a Milena no one else had known: someone more tender and lovable than the bright, glittering, heartless woman everyone else seemed to remember. And that made horrible sense to me: I couldn't imagine Greg having a cold-hearted affair, but I could imagine him falling in love with a woman, and, by his love, transforming her into someone different, better. I used to think he had done that to me.

Gradually the pain in my chest eased. I put away the messages from the anonymous lover and browsed through the in-box. I was about to open a message from Milena's husband when I heard the front door open and Frances hurried down the stairs, looking flushed. 'Hi!' she said, tossing her coat onto the sofa and coming over to kiss my cheek, which felt hot with shame and anxiety. 'Sorry I was away so long.'

'That's OK.'

'What have you been up to?'

'Just clearing things up a bit,' I mumbled. Couldn't she tell that everything was exactly as it had been when she had left, not a single piece of paper moved or dealt with?

She looked at Beth. 'Could you make us some tea, darling?'

Beth pulled a face, got up and left the room with obvious reluctance.

'It's been good having you here,' Frances said, in a subdued tone. 'When Milena died I thought I might give up the business.'

'Really?'

'Even before that things hadn't been going well. Milena had . . .' Frances paused. 'Let's just say that a lot of what brought me into the business seemed to have gone away.' There was another long pause, in which her face took on a troubled expression I hadn't seen before. 'It's all in the past now,' she said finally, 'and it's not what I wanted to talk about. Maybe another time. We could go out for lunch—or dinner, even.'

'I'd like that,' I said.

'To be honest, I need advice. There are things I need to say out loud.'

I didn't know how to respond; I felt my deceit must be written across my face. I made an indeterminate sound and stared at my ringless finger.

'What I was going to say,' Frances continued, 'is that I know David was talking to you but I wanted to ask you formally if you'd think of staying on.'

'I'm just a teacher taking a bit of time out,' I said.

'Don't say no at once. Think it over at least. Are you in tomorrow morning? I'd be grateful if you could manage an hour or so. I've got to go out.'

'All right,' I said. 'Now I ought to leave. Things to do.'

'But before you go, I think I should pay you for the last few days.'

'Later.'

'Gwen! Anyone would think you were doing this for nothing.'

'Don't worry, I'm not a saint.'

'Johnny seems to think you're pretty perfect.' My face burned. 'I've seen the way he looks at you.'

'I'll see you tomorrow,' I managed to say, and dashed out.

I ARRIVED HOME in a restless and agitated state. I made myself a cup of tea and drank it while I paced round the house, my brain tingling uselessly. I took my notebook out of my bag and stared at the addresses. What should I do now? The phone rang and I didn't answer it. I waited to hear the message but there wasn't one. Then it rang again, but still I didn't answer. It rang yet again. Finally I gave up and answered.

'I knew you were there.' It was Fergus.

'Sorry, I was tired.'

'I wanted to ask you for supper. Jemma's put a chicken in the oven.'

'As I said, I'm a bit tired.'

'If you don't come, we'll put the dinner in the car and drive over to you. And if you don't let us in we'll eat on your doorstep and embarrass you in front of your neighbours.'

'All right, all right, I'll come.'

'I'll come, *thank you*.'

I laughed. 'Sorry for being so rude. Yes, thank you for asking me.'

JEMMA WAS VERY, very pregnant. Every so often she winced as the baby kicked. At her invitation, I put my hand on her belly and felt it writhing.

'There are so many things people won't say to me,' I said after two glasses of wine.

'What do you mean?' Fergus leaned forward to top up my glass.

'Well, for example, you two don't talk to me about the baby. You think it might upset me—because of Greg, because we never managed it and now it's too late. And of course it upsets me, but it's much better to say things, otherwise I feel shut out from life. Mary used to go on and on about Robin—his snuffles, the way his fist closed round her finger—and now she barely mentions him. Gwen used to tell me about her love life. Not any more.'

'In that case,' said Fergus, glancing sideways at Jemma, 'we wanted to ask you something.'

'Yes?'

'Will you be its godmother?'

'But you don't believe in God.'

'Well, that's not really the point.'

'Neither do I.'

'Is that a no?'

'Of course I'll be its godmother! I'd love to.' I was crying, tears sliding down my cheek. I held out my glass. 'Here's to whoever-it-is.'

'Whoever-it-is,' they echoed.

Fergus got up and hugged me. 'I'm so sorry about everything,' he said.

CHAPTER SIX

When I got home, I had decided what to do. It would have been easy to send emails from Milena's account, simply replying to the messages she had received, but that felt too risky. Even if I stayed anonymous, they would have to be sent by someone who knew Milena's password. They might even establish a connection with Milena's computer or her office. The safest idea seemed to be to set up a hotmail account. Creating the email address, I simply jabbed randomly at the keyboard and ended up with j4F93nr4wQ5@hotmail.co.uk. I entered my first name as J and my second name as Smith. As a password I wrote out a sequence of numbers and upper- and lower-case letters. When I was done,

I sent myself an email. There was just 'J Smith', the subject line, the date and time and the address.

I entered the first of the email addresses I had retrieved from Milena's computer, wrote 're' beside 'subject', and then typed: 'Dearest Robin, I am LONGING to see you again after all this time. Ring as soon as you arrive, love Jackie xxxxx PS I hope this is your email address and if it isn't will whoever is reading it let me know!!!!!'

I read it over and then again. I pressed SEND and it was gone.

THE NEXT MORNING, when I arrived at the office, Frances was talking on the phone. She was preparing a party for a firm of City lawyers that was being held in an old warehouse by the river. As I switched on Milena's computer, she slammed down the phone and strode over to me. 'They want a Shakespearean theme,' she said. 'I don't even know what that means.'

'Can't you just hire some young actors?' I said. 'They can walk round with the canapés and say lines from Shakespeare. About cakes and ale and, well, there must be some other references to food.'

'And they want Elizabethan food. I mean, honestly! I had this ridiculous woman on the line just now and I said, "What do you mean by Elizabethan food? Carp? Pike? Capon?" She said, "Oh, no. Just normal food with an Elizabethan twist."'

There were shelves of books and magazines in the office for just such a crisis and Frances started to rummage through them. I went to my new account. My new email address and password were impossible to remember. I had to copy them painstakingly from the piece of paper on which I'd written them.

'Sweetbreads are some kind of gland, aren't they?' asked Frances.

'Um, I'm not sure if they're right for finger food,' I said. I had noticed there were two messages for me. The first was welcoming me as a new account holder. The second was from 'gonefishing'.

'Jugged hare,' Frances said. 'Lobster. This is hopeless. We might as well be cooking larks' tongues.'

'You just want little things that have an old-fashioned look to them,' I said. 'Quail's eggs. Bits of bacon. Dumplings. Scallops.'

I clicked on the message. 'Who are you?' it read.

I clicked 'reply' and typed, 'I'm Jackie, as you can see. Have I got the wrong address? Who are <u>you</u>?' I underlined the last word. I pressed SEND.

'That sounds right,' said Frances. 'We can just put Ye Olde English garnishes on the plates. Bits of parchment. Branches of rosemary. Little ruffs.

We can hang tapestries on the wall. Pickled walnuts,' she added, warming to the subject. 'Medlars. Quinces.'

My attention drifted away and I suddenly heard Frances's voice, raised as if she was trying to rouse me from sleep.

'I'm sorry,' I said. 'I didn't hear what you were saying. I was trying to sort something out in my head.'

She looked at me with concern. 'Are you all right? You're rather pale.'

'I'm fine,' I said. 'Maybe a bit tired.'

Frances fussed over me as if she was my granny. She felt my brow with her thin, cool hand. She made me coffee and even asked if I'd like a touch of brandy in it. 'Now, that might be the thing for the end of the party. Did they have coffee in Elizabethan times? They must have had brandy.'

Reluctantly I left my desk and we thumbed through the cookbooks for ideas. As we discussed goujons of sole, devilled whitebait and smoked eel, I heard a ping from Milena's computer. As Frances put the cookbooks down and wandered across to the shelves for an exhibition catalogue, I walked across to Milena's computer.

I clicked on the new message. 'Nobody has this address,' it said. 'How did you get it?'

I collected my thoughts and made myself take on the character of Jackie, a non-existent person conjured up by another non-existent person. 'Maybe I got it wrong,' I wrote. 'I just wanted to try your name to see if I've mixed it up with someone else. But if it's a problem, don't worry about it.'

I sent it and returned to Frances, who had found an old catalogue for an exhibition of Elizabethan miniatures. We leafed through its pages, pausing over men in doublets and ruffs, stockings and breeches; women in cloaks and petticoats, corsets and farthingales.

'If we can dress our young actors in these,' said Frances, 'it should be magnificent. To be really authentic, we should probably have the women played by men as well.'

'I don't think the lawyers would like that,' I said. 'When they asked for Elizabethan they were probably thinking of wenches dispensing ale and behaving bawdily.'

Frances grunted. 'The drama-school girls we employ are pretty unshockable,' she said. 'You know, if they were laid end to end in the garden, et cetera et cetera.'

I heard another ping from the computer. 'What?' I said.

'It's an old joke: if the girls were laid end to end in the garden, I wouldn't be in the least surprised.'

'Oh . . .' I said. 'Excuse me a moment.'

I walked over to the computer and clicked on the new message. 'Sorry for being paranoid,' it read. 'It's a security issue. Just give me your phone number and I'll give you a ring and tell you my name.'

As I read the message, I felt like a person in a foreign country who just about understood what basic words meant but couldn't make out what lay behind them. I found it impossibly difficult to assess what the message meant, its implications. Was it conceivable that this person would ring and tell me who they were and I would know who this lover of Milena's was? Was it possible that whoever it was believed my message had been a mistake? Could that be a security issue? Was it likely they would go to the trouble of phoning to clear the matter up? My thoughts were slow, but in the end, with Frances waiting for me, I decided, no, it was not possible. I had gone too far. I had laid myself open.

My password seemed safe. Certainly it was safe from me, as there was no chance I would ever remember it. But just to be absolutely safe I deleted all the messages I had received and sent, and then deleted the deletions. As far as I could tell, they were as pulverised as anything can be in cyberspace.

I rejoined Frances and we made more Elizabethan plans, then went out to lunch, when we ate a meal that seemed as far from Elizabethan cuisine as it could have been, all tiny slices of tuna carpaccio and miniature heaps of spicy noodles. We also had a small jug of warm sake, which Frances drank quickly and greedily. I remembered the vodka bottles in her desk drawer. She talked about whether we could hire a jester and musicians.

'It's all about money,' she said thoughtfully, as we lingered over the coffee. 'If you're in London and you've got money, you can have anything.' And then she pushed her food, barely touched, away from her and said, 'Except happiness, of course. That's a whole different story.'

I didn't know what to say. In normal circumstances I would have reached across the table and touched her arm, asked what she meant, tried to draw her out. But if she turned to me for support, she would be turning to someone who didn't exist. So I murmured something meaningless.

'Would you say you were happy, Gwen?' she asked.

I stabbed my fork into the final sliver of tuna. 'That's hard to say.'

'I used to be,' she continued. 'When Milena and I first met, before we were married, we were a bit like Beth, I suppose—out every night, lots of men, lots of parties, lots of drink. But then it all changed. You reap what you sow, that's what they say. But I wish I'd understood then what I was sowing. Shall we have a dessert wine?'

'I'm fine,' I said. 'But go ahead if you feel like one.'

'No, you're right. Sorry to ramble on. We should get back to work.'

When we returned to the office, I didn't work on the computer. I sketched our thoughts for the party into a coherent proposal. I had almost finished when David arrived to collect Frances. He was in a bad mood and scarcely glanced in my direction. She made an apologetic grimace. I muttered an excuse and left.

When I got home, I ran up to the computer without even taking off my jacket. I went through the tiresome business of typing in my new email address and password, copying each character one by one. There was a new message and I clicked on it.

The subject line said, 'Who are you?' and the message repeated, 'Who are you?'

I HAD PROMISED to be at the latest Party Animals happening because Beth was away for a long weekend she'd been planning. A very long weekend that was actually one day short of a week.

'You don't need to do anything, really,' Frances had said, the afternoon before. 'Just be in the background and keep an eye on things.' She had examined me dubiously. 'It's that women-in-commerce thing you costed,' she said. 'You know, dozens of high-powered women networking and complaining about men. So if you could . . .' She faltered.

'Wear a suit?'

'Yes. Something like that. Thanks, Gwen.'

I didn't own a suit. There was nothing in the cupboard that Frances might approve of. The only suit there was Greg's green-grey one that he had worn when we married and that, even in my rage-filled binge, I hadn't been able to bring myself to burn. I took it out and examined it. It was lovely, simple and lightweight. It was the most expensive item of clothing either of us had ever bought. I held it against myself: it was a bit long but I could roll up the legs and put a belt round the waist. When I tried it on, I was startled by how different I looked, how jauntily androgynous. I put on a white shirt and tied an old bootlace round my neck in imitation of a tie. A trilby would have completed the effect, but I didn't own one, so I put on a corduroy cap that we'd found in Brick Lane, tucking my hair underneath it and putting studs in my ears. Now I didn't look like Ellie or Gwen, but someone entirely new.

I had time before I needed to leave, so I made myself coffee and had the last of the now-soft cornflakes that Greg used to eat sometimes. The light was flashing on my answering machine but I decided not to listen to the messages. I already knew that half of them would be from Gwen and Mary and say, 'Where are you?' and 'What's going on?' Then, like a crack addict, I went back to the computer and looked at the email I'd received last night. I didn't need to, of course. There were still only those three words: 'Who are you?' I couldn't think of a way to find out the identity of 'gonefishing'. Obviously, I couldn't give him my number, home or mobile. I didn't want to speak to him, to have him hear my voice. But I had to give him some number to ring me on.

I stared at my new hotmail address: j4F93nr4wQ5@hotmail.co.uk. And it came to me: I should simply repeat what I'd done with my email and get myself a new mobile, whose number I wouldn't give to anyone except 'gonefishing'. When he rang, I wouldn't answer, but I would have his number on my phone. That was a step forward, at least.

I had time to buy the pay-as-you-go phone and still be early at the women-in-commerce lunch, which was taking place in a vaulted basement in the heart of the City, a dimly lit, handsome space of ancient brick, cold stone and muted echoes. A fire blazed in the hearth at one end of the room. Slender wineglasses, which nobody used because they drank sparkling water, and silver cutlery glinted. It all felt very old-fashioned and masculine, which, as Frances had explained to me, was the point: this was to be like a stereotypical gentlemen's club taken over by the ladies.

Sure enough, the women, when they arrived, had on the club uniform. They all wore beautiful skirts and jackets and dresses, in black and grey and dark brown, with white shirts, elegant shoes, discreet flashes of gold at their ears and on their fingers. They flowed down the stairs, handing cashmere coats, leather gloves and slender briefcases to the staff, and stood in their massed, discreetly ostentatious wealth. I felt shabby, out of place.

But when Frances saw me she raised her eyebrows. 'You look very fetching,' she said, smiling. 'You certainly have your own style, Gwen.' I didn't know if that was a compliment or a veiled insult.

I drifted from kitchen to dining room, making sure the lunch ran smoothly. By the end I felt in need of fresh air, natural light. When I stepped out onto the street, I gasped and shrank back into the doorway. Joe was walking along the pavement towards me. He seemed deep in thought; there was an angry frown on his face. I felt as though someone had struck me. My mouth was dry and my heart pressed against my ribs. He mustn't see me, not when I was being Gwen, not when, in a few moments, Frances would come up the stairs behind me and witness him greeting me as Ellie. I bent double, pretending to tie up the laces of my shoes, which didn't possess laces, and when I glanced up, he had passed by on the other side of the road. I felt slightly sick with shock. How easy it would be for my two worlds to collide and shatter.

WHEN I GOT HOME, I took the new phone out of its box and plugged it in to charge. Then I opened my hotmail account. 'This is my phone number,' I wrote, and keyed it in. I pressed SEND.

I couldn't put off listening to my phone messages any longer: Gwen, Joe, my bank manager, Joe, Mary, my mother, Fergus, a woman calling about a chest of drawers. I felt a pinch of guilt, but I couldn't talk to anybody until tomorrow. After I'd sorted this latest thing out. It wasn't possible.

Even as I was thinking this there was an insistent knocking at the door. I got up to answer it, then sat down again. No: it would be Gwen or Mary or Joe or Fergus and I wasn't in the mood. If I didn't open the door, they'd go away. The knocking continued. Then it stopped.

I breathed out with relief and stood up. I opened the fridge. A lonely knob of hard cheese, a past-its-sell-by-date packet of butter and a stub of chorizo sat on the otherwise empty shelves. As I stood there, I heard a rustle behind me, coming from the garden and I turned. Someone was staring in at me through the window. Gwen. Her sweet-natured face was transformed by a huge scowl. Another face appeared beside her and the two glared in at me. Then Mary rapped sharply on the glass. 'Let us in!' she yelled.

I opened the back door and stood aside so that they could enter.

'What are you playing at?' hissed Gwen, dumping a large shopping bag on the table. 'Didn't you get my messages? Do you know how worried we've been?'

'I—I was busy,' I mumbled.

'You can't just hide away, you know. If you don't want to see us, fine, but at least tell us you're all right.'

'I'm sorry. I didn't think.'

'Well, you should have done! You should have a bit of consideration.'

Gwen started pulling items out of the bag. Ground coffee, milk, shortbread biscuits, wholemeal bread, salad, carrots, a bottle of wine, eggs. She thumped them down on the table angrily.

'What are you wearing?' said Mary. 'Was that suit Greg's?'

'Yes,' I said shortly.

'You look great.' There was a hint of accusation in her voice. It would have been better if I'd been haggard and red-eyed with grief. 'Doesn't she look great, Gwen?'

'Hmm. Where have you been?'

'Trying to sort things out.'

Gwen snorted. 'Have you dealt with your financial stuff, been to the bank and your solicitor, visited his parents, like you said you would?'

'Not exactly. I will soon.'

'So what have you been sorting out?'

'I—There's a lot of bits and pieces.' It sounded so lame that I blushed.

'What are you up to, Ellie?' Gwen asked.

'I'm not up to anything.' But I couldn't meet her gaze.

The phone rang suddenly and I stiffened. But it was only my landline and we waited in silence as the answering machine picked up and Joe's voice came on: 'Ellie. Ellie, honey? It's me. Come on.' There was a pause, and then he said again, 'Ellie?' before hanging up.

'See? Another anxious friend.'

For a moment I considered telling them everything I had done. But to do that wouldn't I also have to give up my subterfuge and deceits? 'I'm really sorry,' I said. 'Honestly I am. I know I'm behaving oddly. I can't explain it properly. I've been all over the place.'

'We're here to help you,' said Gwen. 'You know that. Don't shut us out.'

'Now we're here, shall I make us tea?' asked Mary. 'Then we can go out. Eric's looking after Robin this evening so I'm free. What d'you say? Film and meal, just the three of us, like it used to be?'

I felt tired and agitated and my heart was bouncing in my chest like a rubber ball and all I wanted to do was wait by the phone, but their two kind faces showed such concern that I said, 'That would be very nice.'

I GOT HOME just after midnight and ran to check the new phone. There were no messages but there was one missed call. I picked up the mobile. Resting in my hand, it felt like a bomb that might go off at any time. In bed, the phone on the table beside me, I could feel myself fizzing with excitement and dread, and when I finally slept, it was fitfully, to taunting dreams.

FRANCES KISSED ME on both cheeks. 'I'm so glad you're here. I've got to dash out in an hour or so and I won't be back until midafternoon. It would be great if you could go through the new brochure for me. I've got to get it to the printers this afternoon and it's littered with errors.'

'It's not that I mind, but what about Beth?'

'Oh, you can show it to her, but she's no use. She studied events management at university, which means she can barely read or write.'

'Fine. I'll do my best.'

There was a hectic air about her: she couldn't sit still, kept taking her glasses off and putting them on again, running her hand through her hair.

'Are you all right?' I asked. 'You seem a bit restless.'

'Maybe I am. Strange times. I'm really glad you're around, though, Gwen. I don't have many women friends I can talk to.'

That she counted me a friend filled me with fresh shame.

'Listen, there's something I need to talk about,' she continued. 'Otherwise this feeling I have, of guilt and disgust with myself, will rot away inside me and poison me. I need to confess.'

What could I say? I gave a small nod for her to continue.

'In your relationships,' she asked, 'have you always been faithful?'

'Yes,' I said, because it was the truth.

'That must be a nice feeling.' She stared into my eyes for a few seconds, then looked away. While she spoke, she gazed at a spot a few inches to one side of me. 'David and I—well, you've seen us together. It's not great. It hasn't been for some time. He was busy, I was busy. Bit by bit we drifted apart. And bit by bit I became lonely—without realising it. It happened too gradually. And one day I knew I was unhappy. My life felt all wrong but I was stuck in it. And then . . .' She stopped and turned her gaze on me briefly. 'It's such a cliché, isn't it? I met a man. A very special man. He made me feel good about myself. It was as if he recognised me, saw someone precious behind the façade I'd built up.' She rubbed her eyes wearily. 'It was such a mess, though. Not just because I was married—for a bit that hardly bothered me. He'd had a thing with Milena first.'

I managed to make a small sound. My heart felt large and painful.

'Just a fling, really, but you know what Milena was like. She didn't take it well that he preferred me. That was putting it mildly. She hated me, really hated me. I felt her hatred would literally scorch me when I walked into the room.' Frances shuddered. 'And then she died.'

'So this man,' I said, 'was he married as well?' I barely recognised my own voice.

'What do you think, Gwen? Yes, he was married.'

'Who was he?'

Her expression hardened. 'That's not what it's about,' she said, in a tone almost of distaste. 'It's over, that's all that matters.' She gave a laugh that wasn't really a laugh at all, closer to a sob. 'Something happened. I still can't make sense of it, Gwen. It's tormenting me. That was why I had to tell someone—otherwise I'll go mad.'

She leaned forward, and at that moment there was a ring at the front door. She straightened. 'That'll be my cab.' She gave me a rueful smile. 'To be continued,' she said, and with that she was gone, tossing her gorgeous coat over her shoulders, picking up her bag, running up the stairs. I heard the front door slam.

I felt as though I had knives in my chest and each inhalation hurt. Thoughts hissed in my brain. Everything was murky and confused.

But I had come here to work and work I did: I went through the brochure and when Beth arrived, I gave it to her to check. While she leafed through it, I filed invoices and receipts; I answered calls; I even tidied the room. And all the time the phone was in my pocket with its single missed call. The more I tried to put it out of my mind, the more it occupied it, so that by the middle of the day it was all I could think about. That, and Frances's secret; the one that had been rotting away inside her and was now out in the open.

I couldn't call the number because what would I say? Yet if I didn't call, what had been the point of going to all that effort?

After lunch I shuffled pieces of paper. I took the phone out of my pocket and laid it on the desk. I put it away again. I made coffee. I fed unwanted mail through the shredder and watered the plants on the windowsill. When Beth left for the day, I couldn't stop myself. I took my phone out once more, pulled up the missed-call window and pressed CALL. I could hear it ringing and closed my eyes, trying to breathe normally in spite of the rushing in my head and the pounding in my ears.

'Hello?' said a male voice down the phone. And 'Hello?' it said, outside the door.

'Who . . .?' I began in confusion, before realisation flooded through me. I jabbed END CALL and slammed the phone on the desk.

'Hello?' said the voice outside the door again, irritable now. 'Are you there? Hello? Hello?'

I was trembling so much I could barely sit upright. The door swung open.

'Hi, Gwen,' said David, pushing his mobile back into his pocket.

I pretended I was so hard at work that I hadn't heard him properly. I stared at some figures and underlined a few. My hands shook and the pen made incomprehensible scrawls across the page. So it was David, I thought.

'Gwen?'

I could barely manage to breathe. But I made myself say something, as if I were a normal human being. 'David,' I said. 'How are you doing?'

He didn't seem to hear my reply. He just wandered restlessly around the office. I tried to make sense of what I had just learned. David was one of

Milena's lovers. Those tender, effusive emails had been from him—he was usually so ironic and amused. How could he have done it? With Frances's friend and colleague? Right under her nose? How could she have done it? Was that part of the excitement? They say that there's no point in gambling for small amounts of money. It has to hurt when you lose. Maybe it's the same with infidelity. Anyone can have a one-night stand on a business trip, at a conference in another country. The real thrill is risking discovery at every moment.

'Is Frances around?'

I felt like someone very, very drunk trying to imitate someone sober and not knowing whether the act was convincing or ludicrous. 'I don't know,' I said, enunciating each word carefully. 'She's seeing the printers some time this afternoon.'

'Don't worry,' said David. 'I can phone her.'

I couldn't stand this any longer. I stood up and reached for my jacket.

David gave me the appraising look I always found so hard to read. 'I'm not driving you away, am I?'

'I've got a meeting,' I said. 'I have to go.'

'At your school?' he asked.

'No,' I said, and stopped myself elaborating. I didn't want to risk any lies I might trap myself inside. 'Could you tell Frances I'll give her a ring?'

Just as I was opening the door, I heard David call my name.

'Sorry, Gwen, I forgot. Do you want to come out to lunch with us tomorrow? Hugo Livingstone's coming. What with Milena, he's in a bad way. We thought it would do him good to meet a friend.'

'That would be great,' I said, my voice trembling. 'Look forward to it.'

All the way home I felt as though I was stained with something. I had turned over a stone and found horrible slimy things. When I got home I had a long shower, trying to wash off all the Gwen-ness, all the deceptions and entanglements. I stood there until the tank began to empty and the water turned lukewarm.

Afterwards I thought of calling Gwen and asking her to come over, but I knew she was with Dan tonight. Mary? She was looking after Robin, and Fergus was with Jemma, waiting for labour to begin. Joe? I could call Joe and he'd be over like a shot, with a bottle of whisky and his gruff brand of tenderness, calling me 'sweetheart' and making me cry. I almost picked up the phone, but then I had a vision of myself as they must see me: poor Ellie, needy and sad, battening onto the lives of others.

I went into the kitchen, and first I made a phone call to Party Animals, knowing Frances would not be there so all I had to do was leave a message saying I wasn't coming back and wishing her luck with the future. That done, I opened the small drawer in the table, where I pushed miscellaneous leaflets, and took out the list that had been given to me all those weeks ago by the policewoman, the leaflet with helpful phone numbers for victims, for the stricken, the harmed, the bereaved, the helpless.

CHAPTER SEVEN

Judy Cummings was a short, stocky woman in early middle age. She had coarse, dark-brown hair with occasional strands of grey, thick brows over bright brown eyes, and was wrapped in a bulky cardigan. Her handshake was firm and brief. I had been dreading the handshake that a grief counsellor might give, which goes on for too long and tries to turn into a condolence; a fake intimacy that would have had me running for the door. But she was almost businesslike. 'Take a seat, Ellie,' she said.

The room was small and warm, empty except for three low chairs and a low table on which, I noticed, there was a discreet box of tissues.

'Thanks.' I felt awkward, tongue-tied. 'I've no idea what to say,' I said.

'Why don't you start at the beginning and see where that takes you?'

So I began with the knock at the door, on that Monday evening in October. I didn't tell her about my amateur-detective work, or about my disbelief that Greg had had an affair. I just talked about losing him.

'I feel so bleak and empty,' I said at last. 'I wish I could cry.'

'I'm sure you will in time.' Her voice was softer and lower now. 'There are so many things going on, aren't there?' she continued. 'Grief, anger, shame, loneliness, fear of the future. And having to see the past differently.'

'My happiness. I thought I was happy.'

'Indeed. Even that must seem unreliable. But by coming here you have taken an important step in your journey.'

'It hurts so badly,' I said. 'The journey.'

We arranged to meet the following week, and I went from her to the shops. I had made myself a promise that I would start looking after myself. No more empty cupboards and midnight snacks, eaten standing up, of cheese and handfuls of dry cereal. Regular meals; honest work. I put pasta, green pesto, rice, Parmesan, olive oil, six eggs, tins of tuna and sardines, lettuce, cucumber and an avocado into my trolley. Muesli. Chicken breasts, salmon fillets. Tonight, I thought, I would make myself a simple supper. I would sit at the table and eat it, with a glass of wine. I would read a book and go to bed at eleven.

It didn't happen quite like that. I listened to my answering machine, called Greg's parents and arranged to see them the following weekend. I checked my mobile and saw there were three messages and two texts from Frances. Basically, they all said the same thing: 'I need you. Beth's away. Please come back.' I turned on my new mobile and saw that there were three missed calls from the person I now knew to be David. I put on a CD, then marinated one of the chicken breasts in coriander and lemon. I got as far as opening the bottle of wine and setting a pan on the hob to heat the oil. But I was interrupted by a knock, so I took the pan off and went to answer.

As the door swung open and I saw who was standing there, I considered slamming it, putting on the chain, running upstairs and pulling the duvet over my head, blocking out the world and all its mess. But even as I thought it, there we stood, face to face, and there was nothing I could do except fix an inane smile in place and hope he couldn't see the panic behind it.

'Johnny!'

'Don't look so surprised—you didn't think I was just going to let you disappear, did you? You can't get away as easily as that.'

'But how did you know where I lived?'

'I heard you give your address to the taxi driver that night. Aren't you going to invite me in?'

'Everything's a mess. Maybe we should go out for a drink,' I said wildly.

'It doesn't look that messy,' he said, stepping over the threshold.

'I was about to go out.'

'It looks to me,' he said, entering the kitchen as if he owned it, 'as if you were about to make a nice little supper for one. Shall I pour us some wine?'

'No,' I said. 'Or yes—yes. Why not? Just half a glass.'

There were envelopes on the table with my name on them and I clutched them, crumpling them in my fist. Sweat prickled on my forehead. My eyes flicked nervously around. On the windowsill, and pushed into the frame, were postcards bearing my name and Greg's. Then, suddenly, there was the sound of the telephone ringing—and if the answering machine picked it up someone would be saying loudly, 'Ellie, Ellie? Pick up, Ellie.'

'Just a minute,' I croaked, and dashed into the hall to pick up the phone.

'Yes?' I said. From where I stood, I could see Johnny examining a photo of me and Greg on the fridge.

'Ellie, it's me, Gwen.'

'Gwen,' I said idiotically. Then, to cover up, I said it again, neutrally, as if I was explaining my identity to the caller: 'Gwen here.'

'What? This is Gwen.'

'Yes, I know.'

'Can I come over?'

'What? Now?'

'It's Dan. I wasn't going to confide in you because of, you know, everything, but then I thought it wasn't fair on you or me, because—'

'Hang on. Sorry. Listen. You have to come over, of course you do.'

'If it's a problem . . .'

'It's not.' Fuck, was he going to look at the postcards now? 'Got to go, my dearest friend. Bye.' I slammed down the phone, but picked it up again and left it off the hook so nobody else could call. Then I tore back to the kitchen. 'I can't be long,' I said to Johnny, putting my hand on his shoulder so he turned away from the windowsill. 'Come and sit in the living room to finish your wine.'

'Who's the guy you were with in that photo?' he asked, as we sat down—he on the sofa and me in the chair, and oh, no, no, no, the chart on the table just beyond him. Couldn't he see? Even from here, Milena's name, in capitals and neatly underlined, throbbed in my field of vision.

'Someone I used to know.'

'Is he why you're so evasive?'

No point in beating about the bush. 'Yes. I'm sorry, Johnny. The thing is—I should have said this before—I'm not ready for another relationship.'

'So that's it?'

'Yes,' I said.

'You think you can behave like that and get away with it?'

'I didn't mean to hurt you.'

'You're all the same,' he said, standing. Now he was even nearer the chart. I willed him to look my way and he did, resentment burning in his eyes.

'I'm not coming back to work,' I said. 'It was all a mistake. So you won't have to see me again.'

'I felt sorry for you. You seemed so sad. I thought you liked me.'

'I do.'

'Women are so good at pretending. Like her. Milena.'

'I don't think I'm like Milena in any way,' I said. 'We're opposites.'

'That's what I thought, too, when I met you,' he said. 'Maybe that's why I liked you—you seemed calm and kind. But I was wrong. You're both actresses. You take on roles.' I stared at him, panic flowing through my veins. 'I've seen the way you are with Frances—Ms Capable. You led her on and made her depend on you; she thinks you're her friend. Milena could do that too—be all things to all people. Everything was a mask. You thought you'd got a glimpse of the real Milena and all of a sudden you understood it was just another mask. I've never forgotten one time when she was talking to a Muslim about Ramadan, which had begun that very evening, and he was explaining how he couldn't eat after sunrise or before sunset. She was so sympathetic and intelligent about it that I thought I was seeing a new side to her. Then, an hour later, when we were together at my flat, she went on this extraordinary rant against Islam and its believers. She was so witheringly contemptuous of the man she'd been so sweet to. It was like a window into her soul. I said to myself then that I should kick her out, that she would only bring me grief. Of course I didn't, though: she stayed all evening and all night.' He laughed bitterly. 'Never believe women. Especially when they're being nice to you.'

'That's not fair,' I began. But I didn't have time to argue with him. Gwen was on her way, the real Gwen. 'You should go,' I said.

'Let me cook that meal for you. You're lonely and I'm lonely and at least we can give each other—'

'No,' I said. 'Stop it. We can't give each other anything. We slept with each other twice. It was a mistake. I apologise. Now you have to go.'

THREE MINUTES after Johnny had left, Gwen arrived. She burst into tears on the doorstep and I pulled her into the house, shut the door and hugged her until her sobs subsided. 'I'm such an idiot,' she said.

'What's he done?'

'Nothing.' And she gave a long, disconsolate sniff.

'Come and tell me about this nothing. I'll make us supper, unless you've eaten already. Wine? I've got an open bottle.'

'Thanks.'

'Tell me, then.'

'He was with this woman for ages and she went off with one of his mates. It took him ages to get over it. You've met him—he's such a big softie. Anyway, she got in touch with him because that relationship's over. He's with her now, "comforting" her. I think she wants him back.'

'Does he want to go back to her?'

'He swears it's me he wants. But I don't know whether to believe him. Am I being an idiot?'

'Who am I to say? All I'm sure of is that he'd be an idiot to leave you—and by the sound of it he's being totally straightforward with you. Plus he seems pretty devoted to you.'

'Yes. Sorry. I don't know what came over me. I was sitting alone in my flat and suddenly I couldn't bear it. It's been so nice, being in a couple.'

'I understand.'

Gwen gave me a hug. We chinked glasses. I cooked the chicken and divided it between us with a bag of salad leaves. It was rather a tiny meal for two emotionally drained and ravenous women, but we finished off with mango and chocolate bourbons, then sat on the sofa with my duvet over us and watched a DVD before I called a cab to take her home.

I WOKE WITH A START and looked at the clock beside me. It was just past five. Something was bothering me, a wisp of a thought I couldn't get a hold of. Something Johnny had said? Just as I stopped trying to remember, and sleep was pulling me down again, it came to me.

I got out of bed and went to the computer and turned it on, and when it came to life, I Googled 'Ramadan'. I knew it always took place during the ninth month of the year; this year it had begun on September 12.

How long did I sit there, staring at the date? I don't know. Time seemed to slow right down. At last I went to the drawer of my desk and pulled out the menu card Fergus had given me, stared at the date at the top and at the scrawled message: *Darling G, you were wonderful this evening. Next time stay the night and I can show you more new tricks!*

The evening of September 12 was the one and only time that I knew for sure Greg had been with Milena. But now I also knew he hadn't, because she had been with Johnny.

I WAS TEMPTED to cancel my next appointment with the counsellor. I didn't, but when I arrived I felt I was there under false pretences, which was how I felt almost everywhere I went and whatever I did. She sat me down and then sat opposite me. 'So, how has your week been, Ellie?' she asked.

'You talked about me being on a sort of journey,' I said. 'I think I've gone backwards a bit. In fact, quite a lot.'

She looked puzzled. 'How do you mean?'

'Last week you asked me if I accepted that my husband, Greg, had been unfaithful. I said I did. That was an incredibly hard step for me to take. Now I've taken another hard step, which is to go back from that. I'm not sure any more. In fact, I think it's possible that he wasn't.'

Judy didn't look cross. I continued before she had a chance to speak. 'It would have been much easier to prove Greg had had an affair with this woman, and in fact I did find that proof. It was a note written on a menu, a menu for a particular date. It looked like evidence that there really had been an affair. But I now know that on that day Milena couldn't have been sleeping with my husband because she was sleeping with someone else.'

I wanted to be as honest as I could, so I told Judy how I had constructed the charts and how, this morning, I had wrapped them up and lugged them into the police station. I had been taken into an interview room by a Detective Inspector Carter, where I had unwrapped them in front of him. Then I had taken him through the details.

'I knew I wasn't going to convince him,' I told Judy. 'What was it someone said? In order to understand me, you have to agree with me. For the police, the most important aspect of the case is that it's closed. They don't care about truth; it's a matter of statistics. If they reopened the case and solved it, their statistics would look the same as they do now, except that they would have done a great deal more work.'

Judy looked at her watch.

'I'm sorry,' I said. 'Am I boring you?'

'I was going to say that our time is up,' she said. 'I make it a rule to be very strict about that. But just this once I'm going to continue for a few minutes. What did the detective say?'

'He said I haven't proved Greg and Milena weren't having an affair. I've just proved they weren't on those particular days. I said I hadn't even found evidence that they knew each other. I tried to point out that there was a note from Milena to Greg, which I had found in Greg's possession, about a sexual encounter on a day when they absolutely couldn't have had one. Didn't he think there was a problem with that?'

'What was his response?' asked Judy.

'You're a psychologist—' I said.

'Actually I'm a psychiatrist.'

'Well . . . You must know that when people have adopted a position in a controversy, if they encounter evidence that contradicts it, that just entrenches them more strongly in the view they already hold. He just said every case had aspects that didn't fit together and it was never possible to dot every *i* and cross every *t*. He saw no reason to reopen the case and he made it clear that he didn't want to see any more of me or my theory.'

'I can understand how you could reconstruct the movements of your husband,' said Judy, 'but how did you compile the chart about Milena?'

I cursed myself silently. 'It wasn't exactly a chart,' I said in desperation. 'I had bits of information from here and there.'

Judy leaned towards me. 'Ellie, are there things you're not telling me?'

'Not relevant things,' I said.

'What would you say if you were sitting listening to you?'

'I'd probably think I was mad,' I said. 'But, in the end, I don't really care about convincing other people. I knew the police wouldn't be interested, but I felt I had a responsibility as a citizen to tell them what I'd discovered. I need to know the truth. It's as simple as that. As long as I know, I don't care what else happens.'

'IT WAS AWFUL,' I said to Joe, who had insisted on taking time off work to pick me up from the station and drive me home, even though it would have been much quicker to catch the Underground. I'd been to visit Greg's mother and father. I'd seen them at the funeral, of course, but I felt that whatever I was going through, it was probably worse for them. No parent should ever bury a child. It was warm and luxurious inside the BMW and I sank gratefully back against the seat.

Joe grinned and put a hand on my knee. I pretended it wasn't there and eventually he moved it to change gear.

'I'll bet it was,' he said. 'And you look tired, Ellie. Have you been OK?'

'Some days are better than others.'

'If you ever want someone to talk to . . .'

'I've talked enough. I just go over and over the same things.'

'Are you working?'

'A little,' I said evasively.

'Good. You need to get back to things. Are you all right for money?'

'Fine, I think. As far as I know. I haven't gone through everything.'

'I can give you some. Lend,' he corrected himself. 'If there's a problem.'

'That's good of you. But I'll be all right.'

The car pulled up outside my house. I went to kiss his cheek but he turned his face and, before I had a chance to pull away, kissed me on the lips. I pushed him away. 'What do you think you're doing?'

'I'm kissing you.'

'Don't be ridiculous. You're my friend. And you were Greg's friend. And you're married to Alison.'

'Sorry, sorry, sorry,' he said, with a groan that was also a half-laugh. 'I don't know what came over me. You're a lovely woman.'

'Do you pounce on every lovely woman?'

He held up his hands in mock-surrender, trying to make it into a joke. 'Just the ones I can't resist.'

'I'm going to forget it happened,' I said. 'Don't ever do that again.'

'I won't. Sorry, sweetheart.'

I looked at him as if he were a strange, exotic specimen. 'Is it easy?'

'What?'

'To have an affair and then go home at night.'

'You make it sound as if I do it all the time.'

'Do you?'

'Of course not! You know me.'

'What about at the moment? Is there anyone?'

'No!' But something in his voice, in his expression, told me he was lying.

'Come on, Joe. I know there is. Is she married?'

'You've got a one-track mind. Ever since Greg died, you've been on the lookout for adultery and deception.'

'Someone from work? Someone I know? It is, isn't it?'

'Ellie.' He was half laughing, as if this was a great joke.

'Oh God, I know who it is. It's Tania, isn't it?'

'No! This is ridiculous.'

'Joe?'

'It's nothing, I promise. But she's so young and eager.'

'Oh God, Joe,' I said. I felt anger well inside me as I gazed at his handsome, rugged face, his smiling mouth. 'She's half your age.'

'Maybe that's the point, Ellie,' he said. 'And maybe you should stop judging everyone.'

'I don't mean to. I just can't bear to think of Alison getting hurt.'

'She won't, I promise. And that—just now—that was wrong of me. Greg's death has left me feeling at a loss. Forgive me.'

After he had driven away I entered my house, but only to dump a bag of photos I'd brought back from Greg's parents. Then I walked to the Underground station, eyes watering in the wind. In spite of everything I made up my mind to go back to Party Animals, and I couldn't bear to wait, even though I wasn't sure what I would do there, except more snooping.

I had three new pieces to add to Life's Most Difficult Jigsaw Puzzle: Milena had been having an affair with Frances's husband; Johnny had been with Milena on the one night when I had evidence to show that she was with Greg; the menu card with Milena's note to Greg was therefore . . . what? Therefore a tease, a slip of the pen, a red herring, a contradiction, a fraud, a mystery—something manufactured to drive me mad.

I RANG THE BELL and, when Frances didn't answer the door, let myself in with the key I still had. I called from the top of the stairs. The basement light was on. I knew Beth was away, so I thought Frances was probably about. I went down, wriggling out of my coat, pulling off my scarf, tossing them over the easy chair as I came into the room.

Frances had obviously been there earlier and was expecting to return. The radiators were warm, the Anglepoise lamp over her desk was turned on, although the rest of the room was in shadow, and there was a mug beside her computer, as well as her glasses and several glossy holiday brochures with exotic destinations.

I prowled restlessly round the office, pulling random books off the shelves. I opened the drawers of Frances's desk and peered inside: a drawer for receipts, one for stationery, another for an assortment of old menus, leaflets and empty bottles. I felt more than usually uneasy now that I knew David had had an affair with Milena, and Frances had had an affair with—with who? The ghastly suspicions I had were eating away at me, although I knew I was probably being ridiculous.

Eventually I sat down at Milena's desk, switched on the side lamp, and turned on her computer, drumming my fingers on the keyboard as I waited for it to boot up. It was very quiet. I could hear the radiators humming and the wind blowing against the windows. Every so often, a car passed or a door slammed, far off. It was dark outside now, and the room was dim apart from the two pools of light cast by the lamps. I had a sudden overwhelming urge to be back in my down-at-heel little house—not on my own, though; I wanted to be there with Greg, blinds drawn, the kettle boiling, him reading out crossword clues that neither of us ever got, putting his arms round me from behind and resting his chin on the top of my head. My world of safety, no matter how scary it was outside.

I shivered and concentrated on the screen, typing in Milena's password, accessing once more her hectic private life. I heard footsteps on the pavement drawing nearer, then receding. A dog barked. I clicked again on the messages from David and stared at them, as if some secret was hidden between the lines.

'Oh God, Greg,' I said out loud, and leaned forward, rolling the chair a bit closer to the desk and resting my head on my arms. My foot touched something solid. I sat up and pushed the chair back again. I bent down, just a little, to see what was there.

A boot, lying lengthways, but a boot wasn't heavy, was it? Two boots, black with elegant pointed toes and small, sharp heels. The room shifted around me; the walls seemed to close in. I bent down further. I heard a gasp, and it had come from me but it didn't sound like me. I stood up, the floor tipping beneath me, sweat prickling on my forehead, and held onto the desk to steady myself. Then I saw. Her body lay bundled under the desk, but her head stuck out and her eyes were looking up at me. I staggered back, my hand over my mouth: how could I have missed seeing her until now?

I don't know how long I stood there, almost gagging, staring into the sightless eyes. But gradually thought returned. First, I had to make sure she was dead. I knew she was but I had to check.

I crouched and dragged the body clear of the desk. It was heavy and awkward. I put my ear against her mouth and felt no breathing; I put my thumb where the pulse should have been and felt nothing. There were bruises on her throat and her lips were faintly blue. The sight struck fresh horror into me, even though I had known from the moment I'd seen the body bundled under the desk that this was no accidental death. And yet she was warm. Not so many minutes ago she must have been alive. I held her head in my hands and gazed at her thin, intelligent face, her blind, open eyes. A thought spiked through me: perhaps the killer was still there. Fear turned me cold and shivery; my legs shook and when I stood up they would barely hold me.

As quietly and calmly as I could, I put on my coat and scarf, eased the front door open, closed it behind me and went out into the street.

My first impulse was to return home, to pretend I hadn't been there. But could I be sure Frances was really dead? Weren't there people who had been revived long after they were apparently dead? As I turned out of Tulser Road onto the main road I saw a phone box. I dialled 999, asked for an ambulance and said that someone was badly hurt, maybe dead, then I gave the address. When the woman asked for my name I hung up.

When I reached the station, my hand was suddenly trembling so much that I couldn't extract the Oyster card from my purse, and when I finally managed it I dropped it. A young man stopped to help me and looked at me worriedly. When he asked if I was all right, I couldn't speak properly. It took a supreme effort to do the simple things, to catch the train in the right direction, to get off at my stop. All the time a thought was repeating in my head, like a dripping tap: Frances is dead, Frances is dead.

When I arrived home I went straight upstairs and pulled off my clothes and got into a bath. I lay there for more than an hour, letting water out as it cooled and refilling it with hot, only my face protruding. If I had had the choice, I would have lain there for the rest of my life, warm and wet and safe. I scrubbed my face, I washed my hair. Finally, reluctantly, I got out and put on what had become my normal domestic outfit of old jeans, baggy sweatshirt and slippers.

When the doorbell rang, I hadn't quite finished my second glass of wine, but I still felt lightheaded. I opened the door. It was Johnny.

'You'd better come in,' I said wearily.

He walked inside. I picked up my glass. 'I'm drinking,' I said. 'Do you want some?'

'All right.'

I poured him some wine and handed it to him. He took a gulp. Then he looked me squarely in the face. 'Frances is dead,' he said. 'She was murdered.' There was a pause. 'You don't look shocked.'

'I knew. I found the body,' I said. 'I called the ambulance.'

Johnny was visibly startled. 'You did? Then why weren't you there when they arrived? Why didn't you talk to the police?'

'I came straight home. I wasn't ready to talk about it.'

'I don't think it works like that,' he said. 'When you find a body, you're meant to stick around, you know, talk to the police, that sort of thing.'

'There's too much to explain.'

'Is there now?' He raised his eyebrows. 'David rang me. One of the things he said was that the police want to talk to everybody involved. Apparently they're having trouble tracking you down. For someone who's been working in the office for several weeks, you haven't left much trace. No address. No phone number.'

'You've got my address,' I said. 'Why didn't you tell them?'

'Is there any reason why I shouldn't?'

'I don't know,' I said. 'I've been thinking about it.'

Johnny frowned at me. 'I don't understand this and neither do I like it. Not one bit. You found the body. What's the problem with talking to the police about it? Don't you want to help them?'

It may have been the memory of Frances's body or the wine or the sheer tiredness, but I couldn't spin any more lies, not just then. I took a deep breath before I spoke, because I felt I was stepping out into a different sort of world and I was scared.

'I'm not Gwen,' I said.

'I don't understand. What does that mean, you're not Gwen?'

'It means that my name isn't Gwen. There is a Gwen Abbott. She's a friend of mine. I borrowed her name. My real name is Eleanor Falkner.'

'You mean you were lying?' he said. 'All the time?'

'Yes. I'm sorry,' I said. 'It got out of hand.'

Johnny gave a horrible laugh. 'Got out of hand? So, *Eleanor*. Why did you do this? Or should I just call the police?'

I told him he could call the police if he wanted, but first . . . And then I told him everything I could. I told him about Greg. I told him about my connection to Milena. When I'd finished he was silent for a long time.

'I don't even know where to start,' he said. 'How could you do such a thing? How could you lie to so many people?'

'I didn't plan it,' I said. 'Really I just wanted to see where Milena worked. She died with my husband. I needed to know everything I could. I got invited in and it developed a momentum of its own.'

'And now someone has been killed.'

'Yes.'

'Perhaps because you came and stirred things up.'

'I've thought of that.'

Johnny put the glass down and then put his hands on my face, ran them down to my neck. I willed myself to stay entirely still, although my skin was crawling with dread. 'So who do you think killed her?' he said at last.

'I don't know.'

'What if it was me?'

'Was it?' I asked.

He raised his right hand from my neck and slapped me across the face so hard that tears came to my eyes. I didn't speak.

'That's for lying to me,' he said. He got up.

'Wait,' I said, as he turned to go. 'I need to show you something.'

'What?'

I went over to the desk, opened the drawer and drew out the menu card. Without saying anything I passed it to him and he stared at it.

'I don't understand,' he said eventually. 'Why have you got this?'

'It was among Greg's possessions. It was what made me believe he was having an affair with Milena. It even has the date on it. But then you said something that made me realise you were with her on the 12th of September.'

'But this is mine.'

'What do you mean, yours?'

'She sent it to me.'

'She can't have done.'

'You think I wouldn't remember?'

'But it's to "Darling G".'

He examined it for a few seconds. 'No. That's just a continuation of the J—you can even see the join if you look closely.'

'How come it was in Greg's stuff,' I asked weakly, 'if she sent it to you?'

'I sent it back. I sent everything that had ever belonged to her back when she finished it—marched round to her house and dumped it in her lap.'

'So how did it get from her house to here?'

Johnny shrugged. 'I don't know and I don't care.'

'Are you going to call the police?' I said.

'I think that's for you to do, don't you?' he said. 'Don't leave it too long. Or I'll make up your mind for you.'

As soon as he was gone, I rang Gwen. I didn't even say hello. 'Have the police been in touch with you?' I asked.

'Ellie? Yes, some policeman rang me. How on earth did you know?'

'I need to talk to you.'

'YOU'RE KIDDING ME.' Gwen was staring at me across the kitchen table. She looked bewildered and accusing all at once.

'No, I'm not.'

'So all this time you said you were—'

'You. Yes.' I poured her a large whisky, neat and ice-less. She took a deep gulp as I poured another for myself. 'Do you feel angry?'

'Angry?' She considered, swilling her whisky in the glass. 'Angry's not the right word, Ellie. I can't get my head round it. You've been using my name, infiltrating this poor woman's business, breaking into computers, like some sort of spy, to find out—what?'

'Something. Anything. I thought I'd go mad otherwise. And, in fact, I did find out something. I found out that Frances's husband was having an affair with Milena and that there was another man who was with Milena the night I thought she was with Greg. Then I found out that the menu card with the love note on it wasn't written to Greg at all.'

'This is all too much to take in. You say this woman—Frances—was murdered. Are you assuming that this has anything to do with Greg?'

'I've no idea. It must have something to do with Milena. Though Frances was having an affair too—that's probably irrelevant.' I sloshed some more whisky into Gwen's glass. 'It's a great relief that you know,' I said.

Gwen opened her mouth to speak, but at that moment there was a loud knocking at the door. My head was swimming as I made my way down the hall and opened the door.

Joe stood there, wrapped in his thick coat, a huge grin on his face, which was rosy with the cold.

'I've brought you a rowing machine,' he said. 'I could hardly get it into the car. I thought it would be good for you, keep you fit through the winter.'

I didn't want a rowing machine. And after our last encounter I didn't much want to see Joe.

'And I wanted to say sorry for—you know—what happened. Aren't you going to invite me in?'

'Gwen's here.'

He stepped past me and walked towards the kitchen, calling out greetings to Gwen.

'Hi there, Joe,' she said.

'You've been drinking,' he said cheerfully

'So would you have been in my position.'

'What position is that?' He took off his coat and slung it over a chair.

GWEN MIGHT NOT have been angry, but Joe was. His blue eyes blazed and his lips turned white. He banged his glass down on the table so that whisky splashed everywhere and told me I'd been very, very stupid and why hadn't I told him what I was doing? Didn't I understand that he wanted to look after me? 'What were you playing at?' he said.

'I don't know. But I don't have to explain it to you.'

'You're upset that your husband dies so what do you do? Weep and mourn? No. Talk things through with friends? No. You pretend to be your own best friend and dabble in half-baked conspiracy theories. And where did it get you? Greg's still dead. He still died in the car with a woman who liked having affairs with married men. Have you unearthed some deep plot?'

'No,' I said.

'And now somebody's died. What are you doing about that?'

'I don't need help. I'm going to the police.'

'You haven't been to the police yet?' said Joe. 'Why on earth not?'

'I was scared and stunned. I know I should. It's all so complicated. I don't know what it all means. Greg and Milena, and then Frances.'

'Why does it have to mean anything except an unholy mess?'

'I'm so tired, Joe.' Tears came to my eyes. 'Maybe that's the reason I haven't been yet—I'm so very tired of thinking about all of it.'

'Oh, Ell.' Joe got up and crouched beside me, taking both my hands in his. 'Of course you're tired. I tell you what, leave it for tonight. Go tomorrow. I'll take you myself, if you want.'

Then the phone rang again and at first I let the answering machine take the call, but when I heard Fergus's voice, I ran to pick it up.

'Fergus? Has labour started?'

'It's not like that, Ellie. I've just seen some news online. It's the weirdest thing. You know that woman in the car with Greg? Well, her partner—'

'Fergus'—I cut him short. 'There's something you should know . . .'

CHAPTER EIGHT

I wasn't sure which police station to go to, but I knew it would be bad either way, and it was. I went to see WPC Darby because I hoped she might be sympathetic to me, knowing me as a grieving widow. She sat me down and gave me some tea. I started to explain why I was there and her expression changed from puzzlement to what looked like alarm. She hushed me and almost rushed out of the room.

Five minutes later, she returned and asked if I would follow her. She led me to a room that was bare, except for a table and three plastic chairs. She sat me down and a detective came in. I recognised him as Detective Inspector Carter, the one I had talked to before.

'WPC Darby tells me that you found the body of Mrs Frances Shaw. And you called it in. Anonymously.'

'Yes,' I said, 'that's right. I—'

He held up his hand to stop me. 'It's not our patch,' he said. 'I need to phone the Stockwell lads. You'll have to wait here, if that's all right.'

WPC Darby brought me a newspaper and another cup of tea, and I flicked through the pages without taking anything in. It was almost an hour before two more detectives, a man and a woman, came in and sat opposite me. WPC Darby left but DI Carter stood to one side, leaning against the wall. The man introduced himself as Detective Chief Inspector Stuart Ramsay and his colleague as Detective Inspector Bosworth. She opened her bag and took out a bulky machine, which she placed on the table between us. She loaded it with two cassette tapes and switched it on. She said the date and time and identified everybody present, then sat back.

'The reason we're being so formal,' said Ramsay, 'is that you have already made admissions that lay you open to being charged with a criminal offence. So, it's important that, before you say anything else, we make clear that you're entitled to legal representation.'

'I'm not bothered,' I said.

'And you need to understand that anything you say in this and any later interviews can be used as evidence and introduced in court.'

'Fine,' I said. 'So how can I help you?'

The two looked at each other as if they didn't know what to make of me.

'For a start,' said Ramsay, 'you can tell us what the hell you were playing at, leaving a crime scene, interfering with a police inquiry?'

I had promised myself I would leave nothing out, make no attempt to justify myself or explain things away. As I meandered through the story, I felt as if I was talking about the misadventures of someone I didn't really know—a distant cousin or a friend of a friend—and certainly didn't understand. When I got on to the subject of Milena dying in the car accident with Greg, and how she had also had an affair with Frances's husband, David, Ramsay's head sank slowly into his hands. I then told him that Frances had confided in me that she, too, had had an affair. 'I wondered if the man she had had her affair with was Greg,' I added.

'What?' He raised his head; there was a glazed expression in his eyes.

'You see, she said this man, I never got to know his name, had also had a fling with Milena, then turned to her. It doesn't sound like the Greg I knew, but by that stage I was so confused I didn't know what to think.'

'I know the feeling,' Ramsay growled. There was a pause. 'Is that all?'

'I think so,' I said. 'I'm not sure if I told it in the right order.'

'It's difficult to know where to start,' said Ramsay. 'For example, as someone who was working for Frances Shaw under an assumed name, you are an obvious suspect in her murder. If you had stayed on the scene, forensic examination might have exonerated you.'

'It might not have,' I said. 'I pulled her out from where she was lying to see if she was still alive. I examined her. I wasn't sure if there was something I ought to do to help.'

'So you moved the body!' said Ramsay. 'And you didn't tell anybody. Our investigation to date has been based on a complete misunderstanding of the crime scene.'

'I'm sorry,' I said. 'That's why I decided I had to get in touch with you.'

'How kind. I still don't understand. Why did you leave the scene?'

'I was scared and confused. I thought the person who killed her might still be there. And maybe a part of me was wondering whether I was responsible for her death.'

'How?' asked Ramsay.

'Perhaps I'd been stirring things up. I'm the one person who didn't believe that Milena's and Greg's deaths were an accident.'

'What on earth has that got to do with it?' said Ramsay.

'It's obvious, isn't it?'

'Maybe we're not clever enough to understand,' said Ramsay. 'Could you explain why it's so obvious?'

'My husband and Milena died in a car crash in circumstances that haven't been explained. And then Milena's work partner is murdered. There must be a connection.'

Ramsay threw his hands up in exasperation. 'I started off saying you ought to talk to a lawyer, but you really need a psychiatrist.'

'I'm seeing one but I haven't told her the details of all of this.'

'What's the point of a psychiatrist if you're not telling her the truth?' Ramsay said. 'And if you're lying to your own doctor, why should I believe you're not lying to us now?'

'It wouldn't be much of a lie,' I said. 'I don't come out of it very well.'

Ramsay switched off the machine. 'There's a bit of me that would like to toss you into a cell right now. If we charged you, you'd be facing six months inside—and that's just for not coming forward sooner. I don't need to tell you there are more serious considerations at stake here. Murder, Ms Falkner.'

I thought suddenly that it would be an immense relief to be sent to prison. It would halt my hopeless, undirected need to do something. Clearly I had done the wrong thing. I had lied to so many people. If I had stayed at home and grieved, as everybody had told me to, this wouldn't have happened and maybe, just maybe, Frances would still be alive. What seemed even more painful was that Frances had thought of me as her friend, as someone she could trust, and everything she had thought she knew about me was a lie.

'I deserve to be punished,' I said. 'I'm not going to defend myself.'

'You bet you deserve it,' said Ramsay. 'And don't pull that pathetic act with us because it won't work. Maybe we will charge you. I'll need to talk to some people about that. In the meantime, you're going to supply any physical evidence you have. The clothes you were wearing would be a help.'

'I've probably washed them.'

'Why was I expecting you to say that?' said Ramsay.

'Were you wearing a jacket or a coat?' said DI Bosworth, speaking for the first time.

'A jacket,' I said. 'I haven't washed that.'

'And shoes?' she continued.

'Yes, and I haven't washed them.'

'When you return home,' said Ramsay, 'an officer will accompany you in order to collect any items that may be relevant to the investigation.'

'So I'm going home?' I said.

'Until we decide differently,' said Ramsay. 'But before that, you're going to give us the mother of all statements.'

'Isn't that what I've done?'

Ramsay shook his head. 'You've only just started,' he said.

I USED TO DREAD Christmas; then, with Greg, I had learned to love it. Now I dreaded it again. In ten days' time I would wake up on my own in this house, which seemed to be on its own downward slide (the heating system was faulty, a window was cracked, a cupboard door was coming off its hinges). For weeks I'd been unable to summon the energy for domestic maintenance and all my organising skills had been used up on Party Animals.

But now I was going to put my life in order. I'd said that before, but this time I meant it. After weeks of murk and madness, I had to make a fresh start. So, I threw myself into clearing up the physical mess of my life. I started each day at six in the morning, when it was still pitch-black outside. I bled the radiators; I called in a heating engineer; I mended a cupboard door; I measured a broken window and bought a new pane of glass, which I fitted with a glow of competence; I painted the walls of the kitchen white and my bedroom pale grey; I bought new bathmats.

I threw out every jar and tin that was past its sell-by date. I stocked the fridge with healthy food, and every day I made myself proper meals. I went to the pool every morning, and swam fifty lengths. I bought myself a new pair of jeans and a grey cardigan.

I put a storage heater in my shed and spent at least eight hours of every day in there, trying to make up for the broken promises of the past months. I replaced the legs on a Queen Anne sideboard, sanded and revarnished a rosewood table. I even put a notice in the local paper advertising my services, and called at the nearby shops with business cards. I went late-night shopping and bought a beret and miniature dungarees for my soon-to-be godchild, and beautiful scarves for Gwen and Mary's Christmas presents.

I did not go back to the counsellor, even though she had made it clear she thought it would be useful, not to say necessary.

I did not take Gwen or Mary or Fergus or Joe up on their offer to talk about what had happened, or describe in detail to them how the police had behaved towards me, particularly during a second interview I had had in Stockwell—their mixture of mounting incredulity and moral disgust. I was attempting to look ahead, not back—because what lay behind and all around me was so scary and inexplicable—and the only way I knew how to do that was to blinker myself, choosing not to see what lay at all sides and behind me.

I did not cry.

I rolled up my two charts very tightly, bent them in the middle and stuffed them into the bin. I gave the menu card with Milena's scrawl on it to the police, who didn't seem very interested, even when I pointed out how the 'J' seemed to have been changed to a 'G'.

ONE THURSDAY MORNING, just as I was about to go out to my shed, the phone rang.

Fergus was gabbling something. I couldn't make out many words, but I got the sense. I was a godmother. Once I'd disconnected, I went and sat for a while in the kitchen. Outside, the sky had turned a dull white, as if it might snow. The house was quiet; the day ahead felt long and empty. I looked down at my hands, plaited together on the table, and told myself to stand up at once, go to my shed, get on with the work I'd planned for the day.

The phone rang again. It was Detective Chief Inspector Stuart Ramsay—and he wanted to know if I would come to the station.

'Why?' I asked. 'What's changed? What's happened?' There was a deep breath at the other end, but before he could answer I interrupted him. 'No, it's all right. I'll come. I can be there in about an hour. All right?'

When I walked into his room, Ramsay had my statement in front of him. He looked tired. 'Is there anything you didn't tell us in your statement?'

I thought back to the long interviews, one in Kentish Town and the other in Stockwell. I had rambled, repeated myself. Had I left anything out?

'I don't think so,' I said eventually.

He shuffled the papers, frowning. 'Tell me, please, did you ever visit the site of your husband's accident?'

'I don't think it was an accident.'

'I'm asking you a question. It's quite simple. Were you ever there?'

'Yes, I went there.'

'And you didn't see fit to tell us?'

'I didn't think it was relevant.'

'Is this yours?'

He took a transparent bag out of his drawer and held it up: my scarf.

'Yes.'

'It has blood on it. Whose blood would that be?'

'Mine! I cut myself, that's all. Look, I went because I wanted to see where Greg had died. It was purely personal.'

'When?'

'It was the day before Greg's funeral and that was on the 24th of October so it must have been the 23rd.'

He wrote the date down. 'And were you alone?'

'Yes.'

'Did you tell anyone you were going?'

'No. It was something I had to do on my own.'

'And afterwards did you tell anyone you'd been there?'

'I don't think so. No, I didn't.'

'Why not?'

'Like I said, it was personal.'

'I see. So there's no one to verify your story?'

'It's not a story, it's the truth. And no, there's no one to verify it, though I don't see why it needs verifying. Why is it so important?'

But even as I said the words, I realised why he thought it was so important. I stared at him and he looked back at me implacably.

'It's just funny you never mentioned it,' he said.

'ARE YOU SERIOUS?' said Gwen. 'What are they playing at?'

I tried to hush her but she wouldn't be hushed. I had arrived at what Fergus had called the baby-boasting party with the miniature pair of dungarees and beret. When I'd bought them, they had seemed impossibly small, but when I peered into the cot I realised they were much too big.

'She'll grow into them,' I said. 'Eventually.'

'She's called Ruby,' said Jemma.

'Oh, great,' I said. 'That's a lovely name.'

Jemma insisted that I hold Ruby. She told her I was her godmother and that we ought to get to know each other straight away. Sensibly enough, Ruby was fast asleep as Jemma showed me her miniature fingernails. Then she woke up and Jemma retrieved her and fed her contentedly.

I went into the kitchen, where Gwen was making tea. Mary had brought a cake and was getting out plates, keeping a watchful eye on Robin, who was asleep in his car seat in the corner. I was still feeling a bit awkward with Gwen, having stolen her identity and everything, but I made an effort to tell her about things, the way I always used to. That was when she erupted in disbelief, and just as she did so, Joe came through and joined us.

'I'm just escaping from Babyland,' he said. 'Not that she isn't beautiful. She's very sweet, isn't she?'

We all agreed that she was.

'To return to what we were saying,' interrupted Gwen, hastily, 'Ellie has to do something to stop the police messing her about.'

'What are they up to now?' asked Joe, raising his eyebrows at me and grinning. I could tell he was trying to make me feel better about the mess I'd caused, turning it into a kind of joke that we could laugh at.

So, of course, Gwen had to explain to all and sundry about my latest encounter with the police.

'What's outrageous,' said Joe, 'is that visiting the scene of your husband's death is something they should find suspicious. Of course you had to go. It would be stranger if you hadn't.'

'Have you thought that you may need legal advice?' said Gwen.

'Legal advice?' Fergus had come into the room. 'What do you mean?'

'Well,' said Gwen carefully, 'if they were talking to Ellie about when she went to the scene, and asking if anybody was with her to corroborate what she was saying . . .' She turned to me. 'It feels awful even to say it but it looks as if they might be thinking . . .' She stopped, unable to say it out loud.

'That I had something to do with Greg's death,' I finished for her. 'Yes. That I was taking revenge on my husband and his presumed lover . . . But I've got an alibi,' I said. I tried to recall the terrible day. 'I'd been working on a Georgian chair. It had taken longer than I'd expected so I had to jump in a cab and take it down to the company who had hired me to do it before they closed for the day. It was a solicitors' office off Lincoln's Inn Fields. It must have been just before six when I arrived. When I handed the chair over, I had to sign a receipt showing that I'd delivered it. I wrote the date and the time on the receipt. So I couldn't have been in East London tampering with my husband's car.'

'But why are they even looking at the scene of the crash?' asked Joe.

'Yes,' said Mary. 'It was an accident. We were at the inquest.'

'God knows,' I said. 'I've caused so much trouble with my blundering around that the police don't know what they think any more. It doesn't bother me. I'm finished with it all. I'm going to do what I should have done a long time ago, which is sort myself out, be good, do some useful work.'

And so I did. Or, at least, I made a start. I helped carry the cake back into the midst of the baby celebrations. I picked up Ruby and held her in my arms, terrified I would drop her. I offered her my little finger to grip in her fist. Then I handed her over for someone else to coo at and left.

The previous day, a man had dropped off six dining chairs. They would give me days of tricky, fiddly, messy, scrapy, lonely, lovely, satisfying work—something to lose myself in, somewhere to escape, or so I thought.

IF I HAD KNOWN who it was, I would never have answered. I had just come in from the shed to make myself a cup of tea and was caught off guard. I picked up the phone automatically, without thinking it might be someone I wanted to avoid, and when I heard his voice I was so shocked that I slopped scalding tea over my wrist.

'Hello.' The voice was cool and uninflected; even now, he wasn't going to show his emotions. I imagined him at the other end: his greying dark hair, his impeccable clothes and manicured hands, his languid air of slightly contemptuous amusement; above all, his watchfulness.

'David,' I said at last. 'What do you want?'

'Straight to the point.' He gave a small laugh that held no mirth. 'I want to see you.'

'I've got nothing to say to you that I haven't already told the police.'

'I, on the other hand, have things to say to you. And I'd prefer not to do it over the phone.'

'I don't want to come to your house.'

'I imagine not.' At last I heard the current of anger in his voice. 'Shall I come to yours?'

'No, I don't want that either.'

'I have a cast-iron alibi, you know, Eleanor.' He gave a light emphasis to my name, to remind me that I had been an impostor. 'If you're imagining that I might be a murderer, you needn't trouble yourself.'

'I wasn't,' I said, although of course I had thought about David murdering Frances, and had found it very easy to picture: he was a cold, clever, ruthless man, rather than a messy creature of conscience.

'We could meet in my club, if you want. There are private rooms.'

'No. Somewhere outside, public.'

'All right, Blackfriars Bridge. North side. In one hour.'

'It's raining,' I said stupidly.

'Indeed. I'll bring my umbrella.'

I ARRIVED WET and cold, dressed in paint-spattered canvas trousers under a streaming waterproof. David was as dry as a bone under his black umbrella.

I stopped a few feet from where he stood on the deserted pavement, and gave him a stiff nod. His beautiful camel-hair coat was familiar, as were the brown shoes that shone like new conkers. I couldn't have pointed to any particular change in his appearance, yet I was struck by a difference in him. His skin seemed to be drawn tighter over his bones, giving him a pinched, sharp expression.

'My wife trusted you,' he said. 'She liked you. For once she showed bad judgment. Catastrophically bad judgment.'

'I didn't kill her.'

David shrugged. 'That's for the police to decide,' he said indifferently.

'Did she trust you as well?'

'You mean, because I was unfaithful to her? I know, of course, what you told the police.'

'I told the police what was true—that you had an affair with Milena.'

'You disapprove of me,' David said. 'You think you're living in a romantic novel where husband and wife marry and live happily ever after, where your precious husband couldn't possibly have deceived you because he loved you so much. If Frances did know, she would have had the good sense not to muddy the waters. We understood each other. We suited each other.'

'You mean you turned a blind eye?'

'That's one way of putting it. Another is to say that we didn't snoop, pry and poke around in each other's worlds, thinking we had a right to know everything about each other. We treated each other like grown-ups.'

'Did you love her?'

Real anger flared in his face. 'You've no right to ask that,' he said. 'You were an outsider who came blundering into our house, putting your nose into business that didn't concern you. Frances was a good woman and Milena was a hard-core, monstrous bitch. She played with people. She lured me, hooked me, pulled me in, and when she was done with me she threw me back into the water. She never loved me. She was only interested in me because she could use me to get back at Frances. Yes, yes. I know there was another man in Frances's life. Milena told me when she dumped me that I had been her revenge on my wife, who'd stolen someone from her.'

As I watched him, he seemed to crumble. His mouth trembled, and for a moment I thought he was going to cry or hit me.

'If you want to know who he was, I can't tell you. I never asked. I didn't want to know. So if this had anything to do with your precious husband, I can't tell you. Nobody can now. Everyone's dead.'

He snapped his mouth shut and we stared at each other.

'I liked her a lot,' I said at last. 'I felt very guilty that I deceived her.'

'Her, me, Johnny, everyone.'

I WALKED ALL THE WAY home in the rain, barely noticing the Christmas lights, and sat in the living room and stared at the empty grate. Greg used to love making fires. He would never use firelighters, saying they were a cheat, but started instead with twisted pieces of paper, then kindling. I remembered how he would kneel and blow on the embers, coaxing them into flames. I hadn't lit the fire since he died and I thought about doing so now, but it seemed too much effort.

Out of the blue a thought occurred to me that was both trivial and irritating. I tried to brush it away, because I was done with my botched attempts at amateur sleuthing, but it clung like a cobweb in my mind: Why hadn't Greg written down his appointment with Mrs Sutton, the old lady I had met on the day of his funeral? I was sure she had told me she'd arranged to see him on the day after his death, but it hadn't been in his diary.

I told myself it didn't matter, it was meaningless. I made myself a cup of tea and drank it slowly, then rang the office. 'Can I speak to Joe?' I asked.

'I'm afraid Mr Foreman isn't here.'

'Tania, then?'

'Putting you through.'

After a few seconds, Tania was on the line.

'Tania? It's me, Ellie.'

'Ellie,' she said. 'How are you?'

'Fine. Listen, Tania, can you do me a favour?'

'Of course.'

'I need the number of one of Greg's clients.'

'Oh,' she said doubtfully.

'I met her at the funeral. A Mrs Sutton—I don't know her first name. She was very nice about Greg and there was something I wanted to ask her.'

'All right.' There was a pause and then her voice again: 'It's Marjorie Sutton and she lives in Hertfordshire. Have you got a pen handy?'

'HELLO?' Her voice was crisp and clear.

'Is that Marjorie Sutton?'

'It is. Who am I speaking to?'

'This is Ellie Falkner, Greg Manning's widow.'

'Of course. How can I help?'

'I know this sounds peculiar, but I was tying up loose ends and there was something I wanted to ask you.'

'Yes?'

'You told me you were going to see Greg the day after he died.'

'That's right.'

'You're quite sure about that? Because there's no record of an appointment in his diary.'

'He'd only arranged it the day before. It must have been just before the accident. He was very insistent that he should come and see me.'

'Do you know what it was about?'

'I'm afraid not. Is there a problem?'

'No problem,' I said. 'Thank you very much.'

CHAPTER NINE

When DCI Stuart Ramsay came to see me in my shed, it felt wrong. The whole point of being there was to pretend that people like him didn't exist.

'I was working,' I said.

'That's fine,' he replied. 'Don't mind me.'

'All right.' I continued with my sanding while he wandered around.

He picked up a plastic squeezy bottle and sniffed at the nozzle, then pulled a face. 'What's this?' he said.

'It's a laminate,' I said. 'It's the sort of thing teenagers sniff.'

He put the bottle down, leaned over one of the chairs I had dismantled. 'This sort of thing would have been put on a bonfire in the old days.'

'I guess you haven't come to hire me,' I said, 'so why are you here?'

'I'm on your side, Ms Falkner,' he said. 'You may not think so, but I am. It's just that you make it difficult for someone to be on your side.'

'You're a policeman,' I said. 'You're not meant to be on anybody's side. You're meant to investigate and find out the truth.'

He looked dubiously at my workbench, then leaned back on it, half sitting. 'I'm not really here,' he said. He consulted his watch. 'I finished work half an hour ago. I'm on my way home.'

'Do you want a cup of tea?' I said. 'Or a drink? If you're not on duty . . .'

'My wife's waiting at home for me,' he said, 'with a drink. Cold white wine, probably. I just wanted to tip you off that things might get a bit messy.'

'Why do you want to tip me off? And why should they get messy?'

'Obviously it's all rubbish. You couldn't have been involved with the death of your husband, could you?'

I stopped sanding and stood up. 'Are you waiting for me to say no?'

'You've been going around making yourself look suspicious but it still doesn't work.'

'It doesn't work because it isn't true,' I said.

'We don't work on truth. We work on evidence. Even so. The death of your husband was recorded as an accident. You were the one who was going around screaming that it wasn't. I've tried to think about it as a double bluff, or a triple bluff, but I can't make it work. And then not only did you claim you didn't know about your husband's infidelity, you kept claiming it was all a mistake, that they weren't even having an affair. Even when you found evidence that they were.'

'But the evidence doesn't work.'

'Evidence is always messy.'

'Not messy,' I said. 'Impossible.'

'Did you have an argument on the day of your husband's death?'

'No.'

Ramsay stood up and walked across the room to look out of the window. 'Do you need planning permission for a shed like this?' he asked.

'No,' I said. 'Is that relevant?'

'I've been thinking of buying one,' he said. 'Somewhere to go that's out of the house. To get back to what I was saying, you'll notice I'm asking you these questions informally, not taking an official statement. If I had been, it might have seemed I was trying to catch you out.'

'How?'

'We've been talking to various people.' He took a notebook from his pocket and flicked through several pages. 'Including people in your husband's office. Mr Kelly, for instance, who was in the office that day doing a software update. He said that early on the afternoon of the day your husband died, he heard one end of an argument on the phone between your husband and someone Mr Kelly assumed was you. Perhaps it wasn't you.'

'He's right. It was me.'

'You said you hadn't had an argument.'

'It wasn't an important argument.'

'What was it about?'

'Something completely trivial.' Ramsay didn't reply. He was clearly wanting to hear more. 'It was about him coming home late.'

'You had an argument about that?'

'All our arguments were about trivial things. Oh, for God's sake, I've still got the text he sent me afterwards.' I picked up my mobile phone and scrolled down to one of the messages I hadn't been able to delete. I handed the phone to Ramsay. He extracted some reading glasses laboriously from his top pocket and put them on.

'"Sorry sorry sorry sorry. Im a stupid fool." That's a lot of sorries. Do you mind if I take this? It'll be returned to you.'

'What do you want it for?'

Ramsay put the phone in his pocket. 'A cynical person would say that your husband doesn't say what he's sorry about. He could be sorry that he's been unfaithful.'

'He wasn't unfaithful.'

'I'm sure you're right.'

'Your wine will be getting warm.'

'I'm not cynical,' he said. 'I'm on your side. I know you've worked hard to incriminate yourself, but you haven't done a good enough job. That crash, with your husband and Milena Livingstone. You couldn't have done that on your own. Besides, who would you do it with? I've talked to her husband as well. He didn't seem like someone to arrange a murder. He seemed more like the tolerant type. And how would you do something like that and make it look like an accident? Tamper with the brakes, the way they do in films?'

'How do you tamper with brakes?' I said. 'Anyway, what would that do, driving in London? You don't kill two people driving along at thirty or forty miles an hour. At least, not reliably.'

'Sounds right,' said Ramsay. 'So what do you do?'

I broke the promise I had made and made myself think about the event once more as I had hundreds of times before. 'They would have to be already dead. And you drive them to somewhere quiet . . .'

'Like Porton Way,' said Ramsay.

'Where you can steer the car over the edge, set fire to it and get away.'

'Making sure you don't leave any traces or drop anything.'

'Do you think I'd have left my scarf behind if I'd committed the murder?'

'You wouldn't believe what people leave at murder scenes. False teeth. Wooden legs. I'm sure it'll never come to this, Ms Falkner, but if you're ever called upon to construct a defence, I wouldn't stress the point that leaving evidence at the scene is an argument that you weren't there. Obviously the case with Frances Shaw is very different. There's no doubt you were there. Traces of your presence were found everywhere at the scene, including on the body. But while there's an obvious motive for you to kill your husband and his lover, there's no motive at all for you to kill Frances Shaw, is there?'

There was a pause because I didn't know what to say.

'We got on well,' I said. 'She thought of me as a friend. I felt bad about deceiving her. I meant to tell her but . . .'

'So you're sticking to your story that you didn't know about your husband's affair and you had no problem with Frances Shaw—although you accuse her husband of having an affair with your husband's lover.'

'He did have an affair with her. And she wasn't Greg's lover.'

'Hmm. You can see why we're so confused, can't you? It's all these negatives, proving that someone didn't know something, that they didn't have a motive. I'm not clever enough for that. A knife with blood and fingerprints. Preferably caught on CCTV. That's what I like.'

'I've got an alibi.' I told him about the delivery on the day of Greg's death. I even went into the house, found the name of the solicitors' office, then wrote out the address and the phone number for him. 'You can check.'

'I will,' he said.

WHEN DETECTIVE Chief Inspector Ramsay came to see me on the Tuesday morning it wasn't anything at all like his previous visit. A younger colleague had come with him, awkward in his shiny new suit, as if Ramsay needed someone to protect him from any hint of informality, of special treatment. There was no suggestion of watching me work. He insisted on going through to the living room, where I felt out of place in my dusty work clothes. Worst of all was his expression, closed off, as if we hadn't met before, as if he was only going by a first impression and it wasn't good. When I offered them tea, he began speaking as if he hadn't heard.

'We sent an officer round to Pike and Woodhead to check your alibi. Unfortunately they didn't have the receipt.' He stopped and looked at me, his expression stiff and unyielding, as if waiting for some justification.

'I remember signing for it but they must have thrown it away,' I said.

'No, they didn't,' said Ramsay. 'But someone had collected it and taken it away before we got there.'

'Who?'

'You.'

For a moment, my vision went dark, dark with little golden speckles, like when you've looked at the sun by mistake. I had to sit down. I couldn't speak. When I did, it took an immense effort. 'Why do you say it was me?'

Ramsay took out his notebook. 'Our officer talked to a Mr Hatch, the office manager. He checked the file, found the piece of paper was missing, but there was a note saying it had been taken by a Ms Falkner. You.'

For a vertiginous moment I wondered whether I really had gone to the office, collected the docket and suppressed the memory of it. Perhaps this was what being mad was like. It might explain everything. Part of my mind had known about Greg's infidelity, had been responsible for other terrible things and had hidden them behind a mental wall. Hadn't I heard about people who had suffered traumas and buried them so they wouldn't have to confront the implications? People who had committed crimes, forgotten them and truly believed they were innocent? It would almost have been a relief to yield to that, but I didn't.

'Where is it?' said Ramsay.

'I don't have it,' I said. 'It wasn't me.'

'Stop,' said Ramsay. He held up his right hand, the tips of his first finger and thumb almost touching, as if he was holding an invisible match. 'I'm this close—this close—to arresting you now. Ms Falkner, I don't think you realise the trouble you're in. Perverting the course of justice is not like crossing the road when the little red man is showing. I can tell you that judges don't like it. They see it as a kind of treason and they send people to prison for a surprisingly long time. Do you understand?'

'It wasn't me,' I said. 'It doesn't make sense in any possible way. If it was me, why would I tell you about the company, give you the address and then take away the evidence before you got there?'

'Because it didn't say what you said it said.'

'But getting rid of the evidence doesn't help. It just makes it worse. Why would I do that? And give my name while I was at it?'

Ramsay gave a snort that was almost a laugh, but then his expression turned serious and when he spoke it was quietly and deliberately. 'If a jury was informed of everything else you've been up to, I don't think they'd have difficulty swallowing one extra piece of insanity.'

He said that in the near future I would be interviewed under caution, which meant there was the possibility of an imminent criminal charge, and that I ought to have a lawyer present. He also muttered about having a psychological evaluation and that it might be my best hope. As they were about to leave he regarded me with a mixture of bafflement and pity. 'I felt sorry for you,' he said, 'but you don't make it easy. I don't understand what you're up to. But we're on your case. Don't piss us around.'

As soon as they were gone, I changed into more businesslike clothes. Half an hour later I was at the office of Pike and Woodhead, whose entrance was in an alley off Lincoln's Inn Fields. A middle-aged woman was sitting at a desk inside the door. I asked her if Mr Hatch was in.

'Darren? Yes, he's around somewhere.'

I asked if I could see him and a minute later he appeared, not in a suit but in jeans and a T-shirt. I hadn't met him when I had delivered the chair.

I had left it at reception, signed a piece of paper, taken a copy and left.

'My name's Eleanor Falkner. I delivered a chair here a few weeks ago.'

His face became suspicious. 'A policeman was here about that this morning.'

'I wanted to check up on it. When I delivered the chair, I signed a receipt. They said I collected it from you. But I didn't.'

He walked over to a filing cabinet against the wall and pulled open the top drawer. He took out a file and flicked through it. 'We have a slip for everything that's collected or delivered. Here we are. It's just a note saying, "Docket retrieved for Ms Falkner".'

'When?'

'That would be yesterday.'

'I don't understand. Who wrote it?'

He examined it more closely. 'Looks like my writing.'

'So was it me who collected the docket?'

'That's what it says here.'

'But can't you remember the woman who collected it?'

'What I mainly do is sort out deliveries. Twenty, thirty, forty a day. That's why I need the pieces of paper.'

'But why did you let someone take a piece of paper away just like that?'

'Because it wasn't important. We keep the receipts for documents. This is just office stuff, pens, photocopying fluid. Every couple of months we chuck it out.'

'So anyone could have walked in off the street, asked for the docket and you would have given it to them?'

He looked back down at the file. 'It says Ms Falkner here.'

'Yes, but . . .' I stopped. I'd realised the futility of pushing it any further.

EIGHT HOURS LATER, or thereabouts, I was drunk. In the afternoon I had phoned Gwen and Mary and left messages. Later in the afternoon, Gwen rang and said that the two of them were taking me out.

They took me to a new Spanish bar in Camden Town where we ate tapas with dry sherry, and then we got into a discussion about what our favourite drink was. Someone said a dry martini and Mary said it should be served with a twist of lemon peel and Gwen said it should be with an olive. So we had one with the lemon followed by one with the olive.

I was given the casting vote as to which was the winner, so I chose the lemon peel and we had to have another of those to celebrate.

It was at that point that Gwen asked how I was. Even in my alcoholic stupor, I realised that this was what the whole evening had been leading up to. My messages on their mobiles must have sounded terrifyingly abject and they had clearly decided something needed to be done.

'I'm all right,' I said.

'No,' said Mary. 'This is us, remember.'

So I told them the events of the previous days in as compressed a way as I could manage. At the end of it, Mary and Gwen exchanged an alarmed, confused glance. I drained my glass. 'I mean, what would be the point of giving the police an alibi that I knew wasn't true, then removing the evidence before they could check it? How would you explain it?'

'There must have been a mix-up of some kind,' said Gwen.

I was now having to concentrate very hard to speak, let alone think. 'I keep trying to think of logical explanations,' I said, 'but all I come up with are illogical ones. For example, I thought that maybe one of you went down there to check whether the alibi was right, found it wasn't and took it away to protect me. But you wouldn't do that, would you?'

'Of course not,' said Mary.

We came out of the bar as it was closing and the cold air seemed to clear my head immediately. I hugged my friends and thanked them.

'You don't think the police will arrest you, do you?' Gwen said.

I pulled my coat tightly around me to protect me from the wind whistling up Camden High Street. Suddenly things came into focus.

'I don't know,' I said. 'I'm not sure if it all fits together. If suddenly I was found dead and it looked as if I'd killed myself, they would be able to close the files on three cases at the same time. A grief-stricken widow, a guilty murderer who felt the net closing over her and couldn't take the pressure any more. If the pieces didn't quite fit, if it didn't make complete sense, well, life's messy, isn't it? But it would be good enough for the police.'

'Ellie,' said Gwen, horrified, 'you mustn't say that.'

I saw a taxi and raised my arm to hail it. 'But if anything happens to me,' I said, 'you'll remember I said it, won't you?'

I WENT TO BED exhausted, but my nerves were jangling, my mind racing and sleep was impossible. I tried every trick I could think of to make my brain forget about trying to go to sleep so that it could just go to sleep. I relaxed, I concentrated, I mimicked a supposedly sleep-like regular breathing. I tried to think of something boring, I tried to think of something interesting. I began to wonder how I had ever managed to fall asleep in the past.

As a deranged way of trying to force myself into unconsciousness, I went for a journey in my head, as if thinking about something was as tiring as doing it. I walked out of the house, turned left, then left again and went down to the canal, past Camden Lock through Primrose Hill, then out into Regent's Park, along Euston Road and back through Somers Town, Camden Town and towards home.

At first I tried to imagine it as a simple walk through the city but then I had the impression I was being chased, but I couldn't see who was behind me, couldn't tell whether I was being pursued by one person or many, or even whether it was a person or a thing. I just had the feeling that people were out there and that they were hostile to me. Suddenly, overwhelmingly, I knew that on my imaginary trek I wasn't being hunted. I was looking for something, following something, and I realised it was you. I wasn't just looking for you but I started talking to you and I wondered whether it made any sense for me to talk to you, whether you existed outside my mind and the minds of people who knew you. Was some remnant of you, Greg, somewhere in some darker dark than the dark in which I was lying?

Suddenly the temptation to yield not only to sleep but to death felt irresistible. To leave the harsh noises and bright lights, the pains and torments of life for the absence, for the nothingness; to join you, to be with you, or at least to share nothingness with you. For a time, as I lay there, listening to sounds from outside, watching the beams of headlights crossing the ceiling, I felt that anyone who killed me would be doing me a favour.

I lay in bed, peacefully, stolidly awake, for what must have been hours, waiting for the curtain edges to grow light, and then I remembered that the shortest day of the year had only just passed and that daylight was still far away. I fumbled for my watch on the bedside table. I got out of the bed, pulled on jeans, a shirt, a sweater, walking boots, then a bulky jacket and a woolly hat. I left the house and started to walk, not as I had in my waking dream but northwards.

Remember in the summer when we walked out on Hampstead Heath late at night? It was so warm that we had been in T-shirts and it was never entirely dark. From the top of Kite Hill we watched the glow in the sky in the east of London, and the office blocks of the City and Canary Wharf.

As I walked up Kentish Town Road I saw a few other pedestrians, stragglers from last night or early birds heading for work. There were taxis and delivery vans and cars, because the traffic never stops, barely even slackens. I turned onto the Heath and walked up the hill so that I could look over the lights of London, distant and abstract and glittering, as if I was flying above it. I went further up the hill and to the right, and walked deeper into the Heath on paths lit only by the moon, finding my way by memory on routes I had taken dozens of times before. The early-morning air felt fierce and good on my cheeks.

Finally I found myself surrounded by the dim skeleton shapes of oak trees. I stopped and listened. There wasn't even the hum of traffic that you hear everywhere else in the city. I was in the centre of London and yet I was in an ancient forest as old as England. I looked up at the branches. Were they standing out more clearly as the sky turned from black to grey? Was the dawn coming?

I started to talk to you, not because I thought you were somehow present in the wind that was shifting the branches—I didn't, not really—but because it was a place we had been together and that had somehow become a part of us. I told you the story of my life since you had gone away. I told you about my strange behaviour, my madness, my distrust of you and then my belief in you. How it had been so hard, how I had wanted to give up.

There was a sudden breath of wind that shifted the branches above me and I wondered what you would have said if you had been there, whether you would have teased me or got cross or said something encouraging, or just put your arms round me and said nothing. Then I told you about the strange things that had happened, the disappearing evidence. I know what you would have said about that. You always wanted to know how things worked. When you didn't know, you found out. And as I told you all that, I realised that I, too, had to know, even if I died at the moment I knew. It didn't matter, as long as I knew, as long as I could tell you.

I looked up at the branches. Yes, they really were standing out more sharply against the greying sky.

CHAPTER TEN

I sat on the sofa in Gwen's living room. I had come round for a cup of coffee. Dan was there, too.

'Are you all right, Ellie?' Gwen asked. 'You seem—I don't know—very thoughtful. A bit subdued.'

'I don't mean to be. I'm fine. Weary. I didn't sleep very well. I've been a bit mad, haven't I? I feel more peaceful now.'

'Do you?'

'I think so. The stages of grief. Are you using your car at the moment?'

'Not that I know of. I never use it if I can help it. It stands there from one week to the next. I'm thinking of selling it.'

'If she does need it, she can use mine instead,' said Dan.

'Can I borrow it? I'm insured. I was thinking of going away for a while.'

'Where to?'

'I don't know. Just for a few days.'

'But it's Christmas.'

'Exactly.'

'Don't go away on your own. Come and stay here, Ellie.' Gwen seemed close to tears.

'That's really lovely of you but I need to go right away. Not for long. I'm sure you understand.'

'As long as you know that there's always . . .'

'I do know. I've always known.'

'Of course you can take the car. Take it now.'

IT WOULD SOON be dark again. So much darkness and so little light. I drove Gwen's car home and parked it outside the gate, then let myself into the house. It was so empty, so silent, so cheerless. I wandered from room to room, picking up objects and putting them down again, running my finger along shelves to collect dust. Perhaps I would move. After I came back from wherever I was going, I would put the house on the market.

I came to a halt in the chilly living room. I closed the curtains. I decided I'd light a fire to brighten it up. The basket contained kindling and some screwed up pieces of paper. We'd got into the habit of doing it with used envelopes, letters we didn't need, scraps of paper. Greg used to talk about identity theft and that it was better than buying a shredder.

I collected a bag of coal from my work shed, then set to work, although I'd rarely lit a fire before—that had always been Greg's task. I made meals, he made fires. I laid several of the homemade firelighters in the grate, then arranged kindling in a wigwam over the top before striking a match and holding the flame against one of the twists of paper. It caught quickly and I immediately felt the comforting warmth on my face.

I sat cross-legged in front of the fire and began to toss the little screwed-up pieces into the flames and watched as they were consumed. Some I unrolled and read. Articles in six-month-old newspapers seem more interesting when you're about to throw them on the fire. Mostly there were useless old envelopes and letters offering to lend us money or telling us we'd won some in a competition. It struck me that these were the last traces of Greg's ordinary daily life that were left in the house; the rubbish that surrounds all of us. I was about to toss another into the flames when something caught my eye. It was just a fragment of handwriting scrawled on the edge of the paper, but it looked familiar and I couldn't think why. I untwisted the paper and smoothed it out.

It had the office letterhead—Foreman & Manning Accountants—but above that, in her flamboyant calligraphy: *I'll ring you about this—Milena Livingstone*. And underneath the letterhead, in a different ink, a name was written over and over. *Marjorie Sutton*, *Marjorie Sutton*, *Marjorie Sutton* . . . about twenty signatures running down the page.

I held the paper in both hands, staring at it. What did it mean? The message was in Milena's handwriting. There was no doubt about that. After my days in the office, I knew it as well as my own. And it was on a piece of paper from Greg's office. It was the thing I had been looking for all this time, the connection. And I was more confused than ever. Why was Marjorie Sutton's name written on it over and over again? What was it doing here?

I tried to remember. I thought so hard it hurt. I looked at one of the newspapers. It was from the day that Greg had died. Yes, that was it. These were the scraps from the tidying I had done that day, just before the knock on the door, before my life changed.

I found Marjorie Sutton's number and dialled it. She seemed confused to hear from me again. She said she had told me everything she remembered.

'Did you know a woman called Milena Livingstone?'

'No,' she said firmly.

I described the piece of paper I'd found. 'Were they your signatures?'

'I don't see the importance of this,' she said, with a touch of impatience.

'I think it's very important,' I said. 'I'm going to take the paper to the police. They may want to ask you about it.'

'I certainly didn't sign any piece of paper in that way.'

'What exactly do Greg's company . . . I mean Foreman and Manning, what do they do for you?'

'I'm not sure that's your concern,' she said.

'I suppose they do your accounts?'

'They handle the money side of things for me, the things my husband used to look after. I couldn't do it myself.'

'Have you had any trouble with the firm? Have they behaved strangely in some way? Had you complained?'

'No, I hadn't. Really, Ms Falkner, I don't know what you're talking about.'

'But there must be something,' I said, in desperation. 'I've found this piece of paper, Greg wanted to see you urgently, just at the time he died.'

'I'm sorry,' she said. 'I can't help you any more.'

'But don't you see—' I realised the line was dead. I couldn't believe it. She'd actually hung up on me.

I walked through to the kitchen. I laid the paper on the table and stared at it. Those signatures. I was sure I'd seen something like it before, but I couldn't think where. *I'll ring you about this. Milena Livingstone.* You? Greg? Milena calls Greg? Greg calls Marjorie Sutton? Had he seen something in the note that I couldn't? Had Milena told him something?

It didn't matter now. I would take it to DCI Ramsay. The professionals could deal with it. I found an old envelope and slipped the piece of paper inside, then I put the envelope into my shoulder bag. As I was pulling on my jacket, the doorbell rang. It was Joe.

He smiled. 'I was worried about you,' he said.

'Everybody's worried about me. I'm fine.'

'One of our clients phoned the office. She's in a state. She said a woman had been ringing her and asking her strange questions.'

'Marjorie Sutton. But you don't need to concern yourself about me,' I said, pulling the door shut behind me and walking towards Gwen's car. 'I was on my way out.'

'The way that woman was talking, I thought you might be having some sort of breakdown. You can't go disturbing old ladies like that.'

I unlocked the car door. 'I can't talk,' I said. 'I've got to go. One of my regular visits to the police.'

'Do you want me to come with you?'

'No, I don't,' I said, and then stopped myself. 'No, thank you.'

'Could you at least drop me at a station? I let my cab go.'

'Sure,' I said. 'So long as you behave yourself.'

As I drove off, I half expected to feel Joe's hand on my knee.

'What are you seeing them about?'

I told him about the piece of paper I'd found.

'Isn't that just a scrap of paper?' he said.

'It's a scrap of paper from Greg's work with Milena Livingstone's handwriting on it.'

'What does that mean?'

'I don't know,' I said. 'But it feels like the thing I've been looking for.'

We drove for a couple of minutes in silence and then I thought, He'll suggest going somewhere else. We continued in silence for several minutes.

'I could drop you over there.'

'It's probably nothing, but why not come back to the office? We could look through Mrs Sutton's file and see if your piece of paper refers to anything. It's not too far out of your way.'

'All right.'

'At least you'd know,' he said.

'That's all I want.'

I felt, almost for the first time, in the midst of all the fog and all the darkness, that I was seeing with clarity. The office was no good to him. If he suggested something else, I'd know. We stopped at some traffic lights.

'There's a short cut ahead,' he said. 'I'll direct you.'

'All right.'

'Turn left along there.'

I drove as if hypnotised, as if someone else was doing the driving and I was just getting a ride and looking around in curiosity. I saw people walking on the pavement and it seemed to me that they were different from me, as if I was a visitor from another world, shortly to depart. I glanced at Joe, who was also glancing around. He rubbed his face. He looked tired. In fact, he looked worn out. Why hadn't I seen that before? I had been so busy looking in the wrong direction. I wasn't afraid. I felt a sense of peace. I wanted to know and after that nothing mattered.

'You turn left just ahead. The second on the left.'

It's funny. Wherever you are in London, however busy it is, you're just a minute or two from somewhere desolate and abandoned. One day it'll all be turned into bijou apartments, but not yet. A left and a right and we were among some abandoned office buildings. There were no cars in sight, and no pedestrians.

'Bloody hell,' Joe said. 'It's a cul-de-sac. I got it wrong. You'll need to turn round. You'd better pull in here.'

'Some short cut,' I said, as I stopped the car.

This was it. This was where it had all been heading. All roads meet here. All stories end here. Now I felt Joe's hand on the nape of my neck, soft, caressing. 'This reminds me of Porton Way,' I said.

'What's that?'

'You know. Where Greg was killed.'

'I don't.'

And now I remembered where I'd seen those signatures.

'I used to play a game when I was little,' I said. 'My friend and me, writing each other's names, copying each other's signature. You could do a lot with Marjorie Sutton's signature. I guess she's not someone who checks her accounts very thoroughly. It was you, wasn't it?'

Joe looked at me stonily. I could feel his hand, hardly more than his fingertips, brushing the back of my neck.

'The thing about Milena,' I said, 'is she had a nose for weakness, for something she could use. She saw it, picked it up, and when you dropped her for Frances, she used it. No wonder you wanted to clear out my house for me. You needed to find it. You must have been frantic. And when Frances guessed—as she must have done, or why would you have killed her—was it easier the third time?'

Joe stared at me, but didn't speak.

'I just wanted to know,' I said.

'So now you do,' he said quietly.

'So this is what it's going to be?' I said. 'Poor Ellie. Couldn't take it. Couldn't live without her husband. There's just one thing.'

'What's that?' said Joe.

'I don't care,' I said, and I pushed the accelerator to the floor so that the rubber on the tyres screamed and the car leaped forward. I heard a shout but I couldn't make out what he was saying. I was in a dream anyway, in the car with this man whom Greg had trusted and loved until he hadn't trusted him any more. Forty miles an hour. Fifty. Then sixty. We were running out of road.

I heard a scream and I didn't know whether it was Joe's scream of terror, or something inside my head, or the tyres against the rough road, and I had a moment to remember that this was Gwen's car I was destroying, and then it wasn't fast and loud and violent, but slow, silent, peaceful. And it was no longer a winter's day pinched by darkness; it was a warm summer afternoon, full of birdsong. There he was at last—oh, I had waited so long—walking towards me over the grass and such a smile on his face, his dear, familiar face. The smile he gave only to me. How I've missed you, I said, I wanted to say. How badly I've missed you. And, Have I done well? Do I make you proud? And I love you, how I love you. I will never stop loving you.

He held me in his arms, wrapped me in his solid warmth. And at last I could close my eyes and rest because I had reached the end and come home.

IT DIDN'T FEEL GOOD to be dead, not the way it should have done. There were bits of me that hurt and bits that felt sticky and bits that were bent in different directions and there was something over my face and there was an insistent electric noise that went on and on. Everything was dim and far away and becoming dimmer. There were presences close to me and hands on me, voices. I was being roughly handled. Didn't they know I was fragile? That I was broken inside? I tried to protest that I wanted to be left alone so I could sleep, but something was forced into my mouth and I couldn't speak. Something was shouted in my ear that I couldn't recognise, and then I did recognise it. It was my name. How did they know? And then I sank without fear or regret into darkness. Not sleep but a state of non-being with no dreams, no thoughts.

I didn't wake up from that nothingness. I gradually found myself in an existence of feverish semi-sleep in which I sometimes saw faces around me. Some were familiar: Mary, Fergus, Gwen. I tried to say sorry about her car but my mouth was full and the words wouldn't come.

The sign of my gradual return to life, to reality, was that I started to hurt in almost every part of my body. In that period when I could still barely tell night from day, sleep from wakefulness, a doctor came and sat by my bed and talked to me about fractures and rib damage and a punctured spleen and operations and about gradual recovery and patience and determination. When he had finished, he paused as if he was waiting for me to ask some question. It took an enormous effort.

'Joe,' I said.

The doctor started talking about how they had tried to revive him and how, unfortunately, they hadn't succeeded, and how they had been waiting until I was strong enough to bear the shock.

One morning I felt for the first time that I was really waking up and that I wasn't stuck somewhere on the brink of unconsciousness. Over by the window a man was standing, looking out. When he turned I saw that it was Detective Chief Inspector Ramsay.

'You were lucky to survive that crash,' he said. 'You were wearing a seatbelt, but Mr Foreman wasn't. I suppose there's a moral there.'

'I'm glad there's one somewhere. So, is the inquiry over?'

'More or less.'

I forced myself to think. My mind felt so slow. 'He must have had help,' I said. 'Who collected the docket from the firm of solicitors? The woman who said she was me. It was Tania, wasn't it?'

'We've interviewed Miss Lucas,' said Ramsay. 'She admitted carrying out tasks on his behalf.'

'Criminal tasks.'

'She claims she had no suspicion of anything criminal.'

'She was pretending to be me.'

'She said that must have been a misunderstanding.'

'Bollocks,' I said. 'They were sleeping together, you know.'

Ramsay coughed. 'I've no evidence of that,' he said. 'Not that it would be relevant. Except possibly to show she was in thrall to him.'

'In thrall? You mean she's a weak woman? So she's not to be charged with being an accomplice to murder, interfering with the course of justice?'

'We're not sure there's a reasonable chance of a conviction.'

'What about the company?'

'In administration, pending investigation of certain irregularities.'

'You mean Joe was stealing from his clients.'

'That has been suggested,' said Ramsay.

'And presumably Tania knew nothing about that either.'

Ramsay shrugged instead of replying. That *was* his reply.

'I suppose at least you accept that Joe killed Frances?'

'Yes, we do. We're assuming that Mrs Shaw knew, or at least suspected, what he had done and was going to expose him.'

'That makes sense.' She was clearly troubled. 'What about the deaths of Milena and Greg?' I asked. 'Do you also accept Joe killed them?'

'We've reopened the file.'

'You don't sound very grateful to me.'

'Your role in the investigation has been mixed,' said Ramsay, 'but at an appropriate time . . .'

'Is that what you meant when you said the inquiry wasn't completely over?'

'Did I?'

'More or less, you said.'

He paused, seeming shifty, ill-at-ease.

'When this accident happened, or shortly before,' he said, 'you had developed suspicions of Mr Foreman's role in the case.'

I suddenly felt under threat. 'How do you mean?'

'What I'm trying to say, Ms Falkner,' said Ramsay, in a deliberate tone, as if he was speaking to a child, 'is that I'm working on the assumption that you had suspicions of Mr Foreman and then he realised you had these suspicions and that there was some sort of struggle while you were driving. Perhaps he tried to seize the wheel. And you crashed. Accidentally.'

I thought for a moment. 'I don't remember,' I said. 'I don't remember anything about the accident. It's a blank. Is that all right?'

'Yes,' said DI Ramsay. 'That'll do.'

I WALKED TO FERGUS'S HOUSE with the box in both hands. It was early, a soft dawn breaking over the rooftops. Even here, in the streets of London, birds were singing all around me.

Fergus was waiting. He opened the door before I knocked and stepped out to join me, kissing me on both cheeks and giving me a small smile.

'Ready?' I asked.

'Ready.'

We didn't talk. After twenty minutes or so we left the road and entered the Heath, making our way along the empty paths to the wilderness. We could no longer see the city glittering in the pale sunlight, or hear the noise of cars. I remembered that other dawn when I had walked there: then it had been winter and I had come alone to talk to Greg. Standing under the boughs of an oak tree, I turned to Fergus.

'It began like this,' I said. 'The alarm went and he woke and kissed me on the mouth and said, "Good morning, gorgeous, did you have nice dreams?" and I muttered something thickly in reply. He got out of bed and pulled on his dressing gown. He went downstairs and made us both a cup of tea, and he brought mine upstairs—which was what he always did, every morning. He watched me struggle up to a sitting position. Then he had a shower. He sang in the shower, loudly. It was "The Long and Winding Road".

'Mornings were always a bit of a rush and that morning was no different. He put on his clothes, brushed his teeth, didn't bother shaving, then went downstairs, where I joined him, still not dressed. He didn't have time for a proper breakfast. He bustled around, making coffee, finding a folder he needed. Then the post arrived. We heard it clatter onto the floor and he went to get it. He opened it standing up, tossing junk mail onto the table. He opened the envelope containing Marjorie Sutton's signatures or, rather, Joe's practice versions of them. He read Milena Livingstone's message. He didn't understand what he was looking at but he was puzzled. He tossed the sheet of paper onto the table, along with the rest of the discarded post, because he was late and in a hurry. The last time I saw him, he had a piece of toast in his mouth and he was running out of the door, keys in one hand, briefcase in the other.

'He drove to work and got there by about nine. He made himself and Tania a pot of coffee, then went through his post and his emails, which he answered. Joe wasn't there—he'd left a message with Tania that he was going to see a client. Then you arrived, to help with the new software that was being installed. Greg sat on his desk, swinging his legs, and talked to you about the IVF treatment I was going to have. He said he was sure it would turn out all right in the end. He was always the optimist, wasn't he? Then he had a meeting with one of his clients. After that, he went out to lunch with you at the little Italian place round the corner from the office, and he ate spaghetti with clams and drank a glass of tap water, because he had just decided that bottled water was immoral.

'You talked about running, compared times. You went back to work and he went into his office and shut the door. The phone rang and it was Milena. She asked if he had received the page of signatures in the post and he replied that he had. She said she was sure that an intelligent man like him must have grasped its implications and Greg responded sharply that he didn't deal in suspicions and implications and put down the phone.'

'Is this all true?' asked Fergus.

It was starting to rain and the drops felt cold and good on my face.

'Most of it,' I said. 'Some of it's the sort of thing that must have happened. The rest of it is what I tell myself in the middle of the night.

'After he had put the phone down he sat for a while, pondering. Then he went into Joe's office to ask him about it, but Joe still wasn't there and he wasn't answering his mobile. So he called up Marjorie Sutton's files and went through them carefully. After he'd done that he rang her and made an appointment to see her the following day. He said it was urgent.

'He was going to go home after that. He'd promised me that we'd have a proper evening together. I was going to make risotto and he was going to buy a good bottle of red wine. We would make love and then have a meal together. But, as he was preparing to leave, the phone rang and it was Joe, saying something odd had just happened concerning Marjorie Sutton and they needed to talk. Greg was relieved to get the call: in spite of himself, he'd been worried about those signatures. He told Joe he'd been trying to reach him about the same subject, but perhaps they could do it the next day. He had a date with his wife. Joe insisted. He said it wouldn't take long, could Greg pick him up at King's Cross?

'Greg rang me. He said, "Ellie, I know I said I'd be home early, but I'm going to be a bit delayed. I'm really sorry."

'And I said, "Fuck, Greg, you promised."

'And he replied, "I know, I know, but something's come up."

'And I said, "Something always comes up."

'"I'll explain later," he said. "I can't talk now, Ell."

'And I should have asked him if everything was all right, and I should have told him to take care, and that it didn't matter if he was late, and I should have said I loved him very, very much. Or no, no, that's not it, that's not it at all. I should have told him to come home at once, to cancel whatever arrangement he had made. I should have shouted and insisted and said I was upset and I needed him. I could have done. I nearly did. A whole other story unwinds from that, the story that never happens and which I'll never get to tell, which is about a long life and happiness. Instead, I said goodbye rather coldly and slammed the phone down, and that was the last time I heard his voice, except on my answering machine.

'You heard the argument, anyway, or at least his end, because you came into his office halfway through. He put down the phone and turned to you, saying I was a bit pissed off with him, and you told him you were sure it would blow over.

'When he was alone again, he thought of me feeling downcast about not getting pregnant, and suddenly his irritation seeped away and he simply felt tender. So he sent me a text. "Sorry sorry sorry sorry. Im a stupid fool."

'He stood up. He put on his jacket. He put his head round Tania's door and said he'd see her tomorrow. He waved at you as he went. He ran down the stairs two at a time, the way he always did. He got into the car and drove to King's Cross. Five minutes, and he'd drive home and barely be late.

'He pulled up and Joe opened the passenger door and climbed in, carrying a bag. He said there was something he needed to show Greg. Of course Greg knew he could trust Joe. He loved Joe, after all, looked up to him and often turned to him for advice. So Greg innocently followed Joe's instructions and they drove east, towards Stratford, towards Porton Way. He would never have suspected anything was wrong. Why should he?

'Greg drove Joe to the disused wasteland. It was dark and cold and there was no one around. He kept asking Joe what this was all about, but he wasn't anxious, just a bit puzzled and slightly amused by the hush-hush air of it all. Joe, being Joe, would have come up with something plausible as they drove along, lots of details. It didn't matter. It would never be checked. Just so long as it kept Greg from becoming suspicious.

'Greg stopped the car when Joe told him to. He looked out of the window, to where Joe pointed. He didn't see . . . what was it? The sort of thing that's called a blunt object. It caught him just above his eyebrow, once and then again. He didn't know that Joe was his murderer—oh, Fergus, I hope he didn't know, and that the last few seconds of his life were not utter confusion and terror. No. He didn't. I know he didn't. Joe's aim was good and death came quickly.

'Joe got out and went to the spot where he had hidden Milena. He dragged her body to the car and lifted her into the passenger seat. He undid

Greg's seatbelt, pulled off the handbrake and, because the car was facing downhill, it didn't take much effort to push it a few feet until it picked up speed, careered off the bend and over the drop. He watched it hurtle to the bottom. Then Joe—who was crying by now, fat tears running down his face because he was always a great sentimentalist, and he did love Greg in his own fashion—Joe clambered down the embankment and set fire to the car and then he stood back while the flames consumed his beloved partner and friend. He was probably still crying. No, he wasn't. He didn't have time to cry. He had to get away before the fire attracted attention. The plan worked perfectly. He left two corpses, total strangers, lying together like lovers.'

I hadn't been looking at Fergus while I spoke, but now I turned to him. A single tear was running down his cheek. I reached up and, with the tip of my finger, wiped it away.

I prised the lid off the box and we crouched under the oak tree and, very slowly, I tipped the box until Greg's ashes flowed over the rim and onto the green grass. We didn't move, but Fergus held out his hand and I gripped it.

You were my best friend, you were my dear heart, my love.

A small breeze stirred the pile. Soon it would be scattered by the wind and rain. It wouldn't take long.

Fergus wanted to walk me home but I told him that today I preferred to be alone. Sometimes being alone is not so lonely as being with other people and, anyway, my heart was full of memories of happiness.

I walked back slowly through the beautiful blue morning, the sun on the nape of my neck, the air soft and warm. People flowed past me on their own journeys. When I unlocked my front door and stepped into the little hall, I almost called out that I was home. I went into the kitchen and stood in the silence that lay all around me. While I was waiting for the kettle to boil, I stepped into the sun-filled garden. I tipped my head back, closed my eyes and saw your face, the smile that was meant only for me.

nicci **french**

The writing team behind the *nom de plume* Nicci French consists of the considerable combined talents of Suffolk-based Nicci Gerrard and her husband Sean French. The couple, married for nineteen years, first met when they were journalists on the *New Statesman*. Nicci was literary editor and Sean a weekly columnist and leader writer who had won *Vogue* magazine's Writing Talent Contest in 1981, going on to become that magazine's theatre critic, as well as the *Sunday Times* deputy literary editor and television critic, and deputy editor of *New Society*.

They forged their creative partnership in 1996, with their first co-written thriller, *The Memory Game*, which became an instant hit the following year. The concept for it, Sean, remembers, had formed simultaneously in both their minds while they were out walking one day. 'I think if it had just been Nicci's idea, then she would have written the novel,' says French, 'but we really did have the idea together. Because we worked in the same area of journalism, we often read the same articles. We'd both seen a long one about the recovered memory controversy and were talking about it.'

Nicci and Sean have both written independently but as individual novelists their sales are not in the same league as Nicci French. There's clearly a very effective chemistry at work during the creative process, which Nicci describes as 'really disconcerting and exposing, like going into a tunnel together. We agree to set off down this path, then in this kind of strange mental space together, we're groping around.'

Recently, they wrote about how they get that initial spark:

Sean: People often ask us where ideas come from, and one answer is that when you're a writer you have a sort of valve attached to your brain through which all your perceptions and experiences are filtered; a valve which constantly asks: Is that something that can be turned into a book?

Years ago, when I used to write a weekly magazine column, I was cycling down a busy road near our house. A woman opened her car door and while I was still in the air a bit of me was thinking, Good, I've got something to write about this week.

I was talking to someone recently who was planning to write a thriller and was preparing for it by reading lots of other thrillers. I couldn't understand that. Of course we read thrillers, because we read all kinds of things, but they aren't much use to us as thriller writers, except negatively. If something is good, then it's been done. If I met a trawler fisherman, I could imagine that encounter becoming the subject of a thriller. When I read Martin Cruz Smith's *Polar Star*, I thought 1) What a terrific book and 2) Damn. He got there first.

Is there a lesson to be extracted from that? Maybe it's that literature and creative courses are all very well (I assume that if you want to be a writer you'll be reading and writing like crazy anyway); but if you have experience of something out there in the real world that is new and exciting, then that could be a very good start.

Nicci: Well, I think that's all true, but I'm not sure that writing makes one feel detached from reality and often feel it does exactly the opposite: makes you—no, makes me—look at life more attentively. It's not only that there's a part of you—sorry, me—that stands back a little, assessing experience as it happens; it's also that there are things that I perhaps wouldn't have paid much attention to if I wasn't a novelist. A tone of voice, a gesture, a phrase. Ordinary life becomes very rich and full of interesting detail. One of the lovely things about collaborating with Sean is that we are looking at the world together; interpreting it together. It's like a shared adventure.

A few months ago, I was invited to a school reunion and went with a mixture of avid curiosity and trepidation. I have lost touch with almost everyone I used to know and so with each face I saw, I was also seeing the face of thirty years ago. Each middle-aged woman was a teenage girl as well. We talked about the past with an urgent, giggly nostalgia; we swapped anecdotes about changing rooms, school dinners, misdemeanors. There was much that I didn't remember, or remembered differently. There was much that wasn't said—no one mentioned the nasty arguments, the bitchiness. After an hour or so, a mild sadness set in—about time passing, about lost friendships.

Then I went away and Sean and I wrote about it, turning the reunion into a crime scene, in which bitter memories surface and past scores are settled.

Things which to other people can seem tranquil and comforting can, if looked at in a certain way (in a Nicci French way, for instance) become dark and disturbing. We often say that any family, however happy, can provide the subject for a dozen thrillers. Come round to our house at breakfast and I'll show you what I mean.

Taken from the Macmillan Minotaur website: www.momentsincrime/nicci_french

DEATH OR GLORY

MICHAEL ASHER

It's June 1942 and Sergeant Tom Caine is in trouble. He's a first-class commando with a reputation for sometimes disobeying orders when he believes he knows a better way.

Now, if he is to avoid court-martial, Caine must lead his men on a suicidal rescue mission. Ranged against him are the rampaging forces of Rommel's Afrika Korps, the scorching sands of the Sahara, and the hard fact that if he can't rescue First Officer Maddaleine Rose, an attractive secret agent stranded behind enemy lines, he'll have to kill her . . .

1

Lieutenant Rowland Green was bleeding to death. He had been hit by a 9mm dum-dum round that had plunged into his armpit and ruptured out through his back in a shower of gore. Sergeant Tom Caine tore open Green's shirt and applied a shell dressing, but it was like trying to stem a dam-burst with blotting paper. Blood soaked into his khaki drill shorts. 'You'll be all right, sir,' Caine said. 'It's not too bad.' He pressed the lieutenant's right hand down on the pad and told him to keep it there. '*Orderly*,' he bellowed. 'I need morphine—*now*.'

Medical Orderly Maurice Pickney heard Caine but was focused on another task. Squatting in a slit-trench, he was trying to prize a Mills grenade from the fingers of Private 'Tinkerbell' Jones, who had been shot in the act of hurling it. Jones had a critical wound in the abdomen and was in shock. Pickney spoke reassuringly to him, holding his wrist in a vice-like grip with one hand, forcing his fingers back with the other. If Jones released the grenade suddenly, they would have about five seconds to live. A moment later Pickney was gripping the steel pineapple tight in his palm, wondering what to do with it. He found the pin lying in the dust and slid it back carefully into place. 'We're out of morphine, Sarn't Caine,' he yelled.

Caine swore savagely. From further down the line, he could hear Corporal Harry 'Cope' Copeland demanding a casualty report from each trench in turn. From Caine's left came the booming voice of Gunner Fred Wallace, a six foot seven regular soldier from Leatherhead. 'I seen a Jerry throwing a potato-masher,' he was saying. 'I shot him, but I didn't mark where the grenade landed, and just as I was squeezing the trigger a second time, it went off. Didn't even know I'd been hit till I saw the blood.'

The attack had been over no more than a minute, but to Caine it already seemed like a dream. The Germans, Panzer Grenadiers of Rommel's 90th Light Division, had launched the assault from about 200 yards. Caine's men—No. 1 Troop, Middle East Commando—had risen to meet them. Time had seemed to stand still. Caine's memories of the fight were a sequence of disjointed images—Lieutenant Green howling as he shot an enemy with his Colt; Fred Wallace dancing madly like a giant marionette, blasting away with his Bren; Harry Copeland, the battalion's champion sniper, drilling shots from his .303; men falling, men thrashing, men entwined together so you couldn't tell friend from foe.

The desert sky was an open furnace. The stones round the trenches were so hot they scorched bare flesh: inside, it was too hot to move, almost too hot to think. The commandos had been awake more than thirty hours, thanks to the Benzedrine they'd swallowed, but the amphetamine haze was wearing thin. Caine felt exhausted. He checked that the drum magazine on his Tommy gun was still firmly in place. He was the only man in the battalion to use this 100-round mag, giving his 'trench-sweeper' more than four times the fire-power of any other. Some of the lads scoffed at his 'Al Capone' shooter, but few of them had the powerful shoulders and biceps that were needed to brace the weapon properly.

Caine wasn't much above average height but seemed top-heavy with muscle. A veteran at twenty-three, his combat experience was reflected in the determined set of his chin and the cool steadiness of his slate-grey eyes. About four miles to the west he could see dust-clouds kicked up by Panzer Army tanks gathering on the edge of minefields that protected the Box. From the ridge behind him there was the continual crash of twenty-five-pounder field-guns, manned by men of the Royal Horse Artillery. Caine knew that Jerry's 88mm guns would open up any minute.

He felt Green's fingers on his wrist. 'Your fannies,' the lieutenant said weakly. 'Ditch them. The enemy will use them as an excuse to execute you.'

The 'fanny' was the combination knuckleduster-dagger issued only to the Middle East Commando, and Caine saw what the lieutenant meant. If the Germans found them—not to mention the cheesewire and explosive charges some of the lads had—they would execute them as 'assassins'.

'Don't worry, sir, I'll tell the men to bury them,' Caine said. Green didn't answer, and Caine saw at once that he was dead. Harry Copeland pivoted into the trench, his face a mask of dried blood and dust. He was a good-looking ex-Service Corps driver, with a prominent Adam's apple. He stared at Green's corpse. 'Poor blighter,' he said and settled back on his haunches.

He licked lips that were cracked with thirst. 'You got water?'

Caine unslung a water-bottle, offered it to him. 'Go steady with it,' he rasped. Cope drank in short gulps, then pulled out two Player's Navy Cut cigarettes and handed one to Caine. 'You all right, Tom?'

Caine touched his face and realised it was smeared with his troop officer's blood. 'Yep,' he nodded. He tilted his head towards Green's body. 'Twenty years old and straight out of OCTU,' he said. 'First time in combat he cops one and lands me with command of the troop.'

'Not new to you, is it, mate,' Cope commented. He was one of the few who was aware that Caine had been an officer in the Royal Engineers; what he didn't know was why Caine had fallen from grace.

Caine shook his Zippo lighter out of its protective rubber condom, and lit the squashed fag. 'What's the damage?' he asked.

'Ammo's down to about ten rounds a man, fifty each for the Brens. Not counting the boys on the outpost, the troop's down to seventeen men. It's not exactly what you'd call a viable fighting unit.'

Caine had almost forgotten the dozen wounded men posted on a ridge a thousand yards to the west. They had all been hit the previous day, and Lieutenant Green had deployed them on the outpost at first light. He had assured them that they wouldn't be abandoned. Caine took a glance over the lip of the trench. He couldn't see the men on the outpost, but he could hear the crackle of their Brens—proof that they were still holding out.

An 88mm shell burst on the escarpment above them, near enough to shower them with rock fragments. A moment later another man pitched into the trench—'Prissy' Hogg, a runner from HQ Troop. 'Where's the boss?'

Caine gestured at Green's body. 'I'm the boss.'

'Orders from the OC,' Hogg said. 'You're to withdraw at sunset, at 1845 hours. The whole Battle Group's being pulled out.'

'What about the wounded lads on the outpost?'

'Commando practice is to abandon the wounded.'

'Mr Green promised them they wouldn't be ditched.'

'Nothing you can do,' Hogg said. 'Leave 'em.'

'I'll be damned if I will. I'm going to pull them out, and I'm coming back with you to get the say-so from the OC.'

'Right you are,' Hogg said. 'We can cover each other.'

The squadron command post lay in a redoubt about 200 yards along the escarpment. It wasn't far but with enemy guns spewing steel it might have been the other end of the earth. Caine and Hogg zigzagged along the ridge at a low crouch, taking turns to run and cover. Twenty yards from the redoubt, Caine felt the waft of a bullet against his cheek. The slug slapped into Hogg, who screamed, waving a smashed wrist, pumping arterial blood. Caine was yelling, 'Get down,' when he heard another bullet hit the runner's chest with a smack like a massive punch.

Caine found Hogg on his back, eyes gaping vacantly. 'Bloody hell,' he grunted. Another round ricocheted off a boulder near by. Caine rolled and dived for cover behind a slope. Then, keeping below the brow, he crawled towards the HQ sangar. It seemed for ever before he made it.

'Sarn't Caine, No. 1 Troop,' he bawled. 'I want to see the OC.'

Major Kenneth Crawford, a chubby man with spectacles, crept to the sangar entrance. 'What's your situation, Sergeant?'

'We've taken heavy casualties, sir. I don't think we can stand another attack.'

'It'll be sundown soon. Jerry won't be back before first light tomorrow. By that time, God willing, we'll be long gone.'

'Very good, sir, but I've got wounded on that ridge to the west. I want your permission to bring them in.'

'Just leave them, Caine. They'll be accorded the rights of war.'

'No, they won't. They're carrying fannies, cheesewire and God knows what else. If the Jerries find commando weapons, they'll shoot 'em.'

The OC didn't seem to be taking in his words. 'Rommel has broken through the Gazala Line. The whole Eighth Army is in retreat.'

At that moment a shell whistled in, striking the redoubt with a direct hit. All Caine remembered later was a flash of orange and black, and several burning bodies being flipped into the air. The next thing he knew he was being shaken by the squadron second-in-command, Captain Robin Sears-Beach, a truculent officer with a gamecock walk and a disturbing absence of chin. 'You're all right, Caine. Get back to your position.'

Caine did a mental body check: other than the familiar scorch of thirst in his mouth, there was no pain anywhere. 'You got water, sir?' he wheezed.

'Use your own,' Sears-Beach snapped.

Caine scrabbled for his bottle, took a blissful gulp. 'The section on the outpost. They're cut off.'

'Leave them. Just get the rest of the troop out when the time comes.'

Caine's eyes smouldered. 'You don't dump your mates,' he said.

The captain gripped his wrist. 'Don't argue with me, Caine. I'm acting OC, and I said leave them. Now, get back to your troop.'

By the time Caine had crawled back to his position the lowering sun cast strange loops of shadow that gave the battlefield a surreal look. The pressure of enemy artillery had eased. Caine threw himself into his slit-trench. Wallace was bracing his Bren gun on its bipod legs, in stand-to position. Copeland, brewing tea on a Primus stove, raised his eyes.

'Was that the HQ position going up?'

'Yep. Whole bunker got wiped. Sears-Beach has assumed command.'

'That turd,' Wallace groaned, waving a saucer-sized hand at the hordes of flies that had invaded the trench the moment the heat had begun to wane.

The tea was hot, sweet and strong, and they drank it crunching desperately on hard-tack biscuits, flapping away flies. Cope relieved Wallace on the Bren and the big man squatted next to Caine. Fred Wallace—rugby-prop, champion boxer and the Commando's best Bren marksman—was so enormous that Caine was surprised that any enemy sniper could ever miss him. When he'd finished his tea, the big man drew out his pet back-up weapon—the twin-barrelled sawn-off Purdey shotgun he carried in a home-made pouch on his belt.

'I don't know why you carry that thing,' Caine commented. 'It's an illegal firearm. If the Boche find that on you, you really will be in trouble.'

Wallace peered happily through both smoothbore barrels. 'Purdey's got me out of more scrapes than I've had hot dinners. I couldn't part with her.'

Cope said, 'A red Very light has just gone up from the outpost.'

'That's the distress signal,' Caine said. 'They can't hold out any longer.'

The sun had gone down and the landscape was drained of its wild sunset colours. The wind had dropped, but trails of smoke and dust still drifted languidly across the desert like gossamer veils. Caine pointed out a gully that ran from the bottom of the salient as far as the outpost ridge. 'I'm going to bring those lads in,' he said.

'I'm with you, skipper,' Wallace said.

Caine shook his head. 'You're wounded.'

Wallace grinned. 'I've had worse than this on a night's boozing in Cairo. Anyhow, you'll never do it on your own.'

Cope sat back on his haunches. 'I think you may have overlooked one small factor. Some of those boys will be stretcher-cases. How's that going to work? You're going to ferry them one by one?'

Caine nodded. It was true that he hadn't considered the stretcher-cases.

Cope pointed down the salient to a knot of lorries. Most were wrecked but not all. 'I reckon there's at least one three-tonner down there that's in good nick. We could drive it up the wadi and shift the lot of them in one bash. If we've got juice, we needn't head back to the Battle Group rendezvous. We could drive straight to the fall-back at Jaghbub. Can you find the way?'

'Yep,' Caine said, 'but I don't know about "we". I'm not having you getting in the shit for me.'

'What d'you mean?' Wallace demanded. 'It's "commando initiative", innit? If those lads get caught with their fannies, they're dog meat.'

'Sears-Beach didn't see it that way.'

'Sears-*Bitch* is a bonehead.'

'And if we *do* get in the shite,' said Cope, grinning, 'We'll just say you ordered us to do it.'

Caine gave in. He knew he shouldn't be putting their lives at risk like this, but their loyalty moved him almost to tears.

There were still a few minutes of light left when they made it to the 3-tonner. Before leaving, Caine had passed command of the troop over to Corporal 'Todd' Sweeney, the next most senior non-commissioned officer after Copeland. He told Sweeney to extract the unit the moment darkness fell, and to make a tactical withdrawal to the Battle Group RV behind the ridge. Sweeney, a balding ex-military policeman, didn't seem happy. 'What am I supposed to say if Captain Sears-Beach wants to know where you are?'

'Tell him the truth,' Caine cut in. 'Say we're missing in action.'

As they reached the wagon, the RHA battery on the ridge launched a walloping barrage. They hurled themselves flat and didn't move until the bombardment stopped. Caine sloped off to make a quick inspection of the vehicle, and was back in five minutes. 'Looks like the driver took a round in the head. I doubt that the lorry was hit, because she's carrying a load of flimsies. They'd have gone off like a rocket.'

'Flimsies' were four-gallon cans of petrol, packed two to a wooden crate, so called because of their notorious tendency to leak. 'That'll solve the juice problem,' Cope said.

'Yep, but we'll need to get rid of some if we're going to fit the boys in.'

They moved to the lorry, where Copeland and Wallace started passing flimsies out of the back. Caine removed the dead driver and laid him in the sand. 'You take the tailboard,' he told Cope. 'Fred, there's a hatchway up in the cab roof. Can you fix the Bren there?'

'I'll have a look.'

Caine was in the driver's seat and about to hit the starter when Cope banged on the back of the cab. 'How are they going to know it's us?' he demanded. 'We don't want 'em opening up on us.'

Caine fumbled in his haversack for the Very pistol. 'Thanks, Harry. I completely forgot. The signal is a blue Very light.'

He stuck the pistol out of the open window and squeezed the trigger.

There was a bang, followed by a flash of brilliant blue light. As if in answer, there were more crashes of artillery fire from the top of the escarpment.

Caine toed the starter and the engine burst into life. Managing a big lorry in the desert at night wasn't easy, but as a sapper mechanic he'd been attached to 7th Armoured Division—the 'Desert Rats'—from the start of the war. He had as much desert driving experience as anyone, and more than most.

He nursed the vehicle slowly into the gully, his eyes pinned on the way ahead. Daylight had faded out completely, and there was no moon—he drove by feel and starlight. The one thing he fervently hoped was that there was no enemy night-patrol hidden in the darkness—with all that petrol in the back, a single round could turn them into a fireball.

Caine drove forward slowly, all his senses alert. The truck grated over rough boulders. Occasional shells whizzed overhead. The ridge was only a thousand yards from where they'd started, but it seemed an age before they arrived. Caine cut the engine and they sheltered for a moment in the lee of an escarpment, watching enemy shells starbursting on the Box behind them. Return fire from the RHA was desultory now, and Caine guessed there was only one gun left, firing for effect. That meant the entire Middle East Commando—or what was left of it—had gone. They would soon be joining the defeated remnants of the Eighth Army limping back to Egypt—the worst defeat the British had suffered since Dunkirk.

'All right,' Caine said. 'We go up spread out five yards apart, and carefully does it. We don't want any accidents.'

The ridge was an easy enough climb, but too noisy for Caine's liking. What if the lads had failed to spot the Very light? Caine broke over the ridge and spotted a faint flutter of white in the darkness. 'Don't shoot!' he screamed. 'It's Tom Caine, Number One Troop.'

A voice came out of the darkness. 'Hell's bells, about bleeding time.'

Caine moved forward and almost bumped into Corporal Jake Campbell. He saw that he was on the verge of collapse and put his arm round the corporal's shoulders to steady him. 'Thank God,' Campbell whispered. 'Mr Green promised, but we thought you wasn't coming.'

'Where are the rest?'

Campbell pointed weakly to a low rise only a few yards away.

'Listen, Jake,' Caine told him gently. 'Go down the slope, and you'll find our three-tonner. Get in the cab. You've done enough. We'll take it from here.'

'Well, you'd best get a move on, because we spotted enemy patrols creeping through the minefield just before last light.'

Campbell staggered off. Caine and the others moved to the bank, where half a dozen commandos sat or lay. Of the twelve men Green had posted on the ridge that morning, only these six were left alive.

'Jesus Christ,' Wallace said. 'What the hell happened here?'

'Hell happened,' someone gasped, and Caine recognised 'Quiff' Smithers, the section medical orderly. He was lying on the ground. 'I tried to patch 'em up,' Smithers said, 'till I took three rounds in the leg.'

Caine realised that Smithers was virtually paralysed. 'You've done a cracking job,' he said. 'You deserve a medal for this.'

'Stuff their medals,' Smithers groaned. 'Just get us out of this shit-hole.'

They had no stretchers, but they scoured the dead men's haversacks for ponchos and used them to ferry the wounded downhill, worst cases first. To spare Wallace's wounded arms, Cope and Caine did the carrying, while Wallace covered them with the Bren. As they ferried the last casualty—Smithers—over the brow of the ridge, the giant said softly, 'There's a light.'

'Forget it,' Caine said. 'Let's get this man in the wagon.' While Cope was making Smithers comfortable, Caine pulled out of his haversack a small surprise he had been saving for this moment—a Hawkins grenade. The flat canister of explosive had a time-pencil attached: Caine half-buried the bomb in the sand and crushed the time-pencil.

Caine hauled himself into the driver's seat and hit the starter. There was a dead click. He tried again: the mechanism failed to respond. He hurled himself out of the cab, wondering what had persuaded him to plant the grenade before he'd even started the engine. If he couldn't start the lorry within five minutes, the bomb would blast the wagon to kingdom come.

He took a deep breath. He'd been working with engines all his life and had an instinctive feel for them. He opened the bonnet. Knowing there would be no second chance, his fingers walked deftly from spark plugs to engine block, feeling for faults, testing connections. Finally, he felt the battery: one of the leads had come loose. As he tightened the screw, he heard Wallace shout, 'Enemy on the ridge!' There was a clatter of submachine gun fire and he rushed back to the cab. He hit the starter. The engine roared.

Caine revved the engine and changed into second gear, aware of the rat-tat-tat of Schmeisser 9mm submachine pistols, the pop of Gewehr 41 semi-autos. He twisted the steering wheel, veering left, then right, already going faster than was safe. There were screams from the wounded men in the back. Above him, Wallace was firing a steady stream of single shots. Caine knew his ammo wouldn't last much longer. At the tailboard, Cope was punching off rounds as steadily as was possible from the bucking vehicle.

Right then, Caine heard a stomach-churning whine, followed by a detonation that seemed to lift the world up and flip it over. The lorry jiggered as a blast wave belched over it. Caine was thinking that it was an awfully big blast for a Hawkins bomb when he heard a second shattering explosion, followed by a third, smaller one. Caine heard Wallace yell, 'The Gunners! God bless the Horse Gunners!'

It struck him that they had just been saved by shells fired by the Royal Horse Artillery, from the last 25-pounder on the Box. The third explosion had been the Hawkins bomb going up. If he had ever in his life made any disparaging comment about the Artillery, he begged silent forgiveness. It was the finest damn gunnery he'd ever seen.

LIEUTENANT GENERAL Sir Claude Auchinleck, Commander-in-Chief, Middle East Forces, stood in his war room, studying one of the huge maps tacked to his wall. The defeat of the Eighth Army on the 'impregnable' Gazala Line was the worst reverse he had suffered in his thirty-year military career. Allied forces were now in full retreat, and the Axis would soon turn its attention to Tobruk, the last Libyan port in British hands.

The 'Auk' had been up until two o'clock that morning, presiding over an agitated conference on the fate of Tobruk. Now, though, his gaze was focused on what appeared to be a green blob on the vast blue expanse of the Mediterranean—the island of Malta. Malta was the key. 'Force and fraud are, in war, the two cardinal virtues,' he recited to himself.

'Thomas Hobbes,' a voice grated behind him. The Auk swung round to see Major General Dorman-Smith, his Deputy Chief of the General Staff.

Dorman-Smith saluted. A lean Anglo-Irishman, he and Auchinleck had been close since they had served together in India. The Auk considered him the most original strategist of his time.

'I was just thinking about Malta,' the C-in-C said. 'This may be the time for fraud. What do you think Rommel will do?'

Dorman-Smith surveyed the map with a penetrating gaze. 'He'll take Tobruk. But then he'll be faced with a dilemma. Does he go for Malta or the Nile? He can't do both, because Malta is a job for the Luftwaffe, and he doesn't have the air power to execute two operations. The Malta option would leave the Panzer Army twiddling its thumbs, and if there's one thing Rommel cannot stand, it's inaction. He'll race for the Nile like a bat out of hell, and try to catch us with our pants down.'

The Auk nodded: as usual, Dorman-Smith's reading of Rommel's character coincided closely with his own. He was about to add something when three staff officers entered: Brigadier Francis de Guingand, Director of Military Intelligence; Lieutenant Colonel Dudley Clarke, chief of the Deception Service 'A' Force; and Captain Julian Avery of the Special Operations Executive's G(R) wing. The brigadier, a tall, black-haired officer said, 'Runefish is outside, sir—shall I wheel her in?'

To full-blooded men largely deprived of the company of women, First Officer Maddaleine 'Maddy' Rose, Women's Royal Naval Service, was a provocative sight. She wore an immaculately starched khaki drill uniform that only served to enhance her striking figure. She possessed an air of elegance that was set off by the officer's rings on her shoulders and the blue and white tricorne hat cocked jauntily on her boyishly cropped golden hair. Her features were expressive, her eyes—an almost supernatural sea-green shade—seemed to conjure depths of solemnity beyond her years.

'Good afternoon, First Officer,' Auchinleck said. 'It's a pleasure to meet you at last.' He sat down at the head of the conference table, but the others remained standing.

Dorman-Smith pointed to the .45 Colt automatic she wore on her webbing belt. 'That's rather ambitious for a lady. Can you use it?'

Rose gave him a shy smile. 'I'm close-quarter-battle trained, sir. I did the Grant-Taylor course at Jerusalem and I qualified as a marksman.'

Dorman-Smith seemed impervious to her charm. 'What else can you do that an *ordinary* officer can't?'

Dudley Clarke, who had selected Maddy for the Runefish mission, looked daggers at the DCGS. 'I think you can safely assume, General, that First Officer Rose is up to the job. She's a qualified parachutist, she's trained in signals and medical skills, and she speaks German, French and Italian fluently.'

Dorman-Smith shot him an amused glance. 'Really?' he said. 'And all that just to escort some dispatches to London?'

'Excuse me, sir,' Clarke said acidly. 'I think we should do well to remember how vital this job is. First Officer Rose is a volunteer, and is exposing herself to considerable risk.'

The Auk gestured to a chair beside him. 'Sit down, Miss Rose. Colonel Clarke tells me that you are fully dedicated to your assignment. Is that so?'

'Absolutely, sir.'

De Guingand produced a slim attaché case and slid it towards Rose. 'This contains the dispatches,' the Auk said. 'You are to take them to London and present them to Prime Minister Churchill himself. They are for his eyes only. If for any reason the documents are endangered, you are to destroy them—the attaché case has a self-destruct mechanism. If necessary you will repeat the message verbally to the prime minister.'

'Very good, sir.'

'You will tell Mr Churchill that there is no longer any chance of holding Tobruk. The Eighth Army has been more fragmented by its defeat at Gazala than the Axis knows. Half of our aircraft are missing. We have lost more than eighty thousand men. Our logistical system is in ruins. Worst of all, more than twenty-five thousand men have deserted, and the Army is a hair's breadth from mutiny. Our assessment is that Rommel is likely to push into Egypt immediately. If so, the Eighth Army will almost certainly be destroyed. You will say that the commander-in-chief therefore requests permission to evacuate Egypt forthwith. That completes the message. Repeat it, please.'

Maddy did so flawlessly.

'Very good,' the Auk said. 'Now, what are the arrangements, Avery?'

Julian Avery stepped forward. He was twenty-six years old, with a pale moustache and straw-coloured hair. The most junior officer present, he smiled encouragingly at Rose, and she beamed back. A close bond had grown up between them during her instruction.

'A staff car will be here to pick you up within the hour. Your aircraft is due to take off at 1830 hours. You will find on board everything you might need in an emergency—parachute, medical kit, survival kit and a biscuit-tin transmitter with details of an emergency SOS frequency. Your personal code, as you know, is Runefish. Do you have any last questions?'

Maddy thought for a second. 'If I am asked why this message was delivered in person, what am I to say?'

Avery nodded with approval; he had anticipated the question. 'You will say we have reason to believe all wireless messages from GHQ are being intercepted and that our codes have been compromised. In view of the grave nature of this message, we could not risk it to the airwaves.'

'Anything else?' Auchinleck enquired.

'No, sir.'

'Then I have one final duty to perform.' He took a small container like a jewel-box from his pocket and picked out what looked like an ancient and slightly yellow molar. He held it up for her inspection. 'Potassium cyanide,' he said, 'Inside a hollow tooth made of Bakelite, fitted to your gum by gutta-percha. Bite hard and the poison kills instantly. If, God forbid, the worst came to the worst, you might wish to do the right thing, rather than let such secrets fall to the enemy.' Auchinleck fixed his clear blue eyes on her.

'I am not ordering you to take it, Miss Rose. That choice is yours.'

The other officers were standing stiffly, their eyes riveted to her. She supposed they were wondering if she would be shocked. In fact, she'd accepted death as her wages for this job the moment she'd volunteered for it. She picked up the box and put it away without ceremony.

The C-in-C rose. Maddy took the attaché case and followed suit. The Auk put his hand out and she shook it. 'The message you're carrying is of crucial importance. I can't tell you, Miss Rose, how greatly I admire your courage. God speed, and the very best of luck.'

Maddy marched out of the room, flanked by Avery and Clarke.

'A remarkable woman,' Auchinleck said to de Guingand. 'Think she can pull it off?'

'She seems a pussycat, but she's got steel claws. She was engaged to an SOE agent, Peter Fairfax, who was dropped into France last year. He was betrayed. The Gestapo gave him the full works—electric shocks, burning cloths on the genitals—horrible business. When he wouldn't talk, they shot him and cut his hands off. Rose is carrying the cross.'

'In times like these, it helps.'

'She won't be overlooked, sir, that's for certain. She stands out like the fairy on a Christmas tree.'

LESS THAN A MILE away, the man who called himself Hussain Idriss was leaning on the radiator of a beaten-up Standard, with a hand-scrawled sign reading TAXI in the windscreen. Hussain had been many things in his life, but today he was a taxi driver. He had borrowed the banger from a friend, and parked near GHQ. He was dressed in cheap European clothes and there was a blue shadow on his chin.

Hussain could pass as a Cairene anywhere, even though he was a German and his real name was Johann Eisner. Born in Cairo of German parents, his education at English schools in Egypt had alternated with spells at boarding school in Germany. When he was called up for military service, the Abwehr—German Military Intelligence—realised they had a unique asset—a German who could pass undetected as an Egyptian. Eisner had passed all tests with flying colours. Not even his closest instructors had divined the one serious flaw in his character that might clash with his excellence as a field agent.

The previous night Eisner had been playing a role that suited him better—a millionaire Egyptian playboy, at the exclusive Kit-Kat cabaret. The club was a magnet for GHQ staff as well as officers on leave, and a place where he frequently picked up information. It was astonishing how rapidly British officers dropped their guard in the presence of half-dressed young women, especially after a couple of cocktails.

One of the cabaret girls, a French blonde called Natalie, was in his pay. She had no idea that he was German. Last night, Natalie had sidled up to his table and asked him to buy her a bottle of champagne.

'You know I have many lovers?' she said in French.

'*Naturellement*,' Eisner said, 'you are the most charming girl in Cairo.'

'Earlier tonight,' she purred, 'I was entertaining a young captain from British headquarters in my flat. He was upset, so I coaxed the problem out of him. He said that he'd been given a most important assignment carrying papers to London, but at the last minute the job had been given to a woman officer of the Royal Navy.'

Eisner's ears pricked up. He poured Natalie a second glass of bubbly. 'Did he mention the nature of these papers?'

'He did not say but he told me that they were for the prime minister himself. That is why he was angry—he felt that his work might have been noticed at last. It would also be his first chance to get back to England since the start of the war. He fell asleep and I went through his briefcase. Among the papers was a schedule entitled "Operation Runefish". I copied it down.'

Natalie paused, opened a small sequinned handbag, and handed him a neatly wadded sheet of paper. Eisner squinted at it in the dim light. It was, as she'd told him, a schedule; detailed instructions and an itinerary for someone called 'Runefish'.

Eisner read it carefully. One item of information caught his attention in particular: '*Cyanide pill to be issued*'. And Natalie had mentioned Mr Churchill. *Cyanide* and *Mr Churchill*: together they indicated something of significance might be happening. 'Where is the date, my dear?'

Natalie grimaced. 'I forgot to write it down. Tomorrow, the 12th of June.'

'Excellent. I don't suppose your lover told you the real name of the woman involved?'

She shook her head. 'No, but I found out *his* real name. He calls himself Richard Ross, but he is really Captain Julian Avery.'

Eisner realised suddenly that this talk of Natalie's lovers had unleashed an urge. He surveyed her sleek legs and gently pouting lips, and pictured her tied to his bed naked—an image so vivid it had him fingering the hilt of the stiletto he carried. He was sorely tempted to invite her back to his houseboat but fought off the compulsion. Natalie was far too valuable an asset to lose.

After leaving the club Eisner had telephoned his two contacts at GHQ—Egyptian clerical workers with Axis sympathies. The first didn't know the name Avery, but the second told him that Avery's department was G(R)—the Cairo wing of the Special Operations Executive. She was also able to confirm that a First Officer of the Women's Royal Naval Service had been seen at GHQ. It was enough to convince Eisner that this case was worth the investment of a little time.

He looked at his watch; it was half past four. If Natalie had been right about the date, then Operation Runefish was an hour behind schedule; according to the information she'd got from Avery, this Runefish was meant to be leaving GHQ at 1530 hours. But had Natalie been right? For all he knew, the schedule might have been dated last week.

He was about to give up, when a Humber staff car rumbled past. Eisner got an impression of a figure in the back seat—blonde hair under a blue and white Wren's hat. He jumped into his vehicle and followed the staff car into the stream of traffic. Luckily it wasn't as busy as usual—the news of Rommel's victory at Gazala had cleared the streets. Eisner felt ambivalent about the prospect of Rommel's arrival in Cairo. It would mean an end to his luxurious life as a spy.

The Humber turned in the right direction for the airstrip at Helwan. GHQ cars normally beetled through the city at breakneck speed, but this vehicle dawdled along. He tagged on behind, never losing sight of his quarry. Soon, the road veered into the narrow, tortuous streets of Maadi. The traffic slowed as the road became congested with donkey-carts and flocks of goats. Two vehicles ahead, the staff car had been brought to a standstill.

It occurred to Eisner that this might be a good opportunity for a photograph. He fished in his bag for his Leica. Balancing it on his knees, he pulled forward in first gear until he was abreast of the staff car's back windows; fortunately the oncoming traffic had also been halted. To his right, he could see the woman through the back window of the Humber.

He was about to lift the camera for a quick shot, when she turned her face towards him. He almost dropped the Leica in shock. He was certain that he had seen her before. It was the face of an exotic dancer he'd once seen in a nightclub.

Eisner looked away instantly; he was almost sure she hadn't noticed anything. He looked back. She was gazing straight ahead now. He raised the Leica, and clicked off a shot. The traffic was stirring, and he let the Humber pull away. In a few moments he was out of Maadi and the staff vehicle was toddling along at the same unvarying pace. Eisner normally had an excellent recall of faces, especially those of pretty girls, but the more he pondered, the less sure he was. He had glimpsed the Wren for only a fraction of a second. Perhaps she only looked like someone he'd seen before. What he could not get over, though, was that instinctive sense of recognition.

The Humber was slowing for the Military Police checkpoint outside Helwan airstrip. Security here was tight. He came to a halt and turned his vehicle round slowly enough to make sure that the staff car had passed through the barrier.

As he headed back towards the city, he decided that, whoever the woman was, her mission was worth reporting to his Abwehr controller, Major Heinrich Rohde. Eisner felt apprehensive about handing him incomplete data, yet he had no choice. For now the girl's identity would have to remain uncertain. He had the photograph, though, and one never knew what a little discreet investigation might turn up.

It was a good five minutes before Eisner became aware that a black Vauxhall was trailing him. Eisner could have kicked himself for his amateurish behaviour in changing direction in sight of a military post. British Field Security would be keeping their eyes skinned. Turning round at a checkpoint, and carrying an expensive camera for no good reason: these were enough to get him bagged.

Eisner was too seasoned a hand to panic, though. He speeded up; the Vauxhall accelerated. He slowed down to a crawl; the Vauxhall slowed. He pulled up by the side of the road; the Vauxhall stopped a discreet distance behind. Peering in the mirror, he could just make out the driver, a lean-faced Egyptian. Eisner moved off hastily. The Vauxhall followed.

They were in the backstreets of Maadi, an area Eisner knew well. For ten minutes he played hide and seek with his pursuer, hanging sharp lefts and rights at the last moment. Finally, having created an interval between them, he turned sharply down an alley he knew to be a derelict cul-de-sac.

He drove as far as he could go, stopped the car, and checked that the place was deserted. A glance in the mirror told him that the Vauxhall hadn't yet entered the alley. He opened the glove compartment, pulled out a length of wire. He jumped out of the car, leaving the door unlocked and the Leica on the passenger seat, and sprinted for the shadow of the nearest doorway. He had just made it when he heard the purr of the Vauxhall's engine.

The car pulled up about six yards from his Standard. The driver emerged—a spindly limbed man carrying a .38 Enfield six-shooter. He moved cautiously over to the Standard, peered through the side window and, bending over the driver's seat, groped with his left hand for the Leica.

Eisner was on the man in three silent bounds, looping his wire garotte round the Egyptian's throat and pulling tight. The man dropped his pistol, attempted to get his fingers under the wire that was already digging into his flesh and failed. Eisner wrenched him to the ground and, planting his knee in the pit of the man's back for purchase, he heaved on the wire with all his weight. The Egyptian thrashed frantically but Eisner held on until an artery in the man's neck popped, shooting blood along the road. He went limp.

Eisner seized the dead man by the armpits and dragged him over to the Vauxhall. He flung the body onto the back seat and trotted back to his own vehicle. He opened his boot and took out a tin of petrol. He sprinkled the interior of the Vauxhall with petrol, doused the tyres and bonnet, then laid a ten-yard trail across the uneven ground. Moving fast so that the petrol wouldn't have time to evaporate in the heat, Eisner returned the empty tin to his boot, got back behind the steering wheel, gunned the engine. He drove past the Vauxhall, struck a match, dropped it on the dark stain. He waited a second to see that it had ignited, then sped off. Just as his car turned out of the cul-de-sac, Eisner heard the whoosh of the Vauxhall bursting into flame, followed by the ear-splitting *karump* of her petrol tank going up.

Forty minutes later, as Eisner was tapping out a coded message to Heinrich Rohde from the hidden cubicle in his houseboat, an RAF Bombay, with First Officer Maddy Rose on board, took off from Helwan.

BY DAY, JAGHBUB was just a sandy depression with a few palms and the ruins of a monastery. By night, when Caine's 3-tonner limped in, it was as teeming as Piccadilly Circus on a Saturday night as a score of Allied units milled around trying to lick themselves into some kind of shape.

Caine had long since transferred his wounded to the 50th Division convoy's field ambulances. The trio's only task now was to locate Middle East Commando lines, and surrender to the blessed luxury of sleep: Caine reckoned he'd had four hours in the last forty-eight. Dog weary, they had almost given up looking when they came across the leaguer—a dismal assembly of lorries, jeeps and tents. They reported to the duty NCO and slept for fifteen hours.

Heat and flies woke them at midday and they found that they were wolfishly hungry. While they were eating, Todd Sweeney appeared. He'd come to report that he'd withdrawn the remnants of the troop to Battle Group RV without a hitch until Captain Sears-Beach had appeared demanding to see Caine. 'I told him you were missing in action,' Sweeney reported, 'but he wasn't convinced. He said he was going to report you to the commanding officer when he got back.'

'That bonehead,' Wallace swore. 'Rear-echelon pen-pusher if ever I saw one. Ex-Pay Corps or sommat.'

Sweeney's face stayed deadpan. 'He's ex-Military Police. Like me.'

'Now, how *could* I have forgotten that?' Wallace drawled, beaming with mock surprise. 'Oh, I remember. Weren't you one of them ex-Redcap boys that Sears-Beach insisted on recruiting, even though the CO said he didn't want the ranks full of dirty, snooping ex-coppers?'

Sweeney glowered at Wallace, then walked away.

'The blighter never even *tried* to cover up for us,' Wallace scoffed.

After lunch, Medical Orderly Maurice Pickney arrived to examine Wallace's shrapnel wounds and told him that they were healing nicely. Wallace went off happily to hunt down a Royal Army Ordnance Corps field workshop. He was back thirty minutes later, rolling a spare balloon tyre with his foot and carrying a replacement windscreen unit. He, Caine and Copeland set about restoring the lorry they'd picked up at the Box. They'd acquired a certain affection for her, christening her Marlene after Marlene Dietrich, and fretting that she would be returned to the King's Royal Rifle Corps—until Wallace painted out her KRRC insignia and stencilled in the ME Commando's 'fanny' badge.

They had just sat down to clean their weapons when they were confronted by the ramrod-straight figure of Staff Sergeant 'Frosty' Greaves.

'Morning, Frosty,' Caine said.

'Afternoon, Sergeant Caine,' Greaves replied. 'You are to present yourself at the battalion command post forthwith, Sarn't, if you please.'

An HQ tent of sorts had been erected inside the monastery yard, but the commanding officer had set up shop in a derelict room opening off it. As Caine and Greaves marched in, Lieutenant Colonel Hilary St Aubin was scrutinising an enormous map pinned on one wall. Behind a table on Caine's left stood Sears-Beach, holding a brass-tipped swagger-stick stiffly under his arm as if on inspection parade. To Caine's right stood a pink-faced subaltern wearing the Royal Horse Artillery badge on his field-cap. Caine had never seen him before.

The CO turned towards them, but neither Caine nor Greaves saluted. It was one of the formalities that the commandos had long ago abolished. Caine knew that the colonel was old-school—a Great War veteran with a hearty manner. Caine's nose for people was usually good, but he couldn't have said whether St Aubin was a man of genuine warmth, or the type who could cheerfully commit his men to a kamikaze mission.

'Sarn't Caine,' St Aubin said. 'Captain Sears-Beach has put you on a charge for disobeying a direct order in battle. That is a very serious breach of discipline—one that could land you in front of a court-martial.'

Caine shot Sears-Beach a piercing glance.

The officer caught the look. 'Don't dare deny it, Caine. We have an eye-witness. Lieutenant Edwards here was with the Horse Gunners on the Box and he saw everything.' He gestured towards the man with the pink face.

Edwards shifted nervously. 'Yes, I did, sir, but I reported the matter only because I thought the sergeant here deserved a medal. It was the bravest thing I've ever seen in my life.'

Caine realised with a gush of gratitude that it was Edwards' crew whose last salvos had saved them. 'That was no mean gunnery, sir,' he said. 'How on earth did you do that in the dark without scragging us?'

Edwards' blush grew deeper. 'Well, we spotted your blue flare and guessed what you were up to. We saw muzzle-flashes from the ridge and identified them as enemy weapons. We already had a range on that ridge so we lowered the elevation a fraction and put our two last shells down at its base. I'm glad it paid off.'

'*Excuse me*,' Sears-Beach cut in furiously. 'Caine is here to answer a charge.' He turned to the CO for support, but St Aubin replied with an irritated look, 'Dismissed, Captain. Escort Lieutenant Edwards and Captain Sears-Beach out please, Staff Greaves, and make sure Sergeant Caine and I are not disturbed.'

Caine fought back a wry smile. He had been marched in like a prisoner, but now it looked as if Sears-Beach was being marched out in his place.

After they had gone, St Aubin said. 'I agree with Lieutenant Edwards that you deserve a medal, Caine, but there's still no way round the fact that you disobeyed a direct order.' The CO pulled at his pipe while Caine waited in suspense. 'I know you, Caine. You have an excellent field record. I've lost a lot of good men, and I don't want to lose another. So I am prepared to make you an offer. I'm looking for someone to lead a search-and-rescue mission behind Axis lines. Do that for me, and you have my assurance that the court-martial business will be dropped. I know you're going to ask what the mission is, but I can't tell you. It's classified. I can only say that it is hazardous and that your chances of survival are about even.'

Caine gasped: the odds weren't encouraging. 'You mean I have to take it blind, sir?'

St Aubin nodded. 'Bear in mind that if you refuse, Captain Sears-Beach will press for a court-martial.'

It was blackmail pure and simple: the choice boiled down to either taking the mission or ending up with five years' hard labour.

Caine swallowed hard. 'All right, sir,' he said in a rush. 'I'll take it.'

Caine imagined he saw a glimmer of triumph in the colonel's eyes. 'Sit down,' St Aubin said. Caine pulled up a camp chair. The CO had moved over to the map again. 'What I'm going to say is for you only. You will need to tell your men something, of course, but what you tell them should be governed by the "need to know" principle.'

'Understood, sir.'

St Aubin pointed the stem of his pipe at the Cyrenaica area of northern Libya. 'Last night an RAF aircraft crossing the Gulf of Bomba was hit by Italian ack-ack fire and went down in the desert here, south of the Green Mountains. The sole passenger, a Royal Navy officer, baled out by parachute. The officer, codenamed Runefish, was a courier carrying top-secret documents for the prime minister. If the documents or the officer fall into the hands of the Boche, there will be hell to pay. These secrets are so crucial, they could change the whole course of the war. Caine, I want you to take twenty-odd men and snatch Runefish from under the Hun's nose.'

Caine let out a low whistle. 'It's going to be like finding a grain of sand in the Great Sand Sea, sir. In any case, there are tens of thousands of Axis troops between here and Cyrenaica—we'll never get through.'

'We have a good idea where Runefish went down, because the plane was being trailed by a Royal Navy Albacore spotter. Runefish was issued with a wireless set and given an emergency frequency on which to transmit an SOS signal. There aren't many Royal Navy officers swanning about behind enemy lines and this one is rather special. As to your second point, there couldn't be a better time for a small patrol to get through. Axis and Allied forces are in confusion all over the desert, each using the other's captured transport. In my opinion, it's most unlikely that you will be noticed.'

'I see, sir.'

'However, I'd be a fool to pretend that this assignment is going to be a pushover. We have word from our agents that a company of the Brandenburg Special Duties Regiment has been deployed in the area.'

'You mean the Jerries know about Runefish?' Caine cut in.

'We have to assume it's likely. So you see, getting in there is one thing. Snatching Runefish and getting out again, evading the Brandenburgers, the entire Panzer Army and the Luftwaffe is quite another. That's why I give you no more than a fifty-fifty chance of survival.'

'No point me asking what these documents are, is it, sir?'

St Aubin's forehead crinkled. 'It wouldn't be violating the "need to know" rule to tell you a little about what you would be risking your life for. These documents concern trials for a weapon the navy has been working on. 'Assegai' is a new type of glider bomb that can be launched from a submarine. It's guided to its target by a combination of radio and radar, and has a range of two hundred miles. The trial results are outlined in the documents being carried by Runefish. You can imagine the devastating effect of this weapon if used on Rommel's tanks, but I'm saying too much. I don't need to tell you what is likely to happen if the Jerries get those specifications. Not only will they be forewarned, they might even be able to reconstruct the glider bombs and use them against us. So there is your incentive, Caine. If you fail in your mission it could tip the whole balance of the war.'

For a moment, Caine stared at the CO in disbelief. 'Why entrust such a crucial mission to me?' he asked. 'Why not send a senior officer?'

Caine thought he saw a flash of irritation in the colonel's eyes but, if so, it was quickly extinguished. 'Believe me, Caine, I've precious few officers left, and none of them could match your skills and experience. Besides, you were an officer once, and you displayed remarkable leadership skills. If it weren't for your peculiar penchant for taking orders as a basis for discussion, you'd be a major by now. You could say that I'm getting an officer's skills for the price of an NCO.' St Aubin chuckled at his own joke. 'We're both members of the desert club, Caine. Unlike *some* . . .' he nodded towards the door through which Sears-Beach had disappeared, '. . . we both know that the best way to survive up the Blue isn't necessarily by adhering rigidly to the rules.'

It was St Aubin's final pitch. In so many words, if Caine had read them correctly, the CO had vindicated his action in retrieving the wounded men and tacitly condemned Sears-Beach as a hidebound fool. But the rest of the speech was so unexpected it set his internal alarm bells ringing—Caine had a nagging hunch that St Aubin had left out something vital. He was tempted to tell the CO where to stick the assignment, but he was aware that he had already given his word. There was no going back on it now.

The colonel was bending over the table, scribbling in a field message pad. 'This is a note to the Regimental Quartermaster Sergeant Major, authorising him to give you anything you ask for in terms of kit, rations, weapons, fuel and transport. You'll need three or four soft-skin vehicles and some armour. You can pick your own men. You start an hour before first light tomorrow, and you have seven days to complete the stunt—I've written down the grid reference of the point where the aircraft piled, and another for the RV where you're to be in a week's time. A Long Range Desert Group patrol is being assigned to escort you from there back to the Wire. Your recon signal is a blue Very flare. Don't be late.'

'I'll file a mission plan with the Squadron office, then, sir.'

St Aubin smiled crookedly. 'Let's keep this one off the books, shall we?'

Caine gave a start. No mission plan meant that if anything happened to St Aubin in the meantime, no one on earth would know where they were. 'Very good, sir,' he heard himself saying. Then it occurred to him that he knew nothing about the officer he was being sent to look for. 'You said Runefish was special,' he said. 'What did you mean?'

St Aubin chuckled again. 'Runefish is special because she is a woman. Her name is First Officer Maddaleine Rose, WRNS—twenty-three, blonde and, I'm told, shapely in all the right places.'

Caine felt his face drop in surprise. 'And there's one other thing I haven't mentioned,' the CO went on. 'If you are unable to extract First Officer Rose, then you are to execute her. Is that clear?'

Caine stammered a 'Yes, sir,' and stumbled out, stunned, unable to decide which appalled him most: the idea of a young woman lost in the endless Sahara, or the prospect of having to put a bullet through her head.

He was about to pass through the gap in the monastery wall when a dark figure barred his way. Sears-Beach was slapping his shin with his swagger-stick in a manner that Caine didn't like. 'What did the CO say to you, Caine?' he demanded.

'With all due respect, sir,' he said, 'that's none of your business.'

Sears-Beach took a step forward, jabbing Caine in the chest with the brass tip of his swagger-stick. 'You had better be careful what you say to me, Sergeant.'

A wave of fury burned through Caine. He was damned if he was going to stand being poked in the chest by a nincompoop, no matter what his rank. Growling with rage, he twisted the swagger-stick out of Sears-Beach's grasp and tossed it hard against the monastery wall. 'Next time you try that, *sir*,' he said softly, 'I will ram that thing so far up your arse you will need to put your hand down your throat to polish it. If you want to know what the colonel said to me, I suggest you ask him.'

Sears-Beach took a step backwards. 'I've got a long memory, Caine. By God you'd better keep your nose clean from now on, because long after the the colonel's posted, I'll still be watching you.'

He picked up the swagger-stick, jammed it under his arm and, with as much dignity as he could muster, swivelled round and marched away.

2

It took Caine twelve solid hours to get everything shipshape for the mission. Wallace and Copeland volunteered, as he'd known they would. Caine had appointed Copeland second-in-command, and Wallace his gunner and general minder. Together, they collected another twenty volunteers, mainly from the fractured Middle East Commando, but also odd stragglers from other units.

By midnight, most of the stores had been loaded on the wagons grudgingly assigned to them by the quartermaster. While the lads were brewing up tea and spooning down bully beef, Caine made a final inspection of the transport with Lance Corporal Henry 'Wingnut' Turner, an ex-Royal Army Ordnance Corps fitter. Apart from Marlene, there were two other 'long-bonnet' Bedfords, christened Vera and Judy; a six-wheel US-built Ford Marmon Herrington 6-tonner, nicknamed Gracie, with a water bowser; a Daimler armoured car; and White and Dingo scout-cars. Caine had ordered all insignia and recognition symbols removed.

Caine would have liked the little snub-nosed Dingo as his command-vehicle for the operation, but as she carried only two men, he'd settled for the White, which had room for seven. Standard Whites were open-top but this one had been modified: an armoured roof had been welded on and the tailboard replaced by rear doors of half-inch steel plate; there were two hatches in the roof of the cab with pintle-mounts for machine-guns. Both the Dingo and the White were now mounted with pairs of Vickers 'K' aircraft machine guns.

The Dingo was a state-of-the-art fighting vehicle, of which only a handful were on issue, undergoing combat trials. 'Beautiful bit of engineering,' Caine commented.

Turner grinned. 'I'm amazed you managed to prize her away, skipper.'

Caine saw Copeland gliding out of the darkness, waving some papers. 'Here's the list of volunteers,' he announced.

'Right, let's let them know what it is they've volunteered for.'

While the volunteers were gathering, Caine scanned the list: it was a good mix, a nice balance of cavalry, infantry and specialist corps men. He considered the bodies before him. They looked pitifully few against the might of the Panzer Army. Caine reminded himself what two years in the desert had taught him—nothing counted a damn against the quality of the men before them. And these were good men: mostly commando trained, all battle hardened, accustomed to the harsh discipline of the desert.

Caine launched into his briefing, and the men listened in grave silence until he mentioned that Runefish was female. This brought whoops and catcalls. He had divided the execution of Operation Runefish into four phases—move out, advance to target area, withdrawal from target area, final RV back to base. 'Friendly forces,' he said. 'None, except perhaps a few Senussi Arabs. Enemy forces: as if the Panzer Army wasn't enough, we know that a company of the Brandenburger Special Duties Regiment has been deployed in our target area. If they have been sent to find Runefish, then we'll just have to make sure we get to her before they do.'

'How are we going to recognise her, then?' asked Maurice Pickney.

'All I can tell you about her is that she's a left-handed, green-eyed blonde who speaks fluent German, Italian and French.'

Caine finished with a few generalities. 'Remember, lads,' he said. 'It's desert rules. Every man carries a map and compass and knows the next RV. No one is ever left on his own. No one goes anywhere without a full water-bottle. Every wagon carries three days' rations of food and water. If a wagon breaks down, you stay with it. If a wagon gets stranded, you stop and work out your position, or wait till someone comes for you. Anyone left alone without a clear grasp of where he is on the map is likely to feel an urge to keep moving. Don't give in to it—the Blue is a damn big place.'

He stared round at them, seeing only shadows like gathering spirits in the darkness. 'All right,' he said, 'that's it. You're volunteers, and I know you'll do a good job. The best of British to us all.'

Before dismissing the boys, Caine ordered Copeland to issue a rum ration all round. While Cope was doling it out, Caine and Wallace unrolled their flea-bags by the White scout-car. Copeland arrived a few minutes later, with a jar two-thirds full of navy-issue rum and poured three fingers into their mugs. 'That ought to warm the cockles of your heart,' he said.

The three of them lit cigarettes. They could just make out each other's faces in the starlight. 'We aren't exactly fearsome,' Copeland grunted, 'but we *do* pack a punch. There's a Bren for every two men, Tommy guns, SMLE .303s and four Lewises. We've got ten boxes of Mills grenades, five Boys anti-tank rifles, three two-inch mortars, thirty landmines and six boxes of Nobel's Number 808 gelignite. We've even some Hawkins grenades.'

'You want to watch them things,' said Wallace. 'That crush-igniter system is unstable.'

'Just the ticket for tanks, though,' Cope said. 'One Hawkins grenade will whack the tracks right off a Mark III panzer.'

'Jerry'll shoot your arse up before you get near enough to throw it.'

'Leave it out, Fred,' Caine cut in. Disagreements between Cope and Wallace had been known to erupt into fist fights. His two mates were as different as Laurel and Hardy, but he liked and valued both for their distinctive qualities—Wallace for his staunch and unswerving loyalty, and Cope for his precise and analytical mind.

Wallace had joined the Horse Gunners straight out of school. He was a good practical soldier, but not the type ever to rise above the rank of private. Even the army hadn't taught him to curb his violent temper, which, coupled with his physical strength, could make him truly formidable. He had appointed himself Caine's protector, but the tables had turned several times when Caine had managed to get Wallace out of hot water.

When Harry Copeland had joined the troop from the Royal Army Service Corps later and become friendly with Caine, Wallace had been jealous. Cope was everything the ex-Gunner wasn't—handsome, educated, cultured. He'd taught history at a boys' school and was a superb organiser, with a mind like a seven-carat-diamond drill-bit. Rumour had it that he had turned down a commission because he was a 'communist', and although this was absurd, it was true that Copeland despised the callous and unimaginative regulars who, he thought, had bungled the Great War.

Wallace explained away Caine's friendship with Copeland as a case of a shared hatred for 'the officer class'; it was a feeling Wallace could identify with himself. The good ones, in his opinion, were few and far between, and it didn't surprise him that Caine had been ejected from their number. Caine was simply too good to be an officer, Wallace thought.

For a long time, Copeland and Wallace had loathed each other. Cope felt physically challenged by Wallace and regarded him as a muscle-bound thug. Wallace was the first to admit that he wasn't an educated man, but he resented Cope's insinuation that he was somehow retarded. They had recently reached an uneasy truce, though, under the influence of their mutual loyalty to Caine.

'So who is this tart we're supposed to be snatching from under Rommel's nose?' Wallace demanded.

Even before the words were out, Wallace knew he'd blundered. If there was one thing Caine was touchy about, it was women. One of the few times Wallace had seen him nettled was in a Cairo bar when two drunken Australians had started abusing a young hostess. Caine had floored both, one after the other, with a volley of snapping knucklebones delivered so fast that Wallace remembered only a blur. Wallace had been shocked: he'd been giving Caine the benefit of his protection for months, never dreaming how smartly the ex-sapper could handle himself—in fact, Wallace had never seen anyone faster in his life.

Caine was staring at him. 'There aren't any tarts or bints on this job,' he said. 'Let's just call her Runefish.'

'Right you are,' Wallace muttered, avoiding his gaze.

Caine guessed his mate was recalling the fight in the Cairo bar, and regretted it. It brought back unpleasant memories of the time he'd broken his stepfather's jaw. There was no doubt in his mind that 'the Butcher', as Caine called his stepfather, had had it coming—he'd been abusing Caine's mother and sister for years—but it had appalled Caine to discover that he was capable of such an attack.

Caine's real father—a blacksmith—had died when he was twelve. From the time Caine was old enough to lift a hammer, he'd been helping his father in the forge, and had developed spectacular shoulder, arm and chest muscles. Even at twelve, though, he'd been astute enough to realise that horse power would soon be a thing of the past. A year later he'd left school and apprenticed himself at a local garage, where he'd taken to tinkering with motors. He'd also talked a retired pugilist into training him as a boxer and had developed a spectacular one-two punch.

It had been this move that he'd relied on the night he'd heard his sister May's terrified screams for the last time. He recalled breaking in on the six foot, fourteen-stone Butcher, who had pinioned May on the couch and was slobbering drunkenly over her. Though Caine could never remember actually hitting his stepfather, he clearly recalled the snap as his jaw broke.

The Butcher had reported the assault to the police. Caine had been arrested. The charge was a serious one, but the constable assigned to his case decided that justice wouldn't be served by Caine going to Borstal. If Caine agreed to join the army, he said, he would not only keep a careful eye on the Butcher, but would also make sure the assault charge was quietly dropped. Caine felt that he was betraying his mother and sister, but there was nothing else for it. A week later he enlisted in the Royal Engineers. His mother committed suicide five years later, writing that she could no longer take the Butcher's conduct. Caine was an NCO by that time and loved the army, but he could never forgive himself for his failure to help his mother when she needed him most.

'Fred's question is still valid, skipper,' Copeland said. 'Why is this

Runefish so special they're launching a search-and-rescue op for her?'

Caine had already resolved to brief the unit once it was on the move. He explained the details of Assegai as St Aubin had revealed them to him.

When he'd finished, Copeland eyed him dubiously. 'Remote guidance to long-range targets? That's far in advance of any gear I've ever heard of.'

Wallace snorted. 'Perhaps Mr Churchill had so much on his plate he forgot to brief you on the latest top-secret gadgetry. After all, as a corporal you must have been well up on his list.'

Caine snickered. Cope said, 'If it's top secret, maybe you can explain why St Aubin revealed the details just before we set off on a dodgy mission with a fifty-fifty chance of getting bagged. Where's the "need to know"? None of us need to know. The whole yarn's as full of holes as a tart's knickers. Why would GHQ choose a Wren for the job? A girl stands out like a sore thumb. Just what you need if you're carrying top-secret documents.'

Caine started cleaning his mug with sand. 'You're right, Harry—my first reaction was that this was all cock and bull. But we're just cogs in the wheel. We follow orders. One thing: whatever Runefish knows, it's so vital that, if we can't get her out, we have to execute her.'

Leaving the other two staring at him in astonishment, he lurched to his feet and marched off towards his sleeping space.

CAINE HAD OFTEN TRIED to imagine how big 'the Blue' actually was. The Western Desert was as large as the whole of India, and that was only one region of the Sahara. It was an ocean of undulating rock and gravel and sand that stretched unbroken to the west for an incredible distance of 3,000 miles. And, as at sea, you had to navigate by the sun, the stars and the moon across a vista without fixed points.

Not that the move-out required any navigation, because the track leading north-west from Jaghbub was marked with oil drums every half-mile. Caine had been impressed to note the quiet sense of purpose about his men when they had mounted the wagons an hour before dawn. It was cold for a June morning, and the commandos were swaddled in coats and stocking-caps, their breath like smoke. Caine had taken the passenger's seat in the lead vehicle, the White scout-car, next to Cope, the designated driver.

When they reached the ten-mile marker, the Military Police motorcyclist accompanying them turned his bike around. 'That's as far as I go, lads. I don't know what crazy mission you're on, but I hope you make it.'

'There goes the only living witness that Operation Runefish ever left base,' Cope said, teasing the wagon into gear.

Caine had also noted St Aubin's absence, and it irked him. 'If anything happens to St Aubin, no one at GHQ will have a clue where we are.'

'That happened to a mate of mine on a Jock column,' Cope grinned. 'They were up the Blue for a month. When they got back the adjutant said, "Who the bloody hell are you?"'

Caine cackled with laughter. 'I can just see that happening to us.'

Copeland flashed a quick glance at him. 'You always look as happy as a pig in shit when you're up the Blue.'

Caine grinned at him. He wasn't a religious man, yet the desert had a sense about it that he could only describe as holy.

They were silent for a moment, then Copeland said, 'You know, Tom, the chances of picking up Runefish are about five per cent.'

Caine was about to agree but stopped himself. 'Just think of that girl alone in the emptiness, surrounded by the whole bloody Panzer Army. Whatever bullshit story we've been fed, we can't leave her there, Harry. I'm going to get her out, if it's the last thing I ever do.'

A quarter of an hour later the sun burst through riffling dust-clouds. Caine waited until it was high enough to provide a clear shadow for the sun compass, then instructed Cope to give three short blasts on his horn—the prearranged signal for 'general halt'.

Land navigation was a meticulous business, but one in which Caine had excelled from the beginning. He was good at it, yet he'd never lost the thrill he'd experienced the first time he'd brought a convoy to within a stone's throw of a point in the middle of nowhere through his own calculations.

As they set off again into the open desert, he felt a surge of euphoria. In the Blue, you engaged with nature's raw dynamics in a way you never could in a city. His eyes worked constantly over the sand. He picked out paths through the void, urging the driver left or right, balancing the compass shadow against the wagon's speed. On the good going the wagons sped along at forty miles an hour. Caine had instructed the drivers to fan out into 'air formation'—a rough arrowhead whose object was to present a more difficult target to marauding aircraft.

By ten o'clock the desert was an inferno. The commandos stripped down to shorts and socks. They had just halted when Caine heard the snarl of engines from beyond the horizon. He knew there was a convoy out there somewhere, but he couldn't see it. Sweeping the landscape with his field glasses, he picked up a string of black beads and told Cope to drive towards them. As his wagons approached, Caine spotted Union Jacks and formation pennants that identified it as an Eighth Army column.

Close up, it was a sorry sight. There were limping trucks with shell-holes shot through their canvas covers, broken-down Bren-gun carriers and wounded men crammed like sardines in the back of captured Axis lorries.

'The face of defeat,' Caine commented.

At high noon Caine let the men brew up tea and open tins of sardines and peaches in the shade of tarpaulins. He walked over to the Dingo, where 'Taffy' Trubman, who doubled as wireless transmitter operator and gunner, was erecting a rod aerial. 'Don't get comms with Group,' Caine said quietly. 'Maintain complete wireless silence unless we hit an emergency.' The Welshman considered him over his thick glasses. 'Standard operating procedure is to get comms at every stop,' he said.

'You'll find a lot that's not SOP on this job.' Caine handed Trubman a page from a message pad. 'I want you to tune into this frequency at each stop and listen for Runefish's SOS signal. If we pick up her transmission it'll solve the problem of locating her. Only, whatever happens, don't acknowledge it. When you pack up the set, tune it back to zero, so there's nothing to betray the frequency if we get bagged.'

The going was classed on the map as 'soft'—the most difficult surface to drive on, apart from a full-blown sand-sea, because it was booby-trapped with pools of dry quicksand that could virtually swallow an armoured car in a single gulp. Copeland drove at a steady thirty miles an hour while Caine directed him to the left of a dune field—a wall of interlocking cut-glass facets with knife-blade crests hundreds of feet high. Caine knew there was no chance of getting through at this point, but he was confident that they would be able to go round. Sure enough a plain of wind-graded gravel opened up on the southern side.

They trolled on silently for an hour, when Wallace suddenly roared, '*Aircraft! Bombers at twelve o'clock!*' Caine squinted through the windscreen, making out three planes raking over the horizon. He made a sober assessment. 'We'll scatter,' he told Copeland. 'When you see the strike pattern, turn sharp out of its path.'

Cope hooted five times—the agreed dispersal signal—then reached for his tin hat. Caine knew that this manoeuvre required stone-cold nerve from the driver; he also knew Cope would deliver. Wallace had removed the dust quilts on the twin Vickers and was glaring at the raiders over the sights.

'Hold your fire,' Caine said, turning to take in the great silver mosquitoes careening towards them. He didn't see the bombs, but he heard the whine as they fell. Sand and stones heaved up with a noise like ripping steel. The earth vibrated. Hot pressure seared Caine's lungs.

He watched the strike pattern approaching with almost detached interest. Copeland swerved out of the bombs' path, so sharply that Caine and Wallace had to grip the hatch covers to stay upright. As the White bumped and shuddered, Caine took a quick dekko over his shoulder. He was satisfied to see that all but Gracie had dispersed to the four winds, each vehicle taking a separate course. None of them had taken a hit. There was a startled yell from Wallace. '*Blenheims!*' he bawled. 'They're *ours*.'

For an instant Caine didn't believe it. He watched the bombers bank and brace for another approach. He recognised the profile of RAF Blenheim light bombers. 'They're dipping into a strafing run,' he hissed.

Caine knew that bomb strikes were always inaccurate, while strafing was likely to be far more deadly. '*Stop*,' he ordered Copeland and the White jerked to a halt. 'Fred, get those recognition panels out. *Now*.'

He shoved open the side door and half tumbled out onto the sand. He waved at Gracie, clocking the drawn face of Sweeney as he pulled up. The other vehicles were still speeding away in every direction.

'They're ours,' Caine bawled to Sweeney. 'Someone help us with the recognition panels, fast.'

Wallace clattered out of the White with a Bren gun slung backwards from his shoulder, grasping a bundle of recognition panels in one hand and a Very pistol in the other. He thrust the pistol at Caine, and together they jogged clear of the convoy. They were joined by Sweeney's co-driver, Gunner Dick Hanley, a bulldog-faced, rugby-playing old mate of Wallace from the Royal Horse Artillery. Caine spun round to see the planes swooping down on them. Shells stitched ladders of dirt and rock fragments across the desert floor.

The recognition signal was one white Very flare. Caine lifted the pistol. There was a dry click: the weapon misfired.

The shadows of the bombers lifted overhead in a concerto of screeching engines and shrieking guns: Caine and Wallace dropped and rolled. Hanley stood his ground, shaking his fist at the soaring aircraft. A second later his body exploded in a gush of blood and tissue.

The shadows passed. Wallace leapt to his feet, gimlet eyes blinking at the gory mess that had been his mate. He lifted the Bren gun to his shoulder, sighting up on the receding planes. 'You bastards!' he roared.

Caine flung himself on the giant. 'Fred! They're *ours*.'

Wallace stared at the Bren in his hands, flashed a glare of pure hatred after the aircraft, then let the weapon drop.

Within minutes the convoy had regrouped. The troops poured out of their vehicles and rushed over to see what had happened. Apart from Hanley there were no casualties. They buried all they could find of the ex-Gunner's remains and built a cairn of stones over the grave. Caine noted its latitude and longitude so that the body could be retrieved later.

He passed round a tin of cigarettes. 'You can't blame the RAF. We're going in the wrong direction, and we don't have ground-to-air recognition markings: if we had, the enemy would be down on us like a ton of bricks. The RAF can't know the positions of every friendly patrol and, in any case, our mission is secret. It's one of the risks we have to take.'

JOHANN EISNER was sitting at the bar of Madame Badia's nightclub. Tonight he was Captain Sandy Peterson, an officer of the General List. He wore immaculate khaki drills, his hair was dyed blond and he sported a trim moustache attached with gum to his upper lip.

Eisner sipped his drink slowly and stared at the half-dozen young women on the stage, clad in diaphanous costumes, swaying sensuously to the Egyptian band. He nodded to the barman for a refill. 'Nice set of girls you've got here tonight.'

The barman, a mild-faced Armenian, winked. 'If there is one you fancy, I can introduce you, sir.'

'The night is yet young, my friend—what's your name?'

'Joseph, sir.'

Eisner took a deep breath. 'I wonder if you could possibly help me, Joseph,' he said. He slipped out of his wallet a two-by-three-inch copy of the photo he'd taken of the blonde Wren officer in the GHQ staff car. He had trimmed the shot carefully so only the face remained. 'I'm looking for this girl. Her name is Betty, and I think she may have worked here.'

Joseph held the photo close to the light, and Eisner looked on, trying not to betray his anxiety. It was only after he'd developed the shot that he'd been forced to admit what part of him had been trying to deny: she was a cabaret girl at Madame Badia's. He had never spoken to her but he did know that she'd witnessed an unpleasant event that had occurred here twelve months ago. The only other living witness to that event was himself.

This was his first visit to the club since that night, and he had returned with some trepidation. His instinct for self-preservation told him that returning to the scene would be suicidal, yet the club was his only lead to the cabaret girl—now transformed into a Wren officer.

In the end, he'd deployed the rational thinking that had always been his saving grace. He had modified the risk by assuming the identity of a British officer—a guise he hadn't used since his early days in Cairo. The service cap with the nondescript badge of the General List was ingenious, he told himself, because it didn't tie him down to any particular unit.

The club was a former private house overlooking the Nile. The doorman had asked him to deposit his Smith & Wesson at the reception and Eisner had handed it over with every sign of resentment. The truth was that he'd worn it only to distract attention from the stiletto strapped to his leg.

Once through the inner door, his confidence had returned. No one had given him a second glance—and why should they? The police had been looking for a well-dressed, clean-shaven Egyptian wearing a tarboosh and dark glasses. There was no reason to identify that man with a respectable British officer on a night out.

The barman was shaking his head. 'I'm sorry, sir, I've never seen this girl. But I've only been here a few weeks. You'd have to ask someone who's been here longer.' He pointed to one of the girls in the floor show—a fair-skinned beauty with glistening black hair. 'Sim-Sim's been working here the longest. When the performance is over, I'll call her.'

Eisner nodded and sat back with his drink to enjoy the rest of the show.

Ensconced with Sim-Sim at a table minutes later, he could see she was even more of a jewel than she'd appeared on the floor—her pale face possessed an aristocratic cast and he regretted that she'd covered her sleek figure with a black cloak. It turned out that she spoke both English and French.

All was going well until he produced the photo. Then her black eyes seared him. 'Why are you looking for Betty?' she demanded.

'So she did work here, then?'

'Yes, but not any more. Why do you want her?'

Eisner related his story: they'd met at an Embassy party a year ago and spent the night together. In the morning she'd vanished, leaving only this photo. Now, after a stint of active service, he was trying to get her back.

By the time he'd finished, he hoped that she'd be less hostile. She wasn't. 'I'm sorry,' she said, 'but I can't tell you anything about Betty.'

'Why not? Where's the harm? I only mean her well.'

She fixed him with a black stare. 'Betty witnessed a terrible crime here,' she said. 'The wife of a British diplomat was murdered in the ladies' room. Her murderer was an Egyptian who'd been her lover, to whom she'd betrayed her husband's secrets. He was selling them to the Germans. When she discovered that he was having an affair with another woman, she denounced him here in the club. He followed her into the ladies' room, raped her and cut her throat. Betty came in while it was happening—she was the only witness. The man might have killed her, too, but he heard the doorman coming and jumped out of the window. The police investigated it, of course—British Intelligence, too. They asked Betty a lot of questions, but up to now, no one has ever discovered the murderer's identity.'

'That's horrible,' Eisner said. 'Though what has it got to do with me?'

'Nothing,' she said. 'But there's at least one person out there who has good reason to want Betty dead. That's why I can't tell anyone about her.'

Eisner shifted in his seat, weighing possibilities. He noticed Joseph watching him from the shadows. 'I understand. You've been a loyal friend to Betty. I'm sorry to have bothered you.' He got to his feet.

Joseph saw him go and picked up the telephone. 'Major Stocker?' he asked quietly. 'Corporal Tankien here. You asked to be kept informed if anyone came in asking about Runefish? Well, someone just has . . .'

Eisner was strapping on his Smith & Wesson by the reception desk. To one side was a dark corridor that he knew led to the ladies' room. He asked himself why its proximity should make him feel nervous. After all, whatever horrific crime had been committed there twelve months ago had nothing to do with him.

ON THE THIRD MORNING out of Jaghbub, Caine's commando hit the ancient slave route that cut across the bulge of Cyrenaica. This, Caine knew, was the frontier of the Axis heartland, and the area where Maddaleine Rose's plane had gone down.

Caine's crews had been driving all night on Benzedrine, mainly because of a stroke of bad luck they'd run into just after last light. Clearing a ridge at full speed, they'd hit an enemy leaguer—an Afrika Korps 88mm anti-tank battery, with about ten trucks. The German camp was directly in front of Caine's column, only a few hundred yards away, and there was no chance of avoiding it. Caine ordered Cope to give three long and two short honks on the horn, the signal to form into line abreast and assume action stations. Alastair 'Flash' Murray, a sandy-haired bruiser from Belfast, at the hatch of the Daimler, manoeuvred the AFV forward. 'Charge!' Caine yelled, but the order was drowned by the crump of a two-pound shell from the Daimler's gun. A gush of yellow lightning torched the half-light: a Jerry truck whamped up in flame.

Caine's wagons were reeling down on the leaguer at forty miles an hour. The machine-gunners opened up almost at the same moment: their guns wove a deadly web of orange tracer that sliced into the Axis vehicles. Two more enemy trucks went up in sears of red and black. In seconds they were into the leaguer. Tracer flew, Jerry small-arms stuttered, rounds blipped across the White's bonnet. Caine saw a German gun-crew working frantically to bring an 88mm gun to bear, then it was lamped by a 20mm incendiary. The shell bang-flashed, and swiped crew and gun to shreds with a blinding light.

Then, suddenly, they were zooming into darkness and open desert. One mile clocked up, then two, then five, until the German column was a chain of bright bonfires along the skyline behind them. Caine told Copeland to give the general halt signal. Slowly his nerves let go as the adrenalin tension evaporated. There had been no serious damage to the wagons, and no casualties. The commandos couldn't believe that they'd got through.

They had pressed on all night. Once his glee at being alive had faded, Caine recognised grimly that Axis patrols would be after them at first light. Their presence was now well and truly known to the enemy.

They were heading north now, towards the Green Mountain massif. This was the country of the Senussi—Bedouin descendants of the great Islamic brotherhood that had once controlled the caravan routes across the whole of Libya. The Senussi were hostile to their Italian colonial masters and therefore classed as friendlies by the Allies.

There was plenty of cover here. Before the heat had begun to kick in, Caine halted the convoy for breakfast in a shallow wadi sheltered by rock overhangs and groves of camel-thorn. There was a gentle breeze, carrying the scent of juniper and wild thyme from the mountains. Caine sat down to eat the breakfast Wallace had whipped up. As Wallace ladled stew from the dixie, Cope was sniffing the breeze. 'I smell burning.'

'It ain't the stew,' Wallace growled.

Caine inhaled air, taking in the distinct odour of fire-ash and smoke. 'We'd better have a look.'

The three men scrambled up the escarpment behind them. Caine spotted a pall of black smoke rising perhaps three miles away. He dug out his field glasses and made out an Arab settlement—a sprawl of mud-brick buildings masked by hillocks and thick acacia groves. He caught the flash of sunlight on the windscreens of trucks.

'There's a Senussi village down there,' he said. 'Looks like they've had a visit from someone unpleasant.'

They crawled off the lip of the hill, sat back among the rocks. 'I think we ought to do a recce,' Caine said.

Copeland made a face. 'It's none of our business,' he said.

'It could be our business,' said Caine. 'This is the area where Runefish went down. Anyway, we ought to know the dispositions of enemy troops.'

Hugging the available shadow, Cope managed to get the wagon to within half a mile of the village. Caine told him to stop under a low butte, and the two of them climbed to the top.

Caine swept the village with his field glasses. The settlement consisted of twenty or thirty wattle houses. Many of them were on fire. The German troops were rousting Arabs from their dwellings, and marching them at gun-point to the village square where most of the activity was focused. Caine handed the field glasses to Copeland.

Cope zeroed-in on the square. 'Jesus wept,' he exclaimed. 'They're hanging the villagers—*Jesus* . . . they're even doing the *children*.'

They stared at each other for a moment. 'We've got to do something,' said Caine. 'If we go in with the AFVs they'll never know what hit them.'

'Let's just think about this, Tom,' Cope said. 'Any action we take can only jeopardise our mission. If we don't get to Runefish before the Hun, it could change the whole course of the war.'

It was an impulse like this, Caine remembered, that had cost him his commission in the Royal Engineers. Then he said, 'I'm not giving up on Runefish, Harry, but this is happening now, and we can stop it.'

Cope snorted derisively. 'These aren't our mates. They're not even really our allies.'

'They're people,' said Caine gently. 'I'm going in, Harry. I'm not ordering you to go with me, but I can't leave this. Not women and children, not even for Runefish. I'd have it on my conscience for the rest of my life.'

Cope let out a long sigh. 'All right,' he said. 'I'll do it.'

It took only minutes to get back to the convoy. Caine called the lads together and explained. He added that no one was obliged to take part. Not a single voice was raised in objection.

THE HANGING in the Senussi village of Umm 'Aijil had been halted by the sudden appearance of the village sheikh on a balcony overlooking the square. The old man, grasping a Mannlicher rifle, had demanded the release of all the prisoners. For platoon commander Oberleutnant Ernst von Karlsruhe, of the Brandenburg Special Duties Regiment, it was an exasperating delay. If Karlsruhe had had his way, he would have rounded up the Arabs and shot them with his Schmeisser MG30, but his instructions had been specific: he was to make an example of this village. His plan was to burn most of the place down, leaving some of the corpses hanging from the walls of the mosque as a reminder to any other Senussi who might be ready to harbour the enemy.

The Oberleutnant was aware that his platoon's situation wasn't tactical. Too many of his troops were concentrated in one place, and he'd put out neither sentries nor forward pickets. This nagged at his sense of professionalism, but there wasn't much to fear from the Allies. The Eighth Army was now scuttling back behind the Wire with its tail between its legs.

When the old man had first appeared on the balcony with his long white beard and tattered shirt, von Karlsruhe's reaction had been to guffaw. His laughter was quickly stifled when the sheikh promptly shot off the face of a corporal standing right next to him, spattering the Oberleutnant with fragments of bone. Von Karlsruhe drew out a handkerchief and began to wipe off the blood, remembering that the Mannlicher was a hunting rifle of celebrated accuracy, and that he was probably the next in its sights.

Von Karlsruhe agreed to negotiate. While he was pretending to do so, two hefty Brandenburgers sneaked up to the balcony and overpowered the old man. The Feldwebel in charge of the hanging detail pointed out that the sheikh's daughter was among the prisoners. He suggested that before stringing the old man up, they should first rape his daughter in front of him, then hang her. It would be a fitting revenge. The officer recoiled. 'Are we animals?' he raged. 'Hang her, yes, but keep it clean. Let's be done with it.'

The girl accepted her fate with remarkable dignity. As the Feldwebel drew the hood over her head, two soldiers on the balcony above forced her father to watch. Another private was just looping the noose around her neck when a .303 round hit him smack in the centre of the forehead. The Feldwebel turned to see three enemy vehicles roiling down the street, machine guns stabbing out long spears of blood-red flame. Two twin Vickers drummed at 1,000 rounds a minute, carving up the troops guarding the prisoners. The Germans reeled in shock, jiggering like puppets. Some dropped their weapons, others leap-frogged for the shelter of doorways and walls. The Senussi prisoners hared off down the street.

The AFVs skidded to a halt. Helmeted commandos scattered, hammering rounds as they ran. Bren-gun crews made cover, lay prone, spritzed double-taps. A dozen Germans went down in the first wave of fire. Flash Murray, in the Daimler's turret, welted a two-pound incendiary at the enemy trucks. The shell stonked a cab: the fuel tank mushroomed.

Copeland, in cover behind the Dingo, clocked the two enemy on the balcony trying to heave the old man over the rail. He got the first of them in his cross hairs. He saw a scarlet blister swell just above the soldier's ear and watched him collapse. He sighted in on the other Jerry, cracked a second slug through his chest.

In the smoke and the dust, Caine found himself looking down the barrel of von Karlsruhe's Walther P38 and felt a round whirr past. He fired his Tommy gun, sowing the officer's broad chest with lead. A round slugged Caine's helmet, ramming him clean off his feet. A German loomed over him with bayonet fixed. In slow motion, Caine saw 'Janka' Cavazzi, a Corsican ex-Legionnaire, take the Jerry in a bear hug, jerking him onto his knife.

A Jerry tried to brain Cavazzi from behind with a rifle butt, but the Corsican dodged, wriggling free to find Bob O'Brian, ex-Royal Ulster Rifles, dragging his assailant off him by the belt. O'Brian swung the German round, and Caine punched a round through his head. Another Jerry came from nowhere, slashing O'Brian's throat with a bayonet. Caine saw the wound gape and shot the German through the chest.

Some of the enemy had taken cover behind a low wall around the mosque and were laying down fire. Caine saw the Feldwebel dragging a Senussi girl away and recognised her as the girl under the gibbet. He was going after them when he heard Todd Sweeney scream, '*Armoured car!*'

He saw the German AFV wheeling through the smoke and dust, registered starbursts of fire from the mounted Schmeisser MG30 and felt its fire shave air. Caine fell flat, knowing this was the critical point in the scrap, knowing the surviving Jerries would now be poised for a counter-attack.

On the White, Cope watched as the enemy AFV rolled towards them. He shouldered his rifle, centred the gunner in the cross hairs and saw the gunner slump. At the same moment the Daimler rolled forward, her turret grating as it rotated. There was an ear-splitting wallop as a tongue of fire licked out and Cope saw the enemy AFV going up like a rocket.

Caine took in the commandos skirmishing forward out of doorways and saw the enemy behind the mosque wall caught in crossfire. The Daimler punched off a shell that dashed the wall into a million little pieces.

As Caine picked himself up, he heard the girl shriek. He spotted the Feldwebel lurking at an open doorway, holding a pistol to her head. Caine ran towards him. The Feldwebel fired, the slug nicking Caine's knuckles. Another round whizzed off his tin lid. He dropped his Tommy gun, drew his Colt. The girl flopped down in a dead faint, giving Caine a clear shot. He shot the Feldwebel smack through the temple.

Small-arms fire was fizzling out. Murray was rotating the Daimler's turret left and right with nothing to shoot at. Todd Sweeney lobbed another grenade behind what was left of the wall. The grenade cracked off. The commandos waited. Their interpreter, Moshe Naiman, a German-born Palestinian Jew, called out in German, ordering anyone left to come out with his hands up. There were no takers.

Caine helped the girl to her feet. The old man with the beard he'd seen on the balcony came running up. He said something in Arabic, pointing at Caine's hand dripping blood. Caine slid a field dressing from his top pocket and tried to apply it. This was difficult with a single shaky hand, and the girl took the dressing from him. Her hands were astonishingly steady for someone who'd just dodged death. She was, Caine couldn't help thinking, a European's dream of an oriental woman—with café-au-lait skin and large dark round eyes.

The old man retrieved Caine's Tommy gun and laid it reverently at his feet—an action that looked remarkably like a tribute. 'I am Sheikh Adud,' he said in fractured English. 'Sheikh of this village. This is my daughter, Layla.' The girl nodded slightly. 'Thank God you came,' the sheikh went on. 'You saved us.' He broke off, evidently overwhelmed by emotion, and Caine looked away, embarrassed.

The square was redolent with the smells of cordite, charred flesh and scorched engine oil. The Jerry armoured car was still crackling from the 20mm incendiary: over to his right, Caine saw the skeletons of the three German trucks melting down in smoke and flame.

There were figures among the enemy dead—Senussi women in rainbow-coloured dresses. He wondered if they were looting the corpses, but a flash of steel told him otherwise. He caught hold of a tall woman who had just slit the throat of a German soldier and tried to wrestle the dagger away from her. She resisted, cursing him roundly. Interpreter Moshe Naiman dashed over and talked with the woman for a moment. 'This soldier was one of those who raped her,' he told Caine. 'These women claim the right of revenge—unless we're taking them with us, in which case the wounded are under our protection.'

He watched Caine with a puzzled half-grin on his face. Both knew that they couldn't take the wounded Germans but killing them was a war crime. 'Just tell them to stop,' Caine said, turning away. 'Anyone found killing a wounded man will be shot.' He knew it was a punishment he'd never be prepared to carry out.

Todd Sweeney gestured at the burning AFV. 'Where the heck did it spring from?' he demanded. 'You said there weren't any armoured cars.'

Caine felt his face glow, knowing that Sweeney was right. The appearance of the AFV might easily have cost them the battle. There was no one to blame but himself. He realised that in his rush to play the white knight there'd been a lot of factors he'd overlooked: what to do with enemy wounded, what to do with his own wounded, what to do if his unit lost so many men the Runefish mission was no longer viable. 'They must have been hiding it,' he answered lamely. 'How's O'Brian?'

'He'll be fine,' Sweeney said. 'The wound wasn't that deep. Jackson copped it in the chest, but it's a cushy one. The worst case is Rigby—he's lost a lot of blood, and Pickney doesn't reckon he'll make it.'

'I want you and Harry Copeland to take a detail of four men each and clear all the buildings that aren't yet on fire.'

'Right,' Sweeney said, with a perceptible lack of enthusiasm.

Caine found Wallace and Trubman leaning on the Dingo's hatch sharing a cigarette. He was mildly surprised: Wallace didn't normally talk to the signaller, and now they looked the best of friends.

'My mate Taffy here saved my life,' Wallace said and Trubman turned pink. That reminded Caine of how the Corsican, Cavazzi, had saved him from being skewered on a Jerry bayonet. He looked around to thank him, but Wallace said he'd gone off with Sweeney's clearing party.

'We need to get moving,' Caine said. 'This whole place is giving off smoke signals.' He asked Trubman if he'd tuned into the emergency frequency. The signaller looked worried. 'I can't get comms, Sergeant,' he apologised. 'It's the mountains—this is signals dead ground.'

Caine nodded. 'Keep trying,' he said. His eyes swept the square for Sheikh Adud and his daughter. He saw them conversing with a group of Arabs who were leading a caravan of donkeys laden with household goods. Caine realised that the Senussi didn't need to be told to evacuate the place. He told Naiman to bring Adud and Layla over, setting out wooden petrol cases for them to sit on.

He took from his haversack a photograph and a letter in Arabic. The photo showed the Senussi leader, Grand Senussi Sayid Idriss, now exiled in Egypt, and the letter was a request from him to all Senussi to assist his British allies. Sheikh Adud examined them with interest.

'Where will your people go now?' Caine asked.

'The sheikh says they'll go up into the Green Mountains,' Naiman translated, 'and stay with relatives.'

'Why were the Germans doing this?' Caine asked.

Sheikh Adud had just opened his mouth to answer when there was a crisp detonation from a nearby street, followed by a salvo of gunshots.

'Grenade!' Caine gasped, grabbing his Tommy gun.

CAINE HAD a good idea what he'd find. In the adjacent street, Todd Sweeney squatted over the twitching body of Janka Cavazzi. 'We were about to clear that house,' Sweeney said, 'when this Jerry drops a grenade right on top of Janka. It went off as soon as it hit him. Whacked his guts right out. We shot the Hun, and the boys searched the house—there wasn't anyone else.'

Caine knelt by the Corsican. 'Do me in, for Christ's sake,' Janka croaked, his breath coming in a rattle. 'Shoot me, *please*, finish me off.'

Pickney began prepping a morphine shot. When he leaned over Cavazzi, though, the Corsican knocked away the syringe, gasping, 'Not that. I'm a soldier. Shoot me, you cowards.'

Caine motioned to the group to move out of the wounded man's earshot. 'Can't you do anything for him?' he said to Pickney.

'Sorry, skipper,' he said. 'Abdominal wounds are excruciating. He's going to die in agony—maybe today, maybe tomorrow.'

'We have to put him out of his misery,' Sweeney said.

Caine stared at the ex-MP. 'All right, Todd, are you ready to do it?'

Sweeney flushed. 'Me? You're the one who got us into this. You wanted to play the big-timer, saving a wog village instead of sticking to our mission. We've got four good men down and a lot of walking wounded. If anyone ought to shoot Janka, it's you.'

Caine was taken aback by the unexpected onslaught. The worst of it was that almost everything Sweeney had said was true. He felt suddenly alone. He took a deep breath and drew his Colt.

Caine knelt down beside the Corsican. Cavazzi focused on the pistol. '*Do it*,' he said urgently. His hands trembling, Caine pushed the Colt's barrel inside the wounded man's mouth. 'Thanks for saving my life, mate,' he said, and pulled the trigger. He felt the recoil and staggered over to the nearest wall for support, and was violently sick.

'It was a brave thing to do,' Sweeney stammered. 'I couldn't have . . .'

'Never mind that now,' Caine snapped. 'I want you to make sure that soldier gets a proper burial.'

Caine found Trubman. 'Did you get anything on the emergency net?'

'Sorry, Sarn't. Not a dickybird. We need to move to higher ground, see.'

Adud and his daughter came over with Naiman, together with the tall Senussi woman who handed him a scrap of paper, an official document, typed in German. He passed it to Naiman, who questioned the woman briefly. 'She found it on the body of the officer you shot,' he told Caine.

'Hey, skipper.' Caine saw Copeland jogging up. 'Look at this.' He held out a flat, round box, painted gold.

Caine opened the catch and caught feminine fragrance. Inside were tiny compartments containing different shades of eye-shadow, face powder and a powder-puff. On the back of the lid was a mirror.

Cope said, 'That's a European woman's make-up compact. Arab women don't use that stuff. And we found these.' He held up a pair of khaki drill trousers, tailored to fit a woman's shape. Inside the band was the familiar British Forces 'arrowhead' label.

'Runefish?' Caine said, and passed the objects to Sheikh Adud. 'Do you know anything about these?' he asked. The sheikh launched into a long explanation. 'There was a European woman here until this morning,' Naiman translated. 'He was about to tell you when that grenade interrupted. She arrived the day before yesterday in a jeep. There was a man with her—a European. The sheikh guessed they were hiding from the Jerries. He was right. A Jerry column arrived this morning and searched the place. They shot the man and took the woman off with their convoy. They left this platoon to punish the village for harbouring them.'

'If this was Runefish, who was the man?' Copeland asked.

'Maybe the pilot survived,' Wallace suggested.

Caine considered it. 'Please ask the sheikh where his body is. It might tell us something.'

Naiman quizzed the old man. 'The Jerries threw it into one of the burning houses.'

'Could you ask what the woman looked like—and what language did she and the man speak?'

'She was blonde, maybe the age of his daughter. She was dressed military style in khaki. She spoke to the Arabs in Italian.'

'Runefish speaks fluent Italian,' Caine said, suppressing his excitement. 'Did the sheikh notice whether she was left- or right-handed?'

The old man said he thought she was left-handed.

'That clinches it,' Wallace said. 'Blonde, spoke Italian and left-handed, wearing military rig. It's her, skipper.'

'Before we start celebrating,' Naiman cut in, 'I think you should consider this.' He held up the paper the Arab woman had just given Caine. 'A movement order for a company of the Brandenburg Special Duties Regiment. Didn't you say that a company of Brandenburgers had been deployed to hunt down Runefish?'

'The idea that it might be searching for Runefish was just speculation.'

'Well, whatever the case, if the lady who was here is Runefish, the Brandenburgers have just pipped us at the post.'

'Can you ask the sheikh how long ago the rest of the column went off?'

The sheikh said, 'I understand. *Tedesci*—Germans—went with girl one hour after sunrise.' He pointed north. 'They go that way—Benghazi.'

'Dammit—that's three hours ago. We'll never catch them now.'

The sheikh shook his head. 'No, no, no,' he repeated. He spoke to Naiman in Arabic. 'The sheikh knows a shortcut,' Naiman translated. 'The road the Boche are taking avoids the Green Mountains, but the sheikh's way cuts through the massif. They call it the Hag's Cleft and it might be dangerous for motor vehicles. He'll guide us personally as a mark of gratitude for what we did here.'

Caine stared at Naiman. 'How far ahead of the enemy will this put us?'

'You get there long before *Tedesci*,' the old man said energetically. 'Long enough you hide and wait—*boom*.' He grinned and drew a hand across his throat. 'You take woman. You kill them all.'

3

It was three o'clock in the morning when Sim-Sim unlocked the door of her flat, exhausted. The flat was dark but she didn't switch on the light in the sitting room. Instead, she went straight to the bathroom to remove her make-up. As she wiped it off with cotton wool, she wondered how long her looks would last.

She detested being 'Sim-Sim', but it was a fitting name for a trade in which it paid to appear more stupid than you were. In fact, she was Rachel Levi, a Palestinian Jew from the Sea of Galilee.

She let down her hair, changed into her dressing gown and walked through to the sitting room. A rough hand grabbed her wrist, twisted her arm sharply behind her: another hand clamped her mouth. Her assailant pushed her down into a straight-backed dining chair and tied her hands to its back. She felt the cold, sharp prick of a knifepoint against her throat. 'I'm going to switch on the light,' the voice said. 'If you make any noise, you're dead.'

Electric light exploded in her face, bringing into focus a strapping man in a black suit. He looked like one of the Egyptian playboys she entertained in the club. Rachel's eyes fell on the slim stiletto in his right hand. 'Who are you?' she stammered.

'Come, my dear Sim-Sim,' the man said, his voice almost unctuous. 'Your memory can't be that bad. It's not very flattering that you've forgotten a nice respectable British officer already.'

Rachel's mouth fell open in shock. 'Captain Sandy Peterson?'

'Not exactly. Captain Peterson is a figment of my imagination. Now, I want to know those things you refused to tell me the first time round.'

Her eyes fixed on him, wide with horror. This was the man who had brutally murdered Lady Mary Goddard at Madame Badia's—the man whom Betty had discovered. What other reason could he have for asking questions about Betty?

'Go to hell,' Rachel said.

In a flash of movement Eisner pinched the lobe of her right ear and sliced it off with his knife. Rachel tried to scream, but once again he stifled her with a big hand. He scrabbled at the neck of her dressing gown and ripped it off her shoulders. He held up the piece of ear he'd just cut off. 'This you won't miss much, but your nose, your lips or . . .' He let the knife blade linger on a perfect nipple.

Rachel shuddered. Blood from her injured ear was dripping on her shoulder. 'What do you want to know?' she asked.

'I want to know about Betty.'

Rachel was aware now what her fate would be if she didn't do what he wanted. In her trade, she'd learned to read men, and this was a man who really did enjoy hurting women.

'All right, I'll tell you. Her name is Betty Nolan. She's British. She was an actress before the war. She got on well with the clients but she never took them home.'

'Why not?' Eisner asked, his voice silky. 'She doesn't like men?'

Rachel tried to clear her head. 'She had a boyfriend, a secret agent in France. He was betrayed. The Nazis murdered him. Betty said she couldn't go with anyone else until she'd laid him to rest in her mind.'

'How long ago did Betty leave Madame Badia's?' he demanded.

'Six months ago. She was never the same after that night I told you about.'

'And what did she say about the man she saw?'

'She didn't say anything,' she stammered. 'She couldn't give any information . . . not enough to identify him. A lot of people saw him in the club—we were all . . .'

'Go on,' Eisner said. 'You were going to say, "We were all there, and we all saw him," weren't you? So you were in the floor show that night.'

'Why do you want to know?' Rachel sobbed.

'I don't,' he snapped. 'What did Betty do after she left Madame Badia's?'

'I don't know. I heard she joined the British Army.'

Eisner surveyed her face, and knew she wasn't lying. 'Where does Betty live now?'

'I don't know . . . really . . . She used to have a flat on the Gezira, in al-Hadiqa Street. Flat one, number twenty-two.'

Eisner doubted that Sim-Sim had much more to tell him. There was something strange going on, and he could almost smell deception.

'What are you going to do to Betty?' Rachel said.

'Your question should be, what am I going to do to you?'

'Let me go,' she said.

'I'd like to do that but, unfortunately, I can't.'

Rachel focused on the stiletto in his hand. A quiver ran down her spine. Betty had said the man who'd murdered Lady Mary used a knife with a long, narrow blade. A knife like this one.

'It *was* you,' she said, her voice dead now. 'You're the one Betty saw. Whatever you do to me, one thing is certain: you're going straight to damnation.'

A tidal wave of fury burst in Eisner's head, overwhelming him. With a sudden movement he cut through Rachel's ropes, snatched her long, beautiful hair and dragged her towards the bedroom.

THEY GLIMPSED the Hag's Cleft from afar, a barely perceptible slit in the wall of the Green Mountains, a warren of heat-weathered hills and steep-sided canyons that rose to 1,600 feet. Caine halted the column at the foot of the cleft.

'We'll never get the wagons through there,' Copeland said.

Caine ignored him and lit a cigarette, holding it in his bandaged hand. Sheikh Adud crouched down by Caine, sketching lines in the dust with a gnarled finger. 'It is narrow,' he confirmed, 'but very steep only in one place. Sometimes Arabs have to drag donkeys up by rope.'

Caine gulped. If donkeys could only get up with difficulty, how would the 3-tonners fare?

'If we get stuck in there,' Copeland said, 'that'll be the end of Runefish.'

Caine was thinking about how his attack on the village had cost the lives of two good men: Janka Cavazzi and Martin Rigby, who'd just died of his wounds. Of the injured, Jackson was still laid up in one of the trucks, but O'Brian, his throat bandaged, was on his feet. Then Caine remembered that the assault on the village had produced clues to the whereabouts of Runefish.

He flicked away his cigarette butt. 'It's a gamble,' he said, 'but no one's going to spot us in the cleft, not even from the air.'

'How do you know we can trust the old man?' Cope asked. 'He might be setting us up.'

'Harry, I don't see that we have a choice. If the Hun get Runefish to Benghazi, we'll never get her out. Don't underestimate the sheikh—he seems pretty switched on to me.'

Cope nodded. 'Let's do it then.'

At first the going inside the cleft was better than Caine had expected. The wadi bed was smooth and the sides wide enough apart for two wagons to pass each other. Most of the men debussed from the vehicles and walked. Caine tramped ahead with Sheikh Adud, Layla and interpreter Naiman.

The wadi sides grew higher and higher until they were soaring hundreds of feet above. Darkness descended like a dead weight, and the wadi floor became increasingly steep. Around midnight, when they'd been climbing for a good five hours without a break, Caine thought he heard the sound of water. 'What's that?' he asked.

'That is Shallal,' Adud said. 'Place of waterfall . . . but no problem. Not much water now.'

Caine called a halt and went forward with Copeland, Adud and Naiman. They began to stumble up the rise. Adud pointed out a narrow channel to one side where they could just make out a slim ribbon of water. A climb of about fifteen minutes left Caine breathless but not disheartened. 'I reckon the gradient's about one in three—steep but not *that* steep,' he told Cope.

Caine sent Copeland with Adud and Naiman to recce the way ahead and then scrambled back down to the White, where Wallace was cooking bully stew in a dixie. By the time Copeland and the others arrived back, they were already digging into it.

Copeland attacked the stew ravenously. 'There's a plateau on top, where the watercourse goes off to one side. On the other side there's a ledge, with the mountain wall on the right and a sheer drop on the left.'

Caine searched his face. 'The width is the crucial factor, Harry.'

Cope wiped his lips. 'I reckon it's just wide enough to take our widest wagon but I can't swear what it's like further on. Adud told me it doesn't get any narrower. You thought how we're going to do this?'

'I'm sending the Dingo up first,' Caine said. 'She's got four-wheel drive so it shouldn't be a problem. She can tow Gracie, and the water bowser. On top, we'll use the winch to haul up the rest of the wagons.'

Caine divided the crews into two parties. One group would go ahead, clearing boulders out of the way. The other would push the wagons, haul on toggle ropes or place chocks under the back wheels if there was any sign of slippage. Wingnut Turner yoked the six-ton truck securely to the Dingo with a towrope.

As the Dingo crawled forward, the towrope tightened and Caine eased the clutch out. The Dingo began to crawl up the gradient and Gracie moved steadily forward. They were about halfway up the slope, when Gracie's engine suddenly lost power. Caine stabbed the accelerator frantically, but a fraction of a second later the lorry stopped abruptly: the towrope snapped, whiplashing his bonnet. A few yards above, Copeland braked the Dingo.

Caine could feel Gracie's wheels grinding, slipping back under the drag of the heavy water bowser. 'Hold her, lads,' he yelled through the open window. The team behind the truck threw in the wooden chocks and Wallace ran forward with the men carrying toggle ropes. They looped the ropes around the winch-bar, and Gracie's backwards momentum was checked momentarily. Then she lurched backwards again, shuddering dangerously. Caine's eye fell on the petrol gauge. The tank was empty, which was why the engine had cut.

Gracie was rolling back even faster now, and Caine saw that Wallace and the others were being dragged forwards on their toggle ropes. Caine switched over to the reserve tank and pressed the starter. The engine coughed. He could feel Gracie's wheels shivering, going out of control. 'Get out, skipper,' Wallace yelled. Caine thought of Jackson lying in the back: if he jumped, it would mean abandoning the wounded man to his fate. He hit the starter again and the engine exploded into action.

Caine put her straight into first gear and Gracie jerked forward. The men behind the lorry cheered.

Holding her in first gear, Caine made a decision. 'I'm going to play the winch cable out. Fred, take the hook and yoke it to the Dingo. Then go up there with Harry, and attach it to a secure rock. Give me the word and I'll winch her up.' A moment later the little scout-car was crunching up the slope taking the cable with her.

It worked better than Caine could have imagined. With the winch reeling in the cable it took only ten minutes to cover the hundred feet to level ground. Once the lorry and trailer were safely on the ledge, Caine turned her round and sited her facing the slope. He jumped out of the cab, to find Cope and Wallace waiting for him.

Just as Cope had said, there were large boulders up there. The three of them worked to secure Gracie to them, then Wallace attached the winch-cable extension. While the big man worked the winch, Caine and Copeland took turns to run down the slope to yoke the cable to the other vehicles. It was painstaking work. By the time the last wagon reached the summit, the men were dropping with fatigue.

Dawn was already firing up in the east, revealing a labyrinth of mountain peaks as far as the eye could see. Caine ordered an hour's rest for breakfast. Cope said, 'You deserve a medal for that, skipper. Nobody's done anything like this since Hannibal crossed the Alps with his elephants.'

Caine was so done in he could barely manage a smile. 'Don't count your chickens, Harry,' he said. 'We haven't got down yet.'

TO THE EAST, 500 miles away, Captain Julian Avery found Sim-Sim's flat cordoned off with tape and crawling with Field Security personnel. Avery was pooped. He'd come straight from an all-night conference at GHQ to discuss the implications of Rommel's imminent attack on Tobruk.

He found the Defence Security Officer, Major John Stocker, in the sitting room, drinking coffee. He saluted, then whipped off his service cap. 'Have some coffee,' Stocker told him. 'What news from Tobruk?'

'Rommel encircled the town yesterday. He'll be through the perimeter this morning, and will probably move in for the kill tomorrow.'

Stocker sighed. 'Will Klopper hold out?'

'I think he'll fold on the first wave of Stukas. Holding it was only viable while the Gazala Line was in place.' Avery gulped the bitter coffee and surveyed the DSO with interest. All he knew about him was that he'd been a professor at Cairo University before the war and had virtually no military training, yet was highly rated as a spy-catcher. 'You said it was urgent, sir.'

Stocker lowered his voice. 'This flat was rented by a young woman known as Sim-Sim, a Palestinian Jew named Rachel Levi who worked as a cabaret girl at Madame Badia's nightclub. She was murdered in the early hours of the morning. The police noticed something familiar in the perpetrator's modus operandi.'

Stocker ushered Avery into a small bedroom. The body had been removed, but Avery's glance was drawn to the bed, where sheets and blankets were caked in blood. 'Levi had been raped in the anus and her throat cut from behind, precisely in the manner of the homicide of Lady Mary Goddard last July. The perpetrator in the Goddard case was never found, even though he was witnessed committing the crime by a woman called

Betty Nolan.' He dropped his voice to almost a whisper. 'I believe this Miss Nolan is of some interest to you?'

'Are you indoctrinated, sir?' Avery whispered.

'Into Runefish? Only in as much as it affccts counter-intelligence.'

Avery managed to suppress his surprise. 'This is connected with counter-intelligence?'

'The man who murdered Mary Goddard was an Axis agent. He was using her to obtain secrets from her husband.'

Avery looked puzzled. 'I can see the rationale for the Goddard murder—she would've been able to identify him—but why a cabaret girl?'

'Levi was present the night Goddard was murdered. So were dozens of others, but Levi was an associate of Nolan's and might have learned something from her. My first conclusion was that this might be a case of the perpetrator eliminating witnesses. Then I asked myself why he should do so after he had gone undetected for a year.'

Avery nodded. 'What was your second conclusion?'

'Two nights ago, a man arrived at Madame Badia's with a recent photo of Betty Nolan. I was tipped off by one of my men, who is working undercover at the club. This man was dressed as a British Army captain. He wanted information about Nolan, and my man directed him to Levi.'

'Who was the officer?' Avery asked.

'He signed his name as Captain Sandy Peterson, General List. There is no such officer. I believe that this Peterson was the killer of both Goddard and Levi. And whatever brought him to the club two nights ago was connected with Operation Runefish.'

Avery stared at him. 'You mean he's rumbled Runefish?'

Stocker beckoned Avery with a finger. They moved back into the sitting room. Stocker pointed to the bloodstains on the carpet and drew Avery's attention to a loop of rope attached to an upright chair. 'Our man interrogates Levi while she's tied to this chair. The bloodstains indicate torture—incidentally, a piece of her left ear was missing—extracting the information he failed to get out of her at the club two nights ago. We have to presume she told him all she knew, which was nothing about Runefish but would probably include the fact that Nolan was recruited into the army. Once he's got the information he wants, he drags her to the bedroom and cuts her throat in the act of raping her, as he did with Goddard.'

Avery frowned, trying to assess the threat to Operation Runefish.

'On the night Runefish departed,' Stocker went on, 'our "Y" Service intercepted an unlicensed transmission from the central Cairo district. The transmission contained the intelligence that a female naval officer, code-named Runefish, was transporting top-secret documents to London for the eyes of the prime minister. That transmission came from an Abwehr agent known as *Stürmer* whom Field Security have been trying to identify for more than a year.'

Avery shifted slightly and said, 'That intelligence was derived from a leak my division deliberately disseminated to known Abwehr assets. Are you saying that *Stürmer* and the Levi–Goddard killer are the same?'

Stocker's bright eyes were on him. 'Let's call it a hunch. The night that transmission went out, one of my agents—Corporal Salim Tanta—was murdered. He was last seen tailing a car spotted behaving suspiciously at the Helwan checkpoint.'

'You mean the person he was shadowing was the same one who sent the transmission? The Levi–Goddard killer—Peterson—*Stürmer*?'

'I think there's a strong possibility.'

Avery saw a flaw in Stocker's thesis. 'The transmission suggests that the sender didn't know that Runefish was Nolan, but the fact that the killer came looking for Nolan at the club suggests that he *did* know. How else would he have made the connection? And he had a photo of her, you said? Doesn't that indicate that the killer and *Stürmer* are two different men?'

Stocker sighed. 'There are other possibilities. Say this man sends his initial report and only later realises from the photo that Runefish is Nolan. Or he knows it all along, but holds back the information because Nolan is also a witness to his murder of Goddard. You're in a better position to judge than I am. I'd suggest, though, that whether we're dealing with one person or two, the Runefish mission is in danger of being compromised.'

CAINE CROUCHED in the cover of an arbutus tree, watching as Gracie began her slow descent from 300 feet above the wadi bed. She was the last of the wagons to come down. The tightness of the spur—only finger-lengths of clearance on both sides—made the operation almost as dicey as the ascent at Shallal in the early hours of that morning. Her driver, Bob O'Brian, had engaged six-wheel drive but, despite her massive load of fuel, and the fact that she was towing the water bowser, Caine felt confident that she would make it without a hitch.

Caine couldn't make out O'Brian's face in the shadows of the cab, but he could clearly see the muscular back of Todd Sweeney, poised on the slope ten feet below the lorry, directing the driver with hand signals. The three 3-tonners and the Daimler were now leaguered under the trees, well concealed from the air, while Caine had sent the Dingo on ahead to recce an ambush site. He would feel much happier when this last vehicle was down.

He wandered back to the leaguer, where the wagon crews were stripping machine-guns, mending punctures and replacing spark-plugs. Wingnut Turner called him over to inspect the repair job he'd just completed—Marlene had suffered a crack in her differential cover-plate on the descent.

'Outstanding job, mate,' Caine told him. 'Especially in these conditions.' He heard roars of laughter from a knot of men in the shade of an ilex tree. Medical Orderly Pickney was straddling the body of Private Ross MacDonald, attempting to shove a grease-gun up his arse. MacDonald, a bearded veteran of the Black Watch, was naked apart from his socks and boots. It dawned on Caine that this was a medical operation. MacDonald had been complaining of painful constipation for the past two days.

Caine was about to tell them to give Mac some privacy when he clocked Todd Sweeney weaving into the cover of the trees. He was surprised to see the corporal so soon. 'Is Gracie down?' he asked.

Sweeney shook his head. 'Nah. O'Brian's competent, so I left him to it.'

Caine was about to ask more, when there was a *crack—crack—crack* of rifle fire from beyond the trees. Caine braced his Tommy gun and whirled round to see that the men were fanning out into the scrub. Caine crouched down next to Sweeney, in time to hear the ex-MP whisper, 'Oh shit.'

Following his gaze, Caine saw Gracie, about a hundred feet up the slope, with both her front wheels hanging over the precipice. This time, Caine could see O'Brian slumped across the steering wheel. 'O'Brian's hit,' Sweeney whispered. 'She's out of control . . .'

For a moment, Caine thought the weight of the water bowser would hold her, but an instant later both her left-side rear tyres were over the rim. The bowser tipped sideways, pulling the truck with it.

'She's going,' Sweeney gasped.

'Jackson's in there,' Caine hissed.

They gaped helplessly as, with exquisite slowness, Gracie tumbled sideways into the abyss. They hurled themselves flat as the air folded and the ground pitched. Engine fragments, spatters of boiling rubber and spurts of liquefied glass all blew outwards, riding a tidal wave of black smoke.

They struggled to their feet, lungs and throats scorched from the blast. Caine, seeing commandos careening through the thickets with fire extinguishers, waved them back. 'There's a sniper out there,' he yelled.

It would have been hopeless, anyway. The wagon was a gutted-out skeleton in a nimbus of licking flames. There was no sign of a body.

'Anybody clock muzzle-flash?' Caine called.

Ross MacDonald padded out of the shadows carrying his rifle; he had managed to slip on a pair of shorts. 'I saw smoke, skipper,' he said. 'Look left down the wadi, about four, mebbe five hundred yards.'

Caine craned his neck but the angle was too acute. Mac had taken one step beyond cover for a better look when gunshots zipped and the back of his head ruptured apart in raw red ribbons.

Commandos ate dirt as another rasp of fire crinkled air. Caine clocked flashes in the scrub 500 paces down the wadi. 'One o'clock,' he yelped. 'Five hundred yards. Enemy in scrub. Fire.'

Nobody fired, and Caine clicked that none of the men had a clear view of the target. Copeland crawled by, peering through his telescopic sight. 'Incoming's stopped, skipper,' he grunted. 'It's a small squad—maybe a two-man sniping team. I reckon they're crawling out through the scrub.'

Caine considered ordering the Lewis gunners to blitz the whole segment, but it would just mean more wasted ammunition. He could hear the Daimler's engine and a moment later she edged out of a thicket with Murray's head popping from the top hatch. 'Get up the wadi after them, Flash,' Caine shouted. 'Go with him, Harry. Take Wallace and . . . where's that Arab? Take him with you as tracker. I want those bastards found. I don't want any sod warning the Brandenburgers we're here.'

Caine yelled for Adud, and a moment later the old man moved into view, his Mannlicher rifle in his hands, his eyes bird-bright. Behind him came Layla and Naiman. 'Go with Cope,' Caine said, gesturing.

The AFV rumbled off. Copeland followed the vehicle at a slow trot, with Wallace, Naiman and the two Senussi close behind him. Caine saw Todd Sweeney hauling Mac's corpse into the cover of the trees and called a couple of the men over to bury the Scotsman's body.

O'Brian, Jackson, MacDonald: all good men. His unit was now down to seventeen—almost a quarter of its strength gone. The loss of so many mates weighed on him like a millstone. He wanted to lash out at the nearest target.

Caine turned on Sweeney with fire in his eyes. 'I told you to guide O'Brian down,' he roared. 'Why did you ditch him?'

'O'Brian didn't need me, so I decided to let him go it alone. How was I to know there'd be a contact the minute I left?'

'It didn't occur to you that O'Brian was a wounded man?'

'Now wait a minute,' Sweeney gasped. 'If he was wounded that bad, why did you let him take the wheel? I was designated driver on that rattletrap.'

It dawned on Caine that Sweeney had put lives at risk through his own resentment. He tasted bile. 'I'm patrol commander on this jaunt, Sweeney, and if you ever fall short in your job again, I shall personally make sure that you never serve with another special-service unit . . .'

Caine's pronouncement was nipped in the bud by the slap of a gunshot from further up the wadi. He groped in his haversack for his field glasses. He saw the Daimler emerge into view in a bolus of dust. The search party was huddled behind the AFV, dragging along with them two prisoners. Even from this distance, he could tell that they weren't Ities or Jerries.

They were Bedouin boys, aged no more than fourteen or fifteen and named Saalim and Said, according to Adud. They looked sullen, contemptuous and completely unafraid.

Copeland shoved them roughly into a sitting position and showed Caine the rifles and cartridge belts he'd taken from them. 'This one took a pot shot at me,' he said, pointing at Saalim. 'Missed me by a hair. See the cartridges? Homemade dum-dums, the lot of them.'

Caine slipped a cartridge out of one of the belts and examined it—a flat-topped round whose soft head was scored deeply with a cross-cut. On impact it would tumble through the vital organs. 'You sure it was them?'

'They admitted it. They told Moshe they thought we were Jerries: said they heard that the Huns were executing Arabs. They thought we were coming to do them in. It was a mistake.'

'Oh, a *mistake*,' crowed Wallace, who had been glowering silently at the boys. 'Come on, skipper, let's get this over with.' He drew his fanny.

'Hold it, Fred,' Caine said, turning to Naiman. 'Corporal, can you ask the sheikh what Senussi custom is in a case like this?'

Naiman exchanged words with the old man. 'He says that the custom is an eye for an eye, even if the death was an accident. He also said that these boys are his relatives. Their father is his second cousin or something. He asks for clemency.'

Wallace pulled out his Colt .45 pistol. 'I'll give 'em clemency. Same clemency they give Mac and Bob and Jacko. I'll shoot 'em in the head.'

'Leave it out, Fred,' Copeland said. 'Whether it was a mistake or not, how do you think the rest of the Senussi are going to feel if you do these lads in? We're in their territory, five hundred miles behind enemy lines. It wouldn't be a great idea to turn them against us now.'

'I'm damned if I come here to worry about a bunch of towel-heads . . .'

Naiman put a firm hand on Wallace's arm. 'The point is that if you bump off the sheikh's relatives, he'll be forced to declare a vendetta against us, and that will extend to the whole family—maybe hundreds of tribesmen.

It's their custom. None of us will get out of Cyrenaica alive.'

Wallace scowled, appealing to Caine. 'Are we going to let this claptrap stop us?' he demanded. 'It should be tit for tat, like the old boy said.'

Caine thought it over. 'To me, the only point is that they're kids. They can't be above fourteen years old and there aren't going to be any children executed while I'm in command. If we do them in, we're no better than those Krauts who hanged women and children at the village yesterday.'

Wallace looked outraged. Finally, he stumped away.

Adud gestured to the boys to stand up and drew out a knife to cut their ropes. 'No,' Caine said. 'They'll have to stay under restraint until after the engagement, so we can be sure they don't warn anyone we're here.' He turned to Copeland. 'Tie them to a couple of trees,' he said, 'but make sure they're comfortable.' He unslung his Tommy gun. 'That's it for this morning's session, ladies. Put Gracie's fire out and then move to your wagons. We've got a date with the Brandenburg Special Duties Regiment.'

BY THE TIME EISNER had arrived at his quay in north Zamalek, the euphoria he'd felt on quitting Sim-Sim's flat had evaporated. The girl's words kept drifting back to him: *One thing is certain: you're going straight to damnation*. He couldn't seem to get that off his mind.

He crossed the gangplank and unlocked the cabin door, making sure that nothing had disturbed the hairpin he always left underneath. He walked through the luxuriously furnished state room and, in the bathroom, cleaned the blood off his knife and hid it behind the cistern. He doused himself with buckets of cold river water and feeling much better, put on a bathrobe, wadded his blood-smeared clothes in newspaper and hurled them through a window into the Nile.

After he'd drunk two cups of coffee and smoked a cigarette, he felt ready to broach the wireless cubicle concealed along the passage. He sat down with his code-book and encryption pad, picked up a pencil, then slapped it down again. He realised that he didn't know what to write.

At Sim-Sim's he'd been convinced that he'd unearthed a high-level decoy plan—a scheme that had the British Deception Service stamped all over it. Now he was nagged by doubt. Sim-Sim's curse—*One thing is certain: you're going straight to damnation*—had at first seemed a shot in the dark. Now, he found himself wondering if it might be the key to a secret agenda. Had the girl known something she'd kept hidden from him—something that he hadn't quizzed her about in his zeal to get the goods on Betty? What did he really know about this Runefish operation, anyway? He'd been handed a schedule and he'd seen a female naval officer riding in a GHQ staff car that had ambled along as if its occupant *wanted* to be shadowed. By an amazing coincidence, the woman in the car had turned out to be about the only person in the world who might be able to identify him as a rapist and murderer. Could that really be random chance?

The Field Security bloodhounds had been after him ever since the Goddard incident. What if this entire plan was their gambit to flush him out? What if he'd been fed the supposed Runefish schedule deliberately?

As for Betty Nolan, he hadn't actually seen her get on an aircraft. He couldn't be sure that she'd gone anywhere: for all he knew, she might be in Cairo still. The more he pondered it, the more it seemed to him that this flaunting of a beautiful blonde in full naval regalia, in a conspicuous staff car, wasn't British style. The British made a fetish of discretion: why send someone who was going to stand out like a nun in a nightclub, unless you wanted her to be noticed? Could Betty Nolan be the bait in a noose that was slowly tightening around his neck?

Eisner had had no feedback from Rohde, his controller, on the initial Runefish report, so it was impossible to say whether the information was significant. Rohde was one of the few men who scared Eisner. He had a disturbingly high-pitched voice and a feminine broadness of the pelvis that gave his posture a look that in anyone else might have been camp, but in Rohde was grotesque. He had long fingers—so spidery that, behind his back, his colleagues called him the 'Black Widow'. Eisner had heard rumours about Rohde's actions in Poland and Russia that made his own private activities look like kindergarten romps. The main difference between Eisner and Rohde, though, was that his boss was fanatically devoted to Hitler. Eisner, who regarded Egypt as his home, wasn't exactly a patriot. It wasn't that Eisner didn't want Hitler to win, only that he'd rather it didn't happen just now, when his life was going so well.

Within ten minutes he had come up with three possible courses of action. The first, to interrogate Natalie, would be simple enough, but he quickly struck it from the list. The French cabaret girl might possibly be working for Field Security. The second would be more tricky: snatch and interrogate the officer from whom Natalie claimed to have stolen the Runefish schedule, Julian Avery. The third course was to investigate Nolan's flat on the Gezira, to find out if it was still being used, and if so, by whom.

The flat job would have to be done at once, before Field Security found Sim-Sim, and he decided to delegate the job to his assistant, Pieter Shaffer. Shaffer was expendable.

He lifted the telephone receiver. 'Pieter? It's Eisner. Are we secure?'

'Yes.'

'Make a note of this address: Flat one, twenty-two al-Hadiqa Street, the Gezira. I want you to find out who's living there, if anyone. Ring the bell. Say you're working for the Red Cross and that you have a package for a Betty Nolan. Treat whoever answers to your most winning smile.'

'What if no one answers?'

'There'll be a concierge. Ask for information.'

'When do you want me to go?'

'Now. The longer you delay, the more chance of compromise.'

Eisner put the phone down, popped four Phenobarbital tablets and, back in the main cabin, threw himself on the divan. Within minutes he was asleep.

Betty Nolan was chasing him through a labyrinth of dark alleys lined with open-fronted butcher's shops, where Heinrich Rohde and other Waffen SS were cutting the throats of lambs hanging from meat-hooks. Betty was pointing a crooked finger at him, and whispering, '*One thing is certain: you're going straight to damnation.*' For a second, Nolan's face was replaced by Sim-Sim's, then Eisner surfaced from the dark river of sleep, gasping for air, and realised that someone was banging on the door.

He rolled off the divan, snatched his Smith & Wesson from under a cushion, and stalked down the passage. Through the spyhole in the door he saw Shaffer—a tall, sandy-haired man wearing a crumpled off-white suit. He was slapping a rolled-up newspaper against his open palm in a rhythmic tattoo—a signal that he hadn't been compromised.

Eisner let him in and Shaffer's eyes fell on the .38 in his hand. 'I was battering on the door for ages. You must be getting past it, old man.'

Eisner forced a grin. 'Long surveillance job last night,' he said. 'Absolute murder.' He was in no mood for Shaffer's manner, but it had to be tolerated. As a South African national with perfect English, it was easy for Shaffer to pass as a South African cotton broker with British sympathies.

Eisner told him to make coffee, and went to dress. When he returned, Shaffer was perched on the divan, his newspaper spread out on the low table. 'Did you see this?' he said excitedly. 'The Luftwaffe launched a massive attack on Tobruk just before dawn this morning.'

Eisner sat down next to him. 'It's up to your lot now, isn't it?' he said. 'Second South African Division. General Klopper.'

Shaffer's blue eyes glinted. 'Klopper will fight to the last bullet.'

'Sometimes I wonder whose side you're on, Pieter,' Eisner chuckled. 'Or maybe you don't know yourself.'

Shaffer put on a hurt look. 'My good man, how dare you? My heart is with the Afrikaners at Tobruk, and ever will be.'

'In that case you've had it. Klopper will hoist the white flag the moment the first panzer enters the town. Rommel will be here in a week.' He offered Shaffer a cigarette from a box, took one himself and lit both.

Shaffer sat back and blew out a jet of smoke. 'Why do I sense that you're not exactly over the moon at the prospect?'

'That's easy,' Eisner said, making a sweeping gesture around the room. 'I've grown accustomed to certain standards. When Rommel gets here, we'll both be out of a job.' There was a moment's silence. 'So, what happened?'

'Well, it turned out to be a first-floor flat. You go through a hallway and up the stairs. The concierge says a girl lives there. He can't tell me her name and he can't say if she's in right now. "What does she do for a living?" I ask. "Nightclub dancer," he says. Anyway, I ring the bell. Nothing happens. I wait a few minutes, and ring again. I'm just about to give up when the door opens, and there she is.'

Eisner stared at him intently. 'What was she like?'

'Beautiful—legs to drive you wild, shortish blonde hair. Twenty-three, twenty-four. Anyway, she's giving me the once-over with these big green eyes, saying, "Can I help you?" and I flash her the lady-killer smile.'

'Pieter, get on with it.'

Shaffer smirked. 'I tell her that I work for the Red Cross and I have a package back at the office for a Miss Betty Nolan. Does she live here?'

Eisner bent forward. 'What did she say?'

'She said, "I'm Betty Nolan, but who'd want to send me a Red Cross parcel?" "I don't know, miss," I say, "but now I know you're here, I'll send it along." She smiles and a second later the door's closed.'

Eisner brought out the photo of Runefish. 'Is this her?'

Shaffer held the snapshot up in a beam of light. 'I'd lay a thousand guineas on it,' he said. 'That's the woman I saw.'

THE DINGO was parked in a pool of shade under a wind-twisted pine. As the convoy approached, Caine told Copeland to stop. He jumped down to meet George Padstowe, a bald ex-Marine, who was clambering out of the Dingo's lower hatch.

'They're on the way, skipper,' the bald man said breathlessly. 'I reckon we've got half an hour at most. There's a top-hole ambush site just on that bend.' He pointed down the track. On the right-hand side lay a gorse-covered plain; the maquis scrub was thick and high enough to conceal men and vehicles, and the steep ground would give them a commanding view. The only drawback was an irrigation trench on the other side of the road, which would provide the enemy with cover when they debussed. From the high ground, though, even that would be susceptible to enfilade fire. 'There's a slope on the other side of the bend,' Padstowe went on. 'That means the wagons will have to change down just as they're approaching.'

'Perfect killing zone,' Caine said. 'How many vehicles in the convoy and what's the composition?'

'Can't rightly say,' Padstowe said apologetically. 'I reckon no more than five, but they were kicking up a dust-cloud. We were going in for a close recce when an Itie kite rolls over: we had to freeze. By the time she'd cleared off, it were too late for a shufti, so I thought we'd better backtrack and report.'

'You did right,' Caine said, sounding happier than he felt. He hustled the commandos over into the shade for a quick O group. It would be a classic ambush—a fire-group in the centre, cut-off groups and an AFV at each side. 'It's going to be a hit-or-miss affair,' he told them. 'You'll hear the wagons change down as they come up the slope. Hang fire till it looks like there's nothing else coming, then give them all you've got.'

'Hold on, skipper,' Copeland cut in. 'We don't know where Runefish is being carried. If we blitz the column, she'll be killed.'

Caine's heart flipped a beat. In the excitement he'd forgotten that they were there to snatch Runefish, not to wipe out an enemy convoy. 'What's your plan, Harry?' Caine said.

'Bluff,' Cope said. 'I suggest we use one of the three-tonners and make out she's broken down. There's so much captured Allied transport around, they'll assume it's spoils of war. Me and you will stick our heads under the lorry's bonnet. Fred will hide in the cab. Give Moshe one of the Schmeissers we liberated yesterday, and let him flag down the first wagon. When she halts, he'll talk to the driver in German. While he's doing that we'll locate Runefish and snatch her.'

Caine nodded. 'They'll keep an important prisoner like that where they can see her, in an open wagon or a cab. If I'm right, we'll sight her in the first minute or so.'

He considered who to put in charge of the fire-group. Sweeney was senior corporal after Cope, but Caine no longer trusted him entirely. On the other hand, the ex-copper had always been dependable in combat, and if Caine gave him a key role it might stump his continuous second-guessing, which, he thought, arose from a sense of inadequacy. 'Todd, you'll take charge of the ambush party. Harry, we'll use Marlene for the decoy. The White and the three-tonners will remain here with the Senussi, and this will be our emergency RV.'

The growl of approaching engines sounded distantly. Caine caught sight of Moshe Naiman. 'Are you up for this?' he asked.

Naiman nodded. 'I can do it. It's a good plan, and I think it might work.'

'Good man. All right, let's get to it.'

Within ten minutes the ambush parties and armoured vehicles were concealed in the maquis. Marlene was parked on the left side of the track, about a hundred yards along from the ambush party. While Wallace curled up in her cab, Caine and Copeland leaned over the engine. Naiman, wearing shorts, shirt and an Afrika Korps peaked cap someone had rustled up, waited tensely by the roadside thirty yards away, the Schmeisser slung muzzle-forward from his shoulder. As they listened to the snarl of motors coming closer, Caine shot a glance at the young interpreter, wondering if he could pull off the ruse. He was the only man in the squad who spoke German, but he didn't look much like an Afrika Korps soldier.

'Here we go,' he said, as a German lorry teetered round the bend.

Naiman raised his hand, assuming a suppliant expression as he strode towards the approaching wagon. Her cab had two occupants—a bare-chested driver and a dark-haired soldier in khaki drills whom Naiman guessed was an officer. He walked casually up to the driver's side, feeling the Germans' eyes on him, reached up and opened the door. 'Morning, friends,' he said, in German. 'We've got a problem. Can you help?'

The Brandenburgers considered him dubiously, and Naiman had a second to register the driver's bull-like chest and football-sized biceps. In that instant he knew they weren't buying it. He snapped the Schmeisser's muzzle towards them but, before he could fire, the huge driver dropped on him with a blood-curdling bellow, knocking him flat. He wriggled frantically, feeling the big soldier's weight suffocating him.

Naiman's fingers found the trigger: his weapon burped. The driver howled as blood palpitated from his thigh. The officer nose-dived from the cab with a hole in his chest, crunching into the ground a foot away. The driver went limp. Naiman freed himself from the heavy corpse and squirmed away from the bodies, clocking the tyres of the staff car crunching gravel. There was a hawk-faced officer standing in the car, pointing a pistol at him, and next to him, her face creased with fear, sat a pretty young woman with green eyes and short blonde hair.

A pistol shot took off a piece of Naiman's right ear as he came up blipping bursts, shearing the flesh off the officer's chest. The car braked, the girl arched forward, bumped her head on the dashboard. Naiman saw the driver groping for a weapon, pumped steel twice, heard his slugs strike flesh. The girl squealed, head in hands.

Naiman was blind to the stutter of small-arms and the tracer. Only the blonde woman existed. He made the car in two bounds, wrenched open the door, snatched the screaming girl, jerked her out. He threw her over his shoulder, hurdled the irrigation ditch on the open side of the road and raced for the cover of a low ridge.

Todd Sweeney watched Naiman's action from the escarpment. Dozens of Germans were swarming from the trucks, humping weapons towards the trench. The Brandenburger gunners were shooting blind up the escarpment. He hung on until Naiman had carried the girl outside the killing zone, then ordered *Fire*. Three Brens blowtorched flame: ball and tracer racked air, punched gaps among the milling Jerries on the track.

Caine and Cope skirmished forward along the track while Wallace laid down covering fire from behind. Caine had a Mills grenade in each hand. Copeland saw him lob the dark pineapples through the window of the forward Jerry truck. The wagon lifted a foot in the air, her bodywork shredded.

Hidden in the maquis 150 yards up the scarp, Wingnut Turner, manning a Bren, saw the truck disintegrate. He observed the rear lorry of the convoy attempting to reverse back round the bend, out of the killing zone. He sighted up on the Jerry driver, put a double tap through the cab. The German's skull imploded like a punctured balloon.

Turner heard a motor gunning and stared in shock as a German AFV chirred into view from behind the bend. 'Hit that bloody wagon,' he gasped.

Gunner's Mate Gus Graveman plumped down next to Turner with the heavy 5.5mm Boys anti-tank rifle and beaded up on the AFV. The round fried air. Graveman clocked no damage to the Jerry wagon. 'Piece of junk,' he swore, firing again, but Turner knew it was useless: the AFV's armour was just too thick. The two watched helplessly as the great ironclad trawled up the verge straight towards Marlene.

Caine and Copeland had run into dense fire from Jerries holed up in the irrigation ditch, and were proned-out on the road shooting back at them. The AFV passed behind them, her 40mm cannon groping towards Marlene. The cannon *kerblunked*: the sky folded, the earth heaved.

Caine clocked Marlene brassing up in sunburst sears of flame. He heard another crump, saw the Jerry armoured car's gun-turret lopped off like the top of a soft-boiled egg. Up the escarpment, Sweeney had seen Marlene go up, and had observed the smoke from the Daimler on his left as Flash Murray took out the German armoured car.

Caine took in the five vehicles burning on the track and realised that it had gone strangely quiet. The Jerries in the ditch had ceased fire too—they were either dead or too badly injured to fight. The spell of silence was fractured by the cries of Sweeney's group moving from their positions on the escarpment. Caine felt the heat of the nearest conflagration on his face, boosted himself to his feet. Wallace, blood oozing from his shoulder, was leaning on Cope. Caine clutched at a wound in his side which was also pumping blood.

Cope scanned the ambush site, took in the five burning wagons, the toppled AFV, the smouldering cadavers. His eyes lingered on the smoking remains of Marlene. 'So the bluff worked then?' he said, drily.

Most of the ambush group was assembled around the Dingo. They had brought with them the bodies of Vic Bramwell and Mick Oldfield, who'd been hit when the Jerries raked the brush. Caine held a dressing to his side. 'Let's grab the girl and get out.'

He beckoned to Copeland and together they limped towards a low bank twenty yards off. They found Moshe Naiman perched in blood-soaked sand with a blonde young woman clad in a khaki drill shirt and trousers. The girl had a cut on the forehead, and both of them were covered in blood from head to foot. Caine stared at the woman. 'Are you Runefish?'

Naiman snorted. 'This isn't Runefish, skipper. Not unless they're recruiting Wrens from the Italians now.'

4

Twenty minutes of bone-shaking brought them back to the arbutus groves where Gracie had crashed. As Cope pulled up, Caine instructed him to get the wagons leaguered. 'Tell the lads not to put down roots. A few minutes to get shipshape and we're off.'

Caine's wound felt like fire. He leaned heavily on the door of the White as Todd Sweeney strode over. 'So it was all for nothing,' the ex-MP said. 'Attacking the village, the casualties, the lost wagons—all wasted. Instead of Runefish, we picked up some enemy civilian bint.'

Caine realised that the olive branch he'd offered Sweeney hadn't worked.

'I suggest you clear off, Corporal, before I look for that grease-gun Pickney used this morning and stick it right up your arse.'

As Caine watched him go, he reflected that, even if Todd's observations were negative, they were true. He was furious with himself: instead of locating Runefish's downed aircraft and making a systematic search around it, he'd got drawn into contacts with the enemy, the very thing he should have avoided. He had no idea what the next step should be.

He forced himself to limp over to where the Daimler was parked. Flash Murray and Trooper Paul 'Shirley' Temple were scouring the Daimler's barrel with a ramrod while Trubman fiddled with the wireless. Caine noticed that the W/T operator had removed his headphones, and enquired if he'd picked up anything on the emergency net. 'Still nothing,' Trubman said, then added, 'I was listening in to Rome Radio on the Phillips short-wave. At 0520 this morning, the Panzer Group penetrated Tobruk's perimeter. Last report puts Rommel himself at King's Cross, overlooking Tobruk town. He'll be inside by last light.'

Caine plumped down heavily on a petrol case, holding his wound. It felt as if he'd been branded with a red-hot iron. Apart from himself and his two close mates, there were only a dozen men left standing. Caine felt momentarily weighed down, not only by the losses, but also by a feeling that there was no hope, even for those who had made it this far.

Copeland was sitting on the White's running board inspecting his rifle.

'Do me a favour when you're finished,' Caine said. 'Go with Adud and cut those Senussi boys free. Give them their weapons back, but no ammo.'

'Got it, skipper.'

Naiman now wore a dressing on his mutilated left ear. He had also sorted out the Italian girl, who displayed a bandage on her temple. Caine waved them over. The woman had high cheekbones, a small nose and full lips that gave her a hint of sulkiness. She was not classically beautiful, but there was a sensuality about her, Caine thought.

'You don't look Italian,' he blurted. 'You look more like a German.'

'Don't call me German,' she snarled. 'I hate those *Tedesci* pigs . . .' She spat venomously onto the sand. 'They killed my brother.'

There was an awkward silence while Caine weighed her up. She sounded genuine enough: her voice had a low, mannish quality and her accent was distinctly Italian. He flushed out a fresh pack of cigarettes. She put one between her lips and her eyes met Caine's. 'You were at the village, no? I saw the headman and a girl here. You bring Carlo's body?'

'Carlo was the man with you at the village? Your brother?'

'Of course. You bring him with you, or you bury him there?'

'The Germans burned his body before we got there.'

'Pigs.'

Copeland arrived with Sheikh Adud and Layla, the Italian girl embracing them like long-lost friends. 'I think this is yours,' Copeland said, handing her the compact he'd found at the village.

'Thank you,' she said, studying her face in the mirror. 'As you see, I am very much in need of it.'

'We don't have a lot of time,' Caine said. 'I want to know who you are.'

He was interrupted by Pickney crouching down to examine his wound.

'Sorry, skipper, but that needs stitches right away.'

As the orderly started to clean Caine's injury, the girl switched her eyes to his face. 'My name is Angela Brunetto. My husband is a communist. He was a soldier in the Italian army, but he didn't like it, so he ran away. There is a band of deserters living in the Jebel. Communists and colonists who lost their farms because of the war, like Carlo. My husband, Michele, is *capo* of all deserters and colonists.'

'What were you doing in that village?'

'Hiding from the *Tedesci*,' she said. 'Carlo and me go to Sirte to buy fish. The pigs find us. They shoot Carlo, and me they take.'

'Why did they kidnap you? I mean why not kill you too?'

She shrugged. 'These soldiers are not ordinary soldiers. I say to myself perhaps they come to hunt Italian deserters, but then why they keep talking to me in English? Then I understand. They think I am someone else. Perhaps the girl you are looking for?'

Caine stiffened. 'I never said we were looking for a girl.'

'You attack them to save me? I don't think so. You, too, think I am someone else. That is why you ask me if I am a fish. It is code, no? I thank you for saving me, even if it is a mistake. Now, why you don't take me back to my camp? You will be safe there and maybe Michele help you find this fish woman. We have many contacts with Senussi all over the area.'

Caine flinched. 'Hell, Maurice. Feels like you're carving the pork.'

'Nearly done, skipper,' Pickney replied.

'I'm sorry about your brother,' Caine said, turning back to Angela again, 'but you're a hostile. I don't know if I even ought to trust you, let alone take you home.'

Angela fluttered her eyelids. 'Me, hostile?' she purred. 'I am civilian, not army. Anyway, we are all against Mussolini.'

Caine examined her face, and guessed that, behind the confident manner, she was scared. She'd seen her brother shot down, been abducted by Brandenburgers, witnessed men being killed horribly and was now in the hands of British troops. He felt sorry for her. As a soldier, he didn't like the idea of deserters, but then, if they were a thorn in the Axis side, they could only be regarded as potential allies.

Angela said, 'We have medical supplies . . . drugs, food, whisky.' Her eyes suddenly lit up. 'What about *benzina*?'

'You mean petrol?' he asked.

'Of course, petrol.'

'Ouch!' Caine spat suddenly. 'Didn't you say you were done, Maurice?'

'That's it, Tom. All over. You'll need sulphonamide pills for infection.'

Caine took the pills but didn't swallow them.

'We have warm springs,' Angela said lamely. 'You can all have a bath.'

Caine's face lit up. 'A bath,' he exclaimed. 'I won't deny that petrol would come in handy. But a bath? How could anyone refuse that?'

After Naiman had taken Angela and the two Senussi away for scoff and a brew, Cope said, 'You weren't serious about taking that woman home? It's always the "women and children first" with you, isn't it?'

Wallace, who had been busy boiling tea, filled three mugs. 'You do come on a bit strong over the ladies and children sometimes. What about them wogs this morning?'

'That's got nothing to do with it,' Caine snapped. He crammed the sulphonamide pills into his mouth, swallowed a mouthful of tea.

'Tom,' Cope said. 'You ever heard of the Sirens? Beautiful women whose singing used to lure sailors to death on the rocks. This area—Cyrenaica—it's named after them.'

'The last thing I need is a bloody history lesson. Look, it's getting late. We need a place to lay up and if that girl is being straight about her deserters, the fact that they're holding out there means that their base must be pretty secure. We also need fuel, and this is one easy way to get it. The boys are knackered. If we take any more hits we'll never pull the mission off.'

Copeland spluttered. 'Skipper, the mission's shot. What we've got to do now is stay alive long enough to get back behind the Wire.'

Caine shook his head. 'While I'm alive one thing is for certain: we're not going back without Runefish—or at least without making sure she's dead.'

Cope sighed. 'What are we going to do, then? We're stuck in the middle of nowhere, with God knows how many Huns on our trail, nothing on the emergency net, and no way of knowing if Runefish even exists.'

'You're wrong, Harry,' Caine said. 'Runefish is out there and going with

Angela is our best chance. Maybe her husband will be grateful enough to give us petrol, or maybe he'll sell us to the Nazis. There are times in your life when you've got to make a leap of faith.'

THE DESERTERS' BASE lay in a vast crater at the heart of the Green Mountains. Caine halted the wagons at the entrance while Angela went ahead. She was back within twenty minutes, declaring that her husband and his band were ready to welcome them with open arms. Wary of a trap, Caine ordered the wagons through the gap with all guns manned. He quickly saw that these precautions had been unnecessary.

As soon as he alighted, a galaxy of lights sprang up in the darkness. A crowd was assembled on a great flat slab of rock, extending like a giant foot from the base of a dark cave. A moment later Caine was mobbed, a horde of excited men, women and children cheered, jabbered at him in Italian, clamoured to shake his hand. After the bloodbath on the road that morning, it felt like a hero's return.

Caine heard a voice rasping orders, and the crowd peeled back to let through a broad-chested, swashbuckling man with a shoulder-length mane of wild hair. He was clad in a sheepskin coat, Afrika Korps jodhpurs and high cavalry boots. The newcomer threw his arms round Caine and kissed him on both cheeks. 'I am Michele Brunetto,' he announced. 'My wife told me everything. Thank you for bringing her back.'

Trubman, Naiman, Pickney and Corporal Barry Shackleton, an ex-Scots Greys farrier, volunteered to stay with the leaguer and Caine gave Trubman instructions to renew his efforts on the emergency net. Adud explained that he and his daughter wouldn't be joining them: some of the Italians here weren't well disposed towards his folk.

Here in the camp Angela and Michele were evidently king and queen. They led Caine and his men up onto the slab, and into the cave-opening. As he entered, Caine caught his breath. It was like some huge Gothic cathedral, lit with dozens of lamps in niches. The rock pillars enclosed recesses that were furnished with old carpets and hung with threadbare drapes. In the open area there stood ranks of trestle tables. Caine noticed another cave that seemed to be festooned with legs of ham and cheeses as big as truck-wheels, and it was stacked with jars of tomato pulp, magnums of olive oil, ten-pound tins of jam and coffee. Caine shot Michele an incredulous glance. 'You do all right for yourselves here, don't you?'

The Italian shrugged. His eyes were shifty. 'This is nothing. We have chickens, pigs, even a few cows for milk. We buy fish and lobsters from the Arabs on the coast, and we have more tinned food than we can eat.'

Copeland frowned. 'British or Axis?' he enquired.

Michele opened both hands wide. 'We trade for some. Some we take. It doesn't matter from which side we take, because property is theft and all are class enemies.' He caught Cope's expression and went on hastily. 'Not you, of course. You bring back my treasure.' He clapped Caine on the shoulder. 'We are blood brothers for ever, and my life is yours.' Michele stared at Angela, his face drained of joviality. 'We will miss Carlo,' he said. 'He was a good man. Tonight, we hold a feast in his memory, to celebrate your safe return, and to honour our guests. We have music and dancing, and we forget the war.'

Noticing that this news wasn't greeted with unalloyed rapture by Caine and Cope, Michele said, 'Angela says you need *benzina*. It is yours. You can take whatever you need. Come, I show you.'

He took a torch from a stone shelf, and led Caine and Copeland back out into the night. Caine got the impression that they were in a huge amphitheatre enclosed by steep rock walls as much as a couple of miles in diameter. On one side, a massive stone tower rose hundreds of feet high, riddled with caves. If ever there was a natural fortress, this was it: with that single entrance it would be almost impossible to take by storm and, even if it were bombed, these caves would make ideal shelters.

Michele explained that the defile was watched around the clock by pickets. 'No one sneak up on us here. Is a good place, no? Very hard to find, hard to see from the air because of the trees. Here . . .' He shone the torch forward and Caine saw among the trees a thirty-foot ziggurat covered in tarpaulins. Michele whipped one of the covers back, revealing hundreds of stacked petrol cases. Caine whistled, while Copeland stared at the British War Office arrowhead on the boxes. 'These look familiar,' he said. 'This is all petrol?'

Michele shook his head. 'Petrol, weapons, ammunition, military clothing, medical stuff, tinned rations. So, how much *benzina* you want?'

'Three hundred gallons ought to do it,' Cope said.

Michele considered. 'OK. It is a small price to pay for my Angela.'

'That's very generous of you,' Caine said, grinning. 'Even if it is our own petrol you're giving back to us.'

Michele laughed. 'You are welcome. It was generous of you to rescue Angela also, even if it was not her you were looking for. My wife told me about the girl you are seeking.'

Caine was serious now. 'She's a British officer. Her aircraft was shot down south of the Green Mountains a few days ago, and she parachuted out. Have you heard anything?'

'I might have heard about a plane coming down. I did not pay much attention. I will send out my people to make enquiries. Now, my wife say she promise you a bath. I must show you our hot springs.'

He led them through the forest and they emerged from the bush to find themselves in a shallow depression filled with a vast rock-pool of inky water. Most of their mates were already bathing up to their chests. 'Come on in,' Wallace yelled when he saw Caine. 'The water's beautiful.' Caine remembered his wound, but it hadn't bothered Wallace, and the prospect of a bath was just too tempting. He and Cope were soon luxuriating in the lukewarm water beside the others.

Caine heard more excited voices and was astonished to see a crowd of Italian girls carrying towels and bundles of brand-new British khaki drills. They laid out their gifts, chattering and bantering with the commandos.

Clad in a clean uniform, Caine felt an entirely new person. The men relaxed, the ugly skirmish of the morning all but forgotten. As they climbed back up the steps to the slab, Caine saw that the fiesta was already in full swing: pigs were being roasted on spits, and the air was full of the smell of roasting pork. Romantic Italian music played on a gramophone, and men and women were locked together on the dance floor. It seemed less a wake for Angela's dead brother than a spontaneous celebration.

The women had dolled themselves up for the occasion in low-cut dresses and arranged their hair in opulent coiffures. There were more than enough women to go around, and almost all of them were beautiful. Caine didn't know whether this was an illusion, exaggerated by the fact that he had lived for years almost without feminine contact. One thing was certain: he and his men had dropped just like castaways into an exotic and sensuous dimension far from the harshness of war.

Michele arrived, carrying two five-litre flagons of red wine. '*Drink*,' he roared. 'To Carlo's memory. To your fallen comrades, and to liberty, fraternity and peace. *Salute*.'

He drained his cup in one draught, and the commandos followed suit. 'By God,' Caine said, putting his goblet down. 'That is *good*.'

The wine flagons were doing their rounds with frantic speed, and Caine noticed that the commandos had entered into the spirit of the party like men reprieved from a death sentence.

The highlight of the feast was fresh lobsters boiled in garlic. 'You must be careful how much lobster you eat,' Michele informed them. 'Too much and you make love all night long.' The commandos ignored Michele's warning and attacked the succulent meat with relish.

The only man who seemed out of sorts was Copeland. Caine saw him hovering morosely and offered him a cigarette. 'What's up with you?'

'I keep thinking I'm dreaming,' Cope said. 'What are we doing here?'

'Drinking good wine, eating good scoff,' Caine said, 'and hoping for news about Runefish. Enjoy it, Harry.'

Just then, Angela glided towards them in a tight red dress. She kissed Caine on both cheeks, then turned to Copeland. 'Do you want to dance with me?' she asked, parting sulky lips.

If Cope was surprised he didn't show it. 'I don't think your husband would like it,' he said.

Angela laughed. 'My husband is pleased to see me,' she said, 'but there are other girls he is also pleased to see.' She nodded towards the floor where Michele was dancing with a pretty girl wearing an almost indecently short dress. The two were wrapped around each other like snakes.

The next time Caine looked, he was amazed to see Copeland and Angela in a slow clinch. A little later they had disappeared. There must be some lesson about the female sex here that had eluded him, he thought. Cope had barely noticed Angela, and yet she'd homed in on him, right under her husband's nose. He had no doubt they were already in her tent.

Caine danced with a dreamy-eyed beauty called Lina. As they floated round the floor, her lips parted, succulent and inviting. When he kissed her she responded with a searing blaze of passion, almost frightening in its intensity. Caine closed his eyes and gave himself up to the feeling. He felt as if he'd been drawn into a parallel universe far away from death and war. 'Why don't you stay here,' she whispered in his ear. 'We need strong men like you.'

Caine felt bewitched. The world beyond this cave seemed to have no meaning—the war, the enemy, the commandos: it all seemed remote. He was about to whisper that he'd stay with her for eternity when there came a tap on his arm and a voice said, 'Skipper, I've got something.'

Caine found himself staring into the unlovely bifocals of Taffy Trubman. 'Let it wait, Taffy,' he groaned. 'Can't you see I'm busy here?'

Trubman didn't move. 'This young lady is very pretty,' he said, 'but is she more important than Runefish?'

It was the name that made the difference. Caine disentangled himself from Lina. Outside, the night air was sobering. 'What is it, Taffy?'

'The emergency net, skipper. I've been picking up a message with

Runefish's signature for the past fifteen minutes. It's coming from a biscuit-tin transmitter, and the signal strength indicates that it's not far away.'

Caine followed Trubman down to the Dingo, whose engine was running to keep the wireless batteries charged, and saw that Trubman had erected a complex antenna. The Welshman plonked himself in the driver's seat and had Caine sit in the passenger's place. He handed him the headphones and adjusted the volume dial on the set. Caine heard the blip-blip-blip of Morse signals. 'You sure it's her?' he asked.

'It's the correct call sign and the signature's very clear, see.'

'But even if it is, couldn't she be sending under duress?'

'Not likely, skipper. There's a security code that would be left out by anyone who didn't know the procedure. In this loop, the code is extant.'

Caine put the headphones down. 'Can you triangulate the signal?'

Trubman hesitated, pulling a wry face. 'It'll require an adjustable aerial, so I'll have to erect the nine-foot poles. I'll need some help to manoeuvre the AFV while I track the signal. In fact, it'd be better with two sets and two aerials, because I can't calibrate both sets at once, and we need to angle the vehicles until we can lock on to the signal.'

Caine listened to the torrent of objections, bemused. 'In other words, you can't do it?' he enquired.

'Oh no, Sergeant,' said Trubman, looking shocked. 'I'm a signalman, first class. It might take a while, but I can do it all right.'

Caine chuckled with relief. 'Good,' he said. 'Get on it right away.' He slipped out of the hatch and waved Naiman and Pickney over. 'Come on,' he said. 'We'll go and round up the boys.'

'From what I saw,' Trubman tittered. 'That's going to take some doing.'

Trubman's warning proved correct. No sooner had they reached the slab than they heard two men and a woman shrieking at each other. The trouble was that one of the voices was Harry Copeland's.

Michele and Angela were at loggerheads outside what Caine took to be their tent. Cope was trying to calm them down, looking embarrassed dressed only in his shorts, and Angela wore a skimpy nightdress that concealed nothing. When Michele saw Caine, he bawled, 'This is how you repay our hospitality? I turn my back and this *stronso*'—he jabbed a finger at Cope—'is with my wife?'

'What about you?' Angela screamed. 'You say, *I missed you, darling*, and the night I get back and Carlo just dead, you are making love with his girlfriend in front of everyone. You would be happy the *Tedesci* kill me, too, so you can go with every trollop in the camp.'

She hurled herself at Michele, scrabbling at his face with broken fingernails. Michele held her off for a second, then belted her in the face, knocking her down. He was about to kick her when Caine cocked his Colt .45. Michele heard the click, and looked up to see that the pistol was trained at his head. 'I don't like to interfere in domestic issues,' Caine said carefully, 'but I'm damned if I'm going to see ladies knocked down.'

Michele halted in his tracks, his face a mask of blind fury. 'You get out,' he bellowed. 'And him'—he gestured at Copeland—'with you.'

'We're going,' Caine said. 'There was just the little matter of petrol?'

Michele spat contemptuously. 'You think I give you petrol?'

Caine didn't lower the pistol. 'Where I come from, a promise is a promise. Either you give me the fuel, or I will make sure the RAF have the coordinates of this place and include it on their next bombing run. My government doesn't take kindly to people stealing material supplied by hard-working tax-payers. Capitalist pigs, you see.'

The Italian tossed his long hair arrogantly. 'All right, but you'—he jabbed a long finger at Copeland—'stay away from her.'

Caine sent Naiman and Pickney to the leaguer with Michele, to collect one of the 3-tonners for the petrol. As soon as her husband was out of sight, Angela threw her arms round Copeland and kissed him. Copeland returned the kiss. 'Give us a minute, skipper,' he said.

Caine waited for him at the entrance to the cave, where he saw that the party had already broken up. Copeland appeared, fully dressed. Caine winked at him. 'What happened to the Sirens, then?'

'Don't start,' Cope snapped. 'She's a . . . she's a very special person.'

'No doubt she is. In case you're interested, though, Trubman picked up Runefish on the emergency net. We're in business.'

It took almost an hour to collect the commandos. A few of them were lying in the recesses of the cave in all stages of undress, mostly in the arms of young women. Caine told them the good news about Runefish, but they didn't seem impressed. 'What's the rush, skipper?' Padstowe demanded blearily, as Caine yanked a blanket off him and his paramour. 'Let's stay a few more days.'

The hardest cases were those who were scattered throughout the tents in the forest and Caine had to frog-march Wallace down to the leaguer at gunpoint. As they arrived, Naiman swept past from the fuel dump at the wheel of the 3-tonner Vera. He gave Caine the thumbs-up from the open window. 'Got it, skipper. All three hundred gallons.'

'Good. Let's get this circus on the road.'

Dawn was creeping across the Green Mountains, the open hillsides smeared with pink candy-floss light. Caine found Trubman in the Dingo. 'How's it going?' he enquired.

'It's not been easy, skipper,' he sighed. 'It's not very accurate. I've only managed to narrow it down to an area of about twelve square feet.'

'Twelve square *feet*?' Caine repeated, wondering if he'd heard right

Trubman handed Caine a map. 'I've marked the spot with an X, about twenty miles from here. I've also marked out a route. I reckon it'll take us no more than an hour to get there.'

'Taffy,' Caine said, beaming all over his face, 'you've just saved the mission. You're worth your weight in gold.'

The plump cheeks pinked out. 'One thing, skipper. Runefish has been transmitting nonstop for nearly two hours. If I've been able to locate her position, the Axis will almost certainly have done the same. There's at least a fifty-fifty chance the Hun will have got there first.'

SIXTY-THREE MINUTES later, Caine, Copeland and Wallace lay scrimmed up in dense maquis scrub on a steep hillside overlooking a sandy dry-wash. Directly beneath them, across the wadi bed, was the narrow opening of a cave. A trickle of smoke from the entrance indicated that it was inhabited. Caine was certain that they had located Runefish at last.

Caine scanned the area with his field glasses, looking out for unwelcome surprises. Nothing stirred. 'That's it then,' Caine said. 'Runefish, here we come.'

He was halted by Wallace. Below them, a German soldier had just emerged from around the bend in the wadi. Another soldier appeared, then another, spaced about three yards apart. Caine would have bet money they were Brandenburgers.

Then Caine became aware of the deep growl of an engine and the rattle of iron tracks. A Mark III panzer slalomed into view round the wadi bend. Caine felt a frisson of dread as the tank rumbled along the wadi directly below him. He knew from experience that a trio of shells from her 50mm cannon would put paid to his entire column.

If Maddaleine Rose was inside the cave, she would have heard the tank, and would now know that the enemy had found her. He wondered why Rose had started transmitting so suddenly, and why she'd kept it up for so long. She must have realised that the Axis would triangulate her signal. Caine could only imagine that either she'd grown desperate, or that she'd somehow discovered his rescue mission was close at hand.

If Michele's men had gone out the night before, it was possible that Rose had discovered from them that a British mobile detachment was on her trail. Was that why she'd keyed in the emergency call so abruptly? But wouldn't it have been more tactical for her to have returned with them? It occurred to him that she might have been injured in the parachute drop. Maybe she'd heard news of the commandos' presence but couldn't move. But then why not send Michele's men back with a message instead . . .?

The tank creaked to a halt a little further up the wadi. At the same moment an entire platoon of Brandenburgers advanced round the bend on Caine's left, led by a stringy subaltern and a bull-faced sergeant. The subaltern detailed five men to accompany him and the group entered the cave.

The single gunshot, muffled by the rock walls, almost made Caine jump. He kept his eyes riveted on the cave entrance and saw the bull-faced sergeant emerge, followed by two men dragging a woman by the arms. She was tall, with the kind of build you might find in a dancer. Her khaki drills were torn and filthy, her crop of short corn-gold hair matted. The holster she wore at her waist flapped empty, and Caine noted that it was worn reversed on her right for a cross-body draw—indicating that she was left-handed. He could make out the light blue WRNS rings of rank on her shoulder straps. '*Maddy*,' he whispered under his breath.

The woman's captors released her arms. Instantly, she let out a deafening screech and burst into a run. She'd made only two paces before the sergeant blocked her way, smashed her in the face hard enough to send her reeling to her knees. Caine forced himself to watch as the Germans hauled the woman up and lashed her hands behind her back with rope. The other soldiers came out of the cave, one of them carrying a wireless transmitter. A second trooper hefted a haversack, and a third what appeared to be the charred remains of a leather attaché case and bits of blackened paper. This explained the smoke issuing from the cave earlier: Runefish had been destroying her documents. From what Caine could see, it looked as if she'd pretty much succeeded. The officer signalled to the squad to move off.

Maddaleine looked remarkably cool considering her position. Her attempt to escape, while futile, had been plucky. The loud, distracting noise, the explosive burst of energy—these were textbook escape tactics. Runefish had been well trained for the job: she was evidently more than just a spare GHQ pen-pusher, Caine thought.

As the party headed for the bend in the wadi, the rest of the Brandenburgers began to withdraw. 'I can take the shot now, skipper,' Copeland whispered, peering through his rifle scope. It took Caine a split second to work out that Cope was talking about execution. Rose had destroyed the documents, but the Hun would soon force her to reveal the secrets of Assegai, or whatever it was that she was carrying in her head.

He found himself casting around for excuses to stop the hit. Copeland was a crack shot: it would only need one round.

'Skipper?' Cope hissed.

Caine felt sick at heart. 'All right, Harry. You can take the shot.'

Copeland lined up his sights. 'What a waste,' he sighed under his breath. 'She's a real stunner.'

Caine took a last peek at Maddy Rose—the woman he and his men had gone through hell to rescue, and whom he would now never meet. As Cope had said, she was a 'stunner'. It wasn't too late. He could stop it. Whatever his orders, he wasn't going to see a brave woman shot down in cold blood. Caine had just opened his mouth so say, 'Don't fire', when an aero engine screeched above them: all three of them ducked.

It was a Storch spotter-plane, skimming the escarpment at about 300 feet. As Caine watched, though, the aircraft looped west towards Benghazi. He let out a breath and squinted down into the dry-wash channel. Maddaleine Rose and her captors had gone.

5

Colonel-General Erwin Rommel, General Officer Commanding the Panzer Group Africa, stood at the door of an abandoned Italian roadhouse, his grey-blue eyes taking in smoke rising in black pencil lines from Tobruk.

His capture of the so-called 'impregnable fortress' of Tobruk in only twenty-four hours should have been the crowning moment of Rommel's career, yet he felt furious. What was gnawing at him was the fact that while his men had captured nearly 2,000 vehicles and 5,000 tons of food, enemy petrol stocks had only amounted to 2,000 tons. Unless he found more petrol soon, he might not be able to continue his advance into Egypt. It was crucial to strike now, he thought, while the Eighth Army was in total disarray.

He turned and marched into the half-derelict building, grateful for the respite from the fierce midday sun. Inside, he found his ADCs tacking up maps and arranging camp chairs round a trestle table for the forthcoming meeting. Rommel had just accepted a cup of coffee when his intelligence officer, Major Friedrich von Mellenthin marched in carrying a sheaf of message forms. Rommel waved them away. 'Just tell me,' he said.

Mellenthin was a stiff-moustached Prussian from an old military family who, like Rommel, had once served as a private soldier. 'One of our agents in Cairo verifies that the Eighth Army has been ordered to take up a fallback position at Mersa Matruh.'

Rommel grunted: this was hardly a surprise. British generals always preferred defensive positions to mobility—it was the same rigidity of thinking that had led to their loss of the Gazala Line. They hadn't yet got the hang of fast-moving mechanical warfare.

'They still haven't learned that any defensive position on the coast can always be outflanked via the desert.'

Mellenthin stepped over to the theatre-map on the wall. 'That's generally true, but not here at Alamein.' He pointed to the map. 'The open flank is guarded by salt marsh and quicksands there. If I were Auchinleck, and wanted to make a stand, that's where it would be.'

'There won't be any stand,' Rommel scoffed. 'The Eighth Army is finished.'

Mellenthin's brow puckered. 'I've got something here from Number Two Company of the Brandenburg Regiment. They've picked up a British courier from Allied HQ Egypt. She's being held at Biska, pending interrogation by the Abwehr.'

'*She*?' Rommel chortled. 'Auchinleck must be hard up. Who is she?'

'A Royal Navy staff officer with the equivalent rank of major. Her aircraft crashed south of the Green Mountains three days ago. We had a tip-off that her mission might be significant—to Churchill in London, no less. Our wireless interceptors picked up communications from her aircraft, and heard her codename—Runefish—being used. We were able to track the plane and shoot her down. The woman bailed out by parachute, and Two Company have been looking for her ever since. It seems that a couple of their platoons may have run into enemy raiding units behind our lines. It's possible that these units were sent to rescue this Runefish.'

Rommel glanced at his watch. 'Can this wait?' he asked. '"Smiling Albert" will be here any minute.'

Mellenthin tried again. 'Sir, Runefish destroyed the documents she was carrying before Two Company found her, but they did manage to retrieve one line in code. That line has been decrypted and it suggests that her mission concerned the condition of the Eighth Army.'

'If she destroyed the documents, she's not much use to us, is she?'

'The intelligence isn't necessarily lost, sir,' he said. 'British standard operating procedure is to have the courier memorise the details. It only requires a skilled interrogator . . .'

'Let me know when you've got something more concrete,' Rommel said. At that moment Field Marshal Kesselring and General Bastico swept in. Kesselring pumped Rommel's hand. 'Well done, General, well done,' he roared, sporting the familiar toothy grin that had earned him the nickname 'Smiling Albert'. 'Today, the eyes of all Germany are upon you.'

As General Officer Commanding the Mediterranean theatre, Kesselring was Rommel's superior. As a pilot who'd been shot down no fewer than five times, and a superb administrator, he was also fundamentally Luftwaffe, and Rommel regarded his knowledge of ground warfare as cursory.

'A thousand congratulations, General,' rumbled Ettore Bastico, a bear-like Italian. 'Today will go down in history as the beginning of the end for the British in North Africa.'

'Perhaps it's premature to tell you,' Kesselring said, 'but our dear Führer has awarded you a field marshal's baton. From tomorrow you won't have to salute me any more.'

Rommel remained pokerfaced. 'The Führer is very generous,' he said, 'but with all due respect, I would rather have had an extra division.'

Kesselring and Bastico laughed. It was the sort of remark expected of the 'Desert Fox'.

As the three generals sat at the table, Kesselring said, 'With the fall of Tobruk, the time has come to carry out the next step of the plan we agreed on at Obersalzberg in March—Operation Herkules—the capture of Malta.'

Rommel fixed him with a glassy stare. 'When we discussed this plan you made it clear that the success of Herkules would require the deployment of all the Luftwaffe squadrons in this theatre. If that is still the case, where am I going to get the air support for my advance into Egypt?'

Kesselring scratched his nose. 'Obviously we don't have enough aircraft to support both the attack on Malta *and* Egypt. But as long as Allied air units and submarines are able to operate from Malta, none of our supply columns is safe. Only one out of every four convoys to Tripoli is coming through intact. Therefore, General, you will await the outcome of the Malta operation. In August, you will be able to advance with full air support.'

'August?' Rommel repeated. 'By that time the Eighth Army will have been reinforced by God knows how many fresh divisions and new tanks. No, no. We have to push across the frontier *now* in a lightning thrust.

The Eighth Army is shattered. We must overtake what's left of it and crush it before it can escape. To go for Malta instead would be the act of a fool.'

Kesselring now bore little resemblance to the mythical 'Smiling Albert'. 'Be careful, General. That strategy was agreed on in March, by the Duce, and by the Führer himself. If there are any fools involved, you are one of them, because I don't remember you making any objection at the time.'

'Things have changed since March. War is fluid. Situations evolve.'

Kesselring leaned back in his chair. 'General, your troops have fought hard, and they are tired. Wouldn't it be more reasonable to rest and refit? You would be in a far stronger position in a month's time.'

'The enemy will be ten times stronger. We must strike today. The Eighth Army is on the verge of collapse. We must go in now.'

'What makes you so certain that the Eighth Army is finished?' the Italian general asked.

'My nose tells me so.'

Bastico smirked. 'With due respect, General, your nose is not always your best advisor. I have great respect for you—you are the only leader we have who truly understands mobile warfare, but this is about logistics.'

'About pen-pushers, you mean,' Rommel snorted. 'About your fat, indolent supply staffs in Rome who wouldn't know a day's work if it got up and punched them in the face. If those blighters put in the same effort my troops in the field put in, then we'd have the supplies you continually promise me here in Tobruk, not a thousand miles away in Tripoli.'

'Are you aware,' Bastico cut in sourly, 'that your eight thousand-ton steamer *Reichenfels* was sunk only this morning by an RAF squadron operating out of Malta? Did you know that, the day before yesterday, the Italian cruiser *Trento* was sunk by the same squadron, and the battleship *Littorio* badly damaged? We can't get supplies to the forward ports, General, because Malta is in our way. To push into Egypt without securing the supply base would be a major strategic blunder. I'm telling you now, that you are to proceed no further than the Egyptian border.'

Rommel laughed. 'You can't give me orders, General. The Panzer Army is under my command.'

'Maybe,' Kesselring grunted, 'but the Luftwaffe is under mine, and I am withdrawing all air units to Sicily. See how far you get without air support.'

Kesselring stood up. Bastico followed. Mellenthin suddenly stepped forward. 'Gentlemen, gentlemen,' he said soothingly. 'There seems to be a misunderstanding here, but I'm sure we can sort it out. Please, Field Marshal, sit down.'

Kesselring considered him for a moment. He knew Mellenthin came from a good Prussian family. He sat down again.

Mellenthin had remained standing. 'It seems to me that the problem all hinges on the state of the Eighth Army. While General Rommel says that Allied forces are on the run, you think that they may still outgun us. What we need, I suggest, is sound intelligence. If General Rommel can come up with proof that the situation is as he says it is, then surely you wouldn't prevent an advance that would bring almost certain victory in only ten days? It would be far more cost-effective than a full-scale offensive against Malta.'

Kesselring shrugged. 'Does such proof exist?'

'This morning our troops picked up a British courier sent by Auchinleck to report directly to Churchill on the state of the Eighth Army. We don't know the content of that report yet, but we hope to in a couple of hours. Could I suggest, sir, that you make no decision until then?'

There was a pause as Kesselring took a deep breath. 'Very well, Major. I will give you twelve hours.'

They stood in silence until the two officers had left the building, then Rommel rounded on his IO. 'How do you know the girl will talk?'

'It was all I could think of to stop them walking out.'

Rommel thought it over. 'I don't see that we have much to lose. Just make sure I have that Runefish report the moment it's available. Who's doing the interrogation?'

'Rohde, sir. He's the top Abwehr man in North Africa.'

Rommel stared at him. 'Rohde—wasn't he one of those scum they deployed to torture women and children illegally behind Russian lines?'

Mellenthin nodded. 'He's not exactly the kind of man you'd want to invite to dinner, sir. But if anyone's likely to make Runefish talk, it's him.'

'Poor Runefish,' Rommel said. 'She won't be fit for much by the time that animal's finished with her.'

CONCEALED HIGH on the hillside, Caine watched Sheikh Adud plodding up the wadi, leading a donkey on whose bony back his daughter was mounted. He wondered how the sheikh had managed to acquire a donkey. Allowing Adud and Layla to go into an Axis-held centre by themselves had been a leap of faith, and he'd felt very relieved when he clocked them emerging from the town twenty minutes earlier.

The town was marked on Caine's map as Biska, and he guessed it had been an important Italian outpost before the war. It had taken them two hours to shadow the Brandenburger convoy. They'd travelled slowly and cautiously, always remaining far enough behind the enemy so that their dust-cloud wouldn't be noticed or their motors heard.

The town itself stood on the edge of an escarpment that swept down into the coastal plain, a cantonment of flat-roofed oblongs on one side of a wide main street and a maze of stone-built Arab huts on the other. Caine had identified a hospital, a town hall and a police barracks. Apart from military patrols, the streets seemed deserted. As far as he could make out, the Brandenburgers' vehicles were leaguered outside the barracks, together with some wagons he guessed might belong to the Italian police.

Caine watched the sheikh and his daughter until they disappeared round the bend, then slithered down to the leaguer to hear the news.

Naiman, Adud and Layla swept in under the scrim nets. 'I've just debriefed them, skipper,' the interpreter said. 'Runefish is in the town-hall building, held in a locked room opening off the reception.'

'What, they actually saw her in there?'

'No, but Adud has a bunch of relatives in the town. One of them works as a servant at the town hall, and he saw them bring Runefish in this morning. She's being guarded by the carabinieri. There are two in the guardroom outside her room, armed with rifles and pistols.'

'What about the Jerries?'

'They're on patrol outside. The sheikh doesn't know how many are on stag at once, but probably four divided into pairs, with another four on standby. The patrols circle the whole admin area in opposite directions, a patrol passing the town hall every five minutes or so. There's a doorman at the town hall—a carabinieri who sits on the porch outside. He's armed with a rifle. The door is unlocked while the sentry's there.'

'How many Jerries and how many carabinieri?'

'The Jerries are the Brandenburg platoon at the wadi, but the carabinieri are at company strength—about a hundred. Adud's relative told him that the Brandenburgers often bring people here for interrogation. They're waiting for an officer to arrive from Benghazi this afternoon to interrogate Runefish. The bloke's name is Major Heinrich Rohde. A regular here, apparently. Intelligence—probably Abwehr. Not a very nice fellow. Adud's relative said he's seen him hang people up with meat-hooks . . .'

'*Jesus*.' Caine closed his eyes for a moment, hoping they could get Runefish out before it came to that. 'Any description of this Rohde?'

'A tall, balding fellow,' Naiman said. 'High forehead, clean shaven, long thin fingers. He's never been known to show mercy—even the local Jerries and Ities are scared of him. Apparently they call him the "Black Widow".'

Caine nodded. 'What time is this "Black Widow" expected?'

'They weren't sure—late afternoon. He always comes by aircraft and lands on the airstrip about five miles outside the town.'

Caine glanced at his watch: it was 1230 hours. 'That means we've got three and a half hours to break her out.' He turned to the Senussi and shook hands with them both gratefully. The gamble he'd taken in sending them in alone had paid off. 'You've done a wonderful job,' he told them. 'By the way, where did you get the donkey?'

'Adud nicked it,' Naiman chuckled.

When the laughter had died down, Caine stood up. 'Moshe, call the boys for an immediate O group. We've got to decide how to go about this.'

He briefed the lads on Adud's information, then threw the field open to 'commando initiative'. Wallace wanted an all-out frontal assault like the one they'd done at Umm 'Aijil but Caine vetoed it. They were facing larger enemy forces this time, and were down to a handful of men. 'No, Fred, it's got to be done by bluff and stealth.'

'Yes, and bluff really worked last time, didn't it?' Todd Sweeney said. 'I can't understand why you didn't bump Runefish off back there in that wadi and be done with it, skipper. Squeamishness, was it?'

'Yes, it was,' Caine rejoindered, 'as squeamish as you were at putting Cavazzi out of his misery.'

Sweeney's mouth clamped tight, and Caine shot him a hard look. Two could play at that game. Yet, as usual, Sweeney had hit the bulls-eye. 'We muffed our orders, skipper,' Cope had told him earlier. 'One shot and we'd be on our way back now, mission accomplished. We may as well accept we missed the boat. The Jerries are going to get whatever it is she knows out of her, so why don't we head homewards?'

Caine shook his head. 'I'm going after her, even if I have to do it alone.'

'I hope you're not expecting gratitude,' Cope had said. 'I know those officer-class bints—they wouldn't spit on you if you were on fire.'

Now, Copeland sat among the lads, brooding over the problem. 'You got any ideas?' Caine asked him.

'All right,' Cope said at last. 'If we're doing this by stealth, in daylight, we're going to need disguise. We could go in dressed as Arabs—two men togged up in Adud's Sunday best, carrying spare clothes for Runefish. We could even take the donkey. We approach the town hall, wait till the patrol's gone by, then gain entry either by bluster or taking out the doorman. Once we're inside, we knock out the guards, dress Runefish up in Arab gear and bunk it. The only real problem is that we're going to need some way of knocking off those guards silently. If any shooting starts, we've had it.'

'Now you're talking,' Wallace boomed, rubbing his hands. 'It's a job for my dear old fanny.'

'No way,' Cope said. 'Cutting the throats of two or three Itie policemen at the same time, without one of them letting out so much as a screech, is too dicey. We need something that's going to shut them up instantly.'

'What about drugs?' suggested Wingnut Turner. 'If we could get Adud's relative to slip something in the guards' food . . .?'

'Too unpredictable,' Maurice Pickney said.

'It's the right idea, though,' Turner said.

'*Abu na'is*,' a female voice said suddenly.

The men wheeled round to see that Adud's daughter had spoken for the first time. '*Abu na'is*,' she repeated, 'is a drug we get from leaves. We shoot it from bow and arrow. It make sleep but not kill.'

Caine stared at Layla in astonishment. She'd evidently followed the entire conversation. 'You speak English?' he asked incredulously.

The girl blushed deeply. 'My father . . . You are all . . . men . . .'

'Oh, I get it,' Wallace said. 'The old boy didn't want us chatting you up.'

Layla smiled. 'I study English in Italian missionary school when I am small. Some I am remember. You excuse me for not talking.'

'Of course we excuse you,' Caine said. 'Now, what is this stuff?'

'*Abu na'is* come from leaf you find here. We make medicine. We put medicine on arrow, we shoot. It is not kill, but make sleep like *that* . . .' She snapped her small fingers.

Adud chimed in with a torrent of Arabic, looking at Naiman. 'The sheikh says that poison is women's work,' he translated. 'So he can't help us make it, but he could make bows and arrows for us. He says that this *abu na'is* works a treat—the victim goes out instantly and stays out for hours.'

There was a pause while Caine weighed it up. 'It *is* the kind of thing we're looking for,' he said, 'but if it doesn't work . . .'

'It work,' Layla cried, clapping her hands in excitement.

Caine smiled at her enthusiasm. 'Let's do it, then. Moshe, ask Adud to make two bows and a bunch of arrows. Layla, you go with Moshe here and collect as many of the leaves as you need . . .'

'You haven't said anything about roles,' Copeland said.

'You're right, Harry. Listen in, ladies. The assault party's going to be me and one other. There's a big risk of capture and we won't be in uniform. That means we'll be regarded as spies, and you all know what the Boche do to spies. I'm patrol commander and this is my responsibility. I'd rather not let anyone else in for it, but I can't do it entirely alone.'

'I'll do it, skipper,' Naiman said. 'You're going to need someone who speaks Arabic and Italian.'

The proposal was met by a chorus of objections, and Caine realised that every man in the squad wanted to volunteer.

'It's got to be me,' Naiman said. 'No one else is qualified.'

'All right, then,' Caine said. He looked at Layla. 'Now, madam,' he said. 'It's all down to your hubble-bubble.'

CAPTAIN HALLER, the Brandenburger platoon officer credited with the capture of Runefish, drove out to the airstrip personally to meet Major Rohde. Haller had encountered only a few men in his life whom he instinctively feared; Rohde was one of them.

They drove along the track from the airfield with Rohde at the wheel. 'I understand you had some trouble overpowering the prisoner,' Rohde said.

'She got off a shot at me, if that's what you mean, sir,' Haller said. 'Missed though. I soon took the weapon off her.'

'Curious that she should miss at almost point-blank range,' Rohde said, chuckling. 'It would have been embarrassing for a Brandenburger captain to have been shot by a dame. You reported that she attempted to escape?'

'That was a farce—only a fool would have tried it with a whacking great tank standing there. She was lucky she didn't get snuffed.'

'Ah yes—the Special Duties troops who needed a Mark III panzer to arrest a girl.'

Haller looked daggers at him. 'The tank was there because of the threat of attack. Two of our platoons have been wiped out by enemy raiding groups in the past two days. One was taking with them a girl whose description was similar to that of Runefish. It might be coincidence, but it sounds as if the British raiding party could have been looking for her.'

Rohde let out a sceptical grunt. 'Since when did the Allies send a search-and-rescue mission to snatch a downed officer? If they *were* sent after her, it suggests that Runefish knows something special. If so, I intend to find out what it is.' He swerved suddenly to avoid an Arab family with a donkey-cart, and let out a string of curses. 'Sub-human trash.'

Rohde was obliged to slow down as the track threaded through the Arab quarter. He said, 'Can you describe the scene in the cave?'

'There was a fire with the remains of some papers and an attaché case on it. One of my boys pulled the papers out of the fire, but there was hardly anything left except a single line in code. There was a sack on the floor with a wireless set on it—what the Tommies call a "biscuit-tin" transmitter.'

'It seems that the girl was transmitting nonstop for more than three hours. You don't find it odd that she should expose herself in that way?'

Haller shrugged. 'Runefish doesn't strike me as being very bright, sir,' he said. 'I got the impression she's out of her depth.'

Rohde considered this in silence, and Haller saw the town hall looming up in front of them. 'Will you see the prisoner now, sir?' he asked.

'Give me a few moments to organise myself.'

'Then we'd better head for the police barracks.'

Rohde turned the wheel sharply. Two Arabs who'd been leading a donkey across the street leapt out of the way. The staff car clipped the donkey's back leg, shattering it instantly. 'Watch where you're going, morons,' Rohde yelled as the car shot towards the police barracks. As she sped away, Haller looked back at the two Senussi crouching over the injured animal. Both men were carrying bows and arrows. Interesting: you didn't see those old traditional weapons around much any more, he thought.

'Was that him?' Naiman whispered to Caine, as the car swept away.

Caine nodded. 'Major's rank, Abwehr insignia. Who else could it be?'

'We haven't got much time then.'

'We'll drag the donkey over by the town hall door,' Caine whispered. 'The guard will almost certainly come over to see what we're doing. Then we'll give it to him.'

Seconds later they had dragged the animal into the shade only yards from the door. As Naiman drew a knife from under his robes, Caine crouched and got ready with one of Adud's homemade arrows. There was a yell from the doorway, and the guard advanced towards them, shouting in Arabic. Naiman remained with his back to the policeman, shielding Caine from view. Caine waited until the guard was no more than six feet away, then nodded at Naiman, who leapt out of the way. The string twanged, the arrow whooshed, and the policeman dropped like a stone.

Almost before he'd hit the ground, Caine and Naiman were inside the porch. Caine tried the handle. It was unlocked. They were in a small atrium with a short passage ending in the open doorway from which came the sound of a voice shouting a name in Arabic. 'He's calling for the guard,' Naiman whispered. 'He heard the door open.'

They both strung arrows and rushed down the passage, through the open door, coming on two carabinieri in the act of getting up from their chairs. Two bowstrings sang, two arrows thwacked. Both policemen slumped instantly. Caine looked round for the ante-room door Adud's friend had described. It was locked, but the key was still there.

First Officer Maddaleine Rose was sitting hunched up in a corner, her hands tied behind her back and a gag on her mouth. She looked filthy, bedraggled and worn out. As Caine stepped into the room her eyes opened wide. Caine held up a hand. 'It's all right, ma'am,' he said in his most soothing voice. 'I'm Sergeant Thomas Caine, Middle East Commando. I'm here with orders to bring you back safely.' He was over to her in a bound, his knife in his hand. As he cut through the rope, he felt a rush of satisfaction. He'd liberated Runefish.

He ushered her quickly into the room where he'd left Naiman. She pulled the gag out of her mouth. 'What in the name of hell do you think you're doing, Sergeant?' she screeched. It was the haughty upper-class voice he'd heard so often in the officers' mess. Cope's words popped into his head: *I hope you're not expecting gratitude. I know those officer-class bints. . .*

'You pair of cretins,' Rose snarled. 'You have just about messed up everything. For Christ's sake, get out of here now.'

'Grab her,' Caine snapped.

They seized one arm each and began to frog-march her towards the door. Rose shrieked at them, kicking and punching.

Caine drew back his fist and was willing himself to hit her with all the force he could muster when there was a thump on the office door, and voices in German. 'They're here,' Naiman said. 'We've shot it, skipper.'

Caine picked up one of the guards' pistols from the desk. 'My orders are to bring you back or execute you. Now you've left me no choice.'

'I don't care what you think you've been ordered to do,' she hissed, 'but if you pull that trigger, you will regret it for the rest of your life.'

He snapped off the safety catch. Afterwards, he was never quite sure whether he would have squeezed the trigger or not. As it happened he never had the choice, because at that moment the door exploded inwards, sending him flying, knocking the weapon out of his hand. Before he could get to his feet German soldiers were swarming round him. Rough hands jerked him up, and a corporal put a size-twelve boot into his balls. The kick doubled him over. Another Jerry whacked him in the side with a rifle stock, slamming his wound.

He was on his knees now, sucking air desperately. The corporal snatched his hair and yanked his head up high enough to see a pair of legs in jackboots striding through the doorway. 'Now, this is a very interesting situation, isn't it?' a voice said in English, and Caine found himself looking straight into the eyes of Major Heinrich Rohde.

THERE WAS a near-naked body writhing in a chair and a fool who wouldn't stop shrieking. Caine's eyelids flickered, the stench of charred meat in his nostrils and it hit him suddenly that the shrieking fool was himself.

Rohde applied the red-hot iron once again to Caine's open wound. It was pain as he'd never known it. Rohde's voice was in his ear. 'Why were you ordered to execute Runefish, Sergeant Caine? What does she know that is so important that you would kill one of your own officers?'

'I'll tell you,' Caine wheezed.

'Don't,' another voice whined. 'Don't tell the bastard anything.'

Caine forced his eyes wide to see Naiman, trussed up five yards away.

'It's all right,' Caine stammered. 'Runefish is carrying a secret.'

'What secret?' Rohde whispered eagerly.

'It used to be common knowledge that Hitler had only one ball,' Caine gasped, 'but the truth is that Hitler has no balls at all.'

He burst into a paroxysm of crazy laughter that ended abruptly when Rohde jabbed the hot iron again into his wound.

It took a dousing of cold water to bring him round. Caine was aware that he'd broken every rule in the book. One thing you never did was antagonise your interrogator. Caine knew he'd messed up, but he didn't care: if he was going to die he wanted these Nazi scum to know what he thought of them.

Rohde was now standing over Naiman, whose eyes were focused on the butcher's cleaver Rohde was holding in his right hand.

Rohde faced Caine. 'In my experience, people will often give information to prevent punishment being meted out to their comrades. I intend to cut off Corporal Hussain's fingers until you tell me what I wish to know.'

Caine wondered who 'Corporal Hussain' was. Then he remembered—they'd agreed that if captured Naiman would give his name as Hussain Musa, an Indian from Calcutta.

'Torture me if you want,' Caine panted. 'He was only following orders.'

Rohde ignored his plea. 'When your comrade is shrieking in agony, you will remember that no one else will be to blame but yourself.'

Rohde croaked an order and a soldier cut Naiman's bonds, then stretched out his right hand until it lay palm-down on the table. Rohde lifted the cleaver. 'The thumb first, I think,' he said.

'Wait,' Caine gasped.

'What information is Runefish carrying? I want the truth.'

'I can't tell you,' he said. 'They sent us with orders to pull her out or kill her. That's all I know.'

Rohde brought the cleaver down on Naiman's hand, shearing the thumb clean off. Naiman vaulted high out of his chair, screaming in agony, letting out a stream of curses in a language Caine didn't recognise. Rohde froze.

'You speak Hebrew? Now where would an Indian Muslim learn Hebrew? Unless . . . you are a Jew. Now that is a surprise.'

Naiman lifted his head. 'Yes, I'm a Jew and proud of it,' he spat.

Rohde raised an eyebrow. 'You know, Corporal . . . I was with Heydrich during the invasion of Russia. We had orders to liquidate every Yid in the operational area—men, women and children. That was what one calls very satisfying work.'

Naiman threw himself out of his chair, got his one good hand round the German's throat and spat in his eye. Before he could do any more, the Brandenburgers leapt on him, one of them whacking his head with a rifle butt. Naiman fell to the ground, his hand and his head pumping blood.

The major kicked Naiman's inert body in the ribs with his jackboot. 'I have a special treatment I keep in reserve for cases like this. I will have you taken to the minefield.'

Rohde ordered the Brandenburgers to dress Caine and Naiman in their shirts and had them marched briskly through the streets. Naiman had lost so much blood that he could hardly walk, and Caine found himself staggering from the pain of his wound.

The minefield lay half a mile from the town hall, sealed off by a barbed-wire fence, intercepted by a narrow path that led up to the rim of a well. Rohde said, 'This is a legacy from you British when they occupied this area. Ironic, isn't it? They must have installed it to stop us using the well.'

He snapped an order and Caine hit the earth with a thump. The Black Widow stood over him. 'This is your last chance to talk,' Rohde said. 'I want to know where the rest of your men are hiding. If you fail to give me this information, I shall force Jew-boy here to tramp around the minefield until he hits a mine. The anti-personnel mines are designed to maim rather than kill and we shall continue until you talk.'

'Don't tell them anything,' Naiman croaked.

As an ex-sapper, Caine knew better than most what anti-personnel mines could do. Naiman had already been maimed once, and the thought of his blundering around in the minefield until his limbs were blown off was horrific. Weighed against Naiman's torture, though, were the lives of his men—Copeland, Wallace and the rest. Neither he nor Naiman had a chance now, but the other commandos did. Whatever Rohde knew about his patrol's actions against the Brandenburgers, he could never be certain that the two of them had been part of that group.

'Well?' Rohde said to Caine. 'Where are the rest of your unit?'

'There are no others,' Caine answered. 'The corporal and I came in by parachute. There only ever were two of us.'

Rohde's grin was an obscene leer. 'So, the two of you wiped out a whole Brandenburger platoon at Umm 'Aijil, and another on the road to Benghazi?'

'It must have been another group.'

'I see, and where exactly did you get that wound in your side, Sergeant? Where did you get the Arab clothes? How did you know that Runefish was in the town hall?'

'The wound was an accident. The Arab gear and the bows—we brought them with us. We got the other information by hearsay from passers-by.'

Rohde shook his head. 'This is getting tedious,' he said. 'For the last time, where are the rest of your men?'

'There are no other men.'

'Throw him into the minefield,' Rohde ordered Haller. The two soldiers holding Naiman pushed him roughly through the gap in the fence. The corporal staggered, clutching his wounded hand, then stood stock still.

Rohde drew his revolver. A single shot cracked and Naiman shrieked as a gaping entry wound appeared in his calf. Incredibly, Naiman didn't fall over. Instead, he hopped forwards into the minefield, hurling curses in Hebrew. The Brandenburgers cackled.

Caine felt more sickened than he'd ever felt in his life and the gorge rose in his throat. As a spectacle of sheer brutality, this would be hard to cap. He watched with bated breath, praying that his mate would be lucky—that a mine would finish him off in one go. There was a heart-stopping *kabuuumfff* and for a second the air was opaque with smoke. When it cleared, Caine saw Naiman lying in a heap, no more than twenty paces from where he had started. His foot had been blown clean off.

Rohde smiled at Caine. 'I think we'll just let him lie there,' he said. 'The vultures will be in around sunset. They don't care if an animal's dead, as long as it can't move. They usually begin by pecking out the eyes.'

Caine gritted his teeth. 'I'll see you in hell,' he spat.

At a nod from Rohde, two soldiers seized him from behind. Rohde lifted his pistol and held it against Caine's temple. 'Go on,' Caine grunted. 'Do it.'

Rohde let the weapon drop. 'Since you insulted my Führer, I'm going to have you thrown into the well. You'll die very slowly. The last Senussi we dropped in there kept going for five days.' Rohde holstered his pistol. 'You will excuse me if I don't wait. I am overdue for a chat with that girl.'

The Brandenburgers dragged Caine along the narrow path to the lip of the well. As they bent him over the rim while they cut his bonds, he got a momentary impression of a dank bottomless shaft. Before he could make any attempt to lash out, the soldiers had sent him plummeting headfirst into the dark abyss.

CAINE OPENED his eyes and found himself lying face up, his head resting against a stone shelf, his body immersed in four feet of water. The well towered above him, a vast black chimney with a cap of wan starlight at the apex. He could hear moans of pain from beyond the well, and knew that it was Naiman. Caine had no idea how long he'd lain there, but guessed from the starlight above it must have been an hour, perhaps two.

Caine's first thoughts were about Runefish. It was probably too late now to stop her talking—Rohde would surely have been interrogating her for the past couple of hours. He couldn't be certain, though. His brief encounter with Rose had given him a glimpse of a character of rigid determination. The problem was that she didn't want to be rescued. No matter—he still had his orders, and before he could carry them out he had to extract himself from his current predicament.

Caine stood up in the water. The stink of rotting meat made him gag, but it was dark and he couldn't make out where the smell was coming from. There was only one way out, and that meant scaling the wall. It looked impossible, but Caine had been trained in climbing cliff faces and knew that few surfaces were without some kind of hand- and footholds. He had always excelled in climbing—his strong shoulders and chest were the ideal physique for it. Still, he'd never encountered anything as difficult as this.

Caine's shirt felt heavier on one side. He grappled in the inside pocket and miraculously his Zippo lighter was there in its waterproof condom. He flicked open the lid and worked the flints. He smelled lighter fuel and caught his breath as a flame licked up. He cast around in the globe of light, and almost jumped out of his skin.

He was sharing the water with a dead man, the bloated corpse of an Arab—the Senussi whom Rohde had boasted about. Caine forced himself to turn the corpse over; the Arab's face was ghostly white. Then Caine noticed there was a hole in the Arab's robe at the belly—a serious knife wound, self-inflicted Caine was sure. The Arab had stabbed himself, which meant he'd had a weapon.

Caine put the Zippo away and ducked under the water, groping along the muddy bed. It was difficult work—twice he surfaced for breath— but the area wasn't large. On the third dive his fingers closed round a Senussi dagger, ten inches long, curved at the end. It might just be his ticket out of the place.

He heaved himself out of the water and stood on the stone shelf, feeling for crevices—as he'd suspected, there were plenty. The wall was full of tiny gaps where he could wedge the knife in firmly and use it to pull himself up. He found such a place at full arm's length, stuck the knife into it, finding a hold for one foot. He'd managed to scale three or four feet up the wall before he missed his footing and fell on top of the floating cadaver beneath. For a second he lay in the water, wondering if it was worth the pain. He could just lie here and die.

Naiman's groans came again, bringing him back to the present. Caine attacked the wall with new determination. He worked the knife with frenzied effort, balancing on inch-wide footholds, thrusting the blade in, securing each step as he'd been trained to do. Slowly, but with increasing confidence, he made progress—ten feet, fifteen, twenty. The moon had come out, casting light straight down the shaft. About five feet above him he sensed another rocky shelf. Beyond that, though, he glimpsed something that excited him much more—a ladder of iron rings climbing from the shelf right up to the well head. Only another five feet to go and he'd made it.

Two more agonising efforts and he had his hand on the shelf. He was dragging himself onto it when something scaly uncoiled out of the shadows—he felt the movement, saw the moonlight reflected off silver scales, saw a flicking fork-shaped tongue. He was so shocked that he let go and plummeted thirty feet down the chimney, crashing into the water like a wrecking-ball.

ERWIN ROMMEL sat at the table in the roadhouse sifting through various reports. He had recovered his normally buoyant spirits. Among the intelligence reports was one suggesting that further east, at Capuzzo, he would find supplies to equip an entire division—more than enough to reach Alexandria and Cairo. Victory was within his grasp. All he needed was intelligence that would convince Kesselring and the High Command that the Eighth Army really was about to disintegrate.

Mellenthin strutted in. 'The Runefish report, sir. It arrived from Rohde in Biska just a minute ago.'

Rommel laid the single sheet on the table and pored over it. 'Listen to this: *The Eighth Army's morale has reached rock bottom. Officers are now openly questioning the High Command. The Army is a hair's breadth from mutiny* . . . This is it—exactly what I predicted.'

'Shall I have it sent to Field Marshal Kesselring immediately, sir?'

'No, he gave us twelve hours. What we must do is get confirmation from our sources in Cairo so that when Kesselring prevaricates, we'll be ready for him. Contact agent *Stürmer* at once and ask for corroboration.'

'We can only contact him via Rohde, sir. Rohde is his controller.'

'Tell Rohde to get on to it immediately. We shall be eating dinner at Shepheard's Hotel in Cairo this time next week. Nothing can stop us now.'

EISNER HAD BEEN apprehensive about breaking into Betty Nolan's flat in daylight, but speed was of the essence. Rohde wanted immediate confirmation of the identity of the girl he had interrogated, whose name he'd given as First Officer Maddaleine Rose. Eisner's reaction had been incredulity. If the major had Runefish in custody 500 miles away, then who was the girl Shaffer had identified as Runefish that morning at Nolan's flat?

Luckily, he had discovered a fire escape at the back of the building with easy access to the first floor. Almost as soon as he'd jumped down inside the bathroom, he'd realised that this flat couldn't be permanently occupied. There was no trace of small personal items—make-up powder, bath-salts, toothbrush. This conclusion was confirmed in the rest of the flat—there were no clothes in the closets, no food in the kitchen, no ornaments. The flat had the impersonality of a spy's safe house.

He was in the kitchen when he heard a key in the lock. He lurked in the shadows and saw a tall woman closing the door. Eisner felt for the knife in his waistband and drew it out slowly. The woman lifted the telephone receiver. She just had time to say, 'Captain Avery, I'm in,' when Eisner was on her, one arm crooked round her neck, his knife at her throat.

She wrenched the throttling arm downwards with astonishing force, flipping Eisner off balance. In an instant she had dodged round and twisted his arm behind his own back. Eisner's mouth fell open as he found himself propelled against the wall, dropping the knife. He recovered in a second, wheeling round furiously. The girl was going for a pistol concealed under her blouse when he clouted her in the jaw with a shattering blow. As she went down, Eisner slipped his Smith & Wesson from its holster and threw himself on her prone body, jamming the pistol under her jaw. 'Try that again, bitch, and I'll blow your chin off,' he spat.

She did look like Betty Nolan, Eisner thought—same height, same lissom figure, same short blonde hair. It wasn't her, though—it was a set-up. Eisner forced her head back savagely with the muzzle of his weapon. 'Who *are* you?' he spluttered.

The girl's sea-green eyes were remarkably steady. 'Betty Nolan.'

'You're lying. I've seen the real Betty Nolan, and you're not her.'

There was a sudden squawk from the telephone mouthpiece, and Eisner froze, realising the person she'd been speaking to—Captain Avery—had heard everything. Wasn't Avery the officer from whom Natalie had stolen the Runefish schedule?

The girl tried to jerk Eisner off her. Blind with rage, he smacked her twice in the face and her body went limp. Eisner ripped the telephone cable out of the wall and picked up his knife. The unconscious girl wasn't Betty Nolan, but she was lovely. Eisner licked his lips, fingering his knife. He had no need to kill her, and in any case the Field Security boys would be on their way. He put the knife away and had taken a step towards the bathroom when the girl moaned. He stopped. *Get out of here now*, hissed a voice in his head. The room lurched abruptly and the light dimmed. 'No,' he protested. 'I'm not going to do it.' Then the sun switched off.

When it came on again, Eisner was standing over the girl's naked body, clutching his knife. A gaping wound like a second mouth stretched across her milk-white throat.

There were footsteps outside the door. He drew out his Smith & Wesson, and backed into the kitchen as the door flew open. He could see two British soldiers—a sergeant in khaki drills and an officer with a pale moustache holding a .45 Colt. This must be Avery, Eisner thought.

The two soldiers saw the dead girl at once. '*Susan*,' Avery said.

As the captain knelt down to feel her pulse, Eisner shot the sergeant twice in the stomach. As Avery came up, Eisner put a slug through his right bicep. The captain gasped and sank back to his knees, his weapon skittering across the room. In a trice, Eisner was looming over him. He brought the handle of his Smith & Wesson down towards Avery's skull but the G(R) man blocked the blow. He clamped Eisner's gun hand, prised apart the fingers, yanked the pistol free. The weapon clattered on the floor, but Avery didn't release Eisner's hand: he bent the index finger until the bone fractured with the dry snap of a pencil. Eisner staggered, tried to pull his hand free. Avery heaved himself up and kicked the German hard in the balls. Eisner doubled up in agony, his eyes bulging. Avery chinned him with a powerful roundhouse punch that sent him sprawling against the wall.

Eisner might never have got up again if, at that moment, the door hadn't suddenly been flung open by the concierge. As Avery turned, distracted, Eisner grabbed the man's discarded Colt and squeezed iron. A round slammed Avery in the shoulder. The concierge took a step back, gabbling in Arabic: Eisner shot him in the face and groin.

Eisner staggered over to Avery's body. Then, taking a deep breath, he bent over, picked him up in a fireman's lift, and heaved him over his shoulder. He lugged the body downstairs. His car was parked only a block away. He knew he was taking a big gamble carrying a wounded officer out into the street, but it was dark now and, in any case, it would be worth the risk. Avery was a prime mover in the Runefish operation: once he'd been persuaded to talk, Eisner would at long last know it all.

CAINE STOOD UP in the water, furious. But for that creature, he'd be on his way up the iron ladder to the surface by now. He let the fury work through him, using its strength. He still had the knife, but he needed a crushing weapon rather than a stabbing one. Within a few minutes he'd found a stone the size of a large grapefruit. He stuffed it with some difficulty into the pocket of his shorts, and once more began the climb.

It was easier this time—the knifeholds and footholds were familiar to him now. He passed the place where he'd paused, twenty-five feet up, and moments later he had his hand on the ledge. Securing his weight, he stuck the knife in his teeth, jerked out the stone. A second later the snake issued out of its lair, hissing ferociously. With a Herculean effort of his enormous arm, chest and shoulder muscles, Caine raised himself and brought the stone down on the snake's head with all the force he could muster.

Suddenly, he was hauling himself up onto the ledge at the thirty-foot mark, grasping the first of the iron rings. Naiman's groans were louder from here, and at once he began to climb the ladder towards the sound. With a last effort of his aching muscles, he burst out into the moonlight.

Caine could see Naiman's body lying not much more than twenty yards away. The groans had ceased, but he could hear wheezing, rattling breaths that told him his comrade was alive. He knew there was nothing he could do to save him, but he wasn't willing to let him lie in agony—it might take him days to die.

Caine knew there was no way he could approach Naiman in safety without clearing the mines. The idea made him shudder. Still, there was nothing for it. He made his way unsteadily to a white-thorn acacia tree he'd spotted. He spent a few minutes breaking off the stiff two-inch-long thorns until he'd collected about a dozen. He reached the gap in the fence and threw himself on the dry ground. He began to probe the earth in front of him with the knife, keeping it at exactly forty-five degrees. His first probes revealed nothing, so he inched forward into the area he'd cleared, then started to probe again. This time the knife struck metal. He dug the sandy earth away with his fingers, exposing a dish-shaped anti-tank mine. Very cautiously, he felt the mine's submerged skin for booby-traps or 'daisy-chain' wires—used to connect mines in sequence. He found none and lifted the mine out of the pit and set it aside. Then he moved into the space he'd cleared and began the process again.

He worked slowly and methodically, crawling nearer to Naiman's body. The young interpreter was lying face down. His left leg had been ripped apart by the same blast that had severed his foot. Caine was astonished that he hadn't bled to death already. Naiman's face was grey in the moonlight, creased with pain lines. His eyes flickered open. 'Do me in, Sergeant,' he croaked. 'Do me like you did Cavazzi.'

Caine cast about him desperately, wondering if there were any other possibilities. Sadly, there weren't. Naiman was going to die: it would happen even if Caine managed to drag him out of the minefield. The only question was how long he was going to suffer.

'All right,' Caine whispered. He considered cutting Naiman's throat, but he knew he couldn't. He looked at an 'S'-type mine he'd just cleared, close to his friend's body and a thought occurred to him. 'Can you roll over?'

'I . . . can . . . try.'

Caine dug a shallow depression in the sand next to Naiman, then set the anti-personnel mine in the hole. He took a deep breath and gently removed the thorn he'd used in place of a safety pin. 'All right,' he said. 'I've laid an "S"-type anti-personnel mine next to you, and I've armed it. All you have to do is make a last effort, roll over on top of it with all your weight, and it will go off. Just give me two minutes to get clear. You got that?'

With huge effort, Naiman extended his maimed hand an inch, touching Caine's leg. 'It has been an honour . . . to serve . . . with you.'

Caine couldn't stop the tears. 'No, brother,' he said, his voice shaking. 'It's been my privilege. I'll see to it that you get the highest decoration.'

'Caine,' Naiman hissed, 'swear the Nazi scum won't win.'

Caine sucked breath. 'Moshe, I swear by the most sacred bond of the commando brotherhood, that I won't stop fighting until every man jack of them gets what's coming to him, or I'll die doing it.'

Naiman's eyes were closed: the faintest glimmer of a smile played round his mouth. 'Goodbye, brother,' Caine said.

He didn't bother crawling back through the minefield, but simply ran as fast as he could along the path he'd cleared, tears streaming down his face. He had passed through the gap in the fence, and was already racing for the streets of Biska, when he heard the mine go off.

6

Half an hour earlier, Eisner had left his car and made for his houseboat. His broken finger was still cucumber-sized but morphine had reduced the pain to a dull throb. He was anxious to get to his wireless transmitter, but was too old a dog in the security game to neglect the customary precautions.

Eisner's interrogation of Avery hadn't been as successful as he'd hoped. At his safe house on Roda Island, the officer had revealed that Betty Nolan was indeed posing as Maddaleine Rose, but on the content of Runefish's message had refused to say anything at all. Eisner, aware that he'd promised Rohde an answer within two hours, had grown increasingly abusive—and careless. While his back was turned, the officer had somehow managed to get free of his bonds. He'd almost made it to the villa's gate, when Eisner had shot him in the back, like a dog.

He consoled himself with the knowledge that he at least had a definitive answer to Rohde's query: First Officer Maddaleine Rose was an impostor.

The houseboat was as peaceful as ever in the light of the three-quarter moon. Nothing looked out of place, but Eisner couldn't rid himself of the feeling that something was wrong. He smelled the jasmine, heard the honk of the bullfrogs, the lap of the water. What was missing? The crickets. There was no sound of cicadas and he suddenly knew with stone-cold certainty that a squad of men was lying in the darkness, waiting.

A voice yelled. 'You there! Stop!' Two men in uniform were running towards him out of the shadows. Eisner pulled out his Smith & Wesson and fired in their direction, left-handed. He fled back the way he had come, made his car in two minutes flat. His escape route had been planned long before. Minutes later he crossed into downtown Cairo, heading by a back-street route to the place where his reserve transmitter was concealed.

MAJOR JOHN STOCKER jogged back to his wireless van and found Pieter Shaffer staring at him expectantly, still wearing handcuffs. Next to him was his MP guard, and behind them a wireless operator, hunched over his set. 'He got away,' Stocker announced, his blue eyes flashing furiously.

'Well, don't look at me,' Shaffer said. 'There's no way I could have warned him, was there? I've been in your custody for the past three hours.'

Stocker addressed the W/T operator. 'Put out an alert to all MP patrols and civil-police roadblocks. He's driving a white Cadillac.' He turned to Shaffer. 'What's the registration number?'

Shaffer told him, and Stocker repeated it to the operator.

'They won't get him, though,' Shaffer said, shaking his head. 'Eisner was brought up here—he's got a map of the bloody place in his head.'

Field Security had picked up Shaffer at his office late that afternoon. It hadn't required much pressure to make him talk. He claimed he was a loyal South African, but the Nazis had arrested his relatives in Germany. When Stocker revealed that Eisner was the brutal sex-murderer of at least three young women, Shaffer had been only too anxious to give up the location of the houseboat and the wireless transmitter.

After finding Sim-Sim's body that morning, Stocker and Avery had worked frantically to close the net on Johann Eisner. Avery's first action had been to send G(R) agent Susan Arquette to occupy Betty Nolan's flat, in case their quarry showed his face there. Avery had long ago groomed Susan as a Runefish lookalike who might be useful if anyone needed convincing that Nolan was still in Cairo. The Field Security surveillance party had arrived too late to observe the first caller that morning but Susan had been able to identify him as South African, and a fast scan of the files had brought up the names of several suspect South African nationals. From their mug-shots, Susan had picked out Pieter Shaffer.

The wireless beeped and the signaller listened carefully to his headphones. 'They've found the safe house, sir,' he told Stocker. 'Captain Avery's body was in the grounds. He was probably shot trying to escape, but his body also showed signs of severe torture.'

Stocker swore. 'Dammit, now we have to assume Eisner knows the lot.'

It was Shaffer who'd given them the address of Eisner's safe house on Roda. If they'd only managed to get to Shaffer an hour earlier, then Avery's death might have been prevented.

Shaffer had been trained in wireless procedure, but it had always been Eisner who'd sent the messages. All Shaffer knew was that the encrypted texts went to an Abwehr controller whose real name was Heinrich Rohde. Eisner's codename was *Stürmer*.

'I suggest you think again about the location of his reserve transmitter,' Stocker told Shaffer. 'The more you help us, the better it will be for you.'

Shaffer made a face. 'There is one place he talked about a couple of times. St Joseph's Church in Imad al-Din Street.'

Stocker picked up the field telephone. 'Please find out as soon as possible the name of the priest at St Joseph's Roman Catholic church in Imad al-Din Street. I'm particularly interested in foreign nationals.'

He listened for a moment and said, 'Thank you.' He looked at Shaffer. 'There's a French priest at St Joseph's. Father Pascal. He's thought to be a Vichy supporter. Did Eisner ever mention him?'

'Nope.'

Stocker picked up the phone again. 'I want two sections dispatched at once to St Joseph's church, Shari' Imad al-Din. One is to throw a discreet cordon round the place and watch out for our man. The other squad is to arrest the French priest, Father Pascal, and search the entire premises for a possible wireless transmitter.'

Stocker turned and bawled to the driver in front. 'St Joseph's Church, Shari' Imad al-Din, and make it snappy.' When he turned to Shaffer again, the South African saw a gleam of victory in his eyes. 'Now,' he said, 'it's just a matter of who gets there first.'

EISNER FELT SAFER after he'd ditched the Caddy in an alley behind Shari' Imad al-Din. The car stuck out like a sore thumb. St Joseph's stood tucked away at the end of a narrow conduit of open-fronted shops. Eisner, clad in his black suit, fez and dark glasses, let himself merge into the crowd.

He pushed open the door of the church, took in the empty pews, deserted altar and pulpit. He opened the door of the vestry and found Father Pascal sitting motionless behind a desk, his furrowed face highlighted by the flickering flame of a tallow candle.

The priest rose when Eisner entered. 'I wouldn't have expected you so late,' he said in French.

'The war waits for no man, Father,' Eisner answered. 'I've got special intelligence to pass on. Can I have the set, please?'

The priest opened a cupboard, brought out the suitcase that held the transmitter and laid it on his desk. Eisner began to set up the antenna. When that was done, he sat down with the code-book and encryption pad. As the priest looked on, he pencilled out his message painfully, using his left hand.

Totally focused on the task in hand, he didn't notice the door behind him open. Neither did he see the dark figures slipping silently through, until he sensed the cold muzzle of a Tommy gun against his neck. 'Move, go on,' a voice goaded him. 'I'd love to blow your bloody block off.' The light was switched on suddenly and he saw that the vestry was full of British soldiers.

Arms rammed him against the wall, and a hand grabbed his broken finger and snapped it backwards: a shock of pain electrified Eisner, an agony so intense that he jumped a foot in the air, howling like a dog.

'Oops, sorry,' the voice said.

Eisner was wrenched round to find himself staring into the spectacles of a dumpy man with a domed forehead and sparkling blue eyes. The man, who wore major's crowns on his shoulder straps, was fingering Eisner's concealed knife. 'I presume this is the weapon you used to murder Lady Goddard, Rachel Levi and Susan Arquette.'

'I don't know what you're talking about,' Eisner stuttered.

'Bloody liar.' It was the voice of the soldier who'd held the gun to his neck. 'You raped those women and slit their throats. You murdered Corporal Salim Tanta and you tortured and killed Captain Avery. If I blew your balls off right now it'd be too good for you.'

'You may yet have the chance, Sarn't Major,' the bespectacled man said. 'It all depends on Mr Eisner here.'

Eisner looked shocked. 'How do you know my name?'

The major smiled wistfully. 'The same way I knew about your houseboat, your car, your safe house on Roda. Your friend Mr Shaffer was a loyal South African after all, or at least enough of one to give you up.'

Eisner stifled a gasp, rocked to the core by the knowledge that Shaffer had ratted on him.

'More crucially for us,' the major went on, 'Mr Shaffer knows your signals procedure—call signs, security codes, that sort of thing. So we will know if you attempt to botch up the message you are about to send. It will read: "Identity of Runefish confirmed: First Officer Maddaleine Rose, Women's Royal Naval Service, staff officer at Allied GHQ Middle East Forces, Cairo. Authenticity of material carried corroborated."'

'No,' Eisner said.

The sharp eyes blazed behind the dense lenses, and Eisner sensed that the major was holding volcanic fury in close check. Very deliberately, the officer drew his Colt .45 and pressed the muzzle hard against Eisner's temple. 'I don't consider myself a violent man, but I hope very much you do not cooperate, as it would give me unspeakable pleasure to send you to the hell where you belong.'

'You're bluffing. I'm too valuable for that.'

'If you refuse to send the message, I will kill you now. I shall simply have Mr Shaffer send it instead.'

Eisner ran his tongue along dry lips. He had no doubt that the major would carry out his threat. If he played along with them, though, he'd survive, and almost certainly be able to escape later. It would mean sending

Rommel a false message, but then, if Rommel captured Cairo, he'd be redundant anyway. What did he have to lose by going along with the British for now?

'All right,' he said. 'I'll do it.'

'Good, but one word of warning. One wrong digit and you won't leave this room alive.'

CAINE HUGGED the shadows in the streets of Biska, hoping that anyone spotting him would take him for a German soldier. His wound was agonising, and he was seething with anger about Naiman—he had half a mind to leave Rose to the mercies of the Black Widow. As it stood, he was faced with the task of extracting her from the hands of an entire Brandenburger platoon armed only with a rusty knife.

As he paused under a tree, he became aware that a small party was making its way across the street. Three Brandenburgers, armed with semi-automatic rifles and bayonets, were shoving ahead of them a gagged and bound prisoner—Maddaleine Rose. The troopers were laughing and subjecting Rose to lewd gestures, whose meaning Caine could not mistake. Evidently she'd blabbed under interrogation and was no longer of use.

By keeping to the darkest places, crouching in the trees, squatting under walls, Caine was able to follow the group unobserved. The Brandenburgers were so focused on what they intended to do to Rose that they'd thrown all caution to the wind. He wondered how he was going to take on three fully armed Jerries with no more than his rusty old blade. He would have to dispose of them swiftly, without allowing them to get off a shot that would alert the rest of the garrison. Surprise was by far his most powerful tool.

The party halted beyond the outskirts of the town in an Islamic graveyard. The Jerries immediately hurled Rose on her stomach, put their rifles down and began to unclip their webbing. Caine closed the distance between them rapidly, ducking behind a thorn bush not two yards away from where they had downed their semi-automatics.

Rose lay facedown in the dust, as if she were resigned to what was happening. Two of the soldiers squatted by her and started pulling down her trousers. Caine saw his chance. He scooped up a rifle in one hand and a bayonet in the other, and swung the rifle like a club. He brought it crashing down on the head of the standing soldier. The pent-up rage of Rose's betrayal, his ordeal in the well, Naiman's horrific death, found expression in that blow. Caine felt the skull cave in, felt the rifle-stock snap.

As the soldier toppled, Caine hurled the bayonet at one of the crouching men. The blade took the man in the neck, the point emerging on the other side in a spume of blood. The third Jerry wasn't even fully on his feet when Caine attacked him with the stump of the rifle. Before the soldier had time to defend himself, Caine had bashed his pate three times, twisted the rifle and thrust the muzzle halfway down his gullet until his windpipe burst.

Caine decided not to take any chances. He picked up a sword-bayonet and cut the second soldier's throat from ear to ear. He moved to the Jerry he'd poleaxed and did the same. The third Hun was already so disfigured that Caine had to force himself to saw through what was left of his neck. He saw Rose lying two feet away, her eyes wide with horror.

He hauled her to her feet by her own bindings. She mumbled something under her gag. Caine ignored her. 'Just shut up and do as you're told,' he growled. He pulled up her trousers, then seized her by one arm and began to hustle her, still bound, in the direction of the leaguer.

ROMMEL HAD MOVED out of the roadhouse, pitching his camp on the plain, where he could enjoy the cool of the moonlit desert night. When von Mellenthin arrived hot foot from the signals detachment, Rommel gestured to a chair. 'Well?' he enquired.

The IO's smile was triumphant. 'Field Marshal Kesselring acknowledges his receipt of the Runefish report,' he said, 'and accepts the confirmation of its authenticity from *Stürmer*, in Cairo. He has agreed not to withdraw his air units, pending approval from OKH/OKW in Berlin.'

'Good,' Rommel said. 'What about the Italians?'

'Bastico, Cavallero and Barbasetti have registered disapproval of your intended actions but I think they can be relied on to toe the line.'

Rommel beamed. 'Signal them that tomorrow I intend to go straight across the Nile and I shall not pause until I have reached the Persian Gulf.'

'Excuse me, sir,' Mellenthin said, 'but may I advise you that it would be prudent to wait for official permission before sending such a message?'

'No, you may not. Those old women have delayed me long enough.'

Mellenthin was about to get up when Rommel continued. 'Tell Rohde he's done a good job, but inform him that I want Runefish sent up to the front on the first available aircraft. I want to talk to her personally.'

A bemused look crossed the IO's face. 'But, General, you said yourself that there wouldn't be much left of her when that swine had done his business. We both know he doesn't wear velvet gloves.'

Rommel's expression turned severe, and Mellenthin guessed that he was experiencing a pang of guilt.

'Whatever state she's in,' Rommel snapped, 'I want her sent here. I do not want her dumped in a shallow grave in the Green Mountains. You tell that piece of horse turd that, grateful as I am for the intelligence he supplied, I am holding him personally responsible for her safety.'

WHEN CAPTAIN HALLER had finished examining the dead soldiers, he flashed Rohde a grim look. 'You'd think they'd been hit by a pack of savages, sir. All three of them have had their throats slit. None was shot and not one of them got a round off, either.'

'Too intent on having a romp with the prisoner,' Rohde said drily. He stared at the captain. 'You lost me my prisoner, Haller—a prisoner that Rommel has asked specifically to see.'

'Sir, you told me that she was of no further use. You announced in front of my men that they could do whatever they wanted with her.'

Rohde's eyes narrowed. 'That's a lie—' he started, but he was interrupted by the arrival of the Senussi police tracker. Haller listened to his report. 'He's sure that this was the work of one man. Whoever it was followed the party from the town and attacked them with their own weapons.'

'One man?' Rohde snarled. 'Who?'

'There's only one person it could have been,' Haller said. 'The sergeant we threw in the well.'

'Caine? Are you telling me you let him *escape*?'

'I followed your orders to the letter, sir,' Haller objected. 'I wouldn't have put money on his even surviving the fall, let alone getting out of a well a hundred feet deep. By God, that joker's tough.'

'He must have had outside help,' Rohde snapped. 'I am going to assemble the entire Senussi population of this town and have them shot, one by one, until I find out who helped him. As for you, Captain, if you don't get that Runefish woman back before noon tomorrow, your next posting will be the Russian Front.'

AS THE SMALL CONVOY crested the last escarpment of the Green Mountains, Caine caught his breath. He had, he told himself, accomplished his mission. The RV with the LRDG escort lay no more than two days' drive away. It glowed as brightly in his imagination as the Promised Land.

The convoy had been moving nonstop for seven hours and Caine had spent almost the entire journey at the White's observation hatch, foiling Wallace's attempts to grill him. For most of that time Maddaleine Rose had been curled up on the floor, still bound and gagged. 'If you don't give her water soon, skipper, she'll croak,' Wallace had observed. 'At least take the gag off and let her breathe. I don't remember you sayin' our orders was to bring her back trussed up like a pound of brisket.'

'Naiman's dead,' Caine had growled. 'It's her fault. She ratted on us.'

'Jesus, what happened in there?'

'I don't want to talk about it, all right?'

As they came down into the labyrinth of dry water-courses in the valley, Caine had Copeland give the three-honk signal to halt and scrim up. While Cope manoeuvred the White under an outcropping, Caine went off to relieve his bursting bladder. He returned to find Cope watching Wallace carry the limp form of Maddaleine Rose into the shade. 'Who told you to take her out of the wagon?' he demanded.

When Caine had hustled Rose into the leaguer the previous night, his mates had clamoured around him shooting questions, slapping him on the back. To their consternation, Caine's only statement had been that Naiman had bought it. He'd confounded them further by issuing orders that no one was to talk to Rose, or remove her restraints.

Now Wallace laid Rose gently on soft ground. 'This ain't no way to treat a lady,' he boomed, 'and you know it—if you was yourself you wouldn't treat a *dog* like that. Now, are you going to cut her loose or am I?'

'Don't touch her,' Caine snapped. 'I told you, she can't be trusted.'

'All right then,' the big man grunted. 'I'll do it myself.'

Caine faced him. 'You want to know what happened? We were doing fine until Runefish here deliberately made a racket that turned out the guard. First, that Black Widow creep applies a red-hot iron to my wound. Then, he chops off Moshe's thumb and when he finds out Moshe's a Jew, he makes him tromp around a minefield until his foot gets blown off. Moshe might have taken days to die if I hadn't got to him first. That was after I'd climbed out of the hundred-foot well they dropped me into.'

'*Jesus*,' Wallace whispered. 'But Moshe ain't the first one we lost, Tom. How long you going to go on blaming yourself and the lass here for something neither of you could do anything about?'

Caine felt almost on the verge of collapse. As Wallace pressed forward, though, he raised a hand to push him back.

'Get out of my way, skipper.'

Caine balled a fist, but Wallace slapped him open-handed across the jaw, hard enough to make Caine's head spin. By the time he'd recovered, the gunner had removed Rose's gag and was cutting through her bindings.

'Let's have a look,' Wallace growled, kneeling in front of her. Caine saw that her wrists had been chafed raw by the tight cords. The wounds looked ugly. 'That's nasty,' Wallace purred, as if he were reassuring a child. 'You'd better call Pickney, Harry. Those wrists could go septic.' He held a water-bottle to her mouth. 'You hurt anywhere else, ma'am?'

She pulled up her trouser-cuffs, showing ankles that were a purple mass of bruises and burns. 'They clamped electrodes there,' she said, her voice soft. 'And here.' She gestured to her armpits. 'They used electric shocks.'

Wallace stared accusingly at Caine. 'And you left her tied up without water for seven hours. You practisin' for a new career with the Gestapo?'

Wallace's words stabbed Caine like daggers. The sight of Rose's injuries, and her mention of electric-shock torture, had brought him back to earth with a jolt. Wallace was right: he'd forced this helpless girl to go through a quite unnecessary torment, without offering her water, medical treatment, or even a word of comfort. Wallace had hit the nail on the head. This was Gestapo treatment. The ordeal had tipped him over the edge into some kind of dark underworld of the soul.

'I'm sorry, ma'am,' he stammered. 'I . . .'

'Sergeant Caine,' Rose said quietly. 'You don't need to apologise. It must have been a shock when I reacted like that at the town hall, and then the terrible loss of your comrade. It might be poor comfort, but I want to say how grateful I am that you risked your life for me.'

Caine could hardly believe his ears. Her statement disarmed him totally. It wasn't only what she'd said that astonished him but the way she'd said it. Her voice was quite devoid of the arrogance he'd heard in Biska.

'I am so sorry about your friend,' she said. 'Believe me, if I could have done anything to stop it I would have done.' Her tearful eyes searched his face for understanding, and it hit him that she held herself responsible for Naiman's death. 'The way I spoke to you back there,' she whispered, 'I was taken by surprise. When you pointed that pistol at me, I didn't know what to do. I'm just a courier. They mentioned the possibility of a rescue in my briefing, but I never took it seriously.'

Copeland spoke. 'I don't quite follow you, ma'am. If you didn't expect us, why did you transmit your emergency call for more than three hours yesterday? If you hadn't done that you wouldn't have been bagged.'

'I suppose I just panicked,' she cut in. 'I'm new to all this.'

Caine felt confused. There had been some kind of cock-up, but he was too tired to work it out. 'I'd almost made my mind up to dump you.'

Rose closed her eyes. He guessed she was picturing his ferocious butchery of the three Brandenburgers. She was a staff courier, not a combat vet.

However grateful she was, she must think him no better than a beast.

'You should have dumped me. You could have saved yourself and your men. I didn't expect to be rescued and it wasn't necessary. I'm expendable.'

She was interrupted by the arrival of Pickney, who slammed his medical box down without ceremony. 'Sorry to break this up,' he said.

Caine was pleased to have an excuse to leave. After the way he'd treated Rose, he felt he wouldn't be able to look her in the eye. That there were unexplained holes in her story no longer troubled Caine. Her mission was top secret, and there could well be security aspects that were beyond his 'need to know'. It really didn't matter now. What amazed him was how he'd started by hating Rose for betraying him and Naiman to the Jerries, yet he'd ended up admiring her, and despising himself.

He marched towards the rock shelter harbouring Vera and Judy to replace his blood-stained kit—he reminded himself to pick up a couple of sets for Rose while he was about it. Vera's crew were cooking stew. There were only three of them left now—Wingnut Turner, Barry Shackleton and Albert Raker, the ex-navvie from the Pioneer Corps. Judy's crew was brewing tea—they were also down to three: Bombardier Dave Floggett, the pugnacious ex-Gunner from Newcastle, Gus Graveman and Todd Sweeney. Caine was accosted by Sweeney, swigging milky tea from a pint mug. 'Got the right one this time, then, Sarn't? Or aren't you certain? Is that why you're keeping her tied up?'

For a moment, Caine considered rearranging Sweeney's face: it was an action long overdue. He thought better of it. 'That was just a temporary precaution until I could make a positive ID.'

'I see. Listen, skipper, I spotted gazelle tracks in the wadi. I fancy going off to bag a couple. Some fresh meat would be just what the MO ordered.'

'The answer's no. Stay with the wagons until further notice.'

Sweeney cocked his brow. 'Did you know we've been short of rations since Marlene and Gracie went up?'

'The answer's still the same, Todd. No one's to leave the leaguer without my orders.'

'I think you're being unduly cautious,' Sweeney said sourly.

Pickney had finished treating Rose, and was now at the Dingo's position. Caine found him crouching over George Padstowe, who was lying on a blanket, half comatose. To Caine's surprise Rose was there with him, kneeling by the ex-marine's head, timing his heart-rate with a finger on his carotid artery. Caine was impressed. 'What's the problem?' he asked.

'Heatstroke,' Pickney announced, screwing up his face in frustration.

'Normally I'd use chilled water or ice, but we're a bit short on those right now.'

'Have you thought of methylated spirits?' Rose suggested. 'It would cause a chill by evaporation.'

'Not a bad idea, ma'am,' Pickney said. 'We've got plenty of white spirit for the cookers. If we swabbed his whole body down, it might do the trick. Have you had medical training, too?'

Rose wiggled her slim shoulders. 'Just the basics,' she said. 'By the way, we can drop this ma'am business. My name is Maddy.'

When she stood up, Caine noticed for the first time how much she differed from Angela Brunetto. While Angela was slim and angular, Maddy's figure was fuller. While the Italian girl's expression had held a hint of hardness, Rose's misty eyes and long lashes gave her a dreamy quality.

The white-spirit trick worked, and when Padstowe started visibly reviving, Caine stuck his head through the lower hatch on the Dingo to find Trubman at the wireless op's post. 'Anything?' he enquired.

The Welshman shook his head. 'Latest report from Rome Radio is that Rommel's forces are moving towards the border. Looks as though he's poised for the invasion of Egypt.'

Rose's face was suddenly transformed. For a split second her whole countenance glowed. '*Yes*,' she whispered.

Caine thought he must have misheard what she said.

Rose and Caine walked back to the White together. He handed her the change of kit and asked how she was feeling.

'I'm fine,' she beamed.

'It must have been bad. I mean . . . the electric shocks.'

'No worse than being dropped in a well, I suppose. Of course, I didn't hold out too long. I spilled the lot.'

'Everyone breaks in the end.' He paused. 'Look, the way I treated you was unforgivable. I deserve to be hung, drawn and quartered for it.'

'So do I. But if we're going to spend the rest of our lives saying sorry, we'll never get anywhere. At least you didn't shoot me.'

'I was a hair's breadth away from it.'

'I don't think so, Tom,' she said, her voice soft. 'You're not a woman-killer. I saw that in your eyes a second before you were knocked down.'

'You seem very sure of yourself.'

Maddy turned towards him, her face grave. 'I once saw a man cut a woman's throat in a nightclub in Cairo. I entered the room just as he was finishing it, and he stared at me. In that instant I knew I was looking into the eyes of a man who got real pleasure out of hurting women. Taking out those three Germans was different—you had no choice. I never had the feeling you were doing it for pleasure. Whatever orders you've been given, you would never have shot me down in cold blood. Not in a million years.'

'You may be right,' he said. 'But if that's the case, why did the brass choose me for the mission?'

'I can think of at least one good reason,' Rose said. 'They didn't want me executed. Anyway, I didn't need an assassin's bullet.' She opened her mouth and pointed to a large back tooth. 'It's a Bakelite insert, contains one hundred per cent potassium cyanide. I have only to bite through it.'

Caine winced and examined the false tooth with concern. 'What if you were knocked over and bit through it by accident?'

'It survived a parachute jump. Anyway, I might still need it.'

They came to the White, where Copeland and Wallace were crouching over a spirit-stove. 'Let me do that,' Rose insisted. Soon she was making a stew of tinned bacon, soya-bean sausages and tinned potatoes.

While she was working, they were joined by Adud and Layla who explained that they'd decided to leave: they had some relatives in the area with whom they intended to seek shelter. Caine asked directions to his final RV on the Maqtal plateau, and Adud spent some time sketching in the dust, showing Caine the best way of approaching it.

Layla took Caine's hand. 'You saved my life,' she said. 'You are always welcome among our people. Wherever we are, our place is yours.' The two Senussi collected their belongings and set off. When Caine looked a few minutes later, they'd already vanished.

'You really scored a hit with that girl, Tom,' Maddy said, as she served them stew.

Wallace and Copeland snorted. Caine attacked his stew vigorously.

When the others had gone off to relieve the sentries, Maddy began cleaning the mess tins and cooking pots with sand. Caine knelt down to help her. 'You said you spilled the beans about your message,' he began. 'I was wondering what the real story is. I was told some pack of lies about Assegai—a new glider-bomb system—but none of us really swallowed that.'

Maddy studied his face, and he suddenly became aware of a flux of energy between them. It was almost palpable. When he'd first met her in Biska town hall, he'd thought her almost nondescript. Now he felt that he couldn't have been more wrong: she was beautiful.

'Tom,' she said seriously, 'you deserve to know, but I can't tell you. Better not to know anything until you're out of it. I promise you one thing, though. If we get through this—and that's still a big if—I'm going to take you to dinner at Shepheard's Hotel to share the whole story.'

'They don't allow sergeants in Shepheard's,' he said.

'Really?' she breathed softly. 'There's a first time for everything . . .'

She was interrupted by three shrill blasts from a sentry's whistle, and when she glanced questioningly at Caine, he was already cocking his Tommy gun. 'We've got visitors,' he said.

In a natural sangar halfway up the screeside, Copeland tried to draw a bead on the pilot of the Messerschmitt 110 that was trawling above them. The twin-engined fighter-bomber was casting a menacing shadow on the pale desert surface. Wallace changed the elevation of his Bren gun. 'Don't move,' Copeland hissed. 'She doesn't know we're here.'

Cope scanned the line of the cliff through his telescopic sights to make sure all the wagons were invisible, the men in cover. They'd done a good job: nestling in the dark cavities along the base of the scarp wall, their scrim nets covered with sand and vegetation, the vehicles would be impossible to discern—even their tracks had been brushed out.

Wallace nudged his arm. 'Who the hell is *that*?' Cope eye-scoped the wadi: a figure was heading straight for the cliff. Cope recognised a barrel-chested man carrying a rifle and something that looked like a furry pack on his back. 'It's Sweeney,' he said. 'He's bagged game.'

Sweeney was entirely oblivious to the enemy aircraft behind him. It was evident to both Cope and Wallace that the pilot couldn't miss him, couldn't help but deduce his destination from his direction of travel. It was too late to warn the ex-Redcap without revealing the leaguer's position.

They looked on helplessly. Before the aircraft's shadow ghosted him, Sweeney seemed to become aware of her presence. He jettisoned his catch and began to run.

They watched in horror as the big bird cruised low towards the running man. They heard the *blatta-blatta-blat* of the machine gun in the aircraft's nose. The man jackknifed, vanished momentarily in a spray of dust-spume, then lay on the desert floor. The Messerschmitt poled towards them on a wide drift-angle. 'She's spotted the leaguer,' Copeland whispered. 'She's coming in for a bombing run.'

Wallace's hawk eyes were on the horizon, where he'd spotted four black smudges at 10,000 feet. 'Stukas,' he grunted. The dive-bombers were homing in on the cliff wall where the vehicles were parked.

Hugging the rock floor of the overhang with Rose close by, Caine was aware of nothing but the squeal of Stuka sirens, the *bumpa-bumpa-bumpa* of 20mm cannon, the droning counter-tenor of fifty-pound bombs, the crumping *barrroooomm* as they hit the deck. The earth quaked and smoke welled into their space like a tidal wave. He pulled himself to his feet. The bombs had exploded in the wadi and, miraculously, none of their cannon-shells had penetrated his overhang.

He peered out across the wadi. Vera and Judy were both on fire. They'd been positioned too close together. He saw bodies on the sand and sprinted towards the burning wreckage, followed by Rose. He clocked Copeland running towards him. 'What's the damage?' Caine demanded.

'Judy and Vera are written off,' Cope panted. 'Two men dead—Floggett and Shackleton—and one wounded.' He pointed to a mud-coloured bundle in the sand about a hundred yards distant. 'Todd Sweeney must have gone out to shoot gazelle.'

'That idiot. I ordered him to stay in the leaguer.'

'When the Messerschmitt came over, the prick kept on going, straight towards the leaguer. It must have been as clear as daylight where the wagons were concealed. Sweeney was hit in her strafing run, but he's still alive.'

'We can't just leave him there,' Rose said. 'He'll be killed.'

Caine and Copeland eyed the fighter-bomber now sailing directly towards them. 'There's nothing we can do,' Caine said.

'Bollocks,' Rose yelled, and was off out of cover into open desert, running towards the inert Sweeney. Caine bounded after her.

Copeland blanched and brought up his SMLE, beading the 110's cockpit through his scope. The plane was still well beyond range.

Rose had reached Sweeney and started to drag him back to cover. Behind her, Caine saw the Messerschmitt looming down, saw the bullets stitching towards Maddy. Then Caine was on her, dragging her sideways. They fell in a jumble of limbs just as a crack rang out from the base of the cliff.

Through his sights, Copeland saw the red rosebud in the pilot's face. The big bird pancaked into the hillside, hung there for a second, then the fuel tanks split apart, sending shrapnel high in the air, streaming down the cliff like dark rain. A hundred yards away, Caine and Rose felt the blast.

Caine had seen the strike pattern hit Sweeney for the second time, blowing him to bits only a second after he'd dragged Rose out of its path. 'He's dead,' he shouted in her ear.

They got back to Cope's position just in time to see the four Stukas go into strafing configuration, and braced themselves for a second onslaught. Instead, the aircraft banked abruptly to the north. 'They must have been recalled,' said Rose. 'That means they want us—me, anyway—alive.'

Wallace came shambling down the scree. 'There's a dust-cloud on the top of the escarpment. I reckon there's a Jerry convoy after us.'

Caine nodded. 'That's why they stopped the attack,' he said. 'You were right, Maddy. They want us alive.'

They stayed in the wadi only long enough to give Sweeney, Shackleton and Floggett a hasty burial, then mounted their three remaining vehicles, headed off along the base of the mountains towards their final RV.

7

Caine coaxed the tiny column along, following narrow goat tracks, crossing lava fields of volcanic clinker and wild expanses of drab camel-thorn. To their right, the landscape dropped away to open desert; to their left it rose towards an escarpment.

Caine halted the wagons and saw the last shards of sunlight mirrored back from the whitewashed walls of a settlement. He told the lads to take a break. The commandos piled stiffly out of the wagons, glugged water, lit up cigarettes. Caine knew they were hungry. Almost all the remaining rations had gone up with the 3-tonners. Caine laid out his map on the White's bonnet. 'Look,' he said. 'There's a colonial scheme marked here. Maybe this is our chance of finding food.'

'The Jerries might find us there, box us in,' Cope said.

'I don't think they'll follow us at night. They'll be too confident of catching us in daylight to bother. They don't know we've got an LRDG squadron coming to collect us tomorrow.'

'I think we ought to have a look, then,' Rose said.

'We'll take the wagons a mile on down the road,' said Caine. 'Then we'll double back and turn off at this junction. We'll brush out our tyre-marks for the first quarter-mile. That should put them off the scent.'

The settlement was eerie in the moonlight. The households were all of a standard pattern, flat-roofed angular blocks, each with its own kitchen-garden and cluster of outbuildings. Close up it was clear that the whole place had been thoroughly looted. Doors hung off their hinges, the yards were littered with broken utensils and sticks of splintered furniture.

Caine ordered the boys to search the settlement and set off for the nearest homestead. There was no sign of life, but Wallace growled. 'Hear that?'

They halted. Caine picked up a deep panting, like someone in the grip of a heavy fever. Holding his Tommy gun at the ready, he inched towards the black aperture of the homestead's door. He was within three yards of it when something the size of a baby rhinoceros charged out of the doorway directly towards him. A single shot snapped out. The creature pitched over with a round drilled cleanly through its skull. It was an enormous pig.

It took four men to lift and hang the pig by an exposed beam in the farm's parlour, where Fred Wallace gutted and butchered it. They broke up furniture and lit a fire. Soon, the room was full of the savoury aroma of roast pork. They squatted on the verandah to eat the fresh meat, washed down with Chianti 'liberated' during their sojourn with Michele's deserters.

Caine and Rose sat a little apart from the others. Caine gave her a cigarette, snapped the Zippo open and bathed the tip in fire. 'See this,' he said. 'This saved my life and yours back in Biska. If I hadn't had this when I was in the well, I'd never have found the Senussi's knife. And without the knife you and I would now be stone dead.' He brought out the Zippo's protective condom. 'Come to think of it, it was this condom that really saved our lives. Funny how your life, future generations, everything, could depend on a rubber Johnny.'

Rose turned away. 'Future generations. What makes you think there'll be any? Why bring children into a world where people treat each other like animals? What's the point?'

'Is that why you said that what happened to you didn't matter?' he asked. 'Why you tried to save an injured man in full view of an enemy aircraft? I saw how you acted when those Jerries were about to murder you in cold blood. It was like you didn't care. Why?'

Rose turned to look at him and Caine stared into the face of the Maddaleine Rose he'd encountered in the guardroom at Biska. 'It's none of your business, *Sergeant*.'

'I see,' Caine said slowly. 'I'm too insignificant to be told what I'm giving my life for. Well, First Officer Rose, *ma'am*, twelve good men have died so far to pull you out of this hell. I don't need the pretence of your friendship to help me do my duty.'

Rose looked away. There was an awkward silence as they smoked their cigarettes. It was Rose who broke the stand-off, her voice low and hollow. 'I was engaged once. He was an agent in the Special Operations Executive. They parachuted him into France. The Gestapo tortured him and murdered him. The day Peter died, I died with him. So, I didn't need you to rescue me. Those Jerries couldn't have killed me, because I'm already dead.'

Caine bit his lip, more confused than ever. Rose had risked her life to courier a secret message to Blighty. That made sense, but it was the only thing that did. Why had she given up all her secrets? If she wanted revenge and an honourable death, why not just spit in Rohde's face and swallow her cyanide pill? Or did she think suicide by poison too clean and easy a way to go? If so, she really did belong in the booby-hatch.

'Listen,' Caine said quietly. 'I don't give a tinker's cuss about your death wish. I'm taking you back alive, and if I have to restrain you again, I will. The odds are that none of us is going to make it, so I want to know now why I was sent on this fool's errand. What was it that you were carrying that was vital enough to justify twelve of my mates getting scragged?'

'All right,' Rose said sourly. 'The dispatches I was carrying concerned the state of the Eighth Army. After Gazala, we're unable to sustain a concentrated attack by the Axis. My message was from the commander-in-chief to be delivered personally to Mr Churchill in London. It was a request for permission to evacuate Egypt and withdraw to Palestine, or even the Sudan. If the Eighth Army remains in Egypt, it will be crushed.'

Caine's mouth dropped open in disbelief. 'Rommel's already heading for the Egyptian border,' he gasped. 'If your message never reached London, and there's no back-up, that means . . .'

'It means the end of the war in North Africa,' she cut in, her voice flat. 'It means that the Nazis have won.'

Caine was too shocked to quiz Rose any further. What made him speechless was the knowledge that she'd actually revealed this vital intelligence to the Hun. That meant that Caine's entire mission had been pointless. Thanks to Maddaleine Rose, the Desert Fox was now aware that his forces would meet zero resistance from the Allies.

If the Eighth Army had been ordered to withdraw, it might be able to regroup for a counterattack. Since Runefish's dispatch hadn't reached Churchill, though, no such permission would have been forthcoming. Unless Auchinleck had decided to act off his own bat, the remnants of his army would be snared like a bunch of jack-rabbits in the open.

'Is it possible,' he asked, a lifetime later, 'that the Auk relied on a single courier to get the message through? Surely there must have been others?'

'I can't answer that,' Rose replied stiffly. 'I only know about myself.'

'Why wasn't it at least confirmed through wireless comms?'

'Because GHQ has been penetrated by Axis agents. They broke our codes long ago. The commander-in-chief couldn't risk—' She never finished her sentence, because at that moment wild figures appeared out of the darkness, converging from all sides. 'Drop your weapons,' a voice hissed.

In the starlight, Caine recognised the untamed black hair of Michele Brunetto, hefting a Beretta .44 magnum revolver in his right hand. Caine glanced around, clocking the horde of bearded bandits who had crept up on them like ghosts in the night. There were at least a hundred men here, and they were well armed. He stood erect, making no move to drop his weapon. 'What are you doing, Michele?' he asked.

The Italian swept back his long hair. 'I am selling you to my friend, Major Rohde of the Abwehr. Lay down your weapons—*now*.'

At the mention of Rohde's name an icy frisson passed down Caine's spine. If Michele had been in contact with the Black Widow, he would have been able to give him vital intelligence about the Runefish mission: arms, strength, intentions. He hoped that none of the lads had let slip to any of Michele's band the fact that they were to meet an LRDG patrol the next day.

Whatever the case, that left only eleven men and a woman against over a hundred. In a scrap, most of his lads would be hit. Their best course of action would be to pretend submission now and tackle the Ities later, when they weren't expecting it—preferably before Rohde turned up. It would be a tall order without weapons, but at least there'd be a chance.

Caine laid his Tommy gun smartly on the earth. Wallace glared angrily at him and there were groans from the lads, but after a brief hesitation, they followed suit. Michele chuckled triumphantly. When the commandos had divested themselves of everything that resembled a weapon, Michele instructed his minions to bundle the hardware into the cab of the Dingo.

He ordered the commandos to form a line, with their hands on their heads, then sauntered up to them cockily. He halted in front of Rose and gawped greedily at her. 'So, you are the famous Runefish. Very nice. I ask myself from the beginning why the British send out a special squad to rescue a girl like you? You must be worth a lot of money. Then last night, I receive a message from Captain Haller of the Brandenburgers. He says you escape from Biska with British commandos. He need my help to get you back, and his boss pay good price and promise no hunting down deserters.'

Caine snorted. 'So, you turned out to be a capitalist, after all. How did you find us, anyway?'

Michele snickered. 'This morning we pick up the old Senussi and his daughter. I threaten to take her virginity and the old man squawks. He track you for us.' Michele turned his attention back to Rose, brushing her breasts with the tips of his fingers. Caine clenched his fists. 'Don't touch her.'

Michele kicked him hard in the groin with a cavalry-booted foot. Caine doubled over, grunting. Michele stood over him. 'You don't give orders here. I welcome you like brothers, and you pull a gun on me in my own camp. You take my *benzina* without thank-you. Your men . . .' He paused as if a thought had just struck him, and his eyes fell on Copeland.

'Here he is, the great lover of women.' He skipped over to Cope and punched him savagely in the kidneys. As Cope bent forward, Michele jammed his revolver into his cheek. 'You, my friend, are *finish*. I'll show you what happens when a man touches my wife.' He pointed a finger at Copeland and ordered two of his men to drag him away. Cope knocked them to the side. 'If you're going to shoot me, shoot me,' he growled. 'I don't need to be manhandled.'

Caine had decided already that he wasn't going to stand by and watch another comrade cut down. He could see from the dark creases on Wallace's granite brow that he wasn't alone.

Michele was arguing venomously with the men he'd detailed to execute Cope. Caine didn't know a word of Italian, but it quickly became apparent that there wasn't a single member of Michele's band who was ready to kill a man against whom they had no personal grudge. Michele could only restore his honour by killing his wife's lover himself. This must finally have dawned on Michele, for with a snarl of rage he pointed his revolver at Cope. 'Down on your knees,' he yelled.

Copeland shook his head stoically. 'You want to kill me, you'll have to do it while I'm standing up.'

Michele's pistol hand shook. He took careful aim. Caine readied himself to spring, noting that Wallace was about to do the same. He was on the verge of jumping, when a voice shouted, '*Stop.*'

Maddaleine Rose was a shapely figure in her loose khakis, her soft blonde hair silvered by the starlight. It was Rose who had spoken. Everyone was looking at her now.

'It's me you want, isn't it?' she asked silkily, her eyes fixed on Michele. 'You can have me. I won't resist. Just let that man go.'

Michele licked his lips. Rose had played her hand perfectly, Caine thought. By offering herself, she'd allowed Michele to preserve a kind of masculine honour, without having to shoot a man dead in the process. Michele holstered his pistol and smiled truculently at Copeland. 'You are a lucky man,' he grunted. He turned to Rose.

Caine's pulse raced. He was glad that she'd intervened but he was no more prepared to let her sacrifice herself than he had been ready to see Copeland shot down. He was half on his feet when a single gunshot blasted out of the night. Caine and his commandos fell flat on their faces: the guards shifted on their feet trying to work out where the shot had come from when a willowy female figure in khaki appeared out of the darkness, stopped in front of Michele, and jabbed an automatic pistol towards him.

Angela Brunetto looked furious. 'Bastard piece of *merda*. These brave men saved my life and you hand them over to the same *Tedesci* who murdered Carlo? You are not a man. You bring shame on us all, and now you make it worse by forcing this woman? Let these English go, or I will shoot you now.'

There was a tense silence. None of Michele's men intervened.

Michele made a grab for Angela's pistol. There was brief tussling match, then Michele howled as a round shattered the bones of his foot.

At almost the same instant Caine heard the growl of engines from further down the wadi. 'The *Tedesci*,' Angela whispered.

Caine's commandos were already poised to leg it, but uncertain whether they'd be shot down by their Italian captors. Caine saw Angela take instant command. 'Get to the vehicles,' she told the deserters. She pointed at the moaning Michele. 'Take that heap of shit with you.'

As the men lifted Michele and jogged towards their wagons, Angela turned to Caine. 'You leave now. I have sent old Adud and his daughter to your vehicles. They wait for you there. Good luck and God go with you.'

The deserters were gunning their engines, and Caine could hear shouts in German drifting out of the darkness from further down the wadi. 'Get going, lads,' he yelled at the commandos. 'Take Miss Rose back to the wagons.' When Caine spun round to thank Angela, he found her wrapped tightly in the arms of Harry Copeland. 'Come on, mate,' Caine hissed.

Cope broke away and Caine saw tears glistening in Angela's eyes. Then, just as the first Jerry silhouettes emerged from the shadows of the wadi, Caine and Copeland dashed off like greyhounds for the cover of the trees.

ALL NIGHT, BLOWN GRIT scoured the convoy like emery-cloth, but at sunup the wind dropped. They halted in the middle of a featureless vanilla sand-sheet and as Caine jumped down from the White, he felt as if a weight had been lifted from his shoulders. Not that he believed they had outrun the enemy, it was just that huge open spaces like this gave elbow room to the spirit. Adud and Layla, who had guided them through the night, seemed to feel the same.

Caine was concerned. If things were as bad in Egypt as Rose had implied, it was possible that the Runefish mission had been ditched. They didn't have enough fuel to get home. Without the LRDG they'd have to foot-slog it back to the Wire. Tabbing 300 miles across sterile desert wasn't exactly what the doctor ordered.

Rose made tea and they were finishing it when Wallace pointed out a faint stain on the north-western horizon. 'It's them,' he said. 'The Huns.'

They started off again. Three times they saw flights of aircraft. The planes made no attempt to strafe them, and Caine decided that either the pilots hadn't seen them, or, as Rose had suggested, that Rohde had given orders to take them alive. Just after midday, they came over a rise and saw a vast purple wall truncating the eastern horizon—the Maqtal plateau, a continuous cliff wall lying directly across their line of advance.

Caine knew that the RV with the LRDG lay along the Maqtal, but his map wasn't detailed enough. He called Adud and the old man pointed out a twin-toothed peak. He explained, with Layla's help, that there was a gap in the rock just to the right of this double peak—a gorge that ascended gradually to the plateau.

It took two hours to reach and Caine realised that they'd shot the RV time by more than an hour and a half. He was sure that the LRDG would give them at least until sunset but as the wagons passed through the jaws of the gorge and began to grind up the rising wadi bed, Caine's spirits sank. The recognition signal—a blue Very flare—failed to show. The LRDG knew their business. If they were here, they would have spotted the convoy.

It took only a quarter of an hour for the wagons to reach the top, but by then Caine knew for certain that no one was waiting to greet them. Leaguering the wagons in a fold in the ground beyond the lip of the scarp, Caine double-checked the coordinates until he was absolutely sure that this was the right place. Then, he and Copeland crawled to the lip of the ridge and surveyed the wadi bed below.

There was a good defensive line about twenty yards from the top where they could pile rocks into sangars and dig shallow shell-scrapes. Caine frowned, knowing that this was going to require enormous effort. There wasn't much time: the menacing brown cloud that signalled the approach of the enemy still lay on the distant horizon.

They withdrew to the leaguer, where Caine held a dispirited O group. The men looked dejected. All the way across the desert they'd anticipated a well-equipped LRDG squadron—wagons manned by fresh troops, bristling with machine guns, their boards crammed with food and drink.

'We've got a problem, boys,' he informed them. 'The enemy is closing in on us, and we don't have the petrol to outrun them.' He took a deep breath. 'As you can see, the LRDG patrol we expected hasn't turned up.'

He let this sink in. 'As I see it, gentlemen, we've got three choices. One, we wait for Jerry and surrender. Two, we break up into small parties and trog back to Egypt on foot. Three, we dig in on this ridge and fight it out. I'm not going to give any orders. I'll give my opinion, but the choice is up to you.'

Pickney broke the silence. 'If we surrender, they have to offer us our rights as POWs. It makes more sense than to get scragged for nothing.'

Pickney's declaration was met by boos. Caine held up his hand. 'If my experience in Biska had been different, I might agree. But this lot behind us aren't Afrika Korps, they're Abwehr troops and under the command of a sadistic war criminal. Frankly, if we surrender to him I don't hold out much hope, especially for Maddy.'

'Leave me out of this, Tom,' Rose said. 'I'll take my chances.'

'What about the escape-and-evasion option?' Flash Murray said. 'When the LRDG got bumped by the Ities near Kufra, one chap walked two hundred miles back across the desert.'

'We'll never make it,' Copeland said. 'We've got hardly any water.'

'I'm for making a stand here,' Wallace cut in. 'Let's whack into 'em with everything we've got, pinch their wagons, head for the Wire.'

'It's not going to be easy,' Pickney said. 'Last time, we had the element of surprise. When the Hun drives up that wadi, he'll be ready for us.'

'What this needs,' Caine declared suddenly, 'is a sapper's solution.'

'Mines,' Cope nodded.

Caine said, 'We've got about thirty landmines and some Hawkins grenades. There's no other way for the Hun to approach us than up that wadi. We'll sow a patch with mines—we could even make a grenade daisy-chain to supplement them. Rohde won't be expecting to hit a minefield.'

Cope's eyes lit up. 'What we need is a decoy. How about posting the Dingo at the mouth of the wadi? The Huns clock her, they give chase, she leads them into the minefield. We'll make a path through it that only the Dingo driver can see.'

'We could dig sangars on this slope, and lay the grenade daisy-chain along the lower skirts,' Wingnut Turner joined in. 'The Huns who survive the minefield blast will rush our position uphill. One of us lies hidden, waits till they've gone past and sets off the daisy-chain just as they go into the assault—boom, bodies fly, we open up on the rest with the Vickers and Brens . . . We'll wipe 'em out just like we did on the Benghazi Road . . .'

'Just a sec,' Taffy Trubman cut in, waving a pudgy hand. 'The column we banjoed on the road didn't have air support. This time they do.'

Caine shook his head. 'I'm not sure about that, Taffy. I think they might want us alive, or at least want Miss Rose alive. Even if they use aircraft, I don't reckon they'll hit us full whack.'

'The question is,' Pickney said, 'who's going to drive the Dingo?'

'It ought to be me,' George Padstowe announced. 'I think Taffy Trubman and I have clocked up the most hours in the Dingo.'

Caine considered it for a moment. 'All right,' he said. 'You and Wingnut will lay the landmines, the Hawkinses and the daisy-chain. You'll do the decoy, George. Wingnut, you'll lie in hiding with the daisy-chain igniter. We'll have to hope that the Huns don't come in waves, though, because we've only got enough ordnance for one good crack.'

Caine searched the men's faces. They nodded in agreement one by one—Pickney alone remained uncertain. 'Listen,' he said. 'How can eleven shagged-out men take on a large force of Axis troops with armoured vehicles and possibly even air support? It's just not on.'

Copeland shook his head at Pickney. 'Ever hear of the battle of Thermopylae, Maurice? Three hundred Spartans used a narrow gorge like this one to hold off a Persian army fifty thousand strong.'

'You're only telling half the story,' Pickney said. 'The way I remember it, every bloody one of them was wiped out.'

The commandos leapt into frenetic activity. As Turner and Padstowe eased the Dingo loaded with mines down the slope, the rest of the men lined up to collect weaponry and ammo. Caine designated a defensive position for each man in a dog's-leg line across the hillside and sent them off to construct sangars.

Flash Murray would man the 20mm gun on the Daimler on the right of the line—there was a clear field of fire directly down the gorge. Wallace had removed the twin Vickers from the Dingo and the White, and set about mounting them on tripods. The White would play no direct part in the battle: Caine decided to hide her in a depression behind the Daimler.

Rose jabbed Caine's arm. 'What about me?' she demanded.

'You're a non-combatant,' Caine told her gruffly. 'I want you to go off with Layla and Adud. Try to reach a Senussi camp, hole up there until you can make contact with British intelligence.'

'A *non-combatant*?' Rose repeated. She grabbed the Bren gun Caine had put aside for himself, cleared the weapon fast and with precision, snapped on a magazine, ratcheted the first round into the chamber and made safe. Caine's face dropped with surprise. 'You've fired a Bren before?'

Rose laughed up at him. 'I'm a marksman with Bren, Tommy gun and .45 Colt pistol—oh, and the Gewehr 41 semi-auto and the Beretta SMG as well. Fully small-arms trained. I'm also a trained parachutist, a medical orderly and a W/T operator.'

'Anything else?' Caine enquired.

'I'm also trained in demolitions, subversion, intelligence-gathering, unarmed combat—and mental techniques.'

'Mental techniques?' he echoed. 'Like how you stopped Michele, just by saying, "Stop"? The way you ordered us around in the guardroom at Biska?'

'They call that the Voice,' Rose agreed softly. 'It's a mental weapon. You can project authority by speaking in a certain tone.'

Caine found himself glowering at her. 'It's a pity you didn't use the Voice on that bastard Rohde instead of flushing the Eighth Army down the toilet.'

'You haven't got a very high opinion of me, have you, Tom?'

'I just don't get you,' Caine said, irritated. 'You've got guts, yet you collapsed under interrogation and blew intelligence that might cost us the entire campaign. You're so taken up in your personal tragedy that you don't seem bothered about ours. If you wanted to die so badly, why didn't you just swallow that cyanide pill and get it over with?'

Rose's face caved in and she put her arms round him. Caine felt the soft curves of her body fitting into his, felt her breath on his face, experienced an explosion of desire that seemed to crash like a tidal wave across his whole body. He felt like making violent love to her right then and there.

'It's been really lonely,' Rose whispered. 'These last two days—being with you—it's made a difference. All right, maybe I am more than what I said . . . maybe I couldn't tell you the whole truth, but I—'

'Where do you want these Vickers placed?' Wallace's voice croaked.

Caine saw the giant towering over him. Desire drained away. Caine broke from Rose's embrace. 'My mission was to bring you back or execute you. I've failed in the first and I'm past doing the second. Get out while you can.'

Rose wiped tears from her eyes. 'The bottom line, *Sergeant*, is that you can't order me to go. For better or for worse, I'm staying here with you.'

'Hey,' Wallace yelled. 'That sounded like a marriage proposal to me, skipper. Anyhow, we could do with anyone capable of handling a weapon.'

Caine shot his mate an exasperated glance. 'Fred, it's against regs for women to fight as combatants in this campaign.'

'I ain't seen no Regulations Manual round here. What I seen is a bint—sorry, ma'am, an *officer*—who knows her way round a Bren gun, and only eleven of us against about sixteen divisions of Jerries.'

His jovial manner vanished and his eyes bored into Caine. 'You spent your life treating women like they was precious flowers, Tom, but you can't go on doing that. Respect means treating 'em like real grown-up people, too. Anyway, seeing as how she's the same rank as a major, and you're a buckshee sergeant, I don't reckon there's much you can do about it.'

Caine looked at the big man in surprise. This simple truth of his mate's words sank in slowly. He nodded at Rose, accepting defeat. 'All right then. Collect your weapons and let's do it.'

Adud and Layla were equally reluctant to quit but Caine insisted that they head for the nearest Senussi settlement. If the worst came to the worst, they wouldn't be implicated. Adud argued, but they left without ceremony.

Half an hour later, Padstowe brought the Dingo back up the slope. 'We laid the mines and Hawkinses about five hundred yards from the base.' He pointed out where Turner was holed up with the daisy-chain igniter. 'Wingnut will stay in cover until most of the Huns have passed by. He'll hit the switch as they come under defensive fire from your position.'

Caine nodded. 'You marked a path through the minefield?'

'Marked by spent cartridge-cases. The Hun'll never see it.' He held up a Very pistol. 'I'll give it a green flare as soon as I see they're after me.'

Caine clapped him on the shoulder. They shook hands. Padstowe said, 'Tom, whatever happens, it's been a privilege—'

'Tell me about it after we've got through it.' Caine cut him short. 'Anyway, George, the privilege is mine.'

A moment later Padstowe was guiding the Dingo back down the slope.

Caine held up a hand. 'They're coming,' he hissed. He blew on his whistle. All eyes were on the Dingo now, as she threaded her way across the wadi bed. She cleared the curve and suddenly the ridge was very still.

Nothing moved. There was silence but for the hum of distant Hun engines. Then a Very flare plopped, coalescing into a streaky green flower. 'That's it,' Caine said. 'They've clocked him.'

Almost at once the Dingo corkscrewed back round the bend, spraying dust, as Padstowe hugged the path through the minefield. Round the curve swept half a dozen German armoured cars, led by a massive SdKfz 231 six-wheeler. The AFVs were racing in two ranks of three abreast, scores of German soldiers hanging onto them. Caine gasped at the size of the enemy force: there were more men here than just the Brandenburger platoon at Biska—they'd been reinforced to at least company strength.

The Dingo raced nearer and nearer to the foot of the ridge. The 231 closed the gap rapidly. Her 20mm gun blazed, a shell sawed past the Dingo, hit the deck in a rumbling *roooomfff*. At the same moment the other Jerry AFVs stonked into the minefeld: the bed of the ravinc heaved up in a head-drumming thunder. AFVs tore apart. Germans shrieked, scarfed up fumes, tumbled off burning wagons. Survivors scuttled for cover, floundered into Hawkins bombs, went up in crimson mousse.

Still Caine's squad held fire. Caine saw smoke clear, clocked the 231 half on her side. He saw her gun pivot, saw the muzzle blowpipe flame. He saw the shell bazooka the rear of the still-retreating Dingo. The little scout-car struck a mine and a second later Caine clocked Padstowe sprinting towards the cover of rocks, slapping at smouldering shorts as he ran.

Caine focused on the Jerries. He saw six or seven soft-skinners, disgorging troops. He heard the clap of Murray's 20mm cannon from the Daimler, and observed a hit on a truck almost a thousand yards away.

He zeroed-in the Vickers, and curveballed tracer down on the Huns. Fire arched down the ravine, stitching sand, snapping bodies. Jerries came uphill in scores, advancing behind supporting machine-gun spritz and mortar shrapnel. To his right, Wallace and Cope squeezed triggers, jack-knifed tracer at the Boche. They pumped slugs until their barrels cooked.

A round ploughed a furrow through Cope's straw-thatched scalp. He touched the bloody groove, gasped at how close it'd come to his skull. He clocked Brandenburgers hobnailing towards his sangar. He grabbed his sniper's rifle, cross haired a Jerry in a coal-scuttle helmet and shot the helmet off. The Jerry stooped, reached for the helmet. Cope cracker-jacked him through the forehead.

Rose, sangared up five yards from Copeland, saw five Huns ranging her. She hand-wove Jerry chests with a pattern of .303 ball. A Boche went to ground behind a rock, and rim-fired her from twenty paces. A slug lumped her flesh where the neck met the shoulder, drilled through muscle, grazed bone. Rose swore through gritted teeth. She waited for the Hun to pop up again, pom-pommed a tight burst, saw his head splat like a watermelon.

Ten yards right, Fred Wallace saw a phalanx of five Brandenburgers coming at him from ten paces. He braced his Bren, let rip a spliff of fire, watched Huns thrashing. He clocked a Squarehead bee-lining him with a Mauser pistol, planted size-thirteen boots, drew his sawn-off from its sheath. He heard the Mauser crack, felt the bullet hopscotch his knuckles: he pulled both handles, smooth-bored the Jerry.

Furthest right, the Daimler's gun blowtorched. Inside the turret, Murray loaded HE shells like a coolie. He sighted muzzle-flash from a Hun MG30 nest down on the wadi side 300 yards away. He swivelled the barrel, blitzed the machine-gunners. Murray was so focused on loading and firing he didn't notice that defensive fire on his left had faltered and the Brandenburgers had broken through. The first Murray knew about it was when a stick grenade sailed through the open hatch and landed in his lap. The blast tore out the turret's guts, fractured the cannon's breech, blew off Murray's legs. Half a dozen Jerries strafed the screaming lance sergeant with fire. Maurice Pickney popped up from nowhere and ripped off bullets from a Tommy gun. A Jerry Schmeissered him. Pickney dropped without a sound. The Germans moved past the burning Daimler, found the White hidden behind a ridge, blew her to shreds.

Caine had seen that the enemy had broken through on the right flank. Where was Turner? What had happened to the daisy-chain? In a few moments the left flank would be overrun and they'd be done for.

Below him, Turner's position was empty. Minutes earlier, Turner had seen his mate George Padstowe emerge from cover further down the wadi, flushed out by Brandenburgers. He'd started limping towards Turner's sangar, thirty yards away. A bullet chugged his shoulder. He fell on one knee, brought up his Colt .45. He hit the first Jerry in the chest, the second in the mouth. Then the rest were on him, bayonets slicking.

Turner ran from his sangar, blunderbussing Jerries with a Bren from the hip. Two Huns blasted him with rounds. Turner felt the hits, saw Padstowe fall in a heap. He fire-gutted Jerries, wiped them out. He crouched by his mate, tried to drag him, gave up the attempt.

Turner saw Germans above him on the slope and realised that they were about to overrun Caine's line. He remembered the daisy-chain. His heart sank. He'd left his post and let down the whole unit. He crawled back towards his position, trailing gore. Rounds whipped sand in his eyes. He kept on crawling. He had to reach the daisy-chain igniter, or the battle would be lost. Bullets spattered around him, but he kept going. He was in the sangar, dragging himself to the switch. Blood spurted from his thigh. He summoned his last dying breath—and pressed the igniter.

Caine felt the daisy-chain shock wave, 200 feet up. He saw detonations all across the slope, right in the midst of the advancing hordes. Jerries skittled over: sawn-off bodies spun and flew. There was an instant loss of momentum in the assault. Everywhere, Germans were turning tail, racing back down the scarp.

On the far right of Caine's line, the Jerries who had just whacked Murray heard the daisy-chain shuttlebang like fireworks behind them. They felt the blast, saw their comrades going down, saw their mates retreating. Three

Tommies pitched at them from different angles: one a giant, another a tall soldier with gore-smeared blond hair, the third a muscular man with unusually broad chest and shoulders. Their lips were drawn back in berserker grins; they were covered in blood and coming on fearlessly.

The last three Jerries reeled: Caine, Copeland and Wallace crashed into them. Wallace brought his blade down on a Hun's chest, piercing his heart. Copeland shot a Jerry in the mouth. Caine snatched a Jerry's rifle, stuck his carotid; the Jerry's blood spritzed out. Wallace shot him in the head.

At last, there was silence. Wallace's bulk swayed dangerously. Caine put an arm round his waist to steady him. Nobody spoke. They studied the charnel house around them—the dead on the escarpment, the retreating Jerries, the smouldering wagons. It felt as though they'd just walked into hell and back. Caine glanced down at his watch; the battle had lasted just half an hour.

Caine didn't kid himself they'd won anything. The Jerries would be back, and there was no way his little band would succeed in fighting them off a second time. He resigned himself to the inevitable, reflecting that his mission would go down in history as the worst ever cock-up behind enemy lines. He knew there'd only been a fifty-fifty chance of success, but if he'd done things differently, they might have succeeded. After all, despite all the odds, they'd snatched Maddy Rose. It was galling to have come so near, and yet still be so far.

As well as Turner, Padstowe and Murray, he'd lost Graveman and Temple—taken out by mortar bombs—and Raker—scatter-gunned in the chest. There were only five of them left now—six if you counted Rose. Trubman and Pickney both had chest wounds: neither could stand properly, but both insisted they could still shoot. When Caine peered into Rose's sangar, he found her grinning back at him. Caine supposed he should have felt resentful that she'd come through when all but four of his boys had got scragged, but he was very glad that she was there.

Not that she, or any of them, was likely to be there much longer. They were alone in the desert, wagons gone, no water, rations or ammo, except what they carried. They had a Bren each, a few mags, some grenades, their personal weapons. They had no means of contacting friendly forces, and they were wounded. They didn't have the energy to escape on foot.

Caine nodded towards the top of the ridge. 'I think we should move up there,' he said. 'That's where we'll make our stand.'

Wallace smirked at the word 'stand', but was too weak to make any rejoinder. Neither Rose nor Copeland said anything; Pickney and Trubman needed all their strength just to stay conscious. The others carried them to the top of the ridge, and set them up in a sangar. Then they sat down behind rocks and boulders to wait for the final act.

Trubman and Pickney's sangar lay on the left flank, with Caine and Rose ten yards away in the centre, and Cope and Wallace on the right. They cleaned and patched up each other's injuries. They glugged water and sucked on cigarettes.

Caine couldn't take his eyes off Rose. He felt a reprise of guilt at the way he'd treated her. 'I'm sorry . . .' he started, but Rose put a finger on his lips.

'Don't,' she said softly. 'You did everything you could, Tom.'

'I didn't do enough. My mission failed.'

Rose took a deep breath. 'Your mission didn't fail. I wanted to tell you before, but I couldn't. Now there's no point me holding back.' Caine put his arms round her. 'These last few days have changed me,' she whispered. 'I wanted to die, to be with Peter. Now I've found you, Tom . . . Funny, isn't it? You want to end it all, and then the minute it looks like curtains, you find someone to live for. I just wish we could have got to know each other . . .'

'Sh, sh,' Caine said. 'I know all I need to know about you . . .'

When he kissed her it wasn't with the death-defying lust he'd felt before: it was as if this was all there ever could be in the universe. The kiss went on—the most passionate kiss of his life. They were going to die but this one priceless moment had been worth all their blood, toil and sorrow.

Rose let go of him. 'You said you know all you need to know about me but you don't. My name is Betty Nolan, and I was trained for the Runefish mission. Maddy Rose is a character I created . . . me and "A" Force. The operation was all dreamed up by them.'

For a moment, Caine thought she was joking. Then the pieces fell into place with an almost audible clang. 'The way you behaved at Biska. Turning us in, giving the griff to Rohde . . . that was all part of a decoy, wasn't it? None of the things you've told me up to now was true.'

Betty smiled crookedly. 'It was true I was carrying a dispatch reporting that the Eighth Army was on the point of collapse, but that message was disinformation. It wasn't intended for Mr Churchill at all, but for Rommel. We made sure that Axis agents in Cairo would find out about Runefish, and that the Axis would track my plane and shoot it down. My pilot was sick. He only had months to live, and he volunteered for the job knowing he'd be killed. When I bailed out the Senussi helped me. They showed me a cave in the Green Mountains. I was sure one of them would snitch—I didn't make much effort to conceal myself, but it couldn't be obvious, either. When the

Huns didn't come for me, I got worried. That's why I sent that three-hour-long SOS. It wasn't meant for you. I just had to make sure the Jerries found out I was there, and I knew they'd triangulate my signal.'

Caine sat up straight, stared at her aghast. 'Do you know how close we came to taking you out? We saw you captured. Harry Copeland had you in his cross hairs. I had orders to snatch you or execute you . . .'

'But you didn't execute me, Tom. I believe they chose you because they knew that, when it came down to brass tacks, you would go against orders. You'd refuse to kill a woman in cold blood.'

'Then why the heck did they order me to do it in the first place?'

'Look, Tom, the Runefish mission was designed to influence strategy. The morale of the Eighth Army wasn't shattered at Gazala. There haven't been any near-mutinies or desertions. By now, the Eighth Army will already have rallied, reinforced by divisions from Palestine. The Eighth Army is strong, but the object of Runefish was to convince the enemy that it was weak, so Rommel would be drawn into invading Egypt. He's walking into a trap.'

Caine's mouth groped for words. 'But surely,' he said, 'Rommel would have done that anyway, without any help from you?'

'No. The long-term strategy of Axis High Command was to take Tobruk, then invade Malta. We had to make sure they went for Egypt first. Of course, Rommel might have wanted to invade Egypt all along. That's in his character, but he's under the orders of Axis High Command . . .'

'Wouldn't the Auk have been happy if the Axis had gone for Malta first?'

'Not at all. The North Africa campaign is a campaign of logistics. It'll be won, not by bravery or aggression, but by supplies. Malta is the key to the campaign, because from Malta our RAF boys can block Axis supply lines, sinking their convoys at will. While we hold Malta, Rommel can't ever be sure of his supplies or reinforcements, and without them, he's done for. The Axis can't invade both Malta and Egypt at once, because they don't have the air power. They can only do one or the other and they had to be deterred from attacking Malta. The only way of doing it was to make Rommel think that the Eighth Army was in such a chaotic state that his few men and tanks would be able to swat us aside like flies. Auchinleck guessed that Rommel would want to advance, even against the orders of his High Command. The Runefish mission furnished him with intelligence that would help him convince his top brass that they could get away with it.'

Caine saw an almost euphoric look in her eyes. '"A" Force needed someone who'd be conspicuous. A female courier would stand out. They needed someone convincing, who could play the role of a snooty British officer. I volunteered. I'm an actress, Tom—I've played Shakespeare. I knew I probably wouldn't survive the mission, but I didn't care. My life in exchange for scuppering the whole Nazi war effort in North Africa? After what those bastards did to Peter? It was a small price to pay. Of course, I didn't really know about you . . . about the side mission . . .'

'*Side mission?*' Caine gasped. 'What the hell do you mean you didn't *really* know? I was sent to rescue you or take you out . . .'

Nolan pursed her lips. 'No, Tom, you were sent to make it look more authentic. When the Hun clicked that GHQ had dispatched a unit to snatch me, it would make what I had to say valuable. Your mission was a decoy.'

'That's why you couldn't come with me at Biska—you hadn't passed on the intelligence. If we'd snatched you then, you'd have failed . . .'

'You've got it,' Nolan smiled apologetically. 'When you walked into my cell at Biska, I just couldn't believe it. Maybe I over-reacted. My job wasn't done. I had to make sure you didn't pull me out.'

Caine saw that her eyes were heavy with tears. 'You were fed the Assegai story as a fragile cover.'

'What does that mean?'

'A fragile cover is one that's meant to be broken. If you talked under interrogation, the weakness of your cover story would look like it was attempting to conceal the real story. No one ever expected a small outfit like yours to get through. What you achieved was incredible, Tom.

'I'm sorry about your men, but be certain of two things: their lives weren't sacrificed for nothing, and you didn't fail. What matters is that we did it. Rommel is going for Egypt, and he'll never get out in one piece. Together, we've helped change the course of the campaign. We might even have changed the world.'

Caine felt himself carried away by her rhetoric. He and his men had been sacrificed, that was certain. Yet he wasn't sure whether being ignorant of the truth hadn't been for the better. He stared at Nolan with new eyes. 'I don't care what your name is,' he said. 'I don't care if you're an officer or a grunt or a civvie. All I know is, you're one bloody hell of a woman.'

He threw his arms around her again. They melted into one another. They might have stayed that way all day if Wallace hadn't called, 'Hey, skipper. They're on their way.'

German soft-skin wagons were trolling cautiously through the burning wrecks on the wadi bed, following at least half a company of Brandenburgers in disciplined formation. This time there were no mines, no daisy-chains, no support weapons. Caine knew it had to be a whites-of-the-eyes job. They had so little ammunition left that it would be pointless to engage the enemy at anything but close range.

'Wait till they're up close, then take as many of the buggers with you as you can.' That, Caine thought, was the last order he was ever likely to give.

The enemy abandoned the trucks at the foot of the ridge. Traversing his barrel, Caine watched them come straight up the slope. There, among the ranks, he made out the figure of Major Heinrich Rohde; there was something about the walk that was familiar—that sidling, feminine gait. He lined up his sights on Rohde's torso, saw the major's arrogant leer. He took the first pressure; he smiled, whispered, *This is for you, Moshe*, and squeezed iron. The weapon burped twice. At precisely that moment a heavy-calibre field-gun bazookered behind him like a volcanic eruption. Caine ducked, looked up to see three spirals of white spume and red dust sand-spouting among the enemy. He saw bodies tossed head over heels, saw the entire Jerry squad hit the deck.

Caine dekkoed over his shoulder, and his mouth fell open. Behind them, a little to the left and no more than fifteen yards away, six stripped-down Ford trucks were raking through sand and gravel straight towards the escarpment edge, throbbing with automatic fire. One of the trucks was hefting a Bofors 20mm gun and a three-inch mortar, while each of the others was manned by four or five men. All but the drivers were crouched intently over machine guns or SMGs, spitting tracer and ball. The men were wearing khaki shirts and shorts, and flowing Arab headcloths, and they looked mean, determined, deadly. There could be no doubt that they were Tommies.

'It's them,' Caine heard Copeland bawl. 'It's the LRDG.'

The trucks screeched to a halt on the lip of the ridge and belted down fire at the Brandenburgers. The driver of the nearest Ford grinned through a mask of fine dust, beckoned to them. Caine heard the drone of aero engines directly above them. High overhead, a brace of RAF Blenheim light bombers were flattening out into a bombing configuration.

Seconds later, Caine, Nolan, Copeland and Wallace were lifting the almost comatose Trubman and Pickney aboard the nearest wagon. Friendly hands pulled them aboard, English voices enveloped them in a bubble of cheeriness. A smiling LRDG man passed Caine a cigarette. He looked back towards the ridge. The last thing he saw was the dark moths of RAF Blenheims going in for the kill. He turned and took Nolan's small hand in his. By the time the crump of the bombs drifted to his ears the tiny column had already been eaten up by the Sahara.

8

Cairo had lost its bustle: shops were bolted and boarded up, offices shuttered. Rommel was only two short hours from the Nile Delta, and Cairenes were hedging their bets.

If there was disquiet, though, Betty Nolan saw no panic. When she'd met Auchinleck soon after their arrival, he'd seemed confident. He'd praised her courage, informed her that he was recommending her for the George Cross. Tom Caine was up for the Distinguished Conduct Medal, and Copeland, Wallace, Trubman and Pickney were all in line for a Military Medal apiece. Nolan was grateful but her main concern was to discover when she could have her cyanide capsule pulled out.

When Caine, Wallace and Copeland had turned up at the LRDG rear echelon base at Abbassia barracks, they'd found St Aubin and his headquarters squadron had vanished without trace, and the camp's admin staff had no time to deal with dislocated units. 'See,' Wallace had grumbled. 'If we'd holed up with Michele's lot, no one would have been any the wiser.'

Two days after their return, Caine and Nolan met for their celebration dinner at Shepheard's Hotel. They were shown to a table decked with roses, where they polished off thick, juicy steaks; they drank wine. Outside, in gilded moonlight, the city's thoroughfares were crammed with tank-transporters and lorries moving up to Alamein.

The restaurant was 'officers only', but Caine was clad for the occasion in Sam Browne belt and service-dress, with lieutenant's pips on the shoulder-straps. He looked the part. Nolan looked charming in a sheer black evening dress. A silk scarf disguised the dressing at the base of her neck.

Nolan studied Caine's uniform, noticed that it was a tight fit round the shoulders. 'Where did you dig that up?' she asked.

He pointed at one of the lapel-badges on his tunic. 'I borrowed these togs off a pal who transferred to the SAS—officially "L" Detachment of the Special Air Service Brigade. They call it "Stirling's Parashots" after the chap who set it up: David Stirling. I've been thinking about applying.'

Nolan took in Caine's tousled hair, the slate-grey eyes, the scarred, freckled features. 'You don't look quite at home in service dress.'

'Since I lost my commission, this is the first time I've worn it.'

'So how did you lose it?'

Caine spoke hesitantly. 'About a year ago, we were being pushed out of Cyrenaica by Rommel. We were withdrawing fast, but kept running into our own minefields. An armoured brigade was held up west of Benghazi, and I was sent with my sapper detachment to pull the mines. We passed through an Italian colonial settlement and the place was being looted by an Allied infantry mob. I won't say who they were.'

Nolan's face dropped in surprise. '*Looted*? That's not like our men.'

'Looting's bad enough, but these boys were beating the Ities to a pulp and gang-raping women and young girls. I tried to stop them, but they told me where to stick myself. I went to the CP to inform the battalion commander—a young half-colonel. He just waved me away as though it was nothing. I got mad.' An embarrassed smile crossed Caine's mouth. 'I pulled my Colt pistol, grabbed him by the throat, and told him that if he didn't order his boys to desist I'd blow his bloody block off . . .'

Nolan gasped, looked appalled. 'And did he?' she asked.

Caine blinked. 'Yes, he did, but by the time I got my detachment to the minefield where we were meant to be, the armoured brigade had been bumped by the Hun. We got them through eventually, but not before they lost some men. I was blamed for that, and I was lucky I only lost my commission. They went easy on me because they reckoned I'd acted with creditable motives. They also felt that I'd treated my orders as a "basis for discussion". But if I hadn't stepped in to protect those girls, who was going to? I had to stop them. I couldn't help it.'

Nolan studied him. 'That's why they roped you in for Runefish. Your record. I knew there had to be something.' She covered his hand with her hers. 'You were ideal for the Runefish mission, because they wanted someone who would second-guess his orders to take me out.'

Caine's revelation of his past had reminded Nolan of recent news she'd acquired. 'Julian Avery, the officer who trained me for the mission, is dead. He was shot by the same psychopath I came across in the act of killing Lady Mary Goddard. It turned out that the killer was a spy for the Abwehr, Johann Eisner. By chance, he picked up the spoof Runefish material Julian fed into the informer network. He tailed me and recognised me as Betty Nolan, the cabaret dancer who walked in on him and Mary Goddard. He even located my old flat on the Gezira, killed a Field Security NCO and a Sudanese doorman there, and kidnapped Julian. He tried to torture information out of him, then murdered him, too. Luckily for us, Field Security picked him up before he could do any real damage.'

Caine attempted a smile. 'We should be grateful he didn't, then.'

'Yes, but in trying to track down my real identity, he murdered two other women. One was my friend Rachel Levi, the other was another female agent, Susan Arquette, who was occupying my flat as my double. I can't help feeling that I was partly responsible for their deaths . . .'

Caine thought of the eighteen good men he'd just left behind on Runefish. 'I know how that feels,' he said. 'If Field Security have picked up this Eisner, he'll get the firing squad for certain . . .'

'No, he won't. A couple of days back, he escaped. He was being transferred to another location when his vehicle was ambushed. His escort were all killed or wounded, and he got away. He's on the loose out there. They say he speaks five languages fluently, and can easily pass as a native.'

Caine shook his head. 'A man like that—a nutter—he's bound to give himself away sooner or later.'

'I hope so,' Nolan said, 'because he seems to have a personal grudge against me. Apparently, the last thing he said to his interrogator was, "I'll see that Nolan bitch in hell if it's the last thing I do."'

For an instant Caine was shocked. 'Did you say he was Abwehr? One of our friend Rohde's men, no doubt.'

This reminded Nolan of something else. 'You know that pot shot you took at Rohde just before we were pulled out? Did you get him?'

'I don't know. I was distracted when the Bofors opened up. Anyway, there's a good chance the Blenheims did. If not, I doubt he's in good odour with Rommel. He let you get away.'

Nolan shivered involuntarily. Caine knew she was remembering her ordeal at Biska. 'Look,' he said, 'if the commander-in-chief was right in his assessment, the Axis are soon to go belly-up. Rommel will get his backside kicked at Alamein, and the Huns will be finished in North Africa. I don't think you need to worry about sadists like Eisner or Rohde. As you told me, we did it. The Runefish mission might never be made public, but you paid them back for murdering your fiancé a thousand times over. That's why the Nazis will never win. Every atrocity hardens people against them: every Peter Fairfax murdered creates a Maddy Rose, ready to give her or his life to get even.' Caine smiled sadly and raised his glass. 'Here's to the lads who gave their lives for freedom.'

She clinked his glass with hers. 'The ladies, too.'

Nolan noticed at an adjacent table a craggy-looking young major, puffing on a pipe. He had a slightly amused expression and was staring at them both intently. What worried her most was the fact that his lapels bore the same insignia that Caine was wearing. 'Do you know that man?'

Caine studied him discreetly. 'No, but he's wearing SAS insignia. He must know I'm an impostor.'

He considered leaving, but decided that he wasn't going to be chased out. They'd planned this evening for a long time. They deserved it.

Nolan saw that he was resigned to staying and lifted her glass again. 'Absent friends,' she said.

The words were hardly out of her mouth when an officer appeared in front of their table. Caine's heart sank. It was his former second-in-command, Captain—now evidently Major—Robin Sears-Beach, and he was shaking with indignation. 'You've really crossed the line this time, Sergeant Caine,' he roared. 'I told you I'd be watching you. Well, there's no Colonel St Aubin here to let you off the hook.'

Caine stood up quickly, noticing that many of the guests at nearby tables were glaring at him. It wouldn't be the first time an enlisted man had been caught in Shepheard's with false insignia: they would enjoy the spectacle of seeing him dragged out by MPs. Sears-Beach was eyeing Nolan's cleavage.

'Who's this tart?' he demanded.

Caine saw red. '*Tart?*' he gasped, clenching his fists. Sears-Beach flinched and veered backwards. Caine might have dropped the Redcap there and then, if Nolan hadn't cut in. 'Don't, Tom . . . he's not worth it.'

Sears-Beach watched him, a hint of triumph on his face. 'Impersonating an officer is a very serious offence . . .'

'But not one that this man is guilty of, Major,' a cultured voice cut in. 'Lieutenant Caine here *is* an officer. He's under my command.'

The pipe-smoking young major from the next table had risen to his feet, and Caine realised that he was very tall—a good six foot three. There was an unkempt look about him and a good-natured expression in his soft brown eyes. His pipe, empty now, was stuck in his mouth upside down.

Sears-Beach was eyeing the officer's long hair, unshaven face and rumpled uniform. 'And who might *you* be?' he enquired.

The tall major removed his pipe. 'How very rude of me. David Stirling. Commanding officer of the Special Air Service Brigade.'

'You must be joking,' Sears-Beach chortled. 'There's no such thing.'

Stirling's smile was deliberately patronising. 'Indeed there is, Major. We are the main special service troops in the theatre now and have absorbed many personnel from the Middle East Commando. You may not be aware of this, but Lieutenant Caine here has just proved himself the most capable desert operator in the business.' He was staring at Caine, his eyes twinkling.

'I should say that he thoroughly deserves the decoration he's just been recommended for.'

'*Decoration?*' Sears-Beach's mouth gaped.

'Indeed,' Stirling said. 'Unless I am mistaken, this lady, too, has been cited for a decoration for the highest gallantry.'

'Lady?' Sears-Beach scoffed. 'What lady?'

Stirling's face lost its good humour abruptly. 'What would you call a woman who risked her life by going alone into the lion's den, endured capture and torture by the Hun, and personally took part in combat?'

'I'd call her an offender,' Sears-Beach said. 'Women are disbarred from combat: it's against King's Regulations.'

A flicker of exasperation crossed Stirling's face. 'Surely, as a gentleman, you ought to apologise for casting aspersions on this lady's character.'

Sears-Beach bristled. 'I'm assistant chief Provost Officer in this town and you have no right to tell me what to do. This is all utter hogwash. I was Middle East Commando myself: if this mob of yours is supposed to be recruiting ex-commandos, how come they never offered *me* a place?'

A thin smile played over Stirling's features. 'The answer to that is simple. You see, in the SAS, we only accept the very best. Lieutenant Caine is one of those excellent people. You, most unfortunately, are not.'

As Sears-Beach groped in soundless indignation, Stirling fumbled in his pocket for a calling-card. He pressed it into Caine's palm. 'Come and see me at my flat first thing tomorrow, will you, old chap? I think we have something of interest to discuss.'

He bowed deeply to Nolan. 'A very *great* honour, miss,' he said, smiled at Caine, gave Sears-Beach an almost insolent nod, and with the eyes of the whole restaurant upon him, turned towards the door.

michael **asher**

RD: What were your early years like?

MA: I grew up in Stamford, Lincolnshire, a picturesque but staid town: I was an avid reader of books about adventure in faraway places, and longed to find some of that in my life. Joining the Paras aged eighteen seemed the best and quickest way to achieve my goal. I wasn't interested in acquiring things, but in acquiring experiences, especially extreme experiences.

RD: Were there any other key influences?

MA: My father served in north Africa in the Second World War and the desert made a big impact on him: his photos and stories inspired me. He was a Sapper sergeant, known for his brilliance as a mechanic, and was decorated for winching an armoured vehicle out of a hole under enemy fire. The desert war was a war of mobility, so anyone who could keep the wheels turning, like my dad, was worth his weight in gold.

RD: Getting selected for the SAS, with their one-in-ten selection rate, was a huge achievement. Can you tell us a bit about that?

MA: It taught me that when the chips were down, I was capable of doing much more than I ever thought possible. I wasn't tough or athletic at school, but commitment is the key, not muscles. You really have to want to get that sand-coloured beret. Big biceps don't matter a damn against determination, speed, firepower, initiative, creativity, and skill in the use of weapons. In the end, it's all in the mind. Or as Peter Ratcliffe (ex RSM 22 SAS) says, selection is 'a battle for a man's mind and a test of his will to win.'

RD: Were there ever any moments when you regretted joining?

MA: Yes, on escape and evasion marches, lost in Denmark, cold, wet, exhausted, nowhere to hide, I've thought, What the hell am I doing here? But then you realise that very feeling—the sapping of your own will to win—is the enemy. It floors most people, but I had passed SAS selection because I was able to override it.

RD: You lived for three years with a Bedouin tribe in Sudan—what led to that?

MA: Disillusioned with the military life, I went there as a volunteer teacher. I found a different world, inhabited by nomads who didn't even know they were part of a nation-state and who believed the earth was flat. They lived by a code of courage, honesty, endurance, loyalty and generosity—and people were respected for what they were, not what they had, so it was an extension of the SAS for me, albeit an extreme one.

RD: How did you meet your wife, Arabist and photographer Mariantonietta Peru?

MA: I was asked by UNICEF to organise a camel caravan to take supplies and a medical team into the remote Red Sea Hills of the Sudan during a terrible famine. Mariantonietta was working as a UNICEF publicist assigned to cover the expedition. We bonded when the guide got lost and we ran out of water. One of the other journalists with us started to scream 'we're all going to die'; Mariantonietta kept her cool. We had something in common because she spoke fluent Arabic: also, she is a photographer, something I've never been. She was also very hot, especially after three years in the desert!

RD: When the two of you made your crossing of the Sahara, was there a worst moment, a low, perhaps?

MA: Yes, towards the end, when we'd spent days with just the two of us, we started to lose track of reality: it was like the 'cabin fever' that Jack London describes in the Arctic: we'd hear people following us, see eyes in the night. Really scary, but we got over it.

RD: What's it like riding a camel?

MA: Easy but it requires energy. A lot of my clients arrive thinking that riding a camel is like sitting in a car: it isn't: it's more like riding a bike, as you have to make the camel go. That said, camels are very gregarious and fall into step with each other, so in a group, with the camels pressing together it feels as if you're floating across the desert.

RD: Do you have any ambitions you'd still like to fulfil?

MA: I want to take up the mantle of Arne Næss, founder of the Deep Ecology movement, who died in January 2009. Næss taught that nature is valuable not because we can make money out of it, but because it is there. It struck a chord with me since the nomads I lived with considered the earth sacred and their society was non-materialist. It is the impulse to *own*, the will to have things, that has ruined the earth. If we wish to save ourselves we need a fundamental change in human values; we need to go back to a life in which status comes from what you are, not what you possess. I'd like to see a new society, neither capitalist nor communist, founded on this principle. We don't have to go back to living in the desert, but we could adopt some of the principles by which the nomads lived. Wouldn't that be better than greed, selfishness and egotism? With my unique experience of living with the nomads and serving in the SAS, I think I can play a serious part in trying to preserve our civilisation for our children.

RD: You now live in Africa. Do you think you'll always stay there, or are there other parts of the world to which you're drawn?

MA: I despair of Africa sometimes, eg what is happening in Darfur. When I lived there it was the most fascinating place on earth, completely unspoilt. The Sahara will always be my first love, but there are many places I'd like to go: Siberia, Canada, Alaska, Mongolia . . .

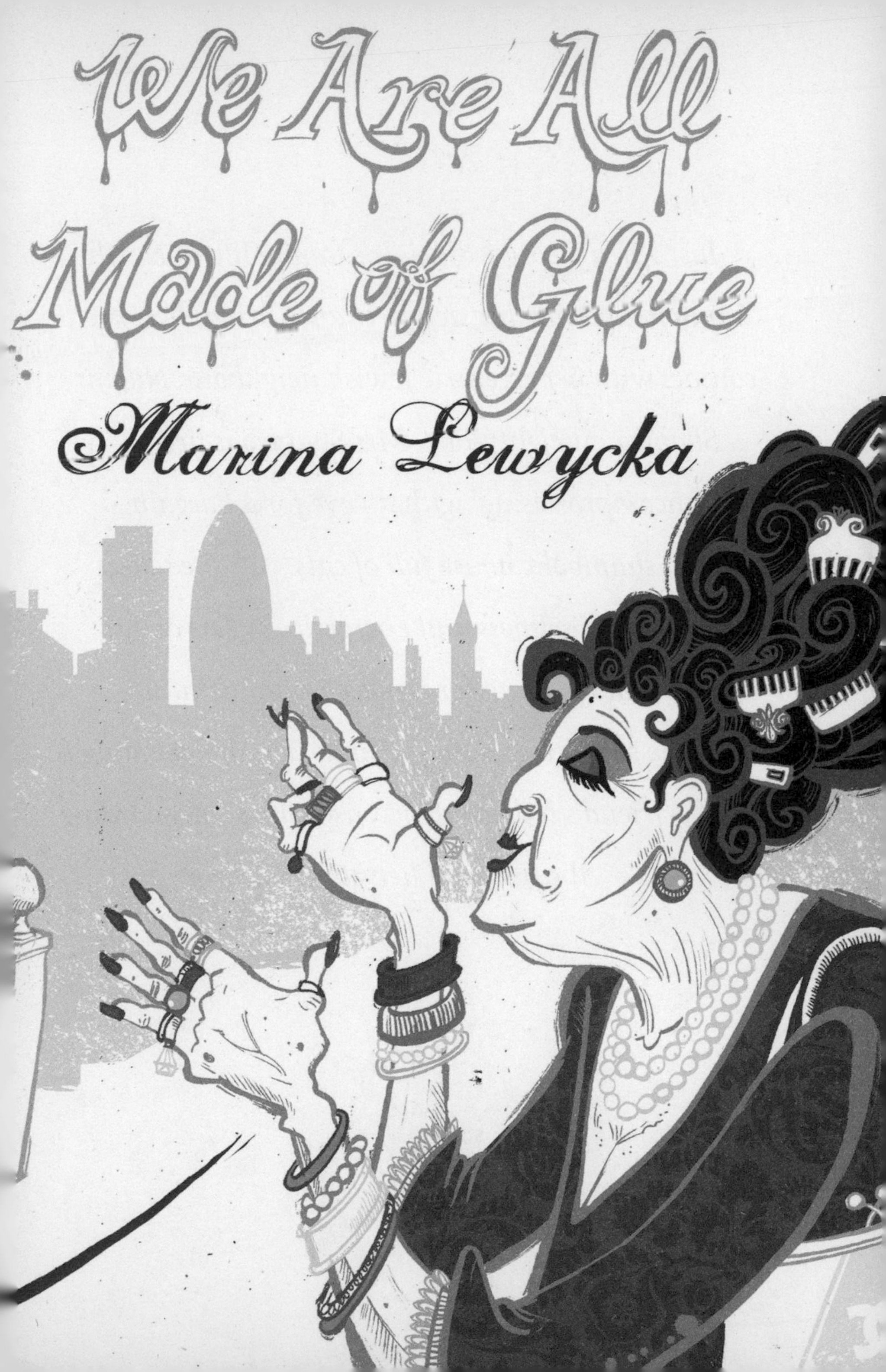
We Are All Made of Glue
Marina Lewycka

Just when Georgie Sinclair's family life in North London is getting her down, chance brings her into contact with her eccentric Jewish neighbour, Naomi Shapiro. At eighty-one, Mrs Shapiro is fiercely uncompromising, with an eye for a bargain and a shambolic house full of cats. But she senses Georgie's loneliness and energetically sets about smartening her up for a more romantic future.

At the same time, Georgie finds herself defending her new friend's independence, as well as safeguarding the future of her home . . .

1

The first time I met Wonder Boy, he pissed on me. I suppose he was trying to warn me off, which was quite prescient when you consider how things turned out.

One afternoon in late October, somewhere between Stoke Newington and Highbury, I'd ventured into an unfamiliar street, and came upon the entrance of a cobbled lane that led in between two high garden walls. After about fifty metres the lane opened out into a grassy circle and I found myself standing in front of a big, double-fronted house, half derelict and smothered in ivy, crouching behind a straggly privet hedge. Something was carved on the gatepost. I pulled the ivy aside and read: Canaan House. A cloud shifted and a low shaft of sunshine made the windows light up momentarily. Then the sun slipped away and the flat dusky light exposed the crumbling stucco, the bare wood where the paint had peeled away and a spiny monkey puzzle tree that had been planted far too close to the house.

Suddenly, a long wailing sob, like the sound of a child crying, uncoiled in the silence. But it was only a cat, a great white bruiser of a tomcat, with three black socks and an ugly face, who emerged from the bushes and came towards me with a purposeful glint in his eye.

'Hello, cat. Do you live here?'

He sidled up, but just as I reached down to stroke him, his tail went up and a strong squirt of eau-de-tomcat suffused the air. I aimed a kick, but he'd melted into the shadows. As I picked my way back through the brambles I could smell it on my jeans—it had a pungent, faintly gluey smell.

Our second encounter was about a week later, and this time I met his owner, too. One evening, at about eleven o'clock, I heard a noise in the street, a scraping and scuffling followed by a smash of glass. I looked out of the window. Someone was pulling stuff out of the skip in front of my house.

At first I thought it was just a boy, a slight, sparrowy figure wearing a cap pulled down low over his face; then he moved into the light and I saw it was an old woman, scrawny as an alley cat, tugging at some burgundy velours curtains to get at the box of my husband's old vinyls half buried under the other junk. Suddenly the box came free and she fell backwards onto the ground, scattering the records. I opened the door and rushed out to help her.

'Are you OK?'

Scrambling to her feet, she shook herself like a cat. Her face was half hidden under the peak of the cap. 'I don't know what type of persons is throwing away such music. Great Russian composers.' A rich brown voice, crumbly like fruit-cake. I couldn't place the accent. 'Must be some barbarian types liffing around here, isn't it? Look! Tchaikovsky. Shostakovich. Prokofiev. And they throw all in a bin!'

'Please take the records,' I said. 'I don't have a record player.' I didn't want her to think I was a barbarian type.

'Thenk you. I adore especially the Prokofiev piano sonatas.'

Now I saw that behind the skip was an old-fashioned pram with big curly springs into which she'd already loaded some of my husband's books.

'You can have the books too.'

'You heff read them all?' she asked, as though quizzing me for barbarian tendencies.

'All of them.'

'Good. Thenk you.'

'My name's Georgie. Georgie Sinclair. I've not lived here long. We moved down from Leeds a year ago.'

She tipped her head in a stiff nod and extended a gloved hand, like a slightly dotty monarch acknowledging a subject. 'Mrs Naomi Shapiro.'

I helped her gather the scattered records and stow them on top of the books. Poor old thing, I was thinking. One of life's casualties, carting her worldly possessions around in a pram. She pushed it off down the road, swaying a little on her high heels as she went. Even in the cold air I could smell her, pungent and tangy like ripe cheese. After she'd gone a few metres I spotted the white tomcat, the same shaggy bruiser with three black socks, trailing her down the pavement. Then I saw there was a whole cohort of shadowy cats slipping off walls and out of bushes, slinking along behind her. I stood and watched her until she turned the corner and disappeared.

From the pavement I could see the light still on in Ben's bedroom window and the computer monitor winking away as he surfed the worldwide waves.

Ben, my baby boy, now sixteen, a paid-up citizen of the web-wide world. The square of light blinked from blue to red to green. What seas was he travelling tonight? Up so late. My gentle, slightly-too-serious Ben. How is it that children of the same parents turn out so differently? His sister Stella, at twenty, had already grabbed life by the horns, wrestled it to the ground, and was training it to eat out of the palm of her hand in a shared rented house near York University which, whenever I phoned, seemed always to have a party going on or a rock band practising in the background.

In the upstairs window the coloured square winked and disappeared. Bedtime. I went in and wrote my husband a curt note asking him to come and remove his junk, and I put it in an envelope with a second-class stamp. First thing next day, I telephoned the skip hire company.

So let me explain why I was putting my husband's stuff in a skip—then you can decide for yourself whose fault it was. We're in the basement kitchen one morning—the usual rush of Rip getting off to work and Ben getting off to school. Rip's fiddling with his BlackBerry. I'm making coffee and frothing milk and burning the toast. Ben is thumping around upstairs.

Me: I've bought a new toothbrush holder. Do you think you might find a moment to fix it on the bathroom wall?
Him: (Silence.)
Me: It's white porcelain. Sort of Scandinavian style.
Him: What the fuck are you talking about, Georgie?
Me: The toothbrush holder. It needs fixing onto the wall. In the bathroom. I think it's a rawplug job.
Him: (Deep manly sigh.) Some of us are trying to do something worthwhile in the world, Georgie. Something that will contribute to human progress and shape the destiny of future generations. And you witter on about a toothbrush.

I can't explain what came over me next. My arm jerked and suddenly there were flecks of milky froth everywhere—on the walls, on him, all over his BlackBerry.

Him: (Furious.) What's got into you, Georgie?
Me: (A shriek.) You don't care, do you? All you care about is your world-changing destiny-shaping bloody work!
Him: (Shaking his head in disbelief.) As it happens, I do care very much. I care about what happens in the world. Though I can't say I care deeply about a toothbrush.

Me: A toothbrush *holder*.
Him: I don't see why I should put up with this.
Me: No one's asking you to put up with it. Why don't you just go? And take your bloody BlackBerry with you.
Him: Your outbursts of hysteria are not very attractive, Georgie.
Me: No, and you're not attractive either, you big fart.

But he was attractive. That's the trouble—he was. And now I've blown it, I thought, as I remembered Mrs Shapiro pootling away up the street with his precious collection of Russian composers tucked in her pram.

I WAS SITTING at my desk, staring at the rain and trying to finish off the November edition of *Adhesives in the Modern World*, the online trade magazine I work for, when the skip lorry arrived. Adhesives can sometimes, I admit, be quite boring, so it was nice to be distracted. I watched it reversing and clanking into position, lowering the chain loops to winch up the overflowing skip, dangling it in the air with the dishevelled papers, limply flapping magazines, the bin bags of clothes and the boxes that contained all the soggy detritus of his Really Important Work, and crashing it down on the back of the truck. When it was ready I went out and paid the skip man, and I must confess I did feel a pang of apprehension as it trundled out of view. I knew Rip would be furious.

When he'd got back from work that day—the day of the toothbrush holder—I'd calmed down but he was still in a rage. He started piling up his stuff in his car.

Me: (Nervous.) What are you doing?
Him: (Stony-faced.) I'm leaving. I'm going to stay with Pete.
Me: (Clinging. Pathetic. Self-hating.) Don't go, Rip. I'm sorry. It's only a toothbrush holder. I'll put it up myself. Tell you what (little giggle), I'll learn to do rawplugs.
Him: (Clenched jaw.) But it's not just that, is it?
Me: What d'you mean? (A terrible truth dawns.) Are you . . .?
Him: (Sigh of boredom.) There's no one else, if that's what you're thinking. (Looking at his watch.) I'd better get going. I told Pete I'd be there at seven.
Me: (Putting on a show of nonchalance.) Fine. If that's what you want. Fine by me. Give my regards to Pete.

Pete Walker was Australian, Rip's squash partner, and a senior colleague on the Progress Project. We called him Pectoral Pete, because he always wore tight white T-shirts and big white trainers. He and his wife Ottoline lived in a tall-windowed house overlooking a square in Islington, with a top-floor flat that they sometimes rented out. I went and stood outside one evening, looking up into the lighted windows with tears pouring down my face.

It lasted for a few weeks, the crying phase. Then rage took over.

'I'll come back for the rest of my things,' Rip had said as he left.

But he didn't. The shoes in the hall, the old clothes in the wardrobe, the back copies of the *Economist* and the *New Statesman* stacked up against the wall, the filing cabinets bulging with progress.

I didn't want him cluttering up my new, independent life with his old discarded stuff so I hired a skip. Perhaps I should have taken it all to Oxfam, but I didn't have a car. Besides, if I had done, this story might never have been written, because it was the skip that brought Mrs Shapiro into my life.

ABOUT AN HOUR after the skip had gone, the doorbell rang. So soon! I stood frozen, paralysed by the enormity of what I'd done. Best not to answer it. But what if he looked in through the window and saw me? I tiptoed into the corridor and lay down on the floor out of sight of any of the windows.

The doorbell rang again and again and again. Obviously he wasn't fooled. Then the letterbox clattered. Then silence.

After a while, a song drifted into my head. 'You thought I'd lay down and die. Oh no, not I! I will survive!' Gloria Gaynor. It was one of Mum's favourites. How did it go? 'At first I was afraid, I was petrified.' I started to sing. 'I didn't know if I could something something without you by my side . . . Something changed that stupid lock . . . I will survive!' I belted the chorus out over and over again.

That's how Ben found me when he got back from school, lying flat on my back in the corridor, singing at the top of my voice. He must have let himself in so quietly that I didn't hear the door.

'Are you all right, Mum?' His eyes squinted with concern.

'Course I am, love. Just . . . enjoying a musical interlude.'

I clambered up from the floor and looked out of the window. The street was empty and it was raining again. Then I noticed a leaflet on the doormat. *The Watchtower*. Ben picked it up.

'What's this about?'

'It's the Jehovah's Witness magazine. It's about the end of the world, when Jesus returns and all the true believers get whisked up to heaven.'

'Hm.' He flicked through it, and to my surprise he stuck it in his pocket and clomped upstairs to his room.

THE DOORBELL RANG AGAIN as Ben and I were about to sit down to eat. Ben answered it. 'Hi, Dad.'

'Hi, Ben. Is your mother in?'

Nowhere to hide this time. I had to face him across the table. Pectoral Pete was with him. They were both wearing their jogging gear. They must have run all the way over from Islington. The kitchen reeked of pheromones and I felt a mortifying stab of lust—my traitor hormones letting me down.

Him: (Pulling back his chair and stretching his legs out.) Hi, Georgie. I got your message. I've come to rescue my stuff.
Me: (Help!) It's too late. They took the skip away this morning.
Him: (Eyes round and blinky.) You're kidding.
Me: Why would I be kidding?
Him: They took the records? My great Russian composers?
Me: (A sly smirk.) Mm-hm.
Him: Why are you being so childish, Georgie?

Childish? Me? I picked up a plate of pasta. I could feel that twitching in my arm again. Then I caught the frightened look in Ben's eyes—poor Ben, he didn't need to see his parents behaving like this. I put the plate down, bolted out of the room and ran upstairs; I threw myself onto my bed, blinking the tears out of my eyes. *I will survive. I will grow strong.* Look at Gloria Gaynor—she turned her heartbreak into a song that sold millions. As I lay there listening to the voices below, and wishing I'd kept my cool, an appealing thought floated into my head: I can't sing, but I can write.

In fact I was already halfway there. I had a working title and a terrific nom de plume. My mind lingered on a seductive image of myself as a published author, jetting around the world.

I got up and went to a drawer where my previous attempts at fiction, twelve and a half full exercise books, were stowed, together with a file of hoity-toity rejection slips.

Dear Ms Firestorm,

Thank you for sending us *The Splattered Heart*. Your book has some colourful characters and displays an impressive array of adjectives, but I was unable to summon sufficient enthusiasm . . .

That sort of thing is bad for morale, and my morale was already low. But it was no use—a seed of optimism had lodged itself in my heart, and the opening lines were sprouting in my head. There was one empty exercise book left.

The Splattered Heart

It was past midnight when Rick rolled exhaustedly onto his broad, ~~muscular~~ slightly podgy back and casually ran his ~~powerful~~ fingers through his thick curly, ~~naturally blond~~ discreetly highlighted hair.

OK, I know it's not your Jane Austen. Maybe Ms Insufficient Enthusiasm had a point about the adjectives. I sat staring at the page. Downstairs I heard voices in the hall and the click of the latch. Then my bedroom door opened a crack. 'Are you all right, Mum? Aren't you having any dinner?'

AFTER RIP MOVED into Pectoral Pete's flat we agreed that Ben should spend half a week with each of us. We broke him in half and divided him between us and he was determined to be fair to his father and to me.

As the rage against Rip congealed in my heart, I was sometimes taken over by a numbness so intense it felt like pain. On the days when Ben wasn't here I found it almost unbearable to be in the house alone. When the silence got too much I'd take a walk, just to get out of the house. Wearing an ancient brown duffle coat with a wide flapping hood and sleeves like bat's wings, I flitted about at dusk, peeping through lighted windows into other people's lives, trying to remember what it felt like to be still stuck together.

One afternoon I went as far as Islington Green, thinking I'd get a few things I needed from Sainsbury's and catch the bus back. It was about four o'clock, and the sticker lady was doing her end-of-day reductions. A crowd was milling around her like a piranha tank at feeding time. Mum had always been a great advocate of past-sell-by-date shopping, and I remembered with a twist of nostalgia how, when I was little, she used to send me scampering along the aisles looking out for the bright red REDUCED stickers that pouted like scarlet kisses on the packaging. Funny how long after you leave home you still carry a bit of your parents around inside you. Now, without the certainty of Rip's salary, I understood that sharp edge of insecurity that Mum must have felt all her life. I pushed forward to join the crush.

No sooner had the sticker lady stuck a new label on something than a hand reached out of the throng and grabbed it from her. I noticed it always seemed to be the same one—a bony, gnarled, jewel-encrusted hand, darting out and snatching. Turning to follow it with my eyes, I spotted an old woman diving in low beneath the shoulders of two fat ladies. Her hair was tucked into a jaunty cap, a straggle of black curls escaping under the brim. It was Mrs Shapiro.

'Hello!' I called.

She looked up and stared at me for a moment. Then, 'Georgine!' she cried. She pronounced it with hard 'G's and an 'eh' sound at the end. Gheorghineh! 'Good afternoon, my darlink!'

'Good to see you, Mrs Shapiro.'

In the enclosed space of the groceries aisle, her smell was ripe like old cheese, with a faint hint of Chanel No 5. I could see the looks on the faces of the other shoppers as they let her through. They thought she was just a bag lady. They didn't know she listened to the great Russian composers.

'Plenty good bargains today, darlink!' Her voice was breathless with excitement. 'One minute full price, next minute half price—same thing, no difference. Always tastes better when you pay less, isn't it?'

'You should meet my mum. She always likes a bargain. She says it's because of the war.'

I guessed she was a bit older than Mum—in her late seventies, maybe. More wrinkled, but more energetic. She was of the age when she should have been wearing wide-fitting bootees held on with Velcro, but in fact she was tottering about daintily on peep-toe high-heeled shoes like a lady of style, the grubby toes of her grey-white ankle socks poking out in front.

'Not only the war, darlink. I heff learned in my life to make the ends meet.'

Her cheeks were flushed, her eyes focused, her brow furrowed with the effort of mental arithmetic as the new labels were stuck on top of the old.

'Come on, Georgine—you must grebbit!'

I squeezed in beside one of the big ladies and grabbed a passing chicken korma, reduced from £2.99 to £1.49. Mum would have been proud of me.

'You heff to be quick! You like sossedge? Here!'

Mrs Shapiro snatched a packet of sausages reduced to 59p out of the hand of a bewildered pensioner and tossed it into my basket.

'Oh . . . thanks.' They looked unappetisingly pink.

Seizing me by the wrist, Mrs Shapiro pulled me towards her and whispered in my ear, 'Is OK. Jewish. No sossedge. You Jewish also, Georgine?' She must have noticed me eyeing the sausages with distaste.

'No. Not Jewish. Yorkshire.'

'Ach, so. Never mind. Can't help it.'

'Have you been playing the records, Mrs Shapiro? Are they all right?'

'Great records. Glinka. Rimsky-Korsakov. Mussorgsky. Such a music. Tek you straight up into heaven.' Her bony hands spread theatrically in the air, the rings glittering, the varnished nails bright like bunches of cherries.

Close up I saw that the red highlights in her cheeks, which I'd mistaken for a flush of excitement, were actually two circles of rouge.

'Shostakovich. Prokofiev. Myakovsky. My Arti has played with them all.'

'Who's Arti?' I asked, but she was distracted by a 79p Quiche Lorraine. 'I don't think I have much of an ear for music.'

'Not all great art is for the messes, darlink. But you would like to learn?' She batted her azure eyelids. 'I will play for you. You like the fish?'

As she said the word, I noticed a fishy undernote welling up through the cheese-and-Chanel. It was coming from her trolley. I saw that among her bargain produce were several packs of fish, all REDUCED. I hesitated. This fish definitely smelled off.

'You come in my house, I will cook them for you.'

I was trying to muster an excuse when she let out a bloodcurdling shriek.

'No, no! You teef!'

The pensioner from whose hand she'd grabbed the sausages had tried to pinch them back out of my basket. Mrs Shapiro snatched them from him and brandished them in the air.

'Teef! You pay for you own sossedge full price if you want it!'

Defeated and humiliated, the pensioner slunk away. She turned towards me, flushed with triumph.

'I am liffing not far from you. Big house. Big garden. Too many trees. Totley Place. Kennen House. You come on Saturday seven o'clock.'

'Have you got a Nectar card?' asked the girl at the checkout, swiping my bargains over the bar-code reader.

I shook my head and muttered something Rip-like about the surveillance society. Behind me, Mrs Shapiro had got into an argument with someone else in the queue and I was planning a quick getaway.

'Bravo, darlink! These surveyors are getting everywhere,' she cried, barging her way towards the exit, bashing the legs of the man in the next queue with her trolley. He was a big man with close-cropped blond hair, built like a rugby player. He turned round and gave her an unsmiling stare.

'Sorry, sorry, darlink.' The blue eyelids fluttered.

The big man shook his head, then made his way through the checkout and out into the car park. I watched him load his purchases into a massive black-tinted-windowed four-by-four parked in a disabled bay in front of Mrs Shapiro's pram. Then he got in, edged forward and stuck his head out of the window. 'Can you just shift your pram, lady, so I can pull round?'

'One moment, please!' Mrs Shapiro cried. She pulled a packet of cigarettes and a box of matches out from under the hood of the pram, offered me one—which I declined—and lit up.

'Just shift your bloody pram, you old bat!' snarled the driver.

'Don't you dare talk to her like that, you big bully!' I hissed back.

Mrs Shapiro turned and fluttered her azure eyelids at him again. 'Sorry, sorry, darlink.' Swaying a little on her heels, she manoeuvred the pram out of the way and tottered off down the road, still puffing away.

WHEN I GOT HOME, I put the kettle on for a cup of tea and phoned Mum in Kippax in Yorkshire to tell her about my pram adventure. She had turned seventy-three in October and time was weighing down on her. Her eyesight was beginning to deteriorate ('immaculate degeneration') and the doctor had told her she shouldn't drive any more. Dad had been struck down with the 'waterworks mither'. My brother Keir, five years divorced, with two sons he hardly ever saw, was posted in Iraq. And now I was splitting up with my husband. Just at the time when Mum should have been sailing into a rosy sunset, everything on her horizon seemed stormy and unsettled. To cheer her up, I launched into a description of my bargains.

'Chicken korma, Mum. Reduced from two ninety-nine to one forty-nine.'

'Oh, lovely. What's a chicken corner?'

Mum isn't stupid, but she's partially deaf. Dad and I tease her because she refuses to wear a hearing aid. ('People'll say I'm an alien if I start going around wi' bits of wire coming out of my head.')

'Chicken *korma*. It's Indian. Sort of spicy and creamy.'

'Oah, I don't know if your dad'd fancy that.' Her voice sounded flat.

I tried another tack. 'Have you read any good books recently, Mum?'

In the right mood, this is her favourite topic. When I was sixteen, she had introduced me to Georgette Heyer and Catherine Cookson, whom I devoured.

'I just finished *Turquoise Temptation*,' she sighed down the phone. 'But it were rubbish. Too much heavy breathing and ripped-up underwear.' A pause. 'Have you seen owt of Euridopeas?'

I knew she secretly hoped we would get together again. I didn't tell her he'd been round to pick up his stuff.

When Rip and I first fell in love, I sometimes used to imagine us as romantic characters in a great tempestuous love story set against the turbulent background of the miners' strike, transgressing boundaries of wealth and class to be together. I was his door into an exotic world where noble savages discussed socialism while soaping each other's backs in t' pit baths. He was my door into Pemberley Hall and Mansfield Park. We were so full of illusions about each other, maybe it was bound to end in a splattering.

After Mum had rung off, I made another cup of tea and picked up my pen and exercise book.

It was a sunny October day, and Rip's ~~mini~~ Porsche ~~nosed its way~~ roared up over the hills still brilliant with dazzling autumn colour. After a few miles the road turned sharply to the right, and Gina saw the entrance to a driveway, with a cattle grid and two stone gateposts, and there at the bottom of the valley, a good mile away, was ~~Holtham House~~ Holty Towers, sailing like a stone galleon in a shimmering red-green-and gold sea. Despite herself, Gina ~~was impressed by~~ found herself inexorably drawn towards the ~~house~~ stately pile and she could not help noticing ~~that these people obviously had a bob or two~~ the stunning period features. So this is how the other half live, she thought.

In fact Rip was always much less troubled by the differences between our two families than I was.

Me: (Whisper.) You never told me they were so posh.
Him: (Murmur.) But when you have money, you realise how little it really matters.
Me: (Loud whisper.) Yes, but it matters if you haven't got enough.
Him: (Quietly confident.) Inequality only matters if it makes people *feel* unequal. (Kisses me tenderly on the lips, then we end up in bed.)

2

It was already dusk on Saturday evening when I made my way up the lane to Canaan House for my dinner date. As I moved out of range of the spooky sodium glow from the street lamp on Totley Place, I felt a tremor of apprehension. What was I letting myself in for?

The night was cold and starry. The moonlight etched silvery outlines of trees and the gables of Canaan House onto the darkness. But even in that ashy light there was something cheerfully eccentric about its hotchpotch of styles: Victorian bay windows, a Romanesque entrance porch with twirly columns supporting chubby rounded arches, exuberant Tudor chimneys, and a mad Dracula turret with pointed Gothic windows stuck on one side. I pulled my duffle coat around me and looked for signs of light up ahead. Had she forgotten I was coming?

The house was dark but I had a sense of eyes watching me. I stopped and listened. I could hear nothing but a faint rustling of leaves that could have been the wind. I took a couple of steps closer, and as I approached the porch a cat burst out of the undergrowth onto the path in front of me. And another. And another. I couldn't count how many cats there were in that soft lithe seething throng, purring and meowing, their eyes glinting gold and green.

The front door had a frosted glass panel through which I could now see a faint sliver of light far away inside. There was a bell to one side. I pressed it and heard it ringing somewhere in the depths of the house. The sliver of light widened into a rectangle as a door opened. I heard shuffling footsteps, then Mrs Shapiro opened the door.

'Georgine! Darlink! Come in!'

It's hard to describe the stench that hit me as I stepped over the threshold, the cats slinking in beside me. I almost gagged at the smell of damp and cat pee and shit and rot and food mould and house filth and sink grunge and, cutting through all that, a rank, nauseating, fishy stink. This last smell, I realised with a sinking feeling, was dinner.

Mrs Shapiro was wearing a long-sleeved dress in carmine velvet, shaped at the waist and daringly cut away at the front. A double string of pearls gleamed around her wrinkled throat. Her dramatic black curls were piled on top of her head with a collection of tortoiseshell combs, and she'd painted on a dash of matching carmine lipstick. I was still wearing my jeans and a baggy pullover under my brown duffle coat. She eyed me critically.

'Why you wearing this old shmata, Georgine? Is not flettering for a young woman. You will never get a man this way.'

'I . . . I don't need . . .' I stopped. Maybe a man *is* what I need.

'Come. I will find you something better.'

She led me into the wide, tiled entrance hall, from the centre of which a polished mahogany staircase curved away to the next floor. Underneath the staircase were piles of black refuse bags, bursting with—I don't know, really, but I could see clothes and books and crockery spilling out where the bags had split. At one side was parked the old high-sprung pram, now apparently full of bundled rags, on which a couple of stripy felines were dozing. She shooed them away and started to root among the bundles. After a few moments she began to tug at a piece of dark green stuff which, when she pulled it out, turned out to be a long-sleeved dress in a silky fabric.

'Here,' she held it up to my chin, 'this I think is more flettering for you.' I looked at the label—it was a size 12—my size—and a Karen Millen. In fact it was a gorgeous dress. Where on earth had she got this from?

'It's lovely, but . . .' Actually, when I thought about it, I guessed that she must have pulled it out of a skip. '. . . but I can't possibly take it.'

Who would put a dress like this in a skip? Then I thought of Rip's clothes, which I'd put in the skip, and in a flash I understood—another heart had been splattered somewhere.

'Is too big for me,' she said. 'Will look better on you. Tek it, please.'

'Thank you, Mrs Shapiro, but . . .' As I shook it out, I could smell the faint sweat and expensive perfume of its previous owner.

'Try it! Try it! No need to be emberressed, darlink.'

Did she expect me to put it on straight away? Obviously she did. She stood over me as I stripped down to my knickers and slipped the dress, still warm from the sleeping cats, over my head. It slid over my shoulders and hips as though it was made for me. Why was I doing this? I asked myself. Why didn't I just put on my own clothes and firmly but politely say good night? I thought of escaping, I really did. Then I thought of the trouble she must have gone to, to prepare the meal, and how let-down she would feel.

'Wait, I will zip it!' I could feel her hands, bony like claws, on my skin as she wrenched the zip up behind me. 'Beautiful, darlink. You already looking much better. You are a nice-looking woman, Georgine. Nice skin. Nice eyes. Good figure. But when you last been at the hairdresser?'

'I can't remember. I . . .' I remembered the way Rip used to look at me, the way he would run his fingers through my hair when he kissed me.

'You want I will put some lipstick on you?'

'No, really, Mrs Shapiro.'

She hesitated, looking me up and down. 'OK. For tonight is OK. Come.'

I followed her through a door into a long gloomy room where an oval-shaped mahogany table had been spread with a white cloth and two places set at one end. In the centre of the cloth, a white cat was curled up asleep.

'*Raus*, Wonder Boy! *Raus!*' She clapped her hands.

The cat stretched and rose to its feet, stretched itself a couple more times, then jumped down from the table and sauntered around the room.

'This is Wonder Boy.' (She pronounced it Vunder Boy.) She reached out and scratched him behind the ears, and he let out a purr like a motorbike starting up. 'He is my darlink. Soon you will meet Violetta and the Stinker. The pram babies you have already met. Mussorgsky is somewhere hiding. He is a little bit jealous of the Wonder Boy. Borodin you will not see. He comes only to take the food. Seven altogether. My little femily.'

I handed her the bottle of wine I'd brought. White Rioja. Nice with fish. She opened the bottle and poured us each a glass.

'To bargains!' she said. We clinked.

'Can I help you with anything?' I was nervous about what was happening in the kitchen, but she gestured me severely to a chair.

'You are my invited guest. Please, Georgine, tek a seat.'

Close up I could see that the tablecloth was not white at all but a sort of mottled greyish yellow, bristling with cat hairs of many colours. The napkins weren't white either, they had pink and red blotches that could be wine or beetroot or tomato soup. While Mrs Shapiro busied herself in the kitchen, I studied the room I was in. The only light was from a single bulb screwed into a brass chandelier whose other five bulbs were defunct. On the wall opposite the door was a marble fireplace, and above it a large gilt-framed mirror so spotted and clouded that, when I stood up to take a peep at myself, I seemed faded and grey, my eyes hollow and too dark, my hair wind-snaggled and too curly, the dress so different to anything I'd worn for ages that I hardly recognised myself. I turned away as if I'd seen a ghost.

On the wall facing me were two tall windows that seemed to be boarded up behind the curtains, and between them hung a photograph: a studio portrait of a young man in evening dress with sharp clean features, fair curly hair swept back from a high forehead, and in his left hand, held up against his cheek, the neck of a violin. He had startlingly pale eyes that held my gaze.

As I studied the photograph I became aware of a faintly fish smell. I looked round and saw that Mrs Shapiro was standing in the doorway carrying a large silver tray on which were two steaming bowls.

'*Soupe de poisson. Cuisine française*,' she beamed, placing one bowl in front of me and seating herself opposite me with the other. 'Don't wait.'

I dipped my spoon into a thin, scummy-looking liquid in which some greyish gobs of matter were floating part-submerged. Probably it won't kill me, I told myself. Across the table, Mrs Shapiro was slurping away, pausing only to dab her lips with her napkin. Ah—that's what those red blotches were. I found that if I held my breath as I swallowed I could manage the liquid. The grey gobs I tried to mash up in the bottom of the bowl so it wasn't obvious how much I'd left.

'Lovely,' I said, trying to find a clean corner of napkin to pat my mouth.

The second course was in some ways better and in some ways worse. It was better because there were boiled potatoes and leeks in a white sauce which looked reasonably edible; it was worse because the fish, a whole fillet of something hard, brown and yellow, smelled so sickening that I knew I would never be able to bring myself to swallow it.

As I was poking away at the potatoes and leeks I felt a sudden sharp prick of claws on my thighs through the silky stuff of the dress. I slipped my hand down under the tablecloth and touched warm fur. Then I had an idea.

'Mrs Shapiro, that photo'—I pointed to the wall behind her—'who's it of?'

As she turned her back, I slid the fillet off my plate onto the floor.

'That is my husband.' She turned towards me and clasped her hands together. 'Artem Shapiro. My beloved Arti.'

From beneath the table came a satisfied chomping.

'Was he a musician?'

'One of the greatest, darlink. Before the Nazis got him into the camp.'

'He was in a concentration camp?'

'Kaiserwald.'

'Where's that?'

'Riga. Besides the Baltic Sea. Many Jews from all over Europe ended there. Even some we knew from Hamburg.'

'Your family was from Hamburg?'

'Left in 1938.'

'But Artem—he got away, too?'

'This story is too long, Georgine. Too long and too long ago.'

The young man in the picture held me with his pale, intense eyes. I noticed how elegantly his fingers were clasped around the neck of the violin. In *The Splattered Heart* the heroine's lover would have hands like this, I thought. Ms Firestorm was already on the prowl, looking out for a romance set against the turbulent background of the Second World War.

'Please tell me, Mrs Shapiro. I love stories.'

'Yes, this is a loff story,' she sighed. 'But I do not know if it will heff a happy ending.'

The story she started to tell me that night did turn out to be a love story of sorts, and though she related it in her funny hobbled English, my imagination filled in the spaces between the words so vividly that afterwards I couldn't remember what she'd said and what I had imagined. Artem Shapiro, her husband, she told me, was born in 1904 in the small town of Orsha in a country that sometimes belonged to Poland, sometimes to Russia, sometimes to Lithuania, and most of the time was just a place where people—Jewish people, anyway—got on quietly with their business, keeping their heads down during the years of wars and pogroms.

'It is our way. We believed if we kept quiet we would survive.'

His father was a violin maker and he thought the boy would learn the trade, too, but one day Artem picked up the instrument and began to play, and it was not long before he began to show real promise as a violinist.

'Darlink, everybody who was listening to this young boy was astonished.'

When Artem was in his teens, the family moved to Minsk, the capital of Belarus. His parents paid for him to have lessons with a violin teacher, and it was the teacher who suggested that the young man should go to St Petersburg, or Leningrad as it was by then, to study at the conservatoire.

'He was tooken to it like a duck into the water!' she said, gobbling up the vile brown-yellow fish with apparent enthusiasm as she talked.

After the revolution, Leningrad was a hub of political and cultural life and many were eager to put their talents to the service of the people. One of these was Sergei Prokofiev, who met the young violinist from Orsha when he conducted the orchestra in which Artem was playing.

By the late 1930s Artem had just started to perform as a soloist with the People's Orchestra. But as Stalin's grip tightened, musicians, too, were booted into line. 'Like poor Prokofiev. He had to repent, isn't it? When I listen to the seventh symphony I think always of how they made him change the ending.' Mrs Shapiro frowned and wolfed down her fish.

Russia did not anticipate the German invasion in the summer of 1941. So when Artem heard that his father was ill, he felt safe enough to set out to visit his family in Minsk in June that year. He hitched a ride on a goods train heading west at exactly the time when every Jew in Europe who could flee was heading east, just as the German armies swept east through Poland into the Soviet Union.

'His parents and two sisters still were in Minsk. But the Nazis were building a wall of barbed wires around the streets where the Jews lived.'

'A ghetto?'

'Ghetto. Prison. Same thing. Too many peoples crammed inside. No food. Potato peels and rats they were eating. And every day soldiers were shooting people in the streets. Some suicided themselves out of despair.'

Mrs Shapiro's voice had grown so quiet that I could hear a tap dripping in the kitchen and the scuffle of a feline scratching itself under the table.

By the time Artem arrived in Minsk, the population was already swollen by the thousands of Jews who had fled eastwards, as well as by German Jews for whom there was no longer room in the German and Polish ghettos or concentration camps. Despite starvation and the typhus and cholera epidemics that raged through the ghetto, and daily summary executions, they just weren't dying fast enough. Shooting them all would use up too much ammunition, so a local Nazi commandant came up with a clever idea to kill Jews efficiently without wasting precious bullets.

One morning some forty Jews were herded to the outskirts of town and forced to dig a pit. Then they were roped together and pushed into the pit they had dug. Russian prisoners of war were ordered to bury them alive.

'But the bolshie Russians refused to do it, so the Jews had to be shot in the end and the Russians also. So even more bullets was used up, isn't it?'

Artem's father was among the forty.

To save bullets, mobile gassing vans were set up, but the munitions factories were struggling to find workers so it was decided that able-bodied Jews like Artem should be made to contribute to the war effort.

'So they sent him in Kaiserwald.'

Kaiserwald was a labour camp, buffeted by cold winds off the Baltic, squatting inside its cage of barbed wire. In this miserable spot, a number of German companies contracted to use the cheap labour facilities. But the Lithuanian guards were lax and lazy. One morning on his way to work Artem came upon a guard pissing against a wall behind the barracks and knew that this was his chance; live or die, he had to take it. He bludgeoned the Lithuanian over the head with a stone, then stole his uniform and papers.

'And he ran away on his fastest legs into the forest, to join the partisans.'

She paused and reached for a cigarette. Beneath the table a fight had broken out over the remnants of my fish.

'*Raus*, Wonder Boy! *Raus*, Stinker! *Raus*, Violetta!' She tried to kick them under the table but her feet got tangled in the tablecloth and she sat back with a sigh of resignation.

'What happened next?' I prompted.

Straightening herself out, she lit her cigarette. 'Ach, Georgine, I cannot tell this story while we are eating good food. Another time I will finish it. Better now I should play you some music. You would like?'

I nodded. Under the table, hostilities had been suspended while the cats waited for their next course. Mrs Shapiro gathered the plates and tottered off into the kitchen, leaving her cigarette smouldering in a saucer. I was beginning to feel a bit strange. Between us, we'd almost polished off the bottle of wine—or maybe it was the images from the terrible story working on my imagination.

After a while I became aware of a sound in the next room, a low mournful sound, like a voice calling from the netherworld. For a moment I thought it was a cat, then I realised it was music—such soft, sad music—that had crept in quietly through the open door. At first it was a single violin, then it was joined by others, and then a tune emerged, throbbing with melancholy and repeating itself over and over, growing louder and higher. I found myself thinking of Rip—of Rip and me together, of Rip and me making love, each time the same yet each time different, repetitions and variations.

Now the tempo of the music changed; it became louder, more violent, the violins racing up and down, faster and faster, arguing with each other, contradicting each other, in a turmoil of sound. I thought of Rip again, and I remembered the terrible fury and churning of our last argument. No, I realised, it wasn't just the music. A gut-churning feeling was building up in my stomach right now. Then Mrs Shapiro reappeared in the doorway with another tray.

'Now we heff a dessert.'

'Er . . .' She placed the tray on the table. It looked like some sort of shop-bought pie, still in its foil dish. I could handle that—I'd grown up on this sort of food. '. . . just a little.'

I tasted the pie cautiously. It seemed perfectly all right.

'You like it?' asked Mrs Shapiro.

'Yes, lovely. Delicious. What is it?'

'Prokofiev. *Symphonic Song*. Wait. It will get better.'

As I listened the tempo of the music changed again. It became graciously flowing and jubilant; the original melody had returned, but with more depths and heights of emotion, as though it was leaping over the contradictions and arguments, into a new world, a new happy world where everything was going to be all right again for ever and ever. Tears welled up in my eyes and rolled down my cheeks.

The music stopped and silence seeped into the room. Across the table from me, I saw that Mrs Shapiro was dabbing at her eyes with her napkin. 'We heff been liffing here in this house together playing music together. I was playing piano, he was playing violin. Such great music we made together. Now I am liffing here alone. Life goes on, isn't it?'

I could feel my tears welling up again. How much better it would be, I thought, to love and be loved like this until parted by death, and even after death, than to feel love shrivel and die while life goes on around you, dreary and loveless. Oh heck, there goes my splattered heart again.

'Why are you crying, Georgine? You have lost someone, too?'

'Yes. No. It's not the same. My husband . . . he walked out on me.'

'You are still young, you will find somebody else.'

I wiped my tears and smiled. 'If only it was so easy.'

'Darlink, I will help you.'

The next thing I can remember is throwing up on my own doorstep. I was still wearing the green dress, with my jeans underneath and my pullover and duffle coat on top. My head was throbbing and I felt terrible. Then I sensed a warm furry presence beside me. It was Violetta. She must have followed me home. 'Hello, cat.' I stretched out my hand to stroke her, and she arched her back and purred, rubbing herself against me.

THE NEXT MORNING, I woke up at about ten o'clock with a horrible taste in my mouth. I must have thrown up in the night, but I couldn't remember anything. A hard beam of sunlight was hammering between the curtains where they didn't quite meet, like a chisel splitting my brain, and the ceiling seemed to be moving back and forth above me. I pulled the covers over my head, but that brought on a panic of suffocation. I staggered into the bathroom and gulped cold water from the tap, then splashed some onto my face. The light was too harsh. I rooted through my drawer for something to cover my eyes and found a pair of black knickers; I slipped them over my head like a hood. The waist elastic just reached the tip of my nose. I lay back down on the bed and let the darkness enfold me. That was better. If Rip had been there he'd have made me a cup of tea and comforted me. I remembered that music, the bounding, soaring, happily-ever-after melody that had carried me in its arms last night. Was that a dream? Yes, it was.

At our wedding, the organist had played *The Arrival of the Queen of Sheba* and Dad overcame his scruples about religion enough to walk me up the aisle on his arm. It was the first time Rip's parents and mine had met, and it was all excruciatingly polite. Rip had discreetly removed the engraving of the Staffordshire coal mine that some ancestor had owned in 1882, and I'd persuaded Dad not to wear his National Union of Mineworkers tie. Mr Sinclair engaged Dad in conversation about rugby, Mrs Sinclair complimented Mum on her hat, and Mum asked her for the recipe for the chocolate peripherals; Mrs Sinclair skirted round the question without revealing that everything had come from a catering firm in Leek. Mum didn't say anything about the olives on the canapés, but I could see her eyeing them with suspicion. It was 1985, remember, and olives hadn't yet reached Kippax.

I must have dozed off, for when I woke up later in the afternoon, I felt much better. I went downstairs to rummage in the fridge for something to eat and ended up pouring myself a glass of wine instead. My stomach was still feeling delicate from its trauma, and probably it would have been sensible to stick to tea and toast, but I needed something to cheer me up. Carrying my glass of wine I went back upstairs, and I noticed that the door to Ben's room was ajar, so for no particular reason I went inside.

It smelled of Ben, or to be precise, it smelled of Ben's socks; and here they were, in a waiting-to-be-washed heap near the door. Also in heaps on the floor were his school clothes, his not-school clothes, the books he was halfway through reading, exercise books, notebooks, a collapsed stack of DVDs, a mound of CDs and various bits of mysterious electronic gear. On the walls were posters of the Arctic Monkeys, Amy Winehouse, and a *Lord of the Rings* poster featuring a close-up of Orc dentistry. My eyes roved around the busy cluttered space and I smiled to myself—dear Ben.

The desk was a tip of crumpled papers, broken pens, bottle tops and ring pulls, gum, wrappers, all splattered with some kind of sticky brown stuff—it may have been congealed hot chocolate—that was also daubed on the keyboard of his computer, and even on the monitor, where a Windows logo was whirling mindlessly around. A small photograph was stuck to the bottom of the monitor with Blu-tack. I leaned forward to look, and my heart squeezed in my chest. It was Ben and Stella. They were sitting on a park bench surrounded by greenery, grinning their heads off.

I bent down to get a closer look at the photo and my sleeve caught the glass of wine, which splashed everywhere, mingling with the congealed chocolate. I took a tissue from my pocket and started to mop, taking care not to disturb anything. As I wiped the mouse, the computer suddenly whirred into life and the screen came up—a black background with a single word flashing in red, animated with dancing flames: ARMAGEDDON: It looked like some stupid computer game.

AFTER THAT DINNER I avoided Mrs Shapiro for a couple of weeks, then I forgot about her. Life carried on with its limping rhythm: Ben, not-Ben, Ben, not-Ben. I was learning to walk with the limp and I slept better with the black knickers. Sometimes, to cheer myself up, I fantasised about revenge. In *The Splattered Heart*, feisty Gina, having discovered Rick's infidelities, was also planning something dramatically unpleasant.

I was sitting at my laptop one dull afternoon, trying to write about adhesives but sneaking back every few minutes to the exercise book, which was open on my desk, when the phone rang.

'Mrs Georgina Sinclair?' An unfamiliar woman's voice.

'Yes. Sort of. Who's speaking?'

'I'm Margaret Goodknee from the Whittington Hospital.'

My hands went cold and my heart started to thump. 'What's happened?'

'We have a Mrs Naomi Shapiro in A and E.'

'Oh dear.'

I must confess, all I felt was relief. Not Ben. Not Stella.

'On her admission form she's named you as her next of kin.'

3

Why me? I wondered, half curious and half irritated, as I made my way down a long busy ward looking for Mrs Shapiro. Doesn't she have anyone closer?

I found her at last, shrunk down into a bed, with only her little face peeping out above the sheet, and her black curls straggling over the pillow. The silver line along the parting was several centimetres wide, but apart from that, without her weird make-up, she actually looked better than before.

'Mrs Shapiro? Naomi?'

Her face lit up with a smile of recognition and she reached out her hand from under the covers to hold mine. 'Georgine? Thenk Gott you come. You heff to get me out of here.'

'I'll do my best, Mrs Shapiro. When you're better. What happened?'

'Slipped on the ice. Wrist brokken.'

She waved her left hand at me, which was plastered and strapped, the fingers protruding from the dressing like bent grey twigs with splashes of chipped nail varnish at the tips.

'You heff to get me out. Food is terrible. They mekking me eat sossedge.'

'Shall I tell them you want a kosher diet?'

'Kosher pick and mix. No hem, no sossedge. But bekkon I like.' She winked. 'A little bit of something does you good, isn't it?'

The sister in charge was a small, brisk, unsmiling woman with scraped-back hair who sniffed at the idea of pick and mix, so I asked her to put Mrs Shapiro down for kosher. She scribbled it in the file, then she added, 'She doesn't seem to be registered with a GP. We need her NHS card or some form of ID to verify her entitlement.'

When I came back to her bedside, Mrs Shapiro was sitting up looking chirpy and trying to get into conversation with the woman in the next bed, who was lying on her back, breathing through an oxygen mask.

'Mrs Shapiro,' I asked, 'are you registered with a doctor?'

'What for I need the doctor?' She was in a fighting mood. 'These young boys, what do they know? In Germany we had Dr Schinkelman—this was a real doctor.' A faraway look had come into her eyes. 'Plenty medicine. Always red. Tasted of cherries. And plenty tablets for Mutti, my mother.'

'But do you have a medical card? Any form of ID?'

She sighed dramatically and passed her good hand across her brow. 'Seventy year I been liffing in this country, nobody ask me for no card.'

'I know,' I soothed. 'But you need something to show how long you've been living here. What about the bills on the house? Council tax? Gas?'

'All papers are in the bureau. Maybe they will find something.' She sat up and blinked rapidly. 'They are looking into my house?'

'I'm sure it's just a formality. I'll go and get them, if you prefer.'

She turned round, gesturing with her strapped-up hand. 'Key to my house is in the coat.'

In the bedside locker was a dark brown astrakhan coat with a turned collar and cuffs, elegantly fitted at the waist, and conspicuously moth-eaten. She saw me examining it.

'You like this coat? You can heff it, Georgine.'

'It's very nice but . . .'

'Please. Tek it. I heff another. What's the matter—you don't like it?'

'. . . I think it's a bit small for me.'

'Try. Try it.'

I made a show of taking off my duffle coat and trying to squeeze myself into it. It smelled of old cheese.

'It suits you good, darlink. Tek it. Is better than your coat.'

True, my brown Bat Woman duffle coat, even in its 1985 heyday, had been in a lower league.

'It's lovely. Thank you. But look, it doesn't fit.' I pretended to struggle with the buttons.

'You must be more elegant, Georgine. And look at your shoes. Why you don't wear mit heels?'

'I'm sure you're right, Mrs Shapiro. But I like to be comfortable.' I slipped my hands into the pockets. 'Where's the key?'

'Always in the pocket. You must be more elegant if you will catch a man, Georgine.'

I rifled through the pockets. The key had slipped through a hole and was shaking around in the hem of the lining.

'Here it is. I'll have a look in your bureau and see if I can find something offcial to keep them happy.'

'You must look only in the bureau. Not everywhere poking, Georgine.' She was smoothing the bedclothes with a nervous movement. 'Darlink, I am worrying about the Wonder Boy. Other cats can catch, but this poor boy he is always hungry. You will please put some food for him? And next time you come, Georgine, you bring some cigarettes mit you, OK?'

'I don't think smoking is allowed in hospital, Mrs Shapiro.'

'Nothing is allowed.' She breathed a dramatic sigh. 'Only sleeping and eating sossedge.'

In the next bed, the woman with the oxygen mask was making a gurgling noise. A couple of nurses rushed up and drew the curtain round the bed.

'You heff to get me out, Georgine.' Mrs Shapiro gripped my wrist. 'Place is full of krankies. Everybody dying.'

I stroked her hand until her grip relaxed. 'You'll be home soon. Would you like me to bring you anything? What about your photo of Artem? Would you like to have it with you? I'm sure they'd allow that.'

She shook her head. 'Too many teefs in here. But if you could bring Wonder Boy nobody will steal.'

Well, she was right about that. Rather than getting drawn into a plan to smuggle Wonder Boy into the hospital, I changed the subject, thinking maybe reminiscence would settle her. And I was curious to know the end of the story she'd started to tell me that night over the fish dinner.

'You never finished telling me the story about Artem. How he got to England. You said he ran away to join the partisans in the forest.'

Letting go of my wrist, she sank back onto the pillow. 'Yes, in Naliboki. Almost six months he was liffing mit the Pobeda partisans.'

Shlomo Zorin and his Pobeda band of partisans had set up a family camp in a clearing in the vast Naliboki forest in Belarus. Here they sheltered any Jews who made their way there, and even sent scouts back into the ghettos to organise escapes. Artem Shapiro undertook several of these missions, using stolen papers; his bright blond hair, inherited from his grandfather, allowed him to pass himself off as a Christian.

'Such a beautiful blondi, he was. He could pass easy.' Mrs Shapiro's voice wavered. 'So one day he made his journey back to Minsk.'

Artem had set out to find his mother and sisters, thinking to lead them back to the forest with him. But the Minsk ghetto, when he arrived, seemed like a ghost town of living skeletons. He learned that his mother had died of starvation, or maybe of a broken heart, shortly after he had been taken away and one of his sisters had died of typhus. No one knew what had happened to the other sister.

After that visit to Minsk, something broke apart inside Artem's heart. He felt himself becoming a drag on the Pobeda camp, undermining everyone's spirits with his own misery. He said goodbye to Zorin and headed east through the forests towards his birthplace at Orsha. When he arrived in the spring of 1942 the Orsha ghetto had already been liquidated.

Artem headed north to join up with a group of Russian partisans who were harrying the German army, which had by now encircled Leningrad. The partisans were trying to open up a supply route into the beleaguered city. Artcm was one of four men who were driving a sleigh loaded with potatoes and beet across the frozen Lake Lagoda when they came under fire from a German patrol. The other three perished, along with their Mongolian pony, but Artem was only wounded in the shoulder. He staunched his wound with a cloth, then crawled under some wolf-skins in the sleigh and waited for his destiny to catch up with him. Either the Germans would take him, or the Russians would rescue him, or he would freeze to death.

'Then started the snow to fall.'

He must have fainted or drifted off to sleep, for he was jerked into sudden consciousness by a sharp jolt. He peeped from under the snow-heavy wolf-skins and saw that the sleigh had been harnessed to what seemed to be another pony, which was trotting over the ice into a whirling blizzard. Seated above and behind him, he could hear two men talking. Were they speaking in German or Russian? He couldn't tell.

'And the pony was walking in the snow and the ice, and the snow was . . .'

She stopped. I waited for her to continue. But after a while I heard a gentle snoring and I realised she'd fallen asleep.

'When do you think Mrs Shapiro might be able to come home?' I asked the sister at the desk on my way out.

'It's too early to say. We'll see how she gets on,' she replied without looking up. 'We don't want her to go back home and have another fall. At her age, she might be better off in residential care.'

'Why, how old is she?'

'She told us she was ninety-six.' She looked up. Our eyes met, and mine must have betrayed my astonishment. 'Isn't she your gran?'

'No, she's just a neighbour. I don't really know her that well.'

Could Mrs Shapiro really be ninety-six?

'Another reason it'd be useful to have some ID.'

I SPOTTED WONDER BOY lurking in the porch of Canaan House as I walked up the path. He was ripping the guts out of a bird he'd caught—it looked like a starling. He bolted off into the bushes as he saw me coming, the bird in his jaws. This cat can well take care of himself, I thought. Usually I'm fond of cats but there was something horrible about Wonder Boy.

The key Mrs Shapiro had given me was only a Yale, in fact any enterprising burglar could have just smashed the frosted glass and put his hand through to turn the lock. I pushed the door open and stepped into the hall, where the stink hit me. I put my handkerchief up to my nose. Out of nowhere, Violetta materialised around my ankles, meowing pitifully. Poor thing—she must have been locked in the house for at least three days.

I followed her through to the kitchen, where a chaos of dirty plates, dead cups with remains of brown fluids, empty tins and greasy ready-meals packaging was spread across every grimy surface. In a cracked sink under the window, a stack of unwashed dishes was soaking in scummy water. The gas cooker was crusted with dark brown grunge. There was an Aga, but it was unlit and seemed to be used for storing old newspapers.

I hunted around and found a dozen cat-food tins in a cupboard. I opened some and spooned the contents of one into a bowl for Violetta. She wolfed it down, almost choking in her desperation. Then I unlocked the back door—the key was on the inside—filled the bowl again and put it out on the step. Wonder Boy appeared, hissed at Violetta, batted her out of the way, and polished it off. A few other scrawny moggies were hanging around too. I fed them all, then locked the kitchen door and returned to the house.

The bureau Mrs Shapiro had been talking about was in a downstairs room that could have been a study. The window had been boarded up behind drawn curtains, so the only light was from a lone surviving candle-bulb in a heavy gilt candelabra. It cast a feeble glow over the old-fashioned floral wallpaper, floor-to-ceiling bookcases and a tiled fireplace above which hung an ornate ormolu mirror. Even in the gloomy light I could see it was a lovely room. There was an armchair and two desks—a mahogany kneehole desk by the window, and a tall oak bureau-bookcase in an alcove.

The bureau was full of papers, mostly bills in the name of Naomi Shapiro, and some older ones in the name of Artem Shapiro, and bank statements from a joint-name account. The most recent of these, to my astonishment, showed a balance of just over £3,000. There was, it seemed, a small monthly income from an annuity, as well as Mrs Shapiro's widow's pension, going into the bank. I chose a selection of statements. In the same drawer, held together with a rubber band, was a bundle of receipts.

There must be something else, I thought; something personal to show a date or place of birth, of baptism or marriage. The kneehole desk was crammed full of stationery, old tickets, train timetables, a library card and assorted out-of-date leaflets. One drawer housed a correspondence with the council about the monkey puzzle tree, which Mrs Shapiro had wanted to cut down, although apparently it had a tree preservation order on it.

In the last drawer was a thick brown envelope stuffed with official-looking papers. This was what I'd been searching for. An odd-looking passport, light blue with a black stripe on one corner. Artem Shapiro; date of birth March 13, 1904; place of birth Orsha; date of issue March 4, 1950, London. Ration book: Artem Shapiro 1947. Driving licence: Artem Shapiro 1948. Abbey National Life Insurance plan, Artem Shapiro 1958. Death certificate: Artem Shapiro 1960; cause of death: cancer of the lung. Knowing his story, I felt a special tug of intimacy as I turned the flimsy, typewritten paper over in my hands. So that was how his journey ended: the ghetto, the barbed-wire camp, the silent forests, the ice-bound lake. I folded the death certificate and put it back, hoping he'd died in his sleep.

But what about her? A Co-op savings book was the only document that had her name on it. Mrs N. Shapiro July 13, 1972. There has to be something else, I thought. I poked through the other rooms. The sideboard in the dining room yielded nothing but plates and cutlery. The sitting room was dark, the bay windows boarded up, and the light switch didn't work. Under the staircase, behind the pram, a narrow door opened onto stone stairs leading down to the basement. A wave of musty air rose up towards me. I felt with my hand along the wall for the light switch and a fluorescent strip light juddered into life, flickering on and off, plunging the low-ceilinged room alternately into light and pitch darkness.

It seemed to be a kind of workshop. A glass-fronted cabinet was fixed to the wall with rows of rusting tools neatly arranged. Below it was a workbench with a variety of clamps. Bits of carved wood were hanging from hooks. I realised that they were panels and necks of unfinished violins. There was a pot of dried-up glue, clear and amber-coloured, still exuding a faint, sickly whiff. Animal glue. Biopolymer. Used for woodworking, veneers and inlays, until modern synthetic glues came along.

My boss, Nathan, once told me that the Nazis had made glue from human bones. Lampshades from human skin; mattresses stuffed with human hair. Nothing wasted . . . I was beginning to feel dizzy. I made my way back up the stone stairs. As my fingers felt for the light switch I turned back towards the workshop, and that's when I saw a flash of colour on top of the tool cabinet—a couple of millimetres of blue. Curious, I went back down and pulled up a chair to have a look. It was an oblong tin, a bit rusty, with a picture of Harlech Castle surrounded by an improbably blue Welsh sky. I lifted it down and eased it open. All it had in it were a few photographs. I slipped the tin under my arm and went back up into the light.

From the hall, a wide staircase led up to the first floor. As I mounted the treads, still clutching the tin, a threadbare Axminster carpet secured by brass rods released clouds of dust under my feet. Nine doors opened off the first-floor landing. One of them was slightly ajar. I pushed it open and two lean stray cats bolted out between my legs. The room was large and light, with a double window overlooking the front garden, and dominated by a massive art-deco walnut double bed on which a tattered-eared tomcat—he had the same moth-eaten look as Mrs Shapiro's astrakhan coat—was curled up asleep. Raising his shaggy head he followed me with his eyes as I came in. The stench in here was terrible. Phew! I opened a window. 'Shoo! Shoo!' He looked at me with contempt, then uncurled himself, jumped down from the bed and sauntered towards the door.

Mrs Shapiro's clothes were scattered everywhere—the baker boy cap, the peep-toe high heels, and on the floor by the bed a pair of peach camiknickers trimmed with cream lace. The walnut wardrobe, carved with art-deco sunbursts, was full of clothes on satin-padded hangers, reeking of mothballs. A matching dressing table stood in one corner, with a triple hinged mirror facing the window. I rifled through decomposing make-up and musty underwear. There was nothing of interest, so I sat down on the edge of the bed, opened the Harlech Castle tin, and spread out the six photographs.

Most were in black and white, but the top one was in sepia. It was a family portrait from the turn of the century: the mother in a lace-collared dress cradling a baby, the other arm round the shoulder of the father with a beard and a tall hat, and two children: a little girl wearing a flouncy dress and a strikingly blond toddler in white pantaloons. There was writing in Cyrillic script on the back. All I could make out was the date: 1905. Artem must have carried it with him, hidden in a pocket or a lining, all that way.

Next, a wedding photograph caught my eye: a tall man, fair and handsome, grasping the hand of a pretty woman with ardent eyes and thick curly black hair. The man I recognised as Artem. But who was the woman? An attractive heart-shaped face with wide-set dark eyes and a generous mouth. I studied it carefully, for people's faces do change as they age, but, really, there could be no doubt. The woman in the photo was not Naomi Shapiro.

Suddenly, I heard voices outside in the garden. My heart thumped. I slipped the photos into my bag, closed the tin and shoved it on top of the wardrobe out of sight. In one of the panes of the triple mirror I could see a reflection of the window and, through it, the garden. A man and a woman were standing on the path, gazing at the house. The woman was a stout redhead, wearing a vivid green jacket; the man was stocky and wearing a blue parka, smoking a cigarette. He stubbed his cigarette out on the path and spoke to the woman. By the time I came down to the door they'd gone.

THERE WAS A DIFFERENT nurse on duty when I went back up to the hospital. She examined the papers I showed her without comment, ticked a box on Mrs Shapiro's notes, then passed them back to me.

'How's she doing?' I asked.

'Fine. She'll be ready to go as soon as we can get her home assessment done.' She flicked through the notes. 'I understand you have the key to her house. I'll get Mrs Goodknee to ring you for an appointment.'

Mrs Shapiro was sitting up in bed, her hair combed back tidily, the green hospital gown covering up her chest and throat. Her cheeks were rosy and her eyes looked bluer—yes, her eyes were definitely blue.

'Hello. You look good, Mrs Shapiro. Are they feeding you well? Are they still making you eat sausages?'

'Not sossedge. Now is better. Now is chickens and fry pottetto. Did you bring the Wonder Boy?'

'I tried, but he ran away,' I lied.

I wanted to ask her about the photographs, but I didn't want to admit that I'd been rifling through her house and had discovered the hidden tin. I would have to find another way of worming the story out of her.

We sipped the thick, bitter tea that came round on the trolley and munched our way through a box of chocolates I'd brought.

'Mrs Shapiro, I'm worried that your house is . . . well . . . don't you think it's a bit big for you to manage? Wouldn't you be happier in a nice cosy flat? Or in a home where you'd have someone to look after you?'

She looked at me with wide-eyed horror, as though I'd put a curse on her. 'Why for you say this to me, Georgine?'

I couldn't find polite words to explain my concern about the smell and the grunge, so I just said, 'Mrs Shapiro, the nurse thinks you might be too old to live on your own.' I studied her face. 'She told me you're ninety-six.'

Her mouth twitched. She blinked. 'I am not going nowhere. What would heppen to my dear cats?' She squeezed my hand. 'So, tell me about your husband—the one who was running away.'

'Oh, it's a long story.'

'But not so long as mine, isn't it?' An impish smile. 'It was a story of loff at first sight?'

'Actually, it was, Mrs Shapiro. Our eyes met across a crowded room.'

In fact it was a courtroom in Leeds, where two miners from Castleford were on trial for a picket-line scuffle. Rip was defending; he was still doing his articles and volunteering at the Chapeltown Law Centre. I was a junior reporter on the *Evening Post*. After the verdict was announced—they were cleared—we went for a celebratory drink. Later Rip drove me home to my parents' bungalow in Kippax, and we made love in front of the fire. We hardly knew each other, yet it was as if we'd known each other for ever.

'And your parents, what did they say? They were a little surprised?'

'Fortunately we were dressed by the time they got back. Mum fell for him at once. He could really put on the charm. Dad thought he was a class enemy. You see Rip was from a moneyed family, and I thought he might patronise my parents. But he was nice . . . respectful.'

She flicked her head impatiently. 'So tell me more about loff.'

'Well'—the memories tightened in my throat—'you could say it's a tempestuous story of forbidden love between an almost-aristocrat and a humble girl from a mining village.'

She nodded. 'This is a good beginning.'

My parents had been out to the Miners' Welfare in Castleford—a retirement do for a fellow pit-deputy. Dad was glassy-eyed and unusually talkative. Mum, who'd drawn the driving straw, was also not stone-cold sober.

Dad: (Mutters to Mum.) What the 'eck's our Georgie brought 'ome?

Mum: (Whispers to me.) You've landed a good fish here, Georgie.

Me: (Embarrassed, to Rip.) Meet my parents, Jean and Dennis Shutworth.

Rip: (All charm and golden curls.) Rip Sinclair. Delighted to meet you.

Mum: (Taking care with her vowels.) Rip. That's an unusual name.

Rip: (A dimply, self-deprecating grin.) It's short for Euripides. My parents had great hopes for me.

Dad: (Whispers to me.) Not your type, Georgie.

Mum: (Getting in quick.) Would you care to join us for some tea?

I looked across at Mrs Shapiro. Her eyes were closed and I realised she'd drifted off to sleep.

When I got home, at about three o'clock, there was a message on the answering machine from Mrs Goodknee. Would I be so kind as to ring her—a tinny, middle-aged voice. I rang, and got another answering machine. I left a message. Then I made myself a cup of tea and carried it up to my room. I'd taken the six photographs out of my bag and spread them across the floor in front of the window. Now, crouching down beside them, I frowned as I tried to puzzle out the story I was sure was there.

First, the Shapiro family in which Artem was the toddler, taken in 1905. Then the wedding photograph—a different woman. Artem Shapiro must have been married to someone else before Naomi. The same couple, Artem and the mystery woman, were pictured in another photograph, standing in front of a fountain. There was something scrawled on the back. *Stockholm Drott* . . . I couldn't make out the rest of the word.

There was a group photo, a man and four women wearing formal clothes seated round a piano. *Wechsler family, London 1940* it said on the back. I looked closely, but the faces were too small to be distinct. In another of the photographs I recognised Canaan House with the monkey puzzle tree, quite a bit smaller than now, in the background. Two women were standing in front of the porch. The taller of the two looked like the dark-eyed woman in the wedding photograph. The other, curly-haired and elfin small, I didn't recognise. I turned the picture over. On the back was written *Highbury 1948*. I looked more closely—although the facial features were indistinct, there was something familiar about the smaller woman. I remembered the slight, boyish figure pulling things out of the skip. Naomi. So they'd been together in Canaan House, they'd known each other.

I recognised the dark-eyed woman in another photo; this time she was alone, standing in an arched stone doorway. On the back was written *Lydda 1950*. That's a pretty name, I thought, for a pretty woman. But who was she?

Downstairs, the front door slammed; the house shook. Ben, coming home from school at half past four. I heard the thud of his school bag in the hall and the *thump-thump* of his footsteps on the stairs. A few minutes later, I heard the Windows welcome chimes on his computer.

Sweeping the photos together into a pile, I went down to the kitchen, made two cups of tea and carried them upstairs. I knocked on the door of Ben's room but he didn't answer, so I pushed it open with my foot. He was sitting at his desk staring at the computer monitor. I caught a glimpse of the screen—a flash of red writing on a black page. A single word leaped out at me: ARMAGEDDON. Then with a click of the mouse the screen changed.

'Ben . . .'

'What?'

'What's the matter, love?'

'Nothing.'

I reached out and ruffled his hair. He flinched under my touch. 'It's OK to feel upset, Ben. It's a hard time for all of us.'

'I don't feel upset.' He was still staring at the screen, his hands resting on the front of the keyboard as if waiting for me to go.

The move from Leeds to London had been hard on Ben. He'd resented being plucked out of his group of friends and having to fight his way into the unwelcoming circles of his north London comprehensive. He never brought any friends home, but a few times he'd come home later than usual and muttered something about having been with someone called Spike.

'What would you like for tea?'

'Anything. Spaghetti. I'll come down later, Mum. All right?' he said without looking up, in a voice that meant 'leave me alone'.

I went downstairs to the kitchen and poured myself a glass of Rioja, feeling my failure sink inside me like a stone. Failed wife. Failed mother. Friendless—for my old Leeds friends were Rip's friends, too. I tried ringing Stella in York, but she was out. I downed the Rioja in a couple of gulps and poured another. Maybe I should get a cat—or seven or eight.

No, I'd just have to pull myself together and make new friends here in London. In fact I'd made one already. Sure, her food hygiene left something to be desired, but we were mates. And I had online work colleagues, too, whom I'd known for years but never met. I'd drop in at the *Adhesives* office in Southwark one day and say hello. I was particularly curious to meet Nathan, the boss. He had a soft, confiding voice when we spoke on the phone. I imagined someone hunkily intelligent, with horn-rimmed glasses and a sexy white lab coat. Penny, the admin manager, told me he was single and lived with his elderly father, which seemed gentle and caring.

Rip's new Progress Project colleagues were frighteningly high-powered. I'd met some of them at a Christmas party last year. He'd introduced me to a couple called Tarquin and Jacquetta, and Pectoral Pete and his wife Ottoline. He was bulging pectorally out of a loud check jacket. She was like a china doll—dainty and expressionless, with a perfect bow-shaped scarlet mouth and a voice that tinkled like cut glass. Rip had spent most of the evening out in the corridor tapping at his BlackBerry.

I went and fetched my exercise book.

'Darling, I have to attend to some really important work on my BlackBerry,' ~~said~~ remarked Rick one evening.

'Of course, beloved,' she ~~said~~ murmured softly. 'Your work is really important and must always take precedence over everything else.'

'How lucky I am to have such an understanding wife,' ~~said~~ he uttered, and kissed her on her cheek before disappearing.

An hour later Gina heard a ringing sound suspiciously like Rick's BlackBerry coming from the study. But Rick was nowhere to be seen.

Suddenly I felt the pressure of a warm hand on my shoulder.

'When's dinner ready?'

Quickly, I closed my exercise book and pushed the almost-empty wine bottle aside.

'Sorry, Ben. Just catching up on a bit of work.'

He frowned. 'You should go easy on that stuff, Mum.'

'What, this?' I giggled. 'It's only a little Rioja.' Was he worried that I would turn into an unfit mother? I caught the anxious look in his eyes, and pulled myself together. Maybe he had a point.

We cooked dinner together. Pasta with anchovies, broccoli and Parmesan. Ben slurped his spaghetti noisily, pulling a goofy face to make me laugh. From the next room, we could hear the television booming, the chimes of the evening news. I wasn't really paying attention; I was still thinking about Rip—his BlackBerry obsession, my toothbrush-holder obsession. How had we let our happiness be ruined by such trivial things?

'Why do they do that?' Ben asked suddenly. His face had clouded over.

'What?'

'Suicide bombers—why do they blow themselves up?'

He was listening to an item on the news.

'It's . . . when people are desperate . . . it's the way they draw attention . . .' The warm glow from the Rioja had worn off. 'It's when you want to hurt someone so much you don't care if you hurt yourself, too.' Desperate. I remembered the frothed milk splattered all over the kitchen.

'But why do *that*? It's gross.' Ben was twirling the remaining strands of spaghetti round his fork. Then he said, without looking up, 'It's like . . . There was this kid at school who cut his arms with a razor.'

'Oh, Ben, why . . .?' I felt a rush of anxiety—I knew the cruelty kids could unleash on each other.

'Dunno. Like you said. Drawing attention.'

My heart lurched. 'Ben, if you're feeling . . .'

'It's all right, Mum. I'm all right. Don't stress.' He smiled fleetingly, loaded his plate into the dishwasher and slouched off upstairs.

THE NEXT MORNING I found myself nursing a headache, worrying about Ben, and wrestling with a chain of polymers. Polymerisation is the key to the chemistry of adhesion—it's when a single molecule suddenly grabs onto two other similar molecules on each side, to make a long chain. A bit like line dancing. Not what you feel like first thing in the morning. Then the phone rang. It was Mrs Goodknee, trying in her squeaky voice to get me to hand over the key so she could do her home assessment. I suggested we meet at Canaan House at noon.

I wanted to give Mrs Shapiro the best chance I could, so I went over there about an hour earlier to prepare for Mrs Goodknee's visit. I'd filled a plastic bucket with cleaning stuff, air freshener spray, and a pair of rubber gloves, and set off at a brisk pace. I was wearing a smart grey jacket that I hoped would make an appropriately serious impression.

The cats must have been waiting for me because as I approached the house they all appeared, clamouring around me, meowing with their pink, hungry mouths. I fed them, then got to work on the kitchen. I took off my jacket, pulled on the rubber gloves and filled up a couple of bin bags with food packaging and the contents of the disgusting fridge. I cleared the sink and poured bleach into it, then swept the floor in the kitchen and hall, removing a pile of cat poo.

Still fifteen minutes to go before midday. I went upstairs to Mrs Shapiro's room, opened the windows, sprayed the air freshener around, picked up the clothes on the floor and shook the bed covers out of the window. I was admiring my handiwork when I heard a woman's voice in the garden. She was talking loudly, the way people do into their mobile phones. It was an ugly, metallic voice, like a rusty gate.

'I'm just going in to have a look.' (A pause, while she listened to the voice at the other end.) 'I'll let you know.' (Pause.) 'It's an old biddy who lives here. She'll be going into a home.' (Pause.) 'I'll get a good valuation.' (Pause.) 'Hendrix.' (Pause.) 'Cash. Five grand.' (Pause.) 'Damian.' (Pause.) 'I'll find out. And I'll ask about the tree. I'd better go.' (Pause.) 'Bye-ee!'

A few moments later, I saw her walking up the path. I recognised her at once as the redhead who'd been in the garden the other day—that toxic-green jacket. Its quilted texture reminded me of lizard skin. She stopped by the gate—she was waiting for me, thinking I'd be coming up the road. I didn't want her to see me emerging from the house so I let myself out of the kitchen door, locked it behind me, and looked for another way out. A mossy path led down through the long back garden to a derelict mews block at the back. Beside it was a gate. It was bolted, but I managed to force it open and found myself in another cobbled alley, now overgrown with brambles, that led back onto Totley Place. As I turned into the lane I could see Mrs Goodknee waiting for me at the gate, flicking through a file.

'Hi. I'm Georgie Sinclair. Sorry I'm late.'

She must have been in her mid-forties, about the same age as me, but she had a stiff, over-groomed style. She was wearing pointy shoes and a green raincoat. She handed me a business card. 'Margaret Goodney. I'm a senior social worker at the hospital. Thank you for coming. Have you got the key?' Her Essex vowels squeezed themselves into a bland corporate dialect.

She followed me up the path. Fortunately I'd fed the cats already and they'd gone off to do their own catty things. Only pretty, friendly Violetta appeared, rubbing herself against our legs.

'Hello, kitty kitty,' Mrs Goodney squeaked. 'Who's a pretty kitty, then?' She took a spiral-bound notebook out of her shoulder bag and turned to a new page. *Canaan House, Totley Place* she wrote at the top. 'A bit of a jungle, isn't it? That tree needs to be cut down.'

'It's got a preservation order on it.'

She made a note.

Seeing Mrs Shapiro's house through Mrs Goodney's social worker eyes made me realise how pathetic my clear-up efforts had been. Her nose wrinkled the moment we walked in through the door.

'Poo! It's like the black hole of Calcutta in here.'

The air freshener had worn off. Her heels click-clacked on the loose tiles in the hall. Her eyes darted around. She made a note on every room we walked into. Her note on the dining room read: *Good proportions. Original fireplace.* Her note on the kitchen read: *Total refurbishment.* She saw me craning to see what she'd written and flicked the page.

'A house this size is a liability,' she said, not unkindly. 'She'd be much happier in a nice care home.' She made another note. 'Mm. No food in fridge. That's a sure sign of self-neglect.'

'I cleared the fridge.'

'What did you do that for?'

'The food was going mouldy.'

'That's what I mean. We have to do what's best for her, don't we, Mrs . . .?'

'Sinclair. Call me Georgie. Doesn't she have any say in the matter?'

'Oh, yes, of course we have to get her consent. That's where you could be very helpful, Mrs Sinclair.'

I felt a flush spreading up my cheeks. Was she going to offer me five grand? But she just smiled her toothy smile.

As we stepped into the bedroom, she quivered and put her hand to her nose. Mussorgsky had managed to get in there ahead of us and had taken up his position on the bed. He raised his head and yowled as we came in. Violetta had sneaked in with us and was lurking in the doorway.

'These cats—they'll have to go.'

'They're her friends. She gets lonely.'

'Yes, companionship—that's another of the advantages of residential care.' She made a note in her book.

On the floor by the bed were Mrs Shapiro's peach silk camiknickers, which I'd overlooked in my whirlwind cleanup. She bent down and picked them up, held them between finger and thumb, then let them fall.

'She fancies herself, doesn't she?'

I saw her wipe her fingers discreetly on a tissue. I can't explain why, but it was that contemptuous finger-wiping gesture that really made me hate her.

The bathroom came as a shock to both of us. The toilet bowl, originally white porcelain patterned with blue irises, was now brown-stained and cracked. The stain had seeped in a damp acrid circle into the rotting floorboards, which had partly collapsed under the toilet bowl, making it lean at an alarming angle. Hanging loose from the wall was a basin in the same iris design, with green-yellow drip-trails beneath the taps. A large enamel claw-foot bath stood under the window. The grime circles inside the bath grew in layers, like trunk rings in an ancient tree.

'It'll all have to come out,' she murmured, jotting in her notebook. 'Shame.' Downstairs in the hall, she stretched out her hand to shake mine. 'Thank you very much, Mrs . . . Georgie. I'll go and write my report.'

'You're going to put her into a home, aren't you?' I blurted.

'Of course my recommendation is entirely confidential.' She pursed her thin lips. 'But I think residential care could be an appropriate option. We have to do what's best for her, not what suits us, don't we, Georgie?'

'What do you mean—"what suits us"?'

'It can be hard for a carer to let go. They like to think they're doing it all for the other person when really they're just being selfish, trying to hang on to their caring role because they want to feel valued.' She smiled a bland professional smile. 'And we wouldn't want to be held responsible if she had another accident, would we?' She turned and click-clacked down the path.

I felt like strangling her with her repulsive reptilian outfit and stuffing her nasty cube-heel shoes into her squeaky creaky gob.

AS SOON AS I got home, I took out the card Mrs Goodney had given me, phoned the number, and asked for Damian Hendrix. There was a pause.

'This is the hospital social work department,' a woman's voice told me. 'Are you sure you don't want the local authority social services?'

I looked up the local authority number in the phone book and tried again.

'Could I speak to Mr Damian Hendrix?'

'I'm sorry, we don't have anyone by that name here. What was it about?'

'It's about an old lady going into a home.'

'Hold on, I'll put you through to Elderly.'

The line crackled.

'Elder-lee!' a cheerful voice chimed in my ear.

'I'm looking for Mr Damian Hendrix.'

'Mm-mm. No Hendrixes here. Are you sure you've got the right name?'

'I'm sure about the Damian. Have you got any Damians?'

'Mm-mm . . .' I heard the voice call to someone else in the room, 'Eileen, 'ave we got any Damians?'

'Only 'im in't store,' said Eileen.

'Only one who works in the resource centre,' said the cheery voice.

'No, it must be someone else. Thanks.'

I put the phone down.

Eileen—that voice—she must be from Yorkshire. I felt a little stab of homesickness, remembering how I'd felt when we moved down from Leeds to London, after Rip was offered the job on the Progress Project. We'd hovered for weeks like lost souls in the limbo of estate agent offices, looking for a place that might one day feel like home. The squat Edwardian semi we finally bought had seemed brighter than most. It had been all done out for a quick sale by the builder and smelled of newness and fresh plaster. I'd liked it at the time—it had seemed like a fresh canvas onto which we'd paint our new life. But that's not how it had worked out. Maybe things had been going wrong for ages and I just hadn't noticed the warning signs.

Later that afternoon, as I was walking down the local parade of a dozen or so shops, I remembered the other reason we'd chosen our house. This little neighbourhood had seemed an intimate island of friendliness in the vast anonymous bustle of London. There was the Turkish bakery, strangely famous for its Danish pastries, the Song Bee, our favourite takeout, specialising in Chinese and Malaysian cuisine, Peppe's Italian delicatessen, the newsagent by the bus-stop, and two estate agents: Wolfe & Diabello on the corner where I was standing and, across the road, Hendricks & Wilson.

Then it dawned on me. Hendricks! Should I barge in and make a scene? Instead, on impulse, I pushed open the door of Wolfe & Diabello. If Mrs Goodney was going to get her little Damian to do a valuation on Canaan House, at least I could get one, too, for comparison.

A small, bosomy girl with sleek blonde hair and careful eyes was sitting at a desk by the window. Her name badge said SUZI BRENTWOOD.

'My aunt's thinking of selling her house. Could you give us a preliminary valuation?'

'Of course.' She flashed her pearly teeth at me. 'I'll make an appointment with one of the partners. Is next Friday all right? What's the address?'

Her eyebrows rose a fraction when I told her.

BY THE TIME Friday came round it was raining again, a miserable December drizzle that stained the streets and rooftops melancholia grey. I left home in a rush without an umbrella, and the hood of my duffle coat kept slipping back as I ran, so I arrived breathless and bedraggled. As I turned the corner into Totley Place I saw a black sports car skulking with predatory menace on the road outside Canaan House. When I came close the driver's door opened, and a long lean form uncurled itself onto the pavement. Tall, dark and handsome. I stopped and caught my breath. There was something oddly familiar about him.

'Mrs Sinclair?' He raised a quizzical eyebrow and proffered his hand, which was warm and firm. 'I'm Mark Diabello.' His smile made rugged creases in his craggily handsome cheeks. His dark, smouldering eyes seemed to gaze right into my soul. 'It means beautiful day, I've been told.' His voice was like black treacle—sweet, with a hard mineral edge.

'Not like today then.' I batted my wet eyelashes. What was happening to me? This man was definitely not my type. 'Er . . . unusual name. Italian?'

I was regretting that I'd worn my batty-woman clothes.

'Spanish. My father was an itinerant mandolin player.'

'Really?' He was still smiling, and I couldn't tell from his face whether he was joking. 'I've got the key,' I mumbled. 'Do you want to look around?'

Wonder Boy, Violetta and their mates had congregated at the door. I let them in and fed them in the kitchen. It was bitterly cold indoors, a dank, pungent chill that hit you with the stink of stale cat food mingled with other, worse odours. Then I became aware of another, more pleasant smell, faint and spicy like expensive soap. That was *him*. Inexorably drawn, I followed along as he wandered around the house. He had a little instrument like a torch with a laser beam that bounced enticingly against the walls of the rooms, to measure the size. He wrote the details on the back of what looked like a crumpled till receipt.

He seemed completely unfazed by the smell. Even when he stepped in a pile of fresh cat poo in the hall, he just bent down and cleaned it off with an immaculate white cotton handkerchief from his breast pocket. I watched, awestruck, as he deposited it in the kitchen bin.

'I could live in a place like this,' he murmured in his deep, mineral-edged voice that spoke directly to my hormones, bypassing my brain completely. I realised now where we'd met before—in the pages of *The Splattered Heart*. He was just as I'd imagined my hero, except that he was an estate agent, not a poet. 'Character. You so rarely get this in the housing market nowadays.'

We were standing together in the entrance porch at the end of his tour.

'Ornate plasterwork; period arches; decorative corbels. I mean, don't get me wrong, Mrs Sinclair, a lot needs doing. You'd have to do it sensitively, of course. Keep all those stunning period features. Get a couple of designers in to give you ideas. You could open up the attic, for instance. Make a fabulous penthouse suite.' A flame flickered in the depths of his eyes.

'Everybody seems to fall for this house.'

'It's the potential. You can see the potential. You'd have to cut that tree down, for starters.'

'It's got a preservation order on it.'

'Doesn't matter. You just pay the fine. The tree gets cut; the council gets its cut. Everybody's smiling.'

'You can't do that!' I hadn't much liked the tree myself, but now it suddenly felt like an old friend.

'So when's your auntie planning to put it on the market?'

'She just wanted an idea of its value, in case she decides to sell. What do you think?'

He looked at the notes he'd scribbled on the receipt, crinkling his eyes and furrowing his handsome brow. 'Half a million, maybe?'

I don't know exactly what I'd been expecting, but our own semi with its three poky bedrooms had cost almost that. He saw the look on my face.

'The area brings it down. And we're looking at a cash buyer, of course, not a mortgage. I'll put it in writing for you.'

I gave him my address. We shook hands. He climbed into his hungry-looking car, and was gone in two puffs of hot air from the twin exhausts.

I walked back home slowly, still feeling slightly giddy from my encounter. As I came up the street, I could see that Ben was already home, the blue square of his monitor winking away through his bedroom window as he navigated the cyber-seas. My mother-heart tightened with a little squeeze of sadness: it wasn't good for him to spend his evenings up there on his own.

I went upstairs and knocked on his door. 'Hey, Ben, shall we go to the pictures tonight? We could go and see Daniel Craig in the James Bond film.'

He opened the door a crack. 'Sounds like crap.'

'It probably is crap, but it might be entertaining.'

'I don't find crap entertaining, Mum? But we can go if you want to?' I noticed there was a new rising inflection at the end of his sentences—questioning, or apologetic.

I wondered whether he was like this when he stayed with Rip. Somehow I imagined that life in Islington would be an endless round of stimulating activities and conversations, and it was only with me that he spent his hours closeted with his computer. I would have rung Rip to ask him if we'd been on better terms, but we weren't, and I didn't.

Instead of going out, we ordered dinner from the Song Bee and ate it in front of a TV cop drama. I'd just been thinking that the male lead looked a bit like Mark Diabello when suddenly Ben turned to me.

'Mum, do you believe in Jesus?'

His question hit me out of the blue. I drew a slow breath. 'I don't know. I'm not sure what I believe, Ben.' What was this all about? 'I believe Jesus was a real person, if that's what you mean.'

'No, Mum. Do you believe Jesus'll save you at the end of the world?'

'Ben, love, the world isn't going to end.'

I had a sudden memory of how I'd been at his age—I believed that nuclear war would wipe out the human race. We'd sat around on Saturdays in the Kardomah café in Leeds, my mates and I, fantasising about how we would spend our last four minutes after the final warning.

'It's like . . . I really love you, Mum. You and Dad. I don't want . . .' He was mumbling, as though his mouth was full of sand. 'All you have to do is accept Jesus into your life?' His eyes, when he looked up at me, were wide, the pupils dilated. 'The signs are there, Mum? All the signs are in place?'

'The world's been around for a long time, Ben. Don't worry.' I pulled him into my arms and hugged him tight. He stiffened against me at first, but I held him close until I felt him relax, his head resting on my shoulder.

THE NEXT MORNING I overcame my pride and phoned Rip. 'I'm worried about Ben. Can we talk?'

'I'm in the middle of something. Can I ring you back in half an hour?'

But he didn't.

Ben spent Saturday on his computer and I spent the day working on *The Splattered Heart*. We took turns to bring one another cups of tea and treated ourselves to Danish pastries from the Turkish bakery. Each time I walked into Ben's room, he minimised the screen he was looking at.

Rip called round at six to pick Ben up in his Saab convertible and they went straight to the cinema—they were going to see Daniel Craig in the James Bond film. After they'd gone, a horrible silence settled on the house.

4

It wasn't until Monday morning that I remembered I hadn't fed Mrs Shapiro's cats. I heard a familiar yowling sound in the garden, and when I looked out of my bedroom window, there was Wonder Boy lurking under the laurel bush. He was staring up with a reproachful look on his face. All around him was a mass of feathers, sodden in the rain. Seeing him here in my garden made me furious—I didn't want him killing my birds; in fact I didn't want him at all. I pulled on my brown duffle coat and my wellies and strode off round to Totley Place. He followed me at a distance.

There were three weird things I noticed on that visit. The first was a pile of fresh cat poo, almost in the same place where Mr Diabello had stepped in it the other day. I was sure that I'd got all the cats out of the house when we left. Who was the culprit—and how had he got in? I cleared it up and counted the cats as they milled round my legs—one, two, three, four, five, six, seven. When I left, I'd make sure to count them out.

As I straightened up, my eye fell on a picture on the wall directly above where the cat poo had been. It was a grainy photograph of an arched stone doorway with a cross on top and Corinthian columns on each side. I must have looked at it dozens of times without really seeing it. What I saw now was that it was the same arched doorway as in one of the Harlech Castle tin photographs, the one with the dark-eyed woman, Lydda.

The third thing I noticed, when I went through to the kitchen to feed the cats, was that the key to the back door, which should have been inside in the lock, was missing. It could only have been taken by Mr Diabello.

I fed the cats quickly and rushed home in a rage, but just as I picked up the phone to vent my fury at Wolfe & Diabello, it rang in my hand. It was Penny, the admin manager from *Adhesives*, wanting to know whether I'd received the press release about the new research into marine biological glues. The truth was, it had come two days ago, and I hadn't even looked at it. I mumbled something vague and apologetic, but she saw through me.

'What's going on, Georgie?' she boomed. 'Something's not right, darling, I can tell. Is it that husband of yours again?'

'No. It's another devious man.'

I explained about the missing key and the dodgy estate agent.

'Hm.' I could hear Penny breathing on the other end of the phone. 'Don't rush into anything, darling. You could be wrong about the key, then you've blown your chances with that sexy man.' How did she know he was sexy? Was I that obvious? 'You should get a second opinion, darling. Two second opinions. One about the price of the house, and one about the social worker.'

I promised I'd get on with the marine biological glues straight away, but first I'd take her advice and try to get another social worker assessment.

Mrs Goodney, I knew, worked at the hospital, not the council, so next day I telephoned the council's social services department again. I explained to the cheery 'Elder-lee!' voice that an elderly neighbour had gone into hospital and needed an assessment before she could go home.

'Mm-mm. Can you hold the line a minute? (Eileen, what's 'er what does 'ome visits?)'

Eileen's voice, muffled by distance, said something that sounded like 'Bad Eel' and 'She's out on 'er tea break.'

'You need to speak to Muz Bad Eel. I'm afraid she's in a meeting. Can I take your number and ask her to call you back?'

Bad Eel. I pictured someone slim and slippery, with scarlet lipstick and a small silver gun tucked inside a frilly garter.

I spent the morning waiting for the Bad Eel to phone me back. I was trying to work on the press release Penny had sent about marine biological glues. Some company was developing a synthetic version of the glue that bivalves such as mussels and oysters use when they cling to the rocks. One of the strongest bonds in nature, apparently. They use fine thread-like tentacles called byssus, which are rich in phenolic hydroxyls. I started thinking about bivalves living down there in the dappled light, how they filter the algae from the water, how they close themselves up against the sea. It must be wonderful to be a bivalve, hanging on to a rock in your own mother-of-pearl-lined world while the waves and tides churn outside. Ms Firestorm showed up to help me out: *Cloistered in their shimmering watery depths, the loyal bivalves cling passionately together* . . . Yes, we could learn a lot from bivalves. I wasn't very interested in commercial applications, and when the other elusive marine creature still hadn't called by lunchtime, I wrapped up warm against the wind and set out for the hospital.

Mrs Shapiro was sitting in the day room when I arrived. She was wearing a hospital gown tied at the back and a pair of woolly socks on her feet. I felt a pang of guilt. Probably it was my responsibility, as her next of kin, to bring in some of her clothes. I'd have to remember next time.

She seemed to be engaged in a fractious and incoherent argument with another old lady sitting beside her.

'But 'er were on this ward when she shouldn't of been,' the old lady was saying vehemently, 'and new sister said it weren't 'er business anyway.'

'Well, if they was no longer there someone must heff tooken them.'

'No, because she weren't supposed to be. That's what I'm sayin' to yer.' She looked up and saw me in the doorway. 'That's 'er there. Ask 'er.'

Mrs Shapiro turned, and stretched out her hands to me. 'Georgine, you got to get me out of here. All this people is mad.'

'She's talkin' tripe,' said the old lady, and heaving herself up out of the chair she minced off to the ward, muttering.

'What's going on?' I asked.

'She is a bonker,' said Mrs Shapiro. 'Brain been amputated.'

I pulled up a chair beside her. 'How are you doing? I thought you'd be going home by now.'

'They say I must go into the oldie-house,' said Mrs Shapiro. 'I tell them I am not going nowhere.' She folded her arms. The argument with the old lady was obviously just a warm-up for a much bigger argument to come.

There was a new sister on duty who looked hardly older than Ben.

'What's happened with the home assessment?' I asked.

'The report's just come. They're recommending residential care.'

'I don't see why she needs residential care. She was managing fine.'

'Yes, but you know, once they start falling, they can very easily lose their confidence.'

'What if she refuses to go?' I persisted.

'We can't discharge her into an unsafe situation. Look, I think you'd better talk to Mrs Goodney. The social work office is over by physio.'

I went back to sit with Mrs Shapiro. 'It's OK,' I said. 'I'll get them to do another assessment.'

'Thenk you, darlink,' she said, gripping my hands. 'Thenk you very much. And my dear cats, how are they?'

'They're fine. But Wonder Boy seems to be killing a lot of birds.'

'Poor darlink, he is upset. Next time you must bring him, Georgine.'

I mumbled something, but then the tea lady appeared with the trolley.

'You heff no *Kräutertee*?' said Mrs Shapiro grumpily. 'OK, I tek this.' Cradling her cup in her hands, she settled back. 'Now then, Georgine, your running-away husband. You heffn't finished telling me.'

'I did tell you. It was so boring you fell asleep.'

She caught my eye and gave a little laugh. 'You told me about your parents. That was quite boring, isn't it? But what about the husband? He was a good man? You were happy in loff?'

'We were happy at first. But then . . . I don't know . . . He got absorbed in his work. I had babies. Two—a girl and a boy. And a miscarriage in between. Then I started writing a book.'

After the miscarriage I'd given up my job and started freelancing. Rip had taken his articles but found solicitor's work tedious and applied for a job in the northern office of a national charity. He was out and about all over the place, so one of us had to be home-based. The freelancing didn't fit easily around children so I decided to try my hand at romantic fiction. I got a couple of short stories published in a women's magazine and after that encouraging start I plugged away at a romantic novel. I thought I'd got the genre spot-on and it grieved me that no one wanted to publish it.

'So, your book. It has been published?'

'Not yet. I've got another job now, writing for online trade magazines.'

'Lane tred? What is this?'

'It's a group—*Adhesives in the Modern World*, *Ceramics in the Modern World*, *Prefabrication in the Modern World*, things like that. I work on all of them, but mainly *Adhesives*. I've been doing it for about nine years.'

'But this is fascinating!'

'Well, it's just for the building trade. It's not exactly world shattering.'

'Too much shettering is going on, Georgine. Building is much better.'

'Glue,' Nathan had said, after telling me I was just the person he was looking for. 'Don't worry, it'll grow on you.'

Romantic it wasn't, but it paid the bills, and it meant I could be at home for the kids and, strangely enough, it did grow on me.

'So that's my story so far. Not very exciting, really.'

'Well, we will heff to see if we can make you a heppy ending.' She raised her teacup. 'To heppy endings!'

ON MY WAY HOME from the hospital, I decided to drop in at Canaan House to do a tidy-up in case the Bad Eel should deign to visit. The wind was still blustering, swirling up leaves and litter on the pavement. Wrapping my coat round me, I turned into Totley Place and saw something brightly coloured at the entrance to the cobbled lane that led up to Canaan House. As I drew closer my heart began to beat with rage and trepidation. Half hidden among the creepers stood a green-and-orange FOR SALE sign, with WOLFE & DIABELLO in bold black letters.

It was stuck in the ground beside the wall. I grabbed the post and heaved. It held firm, so I pushed and pulled it back and forth, to loosen it up. Then I got round behind it and grabbed the post in both hands, arching my back and bending my knees for one last heave. It slid out of the ground and I slid with it, lost my balance and fell backwards into a rose bush. A thorn jagged my cheek and Wonder Boy appeared howling out of the undergrowth.

I'd been all fired up to storm into the Wolfe & Diabello office and demand an explanation, but it began to rain and I called in at home to pick up my raincoat. The phone was ringing as I opened the door. It was Rip.

'Hi, Georgie, I just wanted to have a quick word about Christmas.'

I felt a quiver of dread.

'I was wondering about going up to Holtham with Ben and Stella . . .'

'Fine.' Actually I felt like drowning myself in a tub of lukewarm piss, but I managed to put on a brave show of nonchalance. 'Do that. Fine by me.'

I went up to my bedroom, flung myself on the bed, and sobbed and sobbed for my broken marriage and my broken family, my ailing parents, starving babies in Africa, and the general sorrows of humankind; they all came washing in on the same vast tide of human misery. I thought about the bivalves, the curved pearly walls inside their shells; whatever the extraordinary glue was that enabled them to hold on so tight while the storms swirled around them, that's what I needed now.

BY THE NEXT DAY, the fight had gone out of me a bit, but I decided to walk across to Wolfe & Diabello. There was no one in the office when I went in. I opened and closed the door again, making the bell 'ping', but still nothing happened. The third time I did it, Suzi Brentwood emerged from a door at the back; I thought I spotted a shifty look flit across her face before her professional smile composed itself.

'Hello, Mrs . . . How may I help you?'

'My auntie is thinking of selling her house before Christmas,' I said loudly.

As if by magic, the door at the back of the office opened, and Mr Diabello appeared. He was wearing the same dark stylish suit, a clean freshly folded handkerchief peeping out of the breast pocket.

'Hello, Mrs Sinclair. What can we do for you?'

'The For Sale sign in the garden at Canaan House—you put it there?'

He smiled. 'We have to keep one step ahead of the competition. We heard on the grapevine that Hendricks had sent a valuer in.'

It must have been Damian, I thought. But how did he get in?

'No harm in that, Mrs Sinclair. It's a free market. But, you know, I felt after our chat the other day that you deserve a—how can I put it?—a more focused view of the service we offer here at Wolfe and Diabello.' His eyes smouldered with dark fire. His quizzical eyebrows quizzed.

'You mean you just marched up and stuck a For Sale sign in someone's front garden without their permission?'

'It's a bit cutthroat round here,' he said apologetically. 'Hendricks and Wilson—they aren't the most reputable in the business. Sometimes they even pull our sale boards out. What valuation did he give you, by the way?'

I looked him in the eye. 'He said she should be able to get a million.'

He didn't bat an eyelid. 'I'm sure we could match that for you, Mrs Sinclair. And we could agree a special rate on the commission.' His handsome nostrils flared. A hint of a smile played at the corners of his sensual mouth. 'If your auntie decides to sell before Christmas.'

I could have swooned into his rugged manly arms at that point, but then I remembered my second issue.

'The key. You stole the back-door key. To the kitchen. It was in the door.'

His eyes widened a fraction. 'I think you've made a mistake, Mrs Sinclair, it wasn't me, I assure you. Have you considered the other possibility?'

'What other possibility?'

His mouth tightened. 'Them.' His head jerked to the left. 'Hendricks.'

'It couldn't have been them.'

Then I thought back. Mr Diabello was wandering around scribbling on the back of his receipt. It was raining, so I was in the kitchen feeding the cats. I didn't open the back door. Was it locked? Was the key in the lock? I couldn't remember. Was it when I was showing Mrs Goodney around?

'I'll look into it. If I've made a mistake I apologise,' I said stiffly.

Anyway, all I need to do, I thought to myself, is change the lock. Where do you get a new lock? My mind went blank. Then I remembered a commercial I'd seen on TV. B&Q. For some reason, the thought was pleasantly appealing. The nearest branch to me was in Tottenham.

IT WASN'T TILL the next day, as I made my way in through the sliding glass doors past the displays of Christmas baubles and kitchen units, that I realised what it was that drew me to B&Q: it was the men. Yes, although Rip was both handsome and brainy, he was deficient in the DIY department. There's something deeply attractive about a man with a screwdriver in his hand, I was thinking. These B&Q types were not destiny-shaping men; not even craggily handsome splatter-your-heart-type men; but nice ordinary blokes wearing jeans and pullovers, their pockets bulging with tape measures, sometimes a bit paunchy. Who cares? So long as they weren't always off somewhere to change the world. Maybe one of them might come along to measure me up, be stunned by my period features . . .

I should come here more often, I resolved, as I made my way through the mysterious aisles. At last I found the section that displayed locks. I picked up one or two at random, trying to remember what the one on Mrs Shapiro's door had looked like. It was definitely the type with a big key: a mortise. The trouble was, there were so many different models and sizes.

A man was browsing among the doorknobs at the end of the aisle—a small tubby Asian man. I caught his eye and smiled. He came over at once.

'You need help?' His eyes sparkled darkly. With his neat moustache and beard, he looked like a well-groomed hamster.

'I'm looking for a lock. Mortise. With a big key. Only I've lost the key.'

'You know what type? Union? Chupp? Can you describe?'

'I can't remember exactly. I think it's a bit like this one. Or that one.'

I pointed randomly.

'In my country we have a saying, knowledge is the key. But you have no knowledge and no key.' He sighed, fished in his trouser pocket and handed me a small, dogeared business card.

THERE WAS A MESSAGE on the answering machine when I got home.

'Hello, Mrs Sinclair. This is Cindy Bad Eel from social services, returning your call.'

I rang back immediately, but I just got her answering machine. I left a message asking her to ring me again as soon as she got back.

Next day, she still hadn't rung, so I tried social services again.

'Elder-lee!'

'Could I speak to Mrs Bad Eel, please.'

'May I ask who's speaking, please?'

'It's Georgie Sinclair. I rang about the old lady going into a home.'

('Eileen, where's Muz Bad Eel? It's that woman about t'old woman.' . . . 'She says she'll ring back.')

'Muz Bad Eel's just in a meeting. She'll ring you as soon as she gets out.'

'No—please tell her it's urgent. I need to speak to her now.'

There was a lot of muttering in the background, then a new voice came on the line—a low, smooth, sultry voice with a slight drawl in the vowels.

'Hello-o. This is Cindy Bad Eel.'

'Oh, hello, Mrs Bad Eel. Muz. I really need your help—I mean, a friend of mine needs your help.' I was gabbling, fearful that she would hang up. 'Mrs Naomi Shapiro. She's in hospital. She broke her wrist. Now they won't let her go home. They want to put her in a home.'

'Slo-ow down, please. Who am I speaking to?'

'My name is Georgie Sinclair. I left a message for you.'

'So you did, Ms Sinclair. Take a deep breath. Now, count one, two, three, four. Hold. Breathe out. One, two, three, four. Rela-ax! That's better. Now—would you describe yourself as her carer—an informal carer?'

'Yes—yes, a carer. Informal. That's definitely what I am.' Waves of calm engulfed me. I suddenly felt very caring.

'How old is the lady?'

I hesitated. 'I don't know exactly. Elderly, but she was getting on fine.'

'But you say she had an accident?'

'The accident was in the street, not in her house. She slipped on the ice.'

'And you say she had a home circumstances assessment visit?'

'It was someone from the hospital. Mrs Goodney. The house was a bit untidy, but it wasn't *that* bad.'

There was a long silence, then she spoke again, slowly. 'It isn't for us to judge another person's lifestyle choices. I will visit the house, but I need her permission. Which hospital is she in?'

As soon as I'd put the phone down, I ran into my bedroom and stuffed a few things into a carrier bag—Stella's old dressing gown, a spare pair of slippers, a hairbrush, a nightie—and set off for the hospital. I wanted to forewarn Mrs Shapiro and make sure she said the right things.

I was the only person on the top deck of the number 4 bus as it lurched and swayed along the now-familiar roads, brushing against the trees. When it arrived at the bus shelter outside the hospital there was the usual knot of people huddled over their cigarettes. A voice called to me. 'Hey! Georgine!'

I had to look twice before I recognised Mrs Shapiro. She was enveloped in a pink candlewick dressing gown several sizes too big for her. Beneath it, just peeping out in front, was a pair of outsize slippers—the sort that children wear, with animal faces on the front. I think they were Lion Kings. Her companion was the bonker lady with whom she'd been arguing last time. They were sharing a cigarette, passing it between them, taking deep drags.

'Mrs Shapiro—I didn't recognise you. That's a nice dressing gown.'

'Belongs to old woman next to me. Dead, isn't it?' She grabbed the cigarette from the bonker lady. 'Cigarettes was in the pocket.'

'Nice slippers, too.'

'Nurse give them to me.'

'She give me these,' said the bonker lady, lifting up the hem of her dressing gown to show off a pair of fluffy powder-blue wedgie-heel mules. Her toes were protruding, revealing the most horrible toenails I'd ever seen.

'Them should heff been for me,' said Mrs Shapiro sulkily.

We left the bonker lady to finish the cigarette and made our way back to the ward, where I handed over my carrier bag of things; she took only the hairbrush and gave the rest back to me.

'I have better nightcloth-es in my house. Real silk. You will bring one for me, next time, Georgine? And Wonder Boy. Why you didn't bring him?'

'I don't think they'd let him in. He's not very—'

'They heff too many idiotic prejudices. But you are not prejudiced, are you, my Georgine?' she wheedled. 'I am sure you will find a way.'

'Well, of course, I'll try my best,' I lied.

The ward was busy with visitors, so I pulled two chairs by the window in the day room. It was a square featureless room near the entrance to the ward, with a television high on the wall and green upholstered chairs dotted randomly around. It smelled of disinfectant and unhappiness.

'Mrs Shapiro, I've asked for another assessment from social services. Someone's going to come and visit you. She's called Ms Bad Eel.'

'This is good. Bed Eel is a good Jewish name.'

That surprised me, but what did I know? We didn't have any Jewish people in Kippax.

'Tell her I've got the key and I'll meet her at Canaan House to show her round. She has my phone number but I'll write it down for you again.' I wrote my number on a scrap of paper and she stuffed it into the pocket of the dressing gown. 'If anyone says anything to you about going into a residential home, just tell them you're having another assessment.'

She leaned across and clasped my hand. 'Georgine, my darlink. How can I thenk you?'

'There is one problem. She's certain to ask how old you are. You have to tell the truth.'

She hesitated, then leaned up close and whispered, 'I am only eighty-one.' After a moment she added, 'I told them I am ninety-six.'

'Why did you tell them that?'

'Why? I don't know why.' She shook her head with a stubborn little flick.

I recalled the picture of the two women in front of the house. *Highbury 1948*. She would have been about twenty-three when it was taken.

'Do you know your date of birth?' I probed. 'She's bound to ask you that.'

'Eight October nineteen hundert twenty-five.'

A quick, precise answer. But was it the truth? I wanted to ask her more, but I didn't want to confess that I'd searched beyond the bureau in the study.

'You didn't finish telling me about Artem.'

'You heffn't told me about your running-away husband.'

'It's your turn, Mrs Shapiro. I'll tell you my story next time.'

'Ach, so.' She laughed. 'Where heff I gotten to?'

'The pony . . .'

'Yes, the pony that was trotting on the ice. But you see it was not a pony, it was a reindeer. The reindeer people took him away mit them.'

The men who had hitched up Artem's sleigh were Sami from Lapland. Part traders and part bandits, they made forays down across the ice to exchange smoked fish, reindeer meat and furs for wheat, tobacco and vodka. When they discovered him under the wolf-skins, they debated whether to kill him; but as he opened his eyes, he smiled to find himself still alive, and started to sing a Russian peasant song.

'*Ochi chornye, ochi strastnye . . .*' Mrs Shapiro's voice quavered. 'It is about the loff for a woman mit passionate eyes. He used to sing it often.'

The song saved his life. The croaky voice of the wounded soldier made the men laugh, so they took him with them to their settlement, where he stayed until he was fully recovered. Then the Sami people offered to take him back to Russia. He explained with gestures that he wanted to go the other way, towards Sweden. So they took him to the Swedish border.

'He was looking for his sister. In that time Sweden was full of Jews. But no one knew where she was. Maybe she never was there.'

'So when did you meet him? Did you go to Sweden, Mrs Shapiro?'

She started to say something, then stopped. 'Now is your turn, Georgine. Your husband—why he was running away? There was another woman?'

I hesitated. I didn't want to go into details about the toothbrush holder, but I found myself saying, 'I don't think so. He said there was no one else. He was too obsessed with his work. He wanted to change the world. I think he was bored with domesticity.' There, I'd said it.

Mrs Shapiro wrinkled her nose. 'Ach. This is a typical story. He wants to change the world but he doesn't want to change the neppies, isn't it?'

'Sort of. The children were out of nappies.' I wanted to explain that it was the same roving, inquisitive spirit that had brought him to me in the first place. 'When we met, I was different to the other people he knew. He used to call me his rambling Yorkshire rose.'

'Don't worry, my Georgine.' She grinned merrily. 'When I am mended we will go rembling again.' She sniffed. 'So this husband—when he is finished mit the rembling, you think he is coming back?'

'I don't think so. I threw all his stuff in the skip.'

'Bravo!' She clapped her hands. 'So what he said then?'

'He said'—I put on a hoity-toity voice—'why are you being so childish?'

She rocked back in her chair and shrieked with laughter. 'This running-away husband is quite a schmuck, isn't it?'

It was such a jolly, raucous laugh that I found myself laughing, too. Our laughter must have carried right down the ward, for a few minutes later the bonker lady came waltzing in to see what was going on. She winked at me, pulled a cigarette out of her pocket, and waved it under Mrs Shapiro's nose.

'Look what one of the porters give me. Mind, I 'ad to drop my knickers for 'im inve lift.'

Mrs Shapiro let out another shriek, and that set the bonker lady off, cackling and waltzing around. We were all clutching our sides, screeching and hooting, when the ward sister came along and ticked us off. On the bus home I realised I hadn't laughed as much since . . . since Rip had left.

THE BAD EEL PHONED me back a couple of days later. We made an appointment to meet at the house. As before, I went an hour earlier, with some cleaning things. The Phantom Pooer had been at work again; there were two fresh deposits in the hallway. I cleared them away and did a quick round with a duster and a brush, spraying the air freshener around liberally. Although the weather was dry, I couldn't feed the cats by the back door because I didn't have the key, so I fed them in the kitchen, and counted them again. There were only five. Mussorgsky and Violetta were missing. Violetta appeared at the front door a few moments later, and behind her was a person who could only have been the Bad Eel.

The first disappointment was that she didn't look at all like an eel. In fact she was uninhibitedly, exuberantly plump, with curves that bulged in soft roly-poly layers beneath a tight, stretchy, blancmange-pink outfit. She held her hand out to me. Each finger was like a meaty little chipolata sausage.

'Hello, Mrs Sinclair. I'm Cindy Baddiel.'

She stressed the second syllable. That was the next disappointment. She wasn't a *bad* eel at all. Her honey-gold hair fell in loose curls from two large butterfly clips above her ears. Her eyes were the colour of angelica; her skin was like peaches; she smelled of vanilla.

I must have been staring rudely. Violetta broke the silence between us with a chatty meow. We both bent to stroke her at the same time, our heads touched and we laughed, and after that, everything was easy. She strolled around the house. ('Lo-ovely. Pe-erfect.') In the bathroom she flinched, but her only comment was, 'There's no accounting for cultural diversity.'

'One thing surprises me,' she remarked as we were walking back down the stairs. 'She doesn't seem to be getting any support from the Jewish community. Usually they're good at looking after their elderly.'

The same thought had once occurred to me, but I understood now that Mrs Shapiro was, like myself, someone who'd come unstuck.

'I suppose it's her personal choice.' She'd taken a little notebook out of her bag—it had a picture of a floppy-eared Labrador puppy sitting on a cushion—and was writing something down.

When we were back in the hall, I asked, 'What would happen to her house, if she had to go into a home? Would the council take it from her?'

'Oh no! Where did you get that idea?' She shook her curls. 'If no one else is living there, and the owner is in a home, a house could be sold to cover the fees. But don't worry.' She squeezed my hand. 'I can see no reason for Mrs Shapiro to go into residential care. I'm recommending a means-tested care package that'll support her continuing to live at home.'

I held back my impulse to say I was sure she didn't need a care package and hugged her instead.

After she'd gone, I rushed round to the hospital to tell Mrs Shapiro the good news. We went into the day room again, where the bonker lady kept wandering in and out, making smoking gestures at me.

'She said you can have a care package in your own home.'

'Vat is this peckedge? Vat is in it?' She wrinkled up her nose.

'Well, maybe a home help, to help you keep the place clean. Someone to help with your shopping and cooking.'

'I don't want it. These people are all teefs.'

I tried to persuade her, worried she'd lose her chance to get back home through her own stubbornness, but she looked at me with a little smile. 'You are a clever-Knödel, Georgine. But I heff hed a visitor.'

She produced a card from the pocket of the dressing gown: a garish orange-and-green card, with a bold black inscription across the top: *Wolfe & Diabello*. Beneath, in smaller letters, a name: *Mr Nick Wolfe*.

'Quite a charming man. He has made me an offer to buy up my house.' She turned the card over. On the back was written the figure: *£2 million*.

I felt suddenly out of my depth. The social workers, the nurses, I could handle them; but not men who flashed around those amounts of money.

'It's a lot of money. What did you say?'

'I said I will think about it.' She caught my eye and smiled impishly. 'What for I need two millions? I am too old. I already heff all what I need.'

The nurse—it was the brisk young woman I'd met on my first visit—was happy with the care package and a date was set for Mrs Shapiro to return home. I promised that I'd be there to meet her and would drop in regularly until she was settled. There was one more thing I needed to sort out. I must get that Asian handyman to change the back-door lock. I rang the number on the card and made an appointment with him for the next day.

MR ALI ARRIVED on a bicycle. I'd been expecting a man in a van, so I didn't notice him at first, wobbling up the lane. He was smaller and tubbier than I recalled, and he was wearing a pink-and-mauve-striped woolly hat pulled right down over his ears. It was hard to tell how old he was; his face looked young, but his beard and moustache were flecked with grey.

He jumped off his bike, removed the cycle clips from his ankles, straightened out his trouser bottoms—they were grey flannel, with neat creases down the fronts—and greeted me with a polite nod of the head. I noticed that there was a small leather bag on a long strap slung across his chest, with the head of a hammer poking out at one side.

'I have come to fixitup lock,' he announced. He propped his bicycle in the porch at the front door. 'Jews live here?'

'Yes. How did you know?'

'Mezuzah.' He pointed out something that looked like a small tin roll pinned to the door frame. It had been painted over and I hadn't noticed it.

'Strange thing for me,' he muttered. 'Never mind. Here in London is no broblem.' He took his pink-and-mauve cap off and stuck it in his pocket, along with the cycle clips. 'You Jewish?'

I shook my head. 'Yorkshire. It's almost a religion.'

He gave me a funny look. 'Where you have this broblem lock?'

I led him through to the kitchen. The back door was pine, painted to look like walnut, with two panels of blue engraved glass.

'For this one you have lost the key?'

'That's right.'

'Hm.' He stroked his beard. 'Only way to open must be with force. But usually,' he said, 'usually there exists more than one key for every door.' He turned the door handle up and down. 'You do not have another key?'

'It's not my house. I'm feeding the cats while the owner's in hospital.'

'Better not to break down the door if we can open it by some other way. You have looked for another key?'

I was beginning to feel annoyed. 'Where should I look?'

'How can I know this? I am a handyman, not a detecteef.' He scanned the room, then he started opening cupboard doors and pulling out drawers. In the pine cupboard at the side of the chimney breast was a jumble of crockery, pots, tins and jars. Mr Ali stood up on a chair and went through it all methodically. Inside a silver coffeepot, he found a bunch of keys.

'Try.' He passed them to me. One of the keys fitted the back door.

'So now your broblem is fixit,' he beamed.

'Yes, thank you very much, Mr Ali. But I'd still like you to change the lock, if you can, so the person who took the other key can't use it.'

He rubbed his chin. 'I understand. In that case I must buy new lock.'

He replaced his cycle clips and wobbled off down the road. As soon as he was out of sight, I took the opportunity to continue my investigation of the house. I was driven by the conviction that there must be a stash of documents or letters somewhere that would provide the key to Mrs Shapiro's story, and the identity of the mystery woman with beautiful eyes.

I went up to Mrs Shapiro's bedroom and sat on the bed. My eye fell on another drawer in the dressing table, a curved, concealed drawer without a handle, beneath the mirror. I eased it open. It was full of jumbled jewellery—necklaces, earrings, brooches. As I lifted out a blue bead necklace I saw a photograph at the bottom of the drawer. I pulled it out, but it was only a landscape in black and white of a barren hillside, planted with terraces of shrubby trees. In the valley below was a scattering of flat rooftops. I turned it over. On the back was written *Kefar Daniyyel* and two lines of verse. *I send my love across the sea/And pray that you will come to me. Naomi.*

Daniyyel. Had Naomi had a lover? There was a person-shaped shadow in the foreground—it must be the photographer. So who had taken the photo?

Then I heard the *tink-tink* of a bicycle bell outside and went downstairs. A moment later Mr Ali reappeared. 'Very sorry for delay. I was looking everywhere for right size of the lock. Old-style lock not easy to find.'

It took him less than ten minutes to lever out the old lock and fit the new one. I took one of the new keys and put it back on the key ring in the coffeepot; the other I put in my pocket with a smile. In my imagination, I pictured Mrs Goodney and Damian tiptoeing round to the back of the house at dusk, fiddling and fiddling with the old key, trying to get it to fit.

I settled up with Mr Ali—he asked for ten pounds, plus the cost of the lock, but I persuaded him to take twenty—and thanked him profusely.

MRS SHAPIRO WAS DISCHARGED the next day and returned home by taxi to an ecstatic welcome from Violetta, a languid welcome from Mussorgsky, and a dead pigeon from Wonder Boy. The other four were all there too, rubbing against her legs and purring like trail bikes.

I'd cleaned up the mess in the hall, put a fan heater on to take the chill off the place, brought some shopping in, and put a vase of flowers on the hall table. I'd also replaced the key in the back-door lock. Mrs Shapiro looked in good shape and excited to be home.

I made a pot of coffee and some sardines on toast—probably not a good idea I soon realised—and we sat at the table in the kitchen. The cats circled around, attracted by the smell of the sardines, and I wiped some bread in the oil and put it down for them. They gobbled it up in a flash.

'You heff been a very good friend for me, Georgine. Without you I'm sure they would heff put me away into the oldie-house.'

We clinked our cups together.

'Don't you have a family, Mrs Shapiro? Any sisters? Or brothers? Anyone who could look after you?'

'Why I need someone to look after me? All was OK before this accident.' She bit fiercely into a piece of toast. 'I think I will sue the council. They should be tekking care better of pavements. I am paying rets on this house sixty year. I think they must pay me a compensation.'

'Well, before we get onto that—'

'Yes, I will sue for the compensation. I will go to Citizen Advice this afternoon.'

'I don't think you should go out anywhere just yet, Mrs Shapiro. Wait till you're a bit better. And the lady is coming this afternoon, from the council. Remember? Your care package?'

'Peckedge schmeckedge. I don't want no peckedge. Definitely not.'

Mrs Shapiro's care package was a thin, dour Estonian woman called Elvina. Over the next week or so she did make some impact on the kitchen, and the house looked generally cleaner, but as if in response, the Phantom Pooer redoubled his efforts. Elvina shouted at the cats in Estonian and went for them with the broom. Mrs Shapiro called her a Nazi collaborator and sent her packing.

5

A couple of days before Christmas, I set off for Canaan House to deliver my Christmas present—a little basket of scented soap and body lotion that I thought Mrs Shapiro would like. As I turned the corner, I saw a massive four-by-four, black with darkened windows, tractor-sized tyres, and doubtless a global-warming-sized engine, parked at the bottom of the lane. It looked vaguely familiar, but I couldn't place it. I quickened my step. Violetta was in the porch, her fur fluffed out against the cold. I rang the bell.

There was a silence, then footsteps, then Mrs Shapiro appeared at the door. She was wearing full make-up and a rather stylish striped jersey, with brown slacks and a pair of snakeskin high-heeled shoes with peep toes. Her left wrist was still strapped, and in the other hand she was holding a cigarette.

'Georgine! My darlink!' She grabbed me in her arms, the cigarette waving dangerously close to my hair. 'Come in! Come in! I heff a visitor!'

I followed her through the chilly hall to the kitchen, where the fan heater was on at full blast. A man was sitting at the kitchen table. He was turned away from me, but I could see he was a big man, with close-cut blond hair. He rose to his feet and turned to greet me. He must have been over six feet tall, and heavily built, like a slightly-gone-to-seed rugby player—and then our eyes met. A flash of mutual recognition passed between us and in that moment we made an unspoken pact to forget that we had ever met before.

'Nicky,' said Mrs Shapiro, fluttering her eyelashes at him, 'this is my dear friend Georgine.' She turned to me. 'This is my new friend Mr Nicky Wolfe.' She obviously hadn't recognised him at all.

'Pleased to make your acquaintance.' He gripped my hand.

'Hello, Mr Wolfe.'

'Call me Nick, please.'

'Hello, Nick. You must be from the estate agents.'

'Got it in one. How did you guess?'

'Naomi'—I had to impress on him that we were close—'showed me your card. She said you'd made an offer for her house.'

'An offer I hope she won't be able to refuse.' He leered at her.

'Georgine, darlink. Will you heff a drink?' Mrs Shapiro's cheeks were flushed beneath the two little circles of rouge.

The kettle was hissing away on the gas stove, filling the kitchen with steam. 'A cup of tea would be nice.' Then I saw that on the table, amid all the clutter, was a sherry bottle and two glasses; his full, hers empty.

'I heff only *Kräutertee*. From herbs.'

'That's fine.'

'Why not heff a little aperitif?'

'It's a bit early for me, Naomi. It's not ten o'clock.'

'Is it so early?' She looked round with wide, scandalised eyes, and giggled. 'You are a very notty man, Mister Nick.'

He chuckled, a rapist's chuckle. 'Never too early for a bit of fun.'

I turned the gas off and poured the boiling water from the kettle over a tattered tea bag in a cracked cup. It tasted like not-very-clean pond water. Actually, I could have murdered a glass of sherry.

'Happy Christmas—I mean, festive season—Naomi.' I passed her my little package.

'Thenk you, darlink.' She held it up to her nose and breathed in, closing her eyes with pleasure. 'But I must find something for you!'

Her eyes wandered around the kitchen, resting for a moment on a reduced packet of biscuits on the counter and a half-eaten packaged cake.

'Oh, no. Please. I don't need anything. What will you be doing for . . . for the festive season, Naomi? Will you be all right on your own?'

'Darlink, I will not be on my own. First Christmas we will celebrate, then Hanukkah. Pick-and-mix nonstop festivity, isn't it, Wonder Boy?'

But Wonder Boy was nowhere to be seen.

'Well, I'd better be going. I'll leave you two ladies to your fun.' Nick Wolfe stood up again. 'An estate agent's work is never done.'

Mrs Shapiro saw him out to the front door and minced back into the kitchen with a radiant look on her face.

'Next time I will invite him, you also must come. You must put on a bit of mekkup, darlink. And better clothes. I heff a nice coat I will give you.'

'It's kind of you to think of me, Mrs Shapiro, but—'

'No need to be shy. When you see a good man, you must grebbit.'

THE NEXT MORNING—it was Christmas Eve—I was woken up at seven o'clock by the phone ringing. I guessed straight away who it was.

'Georgine? Come quick. Something is heppening to my votter.'

'Is it leaking? Is it a burst pipe?' I muttered groggily.

'No, nothing. I turn on the tap and nothing heppens.'

'Look,' I said, 'I'm not an expert on plumbing. But I know a handyman. Would you like me to give him a ring?'

There was a pause. 'How much he is charging?'

'It depends what the problem is. He's very nice. His name's Mr Ali.'

There was another silence.

'Is he a Peki?'

'Yes. No. I don't know. Look do you want me to ring him or not?'

'Is OK. I will ring my good friend Mister Nick.'

She put the phone down. I rang Mark Diabello but only got an answering machine. I left a message. A few minutes later Mrs Shapiro phoned back.

'Is not there. Only answering machine in the office. These people are sleeping all morning instead of working. What is the number of your Peki?'

When I went round to Totley Place at about ten o'clock I saw that Mr Ali's bicycle was already propped up in the porch. I found him sitting in the kitchen drinking a cup of the vile pond water. He stood up when I came into the room and greeted me warmly. 'Fixit broblem, Mrs George.'

'What was it?'

'Something peculiar,' said Mrs Shapiro. 'Someone has turned off the votter tap outside. Mr Ali has found it underneath the back door.'

'Water was all off,' nodded Mr Ali, beaming. 'Now back on.'

'But why?'

'How can I know this?' He shrugged. 'I am handyman, not pseecholog.'

'That *is* strange,' I said. Who would do a thing like that?

Mr Ali finished his tea and stood up to go. 'Any more broblem, you telephone to me, Mrs Naomi.' (He pronounced it Nah-oh-me.)

'But wait, I must pay you.' Mrs Shapiro fumbled in a brown bag.

'Is OK. You no pay this time. I did nothing. Only turn tap.' He slung his toolbag over his shoulder and I followed him into the hall. Suddenly he stopped by the framed photograph of the arched stone doorway and leaned forward for a closer look. 'Church of St George,' he said. 'In Lydda.'

'Lydda.' A place, not a person. 'You've been there?'

'One time, I went back. Looking for my family.' He said it so quietly it was almost a whisper. 'I was born nearby to that place.'

'In Greece?' I was surprised. He didn't look Greek.

He shook his head. 'Palestine.'

Before I could think what to say, he'd disappeared through the door. I heard the tink-tink of his bicycle bell as he pushed it down the path.

In the kitchen, Mrs Shapiro was beaming. 'Very good Peki,' she said.

I didn't tell her he was a Palestinian.

My mind was still whirling. Nothing was what it appeared to be. Lydda was a place not a person; Mr Ali was from Palestine not from Pakistan; and someone had turned Mrs Shapiro's water off. Why? The more I thought about it, the more I was sure it must have been Mr Wolfe.

The phone rang and Mrs Shapiro shuffled out to the hall. I could see her through the open door, gesticulating as she talked.

'Nicky! You got my messedge at your office . . . thenk you for ringing . . . Is OK. Votter problem is solved, but you can come . . . Ach, so. Never mind. Yes, and happy Christmas to you, Nicky.' When she put the phone down, she turned to me. 'Very nice man. Would be a perfect husband for you, Georgine. Rich. Hendsome. What you say?'

I laughed. 'Not quite my type.'

'Ach, nowadays you heff too much choices. In the wartime so many men were getting killed. If you seen one you liked, you must grebbit quick.'

I WENT BACK to Kippax for Christmas that afternoon, though I wasn't in a celebratory mood. It was my first Christmas away from Ben and Stella, and there was a cavity in my heart as if from a couple of extracted teeth. Dad had just had a hernia operation and it had knocked him back, but he was determined not to let it show. The Christmas tree lights winked on and off and the TV was on full blast. Mum was wandering around the kitchen wearing a pair of jokey reindeer antlers, wondering what she'd done with the bread sauce and insisting that she had to do Christmas with all the trimmings.

On Christmas Day, we had a traditional-style turkey-breast roast, and Dad made the gravy out of granules mixed with warm water. He put a pinny on specially for the occasion.

'I bet you never thought I'd turn into a new man, Jean,' he said to Mum.

'No, I din't,' said Mum. 'Which are the new bits?' She raised a glass of tepid Country Manor—her third. 'To absent friends! And death to Iraqis.' The antlers had slipped down her forehead and were pointing forward.

'Mum,' I whispered, 'Keir's liberating them, not killing them.'

But it was too late. Dad thumped his hands on the table. 'Got no business to be there at all.' His voice would be heard next door. 'If the government 'adn't shut t' pits, they wouldn't be so mad for oil now, would they?'

'Don't start now, Dennis.' Mum reached out and laid her hand on his arm. 'What d'you think of this turkey breast? It were on special.'

But Dad wasn't to be deflected. 'I'd sooner 'ave 'ad Tony Blair trussed up and roasted.'

Mum leaned over to me and whispered loudly, 'I don't know what it is, but Christmas always gets 'im gooin'.'

I saw Dad wince as he shifted in his chair, and a stab of his pain got to me, too. I thought of Rip, Stella and Ben, spending Christmas at Holtham. The food would be better, the gifts more extravagant, the decor tasteful. Stella would wallow in the jacuzzi and Ben would bring back a gizmo for his computer, which he would hide in his bedroom so as not to upset me.

'Never mind, duck,' said Mum, reading my face. 'There's nowt like being wi' yer own family at Christmas.'

We clinked our glasses together, Mum's filled with the last of the Country Manor, Dad's and mine with Old Peculiar. The mystery of the bread sauce was solved when Dad poured it over the Christmas pudding.

WHEN I ARRIVED in London on the day after Boxing Day, Wonder Boy was waiting for me at the front door. I let him into the kitchen and gave him a saucer of milk, even though I'd previously resolved not to encourage him. Well, it was Christmas. He thanked me by spraying against the dishwasher.

Ben wasn't going to be back for a few days. Even *Adhesives* was having a break—the next issue wasn't due out until late March. Nathan phoned me to wish me a happy New Year and share a joke with me.

'What beats glue when it comes to bonding?' he murmured.

'I don't know. Tell me.'

'Hybrid bond. Glue and a screw. Geddit?'

I imagined him with his white coat casually unbuttoned, chuckling glueily at the end of the phone.

That first night at home, I tossed and turned in my half-empty double bed and wished I was back in my old room in Kippax. Of course, I knew that if I'd been there I'd only be wishing I'd stayed here—it wasn't here, and it wasn't Kippax—the bug was inside me, gnawing away.

A FEW DAYS BEFORE New Year's Eve, the phone rang just before midnight, hauling me up out of a deep sleep. I fumbled for the receiver. 'Hello?'

'It's me. Ben.' The voice sounded muffled and squeaky. 'Will you be in tomorrow, Mum? I'm coming home. I forgot my key.'

His voice sounded unfamiliar—slightly croaky.

'Of course. But I thought you were staying until after New Year.'

'I was. But I'm coming back tomorrow. The train gets in at ten past three.' There was just the hint of a tremor as he spoke.

'Do you want me to meet you at Paddington?'

'No, it's OK. I'll get the bus.'

'But why—?'

'I'll tell you when I see you.'

IN FACT IT WAS half past four by the time Ben got back the next day. I found myself glancing at the clock, waiting with anxious eagerness. Then the doorbell rang and there he was, my boy, standing on the doorstep with his bulging backpack and a carrier bag in each hand. My heart leaped with joy.

'Hi, Mum.'

'Hi, Ben.'

He dumped his bags down in the hall and stood there, grinning stiffly with his arms by his sides, while I hugged him. He looked as if he'd sprouted up an inch or two in the last week, and there was a shadow of a moustache on his upper lip. His hair had grown, too, and he had it tied up in a little red kerchief behind his ears, pirate-style.

'How was your Christmas?' I asked.

'Fine.'

There was something scarily grown-up about the way that Ben had handled the separation between me and Rip. He was fiercely loyal to both of us, which filled me with admiration and awe. But I was burning with spiteful, not-grown-up curiosity to find out what had happened at Holtham.

'So what made you come back early?' I said it very casually.

'Oh, I just got fed up.'

I might have believed him, but I remembered the phone call, his trembling voice at two minutes to midnight. That was more than just fed up.

'And Stella? Was she there?'

'Yeah. But then she left. I think she went to stay with her boyfriend.'

I'd sent a present for her, a handmade silk shawl in different shades of rose—she would look lovely in it. I was hoping she'd ring, but all I'd got was a text message. *Thanx mum great prezzy happy xmas c u soon xxx*.

ALTHOUGH I'D LEFT him a message before Christmas, it wasn't until the morning of New Year's Eve that Mark Diabello phoned me back. I remembered I'd been trying to get to the bottom of Mrs Shapiro's turned-off water and I was sure that either he or Nick Wolfe was responsible.

'Mrs Sinclair. What can I help you with? Did you see your auntie over Christmas?'

OK, I hadn't been quite truthful either.

'Look, Mr Diabello, I just want to know what's going on. You offer Mrs Shapiro half a million for her house. Then you up it to a million, just like that. Then your partner offers her two million—'

'With a unique property like this, Mrs Sinclair, it's difficult to arrive at an accurate valuation, because there's nothing out there on the market to compare it with. At the end of the day, the market value is—how can I put it?—whatever the highest bidder will pay. That's why I suggest we float it on the market and see what offers come in. Does that make sense?'

Actually, it sounded pretty plausible.

'Then he goes round during the night and turns the stopcock off.'

There was a moment's hesitation. 'Nick did that?'

'I'm sure it was him. He'd been round there the same morning, plying Mrs Shapiro with sherry.'

A pause. Then Mark Diabello said, 'I don't think you should jump to any conclusions, Mrs Sinclair. Do you mind if I call you Georgina?'

Did I mind? Didn't I mind? I couldn't hear myself think above the chatter of hormones.

'I'll have a word with him if you like,' he continued. 'Sometimes Nick . . . he does get a bit carried away. He falls for a property and he forgets that it belongs to someone else.' His voice changed. 'You know, this may surprise you, Georgina, but being an estate agent is a labour of love. You go into this game because you're passionate about property. Each place is a dream come true for someone. Our job is to match the dream to the property.' There was a sigh on the other end of the phone. 'Once in a while something really special comes along, something you lose your heart to. Like Canaan House.'

I shushed my boy-racer hormones—he was an estate agent, and probably a crook. 'It's not a property. It's a home. It's not for sale,' I snapped.

It wasn't until he'd put the phone down that I realised the disjuncture in what the two of them had been saying. Mark Diabello had been talking about selling the house at its market value, whatever that was. But Nick Wolfe had wanted to buy it.

'What are you doing for New Year's Eve, Mum?' Ben came and sat down on the arm of my chair, interrupting my thoughts.

'I don't know—I hadn't thought about it. It's tonight, isn't it? I haven't made any plans, Ben. We could cook something special, crack a bottle of wine, watch the celebrations on TV. What would you like to do?'

He shuffled about on the arm of the chair. 'I was wondering about going out with some mates from school . . .'

'Yes, do that. I'll'—I thought fast—'I'll go and see Mrs Shapiro.'

'. . . but I'll stop in if you want. If you're going to be on your own.'

'No, no. Go for it. That's great.' I didn't want him to guess that my heart was crowing. He had friends—he was part of a crowd—he wouldn't spend New Year's Eve sitting at home in front of the TV with his mum.

'Mrs Shapiro and me—we'll down a bottle of sherry and sing raucous songs. It'll be a ball.'

Actually, I was thinking, I'd be happy to have a break from Mrs Shapiro and her smelly entourage, and spend the evening in on my own. Then at about six o'clock the phone rang. It was Penny from *Adhesives*.

'Hiya, Georgie—have you got any plans for tonight?' she boomed. 'I'm having a bit of a bash round at my place. Some of the work gang'll be there. Just bring a bottle and your dancing shoes.' She told me the address, just off Seven Sisters Road. I wondered briefly what to wear, then I remembered the green silk dress. I had intended to get it dry-cleaned, but what the hell.

I COULD HEAR the music as I turned the corner into the street. Penny greeted me at the door with a hug and took the bottle of Rioja out of my hand. She was petite, blonde and curvaceous, in her mid-forties, I would guess, wearing a short black skirt covered with swirls of sequins and a low-cut red top.

'Thanks for inviting me, Penny. It's great to meet you at last.'

I kissed her on each round warm cheek, slipped my coat off and followed her through into a room where the lights were turned off and a PA in the corner was pumping out music at high volume. The room was packed with people all swaying and shuffling and the air was thick with smoke.

'They're all in there.' Penny was swaying her hips as she talked. 'Nathan's brought his dad.' She gave me a little shove and I lurched forwards. I hadn't really been feeling in a party mood, but suddenly the atmosphere caught me, and shuffling in time to the beat I worked my way through the press of bodies.

'This is Sheila.' Penny introduced me to a girl of about Stella's age—wearing the minimum amount of material that you could call a dress—and smooching with a young black guy, about six feet tall, slim and gorgeous. Penny pushed past them and led me deeper into the room.

'Here, meet Paul. Paul, this is Georgie. You know, from *Adhesives*.'

Paul was slightly built and had a tattoo on his forearm. He nodded in my direction and carried on dancing, mesmerised by the tiny dark girl spinning her torso in front of him. When I turned round again Sheila had disappeared and I saw the slim, gorgeous guy thrusting towards me. I felt my knees droop and my pelvis liquefy and found my hips doing unfamiliar gyrations.

'Hi, beauty, I'm Penny's cousin,' he shouted above the boom of the music. 'Darryl Samson. I'm a doctor.'

Having a doctor like that would be enough to keep anybody in bed, I thought. 'I'm surprised any of your patients bother to get better.'

His laugh was deep and juicy.

'I'm Georgie. I'm a . . . writer.'

'No kiddin'!' I could feel his hips pressing close against me.

Then Penny appeared at my side and pulled me away. 'Come on—you need a drink.' She threw Darryl a warning look and he spread his palms with an apologetic smile. 'Don't believe anything that one tells you. He told Lucy he was a gynaecologist and she believed him.'

I stood in the drinks room clutching my glass of red wine and feeling mildly annoyed with Penny, when suddenly she dived into the crowd and pulled someone else towards me. 'Georgie, here's someone you gotta meet.'

I stared. This was incredible. Horn-rimmed glasses. Deep blue eyes. Dark hair swept back from brainy forehead. Yes, definitely hunkily intelligent—all he needed was a white coat. OK, he was a bit short—but was I so shallow that I couldn't fancy a man half an inch shorter than me? I was pondering on this when the small intelligent hunk stretched out his hand.

'Hi. I'm Nathan.'

'I'm Georgie.' I felt myself blush. 'Good to meet you at last.' I noticed he was wearing a midnight-blue silk shirt that matched his eyes, and that the dark designer stubble that shadowed his chin and jaw was attractively flecked with silver.

'Awesome dress.'

'Thank you. It came from—'

'I've been looking forward to meeting you, Georgia.' That low, confiding voice, with maybe just a touch of the mid-Atlantic about the vowels.

'Me, too.'

Then an elderly man I hadn't noticed before, thin and wiry, with a bushy white beard and a glass of red wine in his hand, moved in beside me.

'Aren't you going to introduce me to your young lady, Nathan?'

I thought I saw a flash of annoyance in Nathan's eyes, but he just said, 'Tati, this is my colleague Georgia. Georgia, meet my father.'

'Georgia! Aha! State or republic?'

'Er . . .'

I was saved by the chimes of Big Ben. Putting his glass aside, the old man crossed his hands, took my left hand in his right one and reached the other hand out to Nathan. Then he started to sing: 'Should auld acquaintance be forgot . . .' his voice reverberating deep and mellow. What happened next was a bit like polymerisation. Individual people-molecules milling about in the room grabbed hands and formed a long covalent chain. Soon we were all holding crossed hands and swaying, everybody kissing everybody. I even got a quick snog with Darryl. That was nice. Then the old man pushed in and covered my face with his bristles. I struggled, but his grip was tight. Nathan came to my rescue.

'Happy New Year, Georgia,' he murmured. Our lips met and the room started to spin. But the old man squeezed in between us, coming in for another round, so I pulled myself away, grabbed my coat from a pile in the other room, and was out in the street in a flash.

I didn't put the lights on when I got home. I flung off my coat and shoes, lay down on the bed, and almost immediately fell asleep. I woke up two hours later feeling cold. I had a wash, cleaned my teeth, put my nightie on, and went back to bed. I tried to call Ben, but his mobile was switched off.

Just after dawn I woke again and wandered across the landing to see whether he was back. He wasn't in his bed. A red light was flashing on his computer—it was the screen saver whizzing about. I went to shut it down, and as I touched the mouse, the screen he'd been looking at came up.

It was the same red-on-black text I'd seen before. This time, the single word flashing in red on black in a circle of dancing flames was ANTICHRIST. What was this rubbish he was looking at? I hit the 'back' button, and found myself in a chat forum. There were only two names: Benbo and Spikey.

Spikey: hey benbo happy newyear this is the year of antichrists rein watchout
Benbo: who do you think is the antichrist putin or bush?
Spikey: putin is the king of the north who will join forces with the king of the south at the battle of armagedon daniel 11:40
Benbo: where is armagedon?
Spikey: its in the north of isreal
Benbo: a long way from highbury who is the king of the south?
Spikey: gadafi or sadam hassain or osama binladin take your pick
Benbo: i read somewhere that prince charles is the anitchrist because of the duchy of cornwall bar codes
Spikey: 666 is the mark of the beast check this link Antichrist

Benbo I supposed was Ben. But who was Spikey?

I clicked on the link, which took me to the web page of someone who called himself Isaiah. He was a middle-aged man with a crew cut, drooping eyelids and a chunky wooden cross on a chain round his neck. Beneath the picture was a banner heading:

WHO IS THE ANTICHRIST?

Many Christians used to believe that Communism was the Antichrist, and Armageddon would be nuclear war between Russia and America. However, it seems that now the forces of Islam and Christianity are lining up for a definative battle before the third Temple is rebuilt in Jerusalem and Christ comes back to rule the earth in all His glory.

Infact all the signs are that Antichrist, Satan the great Deceiver, is already stalking the earth. 'Take heed that no one deceives you. For many will come in My name, saying, "I am the Christ," and will deceive many.' (Matthew 24: 4–5)

In Revelation the Mark of the Beast is revealed as 666.

I rubbed my eyes. It was too early in the morning for this sort of stuff. But I was curious about how Ben spent his hours cloistered up here. There was a list of names, each underlined with a link and marked with a little flaming crest. I opened the last link:

> Prince Charles of Wales
>
> This English aristocrat is a surprise candidate—but look at the evidance. His full official name both in English and Hebrew adds up to 666 . . . and his heraldic symbols are based on the beasts of Daniel and Revelution. Also, he really is a prince, as predicted in Daniel 9. Rome is obviously the new Babylon, and the evil European Union is the new Holy Roman Empire. It's constitution is under discussion, and Prince Charles could infact one day be it's ruler . . .

Up to this point I'd been reading with a kind of fascinated horror, but the bit about Prince Charles made me laugh out loud. And how could anyone take seriously anything spelled definative, infact, evidance? I must definately (ha-ha) pull Ben's leg about this.

Smiling to myself, I went downstairs and put the kettle on. When I took my coffee through to the front room, I found Ben there, asleep on the sofa.

He stirred and opened his eyes. 'Happy New Year, Mum.'

'Happy New Year, Ben.'

Before I could ask him about the web pages, he'd gone to sleep again.

The light was flashing on my answering machine. *Georgia. It's Nathan. Tati says sorry about last night. He gets a bit carried away when he's had a drink. Hope you got home all right. Happy New Year.*

He must have phoned really early. That was it, then: Christmas and New Year over. I'd survived.

6

About three weeks into the new year I came downstairs very early in the morning to make myself a cup of tea after a restless sleep. It was cold, the central heating hadn't come on yet. I shivered as I poured the tea, and was about to go back to bed when the phone rang. It was Mrs Shapiro.

'Georgine—please come quick. There is a burglary. Door is brokken.'

Feeling mildly irritated, I got dressed, put on my coat and went round straight away. It had started to snow—miserable powdery stuff flaking down out of the sky like frozen dandruff. Mrs Shapiro answered the door wearing her pink dressing gown and Lion King slippers, her hair dishevelled. She led me through to the kitchen. One of the blue glass panels on the back door had been smashed and an icy draught was whistling through. The key on the inside had been stolen. Nothing else seemed to be missing.

'Maybe it was your Peki. Maybe he is a teef.'

'Why would it be him?' I couldn't keep the irritation out of my voice. 'He didn't even charge you for coming out last time. He didn't steal anything, did he? It could be anybody. A burglar or anybody.' I saw the look of terror flit across her face and wished I'd held my tongue. I hadn't told her that Mr Ali had already changed the lock—I hadn't wanted to alarm her.

'But why they want to frighten me? Why they don't come into the house? Why they just tek the key?' She shuffled across to put the kettle on.

'It might be someone who's planning to come back. You'd better get the glass mended and the lock changed today. You should call Mr Ali. Unless you know of anybody better.'

She started poking around in her cupboards looking for the pond-water tea. 'He is a clever-Knödel, this Peki,' she muttered. Then she looked up at me and said, 'But I think I will ask Mr Wolfe. My Nicky.' She gave me a sly little grin as if to say, I may be eighty-one but I can still wind you up.

She succeeded. 'That's fine. Just the job. You and your Mr Wolfe can sort it out.' I made for the door. I'd had enough of her constant demands and her petty prejudices. Let her sort herself out, I thought.

Once home, I heated the tea up in the microwave and climbed into my bed fully clothed. Outside the window, a feeble dawn was just breaking. I pulled down the black knickers over my eyes to keep the light out, but I was too wound up to drift off. For some reason I remembered the website Ben had been looking at—Antichrist, the deceiver, stalking the earth.

Then the phone rang.

'Don't be engry mit me, Georgine. I am only jokking. I am an old woman. Please, telephone to Mr Ali. I heff lost the number.'

'OK, OK.'

A few hours later she phoned again to tell me that Mr Ali had been and boarded up the back door and changed the lock. He had put a new mortise lock on the front, in addition to the Yale, and had fitted bolts to both doors.

'You will be as safe as prison,' he'd said.

'How much did he charge you?' I asked.

'I give him ten pound. Plus he mek me pay full price for locks and bolts.'

She said it with a grumble in her voice, as though she felt she'd been overcharged.

'You should be grateful,' I said, though she clearly wasn't. 'Especially on a Sunday.'

'You are still engry mit me, Georgine, isn't it? Don't be engry. You are the only friend I heff.'

'No. I'm not angry, Mrs Shapiro.'

And it's true, I wasn't angry with her any more. But I had other things on my mind. Rip had phoned around lunchtime to say he was coming to pick Ben up after work tomorrow. I needed time to get myself into the right frame of mind to face him on the doorstep.

THE DOORBELL RANG earlier than I'd expected on Monday afternoon. I went to answer it with my ready-for-anything smile fixed on my face. But it wasn't Rip on the doorstep, it was Mark Diabello. His black Jaguar was parked by the gate and he was smiling a ready-for-anything smile, too.

'Hello, Mrs Sinclair. Georgina.' The deep creases in his rugged cheeks crinkled craggily. 'I hope you don't mind my dropping round like this. I've been following up on some of the concerns you raised in our last chat and I wanted to bring you up to date.'

Maybe if I hadn't been expecting Rip to appear I wouldn't have asked him to come in. But it seemed too good an opportunity to miss.

'That's kind of you, Mr Diabello. Can I offer you a coffee?'

'Call me Mark, please.'

He followed me inside, looking around him as I led him through to the sitting room. I positioned him on the sofa by the window, where he could be seen from the road, then went downstairs to the kitchen, where I put the kettle on and spooned coffee into the cafetière. When the water had boiled, I poured it into the pot, put everything onto a tray and carried it upstairs.

'Milk? Sugar?'

'Black with four sugars.'

I laughed and handed him a cup. 'It'll taste like black treacle.'

'Mm. That's how I like it.'

Then a car horn beeped—I recognised the distinctive note of Rip's Saab.

'Please excuse me.' I went out into the hall and called, 'Ben! Rip's here!'

A moment later Ben appeared, with his big backpack over his shoulder. I went out to the car with him, my ready-for-anything smile fixed in position again. But Rip just pulled the inside lever to open the boot and sat in his Saab, waiting for Ben to put his backpack in. He didn't even wind the window down. I couldn't tell whether he'd noticed the black Jag or the man sitting in the window. I wanted to kick in the Saab's panels, but Ben was waving goodbye so I blew him a kiss and went back inside.

My face must have been livid when I returned to the sitting room, for Mr Diabello put down his cup and said, 'All going to plan?'

'Not exactly.'

His left eyebrow lifted a fraction and his cheeks tightened, and I realised from that look that he had understood my situation. 'Want to talk about it?' His voice oozed sympathy. 'I can recommend a good solicitor.'

'No. No, it's not at that stage yet.' As I said the words I realised that probably it was at that stage, and probably I did need legal advice. 'Just tell me what you came to tell me.'

'Yes—you were concerned that my partner, Nick Wolfe, might be behaving . . . improperly. I've had words with Nick. He admits he's fallen for the house, and has maybe been a bit too . . . er . . . enthusiastic in approaching Mrs Shapiro. But he denies absolutely having done anything improper.'

'But he admits to plying her with sherry, hoping she'd sign a bit of paper that he just happened to have in his briefcase?' However annoyed I got with Mrs Shapiro I wasn't going to let these two shysters take her to the cleaners.

'I think the sherry was meant as a goodwill gesture. A gift. He didn't mean her to open it up and start drinking it straight away.'

'Oh, come off it! Anyway, why would he bring her a gift?'

'A token of appreciation for a valued client.'

'But she's not a client. He just turned up at her hospital bedside.'

'From what Nick says, she was a willing party. Positively eager. He also told me, by the way, that she's not your aunt.' He looked up at me from lowered eyes, a smile playing around his lips. 'Which does raise the issue of what *your* interest is in the property.'

'I haven't any interest. I just don't want to see an old lady being ripped off. Someone must have told him about the house.' Then I realised. '*You* must have told him.'

Our eyes met. I noticed for the first time that his were not brown, as I'd previously thought, but dark sea-green, with sparks of gold and obsidian.

'I did mention our conversation to him. I didn't expect him to get quite so excited about it. He's a very passionate man, you know.'

'Passionate'—there was something in the way he'd lingered over the word. 'He thought Mrs Shapiro deserved a more focused view of his services?'

'Exactly so.'

'Like me?'

'That's up to you, Georgina.'

'Thank you. It's been nice talking to you.' I stood up abruptly. He stood up, too, brushing past me as he made his way towards the door.

'The pleasure's all mine,' he said.

After he'd gone, I sat down on the sofa and breathed deeply. I knew, in my sensible core, that the last thing I needed was a man like Mark Diabello in my life—a treacle-voiced estate agent with black and gold in his eyes. But I was unhappy and furious and needy. And it was so long since someone had looked at me with desire. And a little voice in the back of my head was whispering—why not?

AS I WALKED past the Islington window of Wolfe & Diabello on my way to the bus-stop the next day, it was still snowing that same powdery snow. I glanced in and saw Nick Wolfe bending over the desk of a young blonde woman who could have been a clone of Suzi Brentwood. On impulse, I pushed the door and went in. They both looked up as the bell pinged.

'Mr Wolfe. I'm glad you're in. Have you a minute?'

He led me into an office at the back and pulled out two chairs. 'What can I do you for, Georgette?' He smiled wolfishly.

I explained my concern about the mains water tap and the back-door keys, keeping my voice neutral and avoiding any hint of accusation.

'You spoke to my colleague Mark Diabello about this, didn't you?' He glanced pointedly at his watch. I ignored the hint.

'What I can't understand is what you and Mr Diabello are up to.' I was smiling sweetly. 'He wants to sell it for half a million. Then he puts it up to a million. Then you go into the hospital with an offer of two million.' I spoke fast, conscious that his eyes were fixed on me in a not-very-friendly way. 'You must admit, it's a bit . . . worrying.'

'Look, Mrs . . . Georgette. I don't really know what it's got to do with you. It's up to Mrs Shapiro what she does with her house, isn't it? I understand she's not even related to you.' He glanced at his watch again. 'I made Mrs Shapiro a very fair offer. And let's get one thing straight.' There was a bullying note in his voice. 'Just because it's floated on the market doesn't mean it reaches its market price. Nor that the person who makes the initial purchase is the ultimate buyer, if you see what I mean.'

'You mean Mark Diabello buys it for half a million and sells it on to somebody else for two million, trousering the difference?'

'I did not say that, Georgette.' He emphasised every syllable forcefully. 'That is not what I said.' He looked at his watch again, and then stood up. 'If you'll excuse me, I have business to attend to.'

I stood on the pavement reeling, then noticed that Hendricks & Wilson was still open. Well, what did I have to lose?

Although the two shopfronts looked similar from the outside, whereas Wolfe & Diabello had been all glass and chrome with laminate flooring, in the style of a city bistro, Hendricks & Wilson had red carpet and leather armchairs in the style of a gentlemen's club. A thin youth with spiky gelled hair was sitting at a computer. He looked up and smiled as I came in.

'I'm looking for Damian,' I said.

'That's me.' He beamed. 'How can I help?'

I hadn't really prepared what I was going to say, so I tried the familiar line about my auntie selling a house in Totley Place. I watched his face carefully, but there was no sign of recognition. It seemed that whatever Mrs Goodney had been planning, she hadn't put it into action.

'I think you need to speak to one of the partners about something like that. Would you like me to make an appointment?'

I hesitated. Did I really need any more estate agents in my life?

'Couldn't you give me just a rough idea?'

'Hm.' He chewed a fingernail. 'Tell you what—I'll drive past on my way home tonight and take a look.'

'Thanks. I'll give you a ring tomorrow. Thanks, Damian.'

'How did you know . . .?'

I quickly made for the door.

WHEN I PHONED Damian the next morning, I was even more convinced that he wasn't involved in the dirty tricks. He wouldn't give me a valuation, but he said, 'A big site like that in the heart of Highbury—it has development potential. You're talking millions. You'll have to speak to Mr Wilson.'

'I don't think my auntie would want it to be developed. But thank you for your help.' I hung up quickly before he could ask me any questions.

If Damian wasn't involved, that meant it must be Wolfe & Diabello. Rage was burning in my head. I tried to calm myself down with Ms Baddiel's breathing exercises, then phoned their office. Neither of the partners was there, so I left a message with Suzi Brentwood.

'Please can you get one of them to ring me back? . . . No, I can't say what it's about. Just tell them I know what's going on. Tell them they're a couple of sleazy double-crossing crooks.'

It was Mark Diabello who phoned me back, within ten minutes.

'I got your message, Georgina. Strong language. What did we do to upset you?'

'It's not what you did, it's what I did. I got another valuation.'

'So you should, Georgina. And?'

'Somebody from Hendricks's said it was a development site with potential. He said it could be worth several millions.'

'The office junior? They always make wild guesses. And you've forgotten that I said I'd match any genuine valuation.'

Had he said that? It's true, I'd forgotten.

'But the other one—your sidekick—he offered her two million.'

'I can't speak for my partner. But *I* said I'd match their valuation. I think you owe me an apology, Georgina.'

'I owe *you* an apology?'

I put the phone down. I was shaking. Yes, maybe I'd been a bit hasty. Even a bit rude. And it's true, Damian did seem to be the office junior. But what he'd said rang true. Actually, what all of them said rang true. That was the trouble. How was I to know who to believe?

'STRESS FRACTURES can occur in adhesive bonds when the materials have different coefficients of thermal expansion.'

I'd been staring at the sentence on my monitor for at least half an hour, thinking maybe that's what had gone wrong between Rip and me. He's slow to get angry, but when he does, he stays hot much longer. I flare up quickly but quickly cool down again. My mind tripped back to that morning's conversation with Mark Diabello—yes, maybe I had flared up too quickly then. What had he said? I couldn't remember. The glue had got to my brain.

It was time to break for lunch. I wandered over to investigate the fridge. In the door was an opened bottle of Rioja. Should I? Shouldn't I?

I was trying to decide when the doorbell rang. Mark Diabello was standing on the doorstep with a bottle of champagne in his hand. It wasn't just any old supermarket champagne, either, it was Bollinger. Maybe it was just a trick of the light, but I could swear his eyes were smouldering.

'A token of appreciation for a valued client,' he murmured.

'I'm not your client.'

'But you could be.'

'I don't think so. But come in.'

I went and fetched two glasses from the kitchen. We clinked.

'Have you come to offer me a more focused view of your services?'

'Would you like that?'

I didn't say yes. But I didn't say no.

We ended up in my bedroom. He led the way. Of course, he was an estate agent, he knew where to go. It all happened astonishingly fast, with the well-oiled precision of a top-of-the-range Jaguar. He gave me just the right amount of champagne, kissed me in just the right way and his hands found their way unerringly to the right places. There was no fumbling with clothes—they just fell away. If I'd had time to think, I might have thought, What the hell am I doing? But I didn't think about anything. My brain was full of bubbles. My skin tingled like electricity. My body purred in his hands. There was something reassuringly impersonal about it all and, actually, it was fantastic. He was the only man apart from Rip I'd slept with in twenty years. It was as though I'd slipped out of my familiar skin and become a different person.

Afterwards we lay together watching the shadows lengthen in the garden and he pulled me into his arms and stroked my hair. He left before Ben got back from school. I thought I might feel used, or disgusted with myself, but I guess I realised that having sex with someone else was part of a sticky repair process I had to go through. 'You get better bonding with glue and a screw,' I think Nathan had once said. Maybe there's something in that.

About half an hour later, I heard the door-click of Ben letting himself in. I pulled my clothes on and went down to greet him in the kitchen.

'You OK, Mum?' He looked at me intently. 'You seem sort of . . . weird.'

'Weird in what way?'

'Sort of hyper. Hyper-manic.'

'Really? It must be all the coffee I've been drinking. I'm having a sticky patch with *Adhesives*. Ha-ha! How about you? How's life in Islington?'

'It's OK. Dad's a bit hyper too.' He poured milk over some Choco-Puffs and sat down with his spoon. 'He says he's starting a new project?'

There was that rising inflection in his speech again. I found it troubling.

'Not the Progress Project?'

'He says it's progressing to a higher level?'

'Yes, he's always had high aspirations.'

A sarcastic note must have crept into my voice. Ben's look warned me that I was in danger of transgressing the subtle boundaries he'd drawn up between his two worlds.

That night, after Ben had gone to bed, I poured myself a glass of wine and reached for my exercise book.

Spurned by her errant husband, heartbroken Gina at last found ~~love~~ ~~fulfilment~~ consolation in the arms of an itinerant mandolin player with ~~obsidian cerulean sapphire amethyst jade~~ lapis lazuli eyes. He brought her beautiful gifts—hand-embroidered Spanish ~~underwear~~ ~~garters~~ mantillas.

As I closed up my exercise book an hour later, I realised that the wine bottle was empty, and I'd opened another one. This was no good. Maybe Ben was right—I should go easy on the Rioja.

Mark Diabello came back again the following Wednesday, this time without the champagne, but with a bunch of flowers—red roses. I was waiting for him, wearing a rather revealing top, which I'd bought the day before, and some lacy panties under a sleek clinging skirt, which I'd also bought the day before. I caught sight of myself in the hall mirror, my flushed cheeks and brilliant eyes, and didn't recognise myself. I could feel myself starting to melt as he kissed me. It took us about five minutes to get to the bedroom.

It was not me, Georgie Sinclair, no, it was someone sexy and shameless, someone whose body melted like warm sugar in the arms of a dark handsome stranger who appeared on her doorstep and made love to her.

Afterwards I couldn't help it, I started to cry. Mark Diabello dabbed my eyes with his hanky and kissed me lingeringly on my throat and neck.

'You're a beautiful woman, Georgina. Has anyone ever told you that?'

I wanted to believe him. I almost believed him; but a cool whisper in my head reminded me that he probably slept with dozens of women and said that to all of them. Then something from another age stirred in my mind, Rip's voice, husky against my cheek: '*If ever any beauty I did see, which I desired and got, 'twas but a dream of thee.*' How long ago was that?

'You'd better go now. It's nearly four o'clock.'

'What happens at four o'clock? D'you turn into a pumpkin?'

'No, I turn into a mother.'

Just after four, the key turned in the latch and I did turn into a mother.

'Hi, Mum.' Ben flung his bag down. He looked tense and pale.

'Everything OK?'

'Fine. Cool.' He wasn't looking at me.

'Do you want a sandwich? Some Choco-Puffs?'

'Nah. I'll just have water.'

He drank resting both elbows on the table, his brown curls falling across his eyes. 'I've been having these weird feelings.'

I could feel my pulse starting to pound, but I kept my voice soft and easy and sat down opposite him. 'What feelings, Ben?'

'Sort of . . . liminal.'

'Liminal?' I had no idea what he was talking about. I waited, listening.

'Like we're living in liminal times. You can see it in the light, Mum—look—it's like it's seeping in from the edges of another world.'

He pointed at the window. I looked round. Between the houses, a low shaft of pinky sunlight was lighting up a bank of purple cumulus from below. The buildings and leafless trees were all backlit, cast in shadow, despite the vivid light. I could see what he meant—it did look unearthly.

'It's winter, Ben. The sun's always low in the sky at this time of year. Further north, in Scandinavia, they don't have any daytime at all.'

He looked up with a flicker of a smile. 'You're so literal-minded, Mum.'

The clouds rearranged themselves and the shaft of light disappeared, but still there was a fiery glow on the underbelly of the sky.

'I keep having these feelings, like the world's going to end soon.' He paused, gulping water. 'Like we're coming to the end of time?'

'Ben, you should have said—'

'So I Googled "End of Time". That's when I realised it wasn't just me?'

That's what they do, his generation, I thought. They don't talk to their parents or friends like we did—they look on the Internet.

'There's like all these signs—predictions in the Bible about the end of time? Wars, earthquakes, floods, plagues and that—it's all starting to come true?' His voice was strained and crackly.

'But you don't believe all that stuff about prophecies, do you, Ben?'

'No, but . . . well, yes, I just think, like, if that many people believe it . . . Floods and earthquakes—there's one every year. And AIDS, SARS, avian flu—all these new diseases. It's all started coming true. Like in the Bible, it's predicted the Jews'll return to Israel, and they did, in 1948. After the Holocaust and that? That was the beginning of all the wars in the Middle East. The invasion of Lebanon. You can read it for yourself, Mum—it's all there in the Bible. And it's not just Jews and Christians? A lot of Muslims think their great prophet is coming? Like they call him the Last Imam?' The rising inflection in his voice seemed to challenge me to disagree.

How could I explain without sounding pompous that just because millions of people believe something, it doesn't make it true. 'Why didn't you tell me, Ben, that you were having these feelings? Or Rip?'

'I thought you'd think it was mad? You wouldn't listen? You and Dad—you never listen to anybody.'

He didn't say it as an accusation, but it stung like one. We were so preoccupied with our own lives and problems that we'd failed to hear our own son's cry for help. 'I'm sorry, Ben. D'you want to talk about it now?'

'Nah, it's all right, Mum.' He grinned sheepishly, swallowing the rest of his water. 'I feel all right now. I think I'll have some Choco-Puffs.'

After he'd gone upstairs, I sat in the kitchen with a glass of wine wondering where we'd gone wrong. We'd brought him up to respect difference—diversity. At his primary school in Leeds, Rip and I, like good middle-class parents, had cheered enthusiastically as the children celebrated Christmas and Eid and Diwali. All belief was equally valid. Christianity, Islam, Hinduism, Judaism, astrology, astronomy, relativity, evolution, creationism, socialism, monetarism, global warming, damage to the ozone layer, crystal healing, Darwin, Hawking, Dawkins, Nostradamus, Mystic Meg, they were all out there vying with each other in the marketplace of ideas. How was anyone to know which was true and which wasn't?

AFTER BREAKFAST the next morning, when Ben had left for school, I sat down and tried to concentrate on an article for *Adhesives*. 'The attraction between surfaces in adhesive bonding.' There was something quite romantic, I was thinking, about the thought of gluey time-enduring forces; bonds so strong that they could outlive the materials themselves. Mmm. My mind started to drift. It was no good. *Adhesives* would have to wait.

I phoned Mrs Shapiro, to see whether she needed anything from the shops. There was no reply, so I pulled on my wellies and my coat and went out anyway. It had snowed overnight and now the sun was low but brilliant, dusting every white surface with a sparkle of gold, but the snow had already started to melt. Wonder Boy followed me down the road.

When I got to Canaan House, I saw that the snow had pulled an end of the gutter down, and melting snow was dripping down the porch. Maybe I would have to get Mr Ali in again. There were footprints in the snow leading away from the house. I knocked on the door but I wasn't surprised that there was no reply. She must have gone out. I went off to do my shopping.

Later in the afternoon I phoned Mrs Shapiro again. Still no reply. This was odd. I began to get worried. Then Ben came back from school and I got on with cooking supper. I'll ring later, I thought. At about seven o'clock, the phone rang. It was an old woman's voice, hoarse and throaty.

'She's in 'ere.'

'Sorry?'

'Yer pal. She's in 'ere. But she ent got 'er dressin' gahn wivver.'

'I'm sorry, I think you've got the wrong number.'

'Nah, I ent. She give it me. You're 'er what comes to 'ospital, int yer? That lady wivve pink dressin' gahn. She says she wants 'er dressin' gahn agin. And 'er slippers.'

I realised in a flash that it must be the bonker lady.

'Oh, thank you for contacting me. I'll—'

'An' she says can yer bring some ciggies wiv yer when yer come.'

The telephone beeped a few times then went dead. She must have been calling from the hospital payphone. I glanced at the clock. There was maybe half an hour of visiting time left. I'd given back the key to her house, so I bundled together my own slippers, a nightdress and Stella's dressing gown.

'I'll see you in a bit, Ben,' I called upstairs as I set off for the bus. The newsagent by the bus-stop was still open and I bought some cigarettes.

When I arrived at the hospital, the bonker lady was in the foyer. I handed her the cigarettes and she pocketed them swiftly. 'Fanks, sweet'eart. She's in Eyesores.'

It took me a while to track Mrs Shapiro down to Isis Ward. I could see at once that she was in a bad way. Her cheek was bruised, one eye almost closed, and her head was bandaged. She reached out and gripped my arm.

'Georgine. Thenk Gott you come.' Her voice was weak and croaky. 'Fell down in the snow. Everything brokken.'

'I've brought the things you asked for.' I took the things out of the bag and put them in her bedside cabinet. 'Your friend phoned me.'

'She is not my friend. She is a bonker. All she wants is cigarettes.'

'What happened? I telephoned earlier to see if you needed anything.'

'Somebody telephoned to me in morning. Said my cat was stuck in tree. I don't know who. I thought it was Wonder Boy stuck.'

'Was he stuck?'

'Don't know. Never seen him. Somebody bumped me, I slipped and fallen. They put me back in the krankie house.'

Visiting time was over and people were making their way towards the door.

'You will feed Wonder Boy again, will you, Georgine? Key is in pocket, same like before. Thenk you, Georgine. You are my angel.'

I must say, I felt rather grumpy for an angel. Still, I took the key out of her astrakhan coat pocket again and joined the tide of visitors flowing towards the exit. Had it really been an accident? I wondered on the way home. Or had someone lured her out into the snow and pushed her over?

Ben was still up when I got back. 'Somebody phoned for you,' he said.

'Did they leave a message?'

'He said can you call him. Mr Diabello.'

'Oh yes, the estate agent.' I kept my voice absolutely expressionless. 'I'm trying to get him to value Mrs Shapiro's house. I'll call tomorrow.'

ON SATURDAY, after Ben had left with Rip, I changed into my old jeans, put a torch and a screwdriver into my bag, and walked over to Canaan House. This was my chance to have another good poke around. I was determined to find out Mrs Shapiro's real age and to discover the identity of the mystery woman in the photo. There were two places I hadn't investigated yet—the front room with the boarded-up bay window and broken light, and the attic. I fed the cats and cleaned up the poo in the hall, then pushed open the door to the front room, shining the torch around with my free hand.

The beam fell on a high ornate ceiling with its defunct chandelier, a huge marble fireplace, two sofas and four armchairs, all draped in white sheets, a carved mahogany sideboard and, over by the window, a grand piano, also under a sheet. The walls were hung with gloomy Victorian oil paintings.

The bay window was covered by heavy fringed brocade curtains; an ugly box-shaped pelmet was sagging away from the wall, and when I looked up I could see why. A huge crack ran from the ceiling above the lintel right down to the floor, with a cold draught whistling through it. At the base, where it disappeared into the ground, it must have been several centimetres wide. It must be the roots of the monkey puzzle tree that had caused the damage, I thought. No wonder she wanted to cut it down.

Seating myself at the grand piano, I raised the dustsheet—it was a Bechstein—and struck a few keys. The melancholy out-of-tune twang reverberated in the silence. There were books of music in the piano stool—Beethoven, Chopin, Delius, Grieg. In the front of the Grieg piano concerto a name was handwritten: *Hannah Wechsler*. In the front of the Delius lieder was another name: *Ella Wechsler*. I remembered the photograph of the Wechsler family seated round the piano. Who were they? As I leafed through the music a piece of paper fluttered to the floor. I picked it up.

Kefar Daniyyel near Lydda *18th June 1950*

My dearest Artem,

Why you do not reply to my letters? Each day I am thinking of you, each night I am dreaming of you. All the time I am wondering if I was doing the right thing coming here and leaving you in London. But I can not undo my decision. For this will be our place of safety, my love, the place where our people gathered from every country where we have been exiles can be living finally at peace. Here in our Promised Land our scattered nation are finally come to rest. We will get old and die here, but we will build a future for our children. They will grow up fearless and free in this land we are making for them—a land without barbed wire, out of which no person will drive us away. If only you would be here, with us, Artem.

At last we are moving from our temporary house in Lydda into our new moshav here at Kefar Daniyyel on a west-facing hillside overlooking the town. A few hectares of a barren wasteland and a trickle of water, an empty abandoned place, but it will be our garden.

In the morning before the sun is too hot we are working outside clearing stones away from the hillside and preparing terraces for autumn planting. Yitzak has obtained some seed-stones for a new type of fruit tree called avo-kado which he believes we can establish here.

My love, I have some big news I hope will persuade you to come. Arti you will be a father. I am with a child. Many evenings when the air is cool I am going up to the hilltop at Tel Hadid and watching the sun setting over the sea, and thinking of you living there beyond the sea and your baby growing here inside me. My dear love, please come and be with us if you can.

With warm kisses,
Naomi

Had the letter been hidden, or lost? I folded it and put it in my bag. Did he go to her in the end? Or was it Naomi who came back? Was he married to someone else? And what happened to the baby?

The light of the torch was beginning to flicker. I switched it off and climbed the stairs to the first-floor landing. The nine doors were all closed. I gathered together Mrs Shapiro's grey-white satin nightdress, pink candlewick dressing gown and Lion King slippers from her bedroom, then I closed the door behind me and opened the door that led up to the attic.

I'd sneered inwardly when Mark Diabello had talked about the penthouse suite, but as I climbed the steep dogleg stair, light poured in from two gable-end windows and a vast light-well in the roof, revealing wide beamed eaves branching off into rooms with sloping ceilings and views over the treetops towards Highbury Fields.

The rooms, however, were full of junk. My heart sank. It would take ages to search through this lot. On my left a narrow doorway opened onto a spiral staircase that led up into a small round room barely large enough to fit an armchair. As I sat down on the blue chair and looked out over the jungly, rain-washed garden, I felt an intense sensation of presence. Whose chair had this been? My restless hands had been stroking the velvet and now I felt something unexpectedly hard against my fingertips—a coin. It was one of those big old-fashioned pennies with a picture of Queen Victoria, pushed down the side of the chair. I carried on feeling with my fingers and pulled out a small crumpled photograph. I smoothed it out. It was a picture of a baby, a beautiful brown-eyed baby.

'Yoo-hoo! Anybody there?'

I jumped. I'd left the front door open, I remembered. Guiltily, I shoved the coin and the photo back down the side of the chair and made my way down the stairs. Mrs Goodney was standing in the hall.

'I thought I'd find you here. Having a good snoop around, are we?'

She was wearing the same pointy cube-heel shoes and an ugly raincoat with a slightly scaly texture in almost the same shade of lizard green.

'Mrs Shapiro asked me to feed her cats. She gave me the key.'

'Feeding them in the bedrooms? I don't think so. Anyway, you can hand the key over now, because we've established that you're not in fact the next of kin. She's got a son.'

I caught my breath—the baby! But there was something about the way Mrs Goodney looked at me that made me think she was bluffing. Or fishing for information. Well, that was a game two could play.

'I don't think he'll be coming over from Israel to feed the cats.'

She blinked, a quick reptilian blink. 'We have our links with international agencies, you know. We'll be inviting him to help sort out his mother's business when the house goes up for sale.' She watched me closely. 'In the meantime, his mother's in the care of social services. She said, by the way, that she doesn't want you to visit her any more.'

Her words sent a tremor through me. Had Mrs Shapiro really said that?

'So,' Mrs Goodney held out her hand for the key, 'I'll be taking over the care of the cats.'

'I'm not going to hand over the keys without her written permission.'

'I can always get a court order, you know,' she snapped.

'Fine. Do that.'

After she'd gone, I locked up the house, putting the new key from the back door onto my key ring, grabbed the carrier bag I'd filled with Mrs Shapiro's stuff and headed straight for the hospital. But when I got to Isis Ward, she'd gone. Someone else was in her bed.

'Where's Mrs Shapiro?' I asked the nurse on duty.

The girl looked vague. 'She's gone into a nursing home, I think.'

'Can you tell me where she's gone? I brought some things for her.'

'You'll have to ask in the social work department.'

Just the thought of the smug smile on Mrs Goodney's face if I went there to ask made my blood boil. Maybe the bonker lady would know. But I hadn't seen her in the lobby when I arrived and now I couldn't find her on the ward. But then, on my way out, I spotted her hanging around outside the main entrance doors. She seemed to be involved in an argument with a couple of youths wearing baseball caps, one of whom had his leg in plaster.

She grabbed me as I came out. 'They've tooken me cigs off of me.' She pointed to the youths, who were both smoking hard.

'You're better off without them,' I tried to console her.

She stared at me silently, a look that combined desolation and contempt.

'OK, I'll get you some more. Do you know where my friend is? Mrs Shapiro? The lady in the pink dressing gown?'

'They've tooken 'er away. This mornin'. They gonna put 'er in ar 'ome.'

'Do you know the name of the home? Where it is?'

'Nightmare 'ouse. It's where they all go. Up Lea Bridge way.'

'Thanks. Thank you very much.'

THERE WAS NO Nightmare House in the telephone directory or on the Internet. I telephoned Ms Baddiel and left a message, but she didn't ring back. Should I go to the police and tell them my friend had been kidnapped by social services? I could just imagine their faces. It came to me that the only person who might be able to help us was Mark Diabello. He had a big interest in making sure Mrs Shapiro's house wasn't sold from under her.

Ever since our last encounter, I hadn't been returning his calls. It's not just that I'd decided he wasn't my type—I'd come to the conclusion that I wasn't his, either. Still, I swallowed my misgivings and dialled his number. It rang just once.

'Hello, Georgina.' (My number must be on his mobile.) 'Nice to hear from you.'

'Mrs Shapiro's disappeared,' I blurted. 'She's in a nursing home, but I don't know where.'

He didn't seem surprised. 'Leave it with me, Georgina. When are we going to—?'

'Thanks, Mark. Got to dash. Someone's at the door . . .'

Before he could get back to me, though, Mrs Shapiro found a way of contacting me herself. One day when I went round to Canaan House, I found a letter on the mat inside the door; I almost didn't pick it out among the junk mail. It was a used envelope, addressed to a Mrs Lillian Brown at Northmere House, Lea Gardens Close. The address had been crossed out, and her own address written in. There was nothing inside the envelope except a scrap of paper torn off from the corner of a newspaper, with two words scrawled in what looked like black eyebrow pencil—*HELP ME*.

7

Northmere House was a square, two-storey institution, purpose-built out of plastered breeze block punctured at regular intervals by square windows that opened wide enough for ventilation but not for escape. The only access to the interior was via sliding glass doors operated by a button behind the reception desk, which was guarded by a fierce middle-aged woman in a corporate uniform.

'Can I help you?' she barked.

'I've come to see Mrs Shapiro.'

She tapped a few strokes on her keyboard and said, without raising her eyes from the screen, 'It says on her notes that she's not allowed visitors.'

'Why not? This isn't a prison, is it? Who made that decision?'

'It'll be up to matron.'

'Can I speak to her?'

She looked up at me finally, a cold, indifferent look. 'She's in a meeting.' She indicated a row of pink upholstered chairs. 'You can wait if you like.'

From a window in the lobby I could see through to a central courtyard. The access was by way of another pair of sliding glass doors on the far side of the courtyard, presumably also button operated. Through the glass, I had a glimpse of a corridor, with doors opening off it. Behind one, Mrs Shapiro would be waiting for me to free her. Somehow I had to get a message to her.

I sat on a pink chair and wondered what to do. The place was eerily quiet, the sounds all muffled by the thick pink carpet and closed double doors, the air dead, with a sweetish, chemical smell. From time to time, a lift discharged someone into the lobby and the guard-dog lady pressed her button to let them exit the building. On a low table beside the chairs was a bowl of polished waxy fruit. I picked up a bright green apple and bit into it, hard.

The sound of my crunching filled the lobby and the guard-dog lady glared at me. When I'd finished it, I placed the core on the reception desk and left.

As soon as I got home, I put the kettle on and while it was coming to the boil I listened to the messages on my answering machine. There was one from Mark Diabello asking me to ring; one from Nathan at *Adhesives in the Modern World*, reminding me of the new deadline; one from Pectoral Pete—no idea what that was about—and a bald peremptory four-word message from Rip: 'Ring me straight away.' Like hell I would.

I put a tea bag into the cup and looked in the fridge for milk. Drat. I'd run out. I hunted around for some powdered milk and ended up pouring myself a glass of wine instead. Then the phone rang. It was Mark Diabello.

'Georgina, I've been making a few enquiries. Shall I come round?'

I should have made an excuse and put the phone down, but the wine had made me weepy and the treacly sweetness in his voice filled me with unexpected longing. No, not for sex—I just wanted someone to be nice to me.

'Sorry I didn't ring you back. I've been feeling . . .'

I didn't get the end of the sentence out. A big sob rose up in my throat and washed the words away. He was round within ten minutes.

I suppose I'd been hoping for a little tenderness, but I could see from the way Mark Diabello looked at me on the doorstep that sex was what was on offer. He led me straight into the bedroom and I surrendered.

As the bedclothes cooled against my skin, he circled me in his arms. 'Georgina, you're a sensitive woman. I like that. I'd like to see more of you.'

'Mmm,' I murmured noncommittally. The touchy-feely talk was probably fake, I concluded. All he wanted from me was sex.

'You know, Mark, I still wonder about Canaan House . . . what you and your partner are up to.'

'I could ask you the same thing, you know, Georgina. Why did you come to me in the first place to have it valued? Mrs Shapiro's not your auntie. It's obvious she doesn't want to sell—so why the sudden interest on your part?' He propped himself up on one elbow, studying my face. 'I keep asking myself—what's in it for you? Why did you start this whole thing?'

I gasped. He thought . . . he thought I was like him.

'I didn't start it.' I had a sudden vivid recollection of the rusty-gate voice talking into the mobile phone. 'It was the social worker who started it. Mrs Goodney. She wanted to put Mrs Shapiro in a home and make her sell the house. She was going to have it valued by Damian at Hendricks and Wilson.'

He sat up. 'You should have told me that before. It's a well-known scam. All the estate agents have their contacts in social services. That's how we get to hear of properties with potential before they go on the market. There might be an investor or a developer waiting for a tip-off.'

My brain was struggling to keep up. Then I remembered something else. 'Actually, that social worker had a man with her the first time. He could have been a builder—I think she was showing him the house. But surely . . . what if Mrs Shapiro has a family?'

'They do a deal with the family, Georgina—cash sale, no questions asked—the family get their hands on the money, and they get the house off their hands. There's always someone in every family that'll take that line.' He kissed me on the forehead in a way that made me feel suddenly queasy.

I sat up. 'You'd better go now. Ben'll be back soon. Anyway, I don't think she has any family.'

He threw me a sharp look, as if he knew I was lying about Ben, and reached for his underpants. 'So the social worker could just be flying solo,' he said.

'You mean, robbing solo?'

'That's one way of seeing it. But look at it from the social worker's point of view—they don't get paid much, do they?' He slipped his arms into his shirtsleeves. 'And it's a pretty thankless job. Then once in a lifetime an opportunity like this comes along. The old lady doesn't need millions, she just needs a nice, safe, clean home. Why not help her and help yourself too?'

I was shocked. 'Aren't social workers supposed to care for the elderly?'

He laughed. 'Nobody cares for anybody in this world, Georgina.' He was buttoning his shirt now. I felt an unexpected pang of pity—poor Mark Diabello, condemned to live in a world where nobody cares.

'I thought you cared for me.'

'That's different. *You're* different, Georgina.' He bent down and kissed me so gently that I was just beginning to think he might mean it. Then he raised his head. 'So, what did Hendricks and Wilson value it at?'

'Seven million,' I hazarded.

He laughed. 'You're lying to me.' Then he left the house and made his way out into the dusk as I retrieved my tangled clothes.

IT POURED WITH RAIN the next day and I sat at my laptop trying to think about adhesives. After a while, I gave up and went round to feed Mrs Shapiro's cats. They were waiting for me as I approached Canaan House, circling disconsolately out in the rain. The porch where they usually waited was one huge puddle. Water was now pouring down from the broken gutter I'd first noticed nearly a fortnight ago, and splashing straight into the porch.

I fed the cats in the kitchen, and shooed them out through the back door.

As soon as I got home I phoned Mr Ali. He was hesitant at first when I described the problem.

'I am a handyman not a builder. Big ladders needed for this job.'

But he agreed to take a look. Next, I rang Northmere House. I was annoyed but not surprised to discover that Mrs Shapiro was barred from receiving phone calls as well as visitors. I phoned Nathan.

'Nathan, I'm sorry, but can you tell me what the deadline is again?'

He sighed and tutted in a way that suggested he wasn't really cross.

'February 25th. Will you be able to have it ready in time, Georgie girl?'

'I think so. Actually, Nathan,' I lowered my voice, 'I keep on getting distracted. Have you ever heard of a place called Lydda?'

'You mean Lydda near Tel Aviv? They call it Lod nowadays. The coast's nice down there. I've got some cousins who live at Jaffa.'

Somehow, it hadn't registered with me before that Nathan was probably Jewish, too. 'I've been visiting an elderly Jewish lady who lives near me,' I told him. 'She's got an old photo in her hall of Lydda.'

'There was a terrorist attack there in 1972. A bunch of Japanese terrorists gunned down a load of people at the airport,' said Nathan.

I searched back through my memory. I would have been twelve years old at the time. 'What did they do that for?'

'They were avenging two Palestinian hijackers who'd been gunned down by the Israelis.'

My mind blanked over. Palestinians and Israelis killing each other—an ancient and inexplicable enmity. Somebody else's problem, not mine.

THE NEXT MORNING I waited for a break in the rain then dashed over and fed the cats in the kitchen of Canaan House. Then, just as I was about to lock up and go home, the rain started again: big heavy drops, presaging a downpour. I could have made a run for it, but getting back to *Adhesives* just didn't seem that appealing. I excused myself by thinking I should check the roof for leaks and made my way up into the attic. The roof was surprisingly sound, except for a place at the front where a couple of slates were missing and water was dripping in. I found a pretty Victorian chamber pot, with a blue-iris design similar to the one in the bathroom, to catch the drips.

In the turret room, the ceiling showed no damp patches. I settled myself into the blue armchair to wait for the rain to pass, and felt round the edges for the baby photo. It was still there. I took it out and studied it. The lovely dark baby-wide eyes gazed out at me. I gazed back at them. This baby must have had at least one dark-eyed parent. Mrs Shapiro's eyes were blue. And so were Artem Shapiro's.

Now my curiosity was truly aroused. With my fingers, I explored the crevice round the edges of the armchair. At last, near the left armrest, I came across what felt like paper. With one hand I held back the blue upholstery, and with the other I dug two fingers in deep enough to catch hold of one end and pull it out.

Kefar Daniyyel, Lydda *26th November 1950*

My dearest Artem,

I am writing with some wonderful news for you. Our baby was born on 12th November, a little boy. Every day I watch him grow a little more beautiful like his father. Truly he has your face, Arti, but he has my brown eyes. I am often talking to him about his daddy in London, and he smiles and lifts up his little hands in the air, as if he is understanding everything. I have called him Chaim after our great new president Chaim Weizmann. Why do you not come, Arti? Why do you not write? Have you forgotten about me?

With all my love,
Naomi

I folded the letter and pushed it back down the side of the chair with the photograph. Naomi must have been the pretty dark-eyed woman—the mother of the baby. But then who was the old lady in Northmere House?

I glanced at my watch. It was three o'clock, almost time for Ben to be back. I resigned myself to getting soaked, and made a dash for home. When I got in, I rubbed my hair dry with a towel, put on dry clothes, and guiltily sat down at my laptop. OK. Concentrate. Glue. 'Adhesive curing is the change from a liquid to a solid state.' Sometimes the science of stickiness can be boringly obvious. I forced myself to focus. *Adhesives in the Modern World* was what paid the bills. Ben was later home than usual . . .

When at last I heard his key in the latch, I went downstairs to greet him. As I came into the hall, I stopped and caught my breath. I saw a stranger standing there—a bald weirdo who'd broken into my house.

'Hi, Mum.' He grinned embarrassedly. 'Don't stare like that.'

'What . . .?'

All his hair had gone. His pale, knobbly skull looked obscenely naked.

'It looks very . . .'

He met my eyes. 'Don't say it, Mum.'

I put my hand over my mouth. We both laughed.

'D'you want some Choco-Puffs?'

He shook his head. 'I don't know why you always get those for me. Dad gets them, too. I hate them.'

He made himself some toast and spread it with peanut butter, a layer of strawberry jam on top of that, then a sprinkling of chocolate powder. I poured myself a cup of tea. Ben, since our liminal conversation, had been drinking only water.

'So isn't it a bit . . . cold?'

He gave me a look of mild reproach. 'Yeah. But when you think Our Lord was crucified, it sort of puts it in perspective?'

The rising inflection made him sound defensive. I felt a flutter of panic.

'Is it something you think about a lot, Ben?'

He opened his school bag, unzipped an inner pocket and pulled out a book. With a shock of recognition I saw it was Rip's old school Bible. He leafed through to a page that was bookmarked with an old bus ticket.

'When ye therefore shall see the . . . Abomination of Desolation . . .' he stumbled on the clunky words, 'spoken of by Daniel the prophet, stand in the holy place, then let those who are in Judea flee to the mountains . . .' He read carefully, looking up from time to time to check I was still listening. 'And then shall they see the Son of Man coming in the clouds of heaven, with power and great glory. And he shall send his angels with a great sound of a trumpet, and they shall gather together his elect from the four winds, from the uttermost part of the earth to the uttermost part of heaven.' When I didn't say anything, he added, 'Mark chapter thirteen? Verses fourteen to twen'y eight?'

'Ben . . .'

In the silence between us, a sweet curly-haired child hovered on the edge of extinction. I wanted to hug him. I wanted him to be my little boy again.

'I'm not saying it's all rubbish, Ben. That language—it's very powerful. But don't you think it refers to things that happened a long time ago?'

'The Abomination that bringeth Desolation in't a long time ago, Mum—it's in the future—soon. Some nutter'll drop a nuclear bomb on the Temple Mount at Jerusalem. The holy place.' He reached over for the cocoa powder and gave his toast another dusting.

'But . . .'

'Daniel predicted it first. In the Old Testament? Then Matthew and Mark picked up on it? They din't know about nuclear weapons, but the way they describe it . . . it's uncannily accurate?' His insistent voice seemed alien. 'And the big guys that run the world—they all know it's going to happen?

George Bush 'n' Tony Blair? Why d'you think they're so, like, totally obsessed with the Middle East? Why are they getting so stressed about Iran going nuclear? They know it's the prophecy of the Second Coming that's working out in our time? Like, we're the last generation?' He slapped two bits of toast together into a sandwich. 'Want to know why America supports Israel? Because in the Bible it says when the chosen people go back to their promised land, like they did in 1948, that's the start of the End Times.' He bit into the sandwich. 'It's sad cases like you and Dad that'll get left behind.'

'Left behind what?'

'The Rapture. The Second Coming? When the elect get taken up to heaven? Don't be so blind, Mum.' He gave me a look that was both angry and pitying, then took a swig of water, got up abruptly, taking his sandwich, his bag and his Bible, and stomped off upstairs to his room.

My stomach clenched into a knot. I finished drinking my tea and went upstairs to my bedroom. I opened up my laptop and typed 'End of Time' into Google, just as Ben said he'd done. There were literally millions of entries. I started opening a few at random, following links, and all of a sudden I found I'd stepped over a threshold into an eerie parallel world, in which war, disease, terrorism, global warming—the scourges of our age—are seized on with glee as signals of the Second Coming. One link led me to a whole page of Christian and Jewish sites discussing the Promised Land. When would God's promise to the Jews be fulfilled? In God's time, in the prophesied future? Or now, in the present-day Middle East? Was the rebuilding of the third Temple in Jerusalem a metaphor for spiritual rebirth? Or was it about bricks and mortar? The cyber arguments raged.

And it wasn't only Christians and Jews who were preoccupied with the Second Coming. Google came up with more than a million links to websites anticipating the imminent return of the Imam Al-Mahdi.

Alone in my dusky room, as I surfed from one link to another, I was beginning to understand why Ben was so rattled. Compared with the vast inevitability of this Rapture machine, the world of our own little secular family seemed puny and insubstantial.

BY SATURDAY the rain had stopped and soft heavy drops dripped from the overhanging trees as I walked along to Canaan House, where I'd arranged to meet Mr Ali to take a look at the gutter. I'd set out a little early, hoping to catch him before he started. I wanted to ask him about Lydda; I wanted to find out about Islam and the Last Imam. But as I turned into Totley Place, I spotted a battered red van parked in the lane that led to Canaan House, and then I heard men's voices in the garden, shouting. I quickened my step.

As I approached the gate, I glimpsed between the trees a terrifying sight—Mr Ali was dangling in the air, hanging on for dear life to a length of cast-iron gutter that had come away from the wall. All that was holding him up was a rusty iron bracket at one end, and a twine of ivy that had clambered over the roof and luckily got a grip on the chimneys. On the ground, floundering among the wet brambles, two young men in white robes and Arabic headgear were grappling with an extendable ladder.

At last they slotted the three sections together and wielded it in Mr Ali's direction. But they swung the ladder too wide, then overcorrected and swung it too far the other way. Mr Ali let out a tirade of furious words. I could see the bracket straining under his weight and the ivy coming away from the bricks. If they didn't get their act together fast, he was going to plummet some thirty feet onto the stone terrace. I held my breath and thought, These young men really are unbelievably useless.

Mr Ali was now balancing with one leg on a windowsill and one thrashing the air, yelling his head off, so I ran over and between the three of us we managed to get the ladder securely up against the wall. Mr Ali climbed down, bawling at the other two. Then, just as his feet touched the ground, all the fight seemed to go out of him and he slumped down.

'This job is for a younger man. Not double excel gentleman my age.'

'But you *did* excel, Mr Ali. Keeping so calm,' I said, though calmness, to be honest, was not the first word that sprang to mind.

'No, size XXL, Mrs George.' He clasped his arms round his hamster tummy. 'My wife feeds me too much. No good for climbing up ladder.'

I laughed. 'Next time, you should get one of the other two to go up it.'

He shook his head with a melancholy sigh, but said nothing.

The other two had got out a packet of cigarettes, and were lighting up. I wondered why they were wearing those bizarre outfits. They looked more like extras out of *Lawrence of Arabia* than any Palestinians I'd seen on TV. They were younger than Mr Ali, taller, and incredibly handsome in a dark-flashing-eyes, white-flashing-teeth kind of way.

'Hello.' I smiled. 'I'm Georgie.'

They nodded their heads and flashed their teeth at me. It was clear they didn't speak a word of English. Mr Ali struggled to his feet. 'Allow me to make introductions. Mrs George, this is Ishmail, my nephew. He is completely useless. This is his friend Nabeel. He is also completely useless.'

The useless young men nodded and flashed their teeth, then went to sit in the porch, where they started arguing and shoving each other off the step.

Mr Ali sighed. 'What a misfortune at my age to have two complete uselesses for my assistants. This house—it needs too much work. I do not know if I can do it with these uselesses.'

'I'm sure you can,' I said. 'There's no hurry. I think Mrs Shapiro will be away for a while.'

'You think? Hm.' He paused and gave me an oblique look. 'You know, Mrs Georgo, I am thinking is a pity so big house must stand empty.' Mr Ali stroked his neat beard. 'My nephew, Ishmail—he sleeping on floor in my apartment. Drive my wife mad. This other useless one, too, sometimes sleeping in there.'

I could see what he meant—they would drive me mad, too.

'Well . . . I don't know what Mrs Shapiro would think . . .' I started. Then it occurred to me that these two might be useless at house repairs, but they could do a great job of keeping the likes of Mrs Goodney and Nick Wolfe at bay. And they could feed the cats. 'It would have to be on the strict understanding that they move out when Mrs Shapiro comes back.'

'No broblem. Even if they stay for short time it will make big difference for my wife. Give her chance to clean it up.'

I wondered what Mrs Shapiro would say if I told her they were Palestinian.

'I am sorry they have no money for paying rent. But everything will be fixitup like new.' He saw the look on my face. 'I supervise, of course.'

I suppose I should have said no, but I was on the scent of another story. 'Where did you learn all your building skills, Mr Ali? In Lydda?'

He shook his head. 'No. We were sent away from Lydda. Do you not know what happened there?'

'Yes, I know about the terrorist attack,' I said, pleased with myself.

'Ha! All of the world knows this.' He seemed annoyed. 'Terrorists shooting on innocent Israelis. But you know why? I tell you. In 1948 all Palestinians were sent out from Lydda. Not only Lydda—many many towns and villages in our country were destroyed. To make way for Jews. People still are living in the refugee camps.' He went suddenly quiet.

'But you learned to be a builder, yes?' I encouraged, wanting to reassure myself that something positive had come out of all that displacement.

'In Ramallah I trained for engineer.' (He pronounced it *inzhineer*.) 'Here in England I must make new examinations. But I am old and time has tipped his bucket on me. This useless one,' he pointed at his nephew, 'he will study for engineering, too. Aeronautical.'

'Aeronautical?' That sounded quite brainy.

'He has a scholarship.' He lowered his voice to a proud whisper. 'Other one, I don't know. Now they are both learning English. First-class English language course—Metropolitan University, next door Arsenal Stadium.'

The Uselesses, realising that they were being talked about, chipped in. 'Arsenal. Yes, please.'

Yes, it would need to be a first-class English course, I thought.

'So why did you come to England, Mr Ali? Wasn't your family over there?'

'You are asking difficult questions, Mrs George.' He hesitated, then continued. 'After my youngest son died, I saw no possibility of end to this conflict. I wanted only to come away from this place. I have a good friend, Englishman, he was a teacher in Ramallah. He helped me to come here.'

'Your son died . . .?'

'He had a burst appendix.' Mr Ali stared at the ground. 'We were in Rantis, visiting wife's family. We wanted to take him to hospital in Tel Aviv but we were delayed at the checkpoint. One soldier, he said we must go back to Ramallah. When we got there it was too late.' His eyes glinted. 'How can I forgive? My son was fourteen years old.'

'So you wanted to leave . . .?'

'Now my daughter is married with this Englishman. I have three grandchildren.' He smiled briefly. 'Drive my wife mad.'

I thought I'd like to meet his wife one day.

The Uselesses had gone off to sit in the van. They must have had a CD player in there, because I could hear strains of Arabic music, sweet and melancholy, drifting incongruously over the lawn and dripping brambles.

But maybe all places have their histories of sadness and displacement, I was thinking. People move in, others move on; new lives and new communities spring up among the stones of the old.

'So, what you say, Mrs George?' Mr Ali interrupted my thoughts. 'They stay here and fixitup the house?'

'I don't know,' I said weakly. My heart ached for sad exiled Mr Ali and his useless assistants, but I owed a duty of care to Mrs Shapiro. 'Maybe if you fix the gutter first, it'll give me time to have a word with Mrs Shapiro.'

SOMETIMES WHEN I TRY to understand what's going on in the world, I find myself thinking about glue. Every adhesive interacts with surfaces and with the environment in its own particular way; the skill in achieving a good bond is to match the appropriate adhesive to the adherends to be bonded.

Acrylics, for example, are fast curing and they don't require as much surface preparation as epoxies, which have high cohesive strength but a slower cure rate. Epoxy adhesives have two components: the adhesive itself, and a hardening agent, which accelerates the process. On Friday, I was sitting at my laptop, pondering this profound philosophical duality, when a thought slipped into my head. What I needed to re-bond with Mrs Shapiro was a hardening agent. And who could be harder than Mr Wolfe?

Flushed with inspiration, I rummaged in the desk drawer for a card and wrote a get-well-soon note to Mrs Shapiro, adding that I was doing my best to visit her and advising her under no circumstances to sign anything until we'd talked. I mentioned that I'd found some builders who might be staying at the house while they did some work there—I freely admit, I didn't go into much detail. I told her the cats were doing extremely well and that Wonder Boy was missing her (well, probably he was, in his own brutal and selfish way). I enclosed a stamped addressed envelope and a blank sheet of paper, put it all in an envelope with the card and sealed it. Then I walked down to the office of Wolfe & Diabello. A quick reconnoitre in the car park round the back told me that Mark Diabello was out and Nick Wolfe was in.

He greeted me with a bruising handgrip and I told him in my specially friendly voice that Mrs Shapiro had been asking after him. On a yellow Post-it note, I scribbled the address of Northmere House and, handing him my envelope, said that if he found the time to call round, would he drop off the card from me, too.

'Fine,' he said.

Then I went home and got on with *Adhesives in the Modern World*. The article I was editing was about the importance of good joint design in bonding. 'Surface atraction is increased, by rouhgening or scraching the surfaces to be bonded.' The article had been written by a young man who knew his glues but seemed to have a total contempt for spelling and punctuation.

What do they teach them in school these days? I tutted to myself. Ben was just as bad. I found myself worrying about how he'd got on in school today. He'd struggled to settle into his new class when we'd moved down from Leeds and I was anxious that his shaved head and religious leanings could make him a target for bullies.

While we were having tea that evening I raised it with him. 'What did they say at school, then, when you turned up with your new hairdo—your no-hair-do? Didn't the kids take the mick?'

He shrugged. 'A bit, but I don't care. Jesus suffered taunts, din't he?'

Yes, and look what happened to him—I held back the thought. 'But wasn't it a bit . . . horrible? I mean, kids can be very cruel.'

'Nah,' he said. 'Don't bother me. Brings me closer to Our Lord.'

When he'd finished his meal, he laid down his knife and fork, put his hands together briefly and closed his eyes. Then he picked up his bag and disappeared upstairs. Maybe I should have been pleased that he wasn't stealing cars or taking drugs, but there was a scary intensity about him that was almost like an aura of martyrdom. I felt a stab of guilt. Was it our failure as parents that had led him to seek out a different kind of certainty?

On impulse, I picked the phone up and dialled Rip's number. A young woman answered—I nearly didn't recognise her voice.

'Stella?'

'Mum?'

The pain of missing her caught me like a thump in the chest. 'Aren't you supposed to be at uni?' (Why was she visiting Rip and not me?)

'I . . . It's reading week. Do you want to speak to Dad?'

Her voice—so sweet—still reedy like a child's, but with an adult's self-assurance. She'd always been a daddy's girl.

'Yes—no. Stella, I'm worried about Ben. Does he seem unhappy to you? Have you noticed anything different about him?'

I realised she wouldn't have seen his haircut yet, but she and Ben were close—they'd fought and loved one another all through their childhoods.

'Ben's cool, Mum. He's got religion in a big way, that's all—like I had Leonardo DiCaprio when I was his age.'

'That's what I mean—religion—it doesn't seem normal for sixteen.'

'I don't know what's wrong with you, Mum. He could be shooting up or nicking cars, and you're stressing about him reading the Bible.'

Maybe she's right, maybe that's all it is, I thought, a schoolboy phase. But there was something terrifying about his intensity, the dilated eyes. 'He talks about the end of the world as though it's going to happen any minute.'

'Yeah, Dad keeps on at him about it. They had a big row over Christmas. Ben started banging on about religion. Something about miring the sanctity of Christmas with alcohol and consumerism. They all laughed.'

'Poor Ben.' I kept my voice even, but I could feel rage boiling up in me.

'It was gross. Grandpa called him a pansy.'

'What did Ben say?'

'He said, I forgive you, Grandpa.' She giggled. I giggled, too.

'Good for him. Stella, it's lovely to talk to you. Have you finished your teaching practice?'

'Yeah. It was nearly enough to turn me into a mass child murderer. I don't know if teaching's really me, but I'll stick with it till the end of the course, then decide. Don't worry about Ben, Mum. He'll be fine.'

When I put the phone down I was filled with a wonderful sense of ease, as if a sack of rocks had just rolled from my shoulders; I burst into Ben's room and hugged him. 'I've just been talking to Stella.'

Ben lifted his head from the computer. 'What did she say?'

'She said she wasn't sure about teaching—whether it was right for her.'

He gave me a long intense look. 'You need to calm down, Mum.'

ON SATURDAY MORNING, after Ben had left for Rip's, I got a phone call from Mr Ali. 'You can come and see, Mrs George. House is all fixitup.'

They were waiting for me when I arrived—all three of them, plus the cats. The Uselesses were wearing jeans and baseball caps. I don't know what had happened to their Arabic gear. Mr Ali was grinning with pride.

'See?'

There was a new gutter running the length of the house, in white uPVC. The brambles had been hacked back to make room for a white uPVC table and chair set and a white uPVC birdbath.

'It's . . . er . . . lovely . . .' I put on a smile.

The Uselesses beamed.

'You let them stay, they will fixitup everything for you,' said Mr Ali.

'Maybe . . . maybe not too many repairs. Just essential things. Maybe the woodwork just needs rubbing down and a lick of paint.'

'Baint, yes,' he nodded enthusiastically. The Uselesses nodded enthusiastically too.

'I'll give you a ring. I need to get a set of keys cut,' I said, playing for time, thinking that maybe Mrs Shapiro would be back soon.

But on Wednesday morning there was a letter for me on the doormat. I recognised my own handwriting on the envelope.

Dearest Georgine,

Thank you for your Card and for you sending my Nicky to comfort me in Prison. He is quite adorable! He was coming with Champagne and white Roses. A real Gentleman! We were talking for Hours about Poetry Music Philosophy the Time was passing too quick like flowing Water under a Bridge and I am always asking myself what matters it if there gives a Gulf in our Ages so long as there gives a Harmony inbetween our Souls. It was like so with Artem he was twenty years my older but we have found Joy together. I wonder if I would ever find such a Joy again with another Man to feel the arms of a Mans around me and the warmth of a good Body close beside mine better than Cats. He has said he will come again now every Hour is dragging too long I wait for him to come and you also my dear Georgine. How have I escaped Transportation and Inprisonment in all my life only to face it now alone in my Older Age? They are wanting me to sign a Confession before I can return to my Home. They are saying I must give the Power of Returning but my Nicky also is saying I must not sign nothing so I am putting a brave resistance.

I must stop the Nurse comes soon with my Injection.

Please help me.

Naomi Shapiro

I read it through a couple of times. Then I phoned Mr Wolfe.

'Thanks for taking my card round. How was she? She looked awful in hospital. I was surprised they let her out so quickly.'

'Bit of bruising. Gash to the head. Nothing serious. We had a good laugh.'

'She seems to be very fond of you.'

'Yes. And you know, in a funny way, I've grown quite fond of her, too.' There was a glibness in his voice.

'Do you know anything about this confession she's been asked to sign? Something about power of returning.'

'Ah. Yes. They want her to sign a Power of Attorney. Whoever she signed it over to would have the power to sign legal documents on her behalf.'

'Like the sale of a house, for instance?'

'Got it in one.'

I felt my heart starting to race. 'What can we do to stop that?'

'I've been wondering that myself.'

Whatever he had in mind, he obviously wasn't going to share it. I needed to find out what he knew, without giving away too much myself. Then I thought of something that would put him on the back foot.

'Apparently her son's coming over from Israel. That'll be a great help.'

I thought I heard a sharp intake of breath. 'Indeed.'

'By the way, did you have any trouble getting in?'

'Oh, yes, they told me she wasn't allowed any visitors. I just told them not to be so bloody ridiculous.'

So that's how it's done, I thought.

An hour or so later the phone rang. It was Mark Diabello.

'Hi, Georgina. Glad I've caught you. Listen, I think I've got the answer to your dilemma about how to avoid Mrs Shapiro having to sell up if she goes into a home. Apparently the council can put a charge on her house. It's like a mortgage—the house is sold after the person dies and that's when the council calls in the debt. The residue, if any, goes to the estate.'

'But the thing is, Mark, she doesn't need to be in a nursing home at all. She's fine at home. She likes her independence.'

'You'd better get her back home as soon as you can, then. Or get someone else to live in the house till she gets back. These things've got a way of picking up their own momentum.'

I HAD ARRANGED to meet Mr Ali and the Uselesses just after two. When I arrived at Canaan House, the red van was parked outside and the three of them were hunched up in the front. As soon as they saw me the Uselesses jumped down, talking excitedly in Arabic, and followed me up the path, carrying their stuff with them in carrier bags. I showed them upstairs, then walked round the house with Mr Ali, pointing out the things that needed fixing.

As his bright hamster eyes explored the details of the rooms he made little murmurs of amazement. 'Hm. Hm,' he said, writing it all down in a notebook. 'All will be fixitup good, Mrs George.' When we went up into the attic, he gasped. 'In here we could make beautiful benthouse suite.'

'Let's just concentrate on the essentials to start with,' I said.

Down in the hall, he stopped once more in front of the picture of the church at Lydda. 'You know, exactly next door to this church was a mosque. Cross and crescent standing side by side in peace.'

'Tell me about Lydda,' I said. 'Is your family still there?'

'Do you not know about *Nakba*?'

'*Nakba?* What's that?'

'Hm. You are completely ignorant.' He said it with a sigh.

'I'm sorry. I'll make some tea if you tell me.' I put the kettle on, rinsed two of the less grotty cups as thoroughly as I could under the tap, then put a *Kräutertee* tea bag into each of them. We sat on the wooden chairs at the kitchen table. Mr Ali drank his pond water with three heaped spoonfuls of sugar, so I put the same into mine. We stirred and sipped.

'You were going to tell me about your family,' I prompted.

'I will tell you how they left Lydda. But you know the history—about British Palestine Mandate?'

'Well, just a bit. Actually, not a lot.'

He sighed again. 'But you know about Jewish Holocaust?'

'Yes, I know about that.'

'Of course, everybody knows about sufferings of the Jews.' He sniffed irritably. 'Only suffering of Palestinian people nobody hears.' Mr Ali blew on his tea and took a sip. 'In the end of the war, after what they have done to the Jews, the whole world was looking for a Jewish homeland. And the British say—look, we will give them this land in Palestine. Land without people, people without land. Typical British, they give away something which does not belong to them.' He looked up and I nodded encouragingly. 'This land is not empty, Mrs George. Palestinian people have been living there, farming our land, for generations. Now they say we must give half of it up to the Jews. Did you not learn about it in school?'

'No.' I was embarrassed by my ignorance. 'In history lessons we learned about Kings and Queens of England. Henry the Eighth and his six wives.'

'Six wives? All at one time?'

'No. He killed two and he divorced two, and one died.'

'Typical British behaviour. Same with us. Some killed. Some sent away into exile. Some died.' Mr Ali shook his head crossly and took a gulp of tea.

'But that was a long time ago.'

'No. Nineteen forty-eight. Same like the Romans did to Jews, Jews did to Palestinians. Chased them out. We call it *Nakba*. It means disaster in your language.'

'No, I mean Henry the Eighth was a long time ago.'

'Before Romans?'

'No, after the Romans, but before . . . Never mind.' I saw the bemused look on his face. 'It's all just history, isn't it?'

This seemed to make him even more annoyed.

'You have learned nothing in school. Apart from a man with six wives. History has no borders, Mrs George. Past rolls up into present rolls up into future. Now young Israelis also are ignorant. In school, their teachers tell them Jews came into an empty land, but not how this land was made empty.'

I thought about the letter in the piano stool. Yes, that's what Naomi wrote—*a barren wasteland . . . an empty abandoned place*.

'But the Jewish people need a homeland, too. And it was their land, wasn't it? Before the Romans sent them away?'

'This land belongs to many peoples. Nomadic peoples wandering here and there, following their sheeps. Palestine, Lebanon, Syria, Jordan, Egypt, Arabia, Mesopotamia. Who knows where everybody was coming from? They will tell you Palestinians left their farms and houses and ran away because their leaders told them. No, they ran away because of terror. Israeli state was made by terrorists. You think only crazy Arabs are terrorists?'

'I'm sorry to be so ignorant. At school we just learned British history.'

'So you must know about Balfour Declaration?'

'A bit. Wasn't it about partitioning the Middle East at the end of the First World War?' I'd seen *Lawrence of Arabia*, with Peter O'Toole. He was great. Those eyes. But I'd never understood who betrayed whom over what.

'Balfour said to meet Jewish aspirations without prejudicing rights of Palestinians.' Mr Ali took a gulp of pond water. 'But Palestinian people still are sitting in refugee camps. They have lost their lands, fields, orchards. They have no work, no hope. So they sit in refugee camps and dream of revenge.' His eyes were glittering with unusual ferocity. 'They have no weapons, so they make their children into weapons.'

I put the kettle on again, wondering about Ben. How had he blundered into this thorny biblical world?

'Isn't there a prophecy, Mr Ali? Don't the Jews have to rebuild the temple in Jerusalem, where the Messiah will come back? The third Temple?'

'Their book says they must rebuild the Temple. But it is not possible at this time, because on this site now stands our mosque—Al-Aqsa Mosque. Next to the Dome of the Rock. One of our most holy places.'

'But is it true that Muslims, too, are waiting for the Last Imam? The Imam Al-Mahdi. Do you believe that, Mr Ali?'

He hadn't struck me as a man of extreme beliefs—beyond an extreme misplaced belief in white uPVC.

'Mostly Shia believe in the return of Al-Mahdi. I am Sunni.' He turned towards me. 'You learned about this in school?

'No. On the Internet.'

I saw now that the hard glitter in his eyes was a trick of the light and his face was gentle and sad.

I took a deep breath. 'Actually, it was my son who told me. He found all these weird sites about the end of time. Antichrist. Armageddon. He's so preoccupied with it . . . I wanted to understand what it was about.'

The kettle whistled and I made us another round of *Kräutertee*. Mr Ali spooned three more sugars into his cup and stirred, looking at me gravely.

'Mrs George, the young are ready to believe anything that will lead them into Heaven. And there are always some whisperers who will say to them that death is the gateway to life.'

I shivered. I had a sudden image of Ben—my lovely curly-haired Ben—his eyes radiant with conversion, his boyish body strapped up to that deadly payload, attempting a little smile or a joke as he said goodbye. The thought made me feel sick.

I could hear the young men thudding about. They must have set up their CD player, for bursts of wild jangling music were swirling downstairs.

'Do not worry about your son, Mrs George. He will grow up before too long. Ishmail and Nabeel used to talk also about these things.'

The thudding upstairs turned into thundering on the stairs, and a few moments later the Uselesses appeared in the hall. They said something in Arabic to Mr Ali and he translated for me.

'They want to say thank you. This is a very good place.'

'There's something else they have to do,' I said. 'They must feed the cats.' I showed them the cupboard in the kitchen where the cat food was kept. They nodded enthusiastically. 'And they have to clear up the mess.' I led them back into the hall and pointed out a deposit the Phantom Pooer had left. I'd spotted it earlier but not got round to cleaning it up.

The taller one—I think he was Mr Ali's nephew, Ishmail—put his hand over his nose and mouth, then went and got a piece of kitchen roll and wiped it up. The other one, Nabeel, said something loud and urgent in Arabic. Mr Ali said something loud and urgent back. It was time for me to go.

I took the keys I'd had cut out of my pocket. 'If anyone comes to the house, anyone you don't know, you mustn't let them in.'

Mr Ali translated it into Arabic and the Uselesses nodded emphatically.

'No in. No in.' They made waving 'keep out' gestures with their hands. I gave them the keys. And I must admit I felt a pang of apprehension.

Mr Ali smiled. 'Don't worry, Mrs George. All will be fixitup good.'

THE FOLLOWING SATURDAY afternoon I made my way down to Sainsbury's at Islington for my big weekly shop. At the top of the end aisle, I spotted a crowd gathering around the sticker lady doing her reductions and out of habit joined them. Without Mrs Shapiro there, it was all much more refined, just a bit of genteel basket-barging when something exciting turned up.

Still, I managed to get some good bargains on cheeses, and a plastic box with three avocados reduced to 79p. I remembered the letter I'd found in the music stool at Canaan House—'avo-kado' she'd called them. They must have been newly discovered at the time.

There were bargains on the fresh produce aisles, too. Bananas, nets of oranges, and plastic-box strawberries flown in from somewhere or other, pretty but flavourless. Where can you get strawberries so early in March? I was wondering as I made my way out of the store.

A young woman was handing out leaflets near the exit. I took one from her hand and was about to stick it in with my shopping when the words jumped off the page at me: BOYCOTT ISRAELI GOODS. Seeing my interest, she pushed a sheet of paper towards me on a clipboard.

'Will you sign our petition? We want the government to make a commitment to stop serving Israeli-sourced products in the Houses of Parliament. Until Israel accepts UN Resolution 242.'

'Isn't that a bit . . .?' I stopped myself.

'It's all grown on stolen land. Watered with stolen water,' she said.

'I know, but . . . it all happened so long ago. It was terrible, I know. But isn't it just—what they had to do?'

'That's crap!' Then she checked herself. 'Sorry, I shouldn't get so worked up.' I realised she was very young—hardly older than Ben. Her hair was cut short and teased up into little spikes on top of her head. 'But it's not just something that happened long ago. It's still happening. Every day. They're stealing Palestinian land. Bulldozing Palestinian houses. Bringing in Jewish settlers. From Moscow and New York and Manchester.' She spoke very fast, gabbling as though frightened of losing my attention.

'That can't be true.' Surely if it were true, somebody would put a stop to it.

'It *is* true. The International Court of Justice says it's illegal. But America supports them. And Britain.'

I turned the leaflet over. On the other side were pictures of Israeli produce. Avocados. Lemons. Oranges. Strawberries. Well, at least I hadn't bought the strawberries.

Suddenly her head swivelled round, and following her gaze I saw a police car draw up and two officers get out—a man and a woman.

'Would you mind moving on now?' said the man. 'You're causing an obstruction.'

'No, we're not,' I said, though I could see he was addressing the girl. She was shuffling her leaflets and her clipboard into a bag. 'We're just chatting,' I said. 'About avocados.'

The policewoman smiled. 'We've had a complaint.'

I looked round to the girl, but she'd disappeared.

There was quite a queue at the bus-stop and a cold wind had sprung up. I was beginning to feel hungry. I hunted round in my shopping bags and broke off a ripe banana—at least they were OK to eat, weren't they? I noticed a couple standing with their backs to me looking into a shop window. The man was tall, fair, solidly built, there was something oddly familiar about him. His head was slightly out of proportion to his body. I realised with a shock of recognition that it was Rip. The woman was small, even in her high heels, with a sleek bob and scarlet lipstick. I stared. I could see her reflection in the shop window. It was Ottoline Walker. What was going on? Where was Pectoral Pete? She was holding hands with Rip, laughing at something, looking up at him. He bent down and kissed her.

Something inside me snapped. A sound rose in my chest, swelled up and forced its way out—*aaah! yaaah!*—a high-pitched wail. They turned. Everybody turned. I lurched across the pavement. The banana pitched forward and mushed into a soft slippery paste on her face. She struggled, but the banana in my hand just kept going round and round, forcing its way up into her nostrils and smearing the slut-scarlet lipstick all round her mouth.

Rip grabbed my arm. 'Georgie! Stop! Have you gone mad?'

Next she turns on me, sputtering. 'What have I done to deserve this?'

You can tell from her voice she's used to getting everything she wants. 'You just thought you could have him, didn't you? You didn't stop to think of me. Me and Ben and Stella. He belongs to us, not you.'

'What d'you mean?'

There's a bit of banana hanging down from her nose. It makes me laugh.

'We were just inconvenient people, getting in the way of your lovely dream.' I'm laughing like mad now, splitting my sides at the sheer symmetry of everything.

Then—this is good—the Scarlet-mouthed Slut scrapes the mush off her face with her hands and starts to smear it over Rip, over his clothes and his hair. And he says, 'Ottie! Stop! What's the matter with you?'

And she says, 'What's the matter with *you*? *You* told me it was OK. *You* told me she didn't mind. You lied to me.' She's wailing, too. 'You told me she'd gone off with another man! In a Jaguar!'

'She did. She is.' He backs away. 'You're both bloody mad. Both of you!' He backs away and breaks into a run. She runs after him, stumbling on her bitch-stilletos. And I run, too, dodging through the startled pedestrians.

In the end, I have to give up. I've lost sight of him. I'm panting for breath, my chest heaving, my throat raw from screaming. I've lost sight of her, too. Still panting, I make my way back towards Islington Green.

The crowd at the bus-stop has thinned out. I look for my shopping bags, but they've disappeared. Someone has picked them up and taken them. The settler avocados. The blood-soaked oranges. All gone.

When I got home I saw that the answering machine was blinking. There was a message from Ms Baddiel. She was sorry she hadn't been in touch before. She'd been on a course. I rang her back but she wasn't there. The second message was from Nathan, wanting to know if I'd like to go to the Adhesives Trade Fair in Peterborough tomorrow with him and his father. I pressed Delete. I know I'm sad, but I'm not that sad. I poured myself a glass of wine. *Casualty* would be on television soon.

Then the reality of three Ben-less days loomed and I started to think that maybe a trade fair in Peterborough was what I needed after all. Maybe Nathan's father would be OK when sober. And the more I thought about it, the more I realised that short men can be incredibly sexy. I dialled Nathan's number. As he picked up the phone ('Nathan Stein speaking') I could hear a familiar theme tune. He'd been watching *Casualty*, too.

8

Nathan arrived at ten o'clock. I'd been trying to imagine what kind of car he would turn up in, but the last thing I'd expected was an open-top sports car, a Morgan, pale blue. He greeted me with a hug. I dropped my knees a bit so our cheeks were just at the same height.

'Sorry, my father couldn't make it.'

'So it's just you and me?' My heart skipped.

''Fraid so. Can you put up with me for a whole afternoon?' (Could I just!) 'You'll need a warmer coat than that.' (I'd already put on my smart grey jacket over my revealing top.) 'And a scarf or something.'

I changed into my brown duffle coat, fastened it up to my chin and tied a scarf down over my ears.

'Sit tight!' he said.

We whizzed up the Holloway Road and out onto the A1, the wind slapping my head, my eyes stinging. Shops. Houses. Trees. Flats. Houses. Trees. *Whoosh!* We couldn't talk. All I could do was watch Nathan's hands on the wheel and gearstick and his hunky profile as he concentrated on the road. His silver-flecked designer-stubbly jaw was clenched in a daredevil look. My stomach was clenched in a knot.

Peterborough emerged suddenly out of a fenland mist, the elegant nave and buttresses of its cathedral swanning above the rooftops. The exhibition centre was on the outskirts, a low featureless hangar of a building. Nathan pulled up near the entrance, switched the engine off, and turned to me with a dimply smile. 'Did you enjoy that, Georgia?'

I smiled weakly. I couldn't bring myself to say yes, even to him.

The exhibition itself was nowhere near as exciting as the journey. It was basically a display of tubes and phials with long technical explanations mounted on card, and samples of things glued together. We seemed to be the only punters, our footsteps click-clacking in the echoing space. The most interesting thing was a car, an old Jaguar, glued to a metal plate on its roof, which was bolted to a chain suspended from the ceiling, so it dangled there, spinning slowly if you touched it, held up by the power of adhesion.

'Wow! That's amazing!' I had a sudden thought. 'Nathan, do you think you could use glue to stick, say, a toothbrush holder onto bathroom tiles?'

'Absolutely. There are a number of purpose-made adhesives. Look for brands with "nails" in the name. No-nails. Goodbye-nails.'

'But you wouldn't use nails in a bathroom. It'd have to be rawplugs, wouldn't it?'

He gave me a sideways grin. 'You mean instead of cooked plugs?'

'What d'you mean?'

'They're called *rawl*plugs, Georgia.'

'*Rawl*plugs?'

'Yes, but they're on their way to obsolescence. Adhesives can do many of the same things nowadays.'

My heart bounced up. Rawlplugs were history!

'Hey, look at this, Georgia.' Nathan had stopped to examine a very distressing full-colour close-up photo of a bottom stuck to a blue plastic toilet seat. It had obviously been taken in a hospital: there was somebody in the background wearing surgical gloves. Just imagine if that was you—having to call for help, and then having blokes with tools break down the door to the toilet, unbolt the seat and rush you to hospital . . . And all the time you'd be wondering who'd put the glue there; in fact you'd probably be able to guess. You'd be fuming, but helpless. Then you'd have to be photographed for medical records. Everyone would be solemn and respectful, but behind your back they'd be laughing their heads off. The explanation card at the side of the picture simply read: *Cyanoacrylate AXP-36C. A practical joke.*

'Deary me,' said Nathan.

Actually, that's not a bad idea, I thought . . .

I kept very close to Nathan, hoping he would slip an arm round my shoulder or take my hand, but he didn't seem to notice me. The next stand was about the history of glue and an intelligent frown was furrowing his brow. He took a notebook and a pen from his coat pocket.

I tried another tack. 'You seem very close to your father.'

'Ah, yes. Tati.'

'Have you always lived with him?'

'Not always, and I'm not sure that I can live with him much longer.'

I brushed against him. Surely my intentions must be obvious?

Nathan had opened his notebook and was busy scribbling. 'Something about the history of adhesion might make a nice article for *Adhesives in the Modern World*, Georgia,' he suggested. 'What d'you think?'

Maybe he just didn't fancy me. Maybe I wasn't intelligent enough for him. Maybe he was involved with someone else.

'Mmm. Good idea.'

'Glue past and present. Or even glue past, present and future.'

'I don't think I could do the future bit.'

I was thinking of Mrs Shapiro. *When you see a good man, you must grebbit*. Should I just grab him?

'You could just speculate. Glue made from recycled carrier bags. Glue made from liposuction by-products. Glue made from stray cats and dogs. Glue made from melted-down social undesirables.' He gave me a grin. 'No?'

'Like you told me once the Nazis made glue out of Jews?'

'Very good glue it was, too. Now Jews are trying to make glue out of Palestinians. But with less success.' He dropped his voice to a whisper. 'They say God told them to.'

I stared at him. How could he joke about that? He saw the look in my eyes.

'Sorry, it's only metaphorical glue. A sticky mess. And I mean the Israeli state, not the Jews. We have to distinguish.'

'Really?' What was he talking about? 'I'm not sure I understand . . .'

'I'm what they call a self-hating Jew. A gay, self-hating Jew.'

Ah! Gay! That explained everything! But why the self-hatred?

'Do you really hate yourself, Nathan?' Maybe it was his height.

'Sorry, Georgia. Self-hating is just a label the neo-Zionists use for people who disagree with them.' He gave me a hunkily intelligent grin.

Gay. What a shame! I thought about the banter of the men in the Miners' Welfare at Kippax. Poofs. Gays. Queers. Pansies. They were the casual everyday slights that were the currency of contempt down our way. I'd never heard Dad threatening to thump someone for using those words.

'What about your father?' I asked. 'Is he rude to your friends?'

'Oh, no. He just sings.'

I laughed. 'That sounds nice.'

'It is. But there are only so many lieder a person can take! Tati moved in with me after mother died, and Raoul moved out. It's sort of put paid to my love life.' He murmured conspiratorially, 'I keep hoping a nice widow will take him off my hands.'

We'd stopped in front of another photo—it was a little girl whose hands were stuck together. She was crying, her eyes screwed up in pain.

'Oh dear. As it says in the manual, one of the disadvantages of adhesive bonding is that disassembly is usually not possible without destruction of the component parts,' Nathan remarked drily.

It was one of the things about adhesives that had always troubled me. I stared. There was something so hopeless about the mess the girl was in.

'I know what you mean by self-hating, Nathan. I hate myself sometimes. I mean, I often feel stupid. I feel I've made a mess of my life.'

The trouble was, I was bonded to Rip; cyanoacrylate; a permanent bond. He was the only man I'd really loved, and I knew I would never love anyone in that way again. I felt tears brimming into my eyes. Nathan slipped an arm round me and gave me a friendly hug. 'Glue can be messy stuff.'

I rested my head on his shoulder, which was at just the right height if I bent my knees a bit, and let the tears roll down my nose. Nathan just stood there and let me cry. After a while, I dabbed my eyes with a tissue.

'Nathan, there's something I'd like to ask you.'

'Fire ahead.'

'Would you mind, on the way home, driving more slowly?'

I WOKE UP the next day feeling full of life. Sitting up in bed I switched my laptop on. The article I was working on was about medical uses of adhesives. Cyanoacrylate (superglue) had been used effectively in emergency battlefield situations in Vietnam to hold wounds together until they could be sutured properly. Now a number of companies were trying to develop specialist adhesives to be used in place of suture. Human bonding. There were two technical problems, it seemed, to be overcome. One, how to get the sides to hold together for long enough for bonding to take place. Two, how to achieve separation without tearing the flesh.

Then I remembered. Cyanoacrylate AXP-36C. I fumbled in the bedside drawer for a scrap of paper to write it down on before I forgot. I tried to picture Rip's face when he realised he was stuck. Who would rescue him? Who would call the ambulance? Ottoline Walker? Or would it be me? Would I laugh? Would I minister gently to his adhered behind?

Hauling myself out of bed, I stood at the window and looked down over the garden. The ground was wet and the leaves of the laurel bush were dazzling with captive raindrops, but the sun kept coming in and out behind the rain clouds, casting fleeting rainbows across the sky. At the far end of the garden, a haze of mauve crocuses had spread almost overnight.

Then I spotted Wonder Boy making his stealthy way towards a blackbird couple. I banged on the window and they flew away. Wonder Boy looked up and gave me a long reproachful stare. I felt a pang of guilt. The *HELP ME* letter Mrs Shapiro had sent was on my bedside table—I'd just scribbled the glue code on it. As I looked at the envelope with its scrawled-out name and address, I had a brainwave.

I dressed myself up in a red jacket, which had belonged to Stella, and a glittery Oxfam scarf, and pulled a woolly hat down low over my hair. I put on bright red lipstick and an old pair of sunglasses by way of disguise, then made my way to the bus-stop on the Balls Pond Road.

However, when I arrived at Northmere House I saw that my disguise was redundant, for there was a different guard-dog lady at the reception desk.

'Can I help you?' she barked.

'I've come to see Mrs Lillian Brown. I'm her cousin.'

She consulted her list. 'Would you sign in, please? Room twenty-three.'

She pressed the button that opened the sliding door. And in I went—into the muted realm of the pink carpet and the rows of closed doors from behind which, from time to time, a television blared eerily. A demented bleeper sounded constantly in the background, reminding the absent staff that behind one of these doors, someone desperately needed help.

I knocked on the door of number twenty-three. There was no reply so I pushed it open. The room was small and overheated and it took me a moment to notice the tiny figure lying motionless on the bed.

'Mrs Brown?'

There was no reply. I shouted louder, 'Mrs Brown? Lillian?'

I tiptoed over to the bed. She was lying there with her eyes closed. I couldn't tell whether she was breathing.

I backed out and let the door close behind me. My chest was thumping. As I turned away, I looked through the glass sliding doors that gave onto the courtyard and saw a hunched figure, wearing a powder-blue dressing gown and matching peep-toe slippers, sitting on a bench. She was puffing away at a cigarette. It was the bonker lady. I banged on the window and waved. She looked up and waved back. I slid open the door and went out to join her.

'Are yer lookin' for yer pal?'

'Mrs Shapiro. Yes.'

'She's in solitary. She int allaared visitors. Bin a naughty gel.'

'Why? What's she done?'

'It's what she ent done. She won't sign the Powah. Keeps refusin'.'

'Do you know which room she's in?'

'Twen'y-seven.'

Mrs Shapiro's room was as small as the other one and just as hot. She was lying on her bed, fully clothed, staring at the ceiling. Her hair was wild and matted, her skin folding in deep wrinkles round her mouth and chin.

'Mrs Shapiro?'

'Georgine?' She struggled groggily to sit up.

'How are you?' I hugged her. She seemed so frail, like a bird. All bones.

'Thenk Gott you come.'

'I'm sorry I didn't come before. I tried, but they wouldn't let me in.'

'Never mind. Good you heff come, Georgine. I do not want to die in here!' She started to cry, her skinny shoulders shaking. I sat down on the bed beside her, stroking her back until the sobs turned to sniffles. Then I passed her a tissue. 'We've got to get you home. But I don't know how.'

'Too much guards in this place. Like in prison.' She blew her nose. 'How are my dear cats?'

'They're fine. Waiting for you. I've got some young men staying there, looking after them. Fixing the house up.' I saw the look of alarm on her face. 'Don't worry. As soon as you're ready to come home, they'll leave.'

The sickly smell in the room was making me feel faint. I stood up and opened a window. The overheated air stirred and Mrs Shapiro took a deep breath. 'Thenk you, darlink.' She squeezed my hand, studying me. 'You looking better, Georgine. Nice lipstick. Nice scarf. You got a new husband?'

'Not yet.'

'Maybe soon I will heff a new husband.' She smiled archly to see the look of surprise cross my face. 'Nicky is saying he wants to marry mit me.'

'Mr Wolfe?' The scheming devil! I remembered how fluttery she'd been when he'd sat in her kitchen plying her with sherry.

'I was thinking he would be for you the perfect husband, Georgine. But maybe this is opportunity for me.' Her smile now was coyly flirtatious. She had cheered up considerably. 'What you think? Should I marry my Nicky?'

'Does he know how old you are?'

'I tolt him I was sixty-one.' She caught my eye and giggled. 'I am too notty for you, Georgine, isn't it?'

'You are a bit naughty, Mrs Shapiro.' Then I thought of something. 'Maybe it's because I told him you had a son.'

A son who would inherit her estate. Unless, of course, she remarried.

She looked at me sharply. 'How you know about this son?'

'The social worker told me. Mrs Goodney.'

'Ach, this woman. All she thinks about is how to shvindel me. I told her I heff a son because she was wanting me to sign the Power of Returning. I said my son will be returning. He will heff the house.'

'But he's not your son, is he?' I said gently.

There was a pause. 'Not mine. No.'

'So who was his mother?'

She sighed. 'It was the other one. Naomi Shapiro.'

Little by little, I drew it out of her. Her real name was Ella Wechsler. She was born in 1925 in Hamburg. Her family was Jewish, but of the pick-and mix variety. Ham but no sausages. Sabbath and Sunday. Christmas as well as Hanukkah—not that all this made any difference to the Nazis, when the time came. Her father, Otto Wechsler, ran a printing business; her mother, Hannah, was a pianist; her two older sisters, Martina and Lisabet, were students. Their house, a large villa in the Grindel Quarter, was a hanging-out place for musicians, artists, travellers arriving or departing, four cats, and a German maid. There was always coffee, music and conversation going on.

She chuckled. 'We were better at being German than the Germans. I thought this life was normal. I did not know such happiness was not permitted to Jews, Georgine, nor what it means to be a Jew until Herr Hitler told me.'

But by 1938, Hitler's message was loud and clear and the Wechslers fled to London. Ella was nearly thirteen years old, Martina was seventeen, Lisabet twenty. They had been able to bribe their way out of Germany, but England did not hold out her arms in welcome. The 1905 Aliens Act meant that they could only come to Britain if they had a job to come to.

Through a cousin, Otto Wechsler had managed to secure a job in a print shop in Whitechapel Road. The owner, Mr Gribb, was a widower from Elizavetgrad who had changed his name from Gribovitch when his family fled the pogroms in 1881. Hannah Wechsler became his housekeeper; Lisabet worked in a bakery; Martina trained as a nurse; Ella went to the Jewish school in Stepney. They lived in a two-roomed flat above the print shop in the East End Jewish community, and counted themselves blessed.

'Tell me about Artem. When did you meet him?'

'In 1944 he arrived in London. Still asking if they had seen his sister.'

He'd fetched up at the Newcastle docks, skeletal and hollow-eyed, on a British merchant ship that had snuck out from Gothenburg. The Seamen's Mission had taken him in and he was passed on, via Jewish relief organisations, to the flat in Whitechapel Road. He stayed with them for a year, helping to run the printing press and sleeping on a camp bed in the workshop. He spoke Russian and a few phrases of German and English, but said little. In his spare time, he started to make a violin with a fret saw and glue. By then, Ella was eighteen, Martina was twenty-three and Lisabet twenty-six. All of them were a bit in love with him.

'Did he finish the violin?'

'Yes. Gott knows where he got the strings. When he was playing, it was like the angels in heaven. Sometimes I or Mutti accompanied mit the piano.'

'Do you still play the piano, Mrs Shapiro? Ella?' Somehow, the new name didn't seem to fit the old lady I'd grown fond of.

'Look at my hends, darlink.' She held them out, bony, with swollen joints. I took them and warmed them in mine. They were so cold.

'And Naomi? Who was she?' I had such a strong image from the photos of the heart-shaped face, the tumble of brown curls, the playful eyes.

When at last Mrs Shapiro spoke, she said, 'Naomi Lowentahl. She was rather tall. And nice looking. Always mit red lipstick. Who would heff thought she would be the type to go away digging in the ground in Israel?' Her mouth twitched. Another silence. She withdrew her hands from mine and started to fiddle with her rings. 'She was in loff with Arti, of course.'

'And he . . .?'

She sniffed. 'Yes. And he.'

Artem Shapiro and Naomi Lowentahl had been married in the synagogue at Whitechapel in October 1945, after the end of the war. Ella, Hannah and Otto Wechsler went to the wedding. Lisabet was away in Dorset on her own honeymoon with a Polish Jewish airman. Martina had been killed by a V2 rocket raid in July 1944.

A rap on the door made us both jump, and a woman in pink uniform barged into the room. 'Teatime, Mrs Shapiro.' She caught sight of me. 'You'll have to leave,' she said. 'Mrs Shapiro in't allowed visitors.'

'I'm not a visitor. I'm a . . .' I thought fast. 'I'm an adhesion consultant.' I stood up and put on a posh voice. 'If you could just leave us now. We've almost finished our consultation.'

'Well, I'll have to report this to matron.' She shook her head. 'We can't just 'ave people wandering in off the streets.'

When we were alone again, Mrs Shapiro gripped my hands. 'You will keep my secret, Georgine?'

'Of course I will. Now, don't sign anything and don't marry Nicky. I'll try to get you out.'

There was a sudden rush of footsteps and voices in the corridor. I kissed Mrs Shapiro on the cheeks and quickly said goodbye, just as they reached the door. The pink-overalled lady was in front, followed by a big green-cardied woman and a security guard. Their faces were flushed with purpose. But before they could say anything they were distracted by a ghastly scream from down the corridor outside number twenty-three. I turned—we all turned—to see the bonker lady waving her hands in the air and yelling, ''Elp! 'Elp! There's a dead body in 'ere!'

They forgot all about me in the ensuing chaos. I slipped out through the sliding doors while someone else was rushing in. All the way home on the top deck of the bus, I was working out a plan to get Mrs Shapiro out.

THE FOLLOWING MORNING, I phoned Ms Baddiel. Amazingly, she answered on the first ring.

'Oh, thank goodness I've got hold of you. Something terrible's happened. Mrs Shapiro's been kidnapped,' I gabbled.

'Ca-alm down, Mrs Sinclair. Take a deep breath for me. Hold. Two—three—four. Breathe out with a sigh. Two—three—four, and rela-ax.'

I did as she instructed. My stomach knot eased and my fists turned back into hands. Then I tried to explain that Mrs Shapiro had been kidnapped and held against her will until she agreed to sign away her house. I tried to avoid directly accusing Mrs Goodney of theft, but Ms Baddiel was more concerned that Mrs Shapiro's lifestyle choices were being violated.

'There are a number of options open to her. If she is to live at home, the house needs to be made suitable. She could install a stairlift . . .'

'Mm. Yes. Good idea.' I tried to picture Mr Ali and the Uselesses installing a stairlift. Mm. No.

'. . . but unfortunately now it usually has to be self-financed,' Ms Baddiel told me. 'Has she got any funds, do you know?'

'I'm not sure. I'll ask her.' Though I knew she wouldn't tell me. My heart sank. Then I imagined trying to persuade her to have a stairlift installed.

'And we could increase her care package.'

'Fantastic.'

We arranged to meet at the house in three days' time. Ms Baddiel undertook to visit Northmere House meanwhile, and to challenge the terms of Mrs Shapiro's incarceration. 'It's a violation of human rights,' she said confidently.

ON WEDNESDAY AFTERNOON I set out to visit Mrs Shapiro at Northmere House again. I must have dozed off on the bus, for when I looked out of the window I realised I'd missed my stop. I rang the bell hastily and when the bus came to a halt I found myself standing near a familiar orange-and-grey building. Another branch of B&Q! It must be destiny, I thought.

A stunningly pretty Asian girl with a sparkling nose stud pointed me in the direction of the adhesives. I pulled the crumpled Mrs Brown envelope with my scribbled note on it from my pocket—*cyanoacrylate AXP-36C*—and started to look at the labels on the packaging. I picked up a few superglues and put them in my shopping basket with a nonchalant air.

By the time I remembered I'd meant to call at Northmere House on the way back, I'd already overshot the stop again.

I got off the bus at my stop and set off home. As I turned the corner into my road, I saw there was a car parked outside my house. A black car. A Jaguar. I stopped. How long had he been waiting for me? As I got closer, the driver's-side door opened and Mark Diabello stepped out.

'Doing a spot of DIY, are you, Georgina?' He was looking at my B&Q carrier bag. 'Have you got time for a quick word? About Canaan House? There are some . . . er . . . developments you should know about.'

'Developments?'

I glanced at my watch. It was Wednesday, just turned three o'clock.

'It'll have to be quick. Ben'll be back soon.'

'I thought you should know . . . my colleague, Nick Wolfe. You were right. His intentions are not honourable.'

'You'd better come in.'

He followed me into the house. I shoved the B&Q bag into a cupboard in the study on my way down to the kitchen, where I put the kettle on.

'Tell me,' I said.

'Yes. Nick's become obsessed with Canaan House. He's commissioned an architect; had plans drawn up to turn it into a gated community. Luxury flats. Plus six mews studios.'

I took a deep breath. 'And what's he planning to do with Mrs Shapiro?'

'He's planning to marry her.'

He delivered his punchline with a slight lift of the eyebrows. 'Apparently they struck up quite a friendship and he sneaked a look at her records in the nursing home. They gave her age as ninety-six. He thought—well, at that age her life expectancy—how can I put it?—a couple of years, at most.'

'Did he tell you she has a son?'

'That's why Nick's in a hurry to tie the knot. If she's married to him, he gets the lot when she pops her clogs. Unless she's made a will, of course.'

'The son's supposed to be coming from Israel. He obviously thinks he's onto a good thing, too. But I don't know if he's really her son. Her husband was married before, you know.'

Before what? That's what I couldn't work out. If Ella Wechsler had married Artem Shapiro, her name would have become Ella Shapiro. But why had she changed her first name from Ella to Naomi?

'If she wasn't married to him,' I was thinking aloud as I poured boiling water over coffee in the cafetière, 'if she was just living with him . . .'

'Mm. Good point. Would she still have a claim on the house?'

'Does it make any difference, who was married to who?' I handed him a cup of coffee. 'Surely, if she's lived there all these years, the house is hers?'

'It depends on how the deeds were drawn up.' He stirred sugar into his cup. 'Do you know where they're kept by any chance, Georgina?'

They were probably among papers in the attic. 'I haven't a clue,' I said.

'It might be possible to find out from the Land Registry,' he said. He drank his coffee quickly and made his way back upstairs. I followed him up in time to see the front door closing behind him.

I went up to my bedroom and lay down on my bed, remembering what we had shared in this room the last time he'd come to see me. Then, riding in on the memory, came a pang of longing for Rip—for his warm solid body, his alert clever mind. In spite of the Progress Project and the destiny-shaping work, in spite of the dereliction of DIY duties and the irritating BlackBerry habits, in spite even of the Scarlet-mouthed Slut, he was still Ben and Stella's dad; yes, and he was still the man I loved. Perhaps it was time to stop messing about and start gluing my marriage together.

BEN AND I had taken to having our supper in front of the gas fire in the sitting room with the television on in the background. So there we were on Thursday, balancing our plates on our knees and watching the seven o'clock news, when we heard the sound of a car pulling up, followed by footsteps on the path and then a knock on the door. I got up and opened it. I didn't recognise the man standing there, but after a moment, I realised he was the driver of the taxi that had pulled up outside in the road. The door of the taxi opened and out clambered Mrs Shapiro.

'Georgine!' she exclaimed. 'Please—do you heff money for the taxi?'

'Of course,' I said. 'How much?'

'Fifty-four pound,' said the taxi driver. He wasn't smiling.

'Isn't that a bit—'

'It should be more than that. We been going round in circles for hours.'

I went to look in my purse. Between us Ben and I rustled together £52.73. The taxi driver took it, mumbled something, and disappeared.

'Come in, come in,' I said to Mrs Shapiro.

'Thenk you,' she said. 'Some persons are in my house. Will not let me in.'

As she stepped inside, Wonder Boy appeared and slunk in beside her.

She sat by the fire cradling a mug of tea in her hands, which Ben had brought on a tray, with some chocolate digestives.

'Thenk you, young man. Charming. I am Mrs Naomi Shapiro.'

Wonder Boy stretched himself out in front of the fire and started rubbing himself up against the Lion King slippers. Through sips of tea and mouthfuls of biscuit crumbs, Mrs Shapiro told us the story of her escape.

After the discovery of the dead body, the bonker lady had become totally bonkers.

'Crezzy. Brain completely rotted away.'

Not content with hanging around in the corridor cadging cigarettes from visitors, she would embellish her patter with an invitation: 'I show you the dead body if you give me a ciggie.'

It came to a head when a party of relatives accompanying their aged mother on an inspection tour were accosted by the bonker lady, who somehow led them to believe that finding corpses was almost a daily occurrence. The staff member who was showing them round lost her rag and tried to push the bonker lady back into her room.

'But she was fighting like a tiger. Clawing and skretching mit the hends!'

In the end the security guard had to be called, but the bonker lady kept struggling and yelling, ''Elp! 'Elp! They gonner kill me!'

In all the kerfuffle Mrs Shapiro managed to slip unnoticed through the sliding doors into the lobby and out into the road, where a passing taxi whisked her to safety.

'And here I am, darlinks!' she exclaimed, flushed with excitement. 'Only problem is some persons are liffing in my house. We must evict them now!'

We all set off down the road, Mrs Shapiro leading the way. As we turned into Totley Place a couple of the other cats appeared out of the bushes and tagged along, too. Violetta was waiting for us in the porch, ecstatic with pleasure at Mrs Shapiro's return. Wonder Boy hissed and sent her packing.

There were lights in some of the windows. I noticed that the front door had been painted yellow and the broken floor tiles in the porch replaced with what looked like bathroom tiles. While Mrs Shapiro was fumbling for her key, I rang on the doorbell.

It was Mr Ali's nephew, Ishmail, who answered the door. Beaming broadly, he gestured to us to come inside.

'Welcome! Welcome!' He'd learned another word.

The inside of the house had been painted, too, in white and yellow. It looked lighter and fresher, and smelled much better. I saw Mrs Shapiro looking around. She seemed to be quite pleased.

'You've been busy,' I said to Ishmail. 'This is Mrs Shapiro. She's the owner of the house. She's come home, so I'm afraid you'll have to leave.'

He smiled and nodded blankly. He obviously had no idea what I was on about. Then Nabeel appeared on the scene, and joined in the smiling and nodding. We were getting nowhere, until Ishmail got his mobile phone out, keyed a number and started talking in Arabic to the person at the other end. After a few moments he passed the phone to me. It was Mr Ali.

'You'll have to tell them to leave,' I said. 'Now that Mrs Shapiro's home. They can't stay. I'm really sorry. I thought we'd have some warning, but . . .'

'Tonight too late. I have no van.' Mr Ali's voice sounded faint and crackly. 'Please let them to stay for tonight. Tomorrow I come with van.'

'OK,' I said. 'I'll talk to Mrs Shapiro. Mr Ali, thank you for the work you've done the painting—it looks wonderful.'

'You like this yellow colour?'

'Very much.'

'I knew you would like it.' He sounded pleased.

Mrs Shapiro had lost patience with our three-way conversation, and had disappeared. Ben had wandered off into the study, where a television had been rigged up with an internal aerial and Nabeel was now watching football. They sat side by side grinning and cheering when a goal was scored. Nabeel pointed to himself and said, 'Hello! Please! Arsenal!' Ben pointed to himself and said, 'Hello, Leeds United!'

I found Mrs Shapiro curled up in bed with Wonder Boy, Violetta, Mussorgsky, and one of the pram babies. Wonder Boy had actually got under the covers with her. They were all purring and Mrs Shapiro was snoring.

THE NEXT MORNING, I woke up with that feeling that I had something important to do, but I couldn't remember what it was. Then the phone rang. It was Ms Baddiel, reminding me of our meeting and asking for directions to Totley Place. After I'd put the phone down, I dialled Nathan's number.

'I wonder whether you could give us some advice . . . About the use of modern adhesives in home improvements . . . This morning . . . Eleven o'clock . . . Good.' I gave him the address. 'Bring your father, too.'

I smiled as I put the phone down. Matchmaking is a game two can play.

I went up there a bit earlier to make sure everything was shipshape for Ms Baddiel, and to supervise the departure of the Uselesses. When I rang on the bell at about half past ten, it was Ishmail who opened the door and invited me in. The house was pleasantly warm and smelled of wood smoke, freshly brewed coffee and cigarettes. I followed him through to the study at the back of the house, where a fire had been lit in the hearth. They were burning some of the boards that had been taken down from the windows.

On the sofa, which had been dragged through from the drawing room, sat Mrs Shapiro and Nabeel. They were smoking and drinking coffee, poured from a silver pot, and watching *The Hound of the Baskervilles* on the television. Mrs Shapiro was wearing her dressing gown and her Lion King slippers. Violetta was curled up on her lap, Mussorgsky was on Nabeel's lap and Wonder Boy was stretched out on the rug.

'Georgine! Darlink!' She swivelled round and patted the empty space at the end of the sofa. 'Come and drink a coffee mit us.'

'Maybe later,' I said. 'We have to get ready. The social worker's coming.'

'What for I need social work?' Mrs Shapiro sniffed. 'I heff my young men.'

'But they're going home now, Mrs Shapiro. They have to go.'

On the screen, the hound started roaring. Wonder Boy pricked up his ears and started swinging his tail.

Mrs Shapiro grabbed my hand. 'This dog is a monster. Same like matron in the Nightmare House. Grrah! I will not go back to this place. Never.'

'No, definitely not. But this social worker is nice. She'll help you to stay at home. It's Ms Baddiel. You met her before. Remember?'

'I remember. Not Jewish. Too fet.'

Ishmail thrust a cup of coffee into my hands. As I was stirring the thick, black liquid, the doorbell rang. The other three were completely gripped by the television so I got up to answer it. Ms Baddiel was standing there. She was wearing a floaty, silk, aquamarine coat and her honey-gold hair was twisted up in a loose braid. Behind her on the porch stood Nathan, with a large attaché case under his arm, and Nathan's Tati looking very spruce in a collar and tie. They had obviously introduced themselves already.

'Nathan's come along to advise us about adhesives,' I said. 'In case there are any urgent repairs that need doing.'

'Perr-fect.' She followed me through to the study, sniffing the air and looking around her, taking in all the improvements. 'Lovely.'

Mrs Shapiro hardly looked up as we came into the room, but Ishmail jumped up and offered Ms Baddiel his corner of the sofa.

'Hello, Mrs Shapiro.' She leaned forward towards the old lady. 'How are you doing? I understand you've had some adventures.'

'Ssh!' Mrs Shapiro held her finger to her lips. 'The hund is killing.'

Half an hour or so later, as the final credits rolled, she turned to us and said in a croaky voice, 'I heff seen this film once before. Mit Arti. When we were still in loff. Before the sickness snetched him away. So long ago.' There were tears in the corners of her eyes.

Ms Baddiel reached in her bag for a tissue. 'It's all right now. You can let it all out. Take a deep breath. Hold. Breathe out with a sigh. There. Perfect.'

Violetta stretched her paws and rubbed her head against Mrs Shapiro's thigh. Tati put a piece of wood—it looked worryingly like an antique chair leg—on the fire and reached down to stroke Wonder Boy, who rolled on his back and started to purr. Nathan and I exchanged smiles. Nabeel went and made another pot of coffee. Ishmail offered round a packet of cigarettes.

'Are you her carer?' Ms Baddiel asked.

'Hello. Yes. Please.' He flashed his lovely teeth at her.

She took out her notebook and wrote something down. Then Nabeel came back from the kitchen with a steaming coffeepot and some fresh cups.

'And you? You're a carer, too?'

'Hello. Yes. Welcome!'

'Well, you may be entitled to claim the Carer's Allowance,' she said. 'One of you. Are you claiming Attendance Allowance, Mrs Shapiro?'

'What for I need attendents?' said Mrs Shapiro.

'Well, you know,' Ms Baddiel said, 'after what you've been through, Mrs Shapiro, I think you deserve a bit of help. Of course it's up to you.'

Then the doorbell rang again. Ishmail was already on his feet so he went to answer it. I heard him talking animatedly and, a moment later, Mr Ali joined us in the study.

He turned to Mrs Shapiro. 'He is saying they want to stay. He is saying they can baint all house and help you make it clean. I will supervise of course. You bay only materials.'

I saw a quick flicker pass through Mrs Shapiro's eyes. She said nothing.

'You know in our culture we have great respect for old people,' Mr Ali pressed on. 'But I think mebbe you do not like to have young men into your house, Mrs Naomi?'

Everyone's gaze now focused on Mrs Shapiro, who looked around cannily.

'I donnow. I donnow.' She put one hand dramatically to her brow, and ran the other through Wonder Boy's shaggy belly-fur. 'Wonder Boy, what you think?' Wonder Boy purred ecstatically. 'OK. We try it.'

There was a general exhalation of breath.

Mr Ali led us on a guided tour around the house to show us the improvements he'd made. The most spectacular change was in the bathroom. There was a rose-pink washbasin and matching lavatory complete with pink plastic seat cover, and under the window an avocado-green bath. The rotten floorboards under the lavatory had been patched up, and a piece of lino in blue-and-white mosaic covered the whole floor. If you were colour-blind, it would have been lovely.

As my eyes scanned the room, they fell on a white porcelain toothbrush holder fixed onto the wall above the basin. I looked more closely. Yes, it was the same one. There was a small chip on one side—must be from where I'd tossed it into the skip. It was quite stylish, but it was just a toothbrush holder. To imagine I'd once got so worked up over it!

Then Mr Ali turned the taps on and off to demonstrate that they all worked. As he flushed the lavatory, steam rose as the clean water from the cistern swirled about.

'Er—isn't it hot, the water?' Nathan observed.

Mr Ali stared into the toilet pan with a puzzled frown.

'But the hot water is much better!' cried Mrs Shapiro. 'You are a very clever-Knödel, Mr Ali.'

He beamed at her. 'Colours you like?'

'The pink is nice colour,' she said. 'Better than the green.'

'Lovely,' said Ms Baddiel, who had seen—and smelled—the original.

'They've developed a new kind of flexible non-crack tile adhesive based on a thixotropic gel,' said Nathan, producing a tub of something from his demonstration pack. 'Should you be thinking of replacing the tiles.'

Mrs Shapiro's bedroom was untouched, the wallpaper a faded-out colourless fawn with small nondescript flowers picked out in muddy taupe.

'We will baint it up next. What colour you like it?' asked Mr Ali.

She pressed her fingers to her brow as she tried to envision a new room.

'What about the penthouse?' I said to Mr Ali. 'Have you started up there?'

'Not yet. Still clearing rubbish. Boys burning it. But slow.'

'They're burning the papers?' I had an image of historical records going up in smoke. 'Mrs Shapiro? Aren't some of your belongings up there?'

'Is all the rubbish belonging previous inhebitants,' she said dismissively. 'Was some type of religious persons liffing here before. Orsodox or Kessolik I don't know. They ren away in the bombing. Yes, eau de nil. Eau de nil is the most charming colour for the bedroom, isn't it?'

'An admirable choice,' murmured Nathan's Tati sonorously into Mrs Shapiro's ear, brushing her cheek with the tips of his whiskers.

As we came back down the stairs, he held out his arm for Mrs Shapiro, and she rested her weight on it lightly. My plan was working!

The last room we went into was the drawing room with the grand piano. Mr Ali had removed the boards from the window and in the daylight we could see a great crack in the bay, so wide that you could see daylight on the other side and the green of the monkey puzzle tree. A trail of muddy paw prints led from the base of the crack across the carpet towards the door. So this explained the mystery of how the Phantom Pooer got in and out—even though I still didn't know which one was the culprit.

Nathan, Nathan's Tati and Mr Ali went over to examine the crack.

'There are new types of heavy-duty fast-setting foam fillers, called structural methacrylates, suitable for construction work . . .' Nathan began.

'But this does not fixitup the problem.' Mr Ali scratched his head. 'First we must find out what causes. Maybe this tree . . .'

They were looking into the break in the floorboards below the ruptured skirting board. 'We could cut the tree down, dig the roots out, then pump the gap full of methacrylate foam,' suggested Nathan.

'What do you think, Mrs Shapiro? Should we cut the tree down?' asked Ms Baddiel.

Mrs Shapiro looked shifty. 'No. Yes. Maybe.'

I remembered her correspondence with the council's tree department. 'It may have a preservation order on it,' I said. 'Shall I find out?'

Everyone seemed pleased with this suggestion. As we stood staring into the crack, a feline head poked up between the floorboards and the Stinker eased himself into the drawing room and made a dash for the door.

Mrs Shapiro moved over to the piano, lifted the cover and tinkled a few notes. Even those out-of-tune keys seemed to come alive under her touch. To my amazement, without any music to read, she started to play the 'Toreador Song', embellishing it with broken chords and little trills, and Nathan's Tati, standing behind her, gave us a full baritone rendition. At the end, Mrs Shapiro sat back, placing her gnarled hands together with a sigh.

'Hends no good, isn't it?'

'Nonsense, Naomi,' said Tati, taking her hands and holding them in his.

Then we all made our way back towards the entrance hall to say our goodbyes. Mrs Shapiro sidled up to me, nodding her head towards Nathan, and whispered, 'He is your new boyfriend, Georgine?'

'Not my boyfriend. Just a friend.'

'Good thing,' she whispered. 'He is too petite for you. But quite intelligent. The father also is charming. Pity he is too old for me.'

After Nathan, his father, Ms Baddiel and Mr Ali had gone, Mrs Shapiro and her attendants went back to sit by the fire, leaving me alone in the hall. That's when I noticed that the framed photograph of Lydda had disappeared. There was nothing but a nail sticking out of the wall to show it had been there. Who had moved it? I was still puzzling over it when suddenly I heard the distinct clack of the front gate.

Coming down the path towards the house was Mrs Goodney, with an important-looking black briefcase under her arm. Behind her came a dark, middle-aged man I'd never seen before. He was wearing a crumpled brown suit. Neither of them was smiling. There was something odd about the way the man was looking at me: his eyes seemed asymmetrical.

Mrs Goodney stopped in her tracks when she saw me standing in the doorway. Then she continued her advance. Now a third person, a tall, spindly youth, appeared on the garden path and made his way towards me. It was Damian, the young man from Hendricks & Wilson.

'Feeding the cats again, are we?' said Mrs Goodney to me. Then she turned to Damian and smiled toothily. 'Glad you could make it, Mr Lee. The gentleman just needs an initial estimate of value at this stage.'

The thickset man nodded. He was looking at the house in frank amazement, his misaligned eyes sliding round this way and that. Then I realised one of them was made of glass.

'Must be vort a bit, eh?' he said. 'Big house like this. Good part of London. I am somewhat impressed.' His English was better than Mrs Shapiro's, if a bit pedantic, with just a slight guttural accent.

'Unfortunately it's not worth as much as you think. I can show you a builder's report, if you like.' Mrs Goodney smiled at the thickset man. 'But don't worry, Mr Lee will quote you a good price. Won't you, Mr Lee?'

Suddenly, her gaze had shifted to a point beyond my left shoulder. I turned round. Mrs Shapiro was there, and behind her, Nabeel and Ishmail.

'Hello, Mrs Shapiro.' Mrs Goodney's rusty-gate voice squeaked with fake cheeriness. 'What are you doing here? You're supposed to be . . .'

'I am come home. Finish mit Nightmare.'

'But this house isn't safe for you, poppet.'

'Poppet schmoppet.' She pulled herself up into her five-feet-tall, chin-out-fighting pose and looked the social worker in the eye. Her cheeks were flushed. 'I heff my Attendents. I will claim the Attendents' Allowance.'

Suddenly the thickset man stepped forward. 'Ella? You are Ella Wechsler?'

Mrs Shapiro drew back. I couldn't see her face, but I could hear her throaty intake of breath. 'You are mistooken. I am Naomi Shapiro.'

'You are not.' His voice was gravelly. 'She was my mother.'

'I don't know what you talking about.' Mrs Shapiro elbowed past me, reached out and slammed the door.

They didn't go away for about half an hour. Standing inside the freshly painted hall, the four of us listened to them ringing the doorbell and rattling the letterbox. Then they walked round the outside of the house and started rapping on the kitchen door. Eventually they gave up.

I didn't leave until I was sure the coast was clear. I walked home, trying to make sense of what had happened. He must be the real Naomi Shapiro's son—the child she wrote about in her letters—this thickset, middle-aged man who had embodied all the hopes of his beautiful mother. But who was she? And how had Mrs Goodney contacted him? Maybe this was why I'd found no documents in the house—Mrs Goodney had got there first.

As soon as I got home I went up to my bedroom and spread the photos out on the floor. Baby Artem; the wedding photo; the couple by the fountain; the woman in the archway; the two women at the Highbury house; the Wechsler family; the moshav at Lydda. At half past four, Ben wandered in to see what I was doing. He picked up the photograph of the woman standing in the stone archway and turned it over.

'It says Lydda.'

'That's a place. In Israel.'

'I know, Mum. It's in one of the prophecies. It's supposed to be where the Antichrist returns.' His voice had gone husky. 'The Muslims call him Dajjal? He's got one eye? He gets killed by Jesus in this massive battle at the gates of Lydda?' There were beads of sweat on his forehead. 'I know there's something in it. I just know. Like, I can feel it coming?'

9

I walked round to Canaan House the next day, hoping to have a chance to speak to Mr Ali. I wanted to ask him about Lydda. After listening to Ben the previous afternoon, I'd logged on to the Internet to look up information about the prophecies relating to Lydda. This story, because of Ben, had now become my story, too, and I knew I had to follow it through.

The sun was shining for once, a hard, clear brightness, with even a touch of warmth—a real spring day. Around the margins of the lawn, daffodils were poking their yellow heads up. Mr Ali was there, standing on a ladder painting the outside of Mrs Shapiro's bedroom window. Wonder Boy was supervising him, sitting on one of the white uPVC chairs in the garden.

'Hello, Mr Ali!' I called. 'Is everything OK?'

He came back down the ladder wiping his hands on a piece of cloth. 'Hello, Mrs George. Nice day! Tomorrow I borrow the van, we take Mrs Shapiro to choose colour of paint for inside.'

'That's good.'

'How is your son?'

'He's OK, but . . .' An image of Ben slipped into my mind, his waxy face, the fear in his eyes. He'd gone off to bed last night without eating anything. I'd knocked on the door of his room, but it was locked from the inside. 'Mr Ali, that picture in the hall—of Lydda. Was it you who took it down?'

'Lydda.' He stuck his brush in a pot of turpentine and swirled it around. 'In the old times this town was famous for its beautiful mosques. But do you know, Mrs George, that this town is a special place to you also? Is home town of your Christian St George. You are named from him, I think?'

'Really? St George the Dragon Slayer came from Lydda?'

'You can see his picture carved above the door of the church.'

But Ben had also talked about a one-eyed devil.

'The picture of Lydda that was in the hall, why did you take it down?'

'Why you are always asking questions, Mrs George?' He wasn't exactly being rude, but the easy friendliness of our previous conversation had gone. 'Everything is OK. Sun is shining. I am working. Everybody is happy. Now you start asking questions, and if I tell you the truth you will not be happy.'

'You were going to tell me about your family, remember? What happened in Lydda?'

He didn't say anything. He was concentrating on cleaning his brush. Then he pulled up one of the white plastic chairs and sat down at the table.

'You want to know? OK. I will tell you.' He folded his arms across his XXL tummy. 'I come from Lydda. I had one brother, born the same time.'

Mustafa al-Ali, the man I knew as Mr Ali, was born in Lydda in 1948. He didn't know his mother's name, nor that of his twin brother, nor even his date of birth, but he reckoned he was a few months old on July 11, 1948.

'Why, what happened then?'

'Have patience. I will tell you.'

Lydda was then a busy town of some 20,000 inhabitants that had grown up over centuries in the fertile coastal plain between the mountains of Judaea and the Mediterranean sea. But that summer, the summer of *Nakba*, the town was filled with refugees from Jaffa and smaller towns and villages all up the coast. 'Everybody was talking about expulsions and massacres.'

One late morning in July, when everything was hot and still, there was a sudden roar of engines overhead. Then the explosions started, as planes began unloading their bombs on the sleepy little town.

'But their purpose mainly was not to kill,' Mr Ali continued, fixing me with his eyes. 'They wanted to drive us out, with terror.'

The next day, as people were emerging from the rubble to inspect the damage and bury their dead, a battalion with mounted machine guns suddenly rolled into town at high speed. As dawn broke, soldiers ran from house to house, banging on the doors with their rifle butts and ordering those inside to leave at once.

The al-Ali family—the women and children, for their father had disappeared—were dragged out of their house onto the street, given only a few minutes to grab their valuables. Everyone was herded towards the outskirts of the town, the soldiers firing shots in the air to make them run. Here, they passed through a cordon where soldiers searched them, stripping them of their possessions. Ahead of them, one of their neighbours, recently married, quibbled about surrendering his savings and was shot dead before his bride.

The al-Ali family were robbed of their money, their gold jewellery, their watches. All they kept was a bundle of clothes, some bread and olives and a bag of oranges. Everyone was forced to make their way east across the stubbly, newly harvested fields. They could see a miserable procession of their fellow townspeople already stumbling towards the stony horizon.

The third day of the march was the worst. The women's sandals were now falling apart, their feet were bleeding and swollen.

'Go,' said his mother to her older son, Tariq. 'Go on ahead and find us some water to drink. Maybe there is a village with a well.'

All along the way people were fainting from thirst and exhaustion. On a rocky scree the boy came across a woman staggering under the weight of a huge bundle. Two watermelons, it looked like; and he thought, If she drops them, I'll pick them up and take them to my mother. But as he drew closer the woman sank to the ground and he saw that she was carrying two babies.

'Help me,' she pleaded. 'I cannot carry my sons.'

The boy hesitated. He already had his mother and sisters to look after; but it was clear this woman was not going to make it.

'Take just one of them,' she said in barely a whisper.

Tariq looked at the two babies, their eyes screwed shut against the light. How could he choose? Then one of them opened its dark bright eyes. The woman, seeing him waver, thrust the infant into his arms.

'Go. Don't wait for me. I'll meet you in Ramallah.'

Mr Ali went silent. I gazed at the green sunlit garden, the busy thrushes in their nest in the tree, the bursting daffodils, but I could feel a desert wind on my cheek, and all I could see was dry rocks and thorn bushes.

'That was you? The baby in the bundle?'

He nodded.

A door opened and from the house I heard the sweet jangle of Arabic music and the noisy patter of television. Then Mrs Shapiro appeared.

'Will you take a coffee mit us?'

Mr Ali didn't reply. 'My name is Mustafa,' he said quietly. 'It means "one who is chosen". My brother Tariq told me this story.'

I wanted to take his hand or put my arm round his shoulder, but there was a reserve about him that made me hold back.

'Did he tell you what happened to the other baby?' I asked.

Mr Ali shook his head. 'He told me only that the soldier who shot at the bridegroom had on his arm a tattoo—a number.'

I found I couldn't join in with the gossip over coffee. I caught Mr Ali's eye once or twice, and I kept wanting to ask him what had happened to the al-Alis; whether they had made it to Ramallah, and whether he, Mustafa, had ever found his mother and brother. But in my heart I knew the answer.

I was troubled, too, by the story of the soldier with the number tattooed on his arm—how could a Jew, who was himself a survivor of the death trails of Europe, act with such casual cruelty against the hapless civilians of his promised land? What had happened to his heart? Then I started to wonder about Naomi—when she had let herself be photographed in the archway at Lydda, did she really not know what had taken place there two years before? Or did she know, and consider it a necessary price?

ON SUNDAY I'D PLANNED to make the most of the fine weather and do some gardening, but I seemed to spend the whole day on the phone, and each phone call left me feeling more upset. The first call was at nine o'clock (would you believe it?) from Ottoline Walker, the Scarlet-mouthed Slut.

'Hello? Georgie Sinclair? Is that you?'

'Who's speaking?' I kind of recognised the voice already.

'It's me. Ottoline. We met. You remember?'

'Yes, I remember. Why are you ringing me?'

'It's about Rip . . . (well, it would be, wouldn't it?) I . . . I just wanted to tell you I had no idea you were still . . . sort of . . . involved.'

'Sort of married, actually.'

'He told me it was over between you two ages ago. He told me you didn't mind. Look, I'm really sorry. I mean, when you're in love, you don't always do the right thing . . . you don't think about the consequences for other people.' She paused. I said nothing. 'I believe in commitment, you know.'

'Like you were committed to Pete. And now you're committed to Rip.'

'That's not what I mean. Ben doesn't know, if you're wondering.'

'What about Pete? Does he know?' I almost called him Pectoral Pete.

'He found out. Poor Pete. It was awful. He was going to kill himself.'

She sounded as though she was sniffling on the phone, and for a moment I felt sorry for her. 'You'll not get much commitment from Rip. He's committed to the Progress Project.'

There was a silence. 'This Progress Project. What is it, exactly? Pete wasn't very good at explaining.'

'Why don't you ask Rip?' I put the phone down.

Grabbing my secateurs, I pulled on my gardening gloves and stomped out into the garden. The sun was shining, but my head was full of dark clouds. Still fired up with thoughts of Rip and the Scarlet-mouthed Slut, I hacked away pitilessly at the ugly laurel bush.

After an hour or so the phone rang again. I carried on snipping and let it ring until the answering machine clicked on. Then a minute later it started ringing again. I put the secateurs down and went to answer it.

'Hello, Georgina, I've been trying to get hold of you.'

Mark Diabello.

'I just wanted to let you know that I've heard back from the Land Registry about Canaan House.'

I took a deep breath. 'And?'

He explained that the house was unregistered, and that if Mrs Shapiro wanted to sell it she would need to register it, for which she would need the deeds. 'What about that son you mentioned, Georgina? The son in Israel? Maybe he knows where they are.' He was still angling for information.

'I met him the other day.' I told him an edited version of our encounter. I also told him about Damian. 'Damian Lee from Hendricks and Wilson.'

'Ah!' Mark Diabello caught his breath. 'That explains the BMW I saw parked round the back of their offices.'

'So Damian's job is . . .?'

'To persuade the son from Israel to let the social worker's friendly builder have the house for, say, a quarter of a million, then disappear back off to Israel with the cash in his pocket.'

'Just like you tried to persuade me?'

'That was different. I wasn't working for the buyer. Tsk. Naughty Damian.' His voice oozed disapproval. 'I told you they were crooks.'

At about five o'clock, just as I was trying to decide what to have for tea, the phone rang again. I listened to Rip's facing-unprecedented-challenges voice leaving a message on my answering machine, telling me to ring him immediately. There was something about the tone of his voice that reminded me of . . . glue. *Cyanoacrylate AXP-36C*. I thought of the B&Q package stowed in the study and smiled to myself. Peace in the world was all very well, but no way was it going to extend to Rip and me. When someone hurts you, what you want is revenge, not peace.

I didn't ring back. I went upstairs and got out my exercise book.

Early next morning, heartbroken Gina made her tearful way to the Castleford branch of B&Q. The sight of the jolly orange-clad building made her broken heart leap. Inside it was vast and creepily echoing like a church, and full of weird men prowling around the aisles, eyeing lovely curvaceous Gina lustfully. She made her way to the extensive adhesives section. At last her eyes lit on a tube of glue that said in large letters: DANGER! AVOID CONTACT WITH SKIN.

I stopped. I couldn't help thinking about the picture of the little girl at the glue exhibition. Messy stuff.

The last phone call came just as I was getting ready for bed. I knew it was Mum—she usually rings about this time—but I was taken aback by the flatness in her voice. 'Your Dad's been took poorly,' she said. 'He's got to have that operation on 'is prostrate.'

The operation date wasn't fixed, but it would be after Easter. My mind went into overdrive, trying to work out the logistics of going up to Kippax, leaving Ben with Rip, and meeting my deadline for Nathan.

I WAS TRUNDLING the vacuum cleaner round the house on Monday afternoon, worrying about Mum and Dad, when the phone rang. I thought it might be Mum with some more news of Dad's operation, but it was Mrs Shapiro.

'Come quick, please, Georgine. Chaim is mekking trouble.'

I realised I'd been half expecting it. Apparently Mrs Shapiro and Ishmail had gone off with Mr Ali in the red van to choose some paint. Nabeel had stayed behind to sand down the woodwork and one of the downstairs doors had been left unlocked. They got back at about four o'clock with their five litres of matt emulsion—'eau de nil—very charming colour—you will see it'—to find Nabeel and Chaim Shapiro wrestling in the dining room.

'Fighting like the tigers. You must come, Georgine, and talk to them.'

By the time I got there, the wrestling, if it had ever really happened, was over and there was an uneasy truce around the dining-room table. Mr Ali was sitting on one side of the table, flanked by the Uselesses, and opposite them sat Chaim Shapiro. Mrs Shapiro sat next to him, smoking. Wonder Boy was sitting on a chair at the head of the table, looking very magisterial.

I came in through the front door, which had been left on the latch for me.

'Hello, everybody!' I said, entering the dining room with a cheery smile. No one smiled back. I sat down at the far end of the table. Mrs Shapiro poured me a glass of water from a jug and introduced the newcomer to me as Chaim Shapiro, adding, 'This is Georgine, my good neighbour.'

He pounced on me at once, demanding to know why I had invited these strangers into his house—I winced at the emphasis—'*my* house'—but before I could get a word out, Mrs Shapiro pounced back.

'Is not your house, Chaim. I been liffing here sixty years paying rets.'

'Shut up your mouth, Ella. You have no feet to stand on, letting Arabs come into your home.'

I started to explain that the house needed repair and renovation and that's why Mr Ali and his assistants had been called in. Then there was the issue of security, I told him, describing the stolen key and the turned-off water main and hinting at Mrs Goodney's involvement. That made him sit up.

'That Goody with her young stick-up-the-hair-nik, they think I am made of short planks. They think I will sell them my house cheap so they can make some quick bucks out of me. But I have a different plan.'

'My house,' hissed Mrs Shapiro. 'When your father died, he give it me.'

'So what's your plan, Mr Shapiro?' I interrupted to move things on.

'My plan is to undertake some major renovations here in *my* house.' There were intakes of breath all round. 'I have already purchased a tool kit.'

'Chaim, darlink, your mother was giving up everything to build the new Israel. Beautiful homeland for the Jews. Why you are not staying there? Why you are coming back now and putting me onto the street?'

'Nobody is putting you onto any street, Ella. You are putting yourself onto the street living with these Arabs.'

'These are my Attendents.'

'Ella, you have lost your screws. All Arabs are the same—they are only waiting for the opportunity to push Jews into the sea.'

'Nobody is pushing me into the sea. The sea is a long way from here, Chaim. Sea is at Dover.' Mrs Shapiro leaned across and whispered to me, 'What is he talking about, Georgine?'

'I am talking about terrorism, Ella. Look at my blinded eye. What I was doing? Minding my own businesses.' He was cracking his knuckles furiously.

'We are in London now, Chaim. Not in Tel Aviv.'

'And you see they have commenced bombing here in London.'

Mr Ali leaned over and translated for Ishmail, who whispered to Nabeel. All three of them were scowling.

'Darlink Chaim, this is a house, not an aeroplane. Please, be calm. And these are my Attendents, not suicideniks. See, they are even animal-lovers.'

Nabeel had reached across and was stroking Wonder Boy behind the ears; the cat's rhythmic purring was a soothing background to the fractious discussion. If only someone would stroke Chaim behind the ears, I thought.

Now Mr Ali spoke, his voice splintering with anger. 'Arabs, Christians, Jews been living side by side for many generations. Making businesses together. No broblem. No bogrom. No concentration camp. Even we selled you some of our land. But this is not enough. You want whole bloody lot.'

Chaim Shapiro ignored him and, turning towards me, explained, 'All Palestinians have same story. They come with some old key, saying this is the key to my house. You must move out! But when my mother came to Israel nobody was living there. All the inhabitants had scarpered.'

'Driven out with gunpoint!' Mr Ali tried to shout.

'If you want to live alongside us in our land, all you must do is to stop attacking us. Is that not fair enough?' Chaim spread his hands theatrically.

'Look, we're not going to solve all the world's problems today,' I said cheerily. 'But it's quite a big house. Maybe everyone can live here together.'

They all turned towards me and I could feel myself turning crimson under their collective gaze. Wonder Boy was swinging his tail from side to side.

'I do not want to share my house with three Arabs,' Chaim grouched.

'Chaim,' said Mrs Shapiro appeasingly, 'the Peki is not living here. He is only a visitor.

'You do not understand the Arab mentality, Ella. You think Israel would exist today if half its population was Arab and trying to destroy it from within?'

I felt a stab of anger, remembering the twin babies, heavy as watermelons, and the soldier with the number tattooed on his arm. 'But you can't expect people to give up their homes and land and not fight back!'

Mr Ali translated for the benefit of the Attendents, who nodded fervently.

'Ha! Then we have the right of self-defence!' Chaim's face was sweating. 'Every time you strike Israel we will strike back harder. You give us home-made rocket-launchers, we give you US-made helicopter gunships. *Bam bam bam!*' He aimed his hands like a gun across the table. '*Bam bam bam!*'

Wonder Boy, who had been sitting on the chair at the head of the table, pricked back his ears at the noise and hissed. Then he leaped up onto the table in fighting pose, his back arched, his tail puffed out, and with a yowl he flew at Chaim, going at his face with his claws. Chaim fought back, trying to pull the big cat off, but Wonder Boy clung tight, his tail thrashing.

Mrs Shapiro shrieked frenziedly at both of them. 'Halt! Chaim! Stop this smecking! Wonder Boy! *Raus!*'

The cat hissed and fled, knocking over the jug of water. Chaim pulled out a handkerchief and dabbed at his bleeding cheek. When he looked up, we saw that his glass eye had swivelled round grotesquely in its socket.

Everyone went quiet, as if shocked at how quickly the confrontation had flared up. It was Mrs Shapiro who spoke first, leaning over to Chaim and patting his arm. 'Darlink Chaim, if you heff no home you can live here mit us. You can tek any room what you like—except of mine, of course. You can make all your beautiful renovations, mit your tool kit. Build in kitchen units, dishwashers, meekrowaves.' She took his hand and gave it a squeeze. 'We will make dinner parties mit cultured conversations. Concerts in the evenings.' I could see his face softening as he pictured these delectable scenes. 'You are my Arti's son, Chaim. This is always your home whenever you want. But my Attendents also must stay here mit me.' Her voice was so seductive that Chaim, I could tell, was already seduced.

'Ella, I can see you are quite a little home-pigeon, and I will gladly accept your invitation to take up my residence with you. And if the Arabs must stay, maybe we can divide the house between us. They keep to the top part of the house, and we stay in our part.' He beamed across the table.

'Hm! Next you will build a wall,' said Mr Ali drily. 'Checkpoint on the stairs. Then you will steal some more rooms for settlements.'

'Have you got a sticking plaster, Mrs Shapiro?' I asked, to diffuse the tension. Chaim's cheek was bleeding badly. She scuttled off to find one.

Mr Ali and the Attendents had convened a separate meeting in the kitchen, so for a few minutes, Chaim Shapiro and I were alone. The eye that looked at me—his good eye—was dark and sad, but it reminded me of the blazing brown eyes of the young woman in the photographs. I was still thinking that someone should stroke him behind the ears, but instead I said, 'You remind me of your mother.'

His face lit up with a smile. 'You knew my mother?'

'I didn't know her,' I said. 'I've seen her photo. You look like her.'

'I wish you could have met her. Everybody who met her loved her.'

'And your father . . .'

'Yes, Artem Shapiro. The musician. She was always talking about him.'

'Why didn't he join her in Israel?' I found myself holding my breath.

'He was sick. Lungs kaput. Ella was looking after him. Here in this house.'

The death certificate had said lung cancer.

'And your mother never came back to him?'

'She wanted to build a garden in the desert—with her own hands. She would not leave until it was finished.' A shadow settled over him. 'Then she got sick. She died when I was ten years old. A few months after my father.'

I remembered the date on the letter from Lydda. Chaim was born in 1950, so she must have died in 1960.

'I'm sorry. To lose your whole family . . . And then your injury . . .'

'But my family was the moshav—father, mother, sister, brother. After she died I stayed there with them.'

It must have been the same moshav she wrote about in the letter.

'Was she from Belarus too?'

'No, she came from Denmark. But they met in Sweden. They were married in London. And I was born in Israel.' He smiled a chubby dimply smile. 'Naomi Shapiro. She was a person who knew how to dream.'

'She dreamed of a promised land?'

'Our homeland. Zion.' His cheeks dimpled again. 'Home sweet home.'

'Then why do you want to make your life here, Chaim?'

'I was a teacher for thirty years. English language and literature.' He shuffled in his chair. 'Now I am retired. Not married. What woman wants to marry a one-eyed man?'

Mrs Shapiro had returned with a rather grubby sticking plaster. 'Well, now your home is mit us, isn't it?' She applied the plaster to his cheek.

'Thank you, Ella. My mother told me you were very solicitous to my father in his illness. And encouraging him to go to Israel upon his recovery. She showed me the letter you wrote.'

I glanced across at Mrs Shapiro.

'It was long ago,' she said. Sometimes it's better to let the past alone.'

'Yes, long ago.' He sat back heavily in his chair. 'You know, Ella, this country, this Israel, it is not the same country she dreamed of. They have spoiled it with their fanaticism.' He gestured with his head towards the kitchen where Mr Ali and the Attendents were chatting in Arabic.

'So what do you think is the solution?' I asked.

'There is no solution. I can see no possibility of peace in my lifetime.' He sank lower in his chair. 'So long as they continue with their attacks, we will continue our defences. We are trapped in tits for tats.'

I NOTICED, as I walked home in the early evening, that the silver buds of the pussy willow had opened out and the air was moist. Everything was cool and green. It was a different world to that of Mustafa al-Ali and Chaim Shapiro, but it was the same world. We all had to learn to live here somehow.

I was almost home when I realised that I'd never asked Chaim how he had lost his eye. Had he been caught up in the revenge attack at Lydda airport? I recalled my conversation with Ben less than a week ago—the ancient prophecy of the battle between Jesus and Antichrist at the gates of Lydda that was supposed to precede the end of the world. An airport is a kind of a gate to a city—isn't it? But surely the terrorists wouldn't have known the words of the prophets? I felt a quake of dread. How could the present reach back into the past? And Dajjal, the devil with one eye? But Chaim Shapiro was no devil, he was a stray soul who had lost his mother too young. Still, I felt as if a voice from another world had whispered, 'Armageddon.'

As I approached the house, I could see through Ben's window that his computer was on, the screen saver flickering. That was strange. Ben was supposed to be with Rip. Maybe he'd come back early.

'Hi, Ben!' I shouted up the stairs as I came in through the door. There was no reply, so I went up and tapped on the door of his room. No answer.

I pushed open the door and there was the screen saver whizzing around in the dusk, hurling its dizzying pattern against the walls. White! Red! Black! White! Red! Black! Then I saw Ben. He was lying on the floor between the bed and the desk, crumpled like a bundle of rags among his scattered clothes.

'Ben!' I screamed.

Then I realised it wasn't just the jerky light; Ben was moving; twitching. Head thrown back, eyes open and rolled back, flecks of foam dribbling from the corners of his mouth. I stumbled towards him, and as I did so, I knocked against the mouse and the screen he'd been viewing came up: ARMAGEDDON.

I screwed up my eyes and reached across to pull the plug out of the socket. The room went dark and I switched the light on. Ben moaned and flailed with his arms and legs. I lay down beside him and folded him in my arms, stroking his cheeks and his forehead, whispering his name, until he was still and his breathing slowed. Then I phoned for an ambulance.

The next stage all happened very fast, in a whirl of brisk paramedics and blue flashing lights. I tried ringing Rip from the ambulance but there was no reply so I sent him a text. After a few minutes Ben came round. He lifted his head from the stretcher, looking around him with a dazed expression.

'Where am I?'

'You're on your way to hospital.'

'Oh.' He seemed disappointed.

I held his hand as we ripped through the evening streets, siren howling.

The ward they admitted Ben to was the same one Mrs Shapiro had been in that first time. The doctor who came to see him seemed hardly older than Ben—in fact he had the same gelled-up hairstyle as Damian.

'It seems your son's had a fit,' he said. His voice had a Liverpool twang.

'What—epilepsy?'

'Could be. We'll have a better idea when we've done the MRI scan tomorrow. Let him sleep it off. We'll keep an eye on him tonight.'

Then the curtain parted and Rip and Stella came in. Rip ignored me and I think I might have done a runner if Stella hadn't come and hugged me.

'What's up with Ben, Mum?'

How pretty she was, but so thin—too thin. I held her and stroked her hair. I wanted to burst into tears, but I forced a cheerful grin onto my face. 'He had a fit, or something.'

Stella squeezed her brother's hand. 'Yer daft little beggar.' She was putting on a thick Leeds voice, the voice of their shared childhood banter.

He opened his eyes and looked around with a beatific smile on his face. 'Hey, everybody!' Then he drifted off again.

Rip stood framed by the curtain, trying to hector the doctor into conversation, demanding explanations and clarifications that the young man was unable to give, and all the time carefully avoiding meeting my eyes. When the doctor left, Rip came and sat on the other side of the bed and took Ben's other hand, leaning over and talking in a sickly, cooey-cooey voice.

I got up and walked out. I went as far as the swing doors, then I stopped. I knew I was being ridiculous. I turned round and went and sat in the day room to calm down, clenching and unclenching my hands. A minute later, the door swung open and Stella came in. Her face was red and blotchy. At first I thought she was upset; then I realised she was furious.

'Mum, you're mental—you and Dad—you've got to stop acting like kids. We're sick of it, me and Ben. We want you to . . . like . . . grow up.'

I stared at her. She was twenty years old and she was telling *me* to grow up. 'Yes, but what about *him*?' I whined.

'Him, too. I've told him, too. Both of you. You've got to stop it. We're fed up of it. *And* it's not doing Ben any good.'

'OK. Well, I will if he will. But I'm not—'

'So just go back in there, and smile at him, and just be *normal*, Mum.'

So I did.

WHEN I THINK of the turning point, the point from which it all started to get better again, I think of that Monday in March, that scene in the curtained cubicle at the hospital, Ben sitting up and trying to remember what had happened, Stella perched on the bed tickling his toes and making him laugh. It reminded me of the glue exhibition, with me and Rip sitting awkwardly on each side of the bed like lumpy, unpromising adherends, and Ben and Stella in the middle holding us together like two blobs of glue.

We sat together like that in the neurologist's office next day, Rip, Ben and me, with Ben in the middle. The neurologist took us through a series of questions, and asked us about the circumstances of Ben's fit.

When I described the whirling screen saver and the flashing flames of the Armageddon website, he said, 'It's possible for photosensitivity to trigger an epileptic seizure. What we can't tell at this stage is whether it will happen again.' He turned to Ben with a smile. 'Try and be more selective about which sites you visit, young man. It's wild out there in cyberspace.'

'Right.' Ben nodded. He was embarrassed by all the attention.

But there must be more to it than that, I thought.

'I can understand the computer flashing could set something off,' I said. 'But what about . . .?' I cast my mind back. 'Sometimes you said you were feeling strange when you got back from school, Ben, before you'd even turned the computer on.'

He blinked and frowned. 'Yeah. It was when I was on the bus. We passed these trees. I could see the sun through the branches.' He described a long road where low winter sunlight flickered through branches of an avenue of trees as he sat on the upper deck. 'That's when I had, like, feelings.'

The neurologist nodded. 'If you find yourself in that situation another time, young man, just try closing one eye.'

So that's all there was to it—the generations of prophets with their obscure and terrifying predictions, the reign of Antichrist, the tribulations, the Abomination of Desolation, Armageddon, the fearsome battle of all the armies of the world, the rebuilding of the Temple at Jerusalem, the end of time with trumpet clarions and fiery chariots, the return of the Messiah—it was all down to a frequency of flashing lights, a temporary short circuit in the wiring of the brain. All you had to do was close one eye.

'So all that religious stuff is nonsense?' Rip's voice was irritatingly smug, but I saw Ben wasn't listening. He was studying a wall chart of the brain.

As we left the hospital, Rip told me, a bit awkwardly, that he'd had to move out of Pete's place and asked me rather sheepishly whether it would be OK if he moved back in temporarily. I replied rather grumpily that it made no difference to me but I was sure Ben would appreciate it. I'd got a life of my own now and I wasn't ready to give it up.

Rip brought his stuff over from Islington later that afternoon and set himself up on a camp bed in the little study. We tiptoed around each other, being excessively polite and considerate.

Stella came home at the end of term, and from being empty, the house suddenly became full. It was Stella who told me, over a quiet cup of tea, that Ottoline had thrown Rip out. That's why Ben had come home unexpectedly on that Monday.

'Ben says he overheard them having a row. Apparently she told him he had a poor attitude to commitment,' she murmured in a grave voice.

Stella made the most of her holiday, sleeping in late and taking long showers. Ben filled the house with techno music and thumped around cheerfully, no longer glued to the computer. Rip and I fell into a pattern of sharing the same space while keeping out of each other's way. We learned each other's habits and avoided unnecessary contact. It wasn't positively amicable, but it wasn't hostile, either.

At Easter, we didn't go to Kippax or to Holtham. We stayed at home, and Rip and I made a tentative stab at collaboration, hiding a trail of miniature Easter eggs around the house for Ben and Stella.

10

On the Tuesday after Easter, I set off for Canaan House. It was a fresh, cold day, with splashes of sunlight spilling through ragged clouds. Nobody answered the doorbell when I rang. I peered in through the letterbox. There were no signs of human life, though a couple of felines were dozing in the pram, which was parked under the stairs. Then I noticed something very alarming—water seemed to be dripping down from a crack in the ceiling and collecting in a pool on the hall floor.

Suddenly Nabeel and Mr Ali materialised, running down the stairs and shouting at each other. I rang the bell again, and Mr Ali came and opened the door. I thought he'd opened it for me, but he raced right past me, out through the door and round to the back of the house. Then Mrs Shapiro turned up, tottering on her high heels, waving a cigarette in her hand.

'Ah! Georgine! Thenk Gott you come!' She flung her arms round me.

'What's going on?'

'Votter creases! I was telephoning to you! They are trying to mek votter pipe diversion into the penthouse suite.'

The trickle of water had become a steady stream and the hall was filling up with steam like a bathroom. Above us, the plaster ceiling was beginning to bow. Now Mr Ali appeared in the doorway. He shook his head and sighed as he gazed at the stream of water, which was fast becoming a torrent.

'It comes out of the tank. Not men's water,' he explained to Mrs Shapiro. Then he shouted something at Nabeel, who bowed his head and slouched off up the stairs. Mr Ali shrugged apologetically. 'Completely useless.'

I was still puzzling over the gender status of the hot water when Ishmail and Chaim came running downstairs, almost colliding with Nabeel.

'Men's now off, but water still coming out,' Mr Ali shouted.

Mrs Shapiro shouted at Chaim. 'Is your fault. You wanted to make votter separation. Jewish votter, Arab votter. So! Now we have pissing votter.'

'Not my fault, Ella. Useless Arabs cut the wrong pipe.'

Then the doorbell rang. I opened the door. It was Mark Diabello.

'Hello . . .' He stared at the scene in the hall, taking in the flushed faces peering through the clouds of steam. 'Georgina, I just wanted to . . .'

'Come in. We're having a bit of a water crisis . . .'

'Who is this?' asked Mrs Shapiro. 'Are you another Attendent?'

'Let me introduce Mr Wolfe's partner,' I said. 'Mark Diabello.'

'My Nicky's partner? How charming!' She fluttered her eyelids at the handsome stranger.

He stepped forward, proffering his hand, his smile-creases crinkling, his green-gold-black eyes flickering nonstop. 'Delighted, Mrs Shapiro. If I could just trouble you for a second, the house deeds—'

There was a horrible wrenching sound above our heads and everyone looked up. One of the ornate Doric-style plaster corbels supporting the Romanesque arch where the water had come through slipped sideways and slid. Mark Diabello seemed to stagger, his knees sagged, then he fell to the ground with a thud. He had been stunned by a stunning period feature.

By the time the ambulance arrived he was sitting up on the wet floor, propped against the wall beneath the grey mark where the picture of Lydda had hung, pressing a white handkerchief to a gash in his head.

Yet after his accident, a strange, exhausted peace fell on the house. The water finally stopped running when the hot-water tank had emptied out. Ishmail got a broom and started sweeping it out of the hall through the front door—there must have been several gallons. Nabeel went into the kitchen to make a pot of coffee. As the door swung open, I overheard a snippet of conversation: *Mr Ali: Where you get your tool kit, Chaim? Chaim Shapiro: B&Q. You want to see it?*

I sat with Mark Diabello until the ambulance arrived.

'I thought you might be here. I came to see you, Georgina,' he murmured. 'I didn't realise your hubby was back.'

'Yes. I should have told you. I'm sorry. It's over between us, Mark.' I squeezed his hand as they led him away to the ambulance. 'But it was fun.'

'MRS SHAPIRO,' I said, keeping my voice casual, 'do you happen to know where the deeds for this house are kept?' We were having a companionable cup of coffee by the fire in the study. 'Apparently the house isn't registered with the Land Registry.'

She looked at me through narrowed eyes. 'On this house I been paying rets sixty years no problem.'

'Mr Diabello said it would better to register in case you want to sell up at any time.'

'I am not selling nothing.'

'Of course there's no reason why you should sell.' There was no point in arguing with her. 'But it would be better for you if the house was registered in your name. Then no one could take it away from you.'

She reached in her bag for a cigarette and stuck it between her lips. 'You think Chaim wants to tek it away from me?'

'Everybody wants it. Chaim. Mrs Goodney. Even Mr Wolfe and Mr Diabello. It's a desirable property.'

'When I am dead, Georgine, darlink, you can heff it.' She said it casually, fumbling in her bag for the matches, not looking at me.

I laughed. 'It's kind of you, but it's too big for me. Too many problems.'

She gripped my hand and suddenly she was intensely serious. 'This house—it belongs to no one. Artem found it empty. Inhebitants ran away. Artem was just new married. He was needing somewhere to live.'

'With Naomi?'

She avoided my eyes. 'It was the wartime. German bombings. People running everywhere.'

'So they moved in?'

'Such a beautiful house, isn't it? Even a piano. Sometimes Mutti and I came to play on it. He played on the violin, we accompanied mit the piano. You know, Georgine, I was only a young girl. I didn't know anything—I knew only that I was in loff.' She pursed her lips and puffed a couple of smoke rings. 'You are not always thinking about the consequence.'

My mind tripped back to my conversation with the Scarlet-mouthed Slut.

'You thought being in love made it OK?'

'I thought only that I could not liff without him. And she was no good for him, that one. Always she was nagging him to go to Israel. Always talking of Zion—of mekking a homeland for all the Jews of the world.' A bit of wood shifted on the fire. 'He wanted only to die in peace.'

'So she went on her own. Didn't you feel . . .?'

She tossed her head in a vague gesture. 'I was looking after him. He was saying he will go there when he is better.'

What I really wanted to ask was—did she feel guilty? For stealing Naomi's husband, and Chaim's father.

'She wrote to him from Israel, didn't she?'

She nodded. 'Yes. Those letters. I burned them all.'

Her face was turned towards the fire, so I could not read her expression.

'Not all of them.'

'WHO WAS THAT MAN?' Stella asked as we were clearing up together after a Thai curry dinner. We were alone together in the basement kitchen. Rip and Ben were watching football upstairs. 'That smooth creepy guy in the Jag who came round while you were out?' Her lip curled with disapproval.

'Oh, he must have been the estate agent. He wants to buy a house from an old lady I know who lives at Totley Place. Why?'

'Daddy answered the door. They both seemed a bit surprised to see each other.' She gave me a hard look. 'He had a bunch of white roses.'

'Really? They were probably for someone else.'

'No, he left them. They're in my room. I told Daddy they were for me.'

'Thanks, Stella. You can keep them. I don't want them.'

On her face was a quick glimmer of a grin.

Next morning Rip gave me a peck on the cheek before he left for work, and maybe that's what made it hard to write about Gina's revenge. I was meant to be working on an *Adhesives* article, but I opened up my exercise book.

> *Disguised as an ~~itinerant window-cleaner rag-and-bone woman~~ Avon lady she made her way to Holty Towers and in the dead of night, she tiptoed through to the luxurious bathroom and got the ~~tube vial~~ phial out of her Avon box and squeezed a thin layer of extra-strong adhesive onto the seat of the ~~toilet~~ lavatory. Then she turned the cold tap on in the basin so that it ran in a steady stream . . .*

Something wasn't right. I was starting to feel a bit sorry for Rick. OK, so he had his flaky moments, but what a pair of idiots Rick and Gina were. Why couldn't they just sort their differences out and stick together? I realised that something inside me had shifted—I was no longer interested in revenge. I was ready to move on.

I closed my exercise book and clicked open the *Adhesives* document on my laptop: 'The Chemistry of Adhesive Bonding.' On New Year's Eve, when we'd joined hands, like molecules grabbing hold of each other, and sung 'Auld Lang Syne', I'd had a flash of insight into polymerisation. Now I discovered something even better—polymerisation depends on sharing. An atom which is short of an electron looks out for another atom that's got the right sort of electron, then the atom grabs the electron it needs. But no theft or nastiness is involved. The two atoms end up sharing the electron, and that's what holds all the atoms together in one beautiful long endlessly repeating dance—the beauty of glue!

Canaan House was still on my mind, and I started thinking about the two Naomis, each trying to grab Artem. Had there been sharing and dancing? Or was it a case of theft and nastiness? Would Artem have made a different choice if he'd read Naomi's letters? Would Ella's heart have been broken instead? Burning the letters seemed such a monstrously wicked thing to do; yet I couldn't think of her as a wicked woman. It's as though love gives you a special licence to do anything you like. In the end death, the ultimate fracture line, split Ella and Artem apart. And Canaan House itself had been part of the dance, too, shared by one couple, then another. But to whom did it really belong? There must be a way of finding out.

THE REFERENCE LIBRARY in Fielding Street, just off Holloway Road, was up on the top floor. The wet weather had brought in all the homeless folk, whose moist, unwashed smell mingled with the musty odour of books.

'I'm trying to find out the history of a house near where I live. It's called Canaan House. In Totley Place.'

The woman at the counter raised her eyes from her computer. 'We've got a small local history section over there on the right.'

Of the twenty or so volumes, the only specifically local book was one called *Walter Sickert's Highbury*. On page 79 was a lithograph of a large house with a tree in front of it. The caption read: *The Monkey Puzzle House, home of Miss Lydia Hughes, whose portrait he painted in 1929 when he was living in nearby Highbury Place.* Had the name of the house been changed?

My eye fell on a slim booklet in a yellow card cover: *A History of Christian Witness in Highbury*. It was obviously self-published. I took it through to the reading room and sat down at one of the desks. Towards the end of the booklet was a short entry that read: 'A Teresian community was established in the late 1930s in a house in Totley Place. It was evacuated following an air raid in 1941 and the community dispersed.'

I felt a rush of excitement—this could be it! The author was a Miss Sylvia Harvey. The book was published in 1977. As I scribbled the details on a piece of paper, you could hear the squeak of my pen. There was no other sound apart from sniffling and rustling and an occasional intermittent gurgle of the water cooler, like a dyspeptic gut. It reminded me that Dad's operation had been due today. I wondered how he'd got on.

Over in the far corner by the magazines and newspapers, a tall, heavily built man was wrestling with the *Financial Times*. He was sitting with his back to me. He had curly blond hair, streaked with grey. I stared. There was no mistaking him. It was Rip. Beside him on the floor were his briefcase and our large blue Thermos flask. He looked defeated. He wasn't even reading the newspaper, I realised. He was passing the time in the library because he didn't want us to know he wasn't at work.

I gathered my things together and tiptoed out through the door.

I'D ALREADY STARTED cooking dinner when Rip came in just before six o'clock. Stella was out and Ben was stretched out upstairs on the sofa with a book. Since his seizure, he'd been avoiding the computer.

'Hi, Ben! Hi, Georgie!' Rip called as he came in, then he went straight into the study.

Half an hour later, I stuck my head round the door. 'Dinner's ready.'

'What's all this, Georgie?' He was holding a B&Q carrier bag in his hand. 'Are you planning a bit of DIY?' He was looking at me intently.

I could feel myself turning red. 'No, not DIY. Collage. You know, sticking things. It's a form of art.'

Our eyes met. He grinned. I grinned. We stood grinning at each other across a bridge of lies. I would never tell him that I'd seen him in the library. In all our years together, I'd never before glimpsed his vulnerability. I reached out my arms and took a tentative step forward. There was a faint crackle and a smell of scorching, and Ben called from the kitchen, 'Come on, you two! The rice's burning!'

I HADN'T TOLD MUM yet that Rip had moved back in—I didn't want to tempt fate—but I rang her after dinner to find out how Dad's operation had gone. She was in an ebullient mood.

'They did a biopic. Doctor says it in't cancer.'

'Oh, that's good. How's he feeling?'

'Full of chips. Food were lovely in 'ospital. Got into a blazing argument with the bloke in the next bed about Iraq. Keir's coming home, by the way.'

'That's good news, too.'

It would be great to see Keir again. Since he'd joined the army, our worlds had drifted apart; nowadays all we had in common was our shared childhood, but Mum resolutely held us together like the family glue.

'She sent us some lovely flowers, by the way, your Mrs Sinclair. And a card. Best wishes for your recovery.'

'I didn't know she knew about Dad.'

'Oh, we keep in touch. She rings up from time to time. Or I ring her.'

'Really?'

This was complete news to me. I tried to imagine what Mum and Mrs Sinclair would talk about. Then I realised they probably talked about us.

I poured a glass of wine and put my feet up on the sofa while Rip and Ben cleared up in the kitchen.Then the phone rang.

'Georgine, come quick! We heff an invitation!'

Mrs Shapiro's voice shrilled down the line, but I was going nowhere. 'What've we been invited to?'

'Wait! Let me see—aha, here it is! We are invited to a funeral!'

My heart lurched. 'Oh dear. Who is it?'

'Wait! It is here! What is this? Looks like Mrs Lily and Brown, ninety-one year old, passes peacefully in the sleep at the Nightmare House. Who is this Brown Lily?'

'She's the old lady you made friends with in the hospital. And at Northmere House. You know—who was always asking for cigarettes?'

'She is not my friend—she is a bonker.'

'But it's nice that you've been invited to her funeral. Her family must have remembered you.'

'What is so nice about a funeral?'

'Don't you want to go?'

'Certainly we must go!'

THE CREMATORIUM WAS in Golders Green. I mentioned this to Nathan and suggested he might like to come along with his Tati.

'He'll enjoy it,' I said. 'There's sure to be plenty of singing.'

Somehow, the four of us fitted into Nathan's Morgan, even though it was really a glorified two-seater. Nathan and Mrs Shapiro sat in front. She was wearing a long black coat that smelled pleasantly of mothballs and a chic little black beret with a veil and a feather. Nathan's Tati squeezed into the back with me. He was wearing a raincoat and a Bogart-style trilby. I had on my grey jacket and a black scarf. It was a warm Saturday morning in April.

Nathan's Tati took Mrs Shapiro's hand to guide her up the steps to the crematorium, and she acknowledged the gesture with a gracious nod. There were only two other people in the chapel when we arrived, a grey wispy-looking woman who introduced herself as Mrs Brown's niece, Lucille Watkins, and her father, Mrs Brown's brother.

'Charlie Watkins,' he introduced himself, lingering over Mrs Shapiro's chipped-varnish fingers which she extended regally to him. 'I think we met at the 'ospital once. Did you know our Lily well?'

'Not well,' Mrs Shapiro replied, fluttering her eyelids. 'Only from smoking. And from slippers. She got the dead-woman slippers.'

I wasn't particularly surprised when Ms Baddiel turned up, too, just as the service was about to start. 'It's always so-o sad when a client passes away,' she murmured, searching in her oversize bag for a packet of tissues.

I felt in my pocket for a hanky and my fingers touched something hard and long. It was a key. I fished it out. Then I remembered the last time I'd worn this jacket. It was when I first met Mrs Goodney at Canaan House.

We spread out around the pews, trying to make ourselves look like more than seven. A thin man in a black suit droned through a short liturgy and disappeared. We all looked around, wondering whether this was all. Then suddenly there was a rustling behind us; the organ music stopped mid-note and gave way to a jolly lilting big-band number. *Ba-doop-a-doop-a!*

You could hear everybody gasp. Charlie Watkins rose to his feet and did a little hip-swing in the pew, then he squeezed out past his daughter and bopped up to the lectern. As the music faded away, he cleared his throat.

'Ladies and gen'lemen, we're 'ere to celebrate the life of a great lady, and a great dancer, Lily Brown, my sister, who was born Lillian Ellen Watkins in 1916 in Bow. She was the youngest of three sisters and two brothers. Now I'm the only one what's left, and all that past life is all washed away on the tides of time.' He fumbled in his pocket for a handkerchief. There was a general shuffling in the pews. This wasn't at all what we'd expected. He blew his nose and continued. 'Even when she was a young gel, our Lily danced like an angel.'

The Watkinses were a music-hall family. Charlie described how Lily enrolled for dance classes and how her breakthrough came when she got a place in the chorus line at Daly's. He leaned forward, snuffling into his hanky. 'I seen 'er up there on the stage, kickin' like she could kick the bollocks off a giraffe.' He blew his nose again. 'Ladies and gen'lemen, I ask you to pray for the soul of Lily Brown. May she dance with the angels.'

The sunlight stung our eyes as we shuffled outside into the Garden of Rest. I wandered along looking at the names on the memorial plaques on the walls: Enid Blyton, Peter Sellers, Anna Pavlova, Bernard Bresslaw . . . It wasn't until I got to the car park that I realised Mrs Shapiro was missing.

It was Nathan's Tati who found her. She'd strayed across the road into the Jewish cemetery. He'd found her wandering among the graves and led her back solicitously, supporting her on his arm.

'She keeps going on about some artist,' he whispered. 'Poor old thing.'

11

It was Mrs Shapiro's idea to hold a housewarming party for the penthouse suite. Mr Ali and the Uselesses had managed to install a functioning shower and toilet and three Velux windows in the attic rooms, without further mishap, and the Uselesses had moved their stuff up there.

We drew up the guest list together one morning over a cup of coffee. Mrs Shapiro was in an effervescent mood. 'We can invite the charming old man from the crematorium. He is good at singing. It will be a musical soirée. Or maybe a garden party. What you think?'

'I think we should be flexible. You can never tell what the weather's going to do.'

'You are very wise, Georgine.' She nodded. 'And, Georgine, this party will be a good opportunity for you to find a new husband. We will invite my Nicky and the other one also, the hendsome one. Maybe more hendsome even than Nicky, isn't it?'

'Yes, very handsome, but . . .' I hadn't yet told her that I was not looking for a new husband.

'You must mek more effort, Georgine, if you want to catch a man. You are a nice-looking woman, but you heff let yourself go. I heff a nice dress, red spotted mit white collar. Will look nice on you. And lipstick. You must wear a nice lipstick in metching colour.'

I smiled noncommittally.

After we'd drawn up the party list, we divided the duties. Mrs Shapiro said she would ring Wolfe & Diabello, and reluctantly agreed to invite Ms Baddiel, too. I was delegated to call Nathan and his Tati. I picked up the phone as soon as I arrived home. 'Your father's made a conquest, Nathan.'

'I think I can guess. It's your old lady, Mrs Shapiro?'

'Has he said anything?'

'He says it's a pity she's so old.'

'That's what she says about him. Anyway, you're both invited to a party.' I told him the day—it was a Saturday, about four o'clock. 'Put it in your diary. It might be a musical soirée or a garden party.'

IN THE END, the party was neither a musical soirée nor a garden party—it was a barbecue. That was Ishmail and Nabeel's idea, and they got so excited about it that no one had the heart to argue with them. They built an improvised barbecue and got a job lot of lamb chops and chicken wings from a Halal butcher.

At one point Chaim, Mr Ali, Ishmail and Nabeel were crowded round the smoking barbecue, puffing and flapping to try to get it lit. Ishmail and Nabeel took turns splashing squirts of lighter fuel onto the smouldering charcoal, then jumping back howling with laughter as the flames flared up. I watched them from the window of Mrs Shapiro's bedroom, where I was trying on the red-and-white spotted dress.

The sun came out after lunch, and stayed out all afternoon. One of the thrushes was up in the tree, his chest puffed out, and all seven of Mrs Shapiro's cats were circling. Mrs Shapiro and I chopped up salads and split pitta breads and set out plates and glasses on the white UPVC table.

Nathan and his Tati were the first to arrive. Tati had brought a bunch of blue irises for Mrs Shapiro.

'Thenk you so much!' Her bright blue eyelids fluttered ecstatically. 'Will you heff a drink?' She was wearing the same striped jersey and brown slacks in which she'd first entertained Mr Wolfe, with her high-heeled sling-backs that kept sticking into the grass. In fact she looked quite elegant.

Ms Baddiel, when she arrived, was wearing a flowing, tie-dyed garment in swirling shades of amber, bronze and gold. It fluttered lightly in the breeze, making her look delicate and ethereal, despite her size. I saw Mark Diabello eyeing her with interest as she came up the path, and felt a small stab of annoyance, even though I'd given him the push.

'Nice dress, Georgina.' He pecked me on the cheek and handed me a packet of sausages and a bottle of champagne. 'Is your hubby coming?'

'Yes, later,' I lied. Actually I hadn't invited him. I just felt I wanted to keep Canaan House and its eccentric inhabitants to myself.

'Nick's coming later, too. He had some . . . er . . . work to catch up on.'

'Mark, there's something you and Nick should know.' If I hadn't had a couple of glasses of wine I might have kept quiet, but I blurted out, 'The deeds to the house . . . there aren't any. The house was abandoned after a bombing raid. Her husband just moved in. Actually, I don't think he was even her husband.'

A strange look came over him, then I realised he was trying to stop himself from laughing. 'No title! Wait till I tell Nick!' He burst into a chuckle. 'No, maybe on second thoughts I won't tell him! Where *is* the old lady?'

Mrs Shapiro and Tati had disappeared into the house. They'd opened the window in the study and moved the old gramophone up to it, so we could hear the music in the garden. You could see them through the window.

'Who's the guy in the brown suit?' Nathan had sidled up to me.

Over by the barbecue, Mr Ali and Chaim Shapiro were cooking and arguing. Seeing them together like that, I was struck by how alike they were. 'Trouble wit you Arabs,' Chaim was saying, 'is you pick bad leaders.'

Mr Ali speared another lamb chop on a skewer and brandished it in the air. 'You Jews put all the good ones in prison.'

Chaim flipped the chicken wings. 'We put only terrorists in prison.'

'Mr Ali, Chaim, this is my colleague Nathan Stein,' I butted in.

'Come! Eat something!' Chaim waved a chicken wing at him.

'We are discussing politics,' said Mr Ali. When he looked round at us, I could see he had a grin on his face and bits of barbecue sauce in his beard. They both looked as though they were enjoying themselves.

Mark Diabello was topping up the glasses. 'I work mainly with old people,' I overheard Ms Baddiel explaining peachily to him. 'Sorting out their housing needs.'

'Fascinating,' he murmured. 'I'm in housing myself.'

Everything that happened next happened very quickly, so I may have got the order of events slightly wrong, but it was something like this. The thrush started it. From his perch in the tree he'd spotted a piece of pitta bread that had fallen onto the ground. Wonder Boy was lurking in the bushes watching the bird. As the thrush swooped down Wonder Boy wriggled into pouncing position and went for the bird. I grabbed the first thing that came to hand—it was a lamb chop—and lobbed it at Wonder Boy. It arced through the air, spinning like a boomerang. Normally I'm hopeless at throwing, but this time I scored a direct hit. Wonder Boy let out a yowl and leaped sideways right under the feet of Nabeel, who was carrying a plate of chicken wings up the garden. Nabeel barged into Ishmail, who lurched and stumbled against the barbecue, which collapsed, scattering hot coals everywhere, setting fire to the lighter fuel that had spilled onto the ground under the open study window, where a curtain was flapping in the breeze. The cats fell on the scattered chicken wings in a frenzy. Wonder Boy grabbed the biggest one and raced off down the path. The wind gusted; the curtains caught and blazed. Outside on the lane there was a screech of brakes and a thud. The flames leaped through the window. Nick Wolfe appeared at the gate, holding up Wonder Boy's limp and lifeless body. Mrs Shapiro screamed and fainted. The fire roared through the study and into the hall. Nathan phoned the fire brigade on his mobile phone, and I just stood there watching, clenching my hands into fists, wishing I could recall the flying lamb chop, and feeling terribly, terribly guilty.

HOURS LATER, after the fire brigade had been and gone, and Mrs Shapiro had been carted off into temporary accommodation accompanied by Ms Baddiel, I walked home through the balmy dusk. When I got to my front door I noticed that Violetta was there beside me.

Ben and Rip were drinking a beer and watching the television.

'Good party?' asked Rip, without looking up.

'Great.' I slumped on the sofa. Violetta jumped up onto my lap, purring.

'Look at this,' said Rip, pointing at the screen. 'Who would have believed it?' Two men were being interviewed in front of a bank of cameras.

'Who are they?'

'Ian Paisley and Martin McGuiness,' said Ben, who'd been watching the item from the beginning. 'They've done a deal in Northern Ireland.'

'Who'd have thought it was possible? Peace has broken out!' Rip turned to face me. He was smiling, then the smile broadened into a lopsided grin. 'What *are* you wearing, Georgie? You've changed. You're different.' He was staring at me as though he hadn't seen me before.

'Oh, I thought I'd dress up for the party . . .' I hesitated. My jeans, jumper and coat had been swallowed up in the blaze.

'It suits you, Mum,' said Ben. 'Sort of retro.'

Later that night, I got out of bed, put on my slippers and dressing gown and walked down to the study. There was a sliver of light under the door. I tapped softly.

'Come in.'

Rip was sitting at the computer in his boxer shorts, staring at the screen.

'You're working late.'

'Got a report to finish,' he said, without looking round.

'Progress Project?'

'No. I'm done with the Progress Project.'

I glanced over his shoulder and I could see quite clearly on the monitor that he was working not on a report but on his CV. I slipped an arm round him. There was something about the way he was leaning forward in his chair, sagging almost, that struck a sudden chime of pity in me.

'You're tired. You should go to bed.' I stroked his hair.

'I need to get this done. It has to be in tomorrow.'

'Shall I make you a coffee?'

'That'd be nice.'

I went down to the kitchen and made two cups of coffee. An hour later, when he crawled into the low canvas camp bed, I crept in beside him.

12

Canaan House is now a building site. After the fire brigade had gone the surveyors checking the damage found an unexploded bomb left over from the war, buried in the roots of the monkey puzzle tree. The street had to be evacuated while the bomb squad carried out a controlled explosion. We stood behind the barrier tape and watched. It was windy and dust blew everywhere—that's all that was left in the end, dust.

Mrs Shapiro was weeping quietly. 'You know, dear Georgine, you were right,' she said, 'this house was too big for me. Too many problems. Too many memories. Like caught in a trap. Now is the time for moving on.'

Fortunately, Mark Diabello had managed to get the title registered in Mrs Shapiro's name, using the evidence of her sixty years as a ratepayer to justify her claim, so she was able to sell the site to a developer for a substantial sum. She has bought herself a lovely apartment in a sheltered housing development in Golders Green—sadly no pets allowed—and she has set up Chaim and Mussorgsky in a flat in Islington. Violetta has stayed with me. The remainder of the money went, with the remaining feline residents, to the Cats Protection League.

IT'S RAINING AGAIN as I make my way across Islington Green to Sainsbury's. I've arranged for Rip to pick me up in the car park at one o'clock. He's gone off to a meeting with the team at the Finsbury Park Law Centre, where he's starting his new job next week.

The Boycott Israeli Goods girl is there, brandishing her clipboard, though she's now collecting signatures on a petition to save the whales. Ben is there with her—he often comes here on a Saturday morning. His hair is twisted into incipient dreadlocks and tied behind his neck with the red pirate-style scarf.

'Hey, Mum!'

I stop to sign their petition, though I've already signed it several times. The girl looks a bit sheepish, maybe thinking I despise her defection, but I just smile, because I understand now that everything—whales and dolphins, Palestinians and Jews, stray cats and rain forests—they're all interconnected, held together by some mysterious force—call it glue, if you like.

While I'm picking up some beer for Rip, I spot Mark Diabello and Cindy Baddiel lingering hand in hand in the wine department.

'Hello, Georgina!' He greets me with a kiss on each cheek, and Ms Baddiel hugs me in her roly-poly arms.

'Thanks for everything you did with getting the house registered,' I say to Mark. 'How's it going?'

A couple of months ago, Wolfe & Diabello mysteriously disappeared from the high street to be replaced by Wolfe & Lee. Mark tells me he is now running a housing association for ex-offenders.

'It's—how can I put it?—more satisfying.'

'I'm glad it all worked out.'

'Take care,' they say.

At the deli counter I bump into Nathan and Raoul, gravely discussing the comparative merits of olive and avocado oils. Nathan has his arm round Raoul's shoulder in that casual gesture with which he once comforted me. They greet me with warm hugs and bring me news of Mr Ali, who has just installed a new jacuzzi at their flat in Hoxton. Ishmail is still living with the al-Alis out Tottenham way and is due to start his engineering course in September, but Nabeel has gone back to Palestine.

'Look out for Tati and Ella,' says Nathan. 'They're here somewhere.'

Sure enough, there they are, pushing the high-sprung pram down one of the aisles, leaning together like a pair of newlyweds. I watch her lift her face up as he bends to give her a whiskery kiss and whisper something in her ear. She laughs, and rests her head against him. The way they're gazing into the pram, you'd think there was a baby in there, but as I get closer all I see inside is a lot of bargains.

marina **lewycka**

RD: Your first published novel, *A Short History of Tractors in Ukrainian*, shortlisted for the 2005 Orange prize for fiction, brought you immediate success. What career were you pursuing before?
ML: I was a teacher. First I worked in schools, then in further education, then I moved to adult education, and in my last job I was lecturing in a university.
RD: Had you been writing secretly all that time?
ML: Well, I started to write at the age of four! It was a poem in English about rabbits. We spoke Ukrainian at home and so I didn't learn English until I went to school. It opened a door into my own new world.
RD: Did you ever submit your poems or any previous novels to a publisher?
ML: I had my first poem, a limerick, published in the Women's Institute magazine when I was about ten. My mother was very proud of me. I wrote my first novel in longhand while at university and no one has ever seen it. The second one I sent out to everyone I could think of and I had thirty-six rejection slips—and that doesn't take into account those who never replied. You have to have a slight grain of madness in you to persist after that.
RD: But you did persist, so did something happen that changed your luck?
ML: I was teaching at Sheffield Hallam, where they let staff members do courses for free. I'd done one on building your own website, and one on Excel spreadsheets and I wasn't very good at either. So I thought I'd go for a creative writing course and just see what happened. At the time I was working on two novels: one was a children's novel and one was *A Short History* . . . I took along a few chapters of each and asked the others which one I should go with. Everyone chose *Tractors*. The course was very good for me because I had to write a certain amount each week and it gave me direction.
RD: Then would your tip to any would-be writer be to sign up for a course?
ML: Definitely. It's a way of admitting to yourself that you are serious about writing, that it's more than a hobby. The most wonderful thing for me was that the external examiner at the end of the course was a literary agent and that's how the book was picked up. I guess that tells you that it's not what you know, it's *who* you know that counts.
RD: Were you worried that the title of your *Tractors* novel might put people off?
ML: Yes, I suppose so. I know that some libraries filed the book under Agricultural

History! And I remember the first review of the book on Amazon said, 'Be warned! This book has nothing to do with tractors. The author should be ashamed of herself!'

RD: *We Are All Made of Glue* is another unusual title . . .

ML: It has at least two meanings, of course. And someone who'd enjoyed *Tractors* came to visit me at work and announced, 'I'm in adhesives.' I thought that adhesives would be a challenge to write about and he helped me a lot with my research. I'd found chemistry difficult at school and had always felt I ought to be able to do better at it.

RD: So you were happy to be expanding your own knowledge . . .

ML: Yes. I became quite hooked on adhesives! I think that's the thing with all the books that I've written: I like to learn something as I write. I often start out with a subject I don't know very much about and finding out more makes the process more interesting.

RD: Presumably you have certain elements in your mind before you start?

ML: The key in *We Are All Made of Glue* is what happens to Mrs Shapiro, which is very similar to what happened to an elderly neighbour. I'd also worked for Age Concern and came to know some things about old people and their estates. But the characters you pick will always lead you on into the story and tell you things that you didn't know at the beginning. It's like entering another world and you just have to surrender to it.

RD: The attitude of social services to Mrs Shapiro was horrifying . . .

ML: Well, some of that was made up, of course. And don't forget that I had a good social worker and a bad one, so it was balanced. Essentially, I do believe in the goodness of human beings, and if there's a message in my books, it is that underneath the surface there is always something good to be found in everyone.

RD: In your books you explore serious issues but lace them with so much humour. In this one, Mrs Shapiro's conversations had us laughing aloud.

ML: Her character is a composite of several people I have met and I know someone who speaks exactly like her. I love to listen to people. I'm a real eavesdropper.

RD: Do you feel sad when you finally finish writing a book?

ML: Yes, because you've been living with the characters for a long time and they're part of your life. I don't know how anyone can write a story in which they hate the characters.

RD: Are you writing a new novel?

ML: I am. And it's all about the credit crunch. I thought, I don't know much about finance—What's going on in the world? Why is it like this? I'm teaching myself, and I hope that readers, who are not experts, like me, will know a lot more about it all by the end.

RD: Are you going to be able to make the credit crunch amusing?

ML: Oh, yes, it's very funny. And, to be honest, even newspaper reporting on the credit crunch, reading between the lines, is very funny. It's all about betrayal, drama, greed, revenge . . . All life is there. I think readers may feel a bit annoyed by the end, too, though.

COPYRIGHT AND ACKNOWLEDGMENTS

Spine lozenge: iStock exclusive. Page 5 (top) and 574 © Ian Phillpott.; 6–8 Imagebank, Riser Images; illustrator Narrinder Singh@velvet tamarind; 158 (top) © Lynn Brubaker Photography; bottom © Ann States; 159 © Getty Images/Paul Morigi/WireImage. 160–162 iStock exclusive; 292 © Mark Read. 294–6 Hulton Archive; illustrator Narrinder Singh@velvet tamarind; 424 © Mariantonietta Peru. 426–8 illustration Richard Merritt@The Organisation.

Printed and bound by GGP Media GmbH, Pössneck, Germany

020-261 DJ0000-1